I Vow. You Vow. We Vow.

Madness

For more information about the author and her books, visit her website — https://shanteltessier.com/
You can join her reader group. It's the only place to get exclusive teasers, first to know about current projects and release dates- https://www.facebook.com/groups/TheSinfulSide

Editor: Jenny Sims
Cover/interior designer and formatter: Booklovedesigns- Melissa Cunningham
Cover model: Kallym Grimmond
Photographer: Lanefotograf

WARNING

For those of you who choose to go in blind, please remember that this dark revenge romance is a work of fiction, and I do NOT condone any situations or actions that take place between these characters. This book is not to teach you BDSM, so please do not take it as a how-to. There is a lot of bondage without aftercare. My FMCs (female main characters) love their Heroes as they are—unapologetic. If you need a groveling Hero, this book is not for you.

With that being said, every character does go through some kind of trauma (physical and emotional) at some point in this story. If you've read any of the previous Lords (highly suggested before reading *Madness* due to spoilers), then you have an idea of what their world is like. But I promise you, they have nothing on the Spade brothers. They wrote the book and then sold it to the devil. So buckle up and get ready for one hell of a ride.

Feel free to continue to the prologue if you're like me and have no triggers and like to be surprised, but just remember that I warned you. If you do NOT want to go in blind, please read the trigger warnings & kinks listed below.

Madness may contain triggers for some.

Trigger Warnings include but are not limited to:

Murder and torture (both in graphic detail), CNC (consent-nonconsent), DUB CON (dubious consent), forced retention enema, predicament bondage, rope bunny, BDSM (no safe word is used or given), anal, face fucking, cockwarming, humiliation, degradation, forced orgasm, praise kink, drugging, alcohol use, spit, forced piercing, branding, forced sterilization, waterboarding, hallucinations, forced proximity, attempted suicide, birth control tampering, talk of miscarriage, rape, blackmail.

If you have any questions, feel free to email me, and one of my assistants or I will get back to you. darkangelcreationsllc@gmail.com

AUTHOR'S NOTE:

Nothing about this is to be taken seriously. It is strictly a work of fiction and for your smut pleasure.

Madness is an all-new dark romance within the Lords world from the USA Today & Wall Street Journal bestselling author Shantel Tessier. *Madness* is based in the #1 Amazon bestselling Lords' world, and it is highly suggested to start with *The Ritual*. If you have not read any previous Lords book(s), *Madness* will contain spoilers for you.

The Lords reading order is as follows

The Ritual
The Sinner
The Sacrifice
Sabotage (the H isn't a Lord but he works for a Lord)
Carnage
Madness

Things to know about ***Madness***

Secret society
MF
J/P (jealous/possessive) Hero
OTT (over the top) Hero
Dark revenge romance
Told in dual POV
Virgin h

Drop your feminism at the door. Haidyn Reeves is going to make you his good little dirty whore in every way.

PLAY

HALLELUJAH
NO RESOLVE

CRADLE TO THE GRAVE
FIVE FINGER DEATH PUNCH

SKELETON LORDS
HALLOW

IN MY MIND
DYNORO AND GIGI D'AGOSTINO

BULLET TRAIN
STEPHEN SWARTZ

PAINKILLER
THREE DAYS GRACE

I CAN HOLD A GRUDGE LIKE NOBODY'S BUSINESS
ADAM JENSEN

BLOODY NOSE
HOLLYWOOD UNDEAD

O.M.W.
MELLINA TEY

THANK YOU FOR HATING ME
CITIZEN SOLDIER

ACID ANNIE
NATALIA KILLS

COMING UNDONE
KORN

DIRTY THOUGHTS
CHLOE ADAMS

YOU ARE THE REASON
CALUM SCOTT

SILENCE
MARSHMELLO AND KHALID

ALWAYS REMEMBER US THIS WAY
LADY GAGA

BROKEN
SEETHER AND AMY LEE

ANYWHERE BUT HERE
FIVE FINGER DEATH PUNCH AND MARIA BRINK

11 MINUTES
YUNGBLUD AND HALSEY

MEET YOU AT THE GRAVEYARD
CLEFFY

Carnage
ENTRANCE
THE CEMETERY

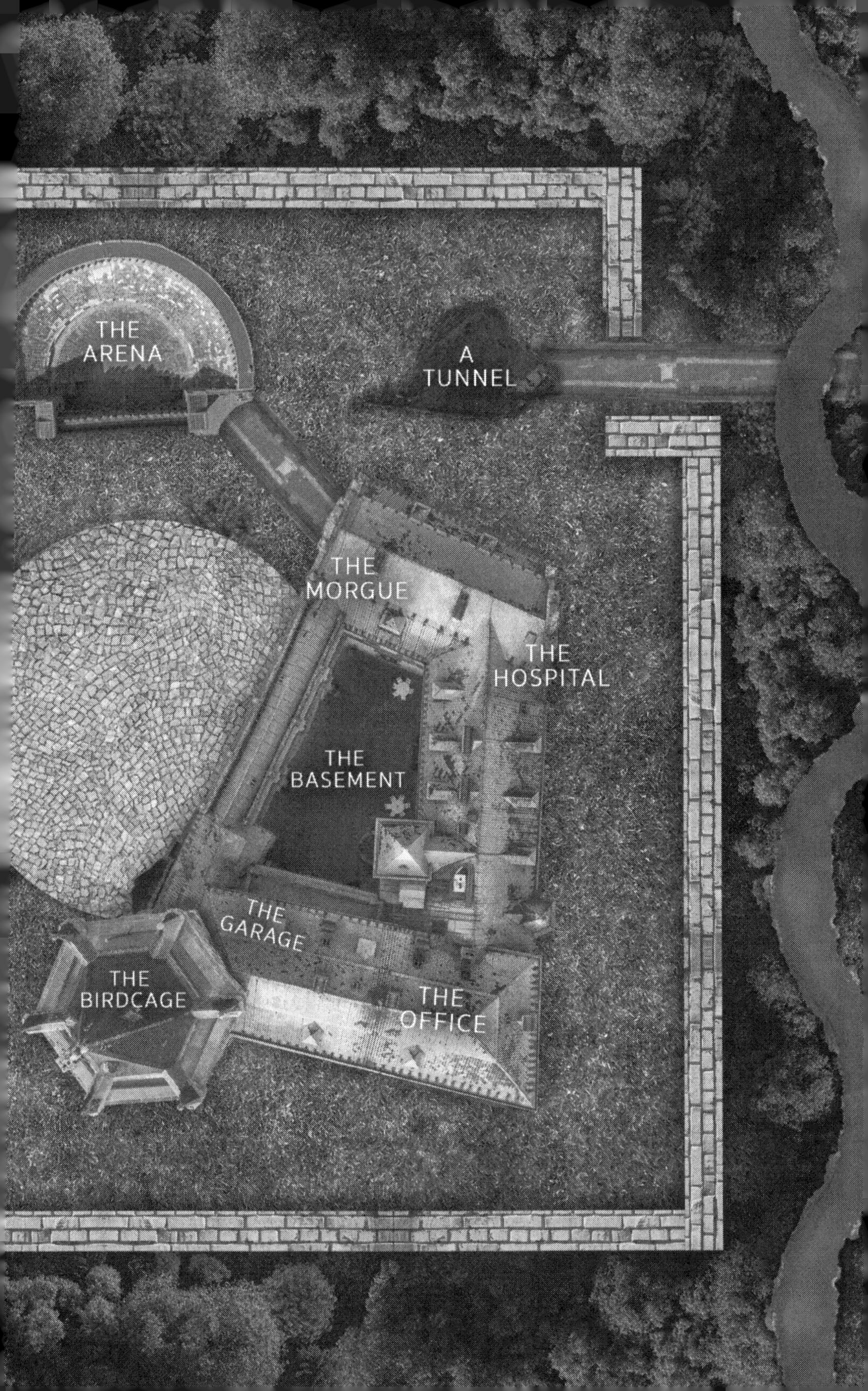
THE ARENA
A TUNNEL
THE MORGUE
THE HOSPITAL
THE BASEMENT
THE GARAGE
THE BIRDCAGE
THE OFFICE

Part One

Prologue

L.O.R.D.

A Lord takes his oath seriously. Only blood will solidify their commitment to serve those who demand their complete devotion.

*He is a **Leader**, believes in **Order**, knows when to **Rule**, and is a **Deity**.*

A Lord must be initiated in order to become a member but can be removed at any time for any reason. If he makes it past the three trials of initiation, he will forever know power and wealth. But not all Lords are built the same. Some are stronger, smarter, hungrier than others.

*They are challenged just to see how far their **loyalty** will go.*

*They are pushed to their limits in order to prove their **devotion**.*

*They are willing to show their **commitment**.*

Nothing except their life will suffice.

Limits will be tested, and morals forgotten.

A Lord can be a judge, jury, and executioner. He holds power that is unmatched by anyone other than his brother.

Chosen one:

A Lord must remain celibate during his first three years at Barrington University. Once he is initiated into the Lords, he is gifted a chosen for his senior year.

A Lady:

After they graduate from Barrington, they are to marry a Lady—a wife to serve him. If he shall die before her, she is then gifted to another Lord to ensure the secrets are kept within the secret society.

A Spade brother:

A Lord is placed strategically out into the world. But no Lord is safe from their own if they break their oath. If you don't believe in hell, the Spade brothers will change your mind. They are a special kind of Lord. They will sit on their thrones and watch you burn to death for eternity with the fire they started. They give no fucks and have no limits. They collect the names they are given, and erase you from the world as if you never existed, and make you wish that was the truth.

Chapter 1

INITIATION

HAIDYN

LOYALTY
FRESHMAN YEAR AT BARRINGTON UNIVERSITY

"*Don't embarrass me.*" My father's words echo in the back of my mind. Like a song stuck on repeat that can't be changed.

"*Yes, Father,*" I told him just before being thrown into a cell.

I'll become a Spade brother—a member of a secret society that is fucked up, for a lack of a better word. Centuries ago, some bored rich men came up with a game.

The story is, they got drunk, branded one another, and then fought each other to see who got to fuck whose wife. Apparently, it got messy—doesn't it always when pussy is involved—and the Lords were invented. Marriage no longer meant what it was supposed to be. Love was a weakness that a man couldn't afford. It became kill or be killed. But like anything else, you have the bad apples. The ones who want more than they are given. They betray their oath and must be made an example of.

That's where the Spade brothers came along. A Spade brother runs their hell. As if any aspect of the society is heaven. We're the minority. There are four of us, and today is my day to begin my journey to becoming a member. My father has reminded me what he expects of me every day of my life. The only reason I bother to show up is to stay alive. I couldn't care less about the Lords. But most don't. The Lords try to make you think you're special. Most of us know the truth and see it for what it is—a curse.

They'll tell you who you can fuck, who you will marry, and what you'll do for a living.

Carnage is my future. I will learn to accept the fight and crave the blood.

"Haidyn Jamison Reeves." My name is called out, and I look up from the spot where I kneel in the center of the arena. I was dragged in here after I spent forty-eight hours in a blacked-out concrete cell. Minimal food and water. They want you to be at your weakest when they test you. "You have been called to serve. Do you wish to proceed?"

Why the fuck would I say no? I don't have a death wish. "Yes, sir."

He nods and takes a step back from the platform. "He's all yours." Turning, he walks out of the arena and disappears through a side door.

"Hands behind your back," a man orders from behind me.

Doing as instructed, I feel the cold metal placed around each wrist as I'm handcuffed. A rope wraps around my neck, and I arch it to try and loosen the pressure, but it does no good.

I tell myself to slow my breathing and not fight the inevitable. I know how this goes, and this is just to get me ready for the show. All the Lords dressed in cloaks and masks fill the seats surrounding the arena's second story to see if I prove myself and pass.

A man comes to stand in front of me and orders, "Open wide."

He shoves a ball gag into my mouth. My breathing accelerates through my nose, knowing what's coming next. He takes the syringe and fills it with the clear liquid before stabbing it into my chest. *Adrenaline.*

My teeth sink into the rubber as pain explodes throughout my body—it feels like hot lava covers my skin.

"He's ready," he calls out and steps back.

My wrists are released from the cuffs, and the rope is removed from my neck as I spit out the gag. I bow my head and close my eyes. My heart pounds in my chest, and my pulse races. I can feel the blood pumping through my veins. My fingers tingle, and I fist my hands.

Fuck! I feel invincible. It's an illusion. They want you to think you're God so they can remind you that you're their fucking servant.

"A well-fed devil is more loyal than a starving saint" has never been a truer statement than when it comes to the Lords.

A door opening and closing has me looking up, and I see a man enter the arena. He's dressed in a bulletproof vest, jeans, and combat boots. All I wear is jeans and my boots.

I slowly get to my feet, taking inventory of my body and liking the way it hums with excitement. As if I was just jump-started—conditioned to fucking destroy whoever comes my way.

He has a chain in his right hand and a knife in the other. They want it to be an unfair match. Just how far are we willing to go to survive?

"Let's see what you've got, big boy." The man laughs just as another man enters and comes to stand next to him. He, too, is dressed the same while holding identical weapons.

In a world of shouting men, be the one who remains silent, my mother used to say all the time. *If they cannot hear you, they won't see you.*

I've always preferred silence to mindless chitchat. Not because I wanted to go unnoticed but because they're just words that mean nothing. No one cares how you feel or what you think. It's about following rules and actions. A servant does as he's told.

I step off the platform, ready to get this shit over with. The room is brighter, the air warmer, and I can feel the sweat running down my back.

The one on the left holds up his right hand and twirls the chain around. *Whoosh…whoosh…*

My ears pick up the sound as if it's right by my head when he's several feet away. Without thought, I go for his legs. *To bring a giant down, you've got to take him out at the knees.*

Rushing him, I bend down and wrap my arms around his knees, picking him up off the floor. He screams out as I carry him backward until we both hit the ground, knocking the wind out of him for just a second. I bet they're both on adrenaline too, so I've got to make this quick before we all pass the fuck out.

The other one takes the opportunity and slams his knife into my side. Although I don't feel it right now, I know I will very soon.

I get off the one on the floor and turn to face the other one. His eyes drop to his knife in my side and he smiles. He goes to lift the chain, and I remove the knife, throwing it at his face. It lands in his right eye, and he drops to his knees as the blood begins to drip from the knife.

I took the knife in order to use it as a weapon. They want us to be defenseless. Sometimes you've got to choose to be the sacrifice.

It's a short victory because the other guy has the chain wrapped around my neck from behind, pulling me backward. Reaching up, I grip the links in my hands—forcing my fingers between the chain and my throat—and bend over, yanking the man over my back and slamming him onto the floor.

He rolls over, and I make my way to the dead guy as the other bounces to his feet. I yank the knife from his face and fling it at the one now standing. He moves at the last minute, and it lands in his vest.

Well, fuck. Now he's got two knives and a chain.

The blood rushes in my ears, and I shake my head, trying to quiet the noise so I can think. Everything is moving so fast. My mind is racing like my heart. Everything goes in and out of sight, and I'm having trouble focusing on one thing for more than a second.

I grab the chain from the dead guy and bend down, whipping the chain to wrap around the other guy's ankles and yank, knocking him to his back once again. I drag him toward me, and he flings one of the knives, barely missing my head. The second lands in my thigh, and I grind my teeth at the sting. The adrenaline is starting to wear off, and the pain is setting in.

He twists onto his stomach and calls out like a little bitch as if anyone is going to help him. I remove the knife from my leg and slam it into the back of his neck, killing the second piece of shit.

Falling to my knees, I place my bloody hands on my blood-covered jeans. *Fuck, I'm fading fast.*

The door to my right opens, and I look over to see my father heading toward me with several other Lords. He doesn't look proud or happy that I passed. He's just glad I didn't embarrass him. The bastard knows I didn't do it for him.

Chapter 2

INITIATION

HAIDYN

Devotion
Sophomore year at Barrington University

Everyone fears something. Whether it be as small as dying alone or as terrifying as drowning to death. It's part of life. Especially the Lords. It's all around us. But I'm not afraid of it. It's inevitable and something that you can't bargain with.

We are raised to know that in our world, it's kill or be killed. So when put in this situation, it's a no-brainer. Have I thought of how I'll die? Sure. A bullet to the back of the head maybe? Or it might be slow and painful—my skin being ripped from my bones? Maybe someone sets me on fire? Who knows. But either way, when it comes, I'll accept it.

So what am I afraid of if death isn't it? I'm afraid of failing those that I love. Of letting my brothers down and leaving them to fend for themselves. I hate being unable to protect the ones who rely on me. And that's the only reason I'm even doing these fucking initiations. Because they need me to help them through this shitty life we've been damned to live until someone takes us out.

I follow my father through the basement of Carnage. He came and woke me up in the middle of the night and told me to get dressed. *It's time.* Another year, another test to prove I'm worthy to have his last name and one day run this hell.

We make our way through the plastic strip curtains and come to a stop when I see two women hanging from the ceiling in the open room. They're a few feet apart, both stripped naked with their arms above their heads, secured with chains wrapped around their wrists. Black hoods cover both of their heads, and large metal collars are around their necks, secured in place to keep them from lowering their heads.

I take a deep breath, trying to calm the nerves. *What the fuck is this?* The initiation is supposed to be for me. My fear. Not anyone else.

A Lord stands between them with his back to me, dressed in his cloak and mask. He's sharpening a knife. The sound wouldn't normally bother me, but right now, it makes the hairs on the back of my neck rise.

My father turns to me. "You have a choice."

"A choice?" I echo his words. Such a foreign concept. Because if I had a choice, I wouldn't fucking be here.

The Lord sharpening his knife turns to face us, the knife in his hand. *It's me or them.* That's the only explanation I can think of. They cut them, or me. "Me." I step forward, not even needing to think about it.

My father lets out a growl, and the Lord wearing the mask makes sweat bead across my head when he speaks. "It's not that kind of choice. One of these women is innocent...the other is not." He places the tip of the knife on the woman hanging on the right and runs it from her hip and along her ribs. She's gasping, her body shaking as she fights the restraints. Her muffled sobs fill the basement, and her feet kick out as she tries to stand on her tiptoes, but they've got her strung up at just the right height that her pink painted toes barely touch. "You choose which one lives or dies."

I look at my father.

"Make a decision, Haidyn." His voice is as cold as the room, as if he knows I'm questioning him. His eyes watch the one on the left.

She's smaller, sickly looking. Shorter in height and she's sobbing in her gag and hood by the way her body trembles uncontrollably.

They're both covered in bruises and dirt. It makes me wonder what happened to them before they were dragged down here in the basement.

"I don't understand..."

"You don't need to understand." My father snaps at me. "You choose which one dies and which one lives."

I run a hand through my hair aggressively. I figured they'd bury me alive...stick me in a pit full of snakes. Not this. It doesn't make sense.

"You have one minute," the Lord behind the mask states, and he turns to flip an hourglass and my heart races as I watch the sand start to fall through the center. "If you don't make a decision by the time the timer is done, they both will die."

The girls start screaming into their hoods and gags, and I take a step back. My eyes go back and forth between them. The Lord taunts them both with the tip of his knife, slowly running it over their flushed skin, nicking them both in various places. Not deep enough to kill them but enough to make them bleed.

My eyes go to the hourglass, and I see it's almost out. I look at my father, and he's still glaring at the girl on the left. I say girl because she looks younger than the other one. Her skin is less touched by years of abuse. The other has tracks along her arms and legs.

I step forward and speak. "Kill the one on my right."

The Lord doesn't even take a second to think about it. He slams the knife into the woman's chest before he yanks it out, and the blood pours down her body as it sags in the chains. He reaches up and allows the other one to fall to the concrete floor. She rolls onto her side, curling up in a ball, and her chained wrists go to her metal collar, trying to get it off, but it's locked in place.

My father walks over to the woman on the floor and kicks her onto her back. His boot steps down on her sweat-covered and bloody chest. He looks her over and then to the Lord. "I don't want to see her again."

"Yes, sir," the Lord says and drags her by the excess chain out of the room and down the hall while she kicks her legs out.

I question that I killed the wrong one. The dead girl who still hangs from the ceiling got off easy. I don't know the fate of the other one. Will she be tortured? Did I sentence her to a life here as a prisoner at Carnage? Doesn't matter. It's too late now. I made a decision, and I told myself a long time ago that I won't have any regrets.

He turns to face me. His eyes narrowed on mine. "You disappoint me, Haidyn."

Good. I made the right decision. "Saying I chose the wrong one?" I picked the one on the right because, for some reason, my father despises the other one.

He steps into me and bows his chest. "You should have let them both die."

The thought never crossed my mind. I was told to make a choice, and that's exactly what I did. "Did I fail?" I ask, arching a brow. Ready to get the fuck out of here.

"Women are no use to you unless you're fucking them," he growls. "They are for your pleasure and reproduction. When are you going to figure that out?"

"I guess when I finally get to fuck one again," I counter. Three years we have to be celibate. It's the stupidest fucking thing I've ever heard of. Maybe it wouldn't be so bad if they weren't always throwing it in our faces. They give you plenty of opportunities to fail.

He huffs, turns, and exits the basement, leaving me alone with the dead woman who hangs by her chained wrists.

I bow my head and take a deep breath. Fuck, here's to another year and another initiation.

Chapter 3

INITIATION

HAIDYN

Commitment
Junior year at Barrington University

I look down at my Patek Philippe watch. We've been on this yacht for four hours. The four of us must work together on this initiation. We each received a card with a name on it, and Saint just finished his. I wanted to get in and out. Obviously, it's going to take all night.

"Clean up," I say, looking over all the blood out on the balcony, and I drop my backpack from my shoulder. "On to the next."

We just helped Saint kill the guy he was assigned to. It got messy. But we were able to take care of him after the poker game, and I ended up taking the dealer out as well. We can't leave any witnesses behind.

"How do you feel, Kash?" Adam asks, rubbing his back. "Doing okay?"

Kashton nods, pushing him away. "The gum the lady gave me helped."

He was feeling seasick earlier. If he hasn't vomited by now, I'd say he'll be fine.

"I'll be right back. I'm going to use the restroom," I tell them.

"Okay. We'll text you when we're done here."

Taking the elevator down, I search for a bathroom. This megayacht is around a hundred meters—three hundred feet—long, so I know I have options. I just have to find one.

I step off, finding myself on the main deck. We're out on the Atlantic, and the lights from the yacht illuminate the night.

The partiers have no clue two guys were just killed and thrown overboard. And by the time we're done at least three more will be at the bottom as well. Along with the Lord who owns it.

He's my initiation. Like the other men who will find their new home at the bottom of the ocean tonight, he fucked up. He took his oath for granted and got greedy. Now, he has to pay the price—his life.

I watch everyone carrying on with mindless conversations about their money market accounts and most recent investments, trying to appear interested in anyone other than themselves. They all scratch each other's backs while fucking each other's wives.

Laughter catches my attention to my right, and I turn to see a woman standing with a couple of others. She wears a white dress. The innocent color makes her skin appear kissed by the sun. It comes up high around her delicate neck and falls to the floor. The slit up the side shows off her lean right leg and a pair of red high heels that wrap and buckle around her ankle.

It's not revealing, but the way it fits her small body shows off the curve of her spine and round ass. Her dark brown hair is up and off her shoulders, showing me a side view of her pretty doll-like face. She hasn't looked my way, so I don't know what color her eyes are, but it doesn't matter. She's stunning. Ever looked at someone and just knew they were too good for you? I don't mean that out-of-your-league shit. I'm talking out of this universe. My brothers and I will be very wealthy and set for life—and so will our children and grandchildren. But even money can't buy you love in our world. I can tell by her demeanor that she's a princess who will live in some high-rise in New York, and I'll be the monster who will live in the basement of a prison no one knows exists. We're not the same.

Throwing her head back, she laughs before taking a sip of her champagne.

My cock is so fucking hard. I've gone three years without sex, and I'm going insane. My hands itch to tangle in her perfect hair, bend her over, and rip the fabric as I fuck her in front of everyone.

That's what we're taught to do—take what we want in front of others. It's to prove ourselves. To show we have power. But do we? Not really.

The Lords allow us to have control in certain areas, but for the most part, we don't. It's like giving a dog a little extra length to their leash. You can go a few more feet, but you're still chained in the same yard. And hungry dogs are never loyal.

That's why they have us—Lords going through initiation—take out the ones who have chewed through them and managed to get away.

A man catches my attention as he walks up to them. He gives the redhead a hug and then kisses the brunette I've been watching on the cheek before he makes his way through the crowd. I follow him with my eyes, watching him talk to a few men here and there before he disappears inside.

I look back at the brunette to see she's no longer where she was. Quickly scanning the deck, I don't see her in the crowd. She most likely went to get another glass of champagne.

Turning, I follow the man and make sure to keep my distance as I watch him shake a few more hands and stop to talk to a few more Lords. Everyone on this megayacht is the best of the best at what they do. The ones at the top.

The one-percenters who own the companies and allow you to survive on a day-to-day basis. Now, they're not looking out for you. They're definitely in it for the money. But if you die, they'll be out of business. So they're going to do the bare minimum to keep you satisfied.

We pull farther away from the crowd, making our way up a set of stairs. He pushes a door open, and I take a quick look to make sure no one sees me following him. I pull my cell from my pocket and send a text to the group chat before returning it.

Then I turn to open the door and step inside. He stands over at the sliding glass door that leads out to his balcony overlooking the dark water. We're close enough to shore that you can see the lights from the land across the way.

I undo the button on my suit jacket and pull it open, wrapping my hand around the handle of the gun.

"Beautiful, isn't she?" he speaks.

And since I'm the only one in his office with him, I guess I did a shitty job at trying to go unnoticed. The brunette had me off my game. I normally don't let pussy get in the way. But it's been so long, and she isn't the type of woman anyone can ignore. She's what a man dreams of—dress her up and show her off to your friends, make them jealous of what you have. And then take her home, tie her down, and make her your dirty little whore. Show her what it's like to be owned.

Pushing those thoughts from my head, I remove the gun and hold it down by my side.

He turns and picks up a glass and fills it with bourbon. "Like a drink?" he asks.

"No thanks," I answer.

He brings the glass to his lips and takes a sip before his blue eyes drop to the gun in my hand, resting against the side of my thigh. Setting the bourbon down, he gives me his back, turning to look out the windows once again. "We're all on borrowed time."

He knows I'm here to kill him. I'm not surprised. A Lord is always aware when he's fucked up—gone too far—and his time is over.

"Yeah." I indulge him in small talk. I feel my phone vibrate knowing it's the guys responding to my previous text. I told them I was handling mine on my own. They're probably searching for me as I stand in this room.

The man picks his drink back up, taking a sip, and smirks as I watch his reflection in the sliding glass door. Turning to face me once again, he throws back the rest of the drink before setting the glass down on the round table. Holding out both of his hands, he speaks. "Take care of her."

Stepping into him, I lift the gun, point it at his chest, and say, "We're going to burn it." And then I pull the trigger.

Chapter 4

INITIATION

HAIDYN

One of them
Senior year at Barrington University

I'm fucking melting. I'm shirtless and tied to a wooden post outside. I can feel the sun beating down on me. I've had a black hood over my head for quite some time now, and it makes it hard to breathe.

I'm sweating and breathing heavily.

The wooden post at my back digs into my exposed skin. My wrists are tied behind it, and there's a rope around my neck and another securing my ankles. They like to restrict movement as much as possible. They say it's for our safety, but I call bullshit. It's for them to humiliate us. Makes us vulnerable.

The smell of smoke fills the air, and I know we're getting closer.

The hood is yanked from my head, and I blink at the harsh sunlight. My three brothers and I are in the courtyard of Carnage. Each tied to our posts with a firepit in front of us.

"Lords," a man calls out, and I swallow against the rope tied around my neck.

He stands on the side of a firepit that has four branding irons in it. They're to mark us. Remind us for the rest of our lives who we are and where we belong. The Lords will own us as if they already don't.

"Today is the day that you take your oath. And with that oath comes great responsibility." He speaks louder than he needs to in order for his voice to carry to the Lords so the ones standing on the balconies can hear him.

They're not wearing their cloaks and masks today. They get to be seen as they welcome their new members to the society. We've earned our place at their table. I'd rather starve.

"As a Spade brother, you will be the ones who must punish those who disobey their oath. You will show them that we do not take our life for granted. You are their jury and executioner. Do you understand?"

"Yes, sir," the four of us say in unison.

I should be glad I've made it this far. *"It's an honor to serve the Lords,"* my father told me once, and I couldn't understand why I didn't share his enthusiasm.

The Lord nods and steps away from the firepit. The fire rages, and the smoke clouds around us, choking me almost as much as the rope secured around my neck.

My father steps in front of me, and I hate that a part of me has accomplished this much. "Haidyn Jamison Reeves, you have completed all your trials of initiation. Do you wish to proceed?"

Fuck no! But as I stand surrounded by my brothers, I answer, "I do, Father." I won't leave them. We're in this together. I take this oath for them and no one else.

His jaw is tight, and his chest bowed. "A Lord must be willing to go above and beyond for his title. He must show strength and have what it takes. If you fail your position as a Lord, your brother will take what you earned."

Dying at the hands of one of my brothers would be an honor that I know I won't deserve.

He turns and walks over to the firepit. I take the time to try and readjust myself in the tight ropes. Fuck, they're itchy, and the sun has me sweating so bad that it's making the rope burn.

Picking up a brand from the firepit, he turns back to me. "Gag him." He orders.

I open my mouth, knowing what's coming as someone pushes something rubber into my mouth from behind me. I bite down on it, getting ready for the inevitable. There's no going back after this. Not like that was ever an option.

"Haidyn Jamison Reeves." The bastard actually smiles as if he's proud of me. Like I'm a son he wants to claim. "Son..." He nods once. "Welcome to the Lords. For you shall reap the benefits of your sacrifice." Then, like a man willing to sacrifice his only heir for his own gain, he places the hot brand into my sweaty chest, giving me something that will remain on my skin until I rot in a shallow grave.

Part Two

FOUR YEARS LATER...

Shhh...

Chapter 5

INITIATION

ANNABELLE

One of them
Junior year at Barrington University

They say we live in a man's world. That if you're a woman, all you have going for you is what's between your legs.

I was born into a secret society that isn't any different. Even more so, really. The women are used and tossed around like we mean nothing. While the men are praised for knowing how to use their dicks.

It's sickening.

I'm not saying I'm out trying to change the world; I'm just trying to change mine. I want to know that kind of power. I want to have women and men fear me. Is it too much to ask that I get a fair chance to prove I can be useful other than in the bedroom?

The Lords have given me the chance. My mother told me not to waste it because I won't be given another one. Mistakes aren't tolerated in our world. If you screw up, you're dead. Life is too short to second-guess yourself. Know your worth and make others see it.

That's what I'm doing.

I'm sitting with a hood over my head, trying to calm my heavy breathing. I have to remind myself that if a Lord can do this, so can I.

This is what the Lords do to you—test you. I'm not fucking weak. I'm a woman who can take on anyone or anything, anywhere.

My hands are zip-tied behind my back. I can no longer feel my fingers.

Someone yanks the hood from my head. I try to blow the hair from my face so I can see, but the back of my neck is grabbed. I'm pushed forward, doubled over where I sit, and the zip tie cut. The hand fists my hair, causing me to cry out as I'm yanked to my feet and shoved forward.

I groan as my hips hit something hard, and I flip my hair back to see it's the Lords altar. I clench and unclench my hands as they begin to tingle—the circulation coming back to my fingers.

My heart pounds in my chest as I slowly turn around to see I'm at the Lords cathedral. It's tucked in the middle of the Pennsylvania woods and serves multiple purposes for the secret society. I'd been here once with my father back when I was younger.

I was sick to my stomach when I left with him because of what I saw. *This time will be different.*

The old wooden pews are lined with Lords. All dressed in their cloaks and masks—white with black lines throughout making it appear to be cracked with black circles around the eyes and matching lips. My legs begin to shake nervously, my throat closing on me.

Breathe, Annabelle. Lift your chin, push out your tits, and give them a smile. Show your teeth before you rip their throats out.

A noise gets my attention, and I spin around to look up at the second-floor balcony. I take a few steps back to the center of the aisle and stand between the third row of pews to get a better view. Someone sits in a chair, wrists tied to the armrests and ankles secured to the legs. She's naked and has a hood over her head. By the sound of her muffled screams, I can tell she's gagged underneath it.

"Annabelle Schults." A Lord calls out my name, and I see him standing from the first pew. "Do you choose to accept your initiation?"

Squaring my shoulders, I swallow the knot in my throat. "I do, my Lord."

His mask nods. "Then you know what to do."

I wait for him to give me further instructions because I have no fucking clue. But instead, I nod and walk over to one of the staircases, making my way to the upper floor. My eyes drop to the baptism pool where the Lords hold their ritual for the vow ceremony, and I see it's currently drained of all the water.

Seniors who attend Barrington University get to fuck in there to prove they're men. I think it's pathetic and barbaric. But it confirms that they made it. So if I have to spread my legs to get ahead in this world dominated by men, then I'll fucking do it. How hard can it be? It's just sex.

Coming up to the chair, I walk around the woman, taking everything in. She already has visible bruises on her pale skin. Her wrists are bleeding from how tight the zip ties are. Her hands are blue from lack of circulation. I see a tattoo on her inner thigh, but it's hard to make out...multiple vertical lines in a row. I've never seen one like it before.

I wonder what she did to end up here, but I can't ask. You follow orders, and that's it. A small rolling cart sits next to her, and it has items placed on a blue napkin.

Scissors, a knife, and a stapler. A small red jug that can only be filled with gasoline sits on the floor next to the metal chair.

"Find her brand," someone calls out, and my head snaps up to look down at the pews below. The Lord who spoke before remains standing, but they always have a distorted voice so you don't recognize them. As if I would know them personally. Thousands of Lords exist around the world, and they're multiplying like rats every day, considering how much they like to fuck.

My eyes drop back to the woman, and I see it peeking out from underneath the overly large hood that covers her head and parts of her upper back. I lift the heavy fabric just enough to see the Lords brand—a circle with three parallel lines through the center. Weird, why would she have it? Only Lords are given those. Unless she belonged to a Lord, and he branded her. That's another thing about Lords—they like to mark what's theirs. Whether they carve it into their women or tattoo it, it's all the same. You're his whore for life, even if he chooses to pass you around to his friends. You'll always be returned to whoever owns you.

Clearing my throat, I call out loudly, "I see it." I'm already a minority here. If you want to be seen, you have to be heard.

Speak up, darling. No one can hear a whisper. That's what my father used to tell me.

The mask below nods. "Either cut it off or give yourself one in the same place."

My eyes widen, and she starts thrashing in the chair.

"You have five minutes." The Lord takes his seat in the first pew.

My hands instantly start to sweat, and my knees begin to shake. I'm trying to catch my breath and not look so weak in front of all these Lords. If I show any weakness, I'll be the next one naked and strapped to a chair.

It's always you or them. I refuse to let it be me.

I rub my hands down my jeans and grab the knife. Even though it's small, it feels heavy in my hand. She's screaming and shaking the chair, but it's bolted down so she can't tip it over.

Grabbing the back of her hood, I shove her head forward, and she fights me, trying to straighten it, knowing what I'm about to do.

Without another thought, I press the tip of the knife to her skin and begin to cut through the brand, ignoring the way she sobs as her blood covers my hands.

It's harder than it looks. Or they made sure the blade was dull for this very reason. I feel bone as I dig too deep, and once I can grab the skin, I cut the rest off as fast as I can.

I walk over to the edge of the balcony and toss the blood-covered skin down to the first floor. It lands at the Lords feet, and his mask looks down at it before it looks back up at me. "Now kill her."

My stomach drops at his words. Why didn't they let me kill her first? Why make her suffer? It's me they want to make suffer. She's the one who's bleeding, but they want me to live with the knowledge I've killed someone.

They set you up. It's how they own you. She fucked up and must pay for her sins. On the other hand, I will have to live with her blood on my hands until they order someone else to kill me someday.

I turn to face the hooded woman once more, and I can hear her gasping for breath around her gag. She's sweating profusely and shaking. Blood runs down her bony shoulders, small breasts, and anorexic stomach. Even in our world, we're always told to look their version of perfect.

We're groomed to be whores but never give it up willingly. Men give us crumbs, and we're expected to survive off that. They prepare us to be thankful for the bare minimum.

How does a woman thrive when she's kept in the dark and never watered? What these Ladies don't understand is that we only have ourselves. I can only rely on myself.

Walking back over to her, I drop my eyes to the cart once more, and I see a gun lying in the lower basket.

I pick it up. *It'll be quick.* I go to pull back the slide, but it's harder than I thought it'd be. My father had guns. Hell, he was always packing. I grew up around them, and he took me to shoot. But I've never just picked up a gun and pointed it at a person before. Taking in a deep breath, I yank it back and see there's a bullet chambered. I walk behind her and face my audience below. Pressing the end of the barrel to the back of her head, I keep my eyes open and on her trembling body as I pull the trigger, knowing they're watching me.

The gunshot echoes through the large cathedral as her head hangs forward, and I feel my soul leave my body. She's dead, and so is a part of myself. I no longer have one. I just sold it in exchange for I don't know what. And deep down, I know it wasn't worth it.

Trying to catch my breath, I make my way over to the stairs to leave, but I pause when I watch as the Lord who gave me the orders stands and so does the one sitting next to him, and then the one next to him.

I take a step back, my legs now shaking for another reason. My eyes go to the dead woman in the chair—it wasn't messy. She's covered in blood, but it's more from removing her brand than shooting her in the head. It was straight through. An extra thin line of blood drips from the hood and onto the floor now that she's hunched over.

I tell myself that they're just coming to get her. To dispose of her body in the cemetery behind the cathedral—where all members who betray their oath are buried. But that voice in the back of my mind says I messed up, and they're coming up here for me.

The three Lords split up. The first takes the stairs to the right, and the other two take the staircase to the left. Slowly, they make their way up to the balcony, and I place the gun on the cart so they don't think I'm going to shoot them.

The two on the left make it to the balcony first. They both come to stand behind me. "On your knees," one of them orders.

I want to run, but my legs give out at the order, and I do exactly as they say, kneeling in front of the baptism pool.

The one who gave the orders comes up beside me and grabs a pair of handcuffs off the cart that I hadn't noticed before. He tosses them to one of the guys standing behind me. "Cuff her."

Before I can say anything, someone slams a foot into my back. Pressing my face to the bloody floor, he smashes my bent legs underneath me, making it harder to breathe. My arms are grabbed behind my back where they cuff them. Then my shirt is ripped and quickly removed from my body. Even though I'm sweating, I shiver at the thought of being so defenseless in front of all these men.

I bite my inner cheek when my hair is fisted, and I'm yanked to sit up in nothing but my bra and bloody jeans as the Lords from below watch. I have a quick thought that at least the baptism pool is empty because I'd rather die by a bullet than drown.

The one calling the shots comes to stand in front of me, and I glare up at him, refusing to let the tears that sting my eyes fall. I will not look weak in front of them.

"You took a brand. Now you've earned one."

The blood rushes in my ears at his words, knowing exactly what's coming. Was that a test? The fact that I hurt her instead of taking the brand myself? If so, I failed.

I close my eyes and try to calm my breathing so I don't pass the fuck out when I hear a blowtorch turn on behind me, heating the branding iron.

This is what you wanted, Annabelle. To be one of them. To be accepted into their fucking cult.

Not every woman in our world gets this opportunity. We're only good for spreading our fucking legs and reproducing. I get to be more than that.

I was raised to understand that the Lords will give you whatever you want. You just have to be willing to give yourself for it.

So be it.

Chapter 6

Haidyn

"Haidyn?"

I look up from my desk at the blonde standing in our office—Saint, Kashton, and I have been running this place for almost four years now. After our fathers passed, it was handed over to us. Well, I guess handed isn't the correct word. We had to undergo "training" to do what we were born to have. The Lords felt we weren't ready to take over this prison. It was a way to punish us. See just how far they could push us. The Lords are notorious for trying to break you.

Her brown eyes tell me everything I need to know. She's been standing there for quite some time, and she's irritated that I chose to ignore her.

She glances at her watch. "We were supposed to start thirty minutes ago."

"I'm busy."

She looks over at Kashton as he sits at his desk across from mine, and he shrugs. What does she expect him to do? He's not my fucking keeper.

"Haidyn—"

"I told you last time you were here and the time before that. You're fired, Lana." I stand from my desk, and she takes a step back, her hand going to her chest as if I'm going to pounce on her. Fuck her or kill her —I'm not sure which one would scare her more.

"The Lords—"

"Tell the Lords that I said they can fuck themselves," I say with a smile.

She gasps, and Kashton rolls his eyes. Lana would never hurt a fly. The woman is in her early fifties and hates her life as a Lady. She's done something to piss the Lords off, and they've put her here for me to fuck with her. Sucks to be her.

The diamond on her left hand tells me she's married to a Lord at the bottom of the totem pole—not a very powerful one but a Lord, nonetheless. So here she is doing her part for the society, and I'm making it difficult. I truly don't give a fuck.

"I'm here to do my job." She speaks softly as if I'm going to yell at her.

I'm not in the mood for that shit today. I just want to be left alone. Meeting her stare, I add, "You have five seconds to get the fuck out of my sight."

She doesn't need to be told twice. She spins around, exits the office, and slams the door behind her.

Kashton shakes his head, chuckling. "You know they'll send someone else."

I tune him out like usual. Life didn't go how it was supposed to. Things went to hell years ago. It only took one woman to fuck everything up. Well, it wasn't her fault. It was mine. But you know what they say—every story worth telling starts with a girl.

Ashtyn Lane Price was the one who changed our paths.

I have secrets that I vowed to take to my grave. I never thought I'd deceive my *brothers*, but it was my only option. Plus, Saint kept a big one from us that I'm sure Kashton doesn't know about.

The door opens, and Saint rushes in. Going over to his desk, he plops down and starts typing on his computer. I exit the office, wanting to be alone. I've always liked my space, which is hard to get as a Lord. You live at the house of Lords for four years while attending Barrington University. After graduation, Lords get to go their separate ways except for us. The Spade brothers all live together at Carnage.

This is our prison. We're chained to this hell. No matter what we do, we'll die here, and we'll be buried here. It's the life the Lords chose for the four of us even though we're down to three already.

I make my way down to the basement. It's my church, in a sense, and where I go to pray. Not to God because I don't believe. But it can be spiritual.

My father thought he had planned my future, but I refused to give him what he wanted.

Senior year at Barrington

We're closing in on the ritual—the vow ceremony that consists of us finally getting to fuck a woman in front of others to show that we have successfully done our part to become Lords.

It's a rite of passage, they say. The senior Lords have served three years of celibacy, and the women are ready to give themselves to us.

The brand is so fresh it rubs against my shirt with every move I make walking down the stairs at my parents' house. I'm going to meet my brothers at a party tonight. I see the door to my father's office cracked.

"She's ready," a male's voice says from inside the room. I know it well and grew up around it. It belongs to one of my father's brothers.

"You sure?" my father asks.

"Absolutely." He scoffs as if second-guessing him is an insult. "Her mother doesn't think so, but I know the truth. Plus, that therapist of hers is a nutcase."

"You're the one who wanted to do business with her." My father chuckles, and I frown. Who are they talking about?

Clearing my throat, I push the door open and step inside his office to see my father sitting behind his desk and Mr. Price relaxing on the couch.

"Haidyn." My father smiles, gesturing to one of the high-back chairs. "Have a seat. We're discussing your future."

Of course, he is. I have no say in my life. If the Lords don't control me, my father does. It's always been this way, and it will continue to go on like this until he dies. That day can't come soon enough.

"You have three weeks before the ritual," my father reminds me.

I want to roll my eyes but refrain. He acts like I don't know how this works. Like I could ever forget I have to take a chosen at the vow ceremony.

"Ashtyn—"

"I'm not choosing her." I interrupt my father.

He looks over at Mr. Price—Ashtyn's father—then back at me. "Son..."

"She doesn't belong to me." Do I want her? No. I've grown up with Ashtyn Lane Price. Our fathers are both Spade brothers. But one of my brothers is in love with her. I can't take her from him. I consider her to be one of my best friends, and things will change if I claim her as mine. And although I hate my life, I love my brothers. I would never do them wrong or betray them, and stealing his girl would be unforgivable in their eyes.

"She belongs to whoever I give her to," Mr. Price states.

"Let me tell you something, boy." My father stands from his desk, buttoning his suit jacket. "You take whatever we want. There is no 'she doesn't belong to me' bullshit. Do you hear me?"

"I don't want her," I say through gritted teeth and look at Mr. Price. "Saint wants her. He can have her."

"No. We have a deal." My father shakes his head. "She's important...which makes you important."

Whatever the fuck that means. It's not changing my mind. Walking over to his desk, I place my hands on the surface and say, "I don't care what kind of deal you've made with him; I will not take her as my chosen." I push off the surface and turn to Mr. Price. He too is now standing. "Make a new deal with Saint. He'll do anything for her." And with that, I exit the office, slamming the door behind me.

I love Ashtyn in a way that even I can't explain. Have I imagined fucking her? Of course, but that's bound to happen when you've been deprived of any sexual activity for three years. I've seen her almost every day of my life. But I'm also a horny bastard. Hell, I went home yesterday and jerked off to a woman who I saw at the gas station because I could see her pink thong peeking out of the top of her jeans.

I'm only human.

If I had my way, I wouldn't take on a chosen at all. I'd rather not get sentenced to fuck one woman. I've seen other Lords do it over the past three years, and it always comes with problems. Just one more thing I don't want to have to deal with. That sounds selfish, but Lords are trained to put themselves first. A woman is nothing more than a toy to use.

The ritual confirms that. We strip a woman naked, tie her to a Lords altar, and fuck her in front of others to prove we are men to the society. She has to bleed for us. A Spade brother only accepts the best—a virgin.

Other Lords get to choose which hole they want to fuck. And she doesn't have to be a virgin. If I was given the choice, I'd pick the ass. There's just something about a woman's ass that gets me off. Any woman can spread her legs, virgin or not. But to bend over and put her ass up in the air, while begging you to fuck it, that takes a different type of woman. Especially since most don't want to do it. They find it dirty, degrading, and taboo.

I PULL MYSELF OUT OF THAT MEMORY. IT DIDN'T MATTER THEN, and it doesn't matter now. She never belonged to me, and I never wanted her.

Making my way off the elevator, I remove the keys from my pocket and approach one of the many cells we have down here. The Lord sits with his back against the wall, his knees pulled up to his chest.

When I turn on the light, he closes his eyes. I smile, in the mood to get bloody. "Good morning," I say, pulling my cell out of my pocket and picking a song. As "Hallelujah" by No Resolve begins to play, my body relaxes. It's my go-to song when I'm in the mood to fuck shit up.

Shhh...

Chapter 7

Annabelle

I sit at a round table with my girlfriends on a gloomy Sunday. We return to Barrington next week for the second half of our junior year. I went through initiation at the beginning of the school year, and it's been heavy on my mind. I hate to say how much sleep I've lost over what I did. I thought I could handle anything they threw at me, but I see that naked woman every time I close my eyes. It's been five months now, and it hasn't gotten any easier.

Hannah gets my attention as she laughs. It's for show. I love her to death, but everything about her is fake. And I'm not talking about what you can physically see. I mean everything else. The part of her that she hides from the world.

She hates her husband. He's a Lord. She was his chosen, and they were forced to marry when he knocked her up. She swears that the baby might not even be his, considering the night of conception lines up with the fuck-fest weekend when he passed her around to his friends. But their parents didn't care. It's whatever you make it look like to the world, not what it really is. I'm not sure what they expected to happen. He wasn't letting her take birth control, and he didn't have his friends use condoms. That's how a baby is made.

He flew her to the Bahamas, had a lavish proposal set up, and made sure someone recorded it all. She posted it on social media the following day with the typical *I SAID YES* post. It was followed with a hundred photos of the trip showing off the happy couple, kissing on the beach, cuddling in the infinity pool, and sharing romantic dinners.

She's gorgeous in a supermodel runway way, and he's hot in that "I wear loafers, drive a Rolls Royce, and work for Daddy" kind of way. They look like real-life Barbie and Ken except they hate one another.

He cheats on her every chance he gets, and she fucks his friends behind his back. A Lord can do whatever and whoever he wants, married or not. But a Lady? She has rules. If he caught her...well, I don't even want to think about what he'd do to her. But then again, maybe he knows and doesn't care. To each their own.

His best friend has a breeding kink, and since Hannah is currently four months pregnant, she meets up with him almost daily and lets him pretend he's the one who knocked her up. Which might actually be true since he was one of the many that her Lord let fuck her that weekend. *Who knows.*

"Were you even listening to what I just said?" she asks, setting down her water.

I nod, eyes meeting hers. "Mm-hmm." *Lie.*

"Then what did I say?" She arches a perfectly shaped dark brow.

"You said that you and your mother-in-law are fighting over where the baby shower will be," Margaret answers.

Hannah narrows her eyes at her. "Thank you, *Annabelle,* for answering." She calls Margaret by my name because she asked me, not her.

"You're welcome." Margaret smiles, picking up her coffee.

"Why are you letting her decide?" I join in on the conversation. "She's not the one going to give birth."

She rubs her growing stomach. "I swear she would if she could, which is creepy. I've never known a woman so obsessed with her son."

"He's a mama's boy. What did you expect?" Margaret laughs.

Margaret is also married. But she and Clint don't want to kill one another. I wouldn't call it love, but he knows she sleeps around and doesn't care. She was also his chosen. Their marriage was already arranged before the ritual even took place. He proposed on her father's yacht after the vow ceremony, and they married the following month. Clint thinks they're trying to get pregnant, but she's still taking the pill behind his back. She's not ready to become a mom. Her words. I give her three months before he figures it out.

Then there's me, midway through my junior year at Barrington. I'm twenty-one, single, and still a virgin. My parents didn't want me to be a chosen. I can't say that I cared either way. Saving myself isn't something that I care about. My mother said I was meant for something greater than spreading my legs in a tub of water for all to see. I know how the ritual works, and although I didn't mind participating, I also didn't really see a bad side to it.

I accepted long ago that I'll live in a loveless marriage to a bastard who will cheat on me and probably pass me around like a piece of cake at a wedding. Some women would be terrified by that thought, but I'm not.

If I can't have love, I want power. I want what a man in our world gets, but I'm going to have to work twice as hard for it because I have a pussy and tits. Fine by me. I'll show them that I can do whatever they throw at me with a smile on my face while bleeding between my legs.

My cell rings, and I pick it up off the table where it sits next to my mimosa. **UNKNOWN** lights up the screen.

"Sorry, I have to take this." I get up and rush outside, hitting answer. "Hello?"

"You have been given your assignment," the voice announces. It's altered so I can't make out who it is. Not like I'd be able to anyway. No one knows who is ever actually in charge. There are rumors, of course, but you can't believe everything you hear.

"Okay." I'm excited and nervous. I've been waiting for this call since I completed my initiation back in August. "What do I need to do?"

"A package has been delivered to your house. You will have three months to prepare before the official assignment begins." The voice continues. "During that time, you will get a new life."

I frown. "A new life?" I figured it would be a quick "kill this person and you're in" type of situation. That's what I get for assuming. The Lords always like to throw curveballs at you.

"New identity. New friends, new occupation. And...a boyfriend."

What the fuck do the Lords have me doing? Why does any of that matter? "O-okay."

"You will remain untouched."

"Wait." I give a rough laugh. "You want me to get a boyfriend but not put out?" Another laugh, thinking I heard him wrong. The Lords world revolves around sex. It's literally all they think about and want.

It's not their fault. It's what we've all been conditioned for. "He won't stay around long." I'm not dumb. I know how relationships work and what men expect. Hell, I'm horny all the time. I'd like to get fucked, but the Lords hold power in sex. They tell you when you can get it and who you get it from.

"*He* likes to ruin his toys," the voice says cryptically.

Ruin his toys? Is he telling me that I have to fuck someone? "Who?" I wonder.

"Three months, Annabelle. If you don't have everything ready to go within that time, you have failed." *Click.*

HAIDYN

"SKELETON LORDS" by HALLOW fills the small concrete room from my phone while the Lord lies on the floor, covered in his own blood, but he's not dead. That's not what we do here.

Death is a luxury we don't supply.

Exiting the cell, I lock him inside and go over to the sink in the corner. I turn on the water and begin to wash his blood off my hands and ink-covered arms.

The sound of someone coming has me looking over my shoulder to see Kashton joining me. Turning off the water, I grab some paper towels and turn to face him.

He's got his head down, staring at the empty pits recessed in the concrete floor while rubbing the back of his neck. Kashton has always been the most expressive out of the four of us. He can't hide how he's feeling. "What's on your mind?" I ask. If he's down here, he wants to talk about something.

"Saint just got a call," he says, and my heart picks up, hoping it's not what I think it's about.

For almost four years, I've lived on pins and needles while Saint has continued to look for Ashtyn, and I've kept quiet. I made a friend a promise.

"And?" I question when he doesn't elaborate.

"And they found a woman...she was restrained with barbwire, and her throat was slit."

"What do they want us to do about it?" I ask.

His eyes meet mine, and he looks hopeful. "It reminded me of our meeting at the house of Lords back when..." He pauses. "Do you think it's Adam?"

Senior year at Barrington

"Over five months last year, twenty girls went missing. Five of those were found raped and murdered," the man tells us—me, Saint, Adam, and Kashton sit down in the basement at the house of Lords. Lincoln called us in for a meeting while we were at the party tonight. We had to wait for Saint to arrive because he had to take home a drunk Ashtyn—Adam's twin sister.

"The other fifteen?" I ask, scanning the picture of a naked woman that he gave us. She's covered in blood. Her head hangs off the side of a bed. Her throat was slit, her ankles tied with barbed wire, and her wrists bound behind her back with barbed wire. Whoever did this to her made her suffer. They must think a Lord did it. But we're not the only sick bastards out there.

"Still missing," the man answers my question.

Adam slams his folder down. "What does this have to do with us?"

"Did they attend Barrington?" Kashton questions before he can answer Adam.

"No." He looks at Kashton. "All were still in high school—seniors—but none of the five were connected to one another. As far as we can tell, they didn't know the Lords existed."

"The ones who are still missing?" Saint questions.

He shakes his head. "Not that we have found."

"I'm with Adam," Lincoln adds, scanning the folder Adam put on the table. "What does this have to do with them?"

"Adam didn't kill anyone." I shake my head, answering his previous question. "Not an innocent woman anyway." We've all got a body count. Just as many kills as we have fucks.

But someone tried to set our brother up, which resulted in his mother being killed and Ashtyn almost dead. Adam's been gone ever since.

"Then why did he leave us?" His soft voice sounds like a little boy asking a mother why his father left. Four years have passed, and Kashton can't seem to accept that our brother isn't coming back.

"You'll have to ask him that." I shrug, knowing the truth, but it's not my story to tell.

He sighs, and we hear the elevator ding, letting us know Saint is about to join us. He storms into the room a moment later. He looks pissed off as usual.

Things changed after Adam left. We took Ashtyn in to protect her, but it was beyond our control by that point.

"What else did they have to say?" Kashton asks Saint.

"They think Adam is in town," he says through gritted teeth.

"He's not—"

"I don't believe he did it either, Haidyn, but you have to admit it looks bad." Kashton interrupts me.

I run my hands through my hair, wanting to scream. I know where Adam is, and he's nowhere fucking close to here at the moment. He's in Las Vegas, where he belongs, but I can't say that. "It's never as it seems," I argue.

Saint snorts. "Yeah, well, until he shows his fucking face, I'm going to assume he's fucking us all over."

Shhh...

Chapter 8

Annabelle

I immediately left the café after my call from the Lord. I didn't even tell my friends that I was going. Pulling into my driveway, I see a box on my front porch. I stop my SUV, get out, and pick it up. Taking it inside, I place it on my kitchen table and open it. It has a laptop, cell phone, Apple watch, and a wallet. Going through it, I find an ID with a new name and birthday on it, but my address is the same. What the fuck is that going to do for me? I feel like I'm going into the witness protection program.

Opening the laptop, I turn it on to see they've given me a new email address to go with my new identity, and I have one in my inbox. In the subject line is **HAIDYN JAMISON REEVES**.

Clicking on it, I read over the information listed in the email.

HAIDYN JAMISON REEVES. Inbox ×

UNKNOWN
to me

Status: Active Lord

Occupation: Spade brother

Residence: Carnage

Parents: Deceased

Chosen: Sierra Ronan

Lady: Denied

Reply Forward

That's it. They didn't give me a birthdate or age. He has to be at least twenty-two because he's an active Lord. That means he finished all three years of initiation while attending Barrington—he wears the Lord's brand. But that also means he could be fifty for all I know.

I don't know much about Carnage, though. I've heard of it, but the Lords keep it under wraps for the most part.

What the fuck does denied mean for Lady? Does that mean that the Lords have denied him a wife, or he denied her? I've never heard of that before. Every Lord has to take a Lady as far as I'm concerned. They have to reproduce. If they don't give back, then they're useless.

Scrolling to the bottom of the email, I click on the attachment. It's a slideshow of pictures. The first one is of a guy on a blacked-out motorcycle. You can't see his face because he's wearing a helmet. But he's got a black T-shirt on with the sleeves cut off, ripped jeans, and combat boots. He's sitting at a stoplight, glove-covered hands resting on his thighs and both boots on the ground, waiting for the light to turn green. He looks tall even sitting on the bike. His arms are ripped as the sun beats down on them, showing off his veins.

The next is of the same man leaning up against a car. This time, there's snow on the ground. Too much for him to even be driving the white McLaren Sabre if you ask me. He's wearing a black leather jacket over a white T-shirt, denim jeans, and combat boots. A black pair of Aviators cover his eyes, but you can get a better look at his face. Sharp jaw, clean-shaven, dark hair spiked on top and shaved on the sides.

The next picture is the same with him and his car, but he's now standing with his back to the camera as he opens the passenger door for a woman. She's dressed in a glittery silver miniskirt and six-inch heels. Her black top has a deep V cut, showing off a large, fake chest.

She's a prostitute. It's the only thing that makes sense due to how she's dressed in the middle of the day with an inch of snow on the ground. He's parked on a corner in what looks to be an abandoned area, and two other women stand farther down in the photo dressed just like her.

The next is of him and three other guys with a girl. She stands in the middle with a bottle of vodka in one hand and a cell in the other. One guy stands behind her with his hand around her neck as she looks down at the camera. Haidyn stands to her left.

I scoot forward, enlarging the picture of him. It's the first one that has a clear shot of his face. His eyes are a pretty blue—like the ocean. It's also the first one that he's smiling in. Straight white teeth and a perfectly lined nose. He's clean-shaven and has a cigarette tucked behind his right ear. He's wearing a long-sleeved T-shirt with the sleeves bunched up around his elbows and a pair of jeans. He's the tallest one out of them all. If I passed him on the street, I'd definitely turn around to watch him walk away.

The next has me blinking. It's him, but it has to be the most recent because he's now covered in tats. And blood. He's got a knife in one hand. Blood drips down it and onto his ripped jeans. His black combat boots stand in a puddle of it as well. His tatted knuckles grip the handle of the knife. Ink covers both arms and chest. He's got a nose ring, and he's shirtless, showcasing his defined bloody abs and deep V.

"Fuck me," I whisper.

What the fuck do they expect me to do with him? Especially a Spade brother? From what I know, they're the devils of hell. The rumors are that Carnage is where the Lords send those who betray their oaths.

Now, from what I grew up believing—Lords who betrayed their oath—was that they were taken to the cathedral and put through what the Lords call confessional. They're tied down to the Lords altar and tortured until they confess what they did wrong, then they're blessed with a bullet in their heads. But as I got older, I overheard my mom and stepdad talking about the Spade brothers. My stepdad had a friend who betrayed his oath and was sent there back when they attended Barrington. My mother assures him that his best friend must be dead by now, but my stepdad doesn't agree. He said Lords don't go there to die. They go to pay for what they did wrong, which means more torture. Typical Lord. Always wanting to make you bleed for the littlest things.

Blood, blood, and more blood until you have nothing else to give them. They enjoy sucking the life out of you. That's why I plan on giving them whatever I must. These Lords want you to go above and beyond and show them what you're worth. The Lords don't give you more than they want you to have. That way, they can hold it over your head or take it away when they decide you no longer need it.

Those who have power were born at the top. And the rest are left to feed off the bottom.

I go on to the next, and it's of a luxurious black house sitting secluded back in the middle of the woods. It reminds me of a modern church. High peak rooftops that look like steeples and a lot of glass windows. Three stories tall and a wraparound porch. Even the outside furniture is black with white pillows. It's gorgeous. The same white McLaren Sabre in the first photo with Haidyn sits in the driveway, but no one is around.

Is this his home? He's supposed to live at Carnage. Maybe it was his childhood home. It did say his parents are dead. He could have kept the house. Or maybe it's a weekend getaway? I guess he could be renting it, and this picture was taken while he was inside with the prostitute in the picture.

I wonder why a man like him needs to pay for sex. The women in our world fall at the Lords feet on any given day. Most want to become a Lady. The girls who attended Barrington do anyway. They want a lavish life with endless shopping sprees. Who cares if their husbands cheat on them? It just means they don't have to put out as much. Plus, higher-ranking Lords are placed with higher-ranking Ladies, so it's not like they're marrying down. We are raised and groomed from an early age to accept what our future holds. It's like anything else in this world —it's all we know.

A new email pops up, and I exit out of the one I'm in to open it. It's of me. A picture that was taken today while I was on my ***UNKNOWN*** call standing outside of the restaurant. Then below is outlined like Haidyn's was.

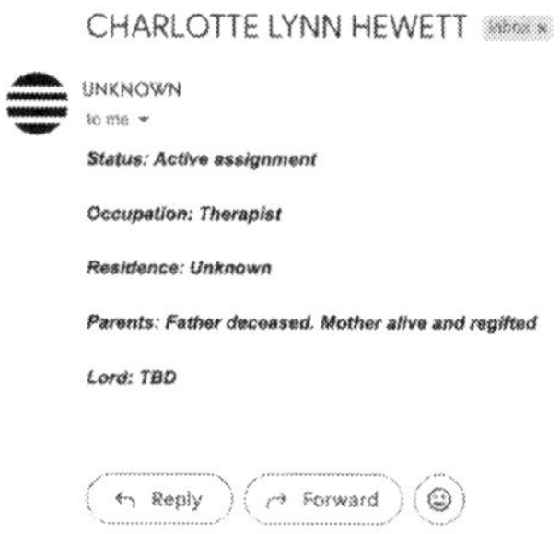
CHARLOTTE LYNN HEWETT Inbox ×

UNKNOWN
to me

Status: Active assignment

Occupation: Therapist

Residence: Unknown

Parents: Father deceased. Mother alive and regifted

Lord: TBD

Reply Forward

I read over it again, wondering what the fuck I'm going to do. A *therapist*? I know nothing about that shit. And *Charlotte*? I sound like an elementary school teacher. I've always hated the name Annabelle. I asked my mother why she named me after a doll that haunts and kills people. She told me it was after her and her best friend…but Charlotte isn't much better if you ask me.

Closing the laptop, I sit back and slump in the chair, trying to wrap my brain around what to do now. I have three months to make a new life, find new friends, and get a boyfriend—who doesn't want to fuck me. This is going to be harder than I thought. Can't I just kill someone instead?

Opening it back up, I type out a response.

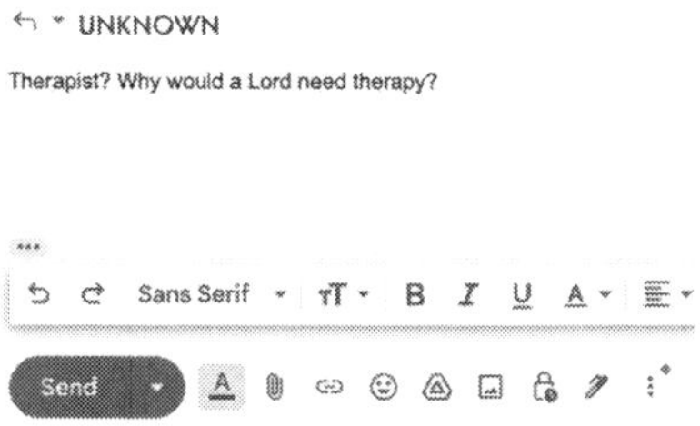
UNKNOWN

Therapist? Why would a Lord need therapy?

Sans Serif

Send

And press send. Chewing on my nails, I stare at the screen,

waiting for a reply. Maybe it's just a cover, and I'm not actually his therapist. That would make more sense, but still...

I have a response and open it.

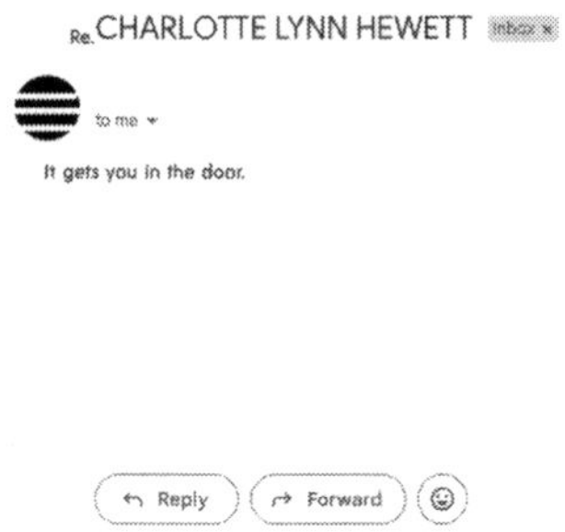

I send the reply. My new phone rings a moment later.

"Hello?" I answer the **UNKNOWN** call.

"Carnage," the altered voice growls in greeting.

"Carnage?" I ask.

"He's a Spade brother," he barks at me as if I haven't read the emails he sent. "Look...you either take the assignment or walk away. That's your choice."

"Yes, of course." I sit up straighter before he can hang up on me. "I...just—am I not allowed to have questions?" I need a little more information than what he's given me, and I don't think I'm asking for the impossible.

"No," he replies. "You have three months to change your life. If you don't get it done, then we'll decide for you."

Click.

HAIDYN

Senior year at Barrington

THE VOW CEREMONY IS QUICKLY APPROACHING, AND MY FATHER IS on my ass. He's mad because I refused to choose my best friend's girl.

No amount of money or power will make me betray Saint like that.

I pull up to my father's house and make my way inside. He spends most of his time at Carnage, so I'm surprised he's here. I already know he's in his office. His doors are closed, but I enter without knocking. He's expecting me.

Entering, I see him sitting behind his desk, a glass of brandy in one hand and a pen in the other, as if he's just signed a deal. "Son." He gets to his feet, motioning me to come have a seat.

I cross my arms over my chest and say nothing.

He gestures to a man who sits on the couch to the left. I immediately know he's a Lord by the way he's dressed and sits there like he fucking owns the world. We're all conditioned to have that mentality.

"I have a proposition for you." The man stands and buttons his suit jacket.

"I'm not interested," I say, stopping him before he goes too far. If my dad is involved, then I want nothing to do with it. Turning, I give them both my back and go to walk out.

"Haidyn," my father growls. "You're lucky I was able to find another one."

I spin back around to face them. "Another what?" I demand, but of course the bastard ignores me and looks at the other Lord. Women are a dime a dozen in our world, so I'm not sure why he's acting like they're limited.

"Let me introduce myself." The guy steps toward me with his right hand out. "I'm…"

"I'm not interested," I repeat, stopping him. I'm not dumb. This man has made some kind of deal with my father, and they both think they can fuck me over. It's not going to happen.

I've done things ordered by the Lords, and until they tell me I have to take this bullshit deal my father is trying to lock me into, it's not going to happen.

Once you get an order, you don't negotiate with them. One day, my time will be up, and the Lords will call for my death, and it will be granted.

I wouldn't say I have a death wish, but I'm not afraid to die.

"Haidyn," my father snaps, slamming his hand down on his desk.

"Sorry you wasted your time," I say, giving the Lord my back. I walk out of the house, not caring if I just pissed off my father or what it cost him.

It's been three months since I fired Lana. And I've been assigned a new therapist. The Lords have ordered me to talk to someone. They act like words fucking matter. They don't. Not in our world. Actions are what make a Lord. You show up, and you do what you're told.

So I sit here in a room at Carnage on the seventh floor, watching the rainfall from the floor-to-ceiling windows. It's been this way for days. I like it, though.

Saint and Kashton are somewhere around, probably down in the basement. Saint lost his mind the day he woke up from Ashtyn shooting him. Kashton tries to hide everything with sarcasm and a knife. Me? I just don't give a fuck. Life is boring. It's the same ole thing every day. Torture and kill. Then repeat. There's no thrill like there used to be.

Where's the challenge? We don't have assignments like other Lords. We run Carnage. Lords are brought in; we initiate them and then place them in a cell to play with later.

My life is missing something, and I'm not sure what it is. But I know it's something that I've never had before. I'm itching to find it.

A door opening behind me has me shoving my hands in the pockets of my jeans when Jessie announces, "Miss Charlotte Hewett, sir."

A soft, "Thank you," follows as I'm guessing he holds the door open for her. Jessie is a gentleman above all. The only one who exists in this prison.

It closes, and I turn around to see a woman bent over the desk to my left. She rummages through a Louis Vuitton bag, oblivious that I'm standing right here.

And a smile tugs at my lips because I've seen her before. It's been years, but I'd never forget her face. She was on the yacht. The girl in the white dress—little Miss Priss. This may be my lucky day, after all.

I clear my throat, and she spins around with a gasp. "Haidyn," she breathes, and my cock instantly hardens. Women see it as a compliment. It's not. My cock stays this way. Fucking is my therapy. Making others feel pain makes me feel better.

I know it's not fair, but I also don't give a fuck. If a woman is willing to crawl into bed with me, then she better be prepared to get fucked—in more ways than one.

She's younger than the other therapists I've had. Chocolate-brown hair pulled tight and secured in a perfect bun at the nape of her delicate neck. I can tell by the blush on her cheeks that she's embarrassed just to be in the room with me. It just furthers the point of my first impression of her—she's too good for me. A woman who probably prefers missionary and doesn't like to mess up her perfect hair or makeup. I bet she'd look even better crying with her face covered with my cum.

Straightening her already straight pencil skirt, she runs her hands down it nervously. "Good afternoon, Haidyn. I'm Charlotte." She walks toward me in a pair of black—very short and professional—high heels, holding out her right hand. "It's great to meet you." Coming to a stop in front of me, she tilts her head up and takes a deep breath for courage when the most beautiful eyes I've ever seen finally meet my stare. They're a deep, dark blue and remind me of two sparkling sapphires.

She can't be over five three. A petite little thing. Like a doll. Or a toy. Either way, I'd chew her up and spit her out. I'm always up for a snack.

My eyes drop to her black button-up blouse, and I imagine ripping it open to see what her tits look like. They don't look to be on the large side, but I know how deceiving a shirt can be.

I cross my arms over my chest, and she drops her hand along with her smile. "Uh...shall we get started?" She steps back and points at the couch like I'm going to lie down and spill all my secrets to this bitch.

"You may leave." I turn and gesture toward the door.

Her dark brows pull together, and she shakes her head. "I'm sorry, but I can't do that." Turning her back to me, she returns to the desk, and I take the opportunity to look over at the pretty brunette.

Her modest heels only give her about an extra two inches, she has on a pair of pantyhose, and there's a short slit up the center of her skirt. My hands itch to rip it all the way off, remove her underwear, and shove them into her mouth while I press her tits to the window and fuck her ass. I bet she'd never let a man near it. Women like her don't like to be treated like a cheap whore. They want the boys who pretend to love them and tell them what they want to hear to get into their pants. I'll tell her she's a pretty whore while I make her crawl to me with a butt plug in her ass and a vibrator shoved up her cunt.

She grabs a notepad and sits down in the high-back chair. She crosses her legs and looks up at me. "The sooner we get started, the sooner I'll leave you alone, and you can get back to work."

I want to laugh at her but decide to play with her instead. I prefer my toys to be dirty. "Tell me about yourself, Charlotte." Did the Lords pick her because they know I've seen her before? I don't believe in coincidences.

"This isn't about me, Mr. Reeves," she says in a tone that tells me she's uncomfortable. The way she shifts in her seat also gives her away.

Mr. Reeves? Isn't that cute. How long before she starts calling me sir? "Then what is it about?" I dig.

"You were ordered by the Lords to seek therapy," she says matter-of-factly. "You've been through what? Four over the last two years?" she inquires, scanning some notes.

I look over her left hand and see no ring. She doesn't have a Lord.

Interesting. Women are married off very young in our world, which makes me question her age and ability to even be qualified for this job. "Five," I answer, not bothering to tell her the term is wrong.Did she not do her homework? Honestly, none of it matters.

"Are you taking any medications?"

I laugh at that, and she looks up, narrowing her blue eyes on mine. Then they drop back down to the notebook. "It says you've been prescribed zolpidem." Her eyes meet mine once again. "Are they helping you sleep?"

"I get plenty of sleep," Another lie.

I'm not one who requires a lot of it. Sleeping slows you down. I have to keep going because something always needs to be done. Plus, I'm not one who dreams. It's always just the past, and I don't like to live there.

"I brought you something..." She walks back over to her purse and pulls a small notebook out of it. "This is for you to keep a log of the hours you sleep. I'll check it at each visit." She smiles at me as she holds it out, but I make no move to take it from her. "Mr. Reeves—"

"We're done here, Charlotte." I interrupt whatever she was about to say and hold the door open.

She lets out a huff and grabs her bag off the desk. Throwing it over her shoulder, she walks toward me. "I'll see you at the same time, same day in two weeks."

"Charlotte?" I call out when she walks out of the room, and she turns to face me. I lean against the doorframe, and my eyes drop to her heels and slowly run up over her legs, thin waist, and chest, letting them linger. When my gaze meets hers, she swallows nervously.

I like the way her breathing picks up, so I slowly make my way toward her in the hallway. She tilts her head up, and I reach out, running the pad of my finger along the buttons on her button-up blouse, letting her know how vulnerable they are. I could rip it open at any second and shred the precious silk. Her pretty blue eyes are wide, and her pouty lips part, but she doesn't dare push me away. "Want me to tell you all my secrets?" I give her a threatening smile and go on. "The only way I'm going to talk to you is if you're naked and on your knees with a gag in your mouth."

She gasps, stepping back, and my hand drops to my side. Turning,

I give her my back and enter the room. I slam the door shut, knowing that the bitch won't show her face here again. No matter how much I want her to.

Shhh...

Chapter 9
Charlotte

I fall into the driver's seat of my white Rolls Royce Cullinan and yank my door shut. I take a few deep breaths, trying to calm myself. God, I knew he'd be a fucking prick. All the Lords are, but damn, I didn't expect him to be this difficult. Or this intimidating.

My pulse races at the way he touched the buttons on my shirt. It was innocent yet threatening at the same time. It was like he was warning me. Then what he said to me—*the only way I'm going to talk to you is if you're naked and on your knees with a gag in your mouth.*

Jesus Christ!

I've never been spoken to like that. I mean, I know how the Lords are and how they treat women, but is it supposed to sound so good? A part of me wanted to call his bluff just to see what he'd do. Would he force me? I'm not sure why that thought excites me, but it does.

I'm not going to leave him alone. I can't. So he can do whatever he wants, but I'll keep returning because he's my assignment. If I want to get to the top, I'll crawl under him. It's that simple.

Digging out the new cell the Lords gave me along with my laptop from my purse, I send an email to the **UNKNOWN** Lord. They know exactly who Haidyn is, and they know that I can't work miracles. They understand it's *going to take time*. They called this a marathon, not a sprint in an email I received last week. Their words, not mine. They've been wanting updates on my *new* life and obviously approved because here I am.

I'm guessing they've got something on him but won't tell me what.

How am I supposed to get information from him if I don't know what I'm digging for?

Starting up my SUV, I pull out of Carnage and head back toward town. It's secluded and out in the middle of nowhere. They don't want the world to see who they are. The Lords are very secretive, and the Spade brothers are even more so. They are the shadow figures who hide in the middle of the night watching you. You know they're there, but you can't see them. Evil always hides in darkness. That's where it feels safe.

Entering my house, I first change into a pair of sweatpants and a T-shirt. Then I get on my bed and pull out my laptop. I open the email I was sent last night and review the photos. They're of him. One shows him standing by a black Lamborghini. He wears dark-wash jeans, black combat boots, and a white T-shirt. He's got a lit cigarette in his right hand and his cell in the other. The second picture is of him on a motorcycle while pulling out of the gates at Carnage. He has no clue that either picture was taken. Why would he, though? They all think they're untouchable and don't pay attention to what's around them.

Haidyn Jamison Reeves. It outlines his life in four words—killer, Carnage, Spade brother. That's it. Like what the fuck? I knew that already.

I'm not a therapist. I have no schooling in that field whatsoever. So I've been watching videos of sessions on YouTube and other sites. I'm not getting much. The only thing saving me is that this isn't a normal situation, so I don't think he expects me to be professional. Especially after the way he spoke to me about being gagged and naked. The Lords use sex for everything. He's a man, and I'm a woman. Of course, he's going to expect me to crawl to him with my mouth open wide, ready to serve. Based on how wet my thong is, I'd say my pussy thinks that's a great idea.

HAIDYN

Charlotte Lynn Hewett is a licensed therapist who graduated from Barrington three years ago. She's twenty-five, five-two, and a hundred and ten pounds. It's amazing what you can find on the internet. It's also very easy for people to put bullshit online.

She's pretty young to have her position, especially since she doesn't belong to a Lord. The lack of a ring on her left finger proves she's not a Lady.

"Where did you guys find Charlotte?" I ask Saint, walking through the basement.

"The Lords recommended her," Kashton answers since Saint currently has a knife in some poor bastard's back while he hangs from the ceiling.

"Suggested?" I question.

He shrugs. "I don't know, man. We were given a list, and she was at the top. Jessie made contact and set it all up."

I run a hand over my face, letting out an annoyed sigh. "Tell them to fuck off. I'm not seeing her." As much as I want to fuck her, I'm not in the mood to deal with another therapist.

The guy hanging from the ceiling has tape wrapped around his head, but it only muffles his screams as Saint runs the tip of the knife down the man's back, right next to his spine. His skin splits like butter, and blood begins to flow down his naked body. The chains rattle from his jerky movements.

"They're not going to let you stop." Saint finally speaks, stepping back and looking proudly at the bleeding man.

"Why don't you two have to seek therapy?" I growl.

"Because we didn't try to kill ourselves."

"I'm not suicidal!" I bark.

There's nothing that I've done that I can't live with. I might not have chosen this life, but I made up my mind when I was younger to make the best of it. I've only ever killed one person who didn't deserve to die, but I don't regret it. It was what was best for *her*.

Kashton arches a brow. "Are you sure?"

Saint snorts. "The Lords think otherwise."

I roll my eyes. "How many times do I have to say this? I don't—"

"Remember how you ended up on the floor with your wrists cut open like a fish." Kashton interrupts me. "However, I remember it perfectly since I was the one who found you." His eyes narrow on mine.

He's still mad at me because he thinks I was leaving him behind. Kashton has abandonment issues. But don't we all? A Lord grows up in a family with more power than God, yet we're literally alone. Kashton and Saint are the only people I can count on, and although I don't remember how he found me practically dead, I know for a fact that I'd never leave them. Not willingly.

"That's better," Saint says happily, spinning the naked guy around to face him.

I give them my back and head up the elevator to my room. I'm not in the mood for that shit today. Coming up to the birdcage—the floor we all share—I scan my thumb for my room and enter, slamming it shut. Sitting on the edge of my bed, I look down at my wrist. You can't see the scar because I have it covered with ink. I know it's there even though I can't remember how I got it.

"HAIDYN?"

I hear my name shouted, but it seems to be far away.

"Haidyn! What the fuck did you do?" Again, with the annoying voice, but it sounds so familiar. "Come on, man."

I just want to sleep. I'm so tired. All of a sudden, it feels like the world is shaking, or maybe it's me.

"Goddammit, Haidyn. Why did you..." It sounds like they're walking away, or maybe I'm finally falling asleep.

It doesn't matter. Either way, I finally have peace and silence.

That foggy memory of Kash finding me was years ago. It was after Ashtyn ran, and we finished our six months of "training." The Lords thought they broke me, but I assure you, they didn't. You can't dish out punishment and not expect to receive it in return.

The professionals say the mind blocks traumatic experiences on purpose. I say it chooses to forget what isn't important. Who knows which one is actually correct.

It doesn't matter to me, just the Lords. They will take you out for betraying your oath, but if you want to take yourself out...that's a different story. They don't like you having any sort of control over your own life.

They own you.

You live for them, and you die for them.

As if I'd give them the satisfaction of killing myself. I'm just not that kind of Lord. I like making others suffer. And if that means staying alive, then I'll do anything to make that happen.

Getting to my feet, I enter my adjoining bathroom. I yank my shirt up and over my head and toss it to the floor. Reaching down, I undo my jeans, but my eyes catch sight of myself in the mirror.

I look like shit. I have dark circles around my eyes, and I look like I haven't slept in days. I haven't, but that's beside the point.

They want me to give my secrets to the pretty brunette. Want me to spill my insecurities and shortcomings so they can use them against me. That's what the Lords do. They use anything they can against you. I won't do it.

She'll give up eventually. Probably quicker than the others have. She seemed innocent. A few comments about fucking her ass and making her cry will get her to run away.

If not, then I'll up my game. I'm always up for a challenge.

shhh...

Chapter 10
Charlotte

I lie in the darkly lit room with a towel over my eyes. The sound of the waterfall to my left is soothing. Today is my *take care of me* day. Once every two weeks, I get a massage, facial, and an IV for rehydration therapy.

My mother suggested these to me when I showed up at our monthly brunch a couple of years back, looking like I had just closed down the club. I had. Although that's not the point, she reminded me I needed to take care of myself. She set me up an appointment with her favorite salon and spa—I've been addicted ever since.

The IVs really do help you feel better. Like a new person. Plus, the man who digs his fingers deep into my muscles takes me to another level of ecstasy that no drug ever has.

My personal cell ringing has me removing the towel from my eyes. I dig it out of my purse, which sits on the small round table next to my chair, then hit answer. "Hello?"

"Hey, honey," my mother says in greeting.

"Hi, Mom." I place the cloth back over my face and lie back, holding the phone to my ear.

"Are you at the spa?" she inquires, already knowing my schedule.

"Yeah." I sigh, getting more comfortable in the seat. The IV takes about an hour, and I feel like I've slept all night afterward.

"I won't keep you. Just wanted to remind you about our brunch tomorrow."

"I'll be there," I assure her.

"Perfect, dear. Enjoy your day, and I'll see you in the morning. Love you."

She hangs up before I can say my goodbyes. Removing the towel from my eyes, I place the cell back in my purse, covering up my face once more and relaxing.

♠

Two hours later, I'm getting into my SUV when I turn both of my phones on ring. After my mother had called, I turned it on silent so no one would disturb me. My body feels like Jell-O, and my hair looks greasy from the oils. But it was amazing.

I see I have an email on my work cell from **UNKNOWN**. Opening it up, it's got a video attached.

It's of a room...looks like a basement—concrete walls and matching floor. A man lies in the center on his back, looking up at the ceiling. He's wearing a Lord's mask and a pair of jeans with a black T-shirt. His arms are fanned out to the sides, palms up, and a pool of blood has gathered below them.

The room is eerily silent. I sit up straighter, looking over the man who appears to be dead. My eyes focus on his chest, and I don't see any movement to show he's breathing. Then I look at his bloody hands to see if his fingers twitch—still nothing.

A door squeaking makes me jump as a man rushes into the room.

I've seen him before...from the pictures the Lords sent me. He was in the picture of the four guys and girl that looked like it had been taken quite a while back.

"What the fuck?" he barks, running over to the dead guy. He drops to his knees next to him and rips off the mask.

I inhale sharply when I see it's Haidyn. I can tell it's an older video because he doesn't have any tattoos. His eyes are closed, and his color looks ashen.

"HAIDYN?" the man shouts, shaking his shoulders. "Haidyn! What the fuck did you do?" He checks for his pulse and lets out a long breath. "Come on, man. Goddammit, Haidyn. Why did you..." He pulls on Haidyn's eyelids, forcing them open.

Haidyn groans in response.

"Wake the fuck up, man! Jesus Christ...Saint?" he screams. "SAINT?"

A man runs in who I'm assuming is Saint—I've also seen him in the group picture. He was the one with his hand wrapped around the girl's throat while he stood behind her.

He pulls out his cell and makes a call while the other continues to look for the source of the bleeding.

It's his wrists. Both have been cut, and once the guy figures it out, he removes his shirt, rips it down the middle, and ties them both around Haidyn's wrists to try to stop the bleeding.

The video comes to an abrupt end, and I see that's all they sent me. What in the fuck was that for? Why send that to me if they're not going to explain it? I mean, the video was self-explanatory, but there was no other direction on what to do next. It leaves me confused more than anything else.

HAIDYN

Senior year at Barrington

I've been out riding all night, needing some fresh air. The vow ceremony is getting closer, and I'm on edge. My father is pissed at me, of course. That's nothing new. He's on the hunt for my new chosen. As if I care who he wants me to fuck.

It's all about what you can get in our world. I guess that's anyone in any type of situation. But you don't see dads out there pimping their daughters out left and right like you do within the Lords. It's sick really. If I have any say, I won't marry or reproduce. The thought of having to watch my theoretical daughter be fucked for the first time in front of an audience makes me want to vomit.

"Cradle to the Grave" by Five Finger Death Punch blasts in my earbuds as I take the exit on the highway and downshift, coming up to the gates at the house of Lords.

Pulling up to the building, I see Adam exiting the front double doors. He storms down the steps and jumps into his G-wagon. As I see his reverse lights illuminate the night, I make a split decision to follow him.

He's been in a mood. I'm not sure what the fuck is going on, but he's been pissy to not only Ashtyn but all of us since we had our meeting with the detective. It's not like him. I love my brothers, but I've always been the closest to Adam. For some reason, he's pulling away from me.

I stay several cars back as he weaves in and out of traffic. He takes an exit, and I can tell when he spots me because he pulls into a vacant parking lot.

Shutting off my bike, I turn off the music and wait as he shoves his door open. "What the fuck, Haidyn?" he barks. "You following me?" He storms over to me.

"If you'd answer your phone, I wouldn't have to." I've been calling him all day, and he's been MIA. Even Kashton brought it up today to Saint and me, and I pretended not to notice.

"I've been busy," he snaps defensively.

"Is this because you haven't had your dick sucked?" I joke. "Because we only have a week left. Then you can fuck whoever you want."

Adam's jaw clenches, and his hands fist to keep from punching me. He's been this way since we met with Lincoln at the house of Lords a couple of weeks ago.

They think a Lord—Adam—is involved, but we all know he's innocent. They can suspect him all they want. They don't have any evidence that he did it.

"I have somewhere to be, Haidyn. Don't follow me," he orders, walking back to his SUV.

"What do you think this means for Ashtyn?" I call out.

He stops and turns to face me but doesn't speak.

I cross my arms over my chest. "They think you're involved. You think they'll try to use her to get you to confess?" It's a reasonable thought. We, as Lords, take whatever weakness we can find when we want something from someone. Why wouldn't the law do the same? Somehow and for some reason, this detective knows about us. How he found out, he won't say. But the fact that he did isn't good by any means. And the fact that Lincoln allowed him to enter the house of

Lords is throwing up red flags. The detective already knows too much about us.

Adam drops his head to stare at the parking lot, rubbing the back of his neck. It tells me he's thought of it too. I think Saint is oblivious to what's going on. All he cares about is finally getting his girl. The last thing he's going to think about is losing her when he's so close to having her.

"It's crossed my mind," Adam admits, his eyes meeting mine once again.

"And what are you going to do about it?" I inquire.

"Why do you think I'm pushing her away?" he questions. "I need her...and you"—he points at me—"to stay the fuck back. Once this is all settled, things will go back to the way they were." With that, he jumps back in his G-wagon and squeals his tires as he leaves the parking lot.

I stay where I'm at, watching his taillights get back onto the highway. I'll give him some time. But if things don't change soon, I'll step in and help him out. We stick together. That's the point of the Spade brothers. We take care of our own.

♠

IT'S JUST ANOTHER DAY, BUT THEN AGAIN, IT'S NOT LIKE THE others. *Ashtyn is here.* Saint found her thanks to fucking Whitney. I've pretended to hate Ash for the past four years because it was the best defense I could come up with.

It's only a matter of time before my brothers find out I lied to them. But I'm not going to say anything. Ash will have to rat me out.

I stand in the room on the seventh floor, facing the floor-to-ceiling windows while the rain comes down. Charlotte sits behind me. I can hear her shuffling around, getting her stuff together for another visit. This will make her third. The woman is persistent, I'll give her that. At this point, I just show up to make her squirm. Seeing her is the highlight of my day.

"Talk to me, Haidyn," she says.

I remain facing away from her with my hands shoved into the pockets of my jeans.

"What are you thinking?" Charlotte goes on.

I snort and turn to face her. She looks so prim and proper sitting in the high-back chair. I decide to walk over to her, getting closer than I usually do, and she sits up straight, crossing her legs as if that'll keep me from getting between them.

Placing my hands on both armrests, I lean over, putting my face in front of hers. "You don't want to know what I'm thinking." My eyes drop to her tits. She's dressed in a fitted button-up white silk blouse.

"I'm…I'm here to help you," she whispers, rubbing her sweaty palms softly down her black pencil skirt.

I can smell the fear, and it makes me hard. "Help me?" I have hundreds of ideas on how she can *help* me. She won't like any of them. "Do you really mean that, Charlotte?"

She swallows nervously, her eyes dropping to stare out the window. Poor thing is scared of me. "Of course."

Bullshit. She's here because she has to be like everyone before her.

I won't lie. She's definitely the most attractive therapist they've sent me, and given the chance, I'd fucking ruin her. "I know what you can do." I smirk. The poor thing asked.

Her wide eyes go to mine. "W-what?"

"Let me rip off your clothes."

She gasps.

"I'll tie you up in a tight little ball, suspend you from the ceiling so that your cunt, mouth, and ass are easily on display for me to fuck." I like the way her face pales at my words. It makes her eyes a brighter blue. "Once I'm done violating you, I'll sit down, have a smoke while I let you hang there, and watch my cum leak from your stretched-out and overused holes like the worthless whore you're meant to be."

She's trembling at just my words. Imagine what she'd do if I got my hands on her.

"I can't promise you'll like it, but it'll make me feel better," I say. "Still want to help me, doll face?" I place my hand on her knee, making her jump, and she whimpers.

"Haidyn," Saint speaks from the open door.

I knew he was there; I just didn't give a fuck. Laughing, I push off the chair, and she runs out of the room, shoving Saint out of her way.

I go back to the window.

"We brought her in to help you." He makes it sound like we had a choice. We didn't.

"She can't." I may not be suicidal like the Lords think, but I'm sure as fuck not going to change who I am.

"You don't even let her try," he growls.

"Unless she's on her knees, she's useless." It's true. But it's not just her. That's how we're raised to see women. It's not her fault she was born without a dick in our world.

"Kash called David."

I'm not even in the mood to fuck a whore at the moment. There's only one woman I'm thinking about right now, and sex is the last thing that comes to mind when I think of her. "Is *she* here?" I ask.

"Yeah." He confirms what I already knew.

FUCK! My hands fist. "You shouldn't have brought her back." My chest tightens at the thought of what will happen now. Everything Kash, Saint, and I went through after Ashtyn ran was all for nothing. And I let a brother down. Just another one I can add to my long list.

"She's here for us to use. You...we all deserve our revenge."

I turn to face him. "I'm going to kill her," I lie, hoping he believes it. Maybe if he thinks she's in jeopardy here, he'll take her somewhere else. "Don't you get that? If I touch her, she's dead." I take a deep breath. "And the worst part of that is she doesn't deserve it." I hang my head. "She's not responsible for what happened once she was gone." I hate what happened to my brothers because of me. But that doesn't mean that Ashtyn deserves the hell Saint will put her through either. She was running to save him.

"She left us," he grinds out, and he's not wrong.

"No. She left you. She never belonged to Kashton or me. She was yours, and you let us borrow her. Big difference." I never really understood why he shared her with us, and we never asked. In a way, I think it was Saint showing how much control he had over her. But no matter how things go down this time, I won't be fucking her in any way. Things have changed.

"Well, she's ours now," he says as Kashton enters.

Fuck this day already. I just want to be alone.

"I sent a car for the girls. They'll be here soon," Kash announces.

I turn and give them my back again and hear them closing the door behind them when they leave.

Placing my forehead on the glass, I close my eyes, hating that Ashtyn is back here at Carnage. I thought *we* did the right thing. Now, I'm not so sure.

Senior year at Barrington

Saint got a text from a fellow Lord that they have Ashtyn. We rushed to save her from Tyson at her parents' home. We've brought her to Carnage to hide her. Our fathers know she's here. Adam is MIA, her mother is dead, and her father is also missing. We're all she has.

She's taking a bath in Saint's bathroom while he went to talk to his father, and Kash said he needed to make a phone call. I'm pacing Saint's room, making sure no one comes in here until they return.

My cell rings, and I pull it out of my pocket to see it's a blocked call. "Hello?" I answer.

"Is she okay?" the voice rushes out.

"What the fuck, Adam?" I whisper, walking over to the double doors and stepping out onto the balcony to make sure no one hears me. "Where the fuck are you?"

"I tried to help her," he rushes out. "Just...just tell me she's okay."

"Your mother is dead. Your father is missing. Know anything about that?" I snap, ignoring his question.

"I need you to trust me, Haidyn." He sighs. "Please. I tried—" He cuts himself off. "I'm trying to fix it."

Looking over at the bathroom door, I can hear her crying while she sits in the bathtub washing off her mother's blood. "What do you need me to do?" He's on my shit list, but I'm doing this for her, not him.

"Just keep her alive. I'll contact you soon." The line goes dead just as Kashton returns to Saint's bedroom.

I pocket my cell before he can see me on it, knowing that things will get worse before they get better.

. . .

STEPPING BACK FROM THE WINDOW, I PULL THE CELL FROM MY pocket and find the number I want. They answer on the second ring.

"Hey, man. What's up?"

"Are you in town?" I ask, my eyes going to the door to make sure no one enters. Privacy isn't a fucking thing when you live with two other men.

"Yeah, why?"

"Ashtyn is here."

A silence lingers over the other end of the phone before he asks, "Here—as in there at Carnage?"

"Yeah."

"Fuck! How did that happen?" he snaps.

"Whitney," I respond. "Some shit went down with Tyson and his wife, and it led to Whitney ratting out where Ashtyn was. Kash and Saint brought her back yesterday."

"Son of a bitch!" he hisses.

Pretty much.

"I thought you were keeping an eye on her?" I demand.

"I've only been in town for a week," he snaps. "What the fuck do we do?"

"Nothing," I answer. "She's back, and there's nothing we can do about it." Shit will hit the fan. We just have to be ready when it does.

Shhh...

Chapter 11

Charlotte

The man is infuriating. The moment I rushed out of the room and got into my car, I had to unbutton my blouse. I was sweating from his words.

"I'll tie you up in a tight little ball, suspend you from the ceiling so that your cunt, mouth, and ass are easily on display for me to fuck."

Goddamn! I have my air conditioner on full blast, trying to cool down.

"Once I'm done violating you, I'll sit down, have a smoke while I let you hang there, and watch my cum leak from your stretched-out and overused holes like the worthless whore you're meant to be."

My hips rock back and forth in the driver's seat, just imagining the picture he painted. Men like Haidyn don't make threats. They're promises.

Is it bad that I can't stop thinking about it? He seemed on edge today. More than the past two times I've come for a session. It's like he's upped his game. He's tired of me returning and wants to get rid of me. I don't care what he says; I'm not walking away.

I killed a woman. I've taken a brand. I can sit there and listen to a few crude comments about how he wants to use my body. He's a Lord after all. Sex is all they think about, and ever since I started seeing him, it's all I think about too.

HAIDYN

Four years ago

I HEAR A GUNSHOT GO OFF, AND I'M WALKING DOWN THE HALLWAY when a small body turns a corner and runs into me. She screams before looking up at me, and my eyes drop to the gun in her hand.

She's shaking, holding on to it for dear life. I can hear Kashton yelling Saint's name. Did she shoot him? Fuck, this isn't going as planned.

"Get the fuck out of here. As far as I'm concerned, you're dead. Do you understand me?" I tell her, not making a move to take her gun. If that makes her feel safe, then she can keep it.

"I...understand." She sobs, nodding her head.

"Saint! Fuck!" Kashton shouts from around the corner.

I step into her, lowering my voice so no one can hear. "We all pay for our sins, Ashtyn. You are no different. You can run from them all you want, but they will catch up with you no matter where you go." Pulling back, I turn and walk back in the direction I came from.

I STAND ON MY BALCONY OVERLOOKING THE ROLLING HILLS behind Carnage. I didn't get any sleep last night, but that's nothing new. That memory from four years ago keeps playing in my mind, knowing she's here.

Picking up the pack of cigarettes on the table outside, I light one up and take a long drag, enjoying the burn of the nicotine as it enters my lungs.

Ashtyn is in the next room, just down the hall, and I'm not sure what to do about that. I've avoided her since Saint returned with her for a reason. I don't want to make things awkward for her.

I pull my phone out of my pocket and hover over Charlotte's number. I want to see her. No, that's a lie. I want to fuck her. She'll think I want a session to talk about my feelings or tell her I'm suicidal and need help.

That's sure as fuck not what I want from her. I want her on her knees while my cock fucks that pretty face. I want her gagging and crying with my hand tangled in her long dark hair, watching her cry. But that won't be happening.

Instead, I texted one of David's girls an hour ago. I'm tired of the same ole pussy, but it's the only option I have right now. Charlotte isn't going to let me near her. Not yet. I saw the way she reacted to my vulgar words. She'll come around, but it'll take time. Until then, I'll fuck what I pay for.

♠

KASH, SAINT, AND I ARE AT BLACKOUT. I NEEDED A NIGHT AWAY from Carnage and Ashtyn. I think we're all on edge since she's returned, but for different reasons, and it's only been a couple of days. I've avoided her other than the one incident when she was crying in the hallway outside my room. I wasn't going to let that dipshit put his hands on her. She belongs to Saint. That's his job now.

We're standing in front of the bar on the first floor while "In My Mind," by Dynoro and Gigi D'Agostino plays throughout the club. The lights flash to the beat of the music, and it's giving me a fucking headache. I wanted to get out and ride a bit tonight, but now I regret it.

Tyson offered us free drinks. I took him up on it. We're on our bikes, so I'm sipping my first one.

My eyes are glued to the woman out on the dance floor. She looks so different from the way I usually see her. She's dressed in a pair of jean shorts that sit low on her hips and cut high up on her legs, with a white T-shirt tied into a knot right underneath her breasts. I knew they were larger than they appeared in her blouse. Her dark hair is up in a messy bun, and she's dancing by herself as if no one is watching. Her ass sways back and forth, and her eyes are closed as if she's feeling the beat.

"You can't be serious, man. She's what? Maybe five-foot-two and a hundred pounds. You're six-seven and like two fifty. You'd destroy her," Kash jokes, seeing what I'm staring at. "Not to mention, I'm pretty sure she's a virgin. You'd scare that poor girl to death."

They haven't been around her. As far as I know, they've never had any real conversations. I'm not sure why he thinks he knows so much about her.

"Isn't that the best part? Seeing how much they can take before they break?" I speak before throwing back what's left of my drink.

I saw her the moment we stepped out of Tyson's office when we arrived. It was like I could feel her presence, and my eyes went right to her. Maybe I'm just that hung up on the brunette. She's probably the only woman I've spent that much time with and haven't fucked. That's why I prefer to pay for sex. They don't need a pointless conversation and to be cuddled afterward.

But fuck, do I want to. I had a whore on her knees with my cock in her mouth when Saint barged into my bedroom after I texted him about Ashtyn earlier this morning. I finished before I helped him take care of the Lord who had manhandled his wife. Then I went back and fucked her some more, but it wasn't enough. It never is. I'm chasing a high that I'm not reaching. And the thought of walking up to Charlotte, fisting her hair, and pulling her out of this place has my hard dick throbbing against my zipper.

I turn, placing my empty glass on top of the bar, and nod to Saint and Kash. "I'll see you guys later." Without waiting for them to reply, I walk out the back door of the club and get on my bike, needing to be alone.

Shhh...

Chapter 12

Charlotte

I'm drunk and extremely horny as the song changes to "Bullet Train" by Stephen Swartz. Haidyn has been heavy on my mind. More so than usual. He's upping his game, and I don't know what the fuck to do about it.

The Lords have me chasing my tail. I haven't received any new information lately about what to do or why I'm seeing him. And I'm not a fucking therapist. I'm running out of things to say to him. He's going to figure out I'm a fraud if I don't come up with something better than "how do you feel?" or "are you sleeping?"

I snort at that thought.

A man walks up behind me, placing his hands on my hips, and speaks into my ear. "You okay, babe?"

I nod and pull back from him, waving off his concern. "I'm ready to go," I shout over the music. I'm sweating and want a shower. I've had enough to drink for the night.

I've been seeing Wesley for a couple of months now. I met him at Blackout of all places. I ordered a drink, and when I turned around to go dance, I ran right into him. We both ended up wearing my drink.

"Okay, come on." He grabs my hand and pulls me through the crowd over to the bar where a few of his friends stand. He tells the rest of his friends goodbye and then leads me out the back door to the parking lot.

I wasn't planning on coming out tonight. I was out with a friend having margaritas when he called and asked if I wanted to go out. I thought, why not?

He opens his passenger door for me, and I fall into it. Shutting the door, I look up, and a black bike catches my attention across the parking lot. It's facing away from the car, and I squint my drunken eyes to see a man straddling the bike.

My heart picks up when I see it's Haidyn. Even my blurry eyes can't miss him. He leans the bike to the right and kicks up the stand before he starts it up. The rev of the engine fills the car as Wesley opens the driver's side door and gets in. As he closes it, Haidyn pulls out of his spot and drives out of the parking lot.

Fuck! I lean back in my seat, blowing the loose strand of hair from my face. Closing my eyes, I run my sweaty hands down my thighs, feeling my skin tingling.

"You okay?" Wesley touches my arm, and I jump.

My eyes spring open, and I take a deep breath. "Yeah." I give him a drunken smile. I can't feel my lips at this point. "Just tired."

The wet spot on my thong tells a different story. I've always been curious about sex, but ever since I started seeing Haidyn, my body has seemed to come alive in ways I've never known before, and I honestly don't know what to do about it. Even getting myself off isn't enough.

"Let's get you home and into bed." He starts up his car.

Haidyn has my mind so fucked. I can only imagine what he'd do to my body if given the chance.

♠

ANOTHER TWO WEEKS HAVE PASSED. I CAN'T DECIDE IF THEY'RE going slow or fast. I feel like the time between my meetings with Haidyn drags on, but then when the day comes, I'm like shit, I just saw him.

It's because I'm letting him fuck with my head. The last time I was here, he told me he was going to tie me up, hang me from the ceiling, and fuck all my holes. My body still hasn't recovered from the visual he gave me.

Parking my SUV, I get out and walk up the steps to the Carnage doors, and the one on the right opens before I reach the last step.

"Miss Hewett?" Jessie looks at me in surprise, dressed in his all-black tux. "Haidyn had me cancel his session today."

"I got your text." I woke up to Jessie's message at seven this morning that Haidyn was canceling. The fucker didn't even bother to text me himself. "Is he dead?" I ask, only half joking.

He frowns but answers, "No."

"Then we're having a session." I start to walk toward the hall where I know there's an elevator that will take me to the seventh floor when he stops me.

"Haidyn isn't up there."

I huff. "Then where is he?" He can't just blow me off. I'm here to do a job, and I'm going to make sure I get it done.

He pulls his cell out of his pocket and places it to his ear. "Sorry to bother you, sir..." I roll my eyes. "But Miss Hewett is here...I know, sir. I did—" He pauses and nods a few times. "Yes, sir." Ending the call, he places his cell back in his pocket and gestures to the elevators. "He'll see you."

I drop my head to hide my smile as I walk toward the elevator and step inside. It's a small win but still a win. I won't let him think he can bully me around. I'm still going to show up. No matter what. He can try and talk about fucking me all he wants, they're just words.

Jessie enters and presses **B,** making me frown. I turn to look at him. "I thought you said he'd see me?" We haven't had many sessions, but they've always been in the same room on the seventh floor.

"He's in the basement," he says.

The door slides open, and we're instantly hit with cold air that makes me shiver and the smell almost knocks me over. "Jesus," I whisper, placing my hand over my mouth and nose. It smells like rotten eggs.

Jessie is unfazed as he steps off the elevator and leads me down a hallway. He stops at a set of plastic strip curtains and pulls them open for me. "Don't want you to get dirty." He nods to my white knee-length dress and pink blazer.

"Thank you," I mumble, turning sideways to make sure I don't get anything on me. They look covered in dirt, but it could be old blood, for all I know.

I can hear "Painkiller" by Three Days Grace off in the distance as we walk past a large open room. It's got recessed rectangular holes in the concrete floor. Reminds me of graves—three side by side. If graves had five metal bars that ran from the top to bottom.

The music gets louder as we come up to another hallway. Doors line either side with metal slots in the center of them that are about hip height.

The smell is getting stronger the farther back into the basement we get, and I try to breathe through my mouth so I don't throw up and embarrass myself.

"Here you are, Miss Hewett." Jessie comes to a stop at what looks to be a jail cell that has bars and opens it for me.

"Thank you," I mumble and step inside. The taste of acid intensifies when I look in the room, and I immediately regret not taking his text message seriously.

HAIDYN

"MISS HEWETT, SIR," JESSIE CALLS OUT OVER MY MUSIC.

I'm in a fucking sour mood and didn't want to put up with Charlotte today. When Jessie reminded me this morning of my meeting with her, I told him to cancel it.

Turning around, I see her standing inside of the cell. Her wide eyes are on the bloody and naked man that lies on the floor.

I take the time to look her over. She wears a white knee-length dress. It's not like the night I first saw her. This one is more professional. Fitted, but not snug enough to show off what I saw when she was at Blackout. She has on a light pink blazer and she's got it buttoned in the middle and her short heels match the dress. Her dark hair in the usual bun at the nape of her neck and her makeup light with a soft pink to match on her cheeks and pouty lips.

She looks so out of place. Prissy, high-class city girl slumming it in the basement filled with nothing but filth. The thought of stripping her naked and chaining her to the wall sounds pretty fucking good. I'd like to see what she'd do—just how desperate she would get when it comes to surviving.

"Watch where you step." I yell at her over the blaring music.

She jumps at the sound of my voice and my eyes drop to her heels.

Hers follow, and she takes a step back, removing her once pristine white designer heels out of the puddle of blood she was standing in.

Fuck, I hate how gorgeous she is.

Her round eyes meet mine again before they go to the guy, and she swallows nervously.

Picking up my cell from the counter, I turn off the music and ask, "What do you want, Charlotte?"

The silence now allows me to hear her heavy breathing. "We, uh... have a session."

It's cute to watch her stumble over her words.

"As you can see, I'm a little busy." I push the guy on the floor onto his stomach with my bloody boot. She says nothing as her large eyes remain on him. "But since you're already here. We'll call this field trip day." I smile at her.

Her eyes come back to mine, and she looks fucking terrified. The fact that my cock is hard pisses me off. I need her to run the other way so I can be done with her and this therapy bullshit.

"Field trip?" she whispers, and the guy groans.

My smile widens. "Perfect timing."

Reaching down, I pick him up and set him in the chair in front of the wooden table. He groans, and his head bobs back and forth. I've been in here maybe thirty minutes beating the shit out of him. Just relieving some stress before Jessie informed me I had a visitor.

I push him forward where his head and chest lie on the table and pull his hands behind his back, securing them in handcuffs. Then I go over to my bag and stand behind him. It gives me a great view of Charlotte across the small room. She stands right inside the open door, wide eyes still on him.

"Open wide," I tell the man and place the gag into his mouth, forcing it wide open and securing it at the back of his head. "Good boy." I tap the side of his bloody face, and then I return to my bag for a few more things.

"What...what are you doing?" she asks in a rush. "Haidyn—?"

"He's a liar," I tell her, and her pretty face pales. "And the only way to punish a liar is to take away his chance at spewing more lies." I put a pair of pliers into his mouth and grab his tongue.

He begins to mumble and gag as I yank it out, stretching it as far as it will go. His wide eyes look up at mine before going to hers. She takes another step back into the hallway.

"She's not here to help you," I inform him. "She's here for me."

Charlotte wanted to see a show, so I'll give her one. The bastard deserves this, but I might be going a little overboard for her. If telling her that I wanted to tie her up in a ball and suspend her from the ceiling while fucking all her holes didn't work...this should do the trick. Maybe she's a visual learner.

Holding his tongue out, I pull his chin down onto the table and shove a nail through the middle of his tongue. He begins to scream and thrash in the chair. Before he can pull his tongue back, I let go of the pliers, grab the hammer and hit the head of the nail. It only takes one time to get the nail into the table good enough to where it holds him captive to the wooden table.

I step back, and he gets to his feet, kicking the chair out from under him. He's bent over the table, screaming and thrashing as he tries to free his tongue with his hands cuffed behind his back. Spit and blood fly from his wide-open mouth.

Looking up, I see her wide eyes on the man, and her small body shakes.

The poor thing doesn't even notice me walking over to her. Coming to stand behind her, I place my bloody hands on her shoulders, and she jumps. Leaning down, I whisper in her ear. "Watch him, Charlotte. He's going to rip his tongue in half." I can feel her trembling against me. "Like a desperate animal that will chew its own leg off to free itself from a trap. Trappers call it 'wringing off'. Some will even break their own teeth as they chew through their limbs."

"Why?" She sniffs, and I'm not sure if she's asking why I'm telling her this or why I'm doing it to the man.

"Because I told you, he lied, and liars must be silenced." I decide to reference the show in front of her.

The man yanks back, his tongue splitting down the center, leaving the nail still in the wooden table and he falls to the floor from the momentum. Rolling onto his stomach, he gets up on his knees and leans forward as blood and drool run from his mouth. He's still got the gag in so he can't close his mouth. He's sobbing and choking.

"Now we wait and see if his tongue swells to the point it cuts off his ability to breathe."

She spins around to face me, and I stand to my full height to look down at her. "Is this what you want to see, doll face?" My eyes drop to the death grip she has on the strap to her purse that's slung over her shoulder and add, "Something new to put in your notebook for next time."

Her tear-filled eyes narrow up on me before she throws her shoulder into mine and storms down the hallway toward the elevator.

"Whoa." Kashton laughs as he comes through the plastic strips curtains and almost collides with her. She shoves him out of the way before she disappears through them. He walks toward me and smiles when he looks into the cell. "Was this a show-and-tell session?" He crosses his tatted arms over his chest. "I want to join next time. I could show her a few things." He wiggles his eyebrows.

I don't know why his words piss me off, but they do. I've been in a shitty mood for a couple of weeks now—since Ashtyn returned.

I've tried to avoid her as much as I can, but it was inevitable when we went to New York for Hooke's show. When we returned, she stayed hidden in her room for a week. Then Kashton gave her a fucking cell phone so she can stay in touch with Jasmine who brought up Whitney missing, and Ashtyn demanded to know what happened to her.

I told Ashtyn that Whitney was the one who ratted her out. She deserved to know. Whitney isn't her friend. Fuck, Whitney isn't anyone's friend. That bitch will backstab anyone she can.

Of course, that reunion didn't go well. Then Tyson and Laikyn showed up and Laikyn offered to fill Ash in on what all she knows. I was done with this fucking day.

"Let's play." Kash slaps my back, getting my attention. "Saint and I are leaving tomorrow for a few days, so you're on babysitting duty." He informs me of what I already know.

I keep telling myself that there's nothing I can do about it. That she's back, and that's not going to change. She was part of our everyday life once. I might as well play nice. I'll take her to dinner tomorrow and let her know she has at least one person on her side.

"Yeah, let's play," I say, ignoring the sobbing man on the floor.

Going over to my cell, I turn on my go-to song, and "Hallelujah" by No Resolve fills the concrete room.

Kashton closes the door and locks us inside with the prisoner. Then he removes the Zippo from his pocket. It's chrome with a black spade in the center, and inside, it has a skull with 666 across the bottom. He pulls a cigarette from the pack I have sitting on the far counter and lights one up, then hands it to me.

I mumble a thanks as thoughts of the brunette fill my mind and the look of horror on her face. I actually feel sad that she won't be returning, not after what I showed her tonight, but it's for the best. My still very hard cock just reminds me that she's too good for me.

Shhh...

Chapter 13
Charlotte

Another fucking visit and another fucking dead end.

"Goddammit!" I shout, storming into my house and kicking my blood-covered heels off in the foyer. I head to the kitchen and grab a bottle of wine but don't even bother pouring a glass. I just down it from the bottle.

I'm still shaking at what I saw.

Slamming it onto the counter, I gasp and run the back of my hand over my chin as it drips onto my dress.

What the fuck are you doing?

What I'm being told to do. I'm following orders from the Lords. I knew the Spade brothers were ruthless, but I guess I never took the time to think how much.

I take another gulp of the wine and head to my bedroom. He made the guy split his own tongue because he's a liar. What the fuck did he lie about? I'm living a lie. What will he do to me if he finds out?

No! Don't think that way. He's not going to find out. I'll either die with this secret or the Lords will kill me before it gets out.

Haidyn wasn't wrong, though. The Lords find a way to silence anyone who goes against them. He was trying to scare me today, and I won't let it work.

I've got two weeks to get my shit together and return with a backbone. To prove to him that I can and will not be pushed away. I grew up in this society too. I know what goes on and how certain situations are handled. I can be just as ruthless, right? I killed a woman. I've got blood on my hands too.

Fuck Haidyn and whatever he was trying to prove tonight. I'll put a smile on my face and show him that I'm not the terrified girl he thinks I am.

HAIDYN

I'm pulling up to the private airstrip and see Adam waiting by his Aston Martin with his arms crossed over his chest. I expect him to be smiling, but instead, he looks remorseful. Things have been turned upside down over the past week. Now our brothers know that we've kept in touch behind their backs.

Kash and Saint left town, and I took Ashtyn to dinner. Well, I was planning on it anyway. We were ambushed. I was shot, and she was kidnapped. Everything went to shit so fast I haven't even had the chance to process most of it.

We board the plane as he speaks. "How are you feeling?"

"Fine." I grunt. My hand on my chest. I wish I was still playing dead if I'm being honest. I didn't feel like shit then. "Did you speak to Ashtyn?" I ask.

"Yeah." He sighs, looking out the window. "Well...I tried to. She wants nothing to do with me. Not like I can blame her," he adds softly.

I want to tell him that she'll come around, but even I can't promise that. And I know he doesn't plan on returning to Carnage.

"What all do they know?" he asks.

"Nothing," I answer.

He nods in understanding. I didn't want to give Saint another reason to hate Adam. Plus, I'm not a rat. I made a decision four years ago, and I stand by it.

His eyes drop to my backpack at my feet. "Did she ask where you were going?"

I rub the back of my neck where my tracker once was. We all had them installed after we finished our training, but they cut Ashtyn's and mine out when they kidnapped her and shot me.

"No." I wouldn't have told her anyway. She came to my room while I was packing my things. Our conversation from an hour ago is fresh on my mind.

. . .

"ARE YOU LEAVING?" I DON'T ANSWER BECAUSE SAYING YES WILL lead to more questions I don't have answers for. "Please, Haidyn... don't." Her voice cracks.

I lean forward and gently kiss her forehead. "Be good, baby girl." With that, I grab my backpack, sling it over my shoulder, and leave her sitting in my room.

I pass Saint standing outside my bedroom door, listening to our conversation, and when I get on the elevator, I turn to face him. The look on his face tells me what I already know. He doesn't care if I ever return.

This isn't about us or what I did. It's about what's to come. This isn't over. We're Lords—Spade brothers. Someone always wants what we have and thinks they can take it. And his biggest weakness sits on my bed.

I don't know why Kashton hasn't ever settled down, but I know why I haven't. It's too risky. Humans are vulnerable. Ashtyn proves that. Even thousands of miles away, she was still reachable. What if Benny didn't have patience? What if he had acted when she first ran and killed her the moment she moved to Vegas? Or decided to kidnap and knock her up at any point over the past four years? He saw Ashtyn as an opportunity to attack us. And that greed is the only thing that saved her.

The door starts to close, and Saint rushes over to it, slamming his hand on it and forcing it to open. I square my shoulders as he steps inside the elevator. His hard eyes go to the strap of my backpack before they land on mine. "Running?"

I don't respond. It's better he doesn't know what I'm doing. It's not that he won't try to stop me. It's that he'll want to go with me, and I won't take him away from her. Not this time. I've seen the man he is without her, and he's much better with her. Plus, Carnage is on lockdown now after what just happened. It's the safest place for any of them to be. I have no doubt Saint will go on a killing spree just like Kash did when he thought I died. There won't be any prisoners alive by the time I return.

He snorts at my silence. "I never thought you'd be like Adam."

My teeth grind. Again, it's not my story to defend. Saint can think what he wants.

Stepping back, he exits the elevator and says, "For her sake, I hope you stay gone." With that, the door closes.

"He'll forgive you," Adam speaks.

"Doesn't matter," I mumble, looking out the window as we taxi down the private runway in the middle of the night.

"We should just tell him the truth." He sighs, running a hand through his hair nervously.

I snort. "It's too late for that."

"I..." He's unable to finish his sentence.

I'm not sure if he was going to say he's sorry or if he wishes we had done things differently four years ago. The truth is, neither matter. He asked me for a favor, and I didn't think twice to give it to him.

He closes his eyes, leaning his head back as the plane picks up speed. I pull my cell out of my pocket, unlock it, and make the call to give the heads-up that we're coming. Then I'm going to pass the fuck out on this short flight. I'm not only tired but my chest is on fire. The fresh bullet hole feels like it's burning. Devin gave me some pain pills, but I refused to take them. I'd rather feel pain than high.

Chapter 14

Haidyn

Less than six hours later, we're pulling up to the most prestigious hotel and casino in none other than Las Vegas.

I hate this city! The people, the noise, it's too much. I prefer the secluded life. Middle of nowhere, hidden in the mountains, woods, and a basement. I thrive in the darkness. It's where all monsters feel most at home.

But here I am. I've been in this town for all of twenty minutes now. I didn't expect to meet with the Kings, but the events that have taken place over the past four days have led me to their doorstep. Literally.

Getting out of the car, Adam and I walk up the fifteen steps and through the double glass doors. A man dressed in a black three-piece suit greets us. He reminds me of Jessie.

"Gentlemen." He nods, walking over to a private elevator. "They're waiting for you in the conference room." The elevator door slides open, and we step inside, where he presses the thirteenth floor.

I look around the mirrored box as it ascends. Glancing at my watch, I see it's almost three in the morning, which means the sun will be rising at Carnage soon.

The ding notifies us that we're stopping, and the door opens. We step out, and the man holds open a glass door for us, and we enter the conference room.

The Kings stand around a large table that sits every bit of twenty people with all eyes on us.

"It's too fucking early," the one I know as Grave mumbles before throwing back a Monster.

The Kings and the Lords have been in bed with one another for years, but we're not close with them. Our fathers had business with theirs back in the day. I don't know how fucked up their fathers were, but I know what ours were capable of. I can only guess how fucked up it got.

Adam walks over to Cross and gives him a handshake hug. "What's going on, man?" Cross asks him.

"Same ole, same ole," Adam jokes.

"Haidyn." Bones nods, gesturing toward a seat at the table. "This is all we were able to recover." He points at the three cardboard boxes that sit in the center of it.

Last time I saw Bones wasn't a friendly encounter. I got in his face in New York, defending Kashton's actions over a friend of his. But I wasn't wrong—he has no clue how far a Lord will go. I'd also like to tell him that there's a lot about his *friend* he doesn't know, but he can figure it out on his own. Eventually, the truth will come out. It always does.

"I appreciate it," I say, looking over the table.

I called as we were taking off, updated them on what little we had to go on, and asked if they could help us out. Adam thought Las Vegas was the best place for us to start, and I agreed with him. "What was it?" I ask, looking at the boxes.

"Fire," Cross answers.

I snort and joke, "Creative."

"As far as I can come up with, I'd say that he had someone ready to torch the place when he didn't return by a certain date," Bones presumes. "But if I had to guess, I'd say he meant for it all to burn anyway."

"Benny wasn't planning on bringing Ashtyn back here." I shake my head.

The words he said less than ten hours ago are still fresh in my mind. *"I'm not going to kill you." He laughs at Saint, his masked head shaking. "I'm going to lock you all up down here in the cells. I'm going to chain her up in the one right next to you. Let you listen to her cry and sob as I fuck her each day. While I feed her just enough to stay alive but not enough to keep your baby alive. Once your baby dies, I'm going to take her with me and leave you all here to rot in this hell that you love so much."*

Benny was adamant that Saint had knocked her up, which could be possible. He wanted her to lose Saint's baby like she did his four years ago when he raped her. And he was committed to making sure it happened.

I rip open one of the boxes and pull out a few things that hold no value whatsoever. It's just a few papers with burned edges. Then there's a set of playing cards.

Opening the second box, I see a set of pictures. My stomach sinks when I realize who they are. Ashtyn. They are Polaroids of her sleeping naked in a bed. Some she's awake, staring at the camera. Kissing the camera. She's got her legs spread, her hand between them, playing with herself and staring at him while he's taking the photos. "Goddammit." I slam them face down so the Kings can't see them, but I'm sure they already have. I can at least spare Adam.

"Told you we should have shredded those," Grave mumbles to Bones.

I reach in and grab an old wicker basket. Flipping it open, I growl when I see more fucking pictures, but looking over them has me curious. "You guys know who is in these photos with Benny?" I ask, showing the Kings.

"No." Titan and Bones both answer. Cross shakes his head, and Grave opens another Monster. There's a fifth guy who stands in the corner—Oliver Nite. I know him even less than I do the Kings, but it can't hurt to ask. Obviously, they are close with him if he's in here. He too shakes his head.

"You?" I put it up to Adam's face.

"Nope."

I go back to digging in the box, and something at the bottom catches my eye. I pick it up and remove the chip before tossing it onto the table. "Where is this from?" I ask, seeing there's more covering the bottom. Maybe five thousand dollars' worth.

"Mason brothers." Adam is the first to answer, looking down at it. I've kept in touch with Adam over the past four years, but I'm not always aware of where he is. Whatever his job is—keeps him busy traveling the world. He comes and goes as he pleases, and I don't ask any questions.

Bones picks it up, and his hard eyes meet mine when his fist tightens around it.

"Are they here in Vegas?" I ask, looking at Adam, and he nods.

Grave explains. "They run the Airport..."

"I want to meet with them." I interrupt him, not really caring what the Airport is.

Bones shakes his head. "We don't do business with them."

"I don't give a fuck what you guys do or don't do with them. I have questions, and they might have answers," I inform him. We flew all this way, and I'm not returning to Carnage until I get what I want. Ashtyn and Kashton have been blowing up my phone. Saint has been dead silent, but I expected that.

Adam made it very clear that Benny wasn't going to speak. I don't doubt my brothers—Kashton and Saint—I can't say that they can make Benny talk, but I can say that Saint will just kill him. He won't do it on purpose. It'll be a heat-of-the-moment sort of situation. Especially after he recently kidnapped and raped Ashtyn for four days.

"Let's go." Adam is already headed to the double glass doors.

"I'll take you guys—"

"Grave." Bones interrupts his brother. The growl in his voice tells me he doesn't want Grave anywhere near these Mason brothers. Again, I don't give a fuck. Grave is a grown-ass adult and can do whatever he wants.

"I'll join them," Cross adds, and Titan stays silent.

I'm not here to start problems, but I'm not leaving until I get what I came for. And the less time I'm in this godforsaken town, the better.

"We don't need babysitters." Adam chuckles.

"Not just anyone can walk in and speak to them," Grave points out. "I can't even guarantee they'll give you what you want."

"I can get us in," Adam states, and everyone turns to look at him as if to silently ask him how he can do that, but he keeps quiet.

Good enough for me. "Let's go." I turn to give them my back and head for the glass double doors.

"This morning?" Cross asks.

I face them, and Grave downs what's left of his second energy drink. "Yes. Now." I rip the door open and exit the conference room. The sooner I speak to them, the sooner I get back home.

♠

The Airport is exactly what I thought it'd be. An actual airport in the middle of the desert. But by the lack of planes, I'd say they're not pilots. I want to ask what exactly this place is but I just can't bring myself to care enough.

We pull into a parking garage and climb out of the back of the SUV, walking with Grave and Cross toward a bank of elevators.

"The Mason brothers don't give information without something in return," Grave informs me.

I nod, placing my hands in the pockets of my jeans. "Nothing worth knowing ever comes free." Lords are always willing to pay in blood. A pound of flesh is the only acceptable payment.

Cross snorts, and Grave nods in agreement while Adam remains quiet.

We enter the building, and the flashing lights and blaring music remind me of a nightclub. But it's got multiple levels and looks exactly like an abandoned airport.

They take us up a flight of stairs and knock on a door before opening it. We step inside, and a guy sitting at a table looks up at us and smiles at the Kings. "Grave, come to fight?"

He laughs. "Not tonight."

One of the guys looks at me and bows his chest. "Bringing in strays, Grave? That's beneath a King." Then he looks at Adam.

I reach into my pocket, and the guy sitting at the table jumps to his feet and removes a gun from his hip, pointing it right at me. Before I can say sit the fuck down, Adam punches him in the face, knocking him back into his seat. He yanks his gun out of the waistband and points it at the guy's head.

"Whoa." Grave raises his hands. "We didn't come to kill anyone tonight." There's laughter in his voice as the guy rubs blood from his face while glaring up at Adam.

I remove the poker chip from my pocket and toss it onto the table.

"You can put the gun away," the one standing orders Adam,

picking up the chip. He flips it over, eyeing it, and then tosses it back to me. I catch it as he speaks. "You can cash in your winnings in the basement."

Adam slowly tucks his gun back into his jeans.

I remove the picture from my back pocket and drop it onto the table as well. "Know either one of them?" I ask.

The guy huffs his annoyance but looks down at the picture before his eyes meet mine. "What's it worth to you?"

"Whatever you want," I answer, and his brows shoot up in surprise. I have a feeling that most don't offer them that, but I also am not like most men.

The one bleeding from the face wipes the blood from his nose. "Not sure what you can give us that we can't get ourselves."

Grave smiles. "Where are my manners? Mason brothers...I introduce you to two of the Spade brothers."

The one sitting in the chair swallows, and the one standing looks down at him, narrowing his eyes. Then he looks back up at Adam for a second. It's as if he recognizes him but wasn't aware he was a Spade brother. I'm not surprised. It's not something we publicly announce. His eyes meet mine when he speaks again. "Let's see what we can do for you guys."

Just then, the door opens, and we all turn around to see a man walk in. He seems to resemble the other two in looks. I'm guessing another brother. He slams the door and speaks, "Christopher just backed out tonight."

The brother who obviously runs the show looks at Grave. "I'm going to need you to fight tonight."

"Fine." Grave sighs as he picks up an open Red Bull that sits on the table and slams it like he's a college student at a frat party. Then he looks at me and Adam. "You two owe me."

Add it to my fucking tab.

Chapter 15

Haidyn

We've been here for two hours and nothing. We've watched surveillance cameras; the brothers let us speak to everyone working at the bar. I don't know if Benny kept a low profile or if the chips found at his place aren't his. Hell, maybe they were Ashtyn's. Who knows where she went in this town? She was here for four years. Maybe she allowed customers to pay her with them when she worked at Glass? The options are endless.

I feel like this trip was for nothing.

We've watched several men get the shit kicked out of them. Grave is coming on in less than twenty minutes, and he's the talk of the Airport. Everyone waits to watch him beat some guy who hasn't lost his last ten fights or some shit like that.

The flashing lights give me a headache, and the music isn't helping. Right now, "I Can Hold a Grudge Like Nobody's Business" by Adam Jensen blares from the speakers.

"We'll figure it out," Adam screams into my ear as if reading my mind.

Not sure *figure it out* are the exact words I'd use, but I'm making it my mission to get the answers that I want.

We stand at the end of the bar. Adam drinks a beer, and I have a water. I'm not in the mood to get fucked up. I look up to see Bones and Titan making their way through the throngs of people. Nite is right behind them. Everyone does a double take when they see who is walking. They're practically royalty in this town. Where we Spades prefer the darkness, the Kings live in the spotlight. From their flashy hotel and casino to all the news coverage about their relationships to Grave's arrests and addiction. They can't escape it, even if they wanted to.

"Thought you weren't coming?" Adam calls out, nodding at him.

"That was before I got a text that Grave was fighting." He stands next to me, facing the bar, and orders a drink.

I don't know the Kings all that well, but I know that Grave has a past with addiction. It doesn't take a lot to see that Bones is protective over his little brother. The fact that he's here proves it.

Just then, a group of women walk up behind him, and a brunette grabs his hand, making him turn around to see who it is. He drapes his arm over her shoulders and pulls her into his side. Obviously, it's his girl.

I look over the other three and recognize one of them. The redhead. Her eyes scan the crowd, meeting mine and then Adam's before lingering on Nite. She steps away, but Adam grabs her upper arm and stops her. She turns around and glares at him. "We—"

"Need to talk." He interrupts her.

"No need." She gives him a smile, but it has "fuck you" written all over it. I'm not sure what the fuck is going on there. They were fighting the last time I saw them together.

I GASP, SITTING UP, AND ARMS INSTANTLY WRAP AROUND ME, squeezing me tightly. I go to push them off but realize who it is. "Ash?" I say.

"Oh my god, Haidyn," she cries, climbing onto my lap. "I thought you were dead."

I wrap my arms around her and hold her tightly. "Baby girl." I breathe a sigh of relief. Last I remember seeing her, we were in the back of a van, and she was sobbing while I lay on the floor bleeding after they ran our car off the road and shot me.

"We can reminisce later." Adam claps his hands and pulls her from me. "We got shit to do."

She rips herself from him and wipes the tears from her face, sniffling.

"How do you feel?" Adam asks me.

"Good." I nod.

"We've got maybe twenty minutes before the adrenaline wears off," he tells me, and I jump down off the metal slab, taking a quick look to see we're in the morgue at Carnage.

"Adrenaline? What the fuck are you into?" Jasmine demands, glaring at him.

He doesn't answer her, and I wonder what the hell she's doing here at Carnage. "What the fuck have I missed?" I ask, stretching my neck and arms. Fuck, I feel good right now, but Adam is right. It won't last long.

"Apparently as much as I have." Jasmine crosses her arms over her chest.

"We don't have time," Adam growls at her.

"How many days has it been?" I look at Ashtyn.

She drops her face to stare at the floor. "Four," she whispers, and I get a pain in my chest that has nothing to do with the bullet Devin removed. "Ash—?"

"Put this on." Adam interrupts me, placing a bag on the slab I jumped off. "The girls are going to help us."

I LOOK BACK AND FORTH BETWEEN ADAM AND THE REDHEAD. That was just yesterday when I woke up in the morgue and tied the girls up and pretended to take them as hostages to fool Benny into thinking we were his men. We needed the element of surprise. We couldn't have pulled it off without them.

"Jasmine—"

"Adam." Her tone further proves my point that she still wants to punch his lights out.

"We should—"

"I have syphilis," she states, and I choke on the water in my mouth.

He smiles at her. "No, you don't."

She rolls her eyes and rips her arm from his hold, stomping off with a bleach blonde following her. She must belong to Cross because he also follows them, finding an open space at the bar to order drinks away from us.

"Man, you must have really fucked up for her to choose an STD over your dick." Bones laughs, finding too much joy in their exchange. Even Titan can't hide his laughter, and Nite smiles.

I lean into Adam. "You know she's been fucking Kash, right?"

He snorts. "Pretty sure I was fucking her first." He steps away, making his way through the crowd, and pushes his way to the bar so he can stand next to her.

I notice Bones and Titan watching the exchange before they both look at me. I shrug, staying the fuck out of that. I have enough problems of my own, and I'm in this godforsaken city to fix one of them.

I'm actually surprised to see her here since she was just at Carnage. She's close with Ashtyn. She probably felt that she and Saint needed their privacy after everything. I don't blame her.

"What the fuck is up, man?" a guy calls out, coming up to me.

I set my water down as he approaches, and we do the half handshake hug. "What are you doing all the way here in Vegas?" I ask. The Lord is a long way from home since he lives in New York.

His eyes slide to one of the Mason brothers helping behind the bar and then back to mine. "Business never sleeps." He smirks, and his eyes find Jasmine at the bar. Hooke went to Barrington with my brothers and me. He graduated the same year as us.

I pick up my water, shaking my head in disbelief. "Ain't that the truth."

The lights turn off, and the crowd screams when the music stops. A spotlight comes on, pointing over in a corner to a hallway, and Grave bounces out of it as "Bloody Nose" by Hollywood Undead plays. The crowd gets louder than I knew possible.

I turn around to the bar and hold up my water, signaling that I want another one. I'm rethinking not having any alcohol because it's going to be a long day. For the first time since the Lords have forced me to start seeing therapists, I wish I had those sleeping pills on me. And the pretty brunette naked in my bed to bury my cock into as I pass the fuck out.

CHARLOTTE

I FEEL LIKE I'M RUNNING CIRCLES AROUND HAIDYN. I PRETEND to know what the fuck I'm doing, and he just tells me that he wants to fuck me. It's getting to the point where I go home, get undressed, and get myself off thinking of him.

It's unbearable. This guy is mentally fucking me, and I'm just supposed to take it. I haven't heard from the Lords in a few weeks. Have they forgotten me? Surely not. I'm not going to give up.

I've done everything they asked me to do.

Sitting up, I run my hand over my face and groan at the pounding headache I have from going out last night.

"You okay?" A hand gently rubs my back, and I nod.

"Yeah." My mouth is dry, and my tongue is heavy. My eyes feel crusty, and my hair is a tangled mess. I went to Blackout last night and got hammered. My mind has been fucking mush since I ran out of the basement at Carnage a week ago. I hate how often I looked around, hoping to see Haidyn there.

Getting out of bed, I manage to make my way to the bathroom and look at myself in the mirror. I'm still wearing my makeup from last night, but it's smeared across my cheeks.

Turning on the sink, I splash my face and decide that only a shower can fix this hungover disaster. I turn on the water and step inside. Falling to my ass, I sit under the sprayer and let the hot water rain down on me.

The door opens, and Wesley smiles at me. "Here, you need to drink something." He places a bottle of water in the corner so the shower doesn't hit it.

I thank him, and he closes the door, so the steam fills the large space. After I spilled my drink on him the first night we met at Blackout, he got my number and asked me to dinner the next day. We've been seeing each other ever since. I wish I really liked him, but it's just part of the job. And I pray to whatever God might exist that the Lords don't forget what I'm doing.

It's happened before or so I've heard. The Lords are a large secret society, and no one knows who is really in charge. It's not like there's a 1-800 number that you can call to reach an operator.

Sure, I have an Apple watch, cell, and laptop, but I'm not reaching out to them. I'll continue to wait to see what directions they give me.

"Your mother just called. We've got lunch with her today," Wesley calls out.

"We?" I ask.

He opens the door once more and smiles at me. "Yeah, I figured I'd go with you. You don't mind, do you? If so...I don't have to go."

"No. It sounds great." Just what I want. My mother to see me hungover.

His smile grows. "I told her noon would be best. That gives you plenty of time to shower and get ready."

"Sounds great," I tell him, and he shuts the door.

I lean my head against the cool wall. He's a good guy, but I like my space. It's hard enough to be someone else when with Haidyn. But having to continue that on a day-to-day basis twenty-four seven is so draining.

My mother knows what I'm doing, and that Wesley is my fake boyfriend. It's not uncommon for the parents of the Lords to know what their sons are required to do for initiations or assignments. I'm really close with my mother and tell her everything. And it's nice to have someone in your corner, wanting you to succeed.

♠

At twelve o'clock sharp, I pull up to my mother's house. My father bought it for her back when she was his chosen. He proposed to her that same day in the backyard. After my father died, my mother was regifted, and my stepfather moved in. He didn't have any kids, and my mother wanted to remain in the house where I grew up. William was nice enough to accommodate her wishes.

Turning off my SUV, we get out and make our way inside. I've taken two painkillers and downed a bottle of water and a handful of crackers. I also put more makeup on than usual to cover up the dark circles under my eyes. She'll still notice, though.

Entering the house, I call out for her. "Mom?"

"Hello, darling." She walks into the foyer, her Louboutins clicking on the white marble floor.

Wesley knows that my family is wealthy. He just doesn't know the truth of how they acquired it. He thinks my mom married into money, and I've never corrected him. It doesn't matter, and he can judge her all he wants. It'll still be better than telling him about the Lords.

His father has money, and his mother was a gold-digging whore—his words—who left his father when Wesley was three. She got the summer villa along with twelve million. The only thing she didn't want...was Wesley. His father raised him and has gone through several marriages since. But he learned his lesson when it came to prenups.

"Hey, Mom." I hug her as she approaches me.

Pulling back, she frowns, looking over my face. "Darling, you have to start getting more sleep," she scolds me with a smile.

I step to the side, and Wesley gives her a kiss on her cheek, telling her how pretty she looks today. She's always done up and looking her best.

"Where's William?" I ask. He always greets me when I come home.

"He had to leave town this morning." She gives me a smile. "He received a work call last night."

I nod. *The Lords.* This is why I could never have a relationship outside of the society. Not like they would allow it anyway. I'd be choosing to walk away, and I'm too deep at this point. The only way out is death.

"I'm going to use the restroom," Wesley announces before he walks down the hallway and into one of the many guest bathrooms.

"Come on, darling. You need to get some food in you. Help that hangover."

I follow her into the formal dining room to see her staff has already set the table. I sit down and wait for Wesley to join us. My mother likes him. She thinks he's a good filler. And that you must do what must be done to get where you want to be in life. And my mother wants nothing more in this life than for me to get ahead with the Lords. Not many women get the chance like I'm getting, and I refuse to let her down.

Chapter 16

Haidyn

I wake up, my head foggy and my eyes heavy. Last I remember I was tied to a cold table, and Devin was injecting adrenaline into my chest. Then he was cutting the bullet out of my chest. I blink, and the room comes into focus. I try to move and can't. "Ashtyn?" I ask, my voice cracking. I clear my throat. "Ashtyn?"

A hand slaps over my mouth, and I can't even fight them. At this point, I hope they just stab me to death. My body has given up.

"Shh." A set of green eyes look down into mine, and I sigh at the familiar face.

It's Adam.

He removes his hand, and I look around to see I'm in a hospital room back at Carnage. How long have I been out? Where did the guys go who kidnapped me and Ashtyn? "I—"

"Shut the fuck up, Haidyn," Adam whispers harshly while he's over at the counter.

My eyes do a quick scan to see he's dressed in all black with a bulletproof vest on. A black mask sits on the counter as well.

"Where is Ashtyn?" I ask, needing to know.

"She's...back here at Carnage," he says, and I don't like the way he says it.

"What do you mean back?"

He turns to face me with a syringe in his hand. "Listen, I don't have a lot of time. Do you want to help her or not?"

I nod. "Of course."

Walking over to the door, he opens it, and I see Gavin enter. They exchange a look that makes my pulse pick up. What the fuck have I missed? How long have I been out?

Gavin comes over to the bed and starts putting cold sticky pieces of tape on my chest and connecting wires to them. "You're going to have to appear dead, Haidyn. But I'm going to bring you back."

I blink, my eyes heavy, but I manage to nod. "O-kay." Licking my busted lips, I add, "Do what you have to do."

Adam looks at Gavin and nods. "See you on the other side, brother." He places the needle into the lead in my IV, and my body instantly feels cold. My heart slows, and I feel like I've been paralyzed before everything goes black.

I SIT STRAIGHT UP, GASPING FOR AIR. ONE HAND GOES TO MY chest, the other to cover my face. "Fuck," I groan at the lingering pain from the bullet I took after the wreck.

"Can I get you anything, Sir?"

I drop my hands and look up at the flight attendant. She's staring down at me with a soft smile on her face.

"No, thanks," I answer, and she looks like she wants to ask again, but instead nods and makes her way to the back of the private jet.

I left Adam behind in Vegas. He said he had something to take care of, and I left it at that. It was a fucking waste of time. I have nothing but a picture of a man that we don't know, and I've barely slept in the past twenty-four hours when I could have been passed out and high on pain meds.

Kashton and Ashtyn are still blowing up my cell, and I continue to ignore them both. Still nothing from Saint. I'm not even sure what to do now. I had a plan, but of course nothing is going as I wanted it to. Like my fucking life.

Sighing, I lean back and close my eyes again, trying to get a nap in before I land back in Pennsylvania. Who knows what shit show I'll return to.

CHARLOTTE

"O.M.W." by Mellina Tey blasts from my earbuds as I round the corner toward my house. It's a muggy morning, and the road is still wet from last night's storm. I'm drenched in sweat. My goal for this morning was two and a half miles, but I went well over three.

Slowing down, I suck in breath after breath coming up to my house. I see the bright red Ferrari backed into my driveway. Wesley stayed the night last night. Again. The guy is becoming more clingy than I like.

I remove the earbuds and hustle up the steps, opening both double glass doors. I try to catch my breath as the smell of bacon hits me.

Making my way down the hallway and through the archway to the kitchen, I see Wesley standing at my stove cooking. "Smells great, babe." I give him a smile as if I'm thankful.

He turns to me with a smile, holding a spatula in one hand and a glass of orange juice in the other. He's wearing nothing but a pair of sweatpants. "I thought you'd be hungry after your run."

I tell myself it's not his fault we're in this situation. He's so thoughtful and a really nice guy. I feel bad for using him the way I do. But the Lords ordered it, so I couldn't not do it.

I lean up on my tiptoes and give him a soft kiss on his lips. "I have to get ready." Then I walk toward the primary bedroom.

He follows. "Babe...you have to eat."

"I'll grab something on my way out," I state, entering my en suite bathroom. I remove my cell holder around my right arm and stop my playlist. Then I peel the nasty sports bra off my sweaty chest and back before shoving my leggings down my thighs along with my thong.

I turn to start the shower and see him standing in the doorway. With both arms above his head, he's gripping the top of the doorframe. His eyes drop to my legs and slowly make their way up to my chest. We haven't had sex. I hate to say I tried one night when I was wasted, but he turned me down.

I wouldn't say he's religious, but he believes in values that people in my world don't even know exist. He's been engaged before, and she cheated on him. She was still going to walk down the aisle. He called it off three weeks before the big day, and he said he couldn't go through that again. I haven't cheated on him, but I'm no better than her. I'm only in this relationship for myself. I told myself the Lords wouldn't know if I slept with one guy. Who knows when I'll become a Lady. It could be years from now.

We made a pact on our third date that we both wanted to wait until we got married. A month into our fake relationship, I threw myself at him, and he told me no. He reasoned that if we couldn't honor something so small, how could we ever honor each other in a marriage? He sees me as the endgame while I'm just playing him.

A part of me says fuck the Lords. How will they know if I'm no longer a virgin? But another part of me knows they see everything, and he isn't part of that world. I refuse to get him hurt because I stepped over the line drawn for me by the Lords. They love making the innocent pay, and the guy I'm pretending to be with is definitely innocent. So I haven't tried since.

"I was thinking about trying out that new restaurant tonight?" He looks away, breaking the silence. "That sushi place that you sent me the link to?"

"Sounds good."

He nods to himself before walking toward me. He kisses my cheek and then turns to leave. "Have a good day today, babe. Call me when you get a chance."

I don't have time to savor the shower, so I hurry to wash my hair and body, already trying to mentally prepare myself for what's to come. That's why I went for a run. I needed to clear my mind.

Once finished, I turn off the water just as I hear a crashing sound. "What the fuck?" I grab the towel on the counter and rush into the kitchen to find the eggs and bacon on the floor. My cat is eating them up. I sigh. "Muffin."

She looks up at me and meows. "Well, one of us should enjoy it."

Making my way back to the bathroom, I proceed to get ready. Drying my hair, I twist it into a tight bun at the nape of my neck. Then I put on very little makeup, just powder and mascara. Entering the closet, I pick my most unflattering tan bra. No push-up, no designs. And then a black button-up shirt. I tuck it into a white pencil skirt that hits my knees and comes high up on my waist, then top it off with a white blazer and a pair of three-inch heels. Not my first choice, but I'm not trying to look too fuckable, just professional.

Then I make a quick coffee, head to the garage, and get into my

SUV. I set out to take the twenty-minute drive to the middle of nowhere. Carnage is a prison of sorts, if you can call it that. Prisoners are treated like kings compared to how the Spade brothers treat the men and women they lock up.

Pulling up to the gates, I roll down my window and punch in the access code. They open, allowing me to enter. I take the winding two-lane road until the trees clear, and the building comes into view. It's an old castle. From just the time I've spent here, I'd say the place is haunted. But if I were locked inside and tortured until they decided to let me die, I'd haunt the fuck out of the place too.

Getting out of my SUV, I take the steps on shaky legs. I'm thankful I decided to wear my subtle three-inch heels and not my hooker ones.

When I push open the doors, Jessie greets me like the last time, dressed in his usual all-black tux. He frowns when he sees me. "Good morning, Miss Hewett. Did no one call you?"

"Call me for what?" I inquire. Dear Lord, not this again. I'm still having nightmares of my last session with Haidyn.

I don't talk to any of the Spade brothers other than Haidyn, and that's only because I'm forced to be in his presence. If I saw him out, I'd drool over him, of course, but I sure as fuck wouldn't have the balls to confront him. Well, maybe if I had enough tequila. But I'd have to be so drunk that I'd probably puke on his combat boots.

"Haidyn isn't here."

My eyes shoot to the staircase as Saint Beckham Carter walks down them. He never speaks directly to me, and I prefer it that way.

"Where is he?" I demand. He cares about no one's time but his own—typical self-absorbed Lord. But I'm a new me. Well, newer than I was when I was here last time. I'm staying no matter what he tries to throw at me today.

"Don't know." He shrugs, coming to stand next to Jessie.

"Saint," a woman calls out, and I look up at the staircase once more to see a brunette coming down after him. She holds a cell in one hand. "He's not answering," she growls. "You said Haidyn—"

"Can the two of you give us a second?" Saint interrupts her.

She stops and frowns at him before her eyes meet mine, noticing they're not alone. It's the girl from the photo with Haidyn and the other Spade brothers. *She's supposed to be dead.* Or so that's what I've found from the research I've done on the Spade brothers. Obviously, that's not the case. My eyes drop to her left hand to see she's wearing a wedding ring, and I glance at Saint's left hand. He also wears one. Interesting.

"Saint..."

"I'll be right up," he says sternly, and she straightens her shoulders before turning and rushing back up the stairs.

Without a word, Jessie turns and walks out of the grand foyer, disappearing down a side hallway.

"May I speak to you privately?" Saint asks, and the hairs on the back of my neck rise.

"Sure," I answer because you don't tell a Spade brother no. I'm honestly surprised he even asked. The Spade brothers I've done research on force you to do what they want. Usually, it involves gags and chains. Just like Haidyn showcased the last time I saw him.

He turns and begins to walk away, and I silently follow him. He enters a room to the left of the foyer and shuts the door behind me. I turn to face him and run my hands down my skirt. It's a nervous habit that I'm aware of but can't seem to stop. "What's going on, Saint?"

"Haidyn has been gone for a week."

"When is he coming back?" I can't not report to them. Although Haidyn doesn't give me shit at our meetings, at least it's something.

"We don't know."

"Well, what do you know?" I bark, getting pissy. My ass is on the line. I wouldn't volunteer to be here if I didn't have to.

"That's all I can tell you," he answers vaguely.

I hold my arms out to my sides. "Then why are we hiding out in here?"

"Things have been...complicated." He avoids my question once again.

"This is ridiculous." I pull my cell out of my purse and call Haidyn's number. It's the first time I've ever needed to call it. Placing it to my ear, I listen as it rings once and goes to voicemail. I hang up and look at Saint. He has a *told you so* look on his face. I call it again. It goes to voicemail after the second ring. "Dammit."

"I'll let you know when he returns." He reaches for the door and opens it for me. "Oh, and Charlotte..."

"Yeah?" I turn and look at him.

"You'll let me know if he contacts you first." It's not a question, but it confuses me even more. Why would Haidyn reach out to me before his brothers? What the fuck has happened that they aren't speaking to one another?

"Of course," I say even though I know it's impossible.

I storm out of Carnage and drop into the seat of my SUV and call him again. Voicemail.

"FUCK!" I hate being ignored. It's one of my biggest pet peeves. I pull up the app downloaded on this cell when the Lords gave it to me. It's untraceable and only contacts one number that's not saved to my contacts. The one person who I think can help me in this situation.

UNKNOWN answers immediately. "Why are you calling?" the altered voice demands. Did they expect me not to use it? They've contacted me before via this phone.

"Haidyn is MIA," I answer. "How do you want me to proceed?" I'm not going to pretend that I know what I'm doing. But I can't do shit if I don't make some kind of contact. So far, just showing up has been enough for the Lords. I report each visit. If I send nothing, then it shows no effort on my end. I'm not getting in trouble because he's shacked up with some prostitute in the middle of nowhere while I'm being forced to go without.

"What do you mean by MIA?" they ask, the altered voice sounding much more concerned.

"I'm sitting in my car at Carnage, where Saint just informed me that Haidyn has been gone for a week. No contact and no information as to where he's gone or when he'll return."

The Lord is silent on the other end for a few seconds before he speaks. "You have two days to find him."

"What—?"

"If you don't have anything to give us in two days, we will have no choice but to believe you've failed your assignment." *Click.*

"Goddammit," I shout, tossing my phone onto the passenger seat. Now what the fuck do I do?

Chapter 17

Haidyn

I sit on the couch in my house back in Pennsylvania, staring at my cell phone. I had to shut it off because I'm tired of ignoring all the calls and texts. Ashtyn has been blowing it up along with Kashton, but again, there's still nothing from Saint.

Charlotte has started calling me too. I didn't forget that I was supposed to see her today. I just don't care. I don't have time for whatever bullshit the Lords are up to with her.

Unless they're handing her to me to fuck, I'm not interested. And as much as I want nothing more than her naked and tied to my bed, I just don't have the energy to listen to her ask me about my feelings right now.

Ignoring my phone, I look at the pictures I have spread across my coffee table. They're of Benny and another guy that I found in the wicker basket back in Vegas. I've never seen him before, but that doesn't say much. We know very little about Benny to begin with, let alone anyone he knew. He obviously worked for the Lords because he worked with Ashtyn's mother and Laura four years ago. But a lot could happen in that amount of time.

Reaching out, I pick up the glass of vodka and take a sip. My body is fucking killing me this afternoon. Everything hurts. I need movement. Standing, I grab my pack of cigarettes and lighter. Making my way to the sliding glass door, I step outside and onto the wraparound porch.

I light up the cigarette and take a long drag, letting the nicotine fill my lungs. Closing my eyes, I hang my head and like a video playing on repeat, the past month of my life flashes in short clips.

"I've always loved you, Ashtyn."

"Haidyn—"

I open my eyes and take another long inhale from the cigarette, listening to the sound of the wind through the Pennsylvania woods. It wasn't a lie. I love her, but how could I not? I love my brothers just as much. I'd do anything for any of them.

For four years, I pretended to hate her whenever someone mentioned her name. Because it was easier than telling the truth that I helped her run away from the life she was supposed to have.

I just wanted one night with her. To take her out to a nice dinner and let her see that her life wasn't over just because Saint dragged her back. I wanted her to know I didn't rat her out. I kept my promise to keep her safe.

Adam was still pretending to be MIA and her parents dead. I needed to make sure that she knew she could count on me. Just like before.

Running a hand through my hair, I bow my head, hating that Benny ruined my plans for that night.

"ASHTYN?" I SHOUT. "ASHTYN. I'M GOING TO PULL YOU OUT."

I grab her arm and yank her through the broken glass of the SUV. "Ash?" She flinches at my tone, and I pull her to a sitting position. Her eyes meet mine, but she's not seeing me. "What hurts?" I demand. My hands push strands of hair from her bloody face. "Breathe!" She tries to push me away, but I grip her face in my hands. "Fucking breathe, Ash. Come on, baby girl. Take in a deep breath for me."

She begins to choke and then cough. "That's it. Deep breaths. One after the other."

"Hai-dyn." Her body trembles in my hands.

"Don't fucking talk, Ash. Just breathe for me."

Her hands go to her chest, and she yanks on her dress. "Burns..."

"You're okay. It's okay." I run my knuckles down her face, wiping away her tears.

"You're bleeding," she whispers.

"I'm fine. Don't worry about me."

"Hai—"

She's yanked from the ground by her hair as she screams. A man pulls the back of her to his front, wrapping his arm around her neck.

I slowly get to my feet and lift my hands in the air. "Let her go."

Her hands dig into his arm, trying to fight him off, but it's useless. She's too weak after the car wreck that we just had. I'm guessing this is the bastard who ran us off the road.

He laughs at her efforts. "Haidyn. It's good to see you again."

Who the fuck is this? "Let her go!" I shout, stepping forward.

He pulls out a gun and presses the end of the barrel into her cheek. "What would Saint say if he knew what you've done to his girl?"

My jaw sharpens, and I look at her before looking at the masked man behind her. How does he know what we've done?

"Get in the van," he orders me.

"I'll go with you, but she stays behind." I nod to a crying Ashtyn.

"Hmm, as tempting as that is, that's not happening."

I run a hand down my bloody face. I'm so over this shit. "Then you can go fuck yourself."

The man laughs once more before he points the gun at me, and I let out a breath since it's no longer pointed at her.

LIFTING MY HEAD, I TAKE ANOTHER HIT FROM THE CIGARETTE before putting it out on the railing. Then I enter the house and take a drink of vodka before making my way to the bedroom, leaving my cell phone off on the coffee table. I'm done for the night. I'm going to finish this drink and then hit my home gym. I need to work out. It's the only thing that seems to help. If I'm going to be sore and have a hard time getting out of bed in the morning, then it might as well be because I did it to myself. Not because that piece of shit shot me.

Then I'll circle back to the photos tomorrow and start all over.

CHARLOTTE

I sit outside the gated entrance to the house that I'm not supposed to know exists. After I spoke to the Lord yesterday, I went home and pulled up the picture of the black house and did a reverse Google search. It led me here. It seemed too easy.

It's got my mind reeling. If I got the photos from the Lords, then why aren't they the ones to confront him? Especially if they know he's here hiding out at this house? What the fuck do they want from him? The unknown is driving me insane.

I have until tomorrow to give the Lords something, or I've officially failed. I had the opportunity to turn them down and walk away, but I accepted my assignment. So now if I fail, I'm useless to them. And I refuse to be the woman naked and tied to the chair who gets killed over a Lord. The women in my world give the Lords too much power as it is. I refuse to give him my life.

As I stare at the gated entrance, I can't bring myself to push the button. What will I say when he answers? How will I explain that I knew he'd be here? What if he's not?

If his brothers can't find him, does that mean they don't know this place exists? So I shouldn't know it's here. It'll bring up questions that I can't afford to answer. Haidyn doesn't know I'm seeing him because I was ordered to do so.

Obviously, he knows I'm part of his world. They would never allow just anyone to enter Carnage. Especially to come and go. Once you're in, you belong to them.

Picking up my cell, I try to call him once again, but it goes to voicemail. I'm getting desperate and very, very pissed.

Letting out a frustrated sigh, I put the SUV in drive and speed off, needing to clear my head and think of a different approach. How can I get in? I need to get his attention. Maybe I could park down the street, jump the fence, and set his house on fire?

That's a little extreme, but that's what the Lords would expect. They put you in situations where it's either you or someone else. We're like rats—claw or eat your way out for survival.

I highly doubt standing in his front yard and saying, "Oh Haidyn, how are you feeling today?" with a smile on my face wouldn't make him suspicious while his house burned behind him. He'd know that I was the one to set it. Then he'd most likely throw me into the flames, so I'd burn with it.

I'm driving down the curvy road when I see a car in my rearview mirror speeding up on me. The flashing lights turn on.

My eyes drop to the speedometer, and I hit the steering wheel. "Dammit!" Haidyn had all my focus, and I wasn't paying attention. The main road doesn't offer a shoulder, so I slow until I come up to a gravel road on my right. I pull off onto it and bring the SUV to a stop.

He gets out and walks up to my driver's side door as I lower my window, taking in a calming breath. "Good morning—"

"License and registration." The officer interrupts me.

I go for my purse in the passenger seat but stop myself. *Don't give him the wrong one.* I open my glove box and grab what he requests. "Is there a problem?" I ask, pretending I wasn't going fifteen miles over.

He looks over my information, and then his dark eyes meet mine. "Get out of the car."

"What?" I ask, sitting up straighter. My heart picks up speed.

He pulls on the door handle and opens the door.

"Hey—"

"I said get the fuck out of the car." He reaches in, grabs my arm, and yanks me out, making me stumble into him.

"Don't touch me," I snap, and he drags me to the front of the SUV, spins me around, and slams the side of my face into the warm hood, momentarily taking away my vision and fight. It gives him the opportunity to place my wrists in handcuffs behind my back. He tightens them down on my bony wrists, and I cry out, finally able to suck in a deep breath.

He grabs the back of my shirt, yanks me from the SUV, and pushes me to his car, putting me in the uncomfortable back seat and buckling me in. Tears run down my face as I try to adjust my body, but it doesn't do any good. They're too tight.

I watch him return to my car and sit in the driver's seat, but I can't see what he's doing. Moments later, he steps out and walks back to his car. Getting in, he drives off with no explanation.

Chapter 18

Haidyn

I enter the garage at my house and jump on my R1. It's a nice day for a ride. I turn my baseball hat on backward, not bothering with a helmet or leather jacket. I don't wear either often. If it's my time, then it's my time. I'm not one of those who try to prepare for the worst. It's going to happen regardless. I've been shot, stabbed, and drowned. I've lost count at this point how many times I've died, yet here I am.

Placing my sunglasses on, I start the bike and rev the engine, then drive out of the garage, leaving my gated property. I take a right, and before I know it, I'm hitting eighty miles per hour. You can't go much faster than that on the straightaways because the road has too many tight curves you have to slow down for.

I didn't get much sleep last night, but that's normal. I worked out until the early hours this morning and then showered. The sun was already rising when I finally crawled into bed, but I was up within a couple of hours and needed to clear my head or at least try to.

It's been repeating the same events over and over to the point I want to fucking knock myself out. From what I can remember anyway...

I can hear voices, but their words aren't registering, and I have no clue where I am. All I know is that I can't move. My heavy eyes open, and I look around, not able to really focus on what I'm seeing, but I feel cold...and wet.

It's hard to breathe, as if someone is sitting on my chest. The voices start to penetrate the fog.

I recognize Devin's voice immediately. "I just need to sedate him."

"No!" a guy barks out, his voice echoing off the concrete walls that I see. Am I back at Carnage? If so, how did I get here, and where is Ashtyn? We were on our way to dinner...had a wreck...I was shot. Where is she?

Devin speaks. "I can't help him unless he's sedated. I have to cut him open—"

"You have two choices." The man interrupts him, pressing the tip of his gun into the side of my head. "You either cut him as is, or you give him a shot of adrenaline."

I try to talk, but my lips won't move. Where is Ashtyn? She was with me.

The sound of cabinets banging and drawers opening and closing fills the room.

"What the fuck is that for?" one of the men asks.

"What you have on him now won't be enough," Devin explains. "Once the adrenaline hits, he'll be hard to keep down. I need him as immobile as possible, especially if I cut him open." He tightens something over my waist and a couple more on my legs. It makes it even harder to breathe, much less move. "Open," he orders.

My eyes find Devin hovering over my face, and I take in a long, shallow breath, forcing my lips to work. I need to know if she's here. Alive. "Ash-tyn?"

One of the guys laughs. "That bitch is as good as dead. You'll be lucky to join her."

I open my mouth to argue, but Devin shoves a mouthpiece into it. Then I feel the familiar pain that takes what little breath I had left away. My body bows up off the table, straining against the restraints. My jaw locks down on the mouthpiece, and my heart races.

The adrenaline makes me feel invincible even when I'm on the verge of dying. I try to fight, but they've got me strapped down too tight. Devin places a hand on my chest, and then I feel pain like I've never felt. My vision fades in and out as if someone is playing with the lights. The voices fade into the background, and it feels like my insides are being ripped out.

Warm liquid covers my skin as if someone is pouring buckets of water all over me. I could be drowning or on fire. Honestly, it all feels the same. Thankfully, my eyes fall closed, and I openly welcome the darkness. Accepting your death is the most peaceful part.

My hand tightens, pulling back the throttle as I adjust myself on the bike, getting ready for a set of curves coming up when I speed past something white that I catch out of the corner of my eye. I pull on the front-brake lever so hard that my back tire comes off the pavement, putting me in a front wheelie—stoppie—position. Once the back comes down and touches the pavement, I spin it to turn tightly in the road. I speed back and come to a stop when I see the back of the Rolls Royce Cullinan parked in the center of a dead-end gravel road. I park behind the SUV. Getting off my bike, I walk up to it. It's still running, and the driver's side door is open. Looking inside, I see a purse in the passenger seat. I know this SUV. I've seen it countless times on the Carnage cameras. It's Charlotte's. I grab her purse and start going through it. Feminine products, lip gloss, a mirror...everything looks to be there except for a cell phone and wallet.

Where the fuck did she go, and what the fuck is she doing out here of all places?

Getting out, I remove my cell from my pocket and call Adam. He answers on the first ring.

"What's up, man?"

"Four years ago...we had the meeting with that detective at the house of Lords," I remind him as if he could forget.

He's silent for a second, and his voice goes cold when he asks, "What about it?"

"The missing high school girl...they found her BMW? What were the details of the scene?" I ask, looking over Charlotte's SUV. It seems oddly familiar.

He sighs. "The news report said it was found on the side of the road. Abandoned. No girl, no phone, and no purse. It was still running, and the driver's side door was wide open."

The rumor was Adam was the last one to see the driver of that car.

He was being set up to look like he killed the senior cheerleader among other women who had gone missing.

"Why all the sudden interest?" he asks.

"I just found a car, and it's similar."

"Similar how?" Adam demands.

"Abandoned on the side of the road, still running, driver's side door wide open. But there's a purse in the passenger seat. No cell or wallet, though."

"Send me the picture of the car, including the license plate."

Placing him on speakerphone, I step back and take a picture, sending it to him. "Done." Charlotte's been calling me, but I've ignored her. Just like Kashton and Ashtyn.

Seeing her SUV here, so close to my house tells me I'm not getting the privacy I want. And it makes me think she set this up. It wasn't a secret what happened to those women. None of them were connected to the Lords—except a single picture that showed Adam and Ashtyn's mother with one of them—so the local news was covering the disappearance of the bleach-blond cheerleader who went missing before it went viral and made national headlines. And she wasn't the only one. If I remember correctly, it was around twenty.

"Got it. I'll see what I can find out." He hangs up.

I immediately call Charlotte. It goes straight to voicemail, so I leave a short message and hang up, return to my bike, and head back to the house, needing to figure out what my next move is.

CHARLOTTE

I FIND MYSELF DRIVING BACK TOWARD THE HOUSE THAT I WAS running from yesterday. I was arrested and had to call someone. I avoided calling my mother because she'll ask too many questions. I'm still unsure what happened. I was thrown into a cell and was granted one phone call. I chose Wesley. He was the only option I had. My fake friends would judge me, and I can't afford to jeopardize that situation. Plus, it gave Wesley a reason to be there for me. To make us feel closer.

Turns out, he didn't have to bail me out. I was just in holding. Who the fuck knew? I sure didn't. I've never been in that situation before. He took me home and ran me a bath. The tight cuffs left bruises on my wrists. I have a knot on the side of my head from it hitting the hood. The police officer's fingers left bruises on my upper arm when he dragged me from my car to his.

Wesley wants to sue the police. I laughed. Men like him think the system is broken. If he only knew the Lords existed, he'd see just how fucked he truly is.

Wesley stayed the night with me. Last night after my bath, he took me to get my SUV, and while he cooked me breakfast this morning, I turned my cell on and had one message. It was from Haidyn.

"Ten o'clock tomorrow. I'll text you the address." He didn't even bother to say his name. Not like he had to. I recognized his voice the moment I pressed play.

Was it coincidence or luck that he wanted to see me all of a sudden? I'm thinking the latter. But it's not like I can turn him down.

Pulling up to the gates that I sat at yesterday morning, I punch in the code that he sent me with the address, and it opens. The house comes into view. The pictures I saw don't do it justice. It's much bigger in person and too pretty to be hidden in the woods.

Coming to a stop, I turn off my car and get out. Walking up the steps to the front double doors, I knock.

One of them swings open, and I look up to see Haidyn standing there. I've never seen him outside of Carnage other than in the photos the Lords gave me. He's got a white towel wrapped around his neck draped over his broad shoulders, dressed in a T-shirt with the sleeves cut off and gray sweatpants. Judging by his wet hair and sweat covered forehead, I'd say I interrupted his workout. So he either forgot I was coming or didn't give a fuck.

"Haidyn." I nod, and he steps to the side. "Thank you," I mumble, entering the house and running my hand through my hair. I wore it down today to try to put on more makeup than usual for daytime wear to cover my bruises. Thankfully, my eyes aren't swollen.

He slams it shut behind me.

He's in a mood. Of course, he is. I don't even know why I keep doing this. *Because you want this.* Do I? I was given a choice, and this seemed like the best one at the time. I'm trying to prove to my family that I'm the daughter they were meant to have. That I'm not a quitter.

All I ever wanted was to make my father proud. Typical woman trying to do the impossible. Especially considering he's dead. Not like he'll know what I end up doing with my life.

"Do I even want to know how your day is going?" I ask, looking up at Haidyn.

His narrowed eyes land on mine, and I can feel my heartbeat in my cheek. "What the fuck happened to you?" he barks out.

"I'm fine," I say defensively. *How the hell can he tell?* Guess I did a shittier job than I thought covering up the marks.

He steps into me and reaches out. I hold my breath when the tips of his fingers run the length of my forehead and gently down the side of my face, pushing my hair back.

I shove his hand away, getting annoyed and self-conscious. "I said I'm fine."

"Does this have to do with your car being on the side of the road yesterday?"

The hairs on the back of my neck rise. "Have you been following me?" The thought has my stomach doing flips. Does he know where I live? Who I am? No. He can't know that much. If he did, he wouldn't be concerned. Instead, he'd be killing me right now. I live in this city too and can drive on the road outside of his house. He can't prove I was stalking him. Shit! Unless he's got cameras out by the gate. No. No. No. I stayed far enough away not to be seen for that very reason.

He doesn't answer. Instead, his dark blue eyes run over my black dress. It's not revealing in any way. It's high on the neck with long sleeves and comes to my knees. I go to step back, giving up some space, but he grabs my wrists. His fingers tighten to the point I cry out. "Haidyn."

He yanks me to him, forcing me to drop my purse. Pushing my sleeves up on my arms, he reveals my bruised wrist. "What the fuck, Charlotte?"

"It's none of your business," I bark out.

If I wanted him to know, I would have called him instead of Wesley. It's not like he would have answered anyway. He's been avoiding me. This makes me question why he called and left me a message. It wasn't a coincidence. He knew something had happened, and he wanted to see me.

Haidyn steps into me, and I tilt my head back to look up at him. My heart hammers in my chest. He never gets this close, and we've never been somewhere alone. When I see him at Carnage at least I know Saint and Kashton are somewhere nearby. Here, it's just him and me. No one will hear me scream or know to look for me. If I don't report to the Lords, they'll just move on and find someone else to do the job I failed. I'm defenseless here and completely at his mercy.

He cups my face, his large hands softly touching my flushed cheeks. "Talk to me, doll face. What happened...who did this to you?"

Wetness pools between my shaking legs, soaking my underwear, and I stare into his blue eyes, getting lost in the depths of what I've always known to be hell. I can't tell him. I can't afford for him to figure out who I am. It'll all be over, and I'll be a permanent resident at Carnage, naked and chained in the basement. I'm committed to this fake life, and I can't afford to chance it.

"Things got a little rough," I lie, hating how breathless my voice sounds. His presence makes me fucking weak. And although his words sounded like he cared, I know it's a lie. The Lords are masters at manipulation.

His eyes harden. "So you're telling me that someone tied you up and fucked you while slapping you around?" He arches a brow, not buying it.

Blood rushes in my ears at the way he explained someone using my body. How I want. I've never had that before. And a part of me is afraid I wouldn't be able to do it. That I'd cry mercy. Another part of me wants to be gagged so they can't hear me tell them to stop.

"Yes." I lift my chin.

He smirks and lets go of me. My arms fall to my sides like dead weight. "Aren't you full of surprises, doll face."

Chapter 19

Haidyn

She's lying. I don't think she's as innocent as she's acting, but she sure as shit isn't what she's leading on to be now.

"I'm not here to talk about me, Haidyn." It's her favorite line to say. She always tries to divert my attention from herself to me. "We're wasting time." Charlotte pretends to look at her watch. I've never paid attention to it until now. It's a Pave Diamond white gold DateJust—woman's Rolex. I've never guessed if she was part of the Lords world. She was sent to me by them. But now I'm questioning everything about her. I notice she has it high up on her wrist so as not to rub the bruise. "Where would you like to conduct your session for the day?" she asks, pushing the sleeve down to cover them up.

I gesture toward the living room, and she makes her way to the couch. My eyes drop to her black heels and look over the back of her tan legs. I wonder if she lies in a tanning bed, gets a spray tan, or uses a self-tanner. I've fucked enough women to know they always have a preference.

She sits down, opens her large Saint Laurent purse, and pulls out a small notebook. It's not her usual one. I can tell she's wearing more makeup than usual as well. She did a shitty job at covering up the situation from yesterday that she doesn't want me to know about.

I'm still waiting for the information I requested, and until I get it, I have to play along with her game. But I know I'm right. My little doll face isn't who she's been pretending to be, and depending on what I'm told will depend on how I handle her.

I mean, I guess she could be telling the truth, and maybe she and some little boy toy were out for a midday drive and got horny and decided to play around. They pulled over, and he chased her into the woods, where he fucked her while the car just sat there waiting for them to return. When you're in the mood, you're in the mood. But I'm not buying that either. The way her SUV was left there had too many similarities to what happened all those years ago.

"I want to see your notebook." She lifts her eyes to meet mine. "The one I gave you to log your sleeping hours."

Reaching up, I grab either end of the towel that's draped over my shoulders and just stare at her.

She sighs. "Haidyn—"

"It's blank." No reason to lie.

She slams her pen onto her notebook and lets out a frustrated sigh. She's usually good at holding back her annoyance, but I like this side of her. She's unprepared. Does it have to do with me or the situation she was in last night? "Where have you been, Haidyn?"

Her question surprises me. She's never so bold. Why does she all of a sudden have confidence? What has changed that she thinks she has the upper hand? Maybe she's desperate for something. The question is, what the fuck is it?

Blue eyes meet mine, and she sits back on the couch. "Why are we here?" She looks around aimlessly, taking in my house before glaring back at me. "Where is here?"

"You tell me," I counter, and her small body stiffens.

"Well..." She licks her painted nude lips. "You sent me this address after you left me the voicemail...I'm guessing this is your place. But why let me see it? Why not meet at Carnage as usual?"

Why would she mention that I gave her my address when she was already here yesterday? She's trying to convince me that she had no clue I was here.

I sit in the chair opposite her and cross my arms over my chest, meeting her stare. She should know by now that I won't tell her anything I don't want her to know.

"I went to Carnage a couple of days ago for our scheduled meeting, and Saint said you've been MIA. Does this have to do with his wife?"

I stiffen but say nothing.

Her pretty nude lips pull into a smirk, thinking she's onto something. What in the fuck is Saint doing speaking to Charlotte? What did he tell her? And how does she know Ashtyn is his wife? I can't see Saint letting that happen unless it was by accident.

I won't ask those questions. No. I'll let Charlotte dig her own grave. She'll keep talking as long as I stay silent. She'll think she's onto something and ramble on, telling me everything that I want to know.

Her eyes drop to the coffee table and look over the empty glasses, pack of cigarettes, and my cell. I cleaned up the photos but didn't bother with the rest. "They all seem very concerned about your sudden disappearance." She looks up at me again and tilts her head to the side. "Are you on an assignment for the Lords? No." She answers her own question. Reaching up with her right hand, she plays with a dark piece of hair, twirling it around her finger. Usually, her hair is up in a low bun. I've never seen it down before, and it's longer than I expected. The big curls fall down over her chest. It looks so soft, and my hands itch to wrap my fists in it while I fuck her pretty face to shut her the fuck up. "The Spade brothers don't do assignments," she adds, still talking to herself.

"I'll tell you what." I can't help myself. "You tell me why you were sitting outside my house yesterday, and I'll tell you why I'm here."

The smirk on her face falls, and her lips part on a deep breath. Her pretty Barbie doll face pales, and I swear the marks on her cheek darken—becoming more prominent than when she first arrived.

I place my elbows on my knees, leaning forward, my hands grabbing the towel wrapped around my neck. "Only a select few know I live here, and that doesn't include Saint, Kash, or Ashtyn. So how did you know, Charlotte?"

Wide blue eyes fixate on mine as she tries to come up with a lie. Saint and Kashton don't know I bought this house four years ago. I did it to help out Adam. I have stayed here on and off but never for more than one night at a time. Until now.

Getting to my feet, I swear her breathing picks up as I walk around the coffee table and come to a stop before her. I reach out and run my hand through her soft curls, unable to stop myself. It feels better than I imagined. "You know more than you should, Charlotte.

The question is what are you going to force me to do to you to get the truth?"

She remains silent, eyes staring at me while her heavy breathing fills the large room. I sit down on the edge of the coffee table to get eye level with her. I smile as panic covers her pretty features. "I would prefer to fuck you, not have to kill you."

Swallowing, she sits there like a statue. As if she can make herself disappear from my sight.

"Why did the Lords send you?" I'm not stupid. She's connected to the Lords, but the question is how? I have my theories, but I want her to tell me who she is. "How about this?" I reach out and place my hands on her knees. She jumps but doesn't pull away. "Tell whoever you answer to that I left Carnage and have no plans to return."

She blinks and licks her lips nervously. "You..." She clears her throat. "You can't leave Carnage." Her voice is soft, but from the way her eyes widen, I can tell I have her attention.

"No?" My eyes drop to her legs, and my hands slowly push the hem of her dress up, showing me her thighs that she has clenched shut. As if that'll stop me from taking what I've wanted since I first saw her. "A Lord can do whatever he wants as long as he's willing to sacrifice something they want."

"What do you have that they want?" she whispers.

"The question is, what do *you* have that they want?"

"No-thing." She jumps when my fingers dig into her soft thighs.

I want to spread them wide and bury myself inside her. "Why me?" I ask through gritted teeth, getting irritated.

"I don't know." She grabs my wrists, but I don't release her legs. "I promise." Her perfectly manicured nails dig into my skin. I feel her legs stiffen as if she can read my mind. "Haidyn..." she breathes, her eyes on mine. I imagine her kneeling before me, begging me to play with her. To fuck her pretty face until I come all over it.

I release her and stand. "Get the fuck out of my house," I command, needing her to go.

She gets to her feet, grabs her things, and runs out the front door, not needing to be told twice.

Walking to my kitchen, I grab a glass and the vodka, needing a drink. That didn't go how I thought it would, leaving me more confused than yesterday. My cock is hard, and my mind is a fucking mess. I don't have time to worry about what the fuck she's up to when I'm in the middle of trying to figure out what the fuck went down with Benny.

Maybe she was telling the truth, and she really doesn't know what the Lords are up to. Or perhaps she's just really good at lying. Just because she has a pussy doesn't mean she can't be a vindictive bitch.

Just then, my cell rings from where it's sitting on the coffee table. Walking over, I see an incoming call from Adam. "Hello?"

"Got what you asked for," he says.

"And?" I walk over to the floor-to-ceiling windows and watch her start her SUV and tear out of my driveway.

"Annabelle Marie Schults."

That name sounds familiar. Where have I heard it before? "I'm confused. What's that have to do with the license plate I gave you?" That's not who I know Charlotte to be. And she didn't deny it when I asked about her being outside of my house yesterday. So I know it was her.

"That's who owns the car."

I frown. "Her mother? Maybe a sister?" I've fucked a lot of women in my life, but other than that, I've never had much of a life outside of Carnage. So to recognize that last name...I know it from somewhere.

"No." I hear him shuffling papers before he speaks again.

The blood rushes in my ears at the information he gives me. I do, in fact, know who that is. My little doll face is in deeper than I could have ever imagined, but now it all makes sense, and I know exactly what I'm going to do to her.

CHARLOTTE

"SHIT!" I SLAM MY HAND ONTO MY STEERING WHEEL. "WHAT the fuck was that?" I whisper, my eyes constantly looking into my rearview mirror to make sure he's not following me. Or I'm not getting pulled over. Now I'm paranoid. He knows more than I wanted him to.

"The question is, what do you have that they want?"

What if he's onto something that I hadn't realized before? What if this is more about me than him? It can't be, right? They've sent me videos of him. Well...one video. When he was lying in his own blood after it was apparent he had tried to commit suicide.

I watched the way his body stiffened when I mentioned Ashtyn. She's a sore subject. He was pissed off at the fact I even went to Carnage. What did he think I was going to do? We had a meeting scheduled. Surely, he didn't think I'd give up.

Probably. That seems to be what the others before me have done. Or fuck, maybe he killed them. I don't know.

What am I going to tell the Lords? I have to lie. If they knew that I was caught, they'd just end it for me. I haven't come this far to give up now. Or to lose to a Spade brother. He may be bigger and faster, but I'm smarter. I just have to get home and regroup. Take a second to figure out where to go from here.

What's that saying? The bigger they are, the harder they fall?

I can do this. I saw the way he looked at me. I'm too close. He won't give me anything because there's definitely something there. I've just got to dig deeper, and I vow right now to do just that.

♠

It's been a week since Haidyn caught me sitting outside his house. I haven't had any contact with him whatsoever, but I've got another week before I have another scheduled appointment with him.

I reported to the Lords that I had my visit with him last week, and when they asked how it went, I said as good as expected. They didn't question me any further. I left out the officer and the holding cell and needing my fake boyfriend. I felt that wasn't important.

They asked how I found him, and I couldn't lie. If I'm searching for shit on my laptop, then I guarantee they can see it too. That makes me nervous because they can see where he is too.

But I remind myself if they want him dead, he'd be dead. I'm a toy. Something they dangle in front of him while something else happens behind the scenes. That's how they are.

I enter my house and make my way through the kitchen. Frowning, I find it odd that I didn't leave the stove light on like I always do. I went out with my fake friends tonight for dinner and let them talk me into drinks afterward at the bar down the street. I stayed out later than I intended to, but I just needed to clear my mind and try to get it off the Spade brother that has quickly consumed my life. I'm dreaming about him now, for fuck's sake. And most nights, he's strangling me because he wants me dead. The others...he's fucking me.

I flip the switch and grab a bottle of water out of the fridge and unscrew the lid. Turning around, I jump, and water splashes on my face when I squeeze the bottle after seeing someone sitting at my kitchen table.

He's got a black cloak on and a devil's mask with horns. *A Lord.* I haven't heard from them since I reported back last week. Surely, they don't know I'm lying. How would they? I haven't been given any actual instructions that I haven't followed through with. "I...I don't know..."

He stands from the chair, and the legs scrape across the floor from his movement, making me flinch. He steps toward me, and I grab a butcher knife out of the wooden block that sits on the counter. "Stay back," I warn, tightening my shaking hand around the handle.

A dark laugh fills the space, making the hairs on the back of my neck rise. My eyes quickly scan the kitchen. Lords rarely come alone. They're like wolves and travel in packs. They're known for their numbers. They like to improve their odds. Even if they don't need the help, they get off on having an audience.

He takes two more steps closer, and I fling the knife, knowing it's my only option. The last thing I need is for him to take it from me and stab me with it.

The knife lands in what I'm guessing is his upper right arm by the way the cloak hangs, forcing him to come to a stop.

I spin around, taking the opportunity to run toward my bedroom. I slam the door shut to give me an extra second to yank open my top drawer in my nightstand, grab the gun, and turn to shoot. But the sight of him rushing in tells me he's faster. The door hits the interior wall as I fire the gun. The safety is off, and there's one already chambered just as my wrist is grabbed. Though I'm momentarily going deaf from firing the gun, I'm slammed into the wall next to the nightstand. The hand gripping my wrists tightens to the point I scream and drop the gun.

His free hand jerks the knife out of his shoulder and holds the tip to my cheek, making me whimper. I try to push myself into the wall, standing on my tiptoes to get away.

"I like to play with knives," he whispers darkly.

"Pl-ease," I gasp. "I haven't seen your face. You can leave..."

He pushes the mask off, and my breath catches in my lungs. It's far worse than I could have ever guessed. "Haidyn?" I ask wide-eyed.

"Surprise, doll face." He yanks me from the wall and drags me back to the kitchen by my hair.

I fight the best I can, grinding my teeth at the sharp pain in my scalp. He shoves me into a chair at the kitchen table. Leaning over my back, I rub my head as he taps the bloody knife on a stack of papers sitting in front of me. "What...what is this?" I read over it, and my stomach drops. Tears fill my eyes, making the typed-out words blur. "How did you...?" I swallow, unable to finish the sentence.

"Find out you're a fraud?" he questions.

I can't speak. My tongue is heavy all of a sudden. The consequences of him knowing what I've been hiding is horrific. I might as well die because my life means nothing now. No purpose. It's over. The Lords promised me this wouldn't happen. That as long as I did my job, they'd protect me. Now I'm as good as dead.

He goes on. "It's very unfortunate for you, I may add. But not for me."

I know where this leads. This is what the Lords do. They find something they can use against you. "What do you want?" I whisper, my stomach sinking at the possibilities.

"You," he answers simply.

"No." I shake my head. He doesn't even need to elaborate. The answer is no.

"Well, see, now that is also unfortunate for you."

"You going to kill me?" I laugh nervously. I've seen people plead for their life when they knew they had nothing to bargain. I never understood it until now. I'd rather die in a fiery car crash than by Haidyn's hands. Lords pride themselves when it comes to torturing someone. I don't want to be his next victim.

I go on when he doesn't answer. "Bury me at Carnage? Put me in a cell? I have a life," I yell, pointing at my fake name and fake age.

"Friends. People will know that I'm missing." It'll be on news outlets. Today, women who go missing are seen everywhere, thanks to the reach that social media has. Most women in my world go missing and Lords are paid off, but they've had me establish a life outside of them. Wesley alone would make a big fuss if I just up and vanished.

"There are break-ins all the time." He pushes the glass bowl on my kitchen counter onto the floor, and the apples and bananas in it roll across the tile when the glass breaks into a million pieces, making me jump. "Say like last Tuesday. After you left the gym, someone could have followed you home." He grabs my purse off the island, unzips it, and removes my wallet. He pulls out my credit cards and ID and puts them in his pocket. I can't see if they're my fake or real ones from where I sit, though. "Monday, someone could have seen you enter your gate code." He picks up a picture off the wall and drops it, shattering it as well. "Or after you left the vet...how is Muffin by the way? Is she feeling better?" *He's been following me.* Watching me. I never suspected anything since my mind has been elsewhere. I should have been paying attention, but I'm not even sure I would have noticed. "And then your morning runs...you're not very observant when you wear your earbuds. Anyone can take advantage of that."

I jump from my chair, taking a step back. "What do you want? Me to go to Carnage with you so you can lock me in the basement and torture me? Rape me?" I'm trying to act like it's impossible, but my mind says he has it all figured out. At any time, he's got a plan to make sure I'm wiped from this world. No one will know where I am. And when I'm not found after days, weeks, and months, they'll just give up. No one is dragged into Carnage and then allowed to walk out. Plus, no one willingly visits Carnage either. Like I did. So no one will think to look for me there. The Lords will give up and move on to someone else. I'll be a lost cause. They'll assign him another therapist to get whatever they want from him while he slowly tortures me to death.

And that makes me wonder...if the news puts Charlotte on TV, will the Lords shut it down because Charlotte will lead them to Annabelle. People will see that I'm missing, but it will also show the world that I'm two very different people.

He gives me a cruel smile that makes my already racing heart skip a beat. Reaching out, he cups my chin and runs his thumb over my trembling lips. The small act paralyzes me where I stand. "I won't have to rape you, doll face. You will crawl to me and beg me to fuck your mouth all on your own."

My breath hitches, and I feel my insides tighten at the thought. Because I've dreamed about him. Giving him what he wants—my body. And imagined what he could do to it if given the chance. But I won't let him see that. Because he wants to make me a prisoner. "Fuck you, Haidyn."

He grabs the back of my neck and shoves me down into my seat. "Either you willingly give yourself to me or I kill you right now. What's it going to be?" He picks up the bloody knife and holds it to my neck. I lift my chin, my eyes downcast as the blood rushes in my ears. The tip pushes into my skin, and I suck in a deep breath, trying to make space, but it just pushes harder as it punctures my skin.

"Fi-fine." I manage to get out. What choice do I have? This is my only bargaining chip.

"Use your words, *Charlotte*. Fine what?" he asks, arching a brow.

Taking in a shaky breath, I whisper, "I'll go with you."

"That's my good girl."

His good girl? Why does that make my shaking thighs clench?

He throws the knife back onto the table, and I suck in a deep breath, rubbing my neck and smearing the blood. I'm not sure how much is mine or his from where I stabbed him.

He picks up a bag on the table and unzips it. He pulls out something that looks like an ear-piercing gun. "Haidyn?" I stand once more and take a step back, but he turns, grips my hair, and bends me over the table.

I moan as he smashes the side of my face to the cold surface. I feel him come to stand behind me, shoving my hips into the edge, pinning me in place. His hand twists my hair in his fist, holding me down. I feel something pinch the back of my neck, making me yelp. Then he releases me.

I slowly get up and fall into the chair as tears well up in my eyes, pushing my tangled hair back from my face.

"That's a tracking device."

"What?" I shriek. My hand goes to the back of my neck, praying he's wrong. My fingers press into the sensitive area, trying to dig it out.

"I'll collect you in five days. In the meantime, live your life like normal. Tell all your friends and family you're going on a vacation and won't have phone service. You're cutting yourself off from the world. I'll be back to get you on Friday." With that, he picks up the bag and tosses it over his shoulder.

I jump to my feet, panic gripping my chest. "Haidyn?" I rush out, and he stops and turns to face me. I'm not sure what to say. He's made up his mind. I will be his, and he'll do whatever he wants with me. I lick my lips as he waits patiently for me to say whatever I need to get off my chest. I can only think of one question. "For how long?" When you face prison time, the first thing you want to know is how long of a sentence you'll have to serve. I need to know how long I'll be his whore for.

He begins to walk toward me, and I go to step back, but the sound of the glass crunching underneath my shoes reminds me there is nowhere for me to go. He sets the bag on the kitchen table once more and places both hands on my jawline, making my pulse race. He shoves my head back, forcing me to look up at him. His thumb runs over my parted lips, and the blood rushes in my ears at the tenderness in his touch. Nothing about the Lords is soft. They are rough with their toys. Then they toss them to the side for others to play with. I've heard stories, and they're all the same.

His dark blue eyes search mine as my heavy breathing fills the room. It's spinning, and I wish I'd just black out.

Lowering his head, he pushes his lips to mine, and he kisses me. Tongue in my mouth and hands on my face, he sucks what little breath I have left from my lungs as if he's a demon come to take my soul.

And like a willing servant, I kiss him back. All the noises go silent, and my eyes fall closed at the taste of his kiss. He's soft yet dominant at the same time. Taking not only my breath away but also my body.

Was it ever a fair fight? I don't think so.

He pulls away, and I open my heavy eyes to meet his. "That depends on you."

"Me?" I whisper. If it were up to me, I wouldn't be handing my life over to a sociopath.

His hand slowly moves from my face and his tatted knuckles run down my neck, feeling my racing pulse to my heaving chest. He lifts his eyes to meet mine when he speaks. "If you're a good girl, you'll walk away sooner rather than later. But..."

I swallow the lump in my throat.

"If you're a bad girl who has to be punished, then you'll be crawling on your hands and knees, begging me to let you go."

His words leave my blood running cold yet my thighs clenching at the same time.

"I'll be seeing you soon, doll face." With that, he lets go of me, grabs the bag, and leaves my house as if he didn't just force me to give myself over to him.

Chapter 20

Haidyn

I straddle the chair backward, my right arm lying across the table next to me.

"Do I even want to know how this happened?" Gavin asks as he sews up my shoulder.

"A woman," I say, and he snorts.

I knew Charlotte would fight. I was in her house waiting for her return for over three hours. I had plenty of time to remove any weapon she could find to use on me, but where would the fun be in that? I wanted her to think she had an opportunity to save herself. And I was proud and turned on to see she used it.

I like a woman who fights. One who thinks she can stand up for herself. It just means I'll have to work extra hard to keep her on her knees. It might require some chains and ropes, but that's okay. Every woman deserves some accessories.

My cell vibrates, and I pull it out with my free hand to see that Ashtyn is calling me. I send her to voicemail. I look at Gavin when I feel he's paused, and he doesn't hide the fact that he's checking my phone.

"I—"

"Save it." I interrupt whatever he was about to say.

"She just misses you," he adds.

"How's she doing?" I bite my tongue the moment the words are out of my mouth. *Why the fuck did I ask?*

"Good." He nods. "If you weren't avoiding Carnage—"

"I'm not avoiding it," I say through gritted teeth. "I have to take care of something."

He nods, not believing a damn word I say. "Mm-hmm."

"I need a favor," I say to Gavin. My mind goes back to the brunette who is the reason I'm here in the first place.

"I figured that was coming." He chuckles.

I pull up the app that allows me access to the cameras in her house. I have them placed everywhere. She's so oblivious to everything that goes on around her. It makes things too easy for me.

Like right now, she's lying in bed, passed out. She's cuddling a pillow, the covers shoved to the footboard, and she's naked. Fuck, I can't wait to show her what that body was made for. To force sounds out of those pouty lips and watch her cry for me to stop, to keep going. For her to be confused and so overstimulated that she can't tell me what day it is, let alone her own name.

She's going to be my newest toy, and I'm going to play with her until she realizes her only purpose in life is to be nothing more than used.

"Name it." Gavin gets my attention, and I lock my cell, dropping my hand.

"I need to use this room and a few minutes of your time." I'm going to make sure she knows what she's in for right off the bat.

CHARLOTTE

I TURN OFF THE WATER IN THE SHOWER AND STEP OUT. Grabbing the towel, I dry off my body and bend over, twisting my hair up into it. Once situated, I straighten and brush my teeth, having to clear the steam from the mirror. I like my showers so scalding hot that my skin turns red. Finishing up, I walk into my closet and pull on a black cotton thong and decide to go make a cup of coffee before I finish getting ready since I got zero sleep last night. I exit my room and walk down the hallway toward the kitchen. I pass the front double doors but come to a stop as something catches my eye through the stained glass. It's blurry, but you can't miss the shape of the black motorcycle in my driveway.

Fuck! I spin around and jump with a scream as my hands instinctively go to my chest. "Jesus Christ, Haidyn," I hiss.

He stands in the foyer dressed in black jeans, a long-sleeved white shirt, and a backward baseball hat. His hands are shoved into his front pockets. "Hello, doll face."

I take a step back, my body hitting the cold door, and I shiver. "I have three more days," I grind out. He was just here two days ago dressed in disguise and ready to kill me if I didn't hand my body over to him.

He ignores me, and his eyes drop to my heaving chest covered with my hands. They then trail down over my stomach to my hips, then the very thin material that hides between my legs before lowering to my bare feet.

He reaches up and runs a hand over his chin as his eyes eat me up. I've never seen a man look so heated in my life, and it has my body on fire as well.

"Haidyn?" I snap, glad my skin is red from the blistering shower I took so he can't see my blush.

"You have nothing I haven't seen, Charlotte," he states, his eyes coming back to mine.

I huff, rolling mine in an excuse to avoid his intense stare. "What do you want?" I get to the point. If he were here to collect me, he would have dragged me out of the house already. I have a feeling that when he shows up to take me to Carnage, whips and chains will be involved. And no heads-up. No, he'll want to know he's got the jump on me. I won't even see him coming. He'll probably take me while I sleep.

"Finish getting ready," he orders. "You have thirty minutes." With that, he turns and walks farther into the house, disappearing into my living room.

"What?" I storm after him. My modesty no longer concerns me. "What do you mean thirty minutes?" Coming to the edge of the living room, I watch him turn and plop down onto the couch. Leaning back, he sinks into it. His legs fall open, and his arms span the length of the cushions.

My eyes fall to his parted legs, and I imagine kneeling while his hands tighten in my hair as I open my mouth, silently begging him to fuck it like the good girl he wants me to be. My pussy throbs like I've never felt before. I've never wanted to be fucked so badly in my life. Why him? Why does he make me feel things that I know any other man on this planet can give me?

"I have dinner plans tonight," I say, clearing my throat and forcing my eyes to meet his stare.

"Dinner plans?" He smirks, and his blue eyes drop to my wrists.

Heat rushes up my spine since I told him things got rough when he questioned the bruises on them. Thinking I let a man use me. *If he only knew...*

"Cancel them. Tell your boy toy something came up. You have an appointment," he states.

I don't know why I thought he'd care if I had a boyfriend. The bastard doesn't give a fuck about anyone but himself. "For what?" I snap.

The corner of his lips twitch, and he reaches up, adjusting his backward hat, and I can't even begin to explain the things it does to my insides. I feel like I'm fucking melting into a puddle before him, and the smirk that graces his gorgeous face tells me he knows exactly what he's doing. "Thirty minutes, doll face. Then we're leaving. I don't care if you get ready or finish getting dressed, I'll carry you out wearing nothing but your underwear and a towel on your head." With that, he pulls his cell from his pocket and starts typing away, dismissing me.

I growl, knowing I can't win with him. I spin around and rush off to my bedroom. Slamming the door, I lock it as if that will keep him out and start getting ready for who the hell knows what.

Chapter 21

Haidyn

I get up off the couch and head to her room. She has one minute before we have to leave. I considered sending her a text about her appointment, but I didn't trust her to go. One of those "you want something done, you have to do it yourself" types of situations. So here I am, taking her to it, even if she kicks and screams.

I go to enter her bedroom, but the door is locked. I smile and shove my shoulder into it, splintering the wood. I could have used my pocketknife to unlock it, but I like the idea of it being broken better.

I look around to see it's empty. I turn to open her bathroom door when it swings open. She jumps back in surprise. Her eyes instantly narrow up at mine. Her dark hair is dried and now up in a high ponytail, showing off her small face, pouty lips, and slender neck. It makes her blue eyes look bigger. I can tell she's put a little bit of makeup on by the way her lashes are darker, and her lips are tinted a soft pink to match her cheeks. Her tits are hidden under a hoodie, and she's got leggings on with tennis shoes.

"Let's go," I command, giving her my back and walking through her house.

"Did you break my door?" she barks, but I ignore her. She can see that's exactly what I did.

Entering her garage, I grab her keys hanging up on the hook.

"What are you doing?" she demands.

"Driving you to your appointment," I answer, opening her passenger door—always a gentleman.

I turn to look at her, and she pushes out her chest, face scrunched with irritation.

It's cute, really. My eyes drop to her leggings, and the thought of her thong comes to mind. She's got a perfect ass. One I just want to bend over my knee and take a belt to. It was red earlier from her shower. I want to see it red from my hand as well while she begs me to stop fucking it.

"Maybe I don't want you driving my car."

"I'm driving," I state. This is not up for debate. "Either I drive you in your car or I put you on the back of my bike."

She nibbles on her lip at my ultimatum for a second before she lets out a huff and storms over to me. She falls into the passenger seat, and I slam the door shut.

It's a little on the colder side this afternoon, but the weather doesn't bother me. I'll ride all year round. I like the freedom a bike gives me, but I knew she'd choose her car.

Getting into the driver's seat, I start it up and open the garage, knowing that she's mad at me right now. But she'll hate me when I drive her back home.

CHARLOTTE

He pulls up to a six-story building with an all-glass front. A set of sliding glass doors reads *entrance*. It's too large to be a house, but there's no sign out front to say what it is or to give me a clue as to why we're here.

He pulls my SUV to a stop, and a man opens my door. "Good afternoon, miss." He smiles at me kindly, then looks over the top of the car and nods. "Haidyn."

"Lance." He acknowledges him, then walks around the back to me. He grabs my hand and pulls me up the six steps. I'm nervous as fuck. My knees are shaking. What could we possibly be doing here?

He didn't say one word to me on the drive and never turned the radio on. We just sat in silence, and I know he did it on purpose. He wanted me inside of my own head. My mind raced with the what-ifs while I tried to calm my breathing.

Entering the building, I see a set of chairs to my right. He lets go of my hand, placing his hand on my lower back, and guides me to one. "Stay," he commands like I'm a fucking dog.

All I'm missing is a collar and a muzzle. Then he disappears down a hallway.

The sliding glass door opens, and a woman enters. She plops down next to me, smiling as she speaks. "You here for David?"

I look over her fishnet stockings, six-inch heels, and red halter top. She reminds me of the woman in the video that the Lords sent me of Haidyn when he was picking up the prostitute. "No."

She throws her hair over her shoulder. "How did you hear about this place?"

I frown, even more confused. It's not like it's hidden in the middle of nowhere. It's beautiful and easily seen from the main road. "My boyfriend brought me," I answer. Because explaining a Spade brother is blackmailing me won't go over well with Haidyn when he finds out. Plus, I doubt she knows what a Lord is. I'd rather not have that conversation with her either.

Her smile widens. "That's nice of him."

I have to hold in a snort at that.

"What are you having done?" she asks.

"Excuse me?"

Her brown eyes drop to my chest. "Is he getting your tits done?"

Mine harden. "No."

Then her eyes roam my face. "Your nose?"

What the fuck? "No," I bark.

Jesus, where the hell did he bring me? Thoughts of someone knocking me out and giving me a new face has me terrified. I've seen those shows of people on the run before. A plastic surgeon great at his job, can make you look like a different person. And I know how easy it is for the Lords to give you a new identity. He could be planning to get rid of Annabelle and Charlotte altogether.

"Don't be offended." She rolls her eyes, sitting back in her chair. "Everyone could use a little help."

I go to tell her to fuck off, but the sound of boots coming down the hallway has all my attention before Haidyn appears.

The girl next to me gasps. "Haidyn. Oh my God. What are you doing here?" she asks excitedly.

He moves to step in front of me, his eyes slowly going to her. I watch her run her hands down her thighs and lick her lips. All of a sudden, she's in heat, and I want to vomit. Do I look that desperate when he's around? Fuck, I hope not.

"Amber." He nods once before looking at me. He grabs my hand, pulls me from the chair, and leads me down the hallway he appeared from.

"Wait?" she calls out, and I try to stop, but Haidyn continues to pull me away from the seating area. "Haidyn Reeves is your boyfriend?" she demands.

I look at her over my shoulder, and her once friendly look has changed to what I can only describe as pure fucking hatred. Her narrowed eyes go from mine to the back of Haidyn, and she crosses her arms over her chest. Scoffing, she shakes her head and storms out of the sliding glass doors, stomping her heels.

"I'm not into labels, but if you want me to brand my name on your ass, I'll be glad to oblige." Haidyn chuckles.

I roll my eyes, letting him pull me into a room. My breath catches when I see what's in it. There's a white table in the center with what look to be medical restraints strategically placed in various spots from one end to the other. A gush of cold air rushes over my face, and I shiver, stepping back. It reminds me of the gynecologist. It smells of disinfectant and the bright lights hurt my eyes. A set of cabinets run the full length of the right wall. There's a sink and a box of gloves along with a biohazard trash can.

Haidyn walks over to the table, and my pulse races. "I'm not getting on that," I say, my voice shaking as much as my knees.

He turns to face me.

I spin around, grab the door handle, and go to pull the door open, but his hand slaps against it above my head, slamming it shut. I'm yanked back by my hair, and I cry out when he shoves my back into the wall next to the door. He steps into me, one hand gripping my chin while the other holds an open pocketknife to my cheek.

I'm gasping for breath, trying to pull my face away, but he's got me pinned in place. "Haidyn," I whisper.

His blue eyes search mine as he speaks. "You either undress yourself or I cut every piece of clothing off you so when we leave this place, you leave with nothing on."

My hands grip his T-shirt, my breathing erratic. Tears sting my eyes. "Please..."

"This is not a negotiation, doll face. I tell you what to do. You either do it or I do it for you. If you pick option two, then you'll be punished afterward. Do you understand?"

The cool tip of the knife slowly glides against my cheek, and I swallow nervously. "Y-yes."

Letting go of my chin, I keep my back to the wall, and he lowers the tip of the knife to the collar of my hoodie. His cold and unforgiving eyes focus on mine. "What's it going to be, Charlotte? Are you going to be a good girl and get undressed, or will I have to cut your clothes off?"

My trembling hands grip the hem of the hoodie, and I pull it up and over my head, sniffling.

"That's my good girl." He closes the knife, putting it away and picks up the gown, holding it out to me. "Undress. All of it. I want you naked. It opens in the front. I'll give you three minutes." With that, he exits the room and closes the door as the first tear runs down my cheek.

Chapter 22

Haidyn

I stand outside the room, giving her a few minutes of privacy to let her mind wander. She knows I'm going to see her naked. The gown is just a false sense of security.

Pulling my cell phone out of my pocket, I give it a quick look before I go back in there. I've had it on silent since I arrived at her place.

I have a text from Kash.

Call me. It's urgent.

Grinding my teeth, I hover over his number but am reluctant to press call. He answers on the first ring. "Make it quick," I say in greeting. This is the first time I've spoken to him since I left Carnage.

"We found out a few things about Benny," he informs me.

Glad I took the call. "And?"

"He was a Lord."

"Was?" I ask, wanting him to get to the point. I'm not in the mood to play guessing games. I have the toy I'm going to play with behind the door I'm leaning on.

"Yeah. He never made it through all the initiations. Failed sophomore year."

Running a hand through my hair, I growl, "Then how did he know so much if he wasn't a fucking Lord?" We had looked for a Lords crest and hadn't seen one, but there was no reasonable explanation for that. And Ashtyn was seeing him while she lived in Vegas. No way would she have willingly dated or fucked a Lord when she was on the run from them.

"We know he was working with Laura and Ashtyn's mother four years ago, but we think he's connected to someone else..."

"Who?" I bark out, hating that he's not willing to give me information. He's the one who said to call him.

"Our guess is Costello."

Like a gunshot to my chest, I stop breathing at the mention of the name. I begin to pace the hallway. "No—"

"It's the only plausible explanation," he growls. "Saint and I have gone round and round on this for days now, and it makes perfect sense. She spent time in Carnage. She knew the system—"

"But Benny had raped Ashtyn before the vow ceremony our senior year with help from Laura and her mother." I interrupt him. "Costello wasn't at Carnage until after Ash ran..."

"That we know of," he snaps, getting irritated with me. "Who knows how long *she* had access before our training."

I sigh, not wanting to believe him but also knowing I don't know enough to argue any of it.

"Look." He softens his tone. "I don't want to believe it either, but what if our dads had something to do with it? We know that Ashtyn's mother was part of Ash being raped because she was trying to make sure that Ashtyn didn't become Saint's chosen. And Laura..." He trails off. "That bitch is fucking nuts. We all know how far she'll go to get her way. And Laura had access to Carnage before our training. So if—a big if—it wasn't our dads, maybe Laura helped Costello get into Carnage after our dads were killed."

"The question is, how did Costello know our fathers were dead?" They weren't even cold, and she was already there.

Senior year at Barrington

I PACE THE HOSPITAL HALLWAY AT CARNAGE WHILE KASHTON SITS in a chair up against the wall, bent over with his hands gripping his hair. "Saint's going to be okay," I tell him.

His head snaps up, and his bloodshot eyes meet mine. "She shot him." Getting to his feet, he steps into me. His chest bumps mine, and I can feel his anger at how much he's shaking. "Ash—"

"Calm down, Kash." I place my hands on his trembling shoulders. "We don't know what happened."

His watery eyes widen. "Are you fucking serious?" he snaps, taking a step back. "She broke my fucking nose and kneed me in the fucking dick! Then she shot our brother."

"Devin is going to take care of him. He'll be okay." He doesn't even mention the fact that our fathers are also dead. The only person he cares about right now is Saint. We carried him up here from the morgue, where Kash found him lying in a puddle of his own blood. Devin just took him back for surgery. Now, it's just a waiting game.

"She's his wife!" he shouts. "What the fuck was she thinking?" He goes on, not expecting me to answer. "And where the fuck were you?"

Saint had called me saying there was a code 26 and that it was for Ashtyn, I pretended to be asleep as if I wasn't the one who helped her run. "I—"

The sound of the elevator dinging gets our attention, and we both turn to face it as the door slides open. A woman steps out wearing a skintight knee-length white dress, showing off her curves and paid-for chest. She's followed by four men, all dressed in black cloaks and white masks.

"What the fuck is this shit?" Kash demands.

"Boys." She smiles, and her dark green eyes go from Kash to me. They lazily take in our sizes and appearances. We're both covered in our brother's blood.

"Hey! I asked you a fucking question, bitch!" Kashton snaps, stepping forward.

I reach out to grab his bloody shirt to keep him back, but he shrugs me off. "Kash—"

"We're going to have so much fun." She gives us both a chilling smile and snaps her fingers.

Two of the guys dressed as Lords step forward, and chains drop from their hands, clanking on the floor.

"Escort them to the arena, boys. I'm going to check on the status of the other."

. . .

"I don't know how she would know they were dead, man." Kash sighs heavily, answering my previous question and pulling me out of that memory. "Are you coming home soon?" he asks.

Hearing someone walking toward me has me looking up to see Gavin. "Have to go," I say.

"Wait," he rushes out. "When are you coming home?"

I end the call without answering and pocket my cell. I'll worry about that later. They're obviously getting some answers, and I'm ready to play with my newest toy.

CHARLOTTE

I sit on the edge of the table dressed in the gown but pulled tightly around the front, tucked under my arms so you can't see anything. I'm naked underneath. My clothes are folded neatly on the counter with my underwear and bra hidden underneath. He's getting ready to see me naked. It's humiliating and embarrassing. I'm sweating, and when the door opens, I startle, seeing Haidyn enter with an older man. *I know who he is.*

Gavin takes care of the Lords and their dirty work. From what I've heard, he's like their father. One they actually trust with their lives and secrets.

"Hello, Charlotte. I'm Dr. Gavin, and I'm going to be running some tests today."

What kind of tests could I possibly need? I notice he calls me Charlotte, not Annabelle, and it makes me wonder if Haidyn has told him who I really am.

Haidyn comes to stand beside me, and I can't make eye contact. Instead, my blurry eyes remain on his T-shirt.

"Lie on your back," Gavin orders softly. His voice would be soothing if my chest didn't feel heavy.

I lie down, the white paper covering the length of the table crinkling at my movement. I look up at the ceiling tiles as my heart hammers in my chest. I hear the opening of wrappers as Gavin moves around on my left. Then he walks over to the table. "Any family history of diseases that you know of?"

"N-o." I clear my throat.

"Any pregnancies?" he asks.

"No." I shake my head as a fresh tear falls out of the corner of my eye. "I'm on birth control," I add. Is that why I'm here? Because Haidyn is going to make me his fuck toy, and he wants to make sure I'm protected? Men like him don't wear condoms. Ever. So I'm going to have to be the responsible one.

"What are you currently on?" Gavin continues.

"The pill," I answer vaguely, knowing there are several different options out there but not knowledgeable enough to go into detail.

My doctor tried to put me on them years ago, but my mother refused. Said there was no need for them. I'm supposed to remain a virgin.

"How many sexual partners?" Gavin questions.

"Two." I don't know why I lied. Actually, I do. I don't want them to know how inexperienced I am. But I have no fucking clue why I chose two—maybe one is not enough and three is too many.

Gavin begins to open my gown. My hand lifts to cover my breasts, but Haidyn grabs my right hand in both of his. It feels like a lover's hold—one on top, the other on the bottom. But I know the truth. Gavin takes my left hand and lifts it above my head to rest on the cold paper while he begins to check my breast and underarm.

You can hear my heavy breathing over anything else in the room, and my nipples harden. Goose bumps cover my skin, and it's freezing in here even though I'm sweating. I feel like Haidyn had them lower the temperature on purpose. I pull my knees up, put my feet flat on the table, and tightly hold my legs closed as I focus on a single spot on the ceiling. I can feel Haidyn's eyes on my body, and I bite my tongue to keep from making a sound.

"All good." Gavin taps my left arm. "You may put your arm back now," he says, then covers me up.

I bite my inner cheek to hold in a sob as Haidyn lets go of my sweaty hand.

"Now...I'm going to give you a pelvic exam." He moves to the end of the table and pulls out the stirrups, making the table rattle.

I allow him to place my shaking legs in them as he instructs. "Scoot your bottom down to the edge."

I try to wiggle my way down, but my skin is stuck to the paper.

"Little more."

I do as instructed, then wrap my arms tightly around my chest, wanting to cover my tear-streaked face.

"You're going to feel some pressure." His glove-covered fingers enter me, and I raise my hips up as he stands between my spread legs and presses down on my lower abdomen. "Doing great, Charlotte," he tells me, and my cheeks flush.

I've had a male gynecologist for years, but to have Haidyn in here with me is humiliating.

Gavin's free hand presses down on my stomach as he feels around before he removes his hand from between my legs, and I sink into the table, letting out a long breath. He takes his gloves off and throws them away. I go to move my legs, but Haidyn's voice stops me.

"Stay," he commands. It's the first word he's spoken since he entered with Gavin, and it sends a chill up my spine.

I take a shaky breath and lick my lips. Gavin walks over to me with a clipboard. He looks over and speaks to Haidyn. "Looks good. I'll go get everything ready and be right back. Should have you out of here within a couple of hours." He exits, closing the door, and I try to take a calming breath, but it doesn't work.

"Haidyn...?" I can only whisper his name and glance up at him.

He's already staring down at me. He gently runs his knuckles down the side of my wet cheek. "Yeah, doll face?"

"What's going to take a couple of hours?" I'm sucking in air but feeling lightheaded. The idea of passing out sounds good.

He doesn't answer. Instead, he says, "Place your arms above your head, *Annabelle*."

The way he calls me by my real name tells me he's serious. My stomach sinks at the order, and I lift my arms, which seem to have gained twenty pounds each, but I manage to lay them above my head, bent at the elbows.

Haidyn steps away from the side, and he grabs my wrist, placing it where he wants it, stretching it above my head. The sound of medical restraints hits my ears before I realize he's secured it to the table. Then he repeats the process with the other.

I try to pull on them, but they're tied down above my head. "Haidyn...please..." My voice trembles, and my legs shake.

He comes back into my view when he stands next to me once again. His hand cups my face as my eyes find his. They don't look amused or intrigued, just empty. I've never seen such pretty blue eyes look so dead. It's scary. There's no telling what kind of initiations this man went through to become who he is today. But I have a feeling he's going to put me through the same humiliation. "I'm not going to hurt you here."

The fact that he said *here* just confirms what I already knew—pain is in my future. But of course, it is. That's how the Lords are taught to treat women. Pain and pleasure go hand in hand in our life.

They're bred to give it, and we're conditioned to like it.

I open my mouth to ask again what he's going to do, but he moves to the stirrups. They're the kind that cover your entire leg, not just for your feet, bending at the knees. He buckles another belt around my upper thigh, then my ankle. He goes and does the other two on the opposite leg.

I'm strapped down to the table from my wrists to my legs secured to the stirrups. I lift my hips the little it allows because that's all I can move. I wish I was face down so I could at least bury it in the table so he can't see me cry. When I pull on my legs, my thighs tighten at the lack of movement. My body heat is rising, and my breath comes in short pants.

We're made to be whores, and I hate that no matter how much I lack in experience in that department, my body still wants to explore it.

The door opens, and I can't see who it is from my position, but I know it's Gavin. The sound of squeaking wheels makes me flinch. He's got a cart of some kind.

"Here you go, Haidyn. Take all the time you need. Once done, I'll return to draw some blood, get a urine sample, and administer the birth control." With that, he exits, leaving me strapped to the table with a man who can do anything to me in this position. Seriously, the options are endless, and my mind runs wild.

Chapter 23

Haidyn

I watch her body tremble while strapped to the table. She's wide open and ready for me to do whatever the fuck I want to her. Gavin is always more than willing to help out a fellow Lord, so when I told him of my plan, he didn't bat an eye. The guy has seen some shit in his day. I'm sure he didn't agree with all of it, but as a Lord, he serves and never asks questions.

I'm not a doctor by any means, but I needed her to be checked. I need tests run to make sure that the information I was sent is true. You can't trust anything in our world. It's all smoke and mirrors. She's been pretending to be who she is. How do I know the information I found out isn't a lie as well? Depending on who she's working for, the shit that's online could be just as fake as the shit she tells me. Thankfully, I can check.

I place a pair of gloves on, then pop the lid on the lube and cover the balloon plug. "Relax, Charlotte." She releases a shaky breath. Smearing it on my fingers, I run them over her puckered ass, and she flinches. "You're okay," I tell her, pushing the tip of one into her, not wasting any time. I brought her for a reason, and I'm in no mood to prolong it.

The sound of her sniffling follows while her body fights the restraints. Pulling it out, I repeat the process, pushing it in a little farther. "You're doing good, doll face."

Her legs tighten as they pull against the leather straps that hold them wide open for me. I apply more pressure and enter a second one, making her whimper as her ass tightens down on me.

Then I remove them and grab the tube. I lube it up once more and push my finger back into her ass first before I pull out and begin to replace it with the deflated balloon. "Deep breath, doll face."

She sucks in a shaky breath, and I begin to slowly glide it into her. "That's it. Doing great."

"Hai-dyn." Her soft voice cracks. The table rattles from her useless fight.

"Shh, you're doing so good for me, Charlotte." I push it farther into her ass. "So good. Almost there."

"Oooooww," she cries, her ass trying to lift off the table.

Watching it slide into her ass, I tell her, "It's in." Then I inflate the balloon just enough to where she can't push it out and turn the valve so the solution flows—slow and steady.

I remove my gloves and throw them in the trash while she struggles in the restraints, causing the gown to fall open some since her arms are above her head.

"It'll take about an hour," I inform her, walking over to the sink and washing my hands. "And then you're going to hold it for thirty minutes." I dry them off and discard the paper towels into the trash can. Usually, they require more time, but we'll start with baby steps. I have plenty of time to test her.

She had her eyes tightly shut until I spoke, and they spring open in horror. "What...no...I can't..."

"Yes, you can." I run my knuckles down the side of her wet cheek. "You can do it, Charlotte."

She shakes her head, sucking in a deep breath.

"Are you hurting?"

"No," she whispers.

Just embarrassed. She needs to get used to this. I'm going to have her in so many situations that will have her blushing and crying. I have endless ideas.

"Please?"

Her little whine has my cock so fucking hard. Hell, I've been hard since the first time she walked into my life. I should have known she was a trap—something so beautiful can only be used as a weapon. I've survived my initiations and being tortured, and that's stuff I signed up for. I'm not going to let pussy be the one thing that does me in.

"What are you begging for?" I ask her.

Her hands fist as she pulls on the belts that secure her small wrists to the top of the table. "I...uh," she moans, her hips twisting from side to side. A soft sob comes from her plump lips, and I reach out, running my knuckles over her flushed cheeks to wipe away the tears from her face.

Her heavy eyes open and meet mine. Dropping my hand, I run them down over her heaving chest, and to test the waters, I gently caress her hardened nipple. Her boobs are perfect just like I imagined every time she sat in the room at Carnage pretending to be someone else. They're bigger than they looked in her blouses that she would wear. Makes me wonder if she was hiding them on purpose. Her pussy is shaved, and she's got a pink diamond belly ring in.

My eyes go back to her face, and she moans, her hips pulling against the belt. "Is this turning you on, doll face?"

She closes her eyes tightly and turns her face into the side of her arm, trying to hide from me.

Wrapping my hand around her fragile neck, I pin it to the table. "Look at me," I command.

She straightens her head, swallowing against my palm as her wet lashes flutter open. "Eyes on me, Charlotte. I want to see you."

She blinks, fresh tears running out of the corner of her eyes. "Talk to me. Use your words," I urge her.

She parts her lips and takes in a shaky breath. Her hips lift off the table, and she whimpers.

Letting go of her neck, I pull out another medical strap from the side of the table and fasten it low across her hips, securing them. "Don't want you to pull it out," I tell her even though I know it's not possible. I move back to hover over her face. "Are you in pain?" I ask. My hand gently rubs her flat stomach, feeling her body tremble.

She shakes her head, sucking in a deep breath. "No...but, what...is it? I—" She closes her eyes again and cries out. Poor thing is already so confused.

"I'm giving you a retention enema, Charlotte. I'm pumping soapy water into you. After I think you've taken enough, I'm going to make you hold it. When I think you've held it long enough, I'll let you relieve yourself."

She arches her neck and lets out a sob at my words. "Please," she cries, fighting harder against the straps that hold her down.

Her nipples are hard, and I slap her inner thigh to see how she reacts to it. The moan that leaves her parted lips tells me all I need to know. "Words, Charlotte."

"Y-es." Her voice cracks, and I smile to myself because I didn't ask her a question.

My hands trail over her heaving chest to her breasts once again, unable to stay away from them. "Your nipples are hard, doll face," I say, cupping her right one and running my thumb over it.

Arching her back, she sucks in a ragged breath.

"Talk to me." I want to make her uncomfortable. I want to humiliate her. I also want her to know that I don't give a fuck what bothers her. I'm going to find her boundaries and push her further. She will have none once I walk away from her.

"Please?" she whispers.

"Please what?" I ask, my fingers now running down her sternum. The cold room is filled with her heavy breathing. I like the way it sounds. I can't wait to see her struggle in the positions I'm going to put her in.

"I..." She licks her lips.

"Tell me." My fingers run down over her stomach, to her pelvic bone over the straps and to her inner thigh. Her legs shake in the stirrups, and I smile. "You're going to have to ask me, doll face."

My eyes go to hers, and they're tightly closed. I slap her inner thigh again in warning, and they pop open, meeting mine.

"Which part is turning you on the most?" I ask, knowing what she's afraid to ask for. An enema isn't normally painful. But of course, this isn't a usual one. I had the water a little colder than normal, and I'm going to fill her with a little more than I think she can hold. I want to make her cry and beg. Not for the reasons she is now, but hey, this is even better. "Is it the fact that you're naked and tied down?" I inquire. "Is it the feel of having something shoved into your ass, filling you full of water? Hmm?" I slap her inner thigh again. Harder.

She cries out, arching her back the little the straps allow. "Please... please touch me."

"Where, Charlotte?" I slap her again. Same spot but with more force to the point my hand stings.

"My pussy," she cries, wiggling her hips on the table.

I run my hand down her inner thigh until I'm cupping her cunt. "This what you want?" My hand rests there, feeling the heat and wetness. I remove my hand and slap it.

She yanks on the restraints, crying out. I slap my free hand over her mouth and lean down into her face as her tear-filled eyes meet mine. "Don't want anyone hearing you, do we?"

She shakes her head. Inhaling sharply through her nose.

"We don't want them to know what a desperate whore you are." I slide a finger into her pussy. She's soaked. Of course, I'm sure some of it is from the lubricating gel Gavin used to check her, but I know some of it's from her arousal as well. She's turned on. "My doll face is a dirty little whore, isn't she?" I ask, entering a second. Blinking rapidly, she arches her neck. I remove my fingers and slap it again, making her nod quickly.

"Good girl," I praise, shoving them back in, and her chest rises and falls rapidly. "You're so tight, doll face." I feel her clench down on me.

I pull them out, and she slumps onto the table, full-on crying now. Tears spill from her eyes like an endless waterfall. I slap it again and again and again. The sound fills the large room as the bag continues to push soapy water into her, filling her stomach like a balloon.

"You're so beautiful, Charlotte. Such a beautiful, desperate whore." Her shoulders shake at my words. "So perfect."

My free hand remains on her face, covering her cheeks and mouth. She will spend a lot of her time with me gagged for many reasons. But one being I like the way she looks when she realizes she has no voice. Vulnerable and a little scared. But also turned on.

I run my fingers over her clit, gently playing with it before pushing one into her really slowly. Her trembling body begs for more. "Do you want to come?" I ask and remove my hand from her face.

"Please...Haidyn. Please." She sniffs.

I remove the one finger and then slap her again. She bites her lip and arches her neck.

"That's a good girl," I praise her. She's such a quick learner. "If you make a sound, I'll stop. Understand?"

She nods quickly and gasps. "Ye-yes."

My eyes drop to her open legs. "Fuck, Charlotte, your cunt is red and swollen. So pretty."

I slap it again, and she turns her face to the side to bury it into her arm. I pinch her nipple. "Eyes on mine," I remind her. "I know it's a lot to keep up with, but you'll learn to follow the rules I give you."

"Yes," she agrees.

I go back to slapping her soaked cunt. I like the way she bites down on her bottom lip to keep quiet. Then I'm burying three fingers into her tight pussy. Reaching up, I find her G-spot. She quits gasping. Instead, she holds her breath as her body goes stiff. Her watery eyes soften in a trance before she comes on my fingers.

CHARLOTTE

I sit in the passenger seat of my SUV staring out the window and silently crying. I'm so mad at myself. What in the fuck just happened? He had me checked, my blood taken, then I was given the birth control shot after an enema.

I've had colonics before. Is that the same thing? I don't think so. I've never had the experience of being turned on with one. Is that a kink? I'm also not sure. I'll have to look that one up once I'm alone. I was exposed and practically sobbing. At first, it started out due to humiliation. Then it turned to need. Now I'm ashamed. Who the fuck gets turned on by that?

I can now say that I do. That's what men like Haidyn want. To make you feel like nothing. They turn you on yourself. I haven't even started serving him yet, and my underwear is already soaked. I've become weak.

After I came, it got even more awkward. I came down from my high, and he stood next to me for thirty minutes while I continued to hold in my enema. A part of me wished he had just choked me out and saved me from the embarrassment. No such luck.

Afterward, he removed it and let me use the restroom. Thankfully, I was allowed to go by myself. I cried while I sat on the toilet. It wasn't necessarily painful, mostly just from shame. I looked over the marks that covered my body from pulling on the restraints. I've never come so hard in my life, and he didn't even fuck me. Thank God he and Gavin don't know I'm a virgin. I was ready to beg him to fuck me right then and there, but he wouldn't have. Lords get off on you wanting them. He gave me just enough to keep me wanting more. A taste. It's like a starving man smelling a steak dinner—your mouth waters and your stomach turns, reminding you how hungry you really are. Then you realize you'll do anything for it.

That was me—desperate and accepting.

He pulls into my driveway and opens the garage. The moment he comes to a stop, I jump out and run into the house. "Charlotte?" he calls out, but I ignore him.

I run through the house to the bedroom. Rushing to the bathroom, I want a shower. I've never felt so dirty in my life.

I slam my broken bedroom door closed behind me, and it's shoved open. I'm spun around with a fist in my hair, and he tosses my weak body onto the bed. The one that betrayed me.

"Get off me!" I shout, my hands swinging and legs kicking. But he easily straddles me and pins my hands above my head.

"Calm down, doll face." He chuckles, thinking this is funny.

"I HATE YOU!" I shout so loud it hurts my own ears and burns my throat. "Fucking...hate you." My throat tightens, and tears sting my eyes. But this is my fault. I had the opportunity to walk away before I accepted my brand and chose to go through with this.

He releases my arms and wraps both hands around my neck. I tilt my head back and grab his wrists, trying to stop him, but he doesn't restrict my air. My fingers dig into his large watch, and it pinches my skin, but I don't let go. Instead, my already wet pussy throbs with need as I try to lift my hips to push him off. It's like I'm tied down to the table all over again.

He lowers his face to mine, and I hold my breath as those pretty haunted blue eyes glare into mine. "That was just the beginning, *Annabelle*." I'm really starting to hate it when he calls me by my real name. "The things I'm going to do to you...some you'll like, others probably not. I'm going to make you my little fuck toy. You'll cry... you'll beg, and you'll crawl on your hands and knees to me, begging to be played with like a mindless toy."

My stomach sinks at his words because it's a promise. And Lords always make good on their promises.

"When I decide I'm done with you, you will have no dignity left. All you will know is me. All you will want is me. I suggest you accept that now rather than later." He lets go of my neck and stands. Without another word, he turns and exits my room.

I stare at the ceiling through my tear-filled eyes as I hear his motorcycle start. Only when I'm met with silence do I roll over, bury my face in a pillow, and let out a sob because I belong to Haidyn Reeves. A Spade brother who knows I'm a fraud. I'm a nobody really. Not in our world. That's why I'm doing what I'm doing—to be someone. I want power. I want to be feared. I guess Lords have to be humiliated, and so do I. He could turn me in. The Lords don't know that he found me out. But what would they say? Probably tell him he can have me. That if I'm no longer valuable to them, then they'd let Haidyn throw me into Carnage. At least now, I'm playing both sides.

He's not going to tell them because then he will no longer have leverage over me. I'm not going to rat myself out because I signed up for this. I knew the risk. Did I, though? I didn't know he was going to find me out.

I sit up when I hear my cell ring. Drying my face, I take in a shaky breath to calm myself and retrieve my cell from my purse on the floor. "Hello?" I say when I see it's my mother.

"Hello, dear. How is your day?"

A laugh bubbles up, but I swallow it. "Great. Yours?" I'm trying to sound cheerful and hoping she can't tell. My mother is very perceptive. I was never that kid who could get away with anything. She always knew.

"Quite wonderful," she says cheerfully. "I was hoping you're free for an early dinner. We can go to your favorite place... you know, since you're going on vacation at the end of this week."

I hang my head and rub the back of my neck, knowing there's a tracker there. "Yeah, of course." Why not? I had to cancel my dinner plans with Wesley.

"Excellent. I'll see you soon." *Click.*

I pull myself together and walk to the shower to start getting ready.

Chapter 24
Haidyn

Senior year at Barrington

"Don't fucking touch me," Kash snaps, pulling away from one of the Lords dressed in cloaks and masks.

We stand in the center of the arena at Carnage. We've been here before for our first initiation.

"What the fuck is going on?" Kash looks at me. "We don't have time for nonsense. Saint—"

"Is still in surgery."

We both spin around to see the brunette bitch is back.

"What the fuck do you want?" Kashton growls. "And why the hell are we here?" He reaches his arms out wide, gesturing to the arena.

I take a look around and see it's empty. Last time, it was packed with Lords to watch us. My eyes drop back to the woman.

She crosses her arms over her chest, pops one hip out, and smiles. "Bring them in."

The back doors open, and I stiffen when eight men are brought in. They're wearing a pair of black pants and that's it. Their ribs are showing and their eyes are sunken in. Hair missing in patches. Bruises and scars cover their ashen skin.

"Fuck," Kashton snaps.

They're prisoners here at Carnage.

"What the fuck is going on?" I step forward, starting to panic. I tried to stay calm for Kash and keep him together while we waited for Saint to finish surgery, but now I'm starting to get a sickening feeling.

"Boys." She turns and addresses them. "Salvation comes with a price." She begins to speak, and the four Lords who brought us in here walk over to the eight prisoners. "You want freedom? You have to earn it."

What is she doing?

"If you kill them, you get to walk free. Today."

"What the fuck do you think you're doing?" Kash steps forward, saying what I'm thinking, and I grab his shirt to keep him back.

She smirks at us. "You're supposed to be the best of the best." Her dark green eyes look us both up and down as her tongue runs across her red-painted lips. "Let's see how good you really are."

The four Lords stab syringes into the prisoners' chests, and the blood begins to rush in my ears.

"One-on-one isn't really fair"—she shrugs—"considering they've been deprived of what their bodies require to be top of their game. Not even two-to-one. But four-to-one." Smiling, she steps to the side. "I gave them a little extra boost. I really do wish you two the best. If you survive, I get to play with you."

I STAND IN MY SHOWER, MY FOREHEAD ON THE COOL WALL AS I let the water drown me from above. My right hand fists my hard cock, and I try to slow my racing heart.

Fuck, the memories are harder to forget than usual. I've become accustomed to fucking them out of me. I could call up David and have him send some girls over, but Charlotte changes things. She's the one I'll use, and I have to have patience. Plus, the longer I wait, the better it will be.

So I'll just do it myself. Although it's never as good, it's at least some kind of release.

I push my hips forward as if she's on her knees for me, and I slide my dick through my fist. My mouth falls open. "Fuck," I groan, my hand picking up the pace.

She was so fucking gorgeous, looking up at me from the table, tears falling from her eyes and her cunt soaked.

Afterward, I left her lying there tied with cum leaking from her pussy while she held in the enema. Showing me how obedient she's going to be for me.

My good girl.

"Soon, doll face," I say. "Soon you'll be mine."

CHARLOTTE

Right on time, I pull into the parking lot and park next to my mother's white Lamborghini. I can't say that I'm not close with my mother because I am, but I was a daddy's girl. My mom tried to make life the best for us after he died. She remarried, and I like my stepdad. He's a good guy from what I know. As good as a Lord can be. Plus, he keeps her happy. She was in love with my father. I won't say they had a perfect marriage, but it was one of the best ones I've seen in our world.

I enter the restaurant and find her already sitting at a table dressed in a black Valentino dress and matching Jimmy Choo heels. She waves me over and stands as I approach.

"Good afternoon, dear." She hugs me before kissing me on each cheek. "Glad you were able to meet up."

I nod. "Me too."

"How are things going?"

"Good." I lie.

My life is over. Okay, maybe I'm being dramatic, but I feel like being Haidyn's fuck toy may kill me. I mean, I never thought I'd beg him to get me off during an enema. I can't imagine what else he'll put me through.

It's been a little over an hour, and my pussy is still swollen and red from his hand slapping it over and over. His fingers hurt but in a good way. It took my mind off the balloon in my ass. My fresh underwear is soaked. It's throbbing as if to ask him for more. Another hit from his hand. Another finger to fuck. Hell, his cock. If he's that rough with his hands and fingers, I can't imagine what he can do with his dick.

"Perfect timing," my mother says, and I look up to see her stand once more.

I follow her line of sight and see her best friend has also joined us.

They exchange hugs, and she sits beside Mother across from me. They've been best friends since they were kids. "What are you doing in town?" my mother asks as if she wasn't sure about whether her friend would show.

"Looking at houses," she answers with a big smile.

"Since when do you want to move here?" my mother inquires. "You hated it here while attending Barrington."

"Things change," she answers vaguely.

I tune them out as my mind wanders back to Haidyn. Surprisingly, my ass isn't sore, but my pussy? My body craves sex more than it ever has. I've always been curious about sex. I've watched porn before, but it always seemed so fake. Like how much can a woman moan and beg for more? Now I realize just how real it can be. I was a puddle for him and so fucking desperate.

When he tied me down, it was like a light switch flipping, and my body came alive. My need took over, and I wanted whatever he was willing to give me.

"Annabelle?" my mother speaks.

"Hmm?" I ask, pulling myself from that thought. I feel my cheeks flush just thinking about it when I meet her stare.

"I asked how things are going with Wesley?"

"Who's Wesley?" her best friend, Anne, asks.

I was partially named after her. When I was old enough to figure it out and asked, my mother said Annabelle just fit me. She took one look at me and knew that's who I was. All I can think of is that scary fucking doll that they made a movie about. I've always hated it.

"Her boyfriend. They've been dating for a couple of months now." My mother fills her in.

"He's good," I tell her.

"Are you guys ready for your trip?"

I don't know why I told her he was going with me. I panicked when Haidyn left me no choice but to fabricate a trip out of thin air. I guess because my mother knows I'd never go somewhere by myself at the last minute like that, and I'm trying to limit her information about my life. "Yep. Already packed and ready to go." Fuck, I feel sick to my stomach. Or that could be the effects of the enema.

"Oh, your backpacking trip." Anne nods, obviously knowing about it. "Sounds exciting."

Reaching out, I take a sip of the water that Mom had ordered for me when she arrived. I'm swallowing when she asks, "How are things with Haidyn?"

I choke on it, the cold water running down my chin. Setting the glass down, I pick up the napkin and blot my face. "Good." I nod, trying to convince both of us. "Going great."

"Haidyn Reeves?" Anne asks, arching a brow.

My mother nods. "I told you she was given her assignment."

Her friend is of course a Lady. My mother wouldn't associate with anyone outside of our world. She was raised that the Lords are everything. Royalty only sits with royalty—her words.

"Yes, but I wasn't aware it involved a Spade brother."

"How are the sessions going?" my mother asks, and I look at her friend, not sure I should answer.

So I shrug and say, "Good." It's a fucking lie.

I've fucked up what little chance I ever had. The Lords sent me on a wild goose chase. I think it's their way of knowing I'll never be enough for the life I'm supposed to have. You have to be born into this world, but they're going to see if you're worthy.

"Sessions?" her friend inquires. "What exactly do you mean by *sessions*?"

"Oh, Annabelle is his therapist." She does air quotes at therapist and her friend laughs.

Pretty much what I thought when I read the email.

"I mean, I see how the Lords would use you for that position." Anne's blue eyes look me up and down in thought. "Men are weak when it comes to pussy."

I choke on my own saliva at her choice of words. "Oh, no. We're not—"

"Fucking?" She chuckles. Her red-painted lips turn up into a smile. "I promise you, honey. He's thought about it."

My cheeks flush because of what he did to me today and what I can only guess is to come.

"Well, that won't be happening," my mother says tightly.

I'm to remain a virgin. She sold my virginity a long time ago to the man she wants me to marry. I don't know who that is, but she'll let me know when the time is right. Again, her words.

"Don't ever underestimate a Lord," her friend says in a tone that has a chill running up my spine. Her eyes search mine from across the table, and the smile that tugs at her lips makes me think she already knows what I've allowed Haidyn to do to me. "Plus," she adds, "those Spade brothers have been through a lot."

I frown. "How do you know?" Placing my elbows on the table, I lean forward. Not many know that Carnage exists, let alone what happens inside Carnage because those who are placed inside never get out.

"My ex," she answers, and I can't tell if she's lying or not. "He knew quite a bit about them."

"What could he possibly have known?" My mother rolls her eyes while taking a sip of her water.

"What did they go through?" I inquire, fully invested in this conversation now. If I can learn more about them, then maybe I can get leverage over Haidyn.

"They say that Haidyn killed their fathers," Anne answers, and I watch my mom stiffen like she knows something about that too.

"Why would he do that? To take over Carnage?" I ask.

"No." Anne shakes her head. "They were going to inherit it no matter what. The rumor is that he killed them for Ashtyn."

"Why would he kill them for her?" After I got the assignment, I did a deep dive into the Spade brothers. There wasn't a lot of information out there. The Lords, in general, are very secretive, but I was able to find old social media pages of Ashtyn and some of her friends.

I found that Ashtyn was Saint's chosen before she was assumed dead. The fact that I just saw her the other day at Carnage tells me that is not the case. It makes me wonder if the Spade brothers started that story to hide her from the world.

Anne's eyes meet mine when she answers. "Because Haidyn loves her."

My mother snorts. "The Lords don't love anyone."

"Not most, but some are weak," her friend argues, keeping her eyes on me.

"Saint was Ashtyn's Lord," I state the obvious.

"True, but she was assigned as Haidyn's chosen. He was supposed to marry her."

"A Lady and a chosen are two very different things." So that's interesting that she was supposed to be both for him.

"The Spade brothers have different rules." Anne waves her hand in the air, refusing to divulge any more information.

"Then why didn't he?" I saw her at Carnage, and she looked so concerned about Haidyn not answering her calls when she was telling Saint. Does she love him too? Did they have a relationship before she and Saint did? I wouldn't be surprised. Maybe they were like my friend and her Lord—slept around on one another.

"Although Haidyn acts like a monster, he's a teddy bear. He's weak." Anne chuckles. "He gave her to his best friend, who was also in love with her."

"Saint," I say, knowing what she means.

My mother snorts once more, bringing the glass of water to her lips and looking away. "Not sure why they're so obsessed with her." She sets it down and looks at me. "She's nothing like you."

Every mother is supposed to love their child unconditionally, but my mother is borderline obsessed with me. I grew up doing no wrong. I've never been grounded or punished in any way. She raised me to believe that I can achieve anything I want. Except freedom. I was born into this world, and I'll die being part of it. That's when I realized that she was lying to me, trying to sell me bullshit. You can't be anything you want. It's a fairy tale parents tell their kids in hopes they believe it.

I don't.

"Like I said, the pussy can be powerful." Her friend shrugs, and I'm not sure if she's referring to Ashtyn fucking Saint's friends or me fucking Haidyn, and I'm not sure I want to know.

My work cell goes off, and I remove it from my purse as my mother calls over to our server. I see it's a text from Haidyn. My heart picks up, and my throbbing pussy begins to sting as if he just slapped it. My eyes snap up to look around the restaurant to see if he's here. Maybe he's listening to our conversation and knows I'm talking about him. When I don't see him anywhere, my eyes drop back down to my phone to read the text he sent.

HAIDYN: Make sure to drink lots of water.

I roll my eyes and type back.

Yes, Lord, Sir.

HAIDYN: Sarcasm will get you nothing more than a face fucking.

The thought of being on my knees for Haidyn has my pulse racing. I'm sure I'd be tied up somehow as he pushes his cock into my mouth. Gagging me...I wonder if he'd slap my face. My hand goes to my cheek as it reddens just thinking about it.

I look up at my mother and find her occupied with the server. So I pick up the water in front of me, bring the straw to my lips and suck on it as I take a quick selfie. Setting the cup down, I send it to him.

HAIDYN: That's my good little whore.

The throbbing between my legs intensifies, and my underwear gets wetter. Looking up quickly, I see my mother's friend's eyes on mine, and my cheeks redden.

Fuck, I'm so fucked!

My phone goes off again, and it's Wesley texting me this time. I sigh. How do the Lords expect me to handle this? Does it mean I can break up with Wesley now since Haidyn knows who I am? I'm not sure what to do, and I can't ask them because then they'll know that Haidyn knows who I am. *Goddammit!* I want to slam my face into the table. Instead, I open his text.

WESLEY: Hey, baby. Sorry you had to cancel our dinner tonight. Tomorrow night, I'm going out with the guys. Want to go with?

Sure.

I respond and turn the phone off, done with this day. I need a margarita, not a water, and I need a fucking nap.

Chapter 25

Haidyn

Senior year at Barrington

"Where's Kash?" I ask, my eyes heavy. My head hangs forward, and blood drips from my busted mouth.

"His fear is being alone, right? Abandonment." The woman laughs. "The Lords were made to be unstoppable. There's power in numbers, but the Spade brothers...you were always meant to be different." Her red-painted nails run along my sweaty chest. I try to pull away, but the chains that tie my wrists above my head prevent it. "You boys were raised together, dependent on one another. Hell, you even shared the same girl," she adds, referring to Ashtyn. "How do you think Saint will feel when he wakes up? Hmm? Will he still love her?"

"Where..." I take a deep breath, and it hurts my aching chest. "Is Kashton?" I ask through gritted teeth. We fought eight prisoners who had been given shots of adrenaline, and when I was done, I saw him lying on the floor next to me. Face bloodied. The only thing that reassured me he was alive was that I felt his pulse on his wrists before they dragged his unconscious body out of the arena.

It's just us at the moment. Adam is gone, and Saint was shot.

"He's learning to live alone," she answers cryptically, and my teeth grind.

She grips my chin with her pointy nails and pushes my head up so I have to look down at her as she stands in front of me. I'm six-seven, and my feet aren't touching the concrete floor. She's maybe five-nine with her heels on.

I spit blood onto her face, and all she does is smile at me. "Funny how the girl you were supposed to have, you gave to your friend, and now he can die because of her."

"He's not going to die," I grind out.

She shoves my head back, and I look up at the chains wrapped around my wrists just to make sure they're still there. I can no longer feel my busted hands from fighting in the arena.

"You killed your fathers because of her." She goes on. "And now I've been brought in to make sure it never happens again."

"They're dead," I state the obvious and joke when my head falls forward to stare at the bloody concrete floor once again. Pretty sure I have a couple of broken ribs since it hurts to breathe. "Can't kill someone more than once."

"The Spade brothers are supposed to be THE Lords. You take care of the ones who betray your oath that you hold so high. But you all went fucking weak over pussy." I hear her heels clanking on the concrete as she walks away from me. "I volunteered my assistance to the society to train you boys. Make you men again. Remind you of who you are. They said I couldn't kill you, but I'm allowed to do whatever is necessary to get you back on track."

"Take me to Kash." I try to take a deep breath, but the pain in my side makes it hard. Where could he be that he thinks he's alone? Have they told him that Saint and I are dead? Maybe they told him I didn't survive the fight.

Her laughter fills the cold room as she comes back to stand in front of me. "I like you, Haidyn, and I'm going to enjoy breaking you."

"Fifty-eight," I breathe. "Fifty-nine." Another breath. "Sixty." Dropping the bar, I step back as the weights hit the padded floor in my home gym.

I fall onto the bench behind me and hang my head, running my hand through my sweaty hair. My chest is on fire. I'm overdoing it, but it is what it is. I'm trying to get back to who I was before I got shot. I'm not lifting heavy, but consistently.

Reaching over, I pick up my cell off the bench and hover over Kashton's number and press call.

He answers on the first ring. "Haidyn—"

"Want to go for a ride?" I stand and walk over to the floor-to-ceiling windows that run the length of the back wall. The sun is just starting to set over the mountains. I love riding at night. It's my favorite time.

"Yeah...wait! Are you in town?"

"For the night," I decide to say. Not a total lie.

"I'll ask Saint..."

"Just you and me," I tell him before he can involve Saint. I'm definitely not in the mood for that argument right now.

"Okay. Where do you want to meet?"

♠

After a quick shower and thirty minutes later, I pull into an empty parking lot and see Kashton waiting for me on his bike—a Ninja H2R. Coming up next to him, I shut mine off.

He wears a backwards hat and no helmet. "What the fuck is going on, Haidyn?" he asks, getting off his bike. "Why are we meeting here like it's off the books? And why the hell wasn't Saint invited?"

I sigh and reach into my leather jacket pocket, pulling out the picture. "Do you know who this is?"

He walks over to my R1 and takes it from my hand. Scrunching his face, he shakes his head. "Only Benny looks familiar. Who is the other guy?" he asks, handing it back to me.

"That's what I'm trying to figure out."

He lets out an aggravated sigh. "And you can't do that from Carnage?"

I could return, but not now. Not with Charlotte. I'm not letting her out of my sight, and it's too risky to bring her into our world. The guys will start questioning her and who she is. As far as they know, I'm no longer seeing her since I'm not there for our session. "I'll come back soon," I assure him.

He runs a hand through his hair.

"Found anything else out since I spoke to you last?"

He shakes his head. "Nothing. The bastard is almost dead by this point. But he's not going to give anyone up."

"And Laura?"

"Nope. Until she has the baby, we're not getting shit from her." He leans up against his bike, crossing his tatted arms over his chest. "We spoke to Sin, and he told us to do whatever needs to be done, even if we have to pull her out of her coma for answers, but we don't think it's worth it. Once the baby is born, we'll find out what we don't have by then."

I nod. "Luke?" I go to the next name on my list.

He gives a rough laugh at that one. "That guy is fucked. He just mumbles nonsense to himself twenty-four seven." His face grows serious, and he rubs the back of his neck. Looking up, he meets my eyes. "They cut your tracker out when they shot you."

I say nothing because it wasn't a question.

"Why haven't you had it replaced?"

"I will."

"When?" he demands.

"When I get back to Carnage," I snap, not liking the direction of this conversation.

His jaw sharpens, and he looks away from me.

"Kash—"

"Ashtyn's pregnant." He interrupts me.

I frown a little, confused by his change of topic. "Well, that's good, right?" We knew it would happen because Saint had her IUD removed when he brought her back. "Didn't Devin test her after Benny...?"

"Yeah, but it was negative. Apparently, Jasmine went out and bought her a fucking purse full of pregnancy tests before she left, so Ashtyn's been taking one every day since. She came into the office this morning crying that it was positive. Saint spoke to Devin, and all he could come up with was his test was a false negative. Or it was taken too early. I don't know how that shit works." His hands slap the sides of his jeans.

Silence falls over the empty parking lot because I'm not sure what else to say. I just wanted to see him. I don't want him to think I left him. Not after I faked my death. It had to look real. I needed my brothers to think I was no longer with them. Too many eyes were inside Carnage that didn't belong, so I had to put on a show.

He pushes off his bike. "Are we going to ride or not?" he asks, straddling it.

I smirk and start my R1. "Yeah."

My phone vibrates in my pocket, and I pull it out to see it's the text I've been waiting for from Gavin. I open it up and read over it.

GAVIN: Your information was correct.

Smiling, I exit out and lock the phone. Looking up, I see Kashton already staring at me.

"Good news?" he asks.

"Something like that," I answer. It's the green light I've been waiting for.

CHARLOTTE

I'M SITTING ON THE COUCH, EATING POPCORN WHILE WATCHING *Slasher,* when my doorbell rings, knowing it's probably Wesley. I bailed on him again. I just didn't feel like going to a sports bar with him and the guys tonight. If I wanted to watch sports, I'd go to a game. If I want to go out, I'm going out to get drunk and dance. Staying home just sounded better than either one.

Getting up, I make my way to the door and open it to see Haidyn standing on my porch, one hand gripping the strap to his backpack and the other shoved into the pocket of his leather jacket. Seeing him still makes my stomach tighten at the possibility of why he's here. "I have another day," I remind him.

He smirks at me, entering and forcing me to step back. "Don't worry. I won't be long. Just dropping by to give you something."

"Aw?" I slam the door shut. I lock the door and want to laugh at myself. The biggest threat I have is already inside. "Did you bring me flowers and chocolate?" I turn around to face him.

His hand wraps around my throat, pulling me up to my tiptoes. "Remember what I said about sarcasm?"

I swallow against his hand, knowing he can feel my pulse pick up at his words. "Yes," I whisper.

He lets go of my neck, and I rub it. He wasn't cutting off my air, but he had a good grip on it.

I follow him into my living room. He stops and looks at the TV for a second before turning to face me. "Strip," he commands, his voice deeper.

My body begins to shake, but my hands go to the hem of my T-shirt without thought. I pull it up and over my head, tossing it to the side. I'm not wearing a bra. I push the thin material of the cotton shorts and underwear down my legs and kick them out of my way so I'm standing before him naked.

He stood at the end of the exam table fingering my ass and played with my breasts just two days ago before I came all over his fingers. There's nothing on my body he hasn't seen.

As shy as I was before, my mother raised me to love my body. She once told me to know my body more than any man. That way, when I'm given to a Lord, I can satisfy myself.

When he steps forward, my breathing picks up. My nipples instantly go hard. Reaching out, he runs his hands down my stomach before they grip my hips, pulling my body flush with his. "How do you feel?"

"Fine," I whisper, looking up at him through my lashes. He's every bit of six-seven, and he's got combat boots on. I'm five-two and barefoot, not to mention naked. He's got an advantage in every possible scenario right now.

He takes my hand and pulls me over to the center of the living room. He grabs a throw pillow off the couch and places it in the center of the large glass coffee table. "Lie on it. Face down," he commands. "I want your hips to rest on the pillow."

"I—"

"It'll hold you."

Crawling onto the table, I take in a shaky breath, nervous it'll shatter into a million pieces and cut me when we both fall to the floor. Doing as he said, I lie down face-first, and the coldness makes me hiss in a breath.

He grabs my hips, lifting them to position the pillow where he wants it under my hips—pushing my ass up in the air.

He kneels in front of me and unzips his backpack. I take a second to push my hair from my face for a better look when he removes rope from it. He quickly ties my left wrist to the leg of the coffee table before doing the same to the right. Then he disappears, and I feel the rope around one ankle and then the other. He's tied me spread eagle face down on the coffee table naked.

I'm moaning, pulling on them. My body was already starting to tingle, but now it's heating up. I pant, trying to reposition myself to a more comfortable position, but it's useless.

"Are you a rope bunny, doll face?" he asks with a chuckle. Then he grabs a small-looking hourglass with sand out of his bag and places it in front of the TV, and I frown, watching the sand start to fall through it.

"I...I don't know what that means," I stammer, trying to ignore my throbbing pussy. If he looks, he'll see I'm already wet.

"It's when a slut likes to be tied up with rope. That you get turned on being helpless...and at someone else's mercy."

I close my eyes, placing the side of my face on the table, hoping he won't see my cheeks turn red.

The sound of him unbuckling his belt makes my heart race and thighs clench. Then the swoop of it being released from the loops. I scream as it lands on my ass, making me pull on the ropes. "That was for your sarcasm yesterday." *Swat.* "That was for your sarcasm today." *Swat.* "And that one was because I can see how fucking wet your cunt is when I play with you."

I'm gasping, body trembling, ass on fire, and sweating. I expected him to fuck my face for my sarcasm, and that was exactly why he spanked me like an unruly child instead. He wants to keep me surprised.

"Hmm? Tell me, doll face. Tell me you're wet and want me to fuck you." His hand goes between my legs, and I arch my ass up in the air even more, wanting his fingers inside my pussy.

"Please?" I'm more than willing to beg. The fact that my body pulls on the restraints proves he's right when a moan escapes my parted lips at how helpless I really am.

Swat. "Don't beg. Tell me."

I sniff, my nose now running as the burning sensation intensifies on my backside. "I need...I need you to fuck me. Please, I need to get off." My clit pulses, begging for his attention. I've been horny for years but never like this. The ache hurts so much I'll do anything for him to soothe it.

"Look at you using your words, such a good girl." His hand massages my stinging ass, and I moan, wiggling it the best I can. "But that's not why I came over tonight. That'll have to wait."

I sag onto the table with a frustrated growl. I try to look over my shoulder to see what he's doing but can't see shit with my hair down. I should have worn it up. It's sticking to my sweat-covered face, chest, and arms. It's itchy.

His hand drops between my spread legs, and he runs his fingers over my pussy and up between my ass cheeks. I clench them even though I know it won't stop him.

His fingers disappear only to come back a second later, and this time, they feel...wet? "Haidyn..."

He pushes one into my ass, and I yank on the restraints, my breath momentarily taken away. "You think I'm only going to fuck your mouth and cunt, Charlotte?"

I whimper as he pulls it out and pushes it back in again. I try to pull away, but he's got me tied too tight. There's not enough give to get away from his touch. It just makes my pussy wetter and my need for him greater.

"Your pretty pussy will be the last thing I fuck." He removes his finger, and I'm gasping, trying to prepare myself for his dick.

I know anal sex takes time. From what I've heard anyway. Surely, he's not going to just fuck me right here right now. Probably. Men like Haidyn want to make women bleed. They like to take what they know they can't have. And I'd never willingly give that up.

I close my eyes when I feel his hand at my ass once again, and he pushes something inside it. My ass gives way even though I try to stop it. It closes around something, and I relax but quickly tense once more when I feel something new being pushed into me. It's bigger, stretching me wider. I lift my head and cry out at the sting of the stretch.

Chapter 26
Haidyn

"Good girl." I rub her reddened cheeks while my eyes stare at the base of the butt plug I just pushed into her ass. I walk to the side of the coffee table and sit on the couch, looking over her shaking, tied-down body.

Her cries have subsided, but her heavy breathing can be heard over the crying woman on TV. I'm going to prepare every hole she has. Fucking her cunt will be a privilege for her. I'll still make sure she gets off because there's power in that, but her body will learn to climax in other ways than having her pussy filled.

"Hai-dyn," she says, her voice trembling. "What...what's in me?" She sniffs.

I reach out and slide the coffee table closer to the couch. Gripping a handful of her hair, I yank her cheek up off the glass and wrap my free hand around her delicate neck as I whisper in her ear. "It's a butt plug, doll face. You're going to beg me to fuck that ass of yours, so I have to stretch it." Not a total lie.

"No..." She tries to shake her head, but my hand prevents it.

"Yes," I tell her. "I'm going to fuck it and then watch my cum leak from it." It's going to be a glorious sight.

She whimpers, knowing it's true. "It hurts." She struggles with the ropes around her wrists.

I smile. "That means it's working."

"What's working?"

I don't answer. "Want me to play with your pussy? Will that help take your mind off it?" The plug is on the smaller side. It's not meant to stretch her this very night, just to keep a little something inside for the time being.

She sucks in a deep breath. "Yes...please?"

"Okay, doll face." I kiss the side of her face, tasting the salt from her tears and sweat. Fuck, she tastes amazing! I can't wait until she shows me how obedient she can be, and I reward her by letting her sit on my face. I'm dying to taste her.

Letting go of her, I gather all of her hair in my right hand and hold her face up once again. "Watch your show," I tell her, and my left hand drops between her open legs. "You're soaked, Charlotte. It's all over the pillow."

She groans, shaking her ass for me as my fingers massage her cunt. She tries to rock back and forth so one will slide in, but I keep them where I want them.

"Please, Haidyn. I need to come. Make me come."

I smile as she rambles. She's getting good at using her words. "This visit isn't about pleasure, Charlotte."

She lets out a frustrated growl, her head fighting for me to release her hair. I don't.

"Oooww," she cries out.

"What hurts?" I ask, already knowing.

"My stomach," she answers. "It's cramping. What-why does it hurt my stomach?"

"This is a punishment, doll face," I say vaguely.

"I'm sorry." Her body shakes, and I push a finger into her pussy, loving how tight she is.

"I know, but it's too late."

"Haidyn." She yanks on the rope. "Please...take it out."

"I'm timing you, and you're not done yet," I inform her.

I placed something inside her before I added the butt plug to her ass. I want my girl prepared for what I'm going to give her, which means I'm going to make sure she's ready. I want her to question everything her body feels and why. Is it me bringing it to meet my needs? Is it her wanting new things? She'll always wonder, and no other man will be able to get her as high as I will.

"How much longer?" she asks breathlessly.

"When the hourglass is done, I'll untie you." Time messes with your head. Being forced to sit and watch it tick by makes the time slower.

"I can't. Oh God, the burn...the cramps."

I slap her pussy, making her cry out. Then I shove two fingers into her. "That better?"

She's panting, unable to speak.

"How about this?" I add another, feeling the plug in her ass and pushing against it.

"Yes, oh fuck..." She rocks back and forth on the table, making it rattle as she tries to fuck my fingers.

I'd give anything to keep her tied like this for a solid twenty-four hours. Just teasing and messing with her until she passes out from exhaustion. And then when she woke up, I'd already be balls deep inside her.

I have many reasons as to why she's my newest toy, but I'll never let her know the main one.

CHARLOTTE

My body moves on its own, but my mind is on my stomach. I have the worst cramps I've ever had. I part my lips to beg him to stop, but a moan comes out instead.

"I love the way your body begs to be used," he says as his fingers fuck my soaked pussy.

I'm panting, and a line of drool falls from my parted lips. I'm unable to swallow due to the position of my neck with his fist in my hair. My fisted hands yank on the ropes, and my heavy eyes stare at the hourglass in front of the TV, but I don't see it. All I hear is the blood rushing in my ears as that sensation between my legs grows hotter.

"That's it, doll face. Concentrate on my fingers. Ride them, Charlotte. Show me how much you want to come."

That cramping returns, and fresh tears sting my eyes. What's happening to me? I feel like I'm being pulled in different directions. Pain, pleasure. Then pain again.

He removes his fingers, and I slump on the sweat-covered table. Then his belt hits my already tender ass, and I cry out.

"I never thought you'd get so turned on from pain, Charlotte. But I'm more than willing to give you what you like."

Swat.

"Please..." I gasp, flinching.

His fingers return to my pussy, and he doesn't stop this time. My breath is taken away completely as he brings me to another mind-blowing orgasm. I'm so far gone that I don't even realize he's untied me until he picks me up off the table. I lie spent across his arms as he carries me out of the living room.

My heavy eyes look around aimlessly as he carries me to the bathroom. He lowers my feet to the floor and guides me to lean over the bathroom counter, and I don't even fight him. I'm ready for whatever he's prepared to do.

"Relax, doll face," he says, gently rubbing my back before his hand lowers down over my stinging ass cheek and falls between my still shaking legs. "I'm going to remove the butt plug."

I'm still trying to catch my breath and my body has no strength left to fight anything. I feel him tug on the plug before my body gives way to the pressure, and he pulls it free. I slump against the counter as the cramping returns.

He pulls me to stand and turns me to face him. With a hand in my hair, he forces my heavy eyes to look up into his. "The butt plug was to make sure you held the suppositories in place."

I blink, my mind trying to comprehend what he's saying, but the pain in my stomach has all of my attention, and I'm shuffling from foot to foot.

His eyes search mine. "You did good, doll face. I'm going to help you to the restroom so you can relieve yourself." Letting go of my hair, he helps sit me down on the toilet, then he steps back, closing me inside. And just like at the doctor's office, I cry once again as my cum runs from my pussy after something my body should not have enjoyed.

Chapter 27

Haidyn

I walk out her front doors and lock them up behind me with the key she doesn't know I have. Knocking when I arrived earlier was a formality. I wanted to see the surprised look in her eyes when she saw me standing on her porch for the second day in a row.

Making my way down her steps, I toss the backpack over my shoulders and get on my bike. Starting it up, I give the house one last look before I kick it into gear and pull out of her driveway.

I'm so fucking hard right now. Fuck, I didn't think that it'd be that difficult to tell her no. When she begged me to fuck her...Goddammit, it took everything not to just do it. But I have restraint. I went three years without it, for fuck's sake. What's a couple of days?

I can tell it's driving her mad. She wants it so bad. The way her voice cracks when she begs. The way she cries when she needs more.

I have to adjust my dick in my jeans to give myself a little room. Getting onto the highway, I speed toward my house while "Thank You for Hating Me" by Citizen Soldier blasts in my ears.

Pulling into my garage, I shut off my bike just as my cell rings. I remove it from my pocket to see it's Bones. "Hello?" I answer, shutting my garage and entering the house.

"Just calling to follow up. Found what you were looking for?"

"No," I answer and walk through my dark house to my office. Tossing my backpack onto one of the chairs, I sit at my desk. "Anything new on your end?"

"No." he sighs. "But I've pulled as much footage as I could from Glass for you. I'm going to send it over for you to go through."

"Thanks." Ashtyn was a dancer at Bones's strip club, and Benny was one of her usual clients. Maybe the guy in the photo was there with him. I could go to Carnage and ask Ashtyn herself, but I know what she's been through. I want her to heal. Not worry about someone who could still be a threat to her. Especially since she's pregnant. She and Saint are finally in a good place, and I don't want to come between that again. I was doing Adam a favor when I intervened last time. I'm not doing it again.

"Sent." Bones gets my attention.

I put in my password for the computer and open up my email. "Got it. Thanks, man," I tell him.

"Let me know if you need anything else." He hangs up.

Placing my cell on the desk, I open my top drawer, pull out my pack of cigarettes, and light one up.

It's a horrible habit I can't seem to stop. But why should I? The Lords aren't cautious in any aspect of our lives.

I pull up the cameras to Charlotte's bedroom and split the screen so I can also look through the footage from Glass. It's going to be another long night.

CHARLOTTE

"DO YOU REALLY MEAN THAT, CHARLOTTE?" HAIDYN ASKS.

I swallow nervously, my eyes dropping to stare out the window. Unable to make eye contact, I softly answer, "Of course."

"I know what you can do." The corners of his lips pull back, showing a shadow of a smirk.

My wide eyes move to his as my breathing accelerates. "W-what?"

"Let me rip off your clothes."

I gasp, but I'm not sure why I'm surprised. That's all men like Haidyn think of—sex, sex, and more sex. That's where they dominate.

"I'll tie you up in a tight little ball, suspend you from the ceiling so that your cunt, mouth, and ass are easily on display for me to fuck."

All the blood rushes from my face at the thought of what he'd do. How vulnerable I'd be. How easily he'd be able to fuck whatever hole he wanted whenever he wanted. The thought makes my underwear wet. But it also terrifies me.

He continues. "Once I'm done violating you, I'll sit down, have a smoke while I let you hang there, and watch my cum leak from your stretched-out and overused holes like the worthless whore you're meant to be."

I'm trembling, pressing my back against the chair. The thought of being Haidyn's sex doll makes me curious. Men like him take what they want. No questions asked. That also goes hand in hand with permission.

"I can't promise you'll like it, but it'll make me feel better," he adds in my silence. Obviously, he likes making me nervous. "Still want to help me, doll face?" He releases the armrest with his right hand and places it on my knee. The soft touch makes me jump, and a whimper escapes my nude-painted lips.

I SIT STRAIGHT UP, GASPING FOR AIR IN MY DARK BEDROOM. "Fuck," I sigh. I've dreamed of him nonstop since he was in my kitchen last week. It's the same dream, the same words, and I wake up soaking wet every time.

Reaching over into my nightstand, I pull out my mini-Body Wand. Pressing the button, I don't even bother to take my underwear off. I also grab the small recorder and press play, laying it next to me. I thought the Lords would want proof that I went through with it, but they've never required any.

It doubles as a pen. I bought it online, and Jessie never even noticed when he searched my things. But why would he? A therapist needs something to write her notes down with.

I never thought it'd come in handy for something like this.

Haidyn's voice fills my room just like it does my head. Over and over, I put it on repeat as I place the vibrator on my clit, close my eyes, and imagine him doing exactly what he said he'd do. Lords don't make false promises. If they say they're going to do something, then they do it.

I arch my back, rubbing the tip back and forth. I need to get off and clear my head. A run isn't going to be enough.

My breath catches, and my hips buck. "Fuuccckkkk." I moan as I come in my underwear. I'm not one of those women who comes very hard—not until Haidyn. I was sixteen the first time I got myself off, and I was so disappointed. All my friends said how amazing it was. Earth-shattering. Not for me. But Haidyn has gotten me off twice now with just his fingers, and I was seeing stars both times. I can't imagine what he can do with his mouth and dick.

Turning it off, I toss it to the floor and stop the recording. I stare up into my dark room, listening to my breathing evening out. My mind is a fucking mess.

It's been six days since he was sitting in my kitchen, where I handed myself over to him. He said he'd be back to collect me in five days, and I'm on pins and needles waiting for him to arrive. A Lord is never late. They are known for keeping their word. So I know he's doing this on purpose. He wants to keep me on edge and make me sweat.

I've told everyone I'm going away for a vacation. Backpacking across Europe sounded stupid but believable. I figured most of my friends thought I was crazy. One, I don't do the outdoors, and two, I'm going alone. A few of them even offered to join me. I only told my mother that Wesley is going with me. He thinks I'm going away on a girl's trip. So many lies that they are all going to figure out if they talk to one another. I feel like any of them finding out will be better than me denying Haidyn what he wanted.

And now I'm not sure how I'll keep up with the facade on social media. I'm not one of those who posts everything I eat or drink. Or when I go out. I'm also not big on selfies. But who knows how long I'll be gone. A few days? Weeks? Over a month? Spending that much time alone with Haidyn terrifies and excites me. He did say to tell all of them that I wasn't going to have any cell service, so maybe I won't have to post anything. Just a few text messages here and there. I can Photoshop myself into any type of picture and send a selfie. I laugh at that thought. I doubt I even get phone time.

Getting out of bed, I make my way to the kitchen. Turning on the light, I come to a stop when I see a glass of water and a pill on the island.

My heart picks up as I slowly step closer. Coming to the edge, I look it over. It's small and round. The hairs on the back of my neck rise, and the air thickens, making it harder to breathe. *He's here.* "You're drugging me?" I ask, my tongue heavy and mouth dry.

He steps up to my back, the roughness of his jeans rubs against the back of my exposed thighs. A hand snakes around my waist, spreading flat on my stomach, while the other wraps around my neck from behind, making my pulse race. "If you're asking me if I'm going to hold you down and force a pill down your throat, the answer is no. I'm giving you a choice."

The thought makes my stomach knot. It doesn't sound any better. "A choice?" I whisper.

"You've always got a choice, doll face."

"There are worse things than dying," I say, trying to calm my breathing. It's so loud I'm practically gasping.

"There are," he agrees. His hand tightens on my neck, restricting my air.

I rise on my tiptoes and croak out, "Hai-dyn."

He loosens his grip, and I look down at the pill. I toss it into my mouth without giving it another thought and take a drink of the room temperature water. No going back now unless I want to shove my fingers down my throat, and I've always hated vomiting.

"Good girl." His deep voice praises me, and I whimper.

Letting go of me, he turns me around. His hands grip my thighs, and he lifts me onto the island, leaving my legs dangling off the edge.

He steps between them. His hands slowly run up my legs to push my T-shirt up in the process. My eyes are on his, but he's staring down at my underwear.

"Did you enjoy coming to the recording of what I'm going to do to you?"

My stomach drops, and his eyes lift to meet mine. He's been in my house, watching me. I should have known there was a reason he's made me wait to come get me.

A smirk graces his lips. "You're so beautiful when you come."

My throat closes, tongue heavy. I'm not sure if it's the way his blue eyes watch mine or the pill kicking in so quickly.

He pulls my ass to the edge of the island as he steps forward, closing the small space. His hands run up over my hips to my waist.

They skate over my ribs, and I lift my arms above my head so he can remove my shirt. He tosses it behind him, and his eyes drop to my chest. I'm gasping for fucking air. It's embarrassing really. My nipples are hard, and my skin is covered in goose bumps.

"So fucking beautiful," he whispers as if in awe.

I blink my heavy eyes. "Haidyn?"

"Yeah, doll face?" He looks back up at me.

I have so many questions. What are you going to do to me? *Whatever he wants.* How long will I be a prisoner at Carnage? *That's up to me.*

All of a sudden, I feel it. My skin flushes, fingers tingling. My lips part, and he cups my face, tilting my head back even more. I stare up at him through hooded eyes. They're the prettiest blue—dark and mysterious. I've been obsessed with him since I first saw him on my computer in the Lords' emails. I was doing as much research as I could on my assignment. It was all over when I saw him at our first session at Carnage. I just didn't know it then. The way he walks, the sound of his voice, the way he stares you down. It's like a lion watching its prey. Ready to attack.

Heat rushes in my face, and I wonder if I'm blushing or having hot flashes. My body leans into him, and his eyes drop to my parted lips. "Kiss me," I whisper, needing to feel them on mine. I want to know what it feels like for him to willingly want me before he turns my body against me. Because I know I'll give this monster anything he wants.

His eyes search mine before he lowers his lips. I open for him, letting him have control. He's soft, delicate as if I'm setting him up for something. I try to lift my arms to touch him, but I can't feel them.

His hands grip my face, and he tilts my head to the side. I moan into his mouth when his tongue meets mine.

I lean into him or fall. Not quite sure. I'm seeing fucking stars, or he's blindfolded me. What's up is down, and what's forward is back. I'm lost, falling down a hole that seems to be endless.

He breaks the kiss, and I gasp, finally able to breathe. I open my heavy eyes, and his face is inches from mine.

When I try to speak, nothing comes out. I can't form a single thought that doesn't involve him on top of me. Sprawled out on this kitchen island while he pins me down and fucks me. What did he give me? Was it supposed to make me beg him to fuck me? Turn me on? The fact that I got myself off while listening to his recording means I didn't need to be drugged to want him. That wasn't the first time I have gotten myself off to it.

"Come on, doll face. It's time to get you ready."

Chapter 28

Haidyn

I pick her up off the island, my hands under her ass as I carry her to her room. She's fading away in front of my eyes. I needed her to take the pill. Not because I want to fuck her. I don't need her to black out for that. But for other reasons. I knew she'd take the easy way out. No one wants to know what's coming if given the option not to have to face it.

I've been in her house for the past three hours watching her sleep. She called out my name while she dreamed of me, and it made me as hard as a rock.

I told her five days, but I've waited six. I've followed her, watched her every move. I've been so close to her that all she had to do was open her eyes, and she would have caught me. But she's been preoccupied. Too worried about what's to come. Her fear is warranted. That's why I just kissed her because soon, she won't want me touching her, let alone looking at her. When I'm done using my new toy, she won't know what to do with her life. She won't know what her purpose is without belonging to me.

I lay her down on her bed. "I dreamed of you," she whispers.

I smile down at her. "I know."

Her heavy eyes open, long dark eyelashes fluttering. "Are you going to fuck me?"

"Not right now." I can't help but run my knuckles over her soft skin and down to her hip bones, dipping my fingertips into her wet underwear.

She raises her hips, a moan escaping her lips. "Please?" she begs desperately.

I didn't give her anything that would make her horny. That's all her. It was just to relax her. Keep her memory foggy so when she wakes up in hell tomorrow, she won't remember how I got her there. "You'll have plenty of time to beg me, doll face," I assure her.

"But I want you." Her hands come up to her chest, and she grabs her breasts.

I grip her wrists and pin them down to her sides. "I'll remember that when you wake up." Letting go of her, she manages to push herself up onto her forearms.

Dilated eyes meet mine, and her lips part on a heavy inhale. "Why do you want me?" she asks.

"Why wouldn't I?" I counter honestly. I've wanted her since I first saw her. Now I have an in. A reason to treat her like the lying bitch she is. I know exactly who she is and who she's working for. I'm going to make sure that when I'm done with her, she's crawling back in tears because I used her in every way possible. I've always been an opportunist. And this is an opportunity that only an idiot would pass on.

She falls onto her back, eyes closing. Mine drop to her chest. They're even more perfect in person. Perky C cup. Her pink nipples are hard, and I reach out to massage them.

She groans, her hips rising once more. Her hands come up to grab her breasts, and I slap them away. "Oh no, doll face. I'll be the only one to touch you."

A soft chuckle comes from her parted lips as if that's not going to happen. I get up off the bed and walk over to the opposite side of the room where I've been watching her sleep. I reach down and pick up my bag and bring it over to the bed. I unzip it and her eyes open, but she looks around aimlessly.

I pull out several leather belts in multiple lengths and sizes. I slide one under her waist, and pull it tight, buckling it above her pierced belly button. I then place the little gold lock on it. Then I grip her cum-covered underwear and slide them down her legs before shoving them into my back pocket. I look over her shaved cunt, and my mouth waters.

I place another belt under her right thigh, pulling it tightly and buckling it in place with the lock. Then repeat it with the other before I connect them with short chains to the belt around her waist so she can't push them down her legs. Then I place one around each small wrist and each arm right above the elbow. These will allow me to secure her in multiple positions. It's endless, really. I have several in mind.

I stand and pull the connecting devices from the bag and secure the ones around her wrists to each thigh, locking her arms down by her side. "Beautiful," I whisper.

"Haidyn?" She pulls on them but has no luck. Even if she wasn't weak, she wouldn't be able to get out of them. It just makes her moan again. "Kiss me." She licks her lips. "Please kiss me like you did in my kitchen."

I smirk, placing my fists on either side of her head. This is going to be easier than I thought. "You want me to kiss you?" What surprises me the most is how much I want to hear her say that again.

Her eyes search mine, but I'm not sure she sees me at all. Nodding, she begs, "Please?"

I grip her cheeks, and she arches her neck, parting her lips. I lower my mouth to hers and spit into it. She doesn't even gag. Instead, she leaves it open like a good girl, and I smile, lowering my lips to hers. I kiss her. My tongue enters her mouth, tasting her, and she arches her body off the bed, begging for more. But that's all she's going to get tonight. Pulling away, I run my fingers over her lips and slide them into her mouth. She wraps her lips around them and sucks as I shove them to the back of her throat, making her gag.

"Fuck, doll face. Look at you begging me to fuck your mouth already." She blinks, and her unfocused eyes start to well with unshed tears. Slowly, I remove my fingers, and her body lowers to the bed, her eyes closing.

"Where do you want my cock the most—your ass, cunt, or mouth?"

"My pussy." She groans, her body rocking side to side. "My pussy, please..."

I chuckle. That'll be the last hole I'll fuck of hers. When you fuck a woman's pussy, it's for her enjoyment. Nothing about this will be about her. It's all about me. She'll learn to please me.

I lower my hands between her legs, and she spreads them for me. I run the tips of my fingers up and down, feeling her wetness from coming on herself earlier.

"Yes." Her hips buck, but I don't push my fingers into her.

My plans with her will take weeks, months even. I'm going to ride this train as long as I can.

I stand and watch her chest rising and falling softly. She's out for now. "Come on, doll face." I slide my arms under her limp body and pick her up, carrying her to her new home. I was telling the truth. How long she stays with me is up to her.

CHARLOTTE

I'M FLOATING, BUT AT THE SAME TIME, I FEEL LIKE A BLANKET IS on top of me, weighing me down. There's a humming in my ears, and my mouth is dry. My heavy eyes open, and I realize I'm lying on my back, staring at a black ceiling. Everything hurts, including my back. I feel like I slept on an uneven rock.

Rolling onto my side, I stop myself when I feel my arm is in the way. I try to move it, but it doesn't work. Did I sleep on it wrong? Has it gone numb?

Sitting up, I look down at it to see black belts wrapped around each thigh and a short chain connected to matching belts that are around each wrist, pinning my arms down.

My breathing picks up, and I start yanking on them, but all it does is pinch the skin on my thighs from the leather. "HAIDYN?" I shout his name, throwing my head back, trying to get my wild hair out of my face so I can see clearly. "Haidyn?"

I'm met with nothing but silence. I manage to get to my knees. It takes a lot of work, but I'm able to get to my feet. My legs feel like Jell-O, so I press my back against a cold concrete wall, trying to take in my surroundings.

The first thing I notice is a small mattress on the floor. No bigger than a twin. It's what I was lying on. It looks dirty, and there's a wet spot from where I was most likely drooling. At least, I hope that's what it is. To my right is a white countertop with six cabinets underneath.

I rush over to them, almost tripping over myself, which would suck because I can't use my hands to keep from slamming my face on the concrete floor. Bending down a little, I position myself to where my right hand can reach the cabinets. I grab the handle and try to open it, but it's locked.

"Fuck!"

I try the other, then another, and another with no luck. All six are locked. "Goddammit." Haidyn is smarter than that.

Blowing my hair out of my face, I look at the far wall, and my heart picks up as I step in front of it. It's a mirror. A large square glass that takes up most of the wall. I see myself in the reflection. I look hungover. Or like I'm coming off a three-day binge of some sort. My eyes are puffy, and my hair is a tangled and wild mess. My chin and cheek are slick from drool.

How long have I been out? I willingly took that pill he offered me. Who knows what it was and how long it affected me. Even now, I feel wobbly. A single bulb that hangs from the low ceiling gives me just enough light to see that my dull eyes look dilated and bloodshot.

I'm also naked. No surprise. My eyes quickly scan my tan skin. I don't see any bruises, but the leather has begun to irritate me. I see two more that I hadn't seen a minute ago. Each one wrapped around my arms above my elbows. Little golden locks get my attention, telling me that I can't remove the belts even if I could unlatch my wrists from my thighs. They've all been locked in place. Another set of belts is wrapped around my ankles. But the ones around my upper arms make me nervous. Why are they in that spot? What could he possibly do with them?

Taking a few steps back, I step on something that digs into my foot. "Ow." I wince and hobble to the side until my ass hits the countertop behind me. I look down to see what I stepped on. It's a large drain in the center of the room. The floor seems to slant toward it. It's not the kind you see in a shower or bath. It's the kind you see on the side of the road—a storm drain.

Walking over to it, I kneel and bend forward, trying to lean over to where I can wrap my right hand around one of the bars and attempt to pull it up. Grinding my teeth, I pull with all I can, but it doesn't budge. "Shit." I hiss, letting go and sitting back.

"HAIDYN?" I shout, starting to get really pissy. My voice echoes in the small room, and I drop my head, trying to catch my breath and slow my racing heart. It won't do me any good. I'm here because he wants me here. I chose to be his. Not like the alternative was any better. The Lords would wipe me off the face of the earth. And I'd still probably end up here at Carnage. That's where those who betray their oath go. I'd be no different.

Fisting my hands, I pull them out to my sides, trying to tear the leather or yank it free, but it only pinches my skin once again on my thighs. They're tight as fuck. I'm sweating, and it's making them itch.

I drop them and suck in breath after breath, trying not to cry. I do that when I'm mad. Throwing my head back, I blow the hair from my slick face and look up at the ceiling. It's so hot in here, and my mouth is dry.

A bright light flips on, and I duck my head, shutting my eyes. A door opening has me shaking where I kneel. It could be Haidyn or any other Spade brother for that matter. Three of them run this hell. And for all I know, he will let them all play with me. They shared Ashtyn, right? And if what my mother's friend said was true, he loves her. I'm nothing to him.

Metal scraping on concrete has me flinching, but I remain where I'm at with my head down. A submissive pose. This is what he wants. A mindless toy he can control.

"Hello, doll face."

His deep voice sends goose bumps over my already heated skin as it fills the small room. I open my eyes and peek up at him through my lashes.

He's sitting in a chair, legs spread wide, hands on his jean-clad thighs. His posture looks relaxed, but his eyes look amused. He's got that fucking baseball hat on backward that makes my stomach do flips, and he wears a white T-shirt that pulls against his hard chest and broad shoulders. He looks like a god, and I'm a chained pet.

Sitting up, he reaches out to push my wild hair from my face, but I pull back from his touch.

He pauses with his hand still inches from my face, and he smirks. "I brought you something." Leaning down, he picks up a water bottle that sits by his feet, and my already dry mouth becomes the Sahara Desert as I look at the condensation on the plastic.

"Thirsty?" he asks, his eyes on mine.

I nod.

Lifting it in front of me, he gives it a little tilt, and it splashes on the drain that separates us. "Hai-dyn!" I shriek, and my voice cracks.

He rights it and arches a brow at me. "I asked you a question, Charlotte." His voice is now a growl, sending a shiver down my spine.

"Yes." I nod again, my arms pulling on the restraints. Those angry tears I try to hold back blur my vision. "I'm thirsty." Taking in a calming breath, I ask, "May I please have a drink?"

Chapter 29

Haidyn

She hasn't been out for long. Four hours. To her, it probably feels like days. I stand from the chair and step onto the drain. I use one hand to move her hair from her face, and the other holds the tip of the water bottle to her cracked lips.

Her head is tilted back, her eyes up on mine, and she greedily swallows the water while some falls down her chin and runs over her naked body to splash on the floor between her legs.

I pull it away, and she's gasping. "Take it easy. Nice and slow, doll face. Don't want you to get sick."

The sedative wasn't a high dosage, but I can't predict how her body will react.

She shakes her head at my words, and I hold the bottle to her lips again. She's like a baby bird begging to be fed. She has no use of her arms, and soon, I'll limit her even more. I'm not sure if I'll need to use the cuffs around her ankles or not. That will depend on her.

She slowly sips on it, and I run my free hand over her matted hair. "That's it. Good girl. Nice and easy."

Pulling away, she takes another deep breath. Sitting back in the chair, I order, "Stand up."

She slowly gets to her shaking legs and stands before me naked, but her head is high and her shoulders back. Fuck, I underestimated her. She would come into Carnage, and her cheeks would redden when I spoke dirty to her, but I could tell by the look in her eyes she'd be into most of the shit I thought of doing to her. She's just another woman deprived of what her body wants and too afraid to ask for it.

"Turn around for me, doll face. I want to see you."

She holds her arms out as far as the connecting chains will allow and slowly gives me her back. The warm room fills with her heavy breathing, and my eyes drop to her bubble ass and run up the curve of her spine. Her hair sticks to her back and shoulders, and I want to put it up for her but refrain. My hands will be in it soon enough.

Turning back to face me, she meets my eyes as her chest heaves. I stand from the chair, and she arches her neck to keep her eyes on me. I'm not going to pounce on her. I was telling her the truth when I said she'd beg me from her knees.

Walking up to her, I cup her face, and her lips part. "Why...why can't I have the use of my hands?" She stumbles over her words, sounding out of breath.

"Because you don't need them," I say honestly.

She pulls on them as if to reassure herself they're secured to her thighs. I didn't buckle them tight enough to cut off circulation, but they aren't coming off unless I unlock them.

She bares her perfect white teeth up at me. "Do you think I'm going to attack you?"

I laugh at that. "No." I run my knuckles down her water-covered chest, and she doesn't flinch. She's becoming accustomed to my touch already. Sooner than I had hoped. "It's also because it turns you on."

She tenses at my words, but we both know they're true. "I think a part of you wants to be forced to be my whore." I lower my face down to hers. Our lips are so close that if I pucker them, I'd kiss her. "Tell me I'm wrong, *Annabelle*."

Her dilated eyes search mine, but she doesn't say anything. She takes a step back, and my hand drops to my side.

"No," she whispers, shaking her head.

"No," I repeat, pulling my cell from my pocket. I pull up an app, and the small TV hanging in the corner of the room turns on.

She spins around and looks up at it as the twenty-five inch shows her bedroom. It's dark, but you can't miss her lying in her bed at her house. She's moaning, her body moving under the covers.

"What is this?" She steps forward to get a better look, but I stay quiet, watching her view herself on the screen.

She wakes up, plays the recording, and gets herself off. Then it skips to the scene in her room where she begs me to fuck her. Begs me to kiss her. I spit in her mouth on the screen, and watching it happen makes her gag.

I step up behind her. My hand brushes the hair off her shoulder, and I wrap my hand around her throat from behind. "See, doll face. Even in your dreams, you're my dirty little whore."

She spins around, eyes glaring up at me. "Fuck you, Hai—"

I wrap my hand around her throat and push her backward, cutting off her words and slamming her back into the glass. Her lips part, but nothing comes out. Her hips buck, pushing into mine as I pin her in place, but her eyes go heavy.

"Spread your legs, beautiful," I command.

She does as she's told, and I loosen up on her neck, allowing her to breathe as my hand drops between her legs. I run my fingers along her pussy, and she pushes it against my hand, wanting them inside her. But instead, I hold them up in front of her face. "Look how wet you are just watching yourself beg me to fuck you. Imagine if I actually gave you what you wanted." I place them in my mouth and suck on them.

Her eyes grow heavy. Fuck, she's panting, and the room grows hotter as my cock presses against the inside of my zipper, begging to push her down to the floor and fuck her right here right now. To forget the plan I've spent two weeks putting together. I wouldn't be a Lord if I didn't have patience.

I take a step back, and she slumps against the glass, gasping. "Get some rest, doll face," I tell her, then turn my back to her. I step out of the room, locking the metal door, making sure she can't escape. Then I take an immediate right and walk into the adjoining room. I sit down on the barstool and watch her through the one-way mirror, knowing this will be her home for however long she decides.

CHARLOTTE

THE BLINDING LIGHT TURNS OFF, LEAVING ME WITH THE DIM bulb that hangs from the center. I manage to get over to the thin mattress and fall onto it. Positioning myself with my back against the wall, I pull my knees up to shield my body, my hands still tied to them at my sides. I know he's on the other side of the glass, watching me. The video he showed me tells me he's always got eyes on me. Whether it be a camera or him hiding in the darkness, he's there.

The TV remains on—adding a little more light to the room—playing the same tape over and over with me being the main character. The sound of my voice begging him to fuck me has my breathing erratic. I can't even lift my arms to cover my ears. *That's the point.*

He's forcing me to watch porn where I'm the slut begging for dick, and he's the one refusing to give it to me.

I remember the dream very vividly. Then waking up and him being there. I even remember choosing to take the pill in the kitchen. It's afterward that's all fuzzy. I don't recall lying in bed asking him to fuck me, him placing the belts on and securing me in place. Or how he got me here to Carnage.

But he's right. I'm so wet right now. I place my forehead down on my bent knees and sniff. I want to cover up my face from humiliation, but I can't. And that makes me angry.

Lifting my head, I glare at the glass with fisted hands. "Fuck you, Haidyn!" I yell. I drop my legs and kick them out, but it won't do me any good. I'm throwing a tantrum in the middle of the store, and I'm being ignored.

Slamming my body down onto the mattress, I turn my back to the glass, forcing a whimper from my shaking lips because of how my arm is tied to my thigh. He's thought of everything.

He wants me to humiliate myself.

The single light turns off, and all that remains on is the small TV, giving me very little light. It's like a jail cell. What did I expect? He's brought me to Carnage. I'm his prisoner. I'll rely on him for food and water. He'll probably only continue to feed me and give me water if he thinks I'm good enough to deserve it.

He said it's up to me how long I'm here. I know what he wants, and as I listen to myself beg him to fuck me on the TV, I'm not sure how long I can hang on without giving in.

My father tried to warn me what would happen. The kind of life I'd live. What would be expected of me if I chose the Lords.

. . .

I look at the clock on my father's dash to see it's almost two in the morning. He woke me up and told me to get dressed. He wanted to take me somewhere.

As we pull down the gravel road, I sit up straighter while he finds a parking spot. The lot is full of expensive cars. "Dad—"

"Put these on." He reaches into the back seat and grabs a black cloak and mask.

"I don't understand," I say, looking at him as he pulls his own over his head.

"You're not allowed to be seen during an offering."

"What am I offering?" I ask, my hands getting sweaty. He's never brought me here before, and we're not religious.

"Nothing." He frowns. "You haven't done anything wrong." Sighing, he looks at the double doors and then back at me. "Your mother wants to prepare you for your future. I want to show you what happens if we fail you."

I'm even more confused than I was five seconds ago. "Does this have to do with being a Lady?"

"Look at me, Anna," he says sternly.

Swallowing, I look over at him in the darkly lit car.

"Your mother wants me to show you what women in our world can do...what you're capable of. You're special."

Every parent tells their child that.

"You will one day marry your Lord, but he will not define you." Giving me a soft smile, he adds. "But a sacrifice must be made in order to get to the top."

"What do I have to sacrifice?" I ask.

He looks away from me, staring out the windshield, and the silence lingers among us before he answers, "Whatever they want."

♠

I didn't get any sleep. I'm not even sure how long I've been awake. Everything still hurts, and I'm thirsty again. My stomach growls, reminding me that I can't remember the last time I ate something.

I'm fidgety and can't get comfortable. If my arms were free, it'd be better. But that's the point. He wants me to be irritated and desperate.

It's fucking working.

"Haidyn?" I call out, sitting up and staring at the glass. "I know you can hear me."

Use your words, doll face. His words echo in my head. "I'm thirsty. May I have a drink, please?" I'll beg for anything at this point. Any kind of contact. He's isolating me on purpose. Carnage has hundreds of cells in the basement. He's got me all alone or in another part of the building. Otherwise, I'd hear other prisoners screaming while the Spade brothers torture them. "Please, Haidyn...I'm—"

The sound of the door unlocking cuts me off, and I almost smile when he enters with two bottles of water in one hand and a bowl in the other.

I stay where I'm at, sitting on the mattress with my back against the wall as he locks us both inside and sits down in the chair that he left in here. He doesn't have to worry about me using it as a weapon because I can't pick it up.

My eyes meet his hard stare, and he sets the waters on the concrete floor. "Come here."

I don't know why, but his voice makes my thighs tighten. Is it because it's the only one I've heard in what feels like days now? Or maybe it's because I've listened to it on the TV that still plays on repeat.

Getting up, I make my way over to him and kneel at his feet. I know my place. I have no control here. Not over my own body. It's just like when I was tied to the table, and he got me off while giving me an enema. Fuck, that thought has my pussy clenching. I close my legs tightly, hoping he doesn't ask me to spread them so he can feel between them.

He unscrews the lid and holds it to my lips. Just like last time, I greedily gulp, and it runs down my chin and chest. I pull away, gasping at how cold it is.

"Take your time, doll face. I have plenty of water for you," he assures me.

At least I know dehydration isn't in my future.

Leaning forward, I place my lips on it again, and he tilts it for me to drink more. It burns my throat, it's so cold, but it's too good to stop. I can feel it running down my chest, stomach, and legs once again.

I pull away and whisper, "Thank you," bowing my head. Whatever the hell it was I took is completely out of my system, and now I feel nothing but shame. I'd do anything for him to knock me out again and just live out my sentence in bliss. Like I was when he spit in my mouth. That Charlotte didn't give a fuck.

"Eyes on me, doll face," he commands, but I can't. Mine remain on the floor. I'm kneeling between his open legs like a dog waiting to be petted. All I'm missing is a butt plug with a furry tail sticking out of my ass. Which I'm sure the fucker has around here somewhere.

He stands, and my breathing picks up while he walks behind me. I hear him unlock one of the cabinets and then slam it shut, locking it back.

His hand grips the back of my hair, yanking my head up. I cry out into the small room as he holds it in place and wraps something heavy and bulky around my neck. He drops my hair, and I hear a click at the back of my neck. Then he comes to sit back down in front of me.

I try to drop my head to look down, but I can't. Something keeps my head up and my eyes on his. I try to reach up and pull it free, but my tied arms don't get far. I bare my teeth at him.

"That's more like it." He reaches out to cup my face, and I try to pull away, but he grabs the thing around my neck, yanking me forward. I fall into the chair, whimpering as it presses into my wet chest. I balance on my shaking knees, the cold concrete digging into me. It's going to leave bruises. "If you're a good girl, I won't have to hurt you."

"And if I'm not?" I grind out through gritted teeth.

Maybe I need to hear him tell me what he's going to do to me word for word. That way, I can hate him. Because right now, I don't. Considering how wet I am between my legs, I don't hate him enough.

"I'll leave that as a surprise." He lets go of me, but my head remains up.

I try to stretch my neck, but my movement is very restricted. I swallow nervously. "What's on my neck?" I ask. It's to keep him talking. I don't want him to leave me alone here, especially since I don't know what's outside of these walls. I'm not sure who all knows I'm here, but the safest person for me to be around is Haidyn.

"It's a posture collar. Keeps your head up and in place. When you learn to follow the rules, I'll remove it."

Rules? Did he give me rules? No. But it's pretty much common sense. *Do as I'm told.*

He pushes the hair from my face, and I lean into his touch. I'm so horny it's fucking pathetic. I'm someone who needs human interaction. I'm affectionate. I need to be hugged and kissed. I blame that on my parents. My father and mother were very affectionate with one another and of course with me. After my father died, my mom always made sure to remind me how much I was loved.

I consider it a curse. Because I was born into a world where that doesn't exist. The fucking, yes. The Lords are all about sex. Even the Ladies are conditioned at a young age to need that. But everything else is not something a Lord will give you.

He reaches into his pocket, removes his cell, and I hear the TV stop. I close my eyes, thanking God that he shut it off only to hear my voice again. But this time, it's different. I open them to meet his stare. "Haidyn," I whisper. "Please..." I beg, not knowing what else there is to do.

He smiles at me and leans forward. "Spread your legs."

Angry tears sting my eyes as I do as I'm told. He reaches down between my shaking legs and touches my wet pussy. I moan and rock my hips forward, wanting more, but he pulls his fingers away and holds them in front of my face to show me that they're wet.

"Ready to be my whore, doll face?"

My lips thin, refusing to give in to him. I don't even know why I'm playing this game. I'll never win.

He wipes his fingers along my lips, and I pull away the best I can. Gripping my hair, he yanks my head back, forcing the collar to pinch the back of my neck. I cry out as he places his face down to mine. "Open your mouth, Charlotte. Taste how wet you are."

I part my lips as the first tear runs down my cheek. He places his finger in my mouth, and I wrap my dry lips around it and begin to suck, tasting myself.

His eyes darken, and I moan, sucking it farther into my mouth and swallowing around it. The urge for him to fuck my mouth is strong as he pulls the finger out, and I leave my lips parted for him to enter it again. He pushes two in this time, and I oblige once more.

"Fuck, doll face. Look at you sucking on my fingers as if it's my cock." He groans, and I rock my hips while I kneel at his feet.

He pushes a third into my mouth, and I open wide for him as he runs them over my tongue and to the back of my mouth. I try not to gag, but it's inevitable. I'd say even though I'm a virgin, I've always loved the idea of being good at sucking dick. I've seen porn where the man is brought to his knees because of how good the women are. Wanting to please a man while watching him fall apart looks like power to me.

He removes them, and I suck in a deep breath, swallowing the saliva that had filled my mouth.

Chapter 30

Haidyn

I'm so fucking hard, and I know she can see it. Her face is right at my crotch, for fuck's sake. Her heavy eyes fall to stare at it while she tries to catch her breath. I get to my feet and head toward the door.

"I need to pee," she whimpers, and I watch her thighs tense as she tries to close them while still kneeling.

I smile. "You may use the restroom," I tell her, and she lets out a sob of relief, "when you suck my dick."

"Wh-at?" she gasps, wide-eyed as if she doesn't want to.

She wants to be put in a position where she seems forced? I'll help her out.

I step into her, cupping her chin and running my thumb over her plump lips. I want to sink my teeth into them, make it bleed and swallow her blood. "When you willingly kneel at my feet, open your mouth, and let me fuck this pretty face, I'll let you use the restroom." This was never part of my plan, but she changed the direction it was going.

Her lips tremble. "Please..."

"The only thing I want to hear from you is you gagging on my dick while you drool all over yourself."

Tears fill her eyes, and I let go of her face. "Good night, Charlotte." I turn to exit the room when her voice stops me.

"Okay."

"Okay, what?" I turn and look at her.

She licks her wet lips and says, "May I suck your dick?"

I smile. I don't know why she continues to be shy and innocent, but I'm going to fix that. I turn my back to her once again and head toward the door.

"Please, Haidyn." She gasps, her voice growing desperate. "Please fuck my mouth."

I stop and turn back to face her. She's scooted forward, her knees now over the drain in the center of the room. I don't even think she's noticed it yet.

Her chest rises and falls quickly with each breath. "Please, sir." I arch a brow at that. "Please let me please you." She licks her lips before parting them in an open gesture.

Such a quick learner.

I walk back to the other side of the room and unlock one of the cabinets. I have them stocked with everything I plan on using. I pull out the two things I want, then lock it. Walking behind her, I order, "Try to pull your elbows behind your back."

She takes her wrists that are tied down to her upper thighs and bends her elbows the best she can, pushing them behind her.

Kneeling, I place one end of the chain on the ring that connects to the cuff that's above her elbow, then secure the opposite end to her other elbow.

She groans, trying to yank on them but the chain that runs across her back stops her from dropping her arms to her sides, keeping them bent in place.

I return to the chair and sit down in front of her. "That's more like it." I reach out and grab her breasts. Locking her arms in place pushes her chest out. Taking her hard nipples between my fingers, I pinch them, pulling her toward me, and she cries out. Letting go, I slap them.

Her moans fill the room, and I pick up the other accessory I grabbed from the cabinet. I take her left breast and place the clamp on over her hard nipple, loving the way her breath hitches. She rocks her hips back and forth while kneeling. I bring the chain through the silver ring in her posture collar and then connect it to her other nipple.

She cries out, and I love the way it sounds. "Every move you make, you'll feel the pinch as it pulls on your nipples."

She gasps, lips parted, her body involuntarily jerking as she tries to ease the discomfort. I unzip my jeans and pull out my cock.

I spread my legs, and her wide eyes fall to my pierced dick. My brothers and I all have the same piercings. A Jacob's ladder with the Saint's cross—two barbells through the head to make it look like a cross. We've had them for about four years now. It was once a punishment. We kept them as a reminder that we're no one's bitch.

I stroke it while watching her, and excitement bubbles in my body. I haven't been this turned on in a long time. "Suck my cock, Charlotte. Show me how much you want it."

She sniffs, bending forward, and her tongue darts out to lick the precum. "Eyes on me while I fuck you."

Opening her bloodshot eyes, she looks up at me through her lashes. She wraps her lips around the head of my cock and sucks the tip. Her mouth feels so fucking warm it takes my breath away. It's been a while since I've been excited about sex. It's been a job for so long. Something I need to get off. This is for pleasure.

She whimpers around my dick, and I know it's because of the nipple clamps pulling tight at her movements. Her shoulders shake, and she tries to reposition herself while she kneels on the drain.

I gently brush the hair off her tear-streaked face and gather it at the back of her head, gripping it painfully. She parts her lips wider with a gasp. "I'm going to show you how I like it."

I push her forward. It's going to be awkward with the posture collar on, but I'm not taking it off. "Open wide and stick out your tongue." She acts like she's never had a dick in her mouth before. But I get it, every guy likes something different, and I'm willing to train her to know what gets me off.

She does as she's told, and her body trembles in my hand.

I hold my cock and guide her mouth down onto it. She begins to suck my shaft as I slowly move her open mouth up and down, allowing her saliva to get it nice and wet. "Look at you being a needy slut."

She closes her eyes slightly, and I pull her head back and slap the side of her face, making her cry out. "Eyes open, doll face," I remind her. "Look up at me. I want to see you cry while you gag on my dick."

She whimpers around my cock, and it makes her throat constrict. A groan escapes my lips, my hands tightening in her hair. "That's it."

CHARLOTTE

Pain...lust...heat...drool...pride...

So many thoughts are going through my head right now. I can't move, and I can barely breathe. He's so big. And the metal...it fills my mouth, runs along the roof of my mouth and tongue. I try to open wider so the piercings underneath his shaft don't hit my teeth.

The collar restricts my breathing, and my nipples feel like they're being ripped off. I look up at him through watery eyes, and he throws his head back, his hand holding my hair while my head bobs up and down.

When he hits the back of my throat, I gag, and his throat works as a deep growl comes from his lips. It's the sexiest sound I've ever heard.

"Fuck, Charlotte. That's a good whore." He's breathless.

I lied. That was the sexiest thing I've ever heard. My pussy thinks so too as wetness pools between my shaking legs.

"Goddamn." He lowers his head, and his heavy eyes land on mine.

Drool runs out of the corner of my open mouth, and he pushes my head farther down. My air is taken away as the head of his cock fills the back of my throat. My body jerks involuntarily, and my eyes blink quickly as I gag.

"You're so pretty on your knees," he tells me, and butterflies fill my stomach. I suck on him harder, as if I can swallow him whole. He smiles down at me. "Are you wet, Charlotte? Hmm? Does that cunt of yours need to be fucked too?"

I try to nod, but the collar prevents it. So I just stare up at him, praying he bends me over and takes my pussy next. He pulls my mouth free from his cock, and I gasp, needing air. I'm starting to feel lightheaded. He pushes me back down. It fills my mouth once again, and he lifts his hips off the chair, my nose almost touching his jeans, and I gag again.

"I'm going to fuck it now," he warns, and my eyes widen. *Isn't that what he's been doing?*

He pulls my mouth free of his cock and then shoves it down before I can even take in a breath this time. He does it again and again.

Gag, drool...gag, drool. I kneel before him like a toy as he fucks my mouth rougher than I thought possible. My eyes and nose run as much as my open mouth, blurring my vision, and the room sways.

"I'm going to come, doll face," he growls, and I try to pull away, but he holds me in place as I mumble around his dick.

The fact that he wants me to swallow makes me nervous. But I have no other choice than to take it. He shoves my head down, pushing his cock deeper than before, and I gag. His cock pulses in my mouth, and I feel his warm cum slide down the back of my throat before he yanks my head back.

I gasp, drool and cum leaks from my mouth as my chest heaves, and I cough it up, choking on it.

He runs his hands through my tangled hair. His hard eyes once again glare down at mine. As if whatever I just did reset us back to hatred.

Reaching down, he undoes one of the nipple clamps, and my shoulders shake from the pain. He pulls the chain through the ring of the collar and undoes the other.

I cry out.

"Shh, you're okay, doll face. You did so good for me."

I swallow roughly and flinch, my throat sore and raw.

He stands and walks around me, removing the chain that connected my upper arms. They fall to the sides, and I've never been more grateful for my wrists being tied to my thighs. "We'll try without this, but if you disobey, it goes back on, understand?"

"Y-yes," I say roughly.

The collar is removed, and I stretch my neck.

"Thank you," I whisper, and my eyes meet his. He smiles down at me, and I have the urge to open my mouth again. I want to be his *good girl*. I want to come so bad. "I need to use the restroom," I remind him.

He nods. "You may use the restroom."

I stay kneeling on the drain. My knees have gone numb, but I remain where I am, waiting for him to come and untie my arms and let me out of the room to use the restroom. But he turns to face me, leans back against the counter, and crosses his arms over his chest.

"You said—"

"I know what I said."

I take a deep breath, starting to get pissy. The high that I got from being a slut for him fades away. "Then let me go to the bathroom." I yank on my secured wrists.

He nods to the drain underneath me. "You'll go right where you kneel."

I drop my head to look at the drain and then back at him. A laugh bubbles up, and I lean back on my heels. "Funny, Haidyn."

"I'm not laughing, *Annabelle*."

His tone and use of my legal name has my laughter dying. "You're serious?" I gasp. "Haidyn—no." I yank on my wrists again. "Take these off and show me to the bathroom."

He turns, giving me his back, and unlocks one of the cabinet doors. Opening it up, he pulls out a miniature hourglass. It's much smaller than the one he used at my house. He sets it down on the counter and looks back at me. "You have until this runs out of time."

I look at the sand falling through the skinny center and quickly filling the bottom part. My eyes slam back to his in horror. "What—?"

"Once you are out of time, I'm going to put an adult diaper on you, and you can piss all over yourself."

This has to be a joke. He wouldn't really make me...would he? I shake my head. "No..."

He opens up the cabinet again and pulls out a fucking diaper. Slapping it on the counter, he speaks. "You have a choice, doll face. What's it going to be?"

I try to hold back the tears, but they fall from my eyes as I watch the time quickly go by. "I hate you," my trembling lips whisper.

He laughs, the sound bouncing off the concrete walls and making the hairs on the back of my neck rise. "You didn't hate me when you were begging me to fuck your mouth."

I lower my head, my blurry eyes on the drain knowing that avoiding eye contact will have him putting the posture collar back on me, but I don't care. I can't face him right now.

"You're running out of time, beautiful. What's it going to be?"

Knowing he's not bluffing, I spread my shaking legs as far as I can and make sure I'm hovering over between a couple of the bars. I close my eyes, shoulders shaking, and I bite my tongue to keep from sobbing as the tears fall from my lashes, and I relieve myself like a stray dog roaming the streets.

Chapter 31

Haidyn

I'm testing her. She thinks this is just to humiliate her, and although it's getting the job done, it's more than that. I want her to fucking loathe the sight of me. I want her to gag at the sound of my voice. I need her to want to stab my eyes out when I look at her.

She kneels over the drain and sits down on it the best she can so she doesn't make a mess on herself. She tries to hide her sobs, but it's impossible.

The hourglass has stopped, so I pick it up and put it back along with the diaper, grabbing a couple of things before I lock the cabinet back.

Once she's finished, I leave the room and come back with a bucket of soapy warm water and a sponge. "Stand up," I order, reaching down and grabbing her upper arm.

I know she needs help. She's spent too much time on her knees on the drain. She gets to her shaking legs but leaves her head down. She'll sleep in her posture collar tonight. Right now, I'll let her think she won.

I kneel before her and take the sponge from the warm water and gently begin to wash her. I start with her feet, then move up her legs. Standing, I clean her cunt and stomach, then her chest and neck, dipping it back into the water when needed. "Turn around."

She quickly gives me her back, thankful not to have to face me as her soft sobs fill the small room. I do the same to her back, legs, and ass. Then I throw the sponge into the bucket and grab the second one. It's got clean water. I slowly pour it over her body, starting at the top, and watch the soap wash away and down the drain. "Face me again."

Sniffling, she does, and I pour what's left of the clean water over the front of her. I grab the towel off the counter and dry her off.

Once done, I tell her, "Lie on the bed, face down."

Keeping her eyes on the floor, she turns and walks over to the small cot. She gets to her knees and then flattens her body, turning her face toward the concrete wall, hiding from me.

"Up on your knees. I want your ass in the air, Annabelle." I want to remind her who she really is and why we're here.

She flinches at my tone but wiggles to where she's up on her knees, legs spread with her ass and cunt on display. Her arms hang from her thighs.

I'm hard again. Her mouth wasn't enough. But I have a plan I have to stick with. I'm proving a point to both of us.

I grab the two things I pulled out of the cabinet and walk over to her. Kneeling behind her, I use my legs to pry hers open more. The room fills with her soft cry, and I pop the top on the lube, pouring it directly over her ass and pussy, not hiding my intentions.

The hourglass wasn't just for her. We're both on borrowed time. I have to escalate this situation to see where we go next.

I run my fingers over her cunt and up to her puckered ass, pushing one into her. She tries to pull away. I slap her ass, and she buries her face into the dingy mattress. "Don't make me tie you down, doll face. I'll leave you that way for the rest of the night."

She stills, and I push my finger back into her ass before entering two. My free hand goes to her pussy, gently rubbing her clit, and she moans. "The body is an amazing thing, isn't it?" I ask, not expecting her to respond. "The way it craves things that your mind tells you is wrong." I pour more lube over her and remove my fingers, only to thrust them in again, adding a third this time.

A whimper turns to a cry, but she doesn't pull away. "Good girl." I pull them out and coat the butt plug with the lube. I then start to push it into her nice and slow, letting her get the feel of it first.

She sniffs. "Almost there, doll face," I say, gently rubbing her ass where I smacked it. "Just a little more." I push the last bit into her and then wrap my lube-covered hand around the bulb and pump it up twice making her voice ring out in a shrill cry. "All done for now."

Getting up, I make my way to the cabinet once again and grab the collar. "On your back," I command. She slowly rolls over, and I kneel beside her, sliding it underneath her neck and buckling it. "I'll be back in a few hours, doll face. Try to get some rest until then." I stand and exit the room, locking her inside.

I go over to the adjoining room and watch her through the mirror as she lets the sobs take over.

CHARLOTTE

MY FATHER AND I ENTER THE CATHEDRAL BOTH DRESSED IN OUR cloaks and masks. The pews are as full as the parking lot, so my father gestures to the back row. I slide in, and he takes the seat closest to the aisle.

Taking a quick look around, I see all the Lords dressed the same and there's an altar at the front of the room, below the second story balcony.

A door opens to the right and all the chatter immediately stops as a woman enters the room from the side door. I've seen her before. Known her all my life.

I stiffen, hoping she doesn't recognize me. My father pats my legs over the cloak as if to remind me I'm hidden. I just have to remain quiet.

Don't draw attention to yourself.

"Bring her in." Her voice fills the large open space.

The door she entered through opens and three Lords carry a woman into the cathedral. She's got a black latex mask over her head, covering her entire face and neck. A black collar is secured around it as well. She's naked.

The Lords, dressed in cloaks and masks, toss her onto the altar and quickly tie her down, spread eagle. She fights, kicking and throwing her arms around, but it's useless. They outnumber and overpower her easily.

The man in the opposite pew of my father reaches across the aisle and goes to hand my father a basket. I see it's full of razor blades. My father waves it off and I get a sickening feeling in my gut.

Why are they passing those out?

My mom's friend steps forward and gestures to the helpless woman, getting my attention. "I'll take ten volunteers," she calls out with a smile.

Most of the Lords get to their feet, and I scoot to the edge of the pew, leaning to the left trying to see over the ones now standing.

I've never seen a woman in charge before. Not like this. The one tied to the altar is more common than the woman standing here in Gucci heels and a Versace dress.

Something catches my attention to the right of me, and I see a girl around my age slide into the pew at the far end. Her green eyes briefly meet mine before she looks away and turns her attention to the show at the front of the cathedral. Why isn't she hidden like the rest of us? And who allows a child in here? I'm only able to watch because I'm covered.

The grunts and moans that fill my ears tell me all I need to know about what's happening.

I CRIED MYSELF TO SLEEP AT SOME POINT. IT COULD HAVE BEEN two minutes or two hours. I'm not sure. But it felt good. Therapeutic almost to cry my eyes out. Even though I knew he was watching, it didn't matter.

My swollen eyes open when I hear the door. I remain on my back, staring at the ceiling. He comes to kneel beside me, and his hand goes between my legs. I part them without having to be told. I chose this. I've been reduced to nothing more than a sex doll. So I'll lie here like one.

"Are you thirsty?" he asks.

I say nothing. I'm not nervous or scared, just determined. A woman uses what she has to get ahead in a man's world. I have a body, and he wants it...so be it.

"You're going to feel some pressure," he says, and my hips rise off the mattress when I feel like a balloon is inside my ass.

I gasp, my hands fisting.

"One more," he adds, and I don't have a clue what he's talking about.

But the balloon intensifies, taking away my breath. I arch my neck and back, my legs tightening, but I don't close them, knowing that will get me punished. I won't give him that satisfaction. "All done," he says softly. "Good girl, doll face."

I lower my body to the mattress, and he moves to hover over my face. He cups my cheek, and his blank eyes search mine. "You have an inflatable butt plug in your ass, Charlotte. It's to get it ready for my cock. I'm going to be back in three more hours to inflate it once more."

The dots finally connect. That's why the enema, the suppositories. He's been preparing my ass this whole time. I just thought it was to humiliate me, which could be part of it, but he really just wants to fuck it.

He stands to leave me once again in this hell when I part my cracked lips and say, "Just fuck it now." Why prolong what we both know will happen?

"You don't mean that."

I sit up, flinching at the tightness in my body, the lack of movement in my neck from the collar, and the plug in my ass. Looking up, I see him by the door. He's got a smirk on his face. Like this is a fucking joke. "Think you'll be the first to be there?" I shake my head, baiting him, and his smirk disappears. "Fuck my ass," I say.

He arches a brow, crossing his arms over his chest. "Charlotte—"

"Want me to beg you?" I push my chest out as if the chain on my arm cuffs is connected. Swallowing the knot in my throat so he doesn't see how much this affects me, I add, "Fuck my ass, please. I need it, Haidyn."

That does it. He pushes off the door and walks over to me. I don't even have to be told. I bend over, placing my face on the cold concrete floor and taking in a deep breath.

"Want your ass fucked, doll face? Then I'll fuck it." He grips my hair and yanks me to my feet.

I cry out at the sting on my scalp.

He pulls me over to the mirrored wall and pushes me into it, my cheek pressing against the cold glass as I pant. My heart races, but I can't back down. That will make me look weak. And I'm not weak. Plus, this was going to happen no matter what. This was always his plan, so we'll do it on my terms, not his.

His boots kick my bare feet open, and I hear him unzipping his jeans over my heavy breathing.

I feel the balloon inside me deflating, and my heart hammers in my chest knowing there's no going back. He pulls it free, and I whimper at the slight pain it causes.

He doesn't give me a chance to recover. Instead, he kisses the side of my face and whispers, "Take in a deep breath, doll face."

I suck in a ragged breath when the tip of his lube-covered cock is at the entrance of my ass. He pulls my body from the mirror a little, bending me at the waist but leaving the side of my face still pressed into the glass. The new position makes it even harder to breathe due to the fucking collar.

I cry out when the tip of his cock pushes into me.

"You're going to take it like the good whore you are, Charlotte." He grunts, pushing farther into me.

I try to pull away to stop the burning sensation, but I have nowhere to go as he pins me in place.

"Beg me for it, doll face," he growls. "Beg me to fuck your ass."

"Pl-ease." A tear falls from my eye.

"Please what?" he demands, pushing deeper. The burning intensifies, and I yank on the short chains that connect my wrists to my thighs.

"Please...fuck my ass." I sob as my smooshed face slides on the wet glass from my tears.

He pushes into me, and I tense as he holds me to him, yanking me from the glass. One hand wraps around my chin from behind while the other drops between my legs. He starts playing with my pussy while his eyes meet mine in the mirror. "Fuck, your ass feels so good, beautiful."

I blink, my heavy eyes on his. My pussy is wet from his hand playing with my clit and the lube he poured all over it. "Please?" I beg, and it's not fake. The smile he gives me tells me he knows it too.

Moving his hips, he pulls his cock slowly from my ass, and I moan before he pushes forward, making me cry out.

"Does it hurt?"

I nod the best I can. "Yes."

"Does it feel good?"

"Y-es."

He chuckles, the sound making my sweaty skin cover in goose bumps.

"Show me how much you enjoy pain, doll face. Come on my fingers while my cock fucks this tight ass."

His fingers get more forceful, making my hips rock back and forth. The motion has my ass fucking his dick.

It's a mixture of torture and pleasure. It feels so good but hurts so much. I'm gasping for breath, my arms pulling on my restraints as his arms hold me captive around my collared neck. It's hard to breathe, and I'm dizzy.

My lips are parted, and drool leaks out of the corners onto his ink-covered arm. He doesn't give a fuck and neither do I.

"All whores love getting their asses fucked. And you're my whore, aren't you, doll face?"

"Your whore," I agree, my eyes growing heavy. Fuck, am I going to come? God, I hope so.

"Ride my dick, Charlotte. Fuck it."

I'm grinding on his cock, faster and faster as his fingers enter my cunt. I'm hanging on by a thread. My muscles are sore, my body exhausted but I can feel it building deep inside me. It's an explosion needing a way out. "Please...Haidyn."

"What are you begging for, doll face? You're the one fucking me." He smirks, his eyes on mine in the mirror.

I lick my lips, and my heavy eyes fall shut.

"Look at me." He slaps my pussy, taking away my breath. My eyes spring open, and he nods to me. "That's it. Tell me how it feels."

"Soooo good," I whisper hoarsely.

It's painful going in but feels good going out. It's a total contradiction, but I can't stop. Instead, I slam backward as if I'm a fucking pro at anal, and he groans. "Goddamn, beautiful."

I do it again and again and that feeling gets bigger, my pussy wetter. His fingers continue to play with my clit, and my entire body stiffens as a fucking storm like I've never felt hits me.

My eyes remain open, but my vision goes black. My legs go limp, but he holds me up by my neck, and my arms rest down by my sides. Blinding light flashes across my eyes. Then everything goes black once again.

Chapter 32

Haidyn

"Good girl." I praise her, but she doesn't hear a fucking word. She's too far gone. I can tell by the look in her eyes in the two-way mirror.

I pull her from it and spin her around. Picking her up, I carry her over to the mattress. I lie her down on her back and kneel between her shaking legs. I spread them wide and lift her hips to position my pierced cock back at her ass.

I smear the tip over her cum-covered pussy before I slide it back into her ass. I groan, going balls deep. "Your ass was made for my dick, doll face," I say, loving the mumbled moan that comes from her parted lips.

Placing my arms behind her knees, I spread her wider, lean over her body and start fucking her ass. I drop my face to hers and kiss her lips.

She kisses me back, but it's soft. Her body rocks back and forth on the mattress as I take what she wanted to give me. I loved that she challenged me. Fuck, the terror in her eyes but the determination in her words was like pure fucking adrenaline.

She challenged me. I knew she'd be this way. And I love it.

Pulling away, I sit up and watch my cock slide in and out of her ass. My hand goes to her pussy, and she arches her back, a soft cry coming from her parted lips.

"I...can't..." she whispers.

I slap her swollen clit, and her body jerks involuntarily. "Come for me again, Charlotte. I want you to show me how much of a whore you are for my cock."

"Pl-ease..." she begs, arching her collared neck.

I slap her pussy again and again. Her cries grow louder, and I slide two fingers into her. Pulling them out, my thumb plays with her clit while my cock slows to an agonizing pace in her ass.

I want to see her come undone again. It was the sexiest sight I've ever witnessed. She earned it.

She's panting, her body covered in sweat, and I'm shaking. I'm so close but trying to hold off. I slam into her ass deep, and she arches her back. I pull out and do it again as my thumb continues to play with her clit.

"Oh...God..."

"That's it, doll face. Give me one more." I pick up my pace once more and enjoy her struggling underneath me. "You look so pretty, Charlotte. Like a used-up toy begging for more."

Her body stiffens, and her pretty blue eyes roll into the back of her head before I watch cum leak from her throbbing pussy. "That's my good girl." I smile.

Running my fingers through her cum, I bring them to my mouth and suck them clean, tasting her. Slowing my pace once more, I spread her legs again with my arms behind them and fuck her ass.

It doesn't take long until I'm coming inside her. Leaning over, I kiss her forehead, trying to get my breathing under control. It was better than I've imagined it to be. "Fuck, you're amazing. You did so good, Charlotte." I praise her.

"Haidyn." She arches her back, and her heavy eyes look around aimlessly.

I kiss her lips, and she opens up for me. "Want another round already?" I chuckle against them.

Her body trembles, and her eyes remain unfocused. She's so close to being a mindless toy and all I've done is fucked her ass.

"You earned a reward, doll face." Getting up off her, I go over to the cabinet and grab the things that I need, then kneel back down beside her.

She's turned her head to the side and closed her eyes; her

breathing is starting to even out. I run my knuckles down the side of her face and smile. "Look at me," I command softly.

Wet lashes flutter open, and her heavy eyes find mine. I smile down at her. "Open for me." My fingers move to her pouty lips before she parts them. "Such a good girl." Pushing the gag into her mouth, I love the sound of her moaning around it. "I'm not going to buckle it. Just bite down on it for me. Can you do that, doll face?" She blinks, and I take that as a yes since the collar restricts her movement, and she can no longer speak. Grabbing the other thing I retrieved from the cabinet, I gently roll her onto her side, facing the concrete wall—away from me. I shove her knees to her chest and hold them in place with my knee while one hand goes to her ass cheek and the other grabs the last thing I need. "Just remember you asked for this, Charlotte."

CHARLOTTE

I WAKE UP, MY HEAVY EYES CLOSING ONLY TO OPEN QUICKLY when I realize I'm back in my bedroom. The curtains are open, allowing the sun to shine into the room. Sitting up, I flinch at how sore my ass cheek is. "Ow..." I go to rub it and flinch when I feel how sensitive it is. Fuck, did he use his belt on me again? I very softly run my fingers over my left cheek and feel something on it...a Band-Aid? Some sort of bandage. There's no telling what happened.

Lifting my hands, I see the belts and connecting chains are gone. I peek under the covers, and they're no longer on my ankles. I reach for my neck, and my skin is tender, but the collar has been removed.

I look over at my nightstand and see my phone. Picking it up, I expect it to be dead, but I'm surprised to find it fully charged. I swipe the screen and skim through all the missed calls, texts, and more notifications than I can count while I was "away" with Haidyn.

I scroll through them trying to ignore the way my body aches. Swallowing, I flinch at the soreness. Fuck, he was so big. I've never seen a dick that size before. I've heard women throughout high school and at Barrington talk about the men they fuck and how some dicks are bigger than others, but I thought they were just exaggerating.

When I started watching porn, I understood what they meant, but Haidyn...was just different. His large size and the piercings...it was intimidating to say the least.

Dropping my cell, I pick up the remote to my left and turn on my TV. My already tense body runs cold when I see it's my bedroom. On the screen, I'm sleeping in my bed with the covers pushed down, exposing my naked body. I moan Haidyn's name before I wake up. Sitting straight up, I open my nightstand and grab my toy.

Why is this playing? I've seen this before. While he had me at Carnage. How the fuck did he get it on my TV?

My heart races as I watch myself get off, then get out of bed. Haidyn walks out behind me from the corner of the room, and my eyes shoot over to where he had been watching me that night. We both return to the screen minutes later, but he's carrying me this time. This was after I had taken the pill he offered.

I beg him to touch me, get me off while he denies me. Then he's securing my arms down by my sides. You can tell in my voice that I'm desperate for him as he watches my body beg him to fuck me.

He picks me up once again and carries me out of my room. The angle changes to the hallway, and I sit up straighter when he opens the door that leads down to my basement. I never go down there. Then he's carrying me down the stairs. He opens a second door, and my throat closes when I see the single cot.

He lays me down on it. "Sweet dreams, doll face. I'll be right here when you wake up." Then he backs out of the room and shuts the door. The camera shows a concrete room, but there's a mirror on the opposite wall where I lie. A light comes on, and he enters the adjoining room, sitting on a barstool where he watches me sleep.

I turn off the TV, and with shaking hands, I throw the covers off. Jumping out of bed, I get to my wobbly legs and rush out of my bedroom, down the hall, and yank the door in the hallway open. Flipping on the light, I race down the stairs to my basement. My heart hammers in my chest when I see the door. Opening it up, I see the cot, the chair in the center with the drain in the floor. The mirrored wall and counter with the cabinets.

What the fuck? How did he...? When did he...? He set this up down here?

My mind is reeling. It makes sense since he had told me in my kitchen that he had been following me. He knew every move I had made and where I was at. He was in my house...was he down here doing all of this while I slept upstairs? While I was out running errands? The room was already here, but the mirror wasn't.

Rushing back to my room, I pick up my phone and call him. He answers on the first ring. "Miss me already, doll face?"

I realize my tongue is heavy when I have nothing to say. Tears sting my eyes as I try to gather my thoughts. "You—"

"I what, Charlotte?" My name sounds like a prayer—sweet and innocent. Like he didn't hold me captive for days, fuck my mouth and my ass until I came so hard, I blacked out.

"You tricked me," I whisper.

"Not sure what you mean, doll face," he says, and I can hear the smile in his voice. This is a game to him. Everything regarding the Lords is a fucking game. They're taught to play with their food.

"My house...the basement..." I swallow. "I thought I was at Carnage." I manage to get out before the first tear falls down my cheek.

"Isn't it funny how easily someone can trick you into believing something that isn't the truth?"

It makes sense now. I made him think I was someone I'm not. He wanted the fear of Carnage to give him what he wanted. I begged him to fuck me because I thought the alternative was worse. "You told me that you were taking me to Carnage," I grind out. The initial shock's wearing off, and I'm getting pissy.

"No. I never said that. You assumed."

Did I? Surely, I heard him say those words. Fuck, maybe he didn't. Maybe I'm losing my mind. That's what men do to you. Gaslight you. Make you think you're the problem when it's them. "Fuck you, Haidyn," I say with trembling lips because it's all my messy brain can come up with at the moment.

His laughter makes me break out in a sweat. I was so fucking stupid. More so than I ever thought I'd be. "I already did that, Charlotte. And although it was good, it wasn't great." *Click.*

I gasp, pulling the cell from my ear, and stare at it. He just hung up on me. *Although it was good, it wasn't great.* What in the fuck?

Growling, I open my laptop that sits on my desk in the corner. Leaning over, I ignore the sting on my ass and send an email to the Lords.

New Message

To **UNKNOWN**

Subject **FUCK THIS SHIT!**

I'm done.

Slamming it shut, I stare at the wall trying to wrap my head around what the fuck happened. I don't even know what day it is or how long I've been here in my house. A prisoner in my own basement.

I fucking peed in front of him. I let him wash me. He humiliated me for his own sick pleasure. I can never face him again. No matter what his body made me feel.

Picking up my cell, I pull up my friends group chat and send a text. The ones who don't know the real me. The friends I had to make with my fake life...for him. At least something good came out of it.

Night out tonight?

I pace my room as I wait for a response. I'll get drunk here by myself tonight if they can't go out, but seeing them would be better. Getting the fuck out of my house knowing that I spent—however long—in the basement while Haidyn hung out here as well.

I've still got the bruises on my knees from the storm drain and his fingerprints on my hips where he held me in place and fucked my ass.

I kneeled and peed in front of him. Does he think he can humiliate me like that and just walk away because it wasn't up to his standards? Fuck Haidyn Jamison Reeves! He's not walking away. I'm walking away. *I'm fucking done!*

My phone dings, and I rush over to the bed to see they responded. My hand instinctively goes to my ass to rub the fucking Band-Aid. Goddamn, why does it hurt so much?

CHELSEA: Absolutely. Let's go to Blackout.

NIKKI: Going out? Aren't you on vacay? What are you doing back so soon?

Shit! I forgot I'm supposed to still be gone. I never gave them a timeframe, but surely, I haven't been gone long enough to be done backpacking through Europe. I look at the date on my cell.

Two days? I was in my basement for two days? What the actual fuck! It felt like at least five. How do I explain two days of being gone? How weak am I that I gave in to what he wanted that fast? What does that say about me? I can say that he blackmailed me—forced my hand—all I want, but I wanted it too. I could have chosen death over being his whore.

Before I can come up with a lame lie, my other friend responds.

CHELSEA: Who the fuck cares why she's back early. I'm glad she's home and ready to party.

She sends another.

CHELSEA: I have Molly. Let's spend the night getting fucked up.

Setting my phone down, I make my way to my bathroom with my

head held high, trying to tell myself not to feel defeated. Women have been doing dumb shit for men long before me.

Flipping on the light, I come to my mirror and gasp as my eyes get a look at myself in front of the his-and-hers sinks. I'm covered in fresh bruises from my neck to my ankles. I look like I got hit by a car. Some are from the belts and collar, and others are from Haidyn's hands. Swallowing the knot in my throat, I turn around to inspect my ass, and my body stiffens when I see there is a large bandage on my left cheek. With shaky hands, I start to remove it.

Chapter 33

Haidyn

I sit in my office at my house, watching her on one of the monitors. She's standing naked in her bathroom, her back facing the mirror as she looks at her ass over her shoulder. Removing the bandage, she hisses in a breath before ripping it off.

She freezes where she stands, the used bandage dropping to her bare feet. Eyes wide and lips parted, she stays silent and unmoving as all the color drains from her pretty face.

I smile to myself as I read the word **HAIDYN** on her ass cheek. I branded her after I fucked her last night. It was the icing on the cake. It was something too good to pass up. In weeks, months, years from now, I want her to remember who the fuck I am.

I may have not been her first, but I will be the one that reminds her who the fuck she is—a pretty little whore that I once used.

The sound of her screaming fills my office as the initial shock wears off at what she sees. Leaning forward, I turn off the monitors and sit back in my seat, placing my hands on my thighs. I fucked my little whore and branded her. She'll never be the same. No matter who she ends up with, he'll see that. Hell, a fucking bikini will show the world that I was there. Nothing she can do will cover it up. I mean, I guess she could tattoo over it. Unless she cuts it off, it'll remain.

My phone rings, and I look down at it, expecting it to be her calling to tell me to go to hell, but to my surprise, it's not.

It's Ashtyn.

I hit ignore and stand. Picking up a pack of cigarettes off the desk, I remove one and my lighter and then turn to the double doors behind my desk. I walk out onto the wraparound porch and light one up, soaking up the sunny day. I'm not ready to talk to her. Not until I have something to give her. She deserves answers. Saint deserves answers. And I haven't heard anything new from Kashton, so I know he and Saint don't have any information.

So I'll continue to look for the man in the picture and see how this plays out with Charlotte. I wanted her pissed and running. If this doesn't do it, then nothing will.

Turning, I walk back into my office and sit down at my desk. I open the top drawer and pull out the information that Adam had found on my little whore.

I look over it.

That's all he was able to find, but honestly it was all I need. This tells me everything I needed to know about her. Who she is and why she was placed into my life. But it also doesn't make me feel sorry for what I did to my doll face. I wanted to make an example of her, and it couldn't get any better than my cum leaking from her ass and my name branded on it.

. . .

CHARLOTTE

I WAS SO TIRED I WAS ABLE TO CRAWL INTO BED AND PASS THE fuck out for five more hours. My brain hurt as much as my body, and I needed to rest it. I hate that I dreamed of Haidyn and what we did down in my basement. It was like I lived it all over again. I woke up and had to remind myself about our phone call. Of course, I'm not good enough for a man like him in bed. I'm an inexperienced virgin. I don't know why I'm letting it bother me so much. Maybe it's the failure. I was born to win. My father raised me to know my limits and push past them. My mother raised me not to underestimate myself.

I may not be a Lord, but that doesn't mean I can't be something in our world. This was my one chance, my assignment, and I blew it.

And not to mention that his name is branded on my ass. It's not big by any means, but it's a reminder that he's laughing at me. That I'm nothing more than a fucking joke.

After finally crawling out of my bed for the second time today, I shower and get ready for my girls' night out. I'm slutting it up.

My black minidress has my tits on display. They're not large, but with the right bra, they look like I paid for them. I know my stilettos will hurt so much that I'll be crawling out of the club when it closes. I've done my makeup dark with black shadow, winged liner, lots of mascara, and the longest fake lashes I own. I have fucking wings on my eyes.

I feel good. Like a new person. One who didn't allow Haidyn Reeves to touch. I scrubbed my skin until it was red and irritated, trying to get rid of his scent. I exfoliated and shaved every inch of my body. The bruises are still there, but I just can't bring myself to care and cover them up. Fuck that. That would let him win.

I fluff my curly hair and apply some red lipstick. I'm going out to make a statement—my pussy may still be a virgin, but I do anal. I'll find a guy, bring him home, and let him fuck me. Then I'll be someone else's whore. My ass will leak someone else's cum. Hopefully, the bastard still has cameras in my bedroom and watches some drunk guy fuck my ass while I cry out the mystery man's name like I'm being paid to do so.

Exiting my bathroom, I pick up my cell just as it rings. I answer without looking at the caller ID, knowing it's my friends. "I'm about to leave..."

"Hello, *Charlotte.*"

The altered voice using my fake name almost has me tripping in my heels.

"Go to your living room," he orders before I can even speak.

It's as if someone threw cold water on me. Numbly, I make it to my living room to see two men dressed in cloaks, masks, and hoods. My stomach drops at the sight of them.

"Place me on speakerphone," the man barks in my ear.

Pulling it away, I do as he says with shaking hands.

"Can you hear me?" he asks.

"Yes, sir." Both men standing in my living room answer. Their voices also altered. I hate that the Lords go-to is to hide who they really are. It makes them fucking cowards if you ask me.

"Good, we'll get started."

I take a step back, expecting them to both rush me, tackle me to the ground, and drag me out of my home.

"I received your email, Annabelle." The man on the other end of my phone starts. "I'm going to give you one chance to change your mind."

I swallow nervously.

"You choose Haidyn, or you choose to quit," he says simply.

It reminds me of Haidyn's ultimatum. *You always have a choice, doll face.* And I know how that turned out.

He continues at my silence. "If you choose Haidyn, these two Lords will leave your house. But if you choose to quit..." The one on the right picks up a duffel bag and drops it on the coffee table. The same one Haidyn tied me to. "They have been given strict instructions to deliver you to the cathedral immediately by any means necessary."

"Cathedral?" I breathe, taking another step back. The memory of me removing the brand from the woman and having to kill her comes to mind. And what if they strip me naked? They'll see Haidyn's name on my ass. Will they remove that one too?

"Yes, Annabelle. They will deliver you to the cathedral where you will fulfill your...duties. You will serve your Lords one way or another."

"Haidyn," I say without thought. It's a no-brainer. "I'll continue with Haidyn," I rush out, feeling my pulse racing. *Duties?* The only thing I can think of when he mentions duties is an offering. Where they take women who have betrayed their Lords, tie them down, and let Lords take their turns with them. They like to cut them, make them pay in blood and screams. The lucky ones die quickly. It's not necessarily about sex. It's about torture in general.

"Did you hear that, Lords?" the man asks.

"Yes, sir," they both answer again.

"You may leave." He hangs up, and I drop my hand to my side.

They both laugh. Then one picks up his bag, and I feel their eyes on me. "She thinks she chose right."

The other one adds, "At least I would have made you enjoy it. You think he's not going to pass you around? That he's not going to use you like the whore you are?" He steps forward, and I take one back. My heel trips me on the rug.

Their laughter grows as they step out of my sliding glass door, and I want to scream because, once again, I'm going to be Haidyn's bitch.

The motherfucker doesn't even want me! What am I supposed to do?

"GODDAMMIT!"

Falling down onto the couch, I rock back and forth as the memory of the cathedral comes to mind.

THE BLEACH BLOND WHO SITS AT THE OPPOSITE END OF THE PEW stands. Before walking away, her eyes meet mine once more before exiting the front double doors.

A man's grunts get my attention as I look back at the altar. We're too far back for me to see anything, so I get to my feet. My father grabs my hand, but I push it away and step out into the aisle to get a better view.

The woman lies naked other than the black latex hood over her head and collar. She fights the rope that binds her to the altar like the sacrifice they've made her.

A man kneels on the altar between her open legs, one hand massaging her large breast while the other runs a razor blade down the middle of her already bloody chest. His hard dick is out of his undone jeans.

Three more are lined up to take their turn.

I jump when a hand is placed on my back. My eyes catch sight of the woman across the cathedral, and I hold my breath as Anne stares at me. Does she know it's me? Will she tell my mother that my father brought me? Will he get in trouble with the Lords?

Turning around, I sprint out of the cathedral and into the cold night.

"Annabelle?" my father calls out, following.

"We should go." I'm gasping as I rip the cloak off my body and the mask, needing fresh air.

"Annabelle," he barks. Grabbing my shoulder, he spins me around to face him as he removes his mask with his free hand.

"Why did you bring me here?" I demand. "Why did you want me to see that?" I point at the old building.

He runs a hand through his hair before releasing a sigh. "Because..." He looks away and sucks in a long breath while I still try to catch mine. When they meet mine again, they're as cold as I've ever seen them, making a shiver run up my spine. "You only see the rewards, Anna. The life me and your mother chose—the money, the cars, the gifts. This..." He points over his shoulder back to the cathedral. "This is what happens if you choose to become a Lady and are unable to be faithful." He cups my face, and his eyes soften. "Your mother and I want very different lives for you. But if this is what you choose, I won't allow you to go in blind. The reward isn't worth the sacrifice unless you know what they demand in payment."

Shhh...

Chapter 34

Charlotte

Blackout is the place to go when it comes to clubs in our city. It recently caught fire, but the Lord who owns it—Tyson Crawford—had it rebuilt from the ground up. Even though he kept it exactly like the original, it's still better than ever.

Like always, it's packed tonight. We've been here for two hours, and I've downed more drinks than I can count. Not like I care. I had an Uber drop me off, and I'll either Uber home or find a man to drive me.

Man? I look around the club as the flashing lights hurt my eyes and the floor vibrates under my heels. I have a rum and Coke in my hands that I'm sipping on.

The only man I'm supposed to be with is Haidyn. Especially now that the Lords gave me an ultimatum, I have to honor my decision. So much for taking a random guy home to fuck my ass.

That thought has me sucking down more of my drink. It doesn't even burn my throat anymore. It slides right down.

I'm out with my friends, and my mind is on Haidyn. It pisses me off, but I knew taking him on as an assignment would control my life.

Making my way to the bathroom, I enter and pull out my cell. I dial his number and hold it to my ear as it rings.

"Yes, Annabelle?" he answers. His voice sounds irritated. As if he is tired of me. Like I'm some obsessed bitch following him around, and for some reason, the way he says my name infuriates me. I like it better when he calls me Charlotte.

"What the fuck do you want, Haidyn?" I bark out but then hiccup.

He laughs lightly. "You called me, doll face."

I stomp my foot. *Fuck!* This is why women shouldn't take their cells out with them. Unable to come up with anything, I hang up and slam the cell down on the counter.

Bowing my head, I take in a shaky breath. My cell beeps, and I grind my teeth. Picking it up, I expect it to be him, but it's a text from **UNKNOWN.**

Tick tock.

I want to scream. Are they watching me? Bugging my cell? Most likely since they're the ones who gave me this one.

I suck down what's left of my drink, then place my cell to my ear, calling Haidyn once more.

"Yes?" he answers. This time, his voice sounds amused.

I straighten my shoulders. "You branded my ass," I snap.

"You're welcome."

I bite my tongue to keep from telling him to go to hell.

"Just giving you a reminder of me, doll face."

Fisting my hand, I take in a deep breath and get this over with. "You said that it's my decision...that it depends on me when we're done."

"I did," he agrees.

"What if I'm not done...?" I bite my numbing lip, hoping he doesn't make me beg him to be his whore. No matter how much my body liked it.

"Done with what, beautiful?"

I roll my eyes, my knees buckling at his choice of words. He's just too good. "You...and me."

"I'm not sure I understand," he says, and I bow my head, running my hand through my hair.

Motherfucker...

Sighing, I lift my head and stare at myself in the mirror. "I want to be your dirty little whore, Haidyn." My chest rises and falls quickly, my breathing accelerating. My face is red, but I'm pretty sure that's from the alcohol I've consumed since arriving.

His silence on the other end of the phone has me panicking. What if he was being serious and doesn't want me? I can't take no for an answer. The Lords have given me an order, and now my life is on the line. If I have to crawl, beg, and spread my legs for him like the desperate woman I am, I will.

The line goes dead, letting me know he just hung up on me, and I toss my phone onto the counter like it's on fire. Gripping my hair, I grind my teeth. "What the fuck?" I hiss. This is why women don't drink and call their exes. They end up regretting it the next day.

I turn off my phone, stuff it into my clutch, and stomp my way out of the bathroom to go down some more drinks. I'll deal with my lack of dignity tomorrow.

HAIDYN

I DROP MY PHONE TO MY LAP. I SHOULD BE HAPPY ABOUT THE call I just received, but I'm not. She was drunk. I'm not surprised about that, but why did she suddenly change her mind?

I kept her at her house because I didn't want her anywhere near Carnage. I can't chance the guys figuring out who she really is. Not until I find out what the fuck it is she's after. I can guess, but that's not good enough.

I want to know, and that will take time. I'm not going to pass up an opportunity to play with her in the meantime.

Looking up, I see Sin and Ryat in the middle of a conversation. I interrupt, not caring what they're talking about. "Ryat?"

"Yeah?" His green eyes meet mine.

"What did Blakely do for her initiation after you two got married?" A Lady has to be initiated, and considering the rank her Lord holds, will depend on how much the Lords require of her to prove her worthy of him.

He sits back on the couch. "They gave her two...the first one was to prove her loyalty to me with divorce papers—she passed by not signing and tossing them into the fireplace." He smiles proudly at the thought. "The second was she had to kill a Lord, but the night of the initiation, she was attacked, so the Lords excused it."

Hmm. That's interesting that they didn't give her a new one. Or at least fulfill the previous one later, but that's all the information he wanted to give so I'll accept it. I look at Sin, who sits next to him. He's typing on his cell. "Sin, what did Ellington have to do?"

His eyes meet mine for a brief second. "They made me put her through hell." Then he goes back to typing to who I can only guess is his pregnant wife.

Tyson gets my attention, sitting behind his desk. "Found a wife, Haidyn?" He smirks.

Tyson's wife didn't have to be initiated. He got to choose who he wanted and when he wanted to make her his. It was something he had negotiated with the Lords in taking over Blackout.

I shake my head. "Just curious." Vague, I know, but I don't want anyone to know anything just yet regarding Charlotte. Plus, the Spade brothers have different rules when it comes to wives and Ladies.

Getting up, I exit Tyson's office on the second floor of Blackout. I walk across the walkway and come to a stop. Curling my hands around the railing, I look down over the packed club.

I spot her immediately. She's hard to miss, dressed in a black minidress and red heels, and standing at the main bar with three shots lined up. She throws each one back and then slams the glasses down. Two women stand next to her doing the same and a man at the end.

I know who they all are. I went through her cell while she was down in the basement. I wanted to know everything I could about my newest toy. They're part of her "fake" life. The question is, why did she come out with them tonight? Just how deep is this second life she has?

It's not hard to figure out, really. She needs to keep up the facade. That's why she called me. The Lords sent her to me, and she can't walk away. No matter what I do to her, she has to take it or else...the real question is, what is the *else*? Am I her initiation? If so, why me? Maybe she's been handed over to another Lord, and they've sent her to me because they think I'll give them inside information about Carnage. Too bad for them, I'm not talking, but I'll make sure to send her back to her Lord with my cum dripping from every hole she has to offer.

Maybe this is about Ashtyn? I don't see that being a possibility, though, because Charlotte was placed in my life before Saint dragged Ashtyn back home. Not by much though. But in our world, you can't rule anything out.

I'm going to do whatever the fuck I can to find out. She'll tell me what I want to know, even if I have to force it out of her. But I'm all for the long game.

"Your latest fuck?"

I look over to see Sin has joined me out on the walkway. Placing his tatted forearms on the railing, he leans over, his eyes looking down over the bar where I was. His eyes immediately come back to mine... then return to her.

Looking over at the door to Tyson's office, I see him and Ryat standing right outside of it in conversation.

"What did you drive tonight?" I ask Sin.

Straightening his back, he turns to look at me. "My car. Do you need it?"

I look back over at her and see her lift a shot up in the air. Her friends clank them together, causing some of the liquid to spill over the edge of hers and run down her arm. Her friend grabs Charlotte's wrist and licks it to lap up the drink spilled as Charlotte throws her head back and laughs.

"Yeah." I dig my hand into the pocket of my leather jacket and hold up the key to my bike. "I'll trade you for the night." I can't put her on the back of my R1. And she's not leaving this place with anyone but me.

He takes it and drops his keys into my hand. "I'll swing by tomorrow and swap them out."

"I'll text you the address."

"I know where Carnage..." He frowns. "You're hiding." It's not a question.

"I'm not hiding." I slap his shoulder. "But this stays between us. And if I find out you told someone, I'll nail your fucking dick to the wall."

He just laughs. Fucker would probably get off on that.

Shhh...

Chapter 35

Charlotte

Chelsea is here with some guy who I've never met before. He's a drug dealer, and when she said she had Molly, she meant he did.

I've done drugs before, but I'm just not in the mood tonight. I'd rather get wasted. We're standing at the bar as the bartender lines up more shots. I'm here to drown out any memory of Haidyn, the Lords, and my future because it's officially over.

A hand reaches up the back of my dress, and I jump, spinning around, about to punch the fuck out of whoever is touching me when I look up into a set of blue eyes.

I have a moment of panic, thinking that I did take a Molly and just forgot, and now I'm hallucinating.

Haidyn steps into me, pinning my back into the bar. He cups my face, and my breathing becomes labored as he lowers his lips to mine.

He kisses me, and my lips part on their own, letting him control the kiss like he did my body in the basement. It feels good to be wanted, even if it's fake. It feels so real.

The taste of his kiss, the touch of his lips, and the dominance in the way his hands hold me in place are more intoxicating than any drink I've ever had. If he wasn't holding me up, I'd fall over. Or float away. Either way, it would end too soon.

He pulls away as if he can read my mind, and I open my heavy eyes to see him staring down into mine. "Hello, doll face."

I can't speak. My body is cold, and my limbs are numb. Does it make me a whore that I want him to place me on the bar top, push up my dress, and fuck me? Make me beg him to come? Show all of Blackout that he owns me and I'm his good girl who begs to be his whore?

"Charlotte?"

My name is shouted over the music, and he lets go of my face. I turn to see my two friends staring at Haidyn wide-eyed. Nikki's boyfriend tilts his head to the side, also staring at the stranger who just swept me off my feet.

"What the fuck happened to you and Wesley?" Nikki asks.

"We broke up." I lie easily. My body may be a little slow right now, but my mind isn't.

"When?" she asks, her eyes finally going to me.

Before I can respond, Chelsea laughs. "Who the hell cares?" She's drooling all over Haidyn.

I can't blame the woman. My eyes go back to his and look over his black T-shirt that has a woman on her knees kneeling in front of an upside-down cross that reads—*devoted*. She's got tape over her mouth and her tied hands in a praying position—ready and willing to serve her Lord.

It fits him like a glove. The short sleeves show off his muscular arms and tattoos. They make my mouth water.

He removes his wallet from his back pocket and pulls out a black card. When he moves to stand beside me, the bartender looks up and notices him immediately. He's hard to miss.

"Haidyn, what's up, man?" he yells over the music.

He holds out the card and tells the guy, "For my girl and her friends."

My girl? Well, I think I earned that, considering his name is on my ass.

"Got it." The guy takes it. "Want anything?"

Haidyn shakes his head. "No thanks."

Haidyn looks toward the end of the bar, and the club owner nods at him. Then he turns to face me and lowers his head to speak into my ear. "Be right back."

I watch him walk through the crowd, and people move out of the way as if he's God. The best thing is that they don't even know who he really is. He says a few things to other Lords that I know of—Sin and

Ryat—before they turn and head toward the exit, and then he and Tyson step into the hallway out of sight.

"Here you go, ladies," the bartender calls out, getting my attention.

I spin around, pick up the shot, and clank our glasses together before I throw it back. After I set it down, the girls start to talk when Chelsea's drug dealer comes to stand next to me. He's looking in the direction of the hallway before his dilated eyes meet mine. "You're dating Haidyn Reeves?"

Does he know who Haidyn is? Surely not. He's a Spade brother. Although the Lords keep their life a secret...the Spade brothers? They're kept even more a secret since they work at Carnage.

Then he speaks again. "He's friends with Tyson?"

Getting irritated happens much easier when I'm drunk. I place a hand on my hip. "Why does it matter who he's friends with?"

"Ryat and Sin?" He arches a brow at me.

The hairs on the back of my neck rise. *What the fuck?* Tyson makes sense. He's the owner of this club, and everyone knows who he is. They don't know him as a Lord, but definitely by name. But to also recognize Ryat and Sin? It's throwing up red flags. I guess he could know them from Barrington, but something tells me that's not it. Kids from all around the world attend Barrington, not just the Lords.

He goes to say something, but Chelsea grabs his arm to pull him toward the dance floor, wanting to dry hump him.

I turn, motion to the bartender, and order another round. I'm already getting drunk, but if Haidyn plans to take me home, I'm getting smashed.

HAIDYN

SHE CLOSES THE PLACE DOWN. NOT THAT I'M SURPRISED. I CAN tell when a woman is on a mission to get drunk, and she has accomplished it.

I have one hand in hers and the other on her back as I guide her out of the back exit to the parking lot. Unlocking Sin's car, I place her in the passenger seat before sliding into the driver's seat. She leans her forehead on the window while I drive out of town. My eyes sneak a quick peek, and I see her minidress has ridden up on her thighs. High enough that I can see her nude lace thong. Thoughts of what I did to her in her basement make me hard.

I watched the video of her getting off while I was balls deep in her ass four times today. Her body was so responsive. I want to see what else her body likes, even if her mind doesn't.

We pull up to my house, and I leave Sin's Zenvo TSR-S in the driveway. Getting out, I remove her from the passenger seat and carry her inside. My eyes catch sight of the blacked-out Aston Martin sitting in my driveway that comes and goes as it pleases.

It's the reason I bought this place four years ago. My brothers don't know I have it. Charlotte changes those plans as well. *She changes everything*. If she can find me, who says someone else can't?

I carry her into my bedroom, where I kick it shut before laying her on the bed. I remove her heels and place them on the couch at the end of the footboard. Stepping next to the bed, I slowly run my fingertips along her tan legs, up over her thighs, and push her mini dress up in the process, taking in the small wet spot that covers her underwear.

The urge to bury my head between her thighs and wake her up with my tongue fucking her sweet cunt comes to mind, but not tonight.

Pushing the dress to her waist, I pull her thong down her legs and toss it to the side. Then I push her dress up over her breasts. It takes me a second to get her arms out of it, and she moans from the movement, but her eyes remain closed as I pull it up and over her head.

Stepping away from the bed, I exit the primary suite and walk through the house to the kitchen. On my way, I grab a bottle of water out of the fridge and some painkillers out of the cabinet.

I'm walking down the hallway back to my room when I hear muffled moaning coming from one of the spare bedrooms. I know the sound of a gagged woman when I hear it. Plus, the slapping of bodies gives them away, along with the sound of the headboard hitting the wall.

Entering the bedroom once again, I find her lying naked on the bed where I left her. "Charlotte?" I run my knuckles along her cheek, looking over her makeup. Her lipstick has worn off from the kiss and the countless drinks she's had tonight. My eyes quickly scan the bruises that I gave her while I had her in her basement. "Wake up, doll face. I need you to take these."

She arches her back and lets out a whimper.

"Come on." I place my arm under her neck and sit her up, ignoring the hard dick pressing painfully against my zipper. Her heavy eyes flutter open and meet mine. "Take these." I prop her up against the headboard and place them in her hand while I pick up her legs and pull down the black satin sheets.

She tosses them into her mouth, and I hand her the water. She gulps some down, swallowing the pills without thought before giving me the bottle.

I help her lie back down under the bedding, covering her up. I go to walk away when her hand reaches out and grabs mine. I turn to see her dazed eyes looking up at me. "Are you going to share me with your friends?"

Her words catch me off guard, but I don't answer. Instead, I sit down next to her and watch her blink a few times as if her pretty blue eyes see several of me.

"Can I"—she hiccups—"ask a favor?" Her words are slurred, but I understand what she's asking.

"Sure, doll face." I indulge her, wanting to know her drunk thoughts. A person can tell you a lot about themselves when intoxicated.

She yawns, and her eyes fall closed as I wait for her to continue. "If you do...will you be my first?" Her words are so soft I wonder if I heard her correctly.

"First?" I ask and wait for her to explain, but the soft snore from her parted lips tells me I'm not getting anything else from her tonight.

Getting up, I pull my cell from my pocket and dial Gavin's number. He answers on the second ring, his voice rough as if I woke him up. "Haidyn—?"

"Is Charlotte a virgin?" I bark out and then look over at her, and she doesn't move. What else could she mean by *first*? Especially when it followed her asking me if I was going to share her?

"I'm not sure..."

"Why didn't you say something to me that day in your clinic?" I demand, exiting my room. I've already fucked her ass and her mouth, so to be her first…? *No*. She's drunk and confused. She doesn't know what she's asking. But then Kashton's words come to mind from when I watched her dance in Blackout a while back.

"You can't be serious, man. She's what? Maybe five-foot-two and a hundred pounds. You're six-seven and like two fifty. You'd destroy her," he jokes. "Not to mention, I'm pretty sure she's a virgin. You'd scare that poor girl to death."

"You can't tell a virgin from an exam," Gavin answers.

I run a hand through my hair, making my way to the living room. I stop at the floor-to-ceiling windows, looking out over the dark woods. "She was on birth control," I argue, trying to avoid what my mind is already telling me. She told us she had two sexual partners.

"Women take birth control for many reasons other than to prevent pregnancy, Haidyn."

Letting out an annoyed breath, I hang up and stuff the cell in my pocket. She's a fucking virgin. That changes things. Why would she allow me to do the things I did? I knew she was inexperienced but never thought she'd be a fucking virgin.

She lied to me when I found the bruises on her, and she said she had rough sex. I knew it wasn't a hundred percent the truth, but I didn't think she was that far off. So why the hell was she so banged up? Bruises on her wrists and on her face…who did that to her? Those were just the ones I could see. Did she have more?

She had told me she'd had anal before when I had her in her basement. And her mouth? I really didn't give her a chance to show me what she could do. I controlled that entire situation.

Pulling out my cell again, I go to the app that shows the cameras I have in her house. Something happened tonight or earlier today. Whatever it was, it had her calling and begging me. *Literally*. No woman begs a man to treat her like trash on purpose. That's why I did what I did to her in the first place. To see just how far I could go with her. I wanted her to run from me. So for her to come back so quickly…?

I watch the screen and see her waking up after I had her in her basement for two days. I start from the beginning, thinking I missed something when I was watching today from my home office. She watches her TV, witnessing the truth that she wasn't at Carnage.

Rushing to her basement, she calls me, then gets on her laptop and slams it shut. I frown, watching her lie down for a nap. I fast-forward until she wakes up. I skip over her getting ready but bring it to a quick stop when I see one of the cameras in the living room shows the sliding glass door open.

Two men enter the house, dressed in cloaks and masks. *Why the fuck are Lords at her place?*

One pulls his cell out of a bag and types a message before putting it back. I pull up two views so I can watch her in the closet getting dressed to go out while the other watches them just stand there. The cameras I have in her house cover every inch of it.

After a few minutes, she's back in her room, and her cell rings. She answers it and comes to a stop. Her face pales before she slowly enters the living room to find the Lords waiting on her.

She places her call on speakerphone, and I listen to the altered voice give her an ultimatum.

She chooses me.

Not like either option is good, but she knew it was better than the alternative.

She hangs up the phone, and the Lords in her house begin to laugh. And my question is answered—*they told her I'd pass her around.*

I might have fucked women who didn't belong to me before, but I won't be sharing what's mine. I've wanted Charlotte from the moment I saw her. The Lords have handed her to me on a silver platter, and I'm a man who likes to feast.

I make my way down to the basement inside my home. Flipping on the light, I go over to the far wall and grab what I want off the shelf, then I open one of the drawers and grab a couple more things. I throw them all into a backpack and make my way back upstairs.

She's still passed out in my bed as I walk through my bedroom and enter my bathroom. I grab a T-shirt from my closet and dress her in it. Then I pick her up in my arms and carry her to my car that's parked in the garage, passing Sin's that I drove home in my driveway as I take her to her house.

I'm going to find out everything I want to know. Whatever she tells me will decide how I move forward.

Shhh...

Chapter 36

Charlotte

My head pounds, and there's a ringing in my ears as if I'm standing in the middle of Blackout with the blaring music.

I swallow and flinch, my throat sore. I try to move, but I can't seem to make my arms work. I have an itch on my face that needs to be scratched.

My head falls forward, and I groan, picking it up. I crack my eyes open, and it takes me a second for things to come into focus. But when they do, I tense. The ringing in my ears intensifies as if an alarm sounding to alert me of danger.

Haidyn stands before me, leaning back against the kitchen island, his arms crossed over his chest. He's dressed in the same T-shirt and jeans as he was at the club. His dark blue eyes stare right at me.

I go to open my mouth to ask him what the fuck he's doing, but I can't. My eyes widen, and I try to look down to see why I can't talk. Panic rises when my face drops, and I see I'm sitting in a chair naked in the middle of my kitchen. My breathing picks up, and I try to move my arms and legs, but all it does is make the chair wobble on the tile.

I try to scream, but it's muffled. *What the fuck?*

My eyes shoot to his, and he doesn't look the least bit concerned. I try to take a deep breath through my nose and allow myself a second to calm my racing heart. This isn't the first time I've been put in front of a Lord, unable to defend myself.

He pushes off the counter, and I glare up at him, hoping he can feel how much I want him dead at this very moment.

Stepping into me, he wraps his hand around my throat, and I tilt my head back. His fingers tighten, holding me in place, and I blink rapidly.

"Good morning, beautiful." He finally speaks, sounding as cool as can be.

I swallow against his hand, and he smiles down at me. "You know..." His hand moves from my throat up to my chin, and his grip tightens, holding it in place when I try to pull away. "You look really pretty wearing nothing but tape."

My eyes widen. *Tape?* Is that why I can't move? He's taped me to a chair? I try to speak but still nothing. His smile just grows, showing his dazzling teeth. It's like he's warming me up before he rips my throat out.

"Is it turning you on as much as the rope does, doll face?" His eyes drop to my heaving chest, taking a second to look over my hard nipples.

I hope he doesn't drop his hand between my legs because I can't hide the fact that I'm wet. I'm unable to close my legs because of how he has my legs tied open.

He laughs at my silence, then lets me go. I lower my head and watch him walk to the island to grab a backpack. He unzips it and pulls out a syringe and vial of clear liquid.

What the fuck happened last night? What did I do? Or did I say something to him to piss him off? I can't remember much other than calling him in the bathroom at Blackout? And then he was there. Did I ask him to come get me?

He sticks the needle into the glass vial, pulling back the plunger to fill it up. Placing it on the counter, he turns to face me.

His blue eyes remain on mine while he slowly walks toward me, and I scream into the tape that I fucking hate him. As if he cares.

"Don't worry, *Annabelle*. This will only hurt for a second." He grips my chin and shoves my face to the side, and I feel a sting in my neck.

HAIDYN

After removing the needle from her neck, I step back and place the cap on it. Then I toss the syringe onto the island, lean back against it, and cross my arms over my chest to wait.

Her chest rises and falls quickly from her heavy breathing, and her nipples are still hard. She looks absolutely stunning tied to the chair. So many things come to mind while having her in this position, and none of them include what I'm about to do to her.

She groans, her head falling back and then forward. *It's working.*

Her legs are spread, each ankle duct-taped to each front leg, and her arms are down by her side, wrists also duct-taped to the back legs of the chair. I made sure to undress her so nothing got in the way. I wanted to see how her body reacted to the situation.

Walking over to her, I grip her chin again and push her head back so she has to look up at me. Her eyes are dilated and heavy. She blinks a few times, looking at the ceiling aimlessly. My hand drops to her neck, and I feel her pulse.

Strong and steady.

Reaching up, I grip the tip of the several pieces of duct tape that I placed over her mouth and rip them off.

She gasps, her head falling forward, her hair covering her face from me. I gather it all in one hand and pull her head up, holding it. "How do you feel?" I ask her.

"What...what did you give me?" she asks, her eyes still unfocused.

I ignore that and let go of her hair. I cup her face and run my thumb over her parted lips. I take in her pretty face. She's still got makeup on from the club last night. The black eye shadow is smeared, her blush has rubbed off, and her lipstick has faded. Her fake lashes clump in various spots. She still looks fucking gorgeous. Like she spent all night on her knees being my good girl.

"Talk to me, Charlotte. How do you feel?" I ask, my eyes searching hers.

"Drunk," she slurs, and her lashes flutter.

"Good." Let's get started. "Why did the Lords send you to Carnage?" I need answers, and this is the best way to get them.

"Assignment." She licks her lips.

"You're on an assignment?" It's not what I thought it was. I figured, at the very most, it was an initiation.

"Y-yes."

Interesting. "Why did they send you to me?"

Her head falls back, and her blue eyes meet mine. "I don't know."

"Bullshit," I hiss, though I know she's telling the truth. Running a hand down my face, I ask, "What do you know about me?"

"I know you're a Spade brother..." She swallows. "Your parents are dead...you killed your father." Her eyes search mine, but I doubt she's seeing me.

The Spade brother isn't a secret to her. She knows that because she's been seeing me at Carnage. My mom being dead isn't a stretch. My father being dead? She can know that because again, Saint, Kash, and I run Carnage. But how he died? "Why would I kill him?"

"Because you love her."

Her answer makes me frown, throwing me off. "Who do I love?"

"Ashtyn."

I've only ever said that out loud to one person. It was recently, but I know she hasn't told anyone. "Who told you that?" I inquire.

"My mother and her friend."

This is what I wanted to know. Now we're getting somewhere. "Been talking to your mother about me?" I know who her parents are.

She goes to roll her heavy eyes, but her whole head makes a circle. "She only knows that I have sessions with you—that you're my assignment."

Well, that wasn't what I wanted to hear. I try to think what else I can ask while I have the upper hand. A thought comes to mind. I gather her hair and push her head forward. "Where did you get this?" I ask, running my fingers over the Lords brand on her upper back. I had seen it the first night I was in her house when I placed the tracker in her neck. I figured she was someone's chosen and they branded her.

"The Lords gave it to me," she mumbles.

With my hand still in her hair, I yank her head back and look down at her. "Why would they brand you?"

"Initiation. I either had to cut a woman's off or give myself the same one. I removed hers, and they ended up giving me one to match."

A brand for a brand.

What the fuck? She's already had an initiation? This doesn't make sense. Women don't get initiated unless they are to be wed to a Lord and I've never heard of one having an assignment.

"What happened to her?"

"They made me kill her," she whispers.

None of this makes sense. I bet it wasn't about Charlotte being initiated but more about the woman she was supposed to kill. No one else wanted that responsibility, so they put it on Charlotte. But that doesn't answer the branding question. Why was the woman branded in the first place? I mean, I know Lords who brand their chosens and Ladies. It's all about claiming their property. But why did they want hers removed or Charlotte to brand herself?

Fuck, I'm getting a headache. This is giving me more questions than answers. "How did you kill her?"

"I shot her," she says softly. "And every time I close my eyes, I see her." She blinks, her heavy eyes looking up at mine through her fake lashes.

"You did what you had to do," I tell her, seeing the uncertainty in her eyes. Her decision haunts her.

She swallows and whispers, "Is that what you tell yourself?"

"I don't have any regrets," I say truthfully. It's kill or be killed in our world.

Releasing Charlotte's hair, I move to stand in front of the chair. "The bruises...when you showed up at my house with bruises, you told me they were from rough sex. Who gave them to you?"

"I was arrested. He was rough..."

"What the fuck were you arrested for?" I demand.

She tries to shrug. "Not sure. He never said."

I'll have someone look into that for me. I reach out and cup her face. "Am I the only guy who's ever fucked you?"

Her pretty eyes look up at me. They're heavier than they were. I'm losing her. "Yes," she answers in her soft voice.

Goddamn.

Lowering my face down to hers, I cup her cheeks with both of my hands, and she licks her plump lips before I press mine to them. She moans into my mouth, her hips rising off the chair, and I lower my hand to her chest, softly playing with her nipple. Teasing her, I love the way her body rocks back and forth in the chair, needing to be fucked.

I pull away as I ask, "Why weren't you a chosen?" If she's a virgin, then she's never belonged to a Lord before.

She blinks, her long, fake dark lashes fanning her cheeks. "I'm having...to save myself for my Lord."

I tilt my head to the side in thought. "Who is your Lord?"

"Don't know. Don't have one." She slurs.

Fuck! I'm getting nowhere and she's not making any goddamn sense. Kneeling in front of her chair, I place my hands on her smooth thighs, and she tries to part them more as if she wants me to bury my face between them. She groans, and her dark blue eyes meet mine, silently begging me to use her.

"So this isn't about revenge?" I have to ask.

Her dark brows furrow, and she gently shakes her head. "Who would I want revenge on?"

She doesn't know.

"Haidyn—" She licks her lips, her thighs clenching under my hands as she tries to pull them farther apart. "Please..."

I stand to my full height and run my hand through her soft curls but don't say anything. I know what she wants, but she's not getting it tonight. Not like this.

Her head falls forward.

Reaching out, I gently cup her chin and push her head back to see her eyes closed. I wait a few seconds to see if they open. When they don't, I remove my knife from my pocket and cut through the tape that secures her wrists to the chair and then her legs. Picking her up, I carry her to her bedroom and place her in bed.

She'll be fine to sleep it off. She'll probably be out most of the day after the night she had last night plus the drugs.

Pulling the covers up to her neck, I leave her room when I catch sight of her desk over by the window. I remember seeing it on the cameras after she called and woke up from her stay in the basement.

I pick up the laptop, tuck it under my arm, then lock up her house, leaving her to rest. Our little truth session is over for now. But it doesn't mean we won't have another one.

♠

I'm sitting on my couch sipping on a glass of scotch when I hear a bike rev its engine. I get up and make my way to the garage. Opening the garage door, I lean up against the wall crossing my arms as Sin pulls my blacked-out R1 inside. Getting off the bike, he tosses me the keys.

"Thanks," I tell him. "Yours are in your car."

He nods. "No problem, man. Nice place by the way." He walks out of the garage toward his car in the driveway.

My words make him stop. "You know her." It's not a question. I saw the way he looked at her last night at Blackout when he realized who it was that I was staring at. He did a double take, and I want to know why.

Sighing, he turns around to face me. "I know *of* her." He corrects me.

My teeth clench. How many more Lords that I know will recognize her? You can't try to sell a lie if everyone already knows the truth. "How?"

"William," he answers.

I frown. "How do you know her stepdad?"

He runs a hand over his messy hair. "Before I gave myself over to you guys, I hired an attorney to help me with Elli."

"Meaning?" I want to know exactly what William did for him.

"I bought her our house, and when I had him bring the papers over for her to sign, I had him slip in a marriage license." His eyes drop to his wedding ring as he absentmindedly spins it around his finger before they meet mine. "And then the morning I turned myself into Carnage I met with him again—off the books—to get all my affairs in order to make sure Elli was taken care of. He had pictures of Annabelle and her mother on his desk. I've never met her face-to-face, and I don't think she knows who I am."

"So Elli knows who William is too?" I make sure I understand him. "Does she know who Annabelle is?"

He shakes his head. "No. I made up a name...introduced him as Mr. Tate. The less she knew, the better. I can't say if she knows Annabelle or not."

I nod, it could be worse. "This stays between us."

"Of course." He agrees. "But I hope you know what you're doing." With that, he gets into his car, starts it up, and drives off.

Shhh...

Chapter 37

Charlotte

It's dark out. The clock on my dash tells me that it's after ten o'clock. I woke up a few hours ago naked in my bed. I felt a little tired and managed to relax in the bathtub, trying to go over what the fuck had happened and how I got home.

Slowly, the pieces came back to me. Last night at Blackout. The call I got from the unknown Lord and then the call to Haidyn. Him showing up at the club, the drinks, the drive to his house. The water... me asking him to be my first. Then there was a gap.

Where had my entire day gone? Did I do ecstasy at Blackout? Had I taken something that I don't normally do?

Then like a fucking baseball bat to the face, it hit me. Waking up taped to the chair this morning, him giving me something, asking me questions, and putting me to bed like a child.

I sat at my desk to log what we had done, only to find my laptop gone. The one that the Lords gave me. It was there yesterday before I went out, so he had to have taken it.

That leads to now and why I'm pulling into Haidyn's driveway and slamming on my brakes. Getting out of my car, I rush to the front doors and shove them both open, not even bothering to knock. For a man who should always be on alert, his door isn't locked.

"Haidyn?" I shout, slamming them shut. "HAIDYN!" I scream, stomping my way to the living room and come to a stop when I see him sitting on the couch, leaning back with his arms across the back cushions. His blue eyes are on mine, and there's a smirk on his face.

"Where the fuck is it?" I demand, my hands going to my hips.

"Hello, doll face—"

"I'm not in the fucking mood, Haidyn. Where is it?" I step forward, my right hand gripping the strap on my purse. I'm not even going to bring up the fact that he drugged me. I'll save that for another day.

"I don't know what you're talking about, *Annabelle.*" He slowly gets to his feet.

The sound of my name just infuriates me more. A reminder that I tricked him. Maybe he shouldn't have been so goddamn stupid and did his homework before he and his *brothers* let me into their home. I huff. "I'm giving you one chance to hand it over. Right now."

He no longer tries to hide his smile. Instead, he lets it light up his face, showing off his dazzling white teeth, and it just makes my skin boil. "Or what, doll face?"

I reach into my purse and pull out what I need. Dropping the Louis Vuitton to the floor, I point my gun at him.

If he's surprised, he doesn't show it. Instead, he takes a step closer to me, and I don't retreat. Get as close as you want, motherfucker. It'll just help my odds.

"Going to shoot me, Charlotte?" He arches a brow, but I can hear the laughter in his voice.

I square my shoulders. "In a world where it's either you or me...I'll always choose me."

He stops as the end of the barrel hits his chest, and I glare up at him. "Pull the trigger, doll face."

"Give me my laptop," I bark out. He knows I can't shoot him because then what will I tell the Lords? I'll be fucked. My assignment isn't to kill him. Will they give me another one? Will they allow the other Spade brothers to throw me in a cell at Carnage? Hell if I know. But I won't allow them to punish me for killing him.

"Go ahead and pull the trigger. Make sure you aim for the heart. I've survived a bullet to the chest before."

I'm not surprised that the bastard has been shot. No doubt a woman who he pissed off. "How about your face?" I arch a brow and lift the gun, aiming right between his eyes.

He just stares down at me, the gun shaking in my hands. I'm not nervous or afraid. I'm fucking pissed. "Haidyn—"

He grabs the barrel of the gun and twists it out of my hand. I grind my teeth at the sharp pain that runs up my arm. Wrapping his hand around my throat, he shoves my back into the wall and presses the end of the barrel to my cheek.

I'm gasping glaring up at him. "Second time I've taken this from you." He laughs, and it pisses me off even more. A burning feeling in my chest that I let him win. *Again.* I just want to stomp my feet and scream at the top of my lungs how much I hate him.

"Third time's a charm," I say through gritted teeth, knowing this isn't the last time I'll want to kill him.

He steps back and removes the gun from my face. His eyes remain on mine as he pushes back the slide, emptying out the chambered bullet and removes the magazine—which he pockets—then holds it out to me. "Never shoot to wound. Always shoot to kill. And don't talk too much. Don't ask questions or explain why you want them dead. Just kill them, doll face."

My eyes drop to the gun and yank it from his hand, and he turns starting to walk away from me. "Where the fuck is it, Haidyn?" He doesn't stop walking toward the couch. "Goddammit, Haidyn," I shout, starting to run after him.

He spins around with a smirk on his face, and I just want to knock it off. So I go to slap him with the gun, but he leans back, forcing me to miss. The momentum spins me around, giving him the perfect opportunity to wrap his arm around my neck, holding my back to his front.

I drop the gun, letting it clank to his marble floor, and reach up, gripping his arm defensively.

"You're really turning me on, doll face." He chuckles. "Did you come over because you need to be tied down and fucked in the ass?"

I wiggle, trying to get free, and I can't miss the feeling of his hard dick pressing against my ass. "Hai—" His arm tightens, cutting off any chance to breathe, let alone talk.

I kick my feet out and try to twist my body out of his hold, but it's no use. My face pounds, my ears ring, and my chest is on fire from lack of oxygen. My body begins to give out on me, losing its fight, and I go limp.

He lets go of me, and I fall to the floor, my side landing on the gun.

I cough, turning onto my back to stare at his high vaulted ceiling with my knees bent.

"Go home, Charlotte," he orders, sounding far away.

"What...do you want?" I ask, getting to my hands and knees. Fuck, this is not going how I wanted it to.

"Nothing from you," he answers, not even bothering to look over at me. I'm no longer worth his time. He's proved his point. Picking up the remote, he turns up the sound on the TV to drown out anything further I might say.

I grab my gun, get to my shaking knees, pick up my purse, and storm out of his house just as fast as I entered, slamming the doors and hoping they fucking break. Getting in my SUV, I begin to cry.

I wipe at the tears angrily because I don't even have control over my own emotions right now. I hate how weak I get when I'm mad. My father once told me, "*Feeling anything is a weakness, darling. No one will take orders from a woman who cries.*"

Taking a deep breath, I throw my head back, staring at the starlight headliner inside my Cullinan as I try to get my emotions under control. Closing my eyes, I count to ten, taking a few deep breaths until I feel like I can think clearly.

Starting up my car, I pull up "Acid Annie" by Natalia Kills on my phone and connect it to my Bluetooth and turn it up all the way. I know what I'm about to do will fucking piss him off, but I no longer care. I'll hit him where it'll count and then face the consequences later.

HAIDYN

"HONEYMOON STAGE OVER ALREADY?"

I look up to see Adam standing in the kitchen with nothing but a pair of black boxer briefs on. "What makes you say that?"

"I walked in on you and your girl fucking around earlier." His eyes meet mine, and he smiles. "I was rooting for her to shoot you," he jokes and wiggles his eyebrows. "I like her."

"Don't," I warn.

"What?" He shrugs.

"I've had enough close calls with death that I don't need any more." At the mention of my close calls to death, my hand goes to my chest, rubbing the tender spot where I was recently shot. It's getting better.

Her words drown out my previous thoughts. *In a world where it's either you or me...I'll always choose me.*

Fuck, she was on fire. I understand it was anger, but it was sexy as hell. The way she barged into my house. The fact that she came prepared to shoot me had me hard as a rock. I wanted to rip off her clothes, pin her down on the floor, and fuck her ass while she held the gun to my face. It's an adrenaline rush that I haven't experienced in a long time.

For someone who has a cunt, she's got balls.

I like it. It's refreshing. She's exactly what I've been looking for in my repetitive life. Giving me something to do.

"Is this what she wants?" Adam asks, looking at the laptop on the kitchen island.

"Yep." It was right there the whole time. She never saw it and didn't even look for it. She thought I had it hidden away where she couldn't find it.

"Find anything on it?" he asks.

"Not that I could see. I was wondering if you could look at it." He nods. "She's receiving emails from an encrypted address. They also seem to be deleted after she views them. I couldn't get far, but I figured you could give it a try." She had a few pictures of me saved, but other than that, there was nothing I could see.

"Of course." He pulls a beer out of the fridge and pops off the cap before taking a sip.

"What do you think they're looking for?"

I run a hand through my hair. "I have no fucking clue."

"It could be Benny," he guesses.

"He's locked up inside Carnage." I shake my head. "I know it's been a while since you've spent significant time there, but we don't allow prisoners to have screen time."

He chuckles. "I mean whoever he was working with. Maybe he had to check in, and now that he's not, they've sent someone to keep an eye on him."

"No. That wouldn't work because I was seeing Charlotte before Saint found and brought Ashtyn back."

"Found anything new with the guy in the picture with Benny that you got in Vegas?"

I shake my head. "Bones sent me some footage from Glass, but he was always solo."

"I'll take a look," he says, giving up trying to guess because it's pointless. We can stand here and try to figure it out until we're blue in the face. We won't know we're on the right track until we get confirmation.

I have an idea of who it is and what they want, but I'm going to keep it to myself for now. It gives me more time with my new toy. Charlotte made me realize I've gone easy on her. I'm more than willing to up my game.

There's a knock on the door, and I look over at Adam. He shakes his head and raises his hands. "Not for me."

Sighing, I make my way to the front doors with a smirk on my face. I knew she'd come back, but I expected her to rush in just like last time. "Hello, doll—"

My words are cut off when I see Saint on my front porch. The smirk disappears, and he pushes his way past me into my house. I slam the door behind him.

He comes to a stop when he sees Adam standing in the kitchen drinking his beer and spins around to face me. Glaring, I cross my arms over my chest.

"Should have known I'd find you two together." Saint shakes his head.

"I'd ask how you found me, but I don't need to." *Annabelle.*

"She's very worried about you," he says in a tone that tells me he's still pissed at me for lying and helping his wife run away from him. But obviously, he couldn't pass up the chance to show me that he knows where I am.

Adam snorts. "Ashtyn didn't seem to worry about him during the four years she was gone."

Saint looks at him over his shoulder. "Charlotte." He corrects Adam, then looks back at me. "Charlotte came to me worried about you."

I can't help the laughter that escapes. *Fuck, she's good.* I told her that Saint, Ashtyn, and Kashton didn't know where I lived, so she ratted me out.

His eyes drop to my wrists, and I stiffen when his eyes meet mine again. "What the fuck do you want, Saint?" I growl, getting to the point. *What the hell did Charlotte tell him?* I hate that they even think I could be suicidal. That I would do that to them.

"Why are you hiding out here?" he demands.

"I'm not hiding," I say through gritted teeth.

"So you left without getting a new tracker put in?" he asks skeptically.

I hate the fact that they removed it when I was shot. They didn't want my brothers to find my body once I was dead. "I needed to do this alone," I say, changing the subject.

He snorts. "Alone?" Then he looks over his shoulder at Adam. "You don't seem alone to me."

Neither one of us says anything, and as the silence lingers, my blood pressure rises. *I'm going to strangle her.*

Sighing, he runs a hand down his face. "I just wanted to check on you."

Fuck that! He wanted to show up to tell me he knows where I'm staying since I've been ignoring Ashtyn's phone calls. I've only spoken to Kash a couple of times. "Well, here I am. I'm alive and well." Walking over to the front doors, I open one. A not-so-subtle gesture to tell him to get the fuck out without physically kicking him out.

He gets the hint and walks out of the house with his head held high and shoulders back. I slam the door shut as he goes to turn around and speak to me.

I look over at Adam, and he just picks up the laptop and disappears into his room. Grabbing a water, I enter mine and catch sight of the notebook she gave me sitting on my long dresser.

Opening it up, I look through the untouched pages and get an idea. Slamming it shut, I smile to myself. *Act like a brat, get treated like a brat.*

Shhh...

Chapter 38

Charlotte

I lie on my couch with my hair up in a messy bun, wearing nothing but a sweatshirt and cotton shorts while drinking wine from the bottle.

I've decided to drink my worries away. Haidyn has my laptop, and I don't know when I'll get it back. Thankfully, I've still got my Apple watch and the second cell phone that the Lords gave me. I haven't received anything new so that's a plus. They don't contact me every day, so I have some time to figure things out.

It's been a week since I stormed into his house, pulled a gun on him, and then went to Carnage. I used my anger for good use.

I PULL THROUGH THE GATES AND UP TO THE DARK CASTLE. GETTING out of the car, there's a smile on my face. I've made peace with my decision, and I'm actually giddy about it.

The front double doors open, and I'm greeted by a man dressed in an all-black tux. "Miss Hewett," he says, sounding surprised. "Haidyn isn't—"

"I know." I interrupt Jessie. "I need to speak to Saint, please."

"Miss Hewett—"

"I need to speak to Saint." I repeat. "Please. It's important. It's about Haidyn."

"What about him?"

I look up to see Saint coming down the stairs. He's got a pair of black sweatpants on and is in the process of pulling a T-shirt over his head. "I know where he is," I rush out.

"Let's talk privately," Saint says, nodding toward the same room he took me into last time. Then I notice he looks over his shoulder as if to see if Ashtyn is following him and has overheard what I said.

Interesting.

Entering the room, he shuts the door behind me. "What's wrong? Is he okay?"

I start to fan my face as if I'm worked up. I am, but not because I give a fuck about Haidyn. But I'm supposed to care, right? I'm supposed to be his therapist and want what's best for him. Instead, I'm here to rat him out like a little snitch. Dropping my hand, I start to rub my hands together and whisper, "Patient-client..."

"Fuck that bullshit." He hisses and demands, "Is he okay?"

This also tells me that Saint hasn't heard from him. What about Kashton? Is Haidyn ignoring them both? If so, why? "I...I'm not sure. He seemed okay, but..." I sniff.

"But what?" He places his hand on my shoulder, and it takes everything in me not to step back.

None of them are overly friendly, but Saint seems to be the hothead out of the three since I've known them. But that could have been because of the story that revolves around his wife. "He called me, wanting a meeting. Said he needed to talk to someone."

He nods. "Well, that's a good thing, right?"

"He just seemed off...you know? He was upset and had been drinking..."

He runs a hand down his face, letting out a sigh. "Where is he?"

I hide my smile by biting my bottom lip and drop my eyes to the floor.

"It's okay, Charlotte. You can tell me. Where is Haidyn?"

I KEPT MY CONCERN VAGUE BECAUSE I DIDN'T WANT TO TELL HIM anything specific. I wanted Saint worried enough to go to Haidyn. And by how fast Saint rushed out of Carnage, I'd say it worked.

I wanted Haidyn to be caught off guard when he saw Saint on his front porch. He'll know it was me, of course, but I don't give a fuck.

Taking another gulp of wine, I relax into the couch, getting comfortable. I've kept my real cell phone off and my one from the Lords on silent because I'm still out of town, according to my social media pages. Wesley gets a text every now and then to update him on my trip, and I send my mother a picture that I have to make on Photoshop with the added *my service is spotty* text. But other than that, I'm MIA, and it's actually been nice. I'm still on the fence about what to do about my fake friends knowing I'm dating Haidyn. I fucking lied about being broken up with Wesley. The only thing about that is they are my friends, not his. I had them before we started our fake relationship.

My door opening has me sitting up and my hand tightening on the neck of the wine bottle.

Haidyn steps into my house, and I roll my eyes, lying back down. "Don't you ever knock?"

He stays quiet as he makes his way into the living room and drops his backpack onto the coffee table. Unzipping it, he removes the notebook that I gave him during my first visit to Carnage and a pencil.

Then he removes the laptop, and I sit up straighter, placing my feet on the floor. "Haidyn—"

"I took the liberty of writing out an email for you." He opens the laptop and spins it around so I can see he's started a new email to the Lords.

New Message

To **UNKNOWN**

Subject

I quit.

"What?" I leap from the couch to grab the laptop, but he slams it shut, yanking it from the coffee table. "What the fuck, Haidyn?" I demand.

He places the laptop next to him on the opposite couch and smiles up at me. "Saint paid me a visit."

I can't help the smile, and his lips thin. "Guessing it didn't go well."

Leaning forward, he places his tatted elbows on his jean-clad thighs. "It went about how you wanted it to go. But it got me thinking..." Reaching up, he rubs his chin, and I notice he still hasn't shaved. I like the facial hair. It makes him look more rugged. More threatening. And somehow, it's a turn-on.

"Don't hurt yourself," I say, rolling my eyes at his silence.

"Oh, the only thing I'm going to hurt is you, doll face."

My pulse races at his threat because I know it's not an empty one. "So..." I try to shrug it off, acting like I don't care. "Go ahead and send the email. I don't care."

He stands, and I swallow nervously. "I think you do care. Otherwise, you wouldn't have picked me last time you tried to quit."

"You know that?" I whisper.

He gives a rough laugh. "I know everything, Annabelle."

My teeth clench, and I look away from his intense stare.

"Do you think they'll give you an option this time? Or do you think they'll just take you in the middle of the night, strip you naked, and tie you to the Lords altar?" Walking around the coffee table, he comes to stand next to me. His hand slowly slides up my back before tangling in my hair.

I moan when he pulls my head back and forces me to look up at him, his free hand wrapping around my neck to hold me in place. His eyes search mine as he speaks. "As much as I'd love to see you tied to the altar, I don't find the thought of you being someone else's whore appealing."

My breathing picks up, and my thighs tighten.

"But you tell me, doll face...do you want to be an offering for the Lords?"

"No." I don't even have to think about it, and he knows that. My father took me to the cathedral that night to make sure I had all the facts...saw all the angles that the Lords work. I knew the night I killed a woman and took my brand that there was no going back. I'm committed to this assignment, and I've come too far to let him give me up. The Lords most definitely won't give me a second chance at picking him.

"So what are you going to do for me, Charlotte?"

"Whatever you want," I answer breathlessly, knowing I'm at his mercy.

Smiling, he releases me. "Strip," he commands, going back to his backpack.

I remove my sweatshirt and shorts along with my thong. I wasn't wearing a bra. I stand naked, trying to calm my racing heart. He makes me nervous, and I hate that my palms are sweating.

"Turn around," he demands, and I gladly give him my back, staring at the TV.

I feel his jeans against the back of my legs, and then he lifts something over my head. "Open wide, doll face."

Licking my lips, I do as he says, and he shoves something hard and unforgiving into my mouth, resting them behind the back of my teeth on both top and bottom. I mumble nonsense as he jerks my head around, fastening it in place.

"On the floor. I want you on your knees and forearms, ass in the air." He slaps my ass cheeks, and I jump at the lingering sting. The brand is still healing and sensitive.

Lowering myself to my living room floor, I get on my knees and forearms just like he said. Drool gathers in my mouth, and my jaw is already getting sore. I feel the cool air from the fan hitting my wet pussy, and I rock back and forth, knowing he's about to fuck my ass.

I knew there would be consequences. I signed up for this when I stormed into Carnage to tattle. If the worst I get is an orgasm, then it was worth it.

He comes to crouch down in front of me and drops the notebook. He opens it to the front page, and I see it's nothing but empty lines. He hasn't been using it. I never expected him to. It was just something I saw when I was doing research on therapists.

Then he sets a pencil on top of it. Placing two fingers in my open mouth, I gag as they hit the back of my throat, and he lifts my face, making me arch my neck painfully. His eyes meet mine. "You're going to write

HAIDYN'S DIRTY LITTLE WHORE

over and over. Until this is done." He sets a bigger hourglass than he had in my basement down in front of the notebook, and my eyes widen.

He removes his fingers from my mouth, and drool runs from my open lips onto the notebook.

"Don't rip the paper," he warns. "Or you'll be punished."

He can't be serious. I try to argue with him, but it's just mumbled nonsense that makes him laugh because he knows that I'm going to lose. If I'm writing with a pencil and the page has drool on it, it will rip. It's paper, for Christ's sake.

"You're wasting time." He smacks my ass once more, and I groan at the sting, rocking my hips back and forth. He chuckles, and I start to write

on the first line.

HAIDYN

I KNEW WHAT I WANTED HER TO DO. I'VE JUST WAITED, LETTING her think she got away with it. I like to keep her guessing when I'll decide to make an appearance in her life. Adam hasn't found anything on her laptop. The Lord she's been assigned to knows what the fuck they're doing. But I knew that already. It just furthers my point of who I think it is.

It just makes this even better.

She's on her knees, rocking back and forth slowly while she drools all over the paper that she's writing on. "Beautiful," I praise her, and she moans.

I smile as she spreads her legs farther. Like a dog in heat, she's assumed the position and begging to be fucked.

When I undo my belt, her breathing picks up as I remove it from my jeans. Doubling it over, I slap her ass with it. She jumps, a scream coming through her mouth gag. "Keep writing," I order, swatting her again.

The two red marks on her ass make me smile and so does the sound of her sniffling while she tries to write in the notebook. I do it again and again, and again until both cheeks are covered in marks from the leather. My name branded on her cheek looks irritated from the leather.

Kneeling behind her, I run my fingers over her cunt and feel how wet she is. "That's my girl," I say. "You're dripping, doll face."

Mumbling around her open-mouth gag, she pushes her ass against me, and I chuckle. "Don't stop writing, Charlotte. No matter what. Understand?"

"Mm-hmm." She nods her head, and I unzip my jeans, pulling out my hard dick.

I rub the tip of my pierced cock against her pussy. Her entire body stiffens, and her hand pauses on the paper. "Keep writing," I order, and the pencil slowly moves across the paper once again.

Pushing the tip into her pussy, she drops the pencil altogether and tries to crawl away from me. I reach out, grabbing the top of her head and digging my hand into her hair, not caring that it pulls on the leather strap that holds the gag in her mouth.

She cries out, spit flying from her mouth. The room fills with her heavy breathing and mumbled protests.

"It's okay, doll face," I say, grabbing my cock with my free hand once again and guiding it into her. "I'm going to fuck your cunt, Annabelle. You're my dirty little whore, and whores get used." My eyes drop to her pussy, and I push my hips forward, my cock forcing its way where no other dick has ever been.

I've thought long and hard about her punishment for her betrayal, and taking her virginity was the only option that fit the crime. She said she was saving it for her Lord. That'll no longer be an option for her.

Her cries grow louder as I sink into her balls deep. Using my hand still in her hair, I tilt her head down and order, "Keep writing." I slap my name where it's branded on her ass, and her already tight cunt clenches around my pierced dick. I grind my teeth to keep from moaning.

She picks up the pencil with a shaking hand and starts up again, and I begin to move. Pulling out, I slam into her. Her crying makes me smile. I release her hair and grip both of her hips, pulling her ass farther up into the air as I pull out and slam forward.

I do it again. And again.

She's sobbing, tears and drool falling onto the paper, and her handwriting is barely legible as I fuck her virgin pussy.

"Fuck, doll face. Feel how wet you are for me?" I pull out and see the first sight of blood. "Aw, that's a good girl—bleeding all over my cock," I tell her over her cries. I wasn't sure she would, considering I've fingered her, and who knows how rough she's played with herself. "I want you to remember this." I slam into her pussy, lean over and wrap my hand around her neck, forcing her head up with my left and take a picture of us with my right. Then I drop my phone to the floor and whisper in her ear, "How's it feel to be my whore, doll face? To know that I'm the first one to fuck every hole you have?"

She's gasping, her small body shaking underneath me. It has my cock twitching inside her.

I sit up, spread her ass cheeks, and let spit fall from my lips. Her gagging makes me laugh. I run my thumb over her ass and push it into her as my hips continue to rock back and forth, slamming into her bleeding cunt. She's so fucking tight.

I groan, throwing my head back. "Gooooddddammmn, Charlotte." It's been a long time since I've fucked a virgin. When you pay for sex, you're paying for experience. Pussy also isn't my first choice when you can have any hole you want. Again, money gives you options. "That's it..." My breath catches when her hips rock back and forth. "Fuck me, beautiful. Show me that you like my cock inside you."

She's sobbing, her head down, and the pencil nowhere to be seen. I let it go for now. Her punishment is bleeding, not writing nonsense.

"Fuck my bloody dick, doll face," I say, stilling inside her.

Slowly, she rocks back and forth, body trembling, but her bleeding pussy is dripping wet.

I lean over and grab her arms, bringing them behind her back, placing them parallel and holding them in place with one hand while the other tangles in her hair, holding the side of her face down onto the drool-covered notebook. I start to fuck her, enjoying the sounds her gagged mouth makes as she comes all over my dick.

Shhh...

Chapter 39

Charlotte

I enter the restaurant and see my friends sitting in a booth. I fall into it next to Hannah.

They are already mid-conversation, and I stare at the salt and pepper on the table. My mind is still on Haidyn and what we did last night. He used my laptop against me and then took it with him when he left. He deleted the email he threatened me with, but now what?

I was supposed to be saving myself for marriage, and he just took it. My mother promised my virginity to a Lord. What does that mean for me now? Should I have taken my chances with the Lords at the cathedral? They would have just lined up to fuck me too.

They did tell me to give Haidyn whatever he wanted. So maybe my mother will understand that my assignment is more important than my future husband. I mean, I'm supposed to be high up. Not just because I marry someone who is important but because *I* am important.

"Earth to Anna?"

I blink, looking up at Hannah, and she's rubbing her huge belly. They didn't know I was going out of town. When I woke up this morning, I needed to get out of my house, so I called both of them up because it had been too long since I saw them. "What?" I ask.

She laughs softly. "Where have you been?"

I don't have an answer to that. Haidyn has kept my mind occupied, so I didn't think to come up with answers to questions they may ask me. "What do you all know about the Spade brothers?" I decide on.

They both go silent, and Hannah's smile drops off her face. She leans forward, lowering her voice as if someone is listening to our conversation. Honestly, at this point, I wouldn't be surprised. "Stay away from them."

It just makes me more interested in what she knows. "I don't know them." I shrug, playing it off. "I overheard my mother talking about them the other day, and it got me curious," I lie.

"Do you remember those women who went missing like four years ago?" Margaret asks.

I frown but vaguely remember. "Not really."

"Not this again." Hannah rolls her eyes.

"What about them?" I ask.

Margaret looks over at me. "Well, the rumor was that one of the Spade brothers was the one kidnapping and killing them."

I get a sickening feeling in my gut. "Which one?"

"Adam," she answers.

I frown. "Who is Adam?" All I know of is Saint, Kashton, and Haidyn.

"They say that's why he ran." She takes a sip of her drink, ignoring my previous question.

Hannah picks up her cell to read a text when it beeps, alerting her of an incoming text. "Lords don't run because they kill someone." She snorts. "Otherwise, he would have never made it as far as he did in our world."

"He ran because he fucked up, and the police were on to him," Margaret argues.

"The Lords are above the law." Hannah laughs, typing away a response. "Trust me, he didn't run." She places her cell down and looks at Margaret. "He was killed by another Lord, and they made up some shit story to cover it up because he was a Spade brother."

"Maybe his *brothers* fucked him over, and he's at Carnage but as a prisoner," Margaret offers.

"Who is Adam?" I ask again, needing to know who the fuck this missing Spade brother is.

Hannah looks at me. "Adam Price. His sister was Saint's chosen."

"Ashtyn?" I question. "She had a brother?" There were four guys in that one picture that the Lords sent me before I started my initiation. I didn't pay that much attention to it, though. Maybe he's the fourth guy. I don't remember finding anything about her having a brother while doing research on Haidyn, but then again, if the Lords took care of him, they could have wiped his existence.

"A twin," Hannah corrects me.

"I think he killed her too." Margaret nods. "He was going down for kidnapping and killing all those women, and his sister caught him, so he got rid of her and their mother. That's why I think Adam is a prisoner at Carnage." Hannah snorts, thinking Margaret's theory is absurd. "Because the brothers were obsessed with Ashtyn. Especially Saint. When Adam got rid of her, they took him prisoner."

I sit back and nibble on my inner cheek. Well, I know their theories are not true because I've seen Ashtyn alive and well. Not sure about the Adam part, but he sure as fuck didn't kill his sister.

"Do you remember Sierra Ronan?" Margaret looks at me.

"The name sounds familiar," I say, but I can't place it.

"She was Haidyn's chosen their senior year. The word was she hated Ashtyn because she was sleeping with both Haidyn and Kashton, and when Haidyn found out, he shared his chosen with another Lord."

Now I remember where I heard it from—the email the Lords sent me with Haidyn's information.

"Hooke," Hannah offers, nodding. "It all went down one night at the house of Lords."

I was never allowed to go to the house of Lords, but rumors traveled all over Barrington about what went on there. My mother said it was no place for someone like me to hang out. I never really understood what she meant, considering we were part of that world. I just figured she wanted me to stay away from temptation. All they ever said went down at the house of Lords were orgies. Lords passing girls around like joints at a party. What she doesn't understand is that happens anywhere you go these days. But it wouldn't have mattered if I was able to go there or not, I wasn't in the same grade as the Spade brothers.

"Hooke fucked her mouth right there in front of everyone while he sat on the couch," Margaret adds.

"What ever happened to her?" Hannah wonders.

Margaret shrugs. "No clue."

I sit back in my seat and let out a huff. That doesn't really answer anything that I was wondering about, but it does tell me that Ashtyn being alive is not public knowledge, and she has a twin brother who is still MIA.

♠

"Mom?" I call out, entering my childhood home. "Mother?"

"I'm in here, darling," she answers faintly down the hall. I enter Bill's office to see her going through some papers on his desk. Her best friend is standing next to her, but I ignore Anne. I came here for a reason. "I'd love to chat, dear, but me and Bill have plans with friends." She pauses and looks up at me frowning. "When did you get back from your vacation?"

"Why am I not married yet?" I get to the point, ignoring her question.

I forgot I'm supposed to still be away. Which also reminds me that I need to touch base with Wesley. He has a key to my house. Wouldn't that be humiliating if he walked in, and I was on all fours while Haidyn fucked my ass?

She drops the papers and stands to her full height. "Anna—"

"I want to know." I interrupt her. I'm not a child anymore. I deserve to know where my life is going that she is planning for me.

Anne clears her throat, and my mom looks at her. It's as if they've had this conversation and her friend warned her, I'd one day have questions.

My mother sighs. "It's not black and white. It never is with the Lords. When I feel you're ready, I'll let you know."

Her answer pisses me off. I've proven to her over the past few years that I can make it in our world. Why keep my future a secret from me? "I had sex," I tell her. She's going to find out eventually when I'm handed to my Lord, and he expects me to be a virgin.

"What do you mean you had sex?" she asks slowly.

"Haidyn fucked me—"

She slaps me across the face, cutting me off. My head whips to the side, and I gasp at the sting on my cheek. She's never hit me before. "Do you understand what you've done?" she screeches.

"The Lords told me to do whatever he wants," I rush out, the tears stinging my eyes from the lingering pain.

"They did?" she asks skeptically.

"Yes," I say through gritted teeth, rubbing my cheek.

"Interesting. I'll call Dr. Lennon and have you put on birth control immediately. In the meantime, I'll have Sally get you the morning after pill." She picks up my stepfather's phone on his desk and begins to dial when I speak.

"I'm already on it."

She eyes me up and down with her hand paused on the phone. "How?"

"He had Gavin put me on the shot."

"Well...that's good at least." She hangs up the phone and runs a hand over her perfectly curled hair. Not really touching it, more of a nervous habit. "I mean it's not really a concern I guess since he wouldn't want to knock you up."

The way she says it makes me want to ask why not, but I don't want her to think I'm trying to get pregnant, so I word it carefully. "Lords need to reproduce." I mean, the Spade brothers are out of Barrington. They should have already settled down and had two or three kids by now. But the email the Lords sent me didn't show him having a Lady. It had said denied. Do they know something that I don't? If he did kill their fathers, is that his punishment? Not to get to have children?

"They were all going to breed with Ashtyn." Anne is the one who speaks.

I don't like the way she says the word *breed*. "She's dead," I challenge. "One of them was her twin brother." That I just found out at lunch. "So...not all of them. Plus, even if she didn't have one with her twin, that would end up making them incest down the line. If she had a girl with one and a boy with another, and those two got together when they were supposed to take over," I blabber, trying to do the math in my head.

Anne laughs. "There are ways to control the sex of the children. If the three Spade brothers each knocked her up with girls, then they would be given to high-ranking Lords after graduation. A new line of Spade brothers would be brought into Carnage to take over." She waves her hand in the air.

"But none of them have kids now." I dig.

"Of course not. Things changed for them when Ash and her brother, Adam, disappeared on them. Their fathers were killed, and their rules...were bent," Anne states.

I frown, not knowing what she means by that but not asking any further. I've heard enough for one day, and my face now throbs. I want a bottle of wine and bed. I look at my mother who stands silently next to her friend. "You still haven't answered my question on who I'm supposed to marry." I circle back around to that. I'm not leaving until I get an answer.

"I don't know—"

"Bullshit!" I shout.

She goes to slap me again, but a hand wraps around her wrist, stopping her. "Give us the room," my stepfather demands.

"Bill—"

"Now," he barks, making her jump. I've never seen him raise his voice to her before.

"We need to leave in ten." With that, she huffs and rushes out with her best friend, slamming the door behind her.

He walks over to his desk that sits in front of the large floor-to-ceiling windows and lights up a cigar. Then he pours two glasses of brandy, offering me one. I shake my head, mumbling, "No thanks."

He nods and sets it on his desk. "A Lord wakes up every day prepared for it to be his last."

I frown. "Meaning?"

"Meaning your father had strict instructions left for me when I was gifted your mother."

I swallow nervously. "What...what were they?" Bill and I get along, but we've never been close, and we sure as fuck have never spoken about my future or my father.

"You were to marry a Lord by the name of Winston Garvey."

Annabelle Garvey...I don't love it. "When?" I ask, not really sure I want to know. Once you have a date, the clock starts ticking. It makes me think of Haidyn's hourglass that he always seems to have with him.

"Well, by your father's orders, over a year ago."

I frown. "Then why haven't we been forced to wed?" Maybe the Lord is refusing me. There are cases when those assigned a Lady end up picking someone else.

"He's not available as of right now."

"I don't understand." Dear God, I hope he's not seventy years old and married, and they're just waiting for his wife to die first. I never stopped and took the time to think that he wouldn't be around my age.

He sighs, taking a puff from his cigar. "I keep in touch with his father...We play golf together."

I stay silent because I'm not sure why that's important.

"But he recently got into some trouble and well..." His eyes meet mine. "He's currently away."

"By *away*, you mean backpacking through Europe, right?" I joke, but he doesn't laugh. He just stares up at me, and I run a hand through my hair. I'm fucking tired, my body sore as fuck, and I don't know if I should scream or drink myself into a coma. "You said we were supposed to get married a year ago, but you just said he's currently away. Is he on an assignment?" Lords start doing assignments after they graduate from Barrington, so an assignment makes sense. Some take a long time to complete, depending on what they have to do. Case in point—my current situation in life. Who knows when mine will be completed.

"Think something more permanent," he answers.

The way he says it makes my stomach drop. I stand, walking to his desk. "You mean he's at Carnage."

He says nothing.

"But Carnage is like death row. You don't get taken to Carnage and then released, so...I just never get married?"

"You don't need a Lord to be powerful, Anna." His eyes drop to glance between my legs, and I take a step back from his desk nervously.

"You overheard our fight." It's not a question. He knows I'm no longer a virgin. *Great!*

"Your conversation, yes."

I snort. That was not a conversation. "She's stubborn."

"She wants what's best for you," he counters and stands from his desk. "Your mother knows where you belong in our world, and she wants to make sure you're given every opportunity to get there."

My eyes widen. "Wait. Are you saying the reason my assignment is Haidyn is because my future Lord is a prisoner there? My mother has something to do with it?" It would make sense. That's why they want me on the inside, and they haven't given me much to do when it comes to Haidyn. Maybe he's just my in to their hell.

He shakes his head. "Your mother doesn't have power over what you do and don't do when it comes to initiations or assignments."

"Then why Haidyn? Why Carnage? It has to be connected, right?" Finally, I feel like I'm getting a little bit of information, but it's only leaving me with more questions.

Bill shrugs. "I can't tell you that because no one knows why the Lords pick what they do for initiations or assignments. But I will say they always have a purpose."

HAIDYN

I SIT AT MY DESK BACK AT MY HOUSE. I'VE BEEN FIDGETY ALL DAY, so I went for a ride and worked out. When neither helped my sour mood, I found myself here, where I've been for the last three hours.

The papers that Adam gave me about the true identity of Charlotte and all the pictures with Ashtyn that I was given when in Vegas are burning in the fireplace to my left. Saint knows where I live, which means it won't be long before Kashton shows up at my door as well. I had to destroy them. I don't want anyone able to find a paper trail that will lead to who she really is.

The hourglass sits in front of me on the wooden surface, the sand running through the center to fill up the bottom. It's a reminder that time never stops. No matter what you can control, time isn't one of them.

I have Charlotte pulled up on my monitor. She lies in her bed like every other night, naked. The clock on my screen shows it's a quarter to five in the morning. She's been tossing and turning all night. I'm keeping my girl awake.

She's frustrated and confused. *Good.* I want her second-guessing everything—even her existence.

I took the one thing she was supposed to be holding on to. Now what? Does she no longer matter? Will her Lord reject her? I want her to think that her future is no longer what she thought it would be.

I'm taking over everything in her life, including her body and mind. I own her. I've made her mine, and she will remain that way until I toss her to the side like a used-up whore that no respectable Lord will want. Which, if I have my way, will be years down the road. Why would I hand over something I've wanted for so long?

She's had my name branded on her ass for all but a week, and I've already taken over her life. I can tell I'm always on her mind. She even watches over her shoulder as if waiting for me to come out of the shadows, tie her down, and fuck her. Make her my dirty little whore who begs in the sweetest way for me to use her.

I love it. Precious and innocent Annabelle to needy slut Charlotte.

She lets out a moan, rolls over, and gives me her back on the monitor.

My eyes drop to the hourglass to see it's run out of time, and I flip it over. Then I pick up my cell, open my messages, and send a picture to her phone. Setting it down, I hear hers go off, and she huffs. Rolling over, she picks it up off her nightstand, and the light from the screen shines on her pretty face.

Her breathing picks up, and her nipples go hard when she sees what I sent her.

It's of her on her hands and knees. The open gag is shoved into her drooling mouth, and I'm behind her with my cock in her bloody cunt. Taking the one thing she had left to offer to our world.

Her face tightens, and she sits up, tossing her phone across the room. She lies back down, grabs a pillow, and places it over her head, letting out a muffled scream.

I smile to myself. Get frustrated, doll face. It just furthers my point that I own you.

My cell rings, and I pick it up to see it's an ***UNKNOWN*** number. I mute my computer and stand, turning to face the floor-to-ceiling windows overlooking the woods. "Hello?"

"Spade," the voice says into my ear. "That guy you're looking for was here in Vegas last night."

My teeth grind. "Then why are you just now calling me?"

"I didn't see him. We had an...issue this evening, and I had to check the cameras. The man in the picture you showed us was in the video."

"Was he involved?" I inquire.

"No. Just a guest walking through. I watched some other surveillance, and he was here for two hours. Played some blackjack and roulette."

"Alone?"

"Nope. He had a woman with him. But by the looks of her, I'd say he was paying for her time if you know what I mean."

I do. Well, that doesn't give me much to go on. "Thanks for letting me know."

"I'll forward you the surveillance. Just in case you can place the woman he's with, but other than that, I don't have anything to give you."

I wasn't going to ask for it, so I'm glad he offered. I know the Mason brothers aren't going to give more than they think you need. "Thanks, man. I owe you."

"Yes, you do." He hangs up, and I return to my screen.

Charlotte is no longer in bed. Instead, she stands in the kitchen with an open bottle of wine and a full glass. She stares down at her cell, looking at the picture of us I sent her as she absentmindedly pets Muffin, who lies sprawled out on the marble counter.

My cell informs me of an incoming email from the Mason brothers. I flip the hourglass over before I open it up.

Shhh...

Chapter 40

Charlotte

It's been three days since Haidyn took my virginity on my living room floor, and my body is still sore. Thankfully, my scheduled "me" day is today. It's exactly what I need.

Walking into the building, I turn my cell off, not wanting to be bothered. It's supposed to be relaxing.

The pretty redhead nurse smiles up at me. "Hello, Annabelle. We've got your room ready." She gestures to the hallway on the right. "You're in number five today."

"Thank you." I return her smile and make my way into the room.

I enter and sit down in the chair, getting comfortable.

The door opens, and my nurse enters. "Hello, Annabelle. How have you been?"

It's so weird to be called that. I have gotten used to being Charlotte. Every time Haidyn calls me Annabelle, it's so spiteful. "Good." I give her a fake smile, leaning back into the chair and closing my eyes. I need a facial, massage, and a night out with endless drinks with my girls. Yes. That sounds amazing. Maybe if I drink enough, it'll knock my ass out, and I'll get a good night's rest.

"Here is your drink...raspberry lemonade just like you like it."

My eyes open, and I take the cup from her, chugging it down. I didn't realize just how thirsty I was until now. Staying hydrated is important, especially if I want to keep up with Haidyn. "Thank you." I hand her the empty glass and close my eyes once again, getting comfortable. A nap sounds amazing.

♠

An hour later, I'm woken up by the nurse as she removes the heating pillow and IV from my arm. I already feel better, but of course that could have been the nap. I didn't mean to fall asleep, but I also couldn't stop it. She hands me a water this time, and just like the previous drink, I chug it down.

I get up off the chair and walk toward the door. Stepping out into the hallway, I bump into someone in my hurry to leave. "Oh, I'm so..." My words die off when I look up into a set of familiar eyes. "Oh, hey." I smile.

"Hello, Anna." He nods his head, returning the smile.

"What are you doing here?" I ask, tilting my head to look behind him to make sure he's alone. His chuckle tells me he knows exactly *who* I'm looking for.

He undoes his cuff links and starts rolling up his sleeve to show me a cotton swab and a single piece of tape. "Your mother has convinced me." He pushes his sleeve back down.

"Well...they do help," I say tightly.

He steps into me and takes my hands. "She means well, Annabelle. She just wants what's best for you. Have you spoken to her?"

I pull my hands from Bill and run them down my thighs nervously. "I'm ignoring her," I answer honestly because I'm sure he already knows. I haven't said anything to her since she slapped me in his office yesterday. For some, that wouldn't mean anything, but I always talk to my mother. There's nothing to say. I have to do what the Lords say, not what she thinks is right.

"Next time she calls, you'll answer." He didn't make it a command, but he also didn't ask.

Bill and I have always had an understanding. He's not my father, and I'm not his daughter. We've lived together without any problems, and I don't want to add any new drama to my life. Haidyn takes up enough of that time.

I nod. "Yes, sir." He smiles at me.

Making my way to the parking lot, I turn my cell back on and go to call Haidyn but stop myself. Why would I call him? What do I have to say? He spanked my ass with his belt like an unruly child while I was on all fours and gagged. Then he fucked my pussy while I wrote I'm Haidyn's dirty little whore in a notebook.

It was humiliating, yet I was so turned on. He got me off twice before he came inside me. A part of me knew it was going to happen. If he planned on only fucking my mouth and ass, he wouldn't have had Gavin put me on the shot. I just didn't think it'd be a punishment.

Then the bastard sent me a picture of it last night. As if I could forget that I'm his dirty little whore. Huffing, I set my phone in the cup holder and look up. My eyes catch sight of a black bike sitting at the back of the parking lot, and my hands fist. I saw it yesterday too while I was out but chose to ignore it. I will not let him ruin my *me* day.

HAIDYN

My cell rings, and I pick it up to see it's a picture of my newest toy on my screen. It's the same one I sent her of us in her living room. She just looked so pretty that I had to put it as her contact. I smile, answering her call.

"Hello, doll—"

"Quit fucking following me, Haidyn," she barks in greeting.

My smirk grows at her attitude. It just gives me another reason to spank her again as if I need one. "I don't know what you're talking about, Charlotte."

She huffs. "Cut the shit. You've been following me for two days now, and I'm over it."

I stand from my couch. My smile drops at her words, and I argue, "I have not."

"Haidyn." She growls my name. "I can see your black bike weaving in and out of traffic behind me."

"Where are you?" I demand.

"You tell me. You're the one who stuck a tracker in my neck."

"Charlotte," I snap, getting pissy now. "I've been home all day. I'm not following you right now. Where the fuck are you?"

"I'm not playing this game with you." She hangs up, and I call her back, but it goes to voicemail. She's turned her cell off.

"Goddammit," I hiss, pulling up the app on my phone. By the look of her current location and the direction she's moving, I'd say she's headed to her house.

Rushing into my garage, I grab the keys to my bike off the hook and speed to her place. I'm pulling into her driveway just as her garage door closes. Getting off, I unlock her front door and barge in. "Charlotte?" I bark out.

I find her standing in her kitchen, pouring a glass of wine. She turns to face me, her dark hair flipping her in the face. She places one arm across her chest, and the other one is bent, holding her glass to her lips. Arching a brow, she gives a soft laugh before taking a sip. "Wasn't following me, huh?"

"It wasn't me," I say through gritted teeth.

She takes another drink before she sets it down on the counter. "Yet here you are standing in my kitchen. You expect me to believe you made record time from your house to mine?" She rolls her pretty blue eyes at her own question.

I walk forward, closing the distance between us. "Who was it?" I demand.

"You." Her eyes narrow up at me.

"What were they driving?" I go on.

She huffs but indulges me. "*You* were on your bike."

I grab her arm and drag her toward the front door. "Haidyn?" she growls, and I pull her through the front door and turn her to face her driveway, where I've parked.

"That bike?" I point at it as if we're in a parking lot with hundreds of vehicles. "How could I have been riding my black bike if I just rode this one from my house to yours?" I have multiple bikes. I chose to drive one that she didn't know I had. I was able to get here in half the time on my white ZX-10R by breaking the law and lane splitting.

I feel her body stiffen against mine as she stares at it. Her breathing picks up, and I grab her shoulders, turning her to face me. Her blue eyes look up at mine, and the color has drained from her face. "You said it was following you yesterday and today?"

She nods slowly and wraps her arms around her chest.

Pulling her back into the house, I shut the door and ask, "Where all did you go?" I could look up her location, but she needs to tell me. I spent too much time going over the surveillance from the Mason brothers of the mystery man I received to watch her.

Her eyes drop to the floor, and her brows pull together as she thinks. "Yesterday, I met with my friends for an early lunch—"

"Which friends?" She lives two lives, and I need to know who she was pretending to be. "Do they know you as Annabelle or Charlotte?"

"Annabelle," she answers softly.

I nod. "Keep going."

"After that, I went to my mother's."

"Straight from lunch?"

"Yeah."

"When was the first time you noticed them?"

She finally looks back up at me again to answer. "I saw them behind me on my way to lunch. Then I noticed them again today while I was at the spa."

"What were they doing? Just sitting on the bike outside of the restaurant yesterday?"

She shakes her head. "It was just the bike. When I left, it was gone, but I saw it on the highway. Then again after I left my mother's."

"And today at the spa?"

"They were sitting on it at the back of the parking lot, wearing a leather jacket, gloves, and a helmet."

I run a hand down my face, releasing a sigh. Why would someone be watching her? Maybe it's Saint thinking he's keeping an eye on me? No. He wouldn't do that. Saint doesn't hide. Plus, he showed up at my house, so he knows where to find me if he needs me. "Pack a bag," I order.

"Haidyn?" Her wide eyes meet mine. "I can't—"

"You're not staying here." I stop whatever argument she was about to give me. "I can't watch you twenty-four seven, and I'm not staying here with you." I have cameras in her house, but I can't control when she leaves the house or where she goes. The only thing a tracker is going to do is tell me where she's been taken. If someone is following her, it will only take them a second to snatch her. I saw that happen with Ashtyn at Carnage after our car wreck, and we were all unprepared. That was when there were three of us watching her. I'm the only one watching over Charlotte. Plus, they can cut it out in a few seconds. "Now." I grab her shoulders, spin her around, and add, "If you're not packed and ready to go in thirty minutes, I'll drag you out of this house with whatever you have on."

Shhh...

Chapter 41

Charlotte

I'm sitting at a stoplight with my windows cracked. My three packed bags are in the back while Muffin is in the passenger seat meowing in her carrier. She hates the car.

"I know," I say, looking over at her yellow eyes. "It'll be okay." A part of me hopes she poops on Haidyn's pillow tonight since he's practically making me move in with him.

So much for my me day. This is not how I saw my day going. I thought I was doing something by calling Haidyn out for following me. My eyes look at the rearview mirror to see him on his bike behind me in the turning lane.

The pictures that the Lords sent me didn't do him justice. Or maybe it's because I know what he's capable of now in the bedroom.

He's got his left boot on the gear, his right one on the pavement, and his tatted hands rest on his jean-clad thighs. He's got a white baseball hat on backward and wears black aviators.

Goddamn! My body heats as if he's staring right at me. He probably is. Men get off on that. Being admired. He probably set this whole thing up and paid someone to follow me, knowing I'd call him, and he'd come running in and save the day. Or at the very least to force me out of my home. Either way, this has a Lord written all over it. I know how they work, and I wasn't born yesterday.

A topless red Jeep pulls up next to me at the light, and I take a quick look. It's occupied with four girls. The one in the passenger seat stands up and spins around, looking right at Haidyn. "You can ride us." She immediately falls into her seat and covers her face, and her friends laugh as if it were a dare.

My hands tighten on the steering wheel, and I adjust myself. My eyes quickly go to him, and he chooses to ignore her. I have the urge to roll down my passenger window the rest of the way and call out *you can't handle him* but refrain. They look like high school girls, for Christ's sake.

Glaring at them, I hope they feel my stare through my sunglasses. I adjust my eyes ahead of me just as the light turns green. I slam on the gas and turn a little too sharp. Muffin meows as her carrier hits the interior door. "Sorry." I reach over to adjust it upright and fix my glasses, letting out a huff.

The thought of being jealous makes me frown. I've never belonged to anyone before. Is this what it feels like not to want to share what's yours? I mean, a lot of women have had him, but it's my turn, even if I have to act like I don't want it. Or for how little time it will last. If someone gets his attention, he'll push me to the side, and I just can't allow that. Not until I've finished my assignment.

My eyes shoot to him again in the rearview mirror as he rides behind me. His right hand on the throttle and left resting on his thigh. He looks relaxed. Much more than I am. But those who are in charge never worry.

He's taking me to his house. I can't decide if that's better or worse than Carnage. At least I know others live at Carnage. At his house, it'll just be him and me. He can do whatever he wants to me, and no one will hear me scream or know to look for me there.

It's the perfect plan to wipe me from this world. You don't need to worry about if the devil is real or not when you know the Lords exist.

I learned at a young age that you don't need a steel cage to be a prisoner. Sometimes all you need is to be left alone in a room by yourself with nothing but your own thoughts. You can drive yourself crazy all on your own. Or at least I know I can.

♠

I NOSE MY SUV UP TO HIS GATE SO HE CAN PULL UP BEHIND ME and press in the security code. Even though I know it. The gate opens, and I pull through and park in front of the garage. He parks next to me and walks to the back of the hatch as I pop it open.

He removes my three bags, and I grab the empty litter box and Muffin before following him into his house.

It feels...awkward. To be here knowing that I don't know when I'll leave. How long will he make me stay? How long will I want to be here?

I don't have the answer to either question. But then again, a prisoner doesn't get to choose how long they serve.

The gorgeous house feels as cold as his eyes look. And it lacks any color other than black and gray. It fits his dark and mysterious personality.

"Which room is mine?" I ask, stepping through the front doors he holds open for me.

"You're sleeping in my room. With me." His response is clipped.

I let out a nervous breath. I knew that was coming, but I just needed confirmation. He walks off the first hall to the right, and I follow him. He pushes the black double doors open to what I assume is his primary suite.

It looks every bit of what a man like Haidyn would have as a bedroom. It lacks any type of decoration. One entire wall is nothing but floor-to-ceiling windows. The dark and thick curtains are open, showing off the woods. His large Alaskan king-sized bed sits up on a platform. It too is covered in a black comforter and two matching pillows. Who the hell only has two pillows?

He enters the adjoining bathroom and returns without my bags. "There's plenty of room in the closet for your things," he tells me, walking over to me.

I take a step back from him, and he comes to a stop. "Did you do this yourself?" I arch a brow, needing to know.

"No." He scoffs as if that question is offensive.

I set down Muffin's carrier and open it up, letting her run free and out of the room. "So you expect me to believe you suddenly care for my safety?" I ask, exiting his room and heading to the kitchen to get Muffin a bowl of water.

His boots on the dark marble floor tell me that he's following. He has a couple of upper cabinets with glass doors, so I open the one with bowls. Looks expensive—crystal—and pick one out. Turning, I face the sink and him, turn on the water, and fill it up before placing it on the floor for Muffin. Then I give Haidyn my undivided attention.

He didn't answer my previous question, so I ask another. "Then why would you care? Are you jealous?" Even I laugh at that thought and continue to dig at his silence. "That another man might be interested in me?" The guy was fucking stalking me. I didn't imagine it.

He walks around the kitchen island, grips my hips, picks me up, and sets my ass on the cold surface. He shoves my knees open, standing between them, and cradles my face. His hands gently hold my jaw, forcing me to look up at him. "It's not about jealousy, doll face. It's about principle. You belong to me."

I snort even though the brand on my ass proves his point. "Tell that to my *boy toy*." That's what he called my fake boyfriend when Haidyn showed up at my house, announcing I had an appointment, and I told him I had dinner plans. The thought reminds me that I still need to text Wesley to let him know I'm at least alive on my made-up vacation.

He gives me a smile, one as cold as his voice. "We both know that boy toy hasn't touched you like I have."

My breathing becomes labored, and he continues.

"If you let another man touch you, I'll string him up and cut off his eyelids so he can't miss you crawling naked on your hands and knees to me. I'll fuck every hole you have, doll face, and let him see you whine and beg to be used like the whore I know you to be. Then after I'm done with you, I'll cut his dick off as well and force it down his throat because he will no longer have any use for it."

My eyes search his, looking for any kind of sign to tell me that he's joking, but all I see is a man who means every fucking word he says.

"Do you understand, Charlotte?" he demands.

Swallowing, I answer, "Y-yes."

"Whose little whore, are you?"

I hate the butterflies in my stomach at his command as I answer, "Yours."

"Good girl." He gently kisses my forehead. "I have work to do." He steps back like he didn't just go into detail about what he would do to another man who thought about me. "Make yourself at home." With that, he walks away leaving me alone as if he didn't just get me wet.

HAIDYN

I enter my office and shut the door, needing a moment to myself. My clothes smell like her, and now my house will too. But this was my only option. A part of me knows this was a setup, but the other part doesn't want to take the risk of being wrong. I've claimed her as mine, meaning I must protect her. She's mine to fuck, mine to ruin, and mine to use. I wasn't lying when I told her exactly what I would do to another man who thinks he can have what belongs to me.

I pull my cell out of my pocket and dial Adam.

"Hey, man."

"Charlotte is at the house," I inform him.

"Everything okay?" he asks, sounding concerned.

"Long story short, she was being followed."

"Need me to run some plates?"

"No. Didn't get a look at them."

He's silent for a second. "Okay. Is there anything I can do?"

Not this time. "Just wanted to let you know I'm not at the house alone. Were you able to find anything out about her being arrested?"

"Nope. Nothing." He pauses for a second. "You think she might have lied to you about it?"

"She couldn't have," I inform him.

"Got it," he says in understanding. "I'll keep digging and let you know what I find."

We say our goodbyes, and I exit the office, going to look for her. I have her right where I want her. In my house, under my roof, she'll sleep in my bed. Instead of watching her on my computer, I can just walk into my room and see her naked. It's like handing candy to a baby. Even I can see the red flags, but I can't not take advantage of them.

I find her on the second story by the railing, staring down into the living room and open kitchen.

I walk up next to her and watch her sigh when she notices me out of the corner of her eye.

"Did you buy this house, or was it your parents?" she inquires.

"You tell me," I counter. I never asked her how she knew where I lived when I taped her to the chair in her kitchen, but I didn't have to. I know how she knew. Only one other person knows I have this house, but she hasn't been here in years.

Charlotte huffs, then pushes off the railing and turns her back to walk away.

"I bought it." I decide to answer. I don't need her to be happy with me. I'm still going to get what I want out of her, but it can't hurt.

Stopping, she turns back to look at me but says nothing, so I continue. "A contractor built it for his wife."

She frowns. "Then why did he sell it?"

"He caught her cheating with his business partner. He beat him to death."

Stepping back over to the railing, she asks, "And his wife...what did he do to her?"

"He dragged her to the cathedral, tied her down, and offered her to the Lords."

She snorts. "Of course he did. Did she survive?"

"No."

Her hands wrap around the metal as she stares out the floor-to-ceiling windows for a long second. "When a Lord dies, his Lady is regifted."

For some. My brothers and I are different. "Yes," I decide to say even though it wasn't a question.

"What happens to a Lord when his Lady dies?"

"He gets a new one."

"So..." She swallows. "You're saying that he killed his business partner and then allowed other Lords to torture his wife before they killed her? And the Lords still rewarded him with another wife?"

"Yes."

She gives a rough laugh. "And let me guess, she was younger and prettier."

I say nothing.

"Was she a virgin too?" Her laughter grows, but when her eyes meet mine, she squares her shoulders. "Unbelievable, but not surprised." Her eyes slowly run up and down my body with disgust before she adds, "You guys get treated like fucking royalty because you have a dick. While those of us with tits should be rewarded for not stabbing you bastards while you sleep." With that, she spins around, and pieces of her hair slaps me in the face before she storms down the stairs.

Moments later, I hear a door slam, and I'm guessing she's in my bedroom. I could go in there, strip her naked, force her to crawl to me, and fuck her until she can't speak. But I won't. I'll save that for later.

Instead, I return to my office downstairs and review the security cameras I have at her house. I go back over the past month. I see myself walking right in her front door while she's sleeping in bed. I make my way down to her basement, where I spent several days getting it ready.

Then I fast-forward through some of it. I rewind here and there, trying to find any kind of hint about who the hell might have been following her today. But no bike other than mine even drives by her place. Plus, a code is required to access her driveway.

I should have put cameras on her SUV. I thought the tracker would be enough.

Three hours later, my head hurts, and I rub my heavy eyes. I turn off my computer and get up. Walking over to the minibar, I pour myself a glass of bourbon, needing something a little extra tonight besides a cigarette. Exiting my office, I stop when the smell of food hits my nose.

I walk down the hall to see the dining room table set for two. She's standing in the kitchen. Her eyes meet mine before they drop to the floor. "I thought you might be hungry," she says softly.

"Starving," I tell her, and she smiles, her eyes meeting mine once again.

"I hope you like Italian."

"I do."

She picks up two plates and walks over to the table, setting them down. "I had to substitute a couple of things, but for the most part, you had what I needed."

"Smells delicious."

She makes her way back to the wine fridge and pops open one, pouring herself a glass to the rim. Then she carries the bottle over to the table with her. Sitting down, she brings the glass to her lips and sucks it down until it's empty. As if she needs the liquid courage to sit through dinner with me. She will need way more than that to sleep in my bed.

When she picks up the wine bottle and goes to refill it, I pick up the glass, causing the wine to spill onto the table and floor. "What the hell?" she barks, glaring up at me.

"One glass is enough," I tell her.

"Haidyn," she growls, and it's so cute.

"After dinner, you're going to undress yourself, and I'm going to tie you to my bed." Her eyes widen at my words. "I'm going to gag you, and I'd prefer you not to be so drunk that you choke on your vomit. But if that's the way you want to go..." I shrug. "That's on you." With that, I pick up my bourbon.

She straightens out her arm, putting the wine bottle as far away from her as possible, and I don't even try to hide my smile.

Shhh...

Chapter 42

Charlotte

He's finished with his dinner, and I pick up his plate along with mine. I didn't even take a single bite. I thought I was hungry, but after he spoke to me about what *I'm* going to do, I no longer wanted pasta. I wanted him.

I'm placing the dishes in the sink when he picks up his bourbon and downs what's left. He sets the now empty glass in the sink as well and shuts off the water. "Leave them," he orders and then walks toward his bedroom.

I follow like a devoted puppy, knowing what's going to happen next. Entering his room, he tells me, "Everything off the bed except for the fitted sheet, and then undress yourself." He slips into his bathroom, and I take in a shaky breath.

I do as I'm told, putting the linens over in the far corner, then remove the two pillows and set them in front of the sliding glass doors that lead out onto the wraparound porch. I slowly toe off my shoes, then remove my socks and unzip my jeans. My breathing is so heavy that I don't even hear him returning from the bathroom.

My eyes drop to both of his hands, and he's got black leather belts in them. Two in each.

"Lie on the bed. Face up." His voice is cold and detached.

Although I'm already half naked, I'm burning up. Quickly removing my shirt and bra, I do as I'm told and lie down in the bed, swallowing nervously as I stare at the dark ceiling.

He sits down next to me and lays my left arm across his thigh. Dropping three belts on the bed, he keeps the fourth one and wraps it around my wrist, buckling it tight enough I can't slip my hand through it. Then he hooks his finger through the silver ring and moves it to where it lies against the top of my hand. He then does the same to the right.

"Arms out to your sides."

Taking in a shaky breath, I run my arms along the cool fitted sheet and fan them both out. He stands and kneels next to the bed, and I lift my head just enough to see him pulling the rope out from under the bed and threading it through the silver ring connected to the leather cuff, securing it to the bed frame. He repeats the process with the other.

He ties them tight, pulling my shoulders, and I arch my neck, biting my lip, not wanting to moan at being at his mercy. I fucking hate him so goddamn much I want to scream, and he knows it. That's probably why he wants to gag me.

Opening the nightstand, he removes a few things, but I can't see what they are. He gets onto the bed, spreading my shaking legs with his knees, and then his hand is on my pussy, making me jump.

His chuckle fills the room. "Relax, doll face."

I want to cry, but I'm not sure why. It can't be from embarrassment; the man has seen every inch of me. Maybe it's knowing how helpless I am and that he's going to make me beg for the slightest touch or to get off.

He slides something under my ass, and I feel liquid being poured between my legs. His fingers are there, rubbing the spot where I want him the most.

I arch my neck and close my eyes. He slaps my pussy, making me gasp, and demands, "Eyes on me, doll face."

His fingers slide down to my ass, and he shoves my legs to my chest, making it hard to breathe. His finger pushes its way into me, and I begin to shake. Pulling it out, he does it again, and I tense.

"Breathe, Charlotte," he orders. "This isn't a punishment, doll face. It's not going to hurt."

I let out a shaky breath.

"That's it." His fingers begin to move again. "In...out...in...out." His finger pumps in and out of my ass while he talks me through my breathing.

I don't even realize I moan until he speaks again. "That's my girl."

I slump when it disappears, already ready to beg for his dick, when I feel something bigger pushing its way into my ass, and I cry out at the burning sensation.

"You're okay, Charlotte. Just relax. It's going to feel good. You're going to be coming all over yourself for me like a good whore."

I suck in a deep breath and whimper as it stretches my ass. Sweat beads across my body.

There's another painful sting before he says, "It's in." He gets off the bed, opens the nightstand once more, and begins to rip off a piece of white tape. I suck in one last deep breath before he places it over my lips. He then rips off a second piece and a third piece. He takes his time placing each piece over the other covering more of my face from my chin up to under my nose and my cheeks as well.

My body fights the restraints, and my pussy clenches.

His eyes search mine, and I look away as my body heats. His hands grip my neck, pinning it to the bed and holding me in place. My wide eyes meet his. "I told you, doll face. I'm going to do a lot of things to you."

I blink rapidly. How could I forget? Letting go of my neck, he trails his fingers over the tape, and the blood rushes in my ears as I pull on my arms, wanting to touch him. I moan in frustration, and he laughs, knowing exactly what I want.

His hands make their way to my pussy, and I lift my hips, spreading my legs wide for him like the good girl he wants me to be. He shoves two deep inside me, making me buck.

"You're so wet, Charlotte. I knew you'd be this way."

I hate how right he is.

"Begging to be used, needing to be fucked." He enters a third, and I close my legs, and he shakes his head in disappointment. I'm still so sore.

"Let's finish getting you dressed." He removes his hands, and I slump into the bed. He places my left ankle in the cuff, yanks it toward the corner end of the bed, and ties it off like my wrist. And then does the same with the right. My legs are spread wide open, and my arms are straight out to my sides. I feel like I'm being ripped apart, and my pussy is wet and ass full. My body likes the fight.

"One more thing," he says, and then he's pushing something new into my pussy that's not his fingers. It hurts, making me cry into the tape.

"It's in, doll face," he says, and I groan at how full I feel. I try to wiggle my hips, move my legs, and do anything to get friction between them, but he's tied me too tight. The leather digs into my wrists and ankles.

He picks up his phone off the side of the bed, and then I scream into the tape, my body stiffening as my breath gets caught in my lungs.

He leans over, cupping my face. "The butt plug in your ass is now fucking you, doll face."

I can feel it. I don't know how it's doing it, but it's going deeper and deeper with each thrust as if he's between my tied legs.

"And this..." He looks back at his cell, and I feel a vibration that has my eyes closing. "The vibrator in your cunt is hitting your G-spot."

My body convulses, pulling on the ropes. My skin grows hot, and my heart pounds.

"It's okay, doll face." He runs his hand through my hair. "I want you to get off. I told you this isn't a punishment."

Fuck...I'm there. My back bows, and my eyes fall closed, and my pussy clenches on the toy shoved inside me while the butt plug fucks my ass.

I'm gasping through my nose when I open my heavy eyes and see his hovering. "That's one. You're going to count for me."

I shake my head, and he nods.

"Yes. Count each one."

Each one? How many is he going to make me have? I already feel it building again, my hands fisting.

"Ride it out," he says, his eyes searching mine. "Come on, doll face. Feel my cock in your ass fucking it."

His cock? I don't know...I groan, my heavy eyes falling closed while his hands play with my nipples. "That's it, Charlotte. Fuck, you're so goddamn pretty when you're coming."

I try to pull my legs closed as another wave washes over me, taking my breath away, and he smiles. "That's two." Leaning down, he kisses my sweat-covered forehead and orders, "Don't stop counting, doll face." Then he pulls away and is out of sight.

. . .

HAIDYN

I STAND IN THE SHOWER UNDER THE SPRAYER. MY HARD COCK IN one hand and the other on the wall. She's in the other room, tied to my bed coming all over herself. I wanted to give her a second—leaving her with her own thoughts. She's going to wear herself out fighting the inevitable. Her body betraying her. Nothing she can do will change the outcome that I want her to have.

She's my fuck toy.

My reward for doing everything the Lords have fucking wanted. This is why they gave her to me. Well…I know they'll want something in return. She's been placed in my life before, and I won't ignore her like last time. This time, I'm taking advantage of the gift they've given me.

My hand tightens on my cock, and I have to remind myself not to jack off. I'm going to come, but it's not in the shower alone. It's inside the beautiful brunette in the other room, squirming and begging for more.

Three years, we waited to get to fuck. And then it was taken away from us again.

Four years ago

"Don't come, Haidyn," the woman says, giving me a smile from her knees. "This is about endurance."

How the fuck can she think I'd come? My cock is in a fucking vise.

It tightens, and I throw my head back, grinding my teeth.

"Small pinch…"

FUCK! Pain shoots up my back and to my neck. It would paralyze me if I wasn't tied up.

"Looks good." She stands to her full height and slaps my cheek.

I suck in a ragged breath. "Your first one is done. We'll leave it in there for twenty-four hours," she says, and the chains keeping my arms above my head are released, and I drop to my knees on the concrete floor.

"This is part of your training, Haidyn," she says as if I fucking care. "Not only is it physical endurance, it's also mental."

They fed me breakfast this morning, and it had Viagra in it. By the time I realized it, it was too late.

"Sex is power." She goes on. "You have the dick; you control when and how it fucks. Women are only good for pleasing you and breeding."

I open my eyes and release my dick. Placing my forehead on the cold wall, I suck in a ragged breath. Lords are controlled by sex. It doesn't matter if you're a woman or a man, it's all the same. You either fuck or get fucked. It can go either way.

Turning off the water, I grab the towel off the hook and dry off. Letting it drop to the floor, I enter my bedroom to see her lying in the center where I left her. The sun has set, but I have the lights on in the room. Her eyes are closed, her chest heaving, and her body is shaking.

She's covered in sweat, and her hard nipples beg me to suck on them. Pinch them and slap them. Anything to get her to open her eyes.

I walk over to the side of the bed and grab each one, pulling on them with a tight grip.

Her heavy eyes slowly open and meet mine. Tears run down the side of her face. "How many times have you come for me, Charlotte?"

She just stares off into space.

"Three times?"

She gives me a faint nod.

"Four times?"

Another nod.

"Five times?" The moment the words leave my mouth her back bows and her eyes roll back into her head. I give her a second to come down before I tap the side of her face forcing her watery lashes to part and look at me. "I asked you a question, doll face."

A slow blink followed by a barely-there nod.

"That's a good girl. But I think six is a better number,"

She arches her neck and mumbles a sob into the tape.

"Let's make it seven," I say, pushing her further.

She's trembling in the restraints.

"I can't help myself," I tell her. "You're so pretty when you look like a mindless toy." Fresh tears fill her eyes and spill over the sides of her face.

Forced orgasm is a fine line to play with. The endorphins the orgasms alone release in the head can alter your perception. That's what I meant when I said mindless. She's lost all train of thought and bodily function. All she can do is lie here and ride it out. One after another. Until I decide she's had enough.

I reach out and remove the tape from her face, knowing she won't be able to hold a conversation. Her lips part, and her heavy breathing fills the room.

Her eyes start to roll back into her head, and I watch her hold her breath as another one hits. "Breathe, Charlotte," I order, slapping her inner thigh when she holds it longer than I like, and she lets out a breath and coughs.

"Don't pass out on me, doll face. If you do, I'll wait until you're awake and start from the beginning."

She just stares up at me through hooded eyes unable to form any words. "One more. Can you do that for me?" I reach between her spread legs and pull the vibrator free from her cunt. It's covered in her cum. I toss it to the floor and undo the rope from the ankle cuffs, leaving them on. I spread her legs and kneel between them. I lick my lips, ready to devour her cunt. I've been dreaming of getting to taste her. Sliding my arms under her shaking hips, I lift her ass off the bed a little. My hands grab her ribs, and I hold her in place while my mouth goes to her pussy.

It vibrates against my mouth from the fucking butt plug still in her ass. Slowly, I lick her pussy, moaning. She tastes like a glazed donut—warm and sweet.

She arches her back, her body continuing to fight my hold due to the forced orgasms. I move my lips to gently kiss her inner thigh. Her skin is so soft. "After you come on my face, doll face, I'll fuck you. And then you can go to bed," I tell her.

More mumbled nonsense comes from her parted lips, and I smile. Moving back to her cum-covered cunt, I devour her like she's a feast laid out for a starving man.

Her hips buck and her body convulses when I sit up between her trembling legs, licking her off my lips. I shove her legs open before sliding my painfully hard dick into her pussy, and I don't waste a second before I fuck her.

Leaning over her, I wrap a hand around her slender throat, pinning her to the mattress while I fuck her into my bed. Heavy eyes stare at mine while her pulse races and her chest heaves. "Can you give me one more, doll face?"

She blinks, and her lips move, but nothing comes out.

I smile. "Poor thing. You're too fucked to even speak." Pulling out, I slam forward, and a strangled moan escapes her lips. "Just one more, Charlotte, and then I'll let you go to sleep?"

Her lashes fall closed, and I let go of her neck to lightly slap the side of her face, forcing them open.

"Eyes on me," I order and pull out of her cunt, making her whimper. I shove two fingers into her, and she arches her back when I enter a third. "What are you going to give me, doll face?" I remove them and slap her pussy, making her body jerk involuntarily. Then I do it again, loving the way her arms pull on the restraints and her legs shake while wrapped around my hips. Tears spill from her heavy eyes, and I ask, "Come on, doll face. I know you have it in you. One more, okay?"

She nods, sniffling, and I smile, sliding my pierced cock back into her. "That's my girl."

My hand goes back to her arched neck, and I fuck her cunt while the vibrating butt plug continues to fuck her ass until I'm coming inside her. I give her exactly what she needs—a reminder that she belongs to me.

Shhh...

Chapter 43

Charlotte

I wake up and moan into the pillow. My body is so sore. Every muscle aches. "Fuck," I groan and sit up. Pushing my wild hair from my face, I look around his bedroom to find I'm alone. No surprise there.

I'm sore in places that I didn't even know existed. I have his handprints on my thighs and my hips where he held me down as if I went through an exorcism and he was trying to suck the demon out of me.

After using the bathroom, I walk through his closet. There's not a lot here, which tells me what I already knew—this isn't where he usually stays. The question is, why is he still hiding out here? Why hasn't he gone back to Carnage yet? Why hasn't he gone home?

I pull on a T-shirt of his and exit the primary suite, deciding not to wear anything of my own. The house is eerily quiet, which makes me nervous.

Padding my way to the kitchen, I look over the kitchen island and out into the open living room. The curtains are open, showing off the woods. It's a sunny day. The clock on the stove says it's almost noon. I'm not sure what time he was done with me or what time he finally allowed me to pass out, but I slept like a baby.

I open Muffin's food and pour it into her bowl, shaking it a little to get her attention.

Meow.

I step out of the kitchen and into the living room to look up at the balcony since I heard her come from up there. "Breakfast time," I say and then whistle. She meows again, but still, she doesn't come down the stairs. "Muffin? Come on, baby. Time to eat."

MEOW.

A cell ringing slices through the quiet house, and I look over at the end of a hallway when I hear Haidyn's voice. "What's up, man...yeah, I can be there. Okay." Then silence blankets the large house once again.

I debate walking over to the open door but think better of it. Instead, I take the stairs and look around for Muffin but don't see her anywhere. "Muffin?" I call out, and I hear her again opposite from the railing to the balcony.

Frowning, I walk over to a set of double doors and place my ear up against it, waiting for her to meow again. She's inside of the room.

Twisting the knobs, I push them open and step inside to see it's another bedroom. Large windows cover the opposite walls to show mountains and more woods. Muffin is laying on a bed, and when she sees me, she jumps up and runs out of the room. "How the fuck did you end up in here?" I wonder, turning to follow her out.

I squeal when I run into a hard and wet surface. "Jesus!" I place my hand on my racing chest when I look up into a set of green eyes.

He tilts his head to the side, his eyes dropping down to my bare feet and slowly run up my exposed legs and then my chest. I feel my nipples harden under Haidyn's T-shirt. I didn't think anyone else would be here. I wrap my arms around myself. At least his shirt is so big that it swallows me up, not leaving much to see.

"Why are you in my room?" His tone is as if he's accusing me of something.

"Why did you have my cat locked in here?" I counter.

He smirks, and I narrow my eyes on him. Something about him seems familiar. I just can't put my finger on it...

"What can I say...I attract pussy."

I roll my eyes and drop my arms. Typical Lord behavior. And the fact that all he has on is a towel wrapped around his narrow hips, allows me to see the Lords crest branded onto his chest. It's old...definitely been there for a while.

Exiting the room, I shoulder past him, and the doors shut behind me. I come to a stop when I see Haidyn standing by the balcony with a set of keys in his hands. His eyes go to the closed doors behind me before they meet mine.

"I'm leaving," he states. Before I can ask where he's going, he adds, "Don't leave this house." With that, he turns and walks down the stairs. I hear the door to the garage shut.

HAIDYN

I knew I couldn't keep Charlotte from running into Adam at the house, but I didn't think it'd happen this soon. A part of me likes that he's there. He'll protect her while I'm away. But the other part didn't like that she was standing in his bedroom dressed in nothing but my T-shirt while he was fresh out of the shower in a towel.

I watched him look her over as if she was some strange woman at a club, and he was trying to decide whether he wanted to take her home, tie her to his bed, and fuck her. That's what I get to do to my doll face. No one else.

But I know I can trust him. I bought that house our senior year for him. So he comes and goes as he pleases. He needed a place to hide when everything was going down and he was on the run. I thought I was doing something good for him but like always, someone is watching.

Four years ago

I'm driving down the road, the woman sits in my passenger seat, sequined mini skirt and matching bra with stripper heels—she's a prostitute that I just picked up on the corner. I really need to let off some steam, and the more you're willing to pay, the more they let you do whatever the fuck you want to them.

Pulling into my driveway, I open her door and enter the house. I flip the light and walk to the kitchen, pouring us both a glass of scotch when I hear the woman scream.

"What—?" I look up and my body tenses when I see a woman sitting on my couch that I hadn't noticed before. This can't be happening. "Get the fuck out," I bark, slamming the bottle down.

Her dark green eyes move to the half-dressed woman standing in my living room. "How much is he paying you, dear?"

"I said get the fuck out!" I walk around the island and over to her.

She reaches into her purse, pulls out an envelope, and stands. Holding out her hand, she speaks to the woman. "Here's ten grand, honey. Take the weekend off."

The door slams shut a moment later, and she smiles up at me. Sitting back down, she lets me know she's not going anywhere.

I run a hand through my hair, wanting a cigarette and my gun so I can blow her brains out. "How did you find me?"

"You've been caged for six months, Haidyn. The three of you scattered like fucking rats after you completed training. Saint is on the search for Ashtyn—he's got a lot of time to make up for. Kashton is probably out getting his dick sucked, just as you were about to get. It wasn't hard to find you. All I had to do was wait and follow you."

Jesus, there's no escaping her.

She tilts her head to the side in thought and asks, "Did you honestly think they wouldn't make you pay for killing them?"

I say nothing.

She stands, her fingers running across my chest, feeling my heart race. "It wasn't all bad, was it?"

"Fucking hell," I answer.

She laughs, and it makes my skin crawl, knowing what she's done to my brothers. I tried to take on as much of her punishment as I could to save them. But she knew that and didn't do them any favors. "Let me make it up to you."

"No thanks."

"They told me you'd be the hardest to break but also the first one to step up...take the fall so to speak." She grabs my arms and turns my hands over—palms up. Her eyes look over my recent scars from the suicide attempt that they accuse me of doing. I yank them out of her hold.

Her eyes meet mine. "Let's see how true that is." She pulls a manila envelope out of her purse and hands it to me.

I take it from her and rip it open, removing the content. It's a picture of Adam. He's in a hotel room. He's standing naked at the end of a bed. A woman lies on it, also naked with rope tying her hands to the headboard and a blindfold over her eyes. Her legs are spread wide as he admires cum leaking from her cunt. I toss it onto the coffee table and look up at her. "You of all people know what sex looks like." Giving her my back, I make my way back to the kitchen for that scotch.

"That was taken last night...in Vegas."

I come to a stop at the island and look up at her, my body trembling at her words. FUCK!

"He's on the run, right? I feel sorry for that poor innocent girl he killed."

My teeth grind. "He didn't do it." She's missing. No body has been recovered.

"I hear there's evidence that he did."

Shit. Shit. Shit. She's got me cornered. Again! Whatever she wants, I have to give her. Adam is in Vegas to watch over Ashtyn. Does she know they're both there or just Adam? I won't rat him out.

"What's it going to be, Haidyn? You...or Adam?"

I pick up the scotch and throw it across the room. It shatters when it hits the wall, and the scotch runs down it to pool on the black marble floor.

When my eyes meet hers again, she's giving me that smile that I've grown to hate so fucking much.

Shhh...

Chapter 44

Charlotte

I've been a prisoner at Haidyn's for a week now. Being his fuck toy isn't as bad as I originally thought it would be. I get fed three meals a day, provided with an endless amount of snacks, and am fucked senseless. What else can a girl ask for?

The Lords have been silent, and I'm starting to think it's because they know I'm no longer seeing Haidyn inside Carnage. My only question is what do they want me to do now? How long until they decide I'm failing my assignment and just take me out?

I'm uneasy, and Haidyn sees it. At least I'm able to blame it on the incident that led me to being his prisoner inside his home.

He's hidden my laptop because I haven't seen it anywhere in this house, and I've looked every chance I get—which isn't much. I swear the guy never sleeps. And he's only left that one time after finding me upstairs in the other man's bedroom.

I haven't heard one word from my mother, and I have this sinking feeling that I've failed her. I'm the only one who can carry on my father's legacy, and I can't even do that right.

I sent a few messages to Wesley. I told him I'm still away, which isn't a lie since I'm not allowed to go home right now. I sent him a few selfies and Photoshopped the background. I felt bad when he told me how gorgeous I looked and wished he could have joined me.

I'm lying in Haidyn's bed. Muffin is curled up on his pillow like she owns the place. She quite likes it here. She loves all of his windows and spends most of her days bird-watching and napping.

The door opens, and Haidyn enters. He's got a towel draped

around his shoulders with a T-shirt and sweatpants on. He's been working out in his home gym. It's part of his daily routine. Sometimes he's in there more than once. Without saying anything to me—doesn't even look my way—he enters the adjoining bathroom and shuts the door to shower.

Waiting for the shower to turn on, I pick up my other cell phone. I chose to leave my real one back at my house. This is the number that Haidyn knows. If he hears another phone going off, he'll start to question why I have two. He's already taken my laptop; I don't want him to know the Lords gave me this too.

Turning on the spare phone, I see it has an email. I open it up to see there's a video attached.

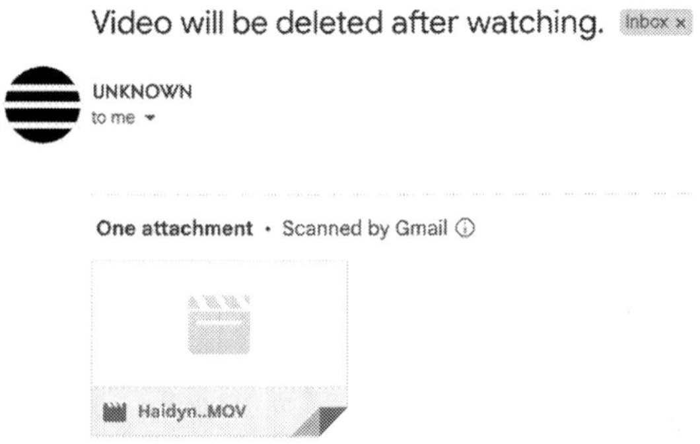

My eyes go to the closed bathroom door quickly before grabbing my earbuds out of my bag. I put one in and leave the other out. That way, I can hear when he's done in the shower.

I wonder if the Lords know he has my laptop. If they can monitor which device I access the emails from?

Getting back into bed, I sink down into it and pull the covers up and over the phone as I open it up and push play.

It's a concrete room. It reminds me of being in my basement, but I have no doubt that it's at Carnage. The camera is positioned high up in the corner, so it shows the entire room. The sound of a squeaky door opening has my eyes looking up at the bathroom door. It's still shut, and the shower is still running, so I drop my gaze back to the video on my phone.

Haidyn enters the room, pulling a gurney inside. Saint pushes the other end. A woman lies on it with duct tape from her jawline to right underneath her nose. A black tube sticking out the center of her mouth makes it possible for her to breathe, and a blanket covers her bottom half.

It's Ashtyn!

I sit up straighter in bed and once again check the door to the bathroom to make sure Haidyn hasn't finished. Then I go back to the screen.

They remove the blanket that covers her, and I gasp, slapping my hand over my mouth when I see she's strapped down to it. Her arms are secured in a straitjacket, and her legs are buckled to the bed. She screams behind the tape and thrashes in the bed that she's secured to.

The bed is adjusted into more of a sitting position, and the belt around her neck pulls tighter on her skin.

It's choking her.

Both Haidyn and Saint go over to the cabinets. "Adrenaline?" The sound of Haidyn's voice makes me jump.

"No," Saint answers. "I don't want to kill her. I'd prefer her to pass out."

What the fuck are they going to do to her? I thought they loved her? How long ago was this taken? A quick look tells me that it's old because neither one of them has any ink.

"And if she doesn't?" Haidyn asks, but his tone doesn't give off any concern. It's more like curiosity.

"She will. Her body won't be able to handle it."

Ashtyn yanks on her arms secured in the straitjacket and begins to choke as saliva shoots out from the black rubber breathing tube from underneath all the duct tape. Saint turns and walks over to her. She's naked from the waist down. He wipes her pelvic bone, and my heart hammers in my chest, wondering what they're going to make her endure.

My eyes go to Haidyn, and he hands Saint a branding iron with the Lords crest on it. "Take a deep breath, Ashtyn," Saint tells her.

"Are you sure?" Haidyn asks once again.

"No," Saint answers. "Go ahead and give her the adrenaline."

Ashtyn shakes her head, and her wide eyes go to Saint, pleading for him not to do it.

Haidyn walks over to the counter, opens a drawer, and fills a syringe from a clear vial. She's screaming into the tape as he walks back to them. Haidyn undoes the belt around her neck to the stretcher, and she goes to lean up, but he grips her taped face, tilts her head back, and pushes the needle into it. She instantly goes limp, and her eyes close.

Then the video goes dark. I close the email and open it again quickly, wanting to see more, but it's gone.

The shower turning off has me yanking the earbud out and shoving it along with my cell between the mattress and box spring.

I lie down and pull the covers up and over my face, praying that he thinks I've gone back to sleep so he won't find me all worked up and wonder why.

I close my eyes, trying to calm my breathing while wondering why the fuck the Lords would send me that. Why do they want me to see that? Haidyn was supposed to give her adrenaline, but it's obvious he didn't. He knocked her out because he didn't want her to go through the pain. Why?

He loves her. My mother's friend's words come back to me. For some reason, they had to brand her, and he couldn't bear to put her through that kind of pain.

The thought makes my Lords brand itch, and I slowly move my neck back and forth, trying to scratch it against the pillow. The one on my ass burns as well. I freeze when I hear the bathroom door finally open and hold my breath.

Seconds later, I hear him exit the bedroom, and I close my eyes, releasing my breath. Fuck. I feel like the Lords are trying to tell me something, but I'm not sure what it is. Or if I even want to know.

HAIDYN

My cell went off while I was in the shower, and it was a text.

SAINT: Come home please...she needs you.

I haven't spoken to him since he stood in the doorway of my house, so I know it must be important if he's reaching out. Running a hand through my hair, I contemplate ignoring it. But the fact that Saint was the one who messaged me makes me think it's important.

Walking back into my bedroom, I go over to the side of the bed that Charlotte is lying on. I gently pull back the covers from her face. "Charlotte?" I place my hand on her shoulder, and her heavy eyes open to meet mine. "I have to run."

"Okay." She yawns.

"Get some sleep, doll face. I'll be right back."

I jump on my bike and pull up to Carnage in less than twenty minutes. Jessie meets me at the main entrance. "They're upstairs in the birdcage, sir," he informs me, knowing I was coming. I guess Saint informed him that he requested my presence.

Making my way up to the birdcage, I exit the elevator just as the door to Saint's room opens. He steps out into the hallway to meet me. His head is down, and he runs his hand through his already disheveled hair. When his eyes meet mine, I feel a coldness run down my spine.

What the fuck happened? "What's going on? Where is she?"

"In our room," he answers, and his voice is hoarse.

I reach out to open the door, but he steps in my way. "Saint—?"

"I..." He pauses, lowering his voice. "I need you to talk to her for me."

"I came, didn't I?" I snap, getting irritated.

He nods to himself a few times. "I just need her to know that I'm here for her."

I frown at his words and go to ask him what the fuck he means by that, but he steps out of the way and opens the door for me. Knowing she'll tell me more than he will, I step inside to find her sitting on their bed, back against the headboard and staring straight ahead. Her eyes are red from crying, and her face is splotchy.

"Ashtyn?" I ask, closing the door behind me.

She blinks, her eyes finding mine. They widen, and she gasps. Scrambling off the bed, she rushes to me and throws her arms around my neck, leaping into my arms. "Haidyn," she whispers before I hear her sniff. Her body trembles in my arms as she begins to cry.

I walk her over to the bed and sit her down on the edge, prying her body from mine. I kneel in front of her. "What's going on, baby girl?"

She sniffs, trying to get her emotions under control, and takes in a deep breath. "I'm pregnant."

I was afraid of this. Kashton had told me that she found out she was pregnant, and all I could think about on the way here was that she lost it. I pretend I don't already know that information because this isn't the first time Ashtyn has told me she's expecting. She had run into me in a hallway here at Carnage. She was upset, and I couldn't get her to calm down, so I snuck her out and took her to see Devin. I didn't want her to worry about being pregnant without proof.

Four years ago

"SAINT..."

"We'll figure it out," I assure her and kiss her forehead. I don't understand why she's so afraid of being pregnant. Saint will take care of her. Hell, Kashton and I will also take care of her. She's not alone here.

The door opens, and her breath catches when she sees Gavin enter. She rises onto her elbows, but I push her down.

"No..."

"This is Gavin," I tell her. She thinks it's Devin—our doctor on call at Carnage—but I understand that. They're identical twins. "He's here to help, Ash."

"Haidyn." He nods to me before placing her in the stirrups and not wasting any time. We've got to confirm the pregnancy and get back to Carnage before anyone notices she's missing.

Her eyes are wide, and her heavy breathing fills the room. I take her hand and give her a reassuring smile, trying to ease her concern.

Gavin begins a vaginal ultrasound, and the sound of a heartbeat makes me smile. She was right. She and Saint are going to be parents. I'm going to be an uncle.

He finishes it up and then stands. "Give me an hour and I'll have a room ready."

"Room?" She jumps up. "What...what do we need a room for?" She's panicking, and her body trembles.

Gavin looks from me to her. "I'm assuming you came here for termination..."

"No," she cries, frantically shaking her head.

"Give us a minute," I tell Gavin, and he walks out.

"Ash—"

"I want this baby," she cries. "Please, Haidyn. I want this baby...We just can't tell Saint."

I run a hand down my face. "You can't hide a pregnancy from him. I can't hide this from him." I cup her face. "He's going to be happy—"

"It's not his child."

I frown, my hands dropping from her tear-streaked face. "What do you mean not his child?"

She drops her head and sniffs. "I was raped."

"Who the fuck raped you?" I snap, and she flinches.

"I don't know who it was." She lifts her eyes to mine and whispers, "But it happened before the vow ceremony."

My mind tries to comprehend everything she's telling me. "No..." I was there. I saw what happened. "You bled—"

"Saint cheated." She interrupts me. "At the ceremony."

I take her hands in mine. It's the same thing she told me when she ran into me in the hallway at Carnage. I didn't understand it then, and I don't understand it now. "I believe you, baby girl, but you're not making any sense."

"Saint knew I was raped beforehand, and he cheated at the vow ceremony to make it look like I was a virgin."

"Fuck." Now it's all making sense. The reason for her overreaction isn't really an overreaction now. Saint will be in deep shit with the Lords if they find out he did something to the vow ceremony. "Who would have known that to tell him?" I ask, trying to think of my next step. I'm now on damage control.

"My father."

"Goddammit," I hiss. "And Laura told you all of this?" Ashtyn had also informed me that the fucking therapist was the one who forced her to take the test during one of her sessions. Right before I ran into her in the hallway at Carnage and I snuck her out to see Gavin. We needed proof other than a test that Laura could have altered. Turns out, she wasn't wrong. We heard the heartbeat. Ashtyn is pregnant.

She nods.

What the fuck? How does that bitch know everything?

There's a knock on the door before it cracks open, and Gavin looks at me.

"I'll be right there." I give him a nod, and he pulls it closed.

"I don't want Saint to get in trouble," she rushes out. "I need you to help me."

I step forward, wrapping my arms around her shoulders, and pull her in for a hug, rubbing her back. "I'll take care of it." Pulling away, I step out into the hallway and shut the door behind me so she can get dressed.

"What the fuck are you doing, Haidyn?" he demands, his eyes going to the closed door and then back to mine. "Is that your child?"

"No."

"Then why the fuck are you here with your brother's girl...who is pregnant?"

"It's complicated, and until I figure it out, I need you to keep your mouth shut."

The door opens behind me, and Ashtyn steps out. I take her hand in mine and exit the clinic. I help her into the car and then send a quick text before getting into the driver's seat.

We've got a problem.

If I'm going to pull this off, I'll need help.

I'M NOT SURE WHY SHE'S SO UPSET THIS TIME, SO I REMAIN silent as I let her continue. I've found the best way to get information from someone is to let them ramble. Silence makes them nervous.

Her watery eyes drop to her bed. "It's twins." She takes another deep breath. "We've been monitoring the pregnancy and running tests…" She sniffles.

"And?" I hate to ask, knowing if she's this upset, then it's bad news. She's already lost one child.

She licks her wet lips. "Devin suggested a DNA test for them." Her eyes meet mine, and fresh tears fill them. "He said we could wait until they're born, but he suggests we do it as soon as possible."

I'm no expert on pregnancies, but I'm not sure why a DNA test would be important to do while she's pregnant. "And you don't want to?" I ask, confused and trying to figure out why she's so upset about that. "What about a second opinion?" I question.

She gives a slight nod. "Gavin was there as well and agreed with Devin. They said they could do it tomorrow and that Saint and I should take the day to discuss it."

If both of them suggested it, then I wouldn't see any harm in it. My eyes go to the closed door, and I'm surprised he hasn't joined us. "Ashtyn—"

"Heteropaternal superfecundation." She interrupts me. "They said it's rare but possible."

"I don't know what that means," I tell her softly. She's going to have to dumb it down for me.

"It means…" She takes in a shaky breath. "That they think I'm pregnant with babies from two different men."

Her tear-filled eyes lower to her legs as she runs her palms down her thighs. Tears spill over her bottom lashes and hit her legs. I swallow the knot in my throat, realizing what she's telling me. When Saint dragged her back, he had Devin remove her IUD. He was going to make her his in every way possible. But he never expected Benny to kidnap and rape her while he held her in the woods for four days, which could have possibly resulted in him getting her pregnant… again.

She sniffs, getting my attention. "I…" Her eyes lift to mine. "Is it bad that I don't want to know?" Her lip trembles. "That I want to believe Saint is the father to both of my babies?"

I straighten before sitting down next to her, wrapping my arms around her and pulling her to my side. "No," I tell her. She turns, wrapping her arms around me, and buries her head into my shirt as her cries fill the room. "There's nothing wrong with that, baby girl."

Shhh...

Chapter 45

Charlotte

I was lucky Haidyn had somewhere to be. I pretended to be asleep when I heard him come back into his bedroom. Once he told me goodbye and left, I immediately turned the cell back on. I've stared at it, hoping the video comes back so I can watch it again and try to decipher what I'm supposed to understand about it.

Was I supposed to focus on Ashtyn, Saint, or Haidyn? What did it all mean, and why did they cut it where they did? What happened after she passed out? They were branding her but why? She looked terrified. I mean, if I was in a straitjacket, strapped to a gurney, gagged and naked from the waist down, I'd be terrified too. But Saint loves her and supposedly so does Haidyn. Maybe it was an initiation for her? Who the hell knows? She was wearing a wedding ring when I saw her at Carnage, and I know once you become a Lady, your Lord will sometimes brand you. So maybe it was because of that?

The phone vibrates in my hands, and the email icon appears, making me drop it on my face. "Fuck," I groan, rubbing my nose and then holding it up. My eyes dart to the bedroom door to make sure Haidyn isn't standing right outside or coming in to check on me.

When I think the coast is clear, I open the email. It's another video. I push play, and it's in the same concrete room as before, but this time, Ashtyn and Saint are gone and so is the gurney. Haidyn enters, pocketing his cell, and looks around as if he expects someone to be there with him.

The door opens once more, and I lower the volume since I don't have my earbuds in. I sink further down into the bed, holding the phone right in front of my face once more.

Haidyn leans back against the counter, crossing his arms over his chest.

"What the fuck do you think you were doing?" the man barks, stepping farther into the room.

Haidyn just stares at him. The look on his face and his relaxed stance say he's unbothered.

The man snaps his fingers, and the door opens again, and three men enter the room.

My heart picks up, knowing this won't end well, but Haidyn still looks unbothered.

"We gave you specific instructions," the man shouts.

"You didn't give me shit," Haidyn speaks.

The guy snaps his finger once more, and one of the guys dressed in a cloak and mask walks over to Haidyn. The moment he gets close enough, Haidyn swings. His fist hits the Lords mask, knocking him back.

All hell breaks loose in the concrete room. Haidyn holds his own until one of them places a stun gun to his neck, forcing him to his knees.

He hunches over, breathing heavily and worn out as the three men start to remove his shirt. They drag him to the center of the room, cuff his wrists in front of him and then string him up to the ceiling by a chain until the toes of his combat boots barely touch the floor. His eyes look around aimlessly, trying to get his bearings straight as they shove a rubber ball gag into his mouth, and then a hood over his head, securing it around his neck.

The man without a mask comes to stand in front of him and crosses his arms over his chest. "You will learn, Son, that the Lords always come first. Over any woman. No matter who she is, you will do as you're told. Even if I have to beat it into you." With that, the guy turns and slams the door shut, and the video stops.

I realize I'm biting my nails and drop the cell to my lap. *What the fuck was that?* He called him Son? Was that his dad? Was Haidyn being punished for knocking Ashtyn out to brand her?

I have so many questions, but it makes sense as to why I keep being told that Haidyn killed their fathers. But was it to save Ashtyn from them, or was it to save himself?

HAIDYN

I STEP OUT OF ASHTYN'S ROOM AND SOFTLY CLOSE THE DOOR behind me. Saint is pacing the hallway but stops and looks up at me.

His eyes go to their bedroom door and then back to mine. "How is she?"

"Upset."

He runs a hand through his hair and gives me his back. "Fuucck-kk," he whisper-shouts.

"She doesn't want to know," I tell him.

Whirling around, he narrows his eyes on mine. "Devin and Gavin—"

"You asked me to talk to her." I interrupt him. "I did. That's what she told me."

He nods his head a few times as if convincing himself.

"Will it make a difference to you if one isn't yours?" I ask.

"Fuck no," he growls. Stepping closer to me, he lowers his voice. "Just like it wouldn't have mattered to me that her first child wasn't mine." His green eyes search mine, and I can feel the heat radiating off him. He wants to hit me, possibly shoot me. I understand he's going through a lot right now. And I can't argue that I don't deserve it. Taking in a deep breath, he adds, "But I didn't get that choice then, did I?"

He expects me to apologize for this shit show I've put us in, but I'm not going to. I did what I thought was best at the time. Things didn't go as planned, then when he woke up, we were already in "training." By the time we finished that, six months had passed, and I didn't have the heart to tell him. Or maybe I just wanted to think she was better off.

"Go be with your wife, Saint." I step around him and head toward the elevator.

He grabs my upper arm, stopping me. "You're leaving again?" His words make it seem like he cares, but his tone says otherwise.

I turn to face him. "I have somewhere to be," I say vaguely.

I can't bring Charlotte here. Not with me. They'll ask too many questions, and I'm having too much fun with my newest toy not to play with her. It wouldn't be like it was—her showing up for one of our sessions and ending with her running out of the room after I gave her a visual of how I was going to fuck her. Pulling my arm free, I step into the elevator before the door shuts.

"She misses you, ya know," he speaks softly.

"Anything from Benny?" I ask, ignoring what he said. I don't have the energy for that conversation right now. I haven't spoken to Kash, so I haven't been updated on anything, and I've had shit luck trying to figure out who the guy in the picture is with him.

He shakes his head. "The guy is begging for me to cut his goddamn head off."

I snort. "If you need help, let me know." That's what I need. Torture and kill some sorry bastard. Who better than Benny?

The door starts to shut when he speaks, "This is your home, Haidyn. You're always welcome here."

Shhh...

Chapter 46

Charlotte

For the past hour and a half, I've just been lying here on my side, staring out of his floor-to-ceiling windows and waiting for the sun to rise. My mind is running a hundred miles an hour.

I'm so confused.

The conversation I had with my friends at lunch, then the conversations I had at my mom's...the videos from the Lords. What does it all mean? Where do I fit into this world if the man I'm supposed to marry is no longer an option?

Will they hand me over to someone new? If so, when?

Marrying a Lord isn't something a Lady has control over. You are called to serve, and you serve, so they could tell me to walk down the aisle at any time. But I won't get that order until I finish this assignment. But again, what is the endgame?

Do the Lords want me to find my future husband at Carnage and then report back...whether he's a prisoner or he's dead?

I'm literally giving myself a headache with all the possibilities.

Sitting up, I stretch my sore body and see the room is dark, letting me know it's still early. This has been the longest night of my life. I watched my cell forever, waiting for another video, but it never came. I have to know what happened to Haidyn.

My mouth is dry, and I'm dying of thirst. Getting out of bed, I pick up a T-shirt of Haidyn's and pull it on before I exit the bedroom. Making my way down the hallway, I go to enter the kitchen when his voice stops me.

"You look like shit." Haidyn chuckles.

Pressing my back into the wall, I slowly look around the corner to see him in the kitchen, drinking a bottle of water as a man enters from the other side. It's the same one who was in the bedroom upstairs when I was looking for Muffin.

"Your bike woke me up. Where the fuck have you been all night? Isn't your girl in your room?"

"I had to run to Carnage," Haidyn answers but ignores the question about me.

"Had to run to Carnage?" he repeats with a snort. "I can only think of one reason you'd rush back to the one place you're avoiding."

"I'm not avoiding Carnage," Haidyn argues.

"But you're also not arguing why you ran back to it."

Haidyn rolls his eyes. "Don't you have a woman in your room to fuck?" He avoids the man's statement.

"She's...marinating."

Haidyn throws his head back, laughing. "Is that what you guys call it these days?"

I don't know why, but the thought of a woman marinating makes me think of her tied up in a bathtub filled with barbecue sauce. With a Lord, anything is possible.

The man jumps up to sit on the counter, his sharp face growing serious. "What did *she* want?"

Haidyn stares at him, taking a drink of his water, but remains silent.

The man sighs. "You can't let her keep doing this to you."

"Don't." Haidyn growls.

"Look, it wasn't your fault." He runs a hand down his face, and I have no clue what they're talking about. "The past can't be changed," the man adds. "But she was never your responsibility."

"We all looked after her," Haidyn states.

"It was my job." The other stabs himself in the chest. "Her marrying Saint doesn't change that."

Ashtyn! They're talking about Ashtyn. My eyes go back to the other guy, and I realize he was in the photo the Lords sent me. It's *Adam*. He's here and alive, which means my friends know less than I thought. I knew they were wrong about Ashtyn being dead, and here's her brother in Haidyn's house. Who is he hiding from?

"You need to lay low," Haidyn tells him.

He shakes his head and demands, "What happened?"

Haidyn takes a deep breath before answering. "Saint messaged me—"

A cell ringing interrupts whatever he was about to say, and Adam jumps off the counter, placing it to his ear and exiting the kitchen. "Yeah?" His voice fades as he walks down the hallway.

I stand and watch Haidyn take another drink of his water before he just stares across the open living room and out the floor-to-ceiling windows. I go back to Haidyn's bed, lie down, and close my eyes. I'm pretending to be asleep for the second time tonight, and I'm more confused than I was an hour ago.

HAIDYN

I HEAR THE FAINT SOUND OF A BEDROOM DOOR SHUTTING, AND I look up toward the hallway that leads to my bedroom. Was Charlotte listening to our conversation? I mean, nothing important was discussed, but I figured she'd be asleep.

I'll have to be more careful. It's no longer just Adam and me in this house, and there's a lot of shit I don't want her to know about.

My cell vibrates in my pocket, and I pull it out, expecting it to be either Saint or Ashtyn at this time of night, but it's a text from an **UNKNOWN** number. Opening it up, I read over it.

Cathedral. Friday 3 a.m.

Backing out of it, I set my cell on the counter and sigh. *What the fuck now?*

Just then, Adam returns to the kitchen. He comes to a stop and crosses his arms over his chest, waiting for me to continue our previous conversation. Taking a deep breath, I fill him in on what I know.

Shhh...

Chapter 47

Charlotte

I was finally able to fall asleep after I heard Haidyn and the man talking in the kitchen. But when I woke up, I realized it was only a few hours. I guess it's better than nothing.

Entering the living room, I stop when I see things lying on the coffee table. There are two items, but they make my body heat rise. One is a black rope, and the other is a large silver-looking hook. It has three balls that vary in size on the curved end, and on the opposite end is a large opening that resembles a ring.

"Good morning, doll face."

I jump at the sound of Haidyn's voice in my ear. Spinning around, I see him standing behind me. He straightens and reaches out, brushing my hair from my face. His knuckles gently brush my cheek. *Did he ever go to sleep last night?*

"Good morning." I clear my throat, trying to act unfazed. I don't know why he still gets to me. Watching that video of him last night reminds me just how deep with him I am. His father told him that he'd beat it into him that women mean nothing. That includes me, and he will take every opportunity he gets to remind himself of that.

"How did you sleep?" he asks.

"Good. You?"

His eyes search mine, and my heart hammers in my chest, wondering if he can tell I lied. After several seconds, he answers, "Good."

It's also a lie. He left to go to Carnage last night. And then when I found him in the kitchen with that guy, I rushed back to bed, and he went to the bathroom to take another shower. I eventually fell back to sleep. And when I woke up, he was gone again.

"Remove your clothes."

The order is no surprise, but the way his voice changes to something so cold sends a shiver down my spine.

Licking my lips, I look around the room. It's still early. A little after nine, but it's a cloudy, rainy day. All you can see are trees and mountains outside the floor-to-ceiling windows. The TV is on ESPN, but the volume is low.

"Problem?" he asks.

It's a test. He knows I saw him and the guy in the kitchen. I want to ask if we're alone, but I won't. I'm committed to dying on this hill. "No," I answer, reaching down and grabbing the hem of his T-shirt that I'm wearing. I pull it up and over my head, tossing it to the floor. Then I slide my hands into my underwear and push them down my hips, letting them fall to my feet before I step out of them.

Standing in front of him naked while he's dressed in jeans and a plain white T-shirt.

"Beautiful," he whispers. His eyes drop over my heaving chest, and my nipples harden at his praise. I hate how much my body enjoys him. Just his presence makes me wet. His words make me weak, and his touch...fuck, my body craves it in the most delirious way.

He steps around me and walks over to the coffee table. He picks up something I hadn't noticed before that was sitting next to the rope, and his eyes meet mine. "Come here."

My feet move on their own, my body wanting to obey, knowing it'll be rewarded.

Stopping in front of him, he places his hands on my shoulders and turns me to face away from him. Lowering his hands over my face, he brings something around my neck. "Hold your hair up for me."

I gather it up to the top of my head with both hands before shuffling it into just one. The leather tightens around my throbbing pulse, and then he buckles it in place. It's a collar.

Something that just further proves I'm a pet. Put a bell on me and call me kitten. I'll purr for my Lord.

"Face me," he commands, and I do as I'm told, letting my hair fall back down over my back. "Arms out in front of you, both hands making a fist." He doubles the rope and drapes it over my arms. Bringing it across both wrists, he wraps the rope around them twice before tucking it through the middle and tying it off in a tight knot. "Face the couch and kneel. Rest your forearms on the cushion."

Taking in a shaky breath, I turn to face the couch and drop to my knees. My chest is on the edge, and my arms are out in front of me along the cushions.

His hands are on my back, pushing me farther down into it. "Spread your legs as much as you can and arch your back."

I wiggle my ass to spread them on the dark rug and then turn my head to the side so I don't suffocate in the cushion. My hair covers half my face, disrupting my view of the house. If his friend is still in the house watching, I'm not even able to see him.

The sound of a lid popping open makes my breathing pick up. It's lube. He's going to fuck my ass. This is a punishment for eavesdropping last night. No matter what, I refuse to admit it.

He runs his wet fingers over my ass, and I try to calm my racing heart. I whimper when one enters me. "Relax, Charlotte," he orders. "It's going to happen. You might as well let it slide right in."

I turn my head, bury my face into the cushion, and bite into the soft fabric. As I fist my tied hands, my body betrays me and pushes against him when he removes it. I close my eyes tightly and hold my breath when he thrusts in again deeper, forcing my open legs to shake.

"That's it, doll face." He pushes another into me. My body gives way no matter how much my mind screams to stop. I lift my head, needing air, and gasp, my hair getting in my mouth.

He removes his fingers and pushes them inside me again, all the way to his knuckles, and I cry out, unable to help it as my body rocks back and forth.

"Haidyn." His name is breathless as his fingers begin to fuck my ass. He goes slow but deep, forcing their way inside me. I bend my arms, my tied hands gripping my hair.

He removes them, and I slump against the side of the couch. My body once again relaxes, and I take in a calming breath, then I feel something cold and hard against my ass. A hand lands on my lower back, holding me down to the couch.

"Take in a deep breath," he orders, and I suck one in. "Let it out."

I let it out, and something much larger than his fingers pushes against me. "Haidyn—" My voice rises this time.

"You're doing great, Charlotte," he assures me as my ass stretches wider. "Almost done."

My body fights the intrusion, but he stands behind my kneeling body, one hand holding me down and the other pushing whatever the hard object is into my ass. I'm powerless against him. My ass burns as it stretches, and when I think I'm going to pass out from holding my breath, it closes around a smaller but still very hard surface.

"Good girl, doll face. You're doing so good." He rubs my back, and I realize I'm crying. "Almost done." He grabs the rope that binds my hands and pulls them over the back of my head. It's pulling my face and chest off the couch and into a sitting position on my knees with my legs tucked under me. Tears fall from my eyes, and my hair sticks to my wet face.

The rope around my wrists and whatever is in my ass is pulled tighter, and a moan escapes my shaking lips.

"That's it, Charlotte. That's the sound I want to hear come out of that perfect mouth of yours."

I can't see much but shapes out of my blurry, covered eyes. Seconds later, his hands are on my face, and he's pushing my hair back. I blink rapidly, letting the fresh tears fall to see he's now sitting on the couch in front of me while I remain kneeling between his now open legs. My arms are still up above my head, bent backward, my tied wrists rest at the back of my neck.

I pull on them only to cry out as it moves whatever is in my ass. "What...what did you do?" I try again but nothing.

His lips pull slightly at the corners as his hands drop to my neck. Hooking his finger into the ring of my collar, he pulls me forward while he leans into me.

HAIDYN

I PLACE MY FACE IN FRONT OF HERS, AND SHE'S GASPING WITH her plump lips parted. I hold her in place as I say, "Your arms are tied behind your head, and the rope is attached to the anal hook that I inserted into your ass."

Her tear-filled eyes widen. I pull her closer, closing the short space, and place my lips on hers. She kisses me back immediately. No hesitation, just a woman begging to be fucked and needing to be taken. She's so submissive it's the sexiest thing I've ever seen. I've had a week with her in my home, and I take advantage of it any chance I get.

My free hand reaches out and rubs her left breast. I tied her arms this way on purpose. She moans into my mouth, and I roll my fingers around her hard nipple, pinching it. She tries to pull away, but I yank harder, and I swallow the cry that follows.

Pulling away, she gasps as she kneels before me. I release her collar and run my knuckles down her heaving chest to where both hands grip her nipples. "Fuck, you're so sexy."

"Haidyn," she whispers my name. Her head falls back, and I watch her neck work when she swallows.

I slap her breast, and her body jerks as another cry echoes through the house. Every little movement she makes has the anal hook moving inside her ass. She has a choice—release the tension on the anal hook in her ass, which means she has to push her arms farther back, or let her arms relax and pull on the hook.

I slap it again and then again, harder each time until she's screaming my name. Her chest is red, and she lowers her head as more tears fall from the prettiest eyes I've ever seen. They're a rich royal blue—they look like sapphires.

"Please," she begs, body trembling.

"Please what, doll face?" I pinch her nipple again. She knows how to use her words.

She yanks on her arms, making herself cry out once more.

I smile at her lack of thinking. I want to see my girl confused. Overwhelmed.

I release her and sit back into the couch. My hands rest on my jean-clad thighs while I allow her a second to get herself together.

My hands go to my belt, and I unbuckle it. She licks her lips, already knowing where this is going, and I'm so fucking hard at how quickly she's learning.

Unzipping my jeans, I pull my cock out and stroke it. Her heavy eyes are on it. "I'm going to sit here and watch the game while you hold my cock in your mouth."

She blinks before her eyes lift to meet mine, but she looks dazed. "What are you going to do, doll face?" I ask, still stroking my cock, jealous of the anal hook that's currently buried deep in her ass. I want to be there right now.

"Hold your cock in my mouth..." Her words are breathless, and I know her pussy is soaked.

"That's a good girl." I run the pad of my thumb over her parted lips, and she opens them wider to let me slip it in. She wraps her lips around it but doesn't suck. "That's it..." I smile at her. "That's what a good whore does."

Her eyes fall closed, and I pull it free from her mouth. "Do as you're told, doll face," I command, sitting back into the couch.

Her eyes open, and she leans forward. A soft cry comes from her parted lips when she realizes that leaning over the edge of the couch will pull the rope taut, yanking on the anal hook. Her lips wrap around my dick, and I watch her eyes shut.

"Eyes on me, Charlotte," I command. "When my cock is in your mouth, your eyes are open."

Her wet lashes flutter open, and she looks up at me through them. I push her head down farther, forcing more of my cock into her warm mouth, and she mumbles around it. "How's your ass feel?" I smile, watching the tears run down her cheeks. "Is your pussy as wet as your face? I bet it's begging to be fucked."

She blinks again and mumbles around my dick. The vibration makes my cock twitch inside her mouth.

I let go of her hair and pick up the remote beside me. I turn up the volume to the TV as I let her kneel before me with my cock shoved into her mouth. She lied to me. She'll learn I don't tolerate being lied to.

Shhh...

Chapter 48
Charlotte

I blink, clearing my vision as drool runs from my mouth while his cock is shoved into it. My arms have gone numb tied up and behind my head, and kneeling over at this angle pulls on the hook in my ass and every little movement makes me moan. It's uncomfortable but no longer painful. It feels…good.

I adjust my bent knees; my thighs are sweaty, and my toes tingle from the kneeling position.

One of his hands rests on the back of the couch while the other gently plays with a strand of my hair. His blue eyes are on the TV. I'm guessing the game is still on, but I can't hear anything over the blood rushing in my ears.

The zipper to his jeans digs into my chin and cheeks. He remained dressed on purpose. I still haven't seen him naked. It's another sign of dominance. I've seen enough porn where the Dom is in a suit and tie, and their submissive is crawling on all fours—naked, collared, and leashed. She's his toy, his property. His to do whatever he wants with.

Haidyn was right when he said my pussy is wet. It's running as much as my open mouth. He moves his hand to slide into my hair at the crown of my head, and he pushes my mouth down farther while he lifts his hips. I gag as his new position forces me to readjust on my knees. My arms pull on the rope, and I moan as it pulls on the hook.

His eyes drop to mine, and he gives me an innocent smile. "Enjoying yourself, doll face?"

I stare up at him with heavy eyes, rocking my hips back and forth.

My hard nipples rub against the edge of the couch cushion. "Leave your mouth open," he commands, and I wonder what the hell he means by that when his cock is down my throat.

He yanks on my hair, ripping his dick from my mouth, and I gasp, leaving my mouth open like he told me to. Instead, he places two fingers at the back of my throat, making me gag once more. My shoulders jerk forward and pull on the rope, forcing a whimper from my full mouth.

"You're so fucking beautiful, Charlotte."

I whimper again, trying to swallow the drool, but it just runs out of the corner of my lips. He removes his fingers. "Are you wet?"

I nod, and he grabs my bent elbows, yanking them forward. I scream out as the rope yanks on the hook, sending a sharp tingle up my spine that is full of pain and pleasure. It takes away my breath.

"Words, doll face." He tsks with a sinister smile.

"Y-yes." I nod. "Yes, I'm wet." I lick my lips.

"That's a good girl." He grips my hair again and shoves my head down, and I manage to take in a deep breath before his pierced cock fills my mouth once more. "Suck on it, doll face. Be my naughty little whore and put that mouth to good use."

HAIDYN

My plan was to make her kneel with my cock in her mouth until the game was finished, but I can't wait that long.

I don't take my time as I fuck her mouth. And within minutes, I'm coming down her throat. Yanking her head up, I watch the drool and cum run from her swollen lips. She's gasping for breath, and I lean down, grabbing her hips. "Stand up," I order.

She softly cries but manages to get to her shaking legs. I close mine and pull her onto my lap to where she straddles me.

Leaning forward, I pull a hard nipple into my mouth and suck on it before letting my teeth sink into it. She screams, trying to pull her nipple free of my teeth, but her hips push into me.

I let it pop free, and I grab my cock. "Spread your legs," I command, slapping her thigh.

"Haidyn." She gasps. "Please…"

I slap it again. "Rise up." She wiggles her way up enough that I can rub the tip of my dick along her cunt. "Fucking soaked." Just like I knew it would be. "You're becoming such an obedient whore for me, aren't you?"

She nods. I lift my hand to slap her breast, and she adds, "Yes, I am."

I push my cock forward at an angle and push down on her, letting her cunt suck me inside.

She throws her head back, chest heaving, and a cry rips through the room. "I…Haidyn!" She lowers her head so her watery eyes meet mine.

My hands grip her hips, and I dig my fingers into her skin, pushing her body down on top of mine. "You're doing so good, doll face."

"Oh my…" She gasps.

I stop and hold her in place. She can't do much since she doesn't have use of her hands, and the anal hook in her ass keeps her from making any sudden movements. I mean, the fact that her ass has steel balls in it does make it a little more difficult and tighter space, but it's very doable.

I lean forward and kiss her wet lips, tasting her salty tears. "I'm going to fuck you now, Charlotte, so just relax and let me in. Can you do that for me, doll face?"

She nods, and her body relaxes, allowing her soaked pussy to slide farther down onto my dick. She pulls on the rope with her shaking arms, and I grind my teeth as I slip all the way into her. The balls in her ass make her pussy walls even tighter.

"Goddamn, doll face." I groan, ignoring her cries of pain and pleasure. I reach up and grab the loop in her collar, pulling her forward and smiling when I feel her hips start grinding back and forth. "Ride my cock, Charlotte. Show me how bad you want it."

My free hand slaps her breast, and she jerks. I do it again and again, loving the way she screams my name while her pussy grinds on my dick that twitches inside her tight cunt. "You're shaking, doll face." I run my knuckles down her chest, enjoying the red mark on her breasts from my hands. "How's your ass feel?" I pull on her restrained arms, and she sobs, but her hips don't stop rocking back and forth. "Words, Charlotte."

"It...hurts." She sniffs.

I drop my hands and grip her ass cheeks as I lower myself into the couch. I lift her to fuck my dick. Her tits bounce in front of my face, and I know each thrust forces her arms to yank on the anal hook. "You're so fucking good at being my whore, doll face."

"Pl-ease," she begs.

"Please, what?"

"May I come?" she pants. "Please? I need to come."

"You can come, doll face," I say, wanting her to come all over my cock. She's earned it. I've always been an ass guy, but that doesn't mean I forget how good a pussy can be. Especially hers. I'm the first man to ever be there, and I want to make sure that any man she fucks in the future leaves her unsatisfied.

She throws her head back, and I grip her collar, yanking her forward. "You'll look at me when you come," I command.

Her heavy eyes open, and her mouth parts, but nothing comes out as I feel her pussy clench down on my dick. So tight it takes my breath away.

♠

I PULL UP TO THE CATHEDRAL AND SHUT OFF MY BIKE. GETTING off, I notice a car parked by the entrance. A black Rolls Royce Wraith. The driver gets out and buttons his suit jacket before walking up the stairs and opens the door for me.

His eyes meet mine as I pass, and I give him a nod that he returns.

The door closing squeals throughout the vaulted ceilings. The cathedral is old, and although the Lords love flashy, they refuse to upgrade this place. They want it to be a reminder that anything they give you can be taken away at any time.

I walk down the aisle, past the pews, and see a man sitting in the front row, his back facing me as he faces the Lords altar. I see two guns sitting on it. I remove the gun from the waistband of my jeans and the pocketknife, placing it beside my gun, and turn to face the man who called me here.

William Marks sits before me. The last fucking Lord I expected to invite me here. It's been years since I saw him last. "Bill." His father was also a William, so he prefers to go by Bill.

"Annabelle Marie Schults." He states his stepdaughter's name.

"I know who she is." I'm not going to hide the fact that I know who Charlotte really is. If he's here, he already knows that I know.

His laughter fills the large cathedral. "I assure you; you have no clue who she is," he states, getting my attention.

"Enlighten me." I bite. The man brought me here at three in the morning because he wants to tell me something, so I might as well let him talk.

The smile that takes over his face tells me he's more than willing to fill me in on what he thinks I don't know. "Do you know the founders?"

Now it's my time to laugh out loud. "No one knows who the founders are." It's to keep them protected from other members of the society.

"What if I told you that Annabelle was from a founder?"

I stiffen.

He smirks. "Now I have your attention."

"Bullshit." I push off the Lords altar and turn around and pick up my gun and pocketknife.

"I promised her father that if anything happened to him, I'd protect her."

"Well, you failed." I turn back around and shove my gun into my jeans, ready to leave.

"I tried to come up with reasons as to keep her from being initiated, but her mother wanted her to be great." He does air quotes. Getting to his feet, he walks over to the end of the Lords altar. "Have you heard of an offering?"

I snort. "Of course I have." All Lords are required to watch at least one offering. It's to desensitize us—a woman being stripped naked and tied down to the Lords altar and then offered up to other Lords—and tells the men that they are what's important. Women are nothing in our world.

"Have you heard of a breeder?" he asks.

"Sounds pretty self-explanatory." I know several Lords who have that kink.

He smirks. "Follow me." Turning, he begins to walk up the far-right staircase to the top floor where the vow ceremony takes place every year for the ritual. I follow him to the second-floor balcony.

I come to a stop when I see the woman I wasn't aware was up here. She's tied up, of course. Face down with her ass and cunt exposed. Head completely covered with a hood that's buckled around her neck, and by the sounds of her muffled screams, she's gagged.

Walking over to her, I see she's got a butt plug in her ass and another one in her cunt. Bruises cover her pale skin. Some look like they're from belts, others from hands and fingers.

"She's a breeder," Bill says, looking down at her. "She failed her assignment."

"What do you mean by her assignment?" I've never heard of a woman having one in our society until Charlotte told me she was given one.

"She's from a founder."

My body tenses as his words start to make sense.

He nods down at her. "See, Haidyn. A woman who fails her assignment after she's been initiated into the Lords isn't completely useless. They may have failed, but they still have something to offer."

"What if they can't have children?" I inquire.

He laughs as if that's an absurd concept. "I guess it's possible, but the Lords take matters into their own hands to make sure they are able to reproduce. Supplements are given..."

"So I've heard."

"She's twenty-one." *Same as Charlotte.* He begins to walk around her. "Her first session was tonight. She'll remain tied here like this for at least forty-eight hours. Ass up in the air stuffed with a lockable plug so the Lords can't use it. And her cunt plugged to retain all their cum. It will be removed for her next session in the morning. Once her forty-eight hours are up, she'll go to the clinic where she will be closely monitored twenty-four seven until she has a positive pregnancy test, and a DNA test will determine which lucky Lord was successful."

"Then what?"

"She'll be kept at the clinic until she's thirty-eight weeks, at which time the baby or babies will be taken and given to the father for him to raise."

"What if this session doesn't take, and she doesn't have a positive pregnancy test?" Forty-eight hours doesn't sound like much time.

"Then she's brought back here for another *session*. Repeat the process until the Lords get their desired results." He points at her. "This is her life from here on out. After she gives birth, she will find herself back here for another round...then another. Until the Lords feel she's served, and then...well, then they will put her out of her misery."

Rinse and repeat. Running my hands through my hair, I sigh. "So you're saying...if Charlotte fails, this is her future?"

He looks up at me, and his silence answers my question. A sickening feeling has my mind reeling. The video I watched of Charlotte's exchange with the Lords in her living room comes to mind. *They will deliver you to the cathedral where you will fulfill your...duties. You will serve your Lords one way or another*. She thought it was an offering and so did I. It was worse than that. "What is her assignment?"

"I don't know."

"BULLSHIT!" I shout before taking a deep breath, and the woman tied face down to the wooden bench cries harder to get my attention. Ignoring her, I keep my eyes on Bill. As awful as it sounds, I'm not here to save her. "I find it hard to believe that no one knows what her assignment is. Not even her."

"She doesn't even know what she's doing it for."

"What does that mean?" I say, trying to wrap my brain around this new information. The Lords have layers. And I know they run deep. But breeding? I mean, the truth is right in front of me, but the question is why? The ones at the top are powerful, and they're always married off. So why would they need a child from someone else other than their Lady?

"Ever heard of Dollhouse?"

I grind my teeth but answer. "No. What the fuck is it?"

"Annabelle thinks she'll take over her family's business. But it's not what she thinks it is."

"Look, I'm tired of your fucking riddles. You had me meet you at three in the morning to see this shit..." I point at the woman while she fights her restraints that hold her in place. "For fucking nothing." Turning, I give him my back. "Thanks for nothing."

"Annabelle isn't going to like the life she gets if she completes her assignment."

"None of us do," I throw over my shoulder as I approach the stairs. I start to descend when he speaks again.

"Very few people in our world are truly innocent, Haidyn."

I stop and turn to face him. He remains standing by the naked woman with his hands shoved into his dress slacks.

"I can say without a doubt that Annabelle is one of them."

"It's too late," I say, shaking my head. I've already made her mine. I've branded my name on her ass. I'm too far in with her to toss her to the side. And if he's right...she's innocent—just another woman caught up in a life that will destroy her.

"Is she in your bed right now?" He goes on as my mind runs wild with the new information.

I don't answer, and he walks toward me. My silence is answer enough. Coming to a stop at the top of the stairs, he speaks, "Go home...grab your gun and put a bullet in her head while she sleeps." He takes the first step off the stairs, getting closer. "I love Annabelle like she is my own, but I promise you, that's the best outcome she'll get." With that, he walks down the stairs, passing me.

Chapter 49

Haidyn

I pull up to my house and push the garage door opener. I start to enter, but I pause when I see her SUV. I knew it was going to be here, but it's weird seeing it.

Pulling in, I park next to her Cullinan, turn off my bike, and get out, closing the garage door before I enter the house. It's dead silent and pitch black since the sun hasn't come up yet. Making my way to the primary suite, I open the door and enter, closing it behind me.

The curtains are open so there's a little light in here from the sconces that hang on the outside of the house. She's lying in my bed. Her back to the window, her arm stretched out on my side of the bed. Her cat lies on my pillow like always.

Walking over to the nightstand, I remove my gun from the waistband of my jeans and go to put it on the surface but pause, looking back at her. She looks so pretty and peaceful.

Her dark lashes laying on her cheeks, her pouty lips are parted, and she softly snores. I release the gun and get undressed. Picking up the covers, I lie down next to her and pull them back up to cover us both as Muffin meows and jumps off the bed.

I run the back of my knuckles along her cheek, over her jaw, and down her neck. Her pulse is strong and steady.

"Haidyn?" she whispers, her eyes remaining closed.

"Yeah, doll face. It's me," I tell her, my thumb running over her bottom lip.

She gives me a faint smile, then she does something I don't expect.

She moves closer, pressing her soft body into mine and draping her left arm over my side and her left leg over my hip.

It makes me tense for just a second before I melt into her warm embrace. Lying down on the bed on my side, I run my right hand up her back, feeling the curve of her spine and over the nape of her neck. I can feel her Lords crest that they branded her with before I allow my fingers to slide into her soft hair and cup the back of her head. I hold her as if she's a dream I don't want to wake up from as I remember part of our "training."

Four years ago

"I HAVE SOMETHING TO SHOW YOU," THE WOMAN SAYS WITH A smile.

I grind my teeth. "I'm not in the mood for games," I inform her, stepping into her. The four guys rush forward, and she raises her hands to stop them.

"No worries, boys. We're just talking."

I need to check on Saint. This is the first time she's let me out of my basement cell in days. "What the fuck do you want?" I still don't know where the fuck Kashton is.

"I want to show you something." She steps forward.

Throwing my head back, I take in a deep breath, trying to calm my fucking temper. I've had enough of this bitch. "What is it?"

Giving me an evil smile, she turns, and I follow her like the good boy she's trying to make us into. It'll never happen. But I can play the game just as well as she can.

We make our way outside, and I look over my shoulder to see her four guys following us. I shove my hands into the pockets of my jeans and wish I had my sunglasses. There's not a single cloud in the sky; it's the middle of the day, and it's hotter than usual for this time of year. It was snowing just last week.

As we approach the back fence surrounding Carnage, she steps to the right, and I stop at what I see.

A woman stands with her back pressed into the ten-foot chain-link fence, on her tiptoes, spread-eagled. Each wrist and ankle are secured with barbed wire, and it's also wrapped around her neck twice. Blood runs down her naked body from her struggles to get free. And there's a fresh scar—horizontal on her lower stomach. Her once flawless skin is sunburned. "How long has she been out here?" I demand, stepping forward, knowing exactly who it is.

The sound of my voice has her body thrashing, and her muffled voice from being gagged fills the black hood that covers her face.

"Two days," the bitch answers.

I turn to face her. "Why is she here?" I bark. "Let her go. She has nothing to do with this," I shout, panic gripping my chest.

She tilts her head to the side. "I think she has everything to do with this...with you." She smiles. "You brothers share everything. Including women."

Crazy fucking bitch! "Let her go!" I shout, stepping forward, but she doesn't retreat.

She frowns. "Women are supposed to mean nothing to you. And her." She points at the sobbing woman. "She belongs to you. So what are you going to do with her?" Walking over to the woman tied to the fence, she rips the hood off her head.

Wide, bloodshot eyes meet mine, and she screams around the duct tape placed over her mouth.

I walk over to her and rip it off her face. "Hai-dyn," she sobs, her body shaking, yanking on the barbed wire, trying to get free.

"Shh," I say, placing my hands on her tear-streaked face. Her skin is hot and clammy. Two days? They probably haven't given her anything to eat, let alone water. "Calm down, baby," I tell her, and she closes her eyes tightly. "Can you do that for me?" I ask, and she nods the best she can. "That's my good girl," I say, and she whimpers at the praise.

"See, Haidyn, you always have a choice," the bitch adds cryptically.

I release Sierra and turn to face her. "Why is she here?" I demand.

"She's your chosen, Haidyn. The Lords gave her to you as a reward for all of your devotion and hard work. She belongs to you until you're done with her. So she will stay here with you at Carnage and go through training with you. Everything I do to you...I'll do to her. And as long as she survives, I'll let you still fuck her. Oh, and don't worry about the possibility of pregnancy. She's already been given her hysterectomy."

Sierra cries and now the fresh scar makes sense. Sterilization is a requirement here at Carnage. Doesn't matter man or woman, whoever is brought in as a prisoner is to be made sure they can never reproduce. How long have they had her hidden here if they've already done that to her?

"But..." The bitch continues, getting my attention and pointing at her four men who followed us out here. "If you choose to be done with her, then you give her to them."

"No," I snap as Sierra's cries turn to sobs, knowing exactly what she means. Either I keep her here for me and allow the bitch to torture Sierra or I hand her over to her men to let them rape her. "Absolutely not."

The woman's frown deepens.

"Haidyn...please..." Sierra sobs, and I turn back to face her.

My eyes quickly scan the barbed wire around her wrists, neck, and ankles. She's been cutting herself trying to get free. There's no way for me to get it off unless I cut it, and I have no way to do so.

"PLEASE..." Sierra screams, her panic rising at what's to come. "Don't let them do this to me!" She yanks on the barbed wire, and it cuts deeper.

I've shared her before, but this is different. Things have changed since Ashtyn ran, and I'm not about to let these sick bastards rape Sierra because I'm being tested. Or let them punish her for nothing she's done.

"What the fuck do you want?" I shout at the woman, losing my patience. We both know it. I'm powerless here, and I hate it. I don't love Sierra, but I also don't want to see her being tortured or raped by these men. She has nothing to do with Carnage. She's here because of me. I turned down Ashtyn as mine, and then I helped her escape. Sierra was stuck with me as her Lord because of my father. After I refused two different chosens, my father decided for me. It was no longer an option. We were forced into each other's lives. She didn't choose me. Everything leads back to me.

"My men work hard, Haidyn. And I believe that hard work should be rewarded. Like yourself." She reaches out and one of them hands her a pair of pliers. "Cut her free and let them play."

My eyes drop to the pliers as my heart races at her words. Sierra won't stand a chance. Two days with no food or water...she's exhausted and bleeding. Even if I could take all four of them on, she wouldn't be able to get far.

This bitch has taken over Carnage, and there's nothing I can do about it. Saint is still in the hospital with no word on his condition other than they've got him sedated for a better chance at recovery. I don't believe that shit. I haven't seen Kash in days. I can only save one person at a time.

Taking them in my hand, I turn back to Sierra. She shakes her head, fresh tears falling from her eyes. "Please...no..."

I pocket the pliers and place both hands back on her face, gripping her tear-streaked cheeks. "Shh, calm down. Deep breath, baby."

She sniffs, snot running from her nose.

"Good girl."

"Please," she whispers. "Please...please...Haidyn...don't let them..." She sobs, unable to finish her sentence.

My chest tightens. I've done some fucked-up shit in my life, but I don't kill the innocent, especially women.

"Don't let them rape—"

"Calm down." I interrupt her. "Relax." I nod my head as my eyes search hers. "Can you do that for me?"

I feel her trembling body relax into the fence the best she can and give her a reassuring smile. Gently, I turn her head side to side to see how much movement the barbed wire wrapped around her neck allows. "That's it. You're doing great, baby."

Taking a second, I place my forehead against hers, feeling my heart pound in my chest. "I'm sorry..."

A soft sob leaves her cracked lips before she whispers, "Thank you." Is she accepting her fate, or does she think I have a plan to save her? Because I can't think of one. Whoever this bitch is that's running the show here now has an army. She's brought in her own men. I have no control. None of us Spade brothers do.

I pull back; her bloodshot eyes meet mine, and she gives me a soft smile as fresh tears fall over her bottom lashes. Without another thought, I snap her neck.

Sierra's body goes limp against the fence, and I gently lower her head. Stepping back, I release her and see her hanging there like a sacrifice that didn't need to be made.

My heart is heavy, and my pulse races. I'm fucking gasping for breath. I killed her. We both knew that was the only option she had. Who knows what they would have done to her or how long she would have been a prisoner of Carnage. She didn't belong here.

"I'm disappointed in you, Haidyn." The bitch sighs dramatically.

I give a rough laugh. "Get in line." It's a long one.

"Cut her down and leave her for the wildlife to eat," she orders her men.

I turn to face them, giving my dead chosen my back, protecting her body. "We'll be taking her with us." She deserves to be laid to rest.

The brunette steps into me, her green eyes on mine—they're contacts. She's trying to hide her true identity from us. I'm just not sure why. Eye color doesn't make a fucking difference. "You don't call the shots here, Haidyn. You were being tested, and you failed."

I snort.

"You will see. It's for the best." She turns to her men once again. "Leave her and bring him back to the basement. He earned a punishment, and you guys deserve to give it." With that, she walks back to Carnage.

I turn around and grab the pliers out of my pocket and start to snap the barbed wire that holds her in place, catching her body as it falls into me. Before I can turn around, I'm knocked forward and we both fall to the ground. Motherfucker... Leaving her on the ground, I don't even get the chance to turn around to face them before they jump me.

I LOOK OVER A SLEEPING CHARLOTTE. I HOPE BILL WAS LYING about who she is and what they want from her. Because she was right when we stood in her kitchen. There are worse things than dying. That's why Bill suggested I kill her because he knows exactly what her future holds.

My eyes scan her soft features. Could I kill her? No. Even though I know deep down that she's innocent, I can't kill her or walk away. She's mine. I've wanted her for years. Why would I deprive myself of something that already belongs to me?

My cum leaks from her lips, her cunt, and her ass. It's my name she moans in her sleep. And it's my bed she wakes up in. I'll ride this train until it falls off the tracks. And then, I'll do whatever it takes to make sure she remains mine. Forever.

Taking a deep breath, I let it out and close my eyes.

♠

DO YOU EVER GET THAT KIND OF SLEEP WHEN YOU FEEL LIKE you've slept for days? Like your body needed a reset. I never have. Until now.

Opening my eyes, I'm greeted with a set of pretty blue ones. I blink, looking around to see we're in my room, in my bed, and the sun is up. "What time is it?" I ask. My voice sounds rough.

"Almost noon."

"What the fuck?" I sit up quickly, rubbing my eyes. No way I slept that long.

"What's wrong? Do you have somewhere to be?" she asks. I feel her hand on my back, rubbing it. I stiffen at the touch, and she removes it.

"I never sleep that long."

"I never see you sleep at all." She laughs.

I look back over at her, and she's now on her back, hands under her neck, and she's staring up at me. My eyes drop to her body since I pulled the covers off her when I sat up. I don't miss the way her soft pink nipples harden when my eyes linger on them. Then they drop to her pierced belly button. I find myself lying down next to her, on my side, my hand propping my head up as the other goes to her stomach.

"Do you want kids?" I'm not sure why I ask, but the conversation I had last night is still fresh on my mind.

"Of course," she replies as if it wasn't an odd question. Then she gives a little laugh. "If I had married my Lord, I would probably have at least one by now."

I frown. "You said you didn't have a Lord yet."

She rolls her eyes. "I recently found out that I have one. He's just...unavailable."

"What's that mean?" Who told her this?

"He's dead." She turns her head to look up at me, and I know she's lying. But I don't push it. As long as she's in the process of her assignment, she won't be given to anyone. The Lords have given her to me, and I'm starting to appreciate that. "What about you? Do you want kids?"

"No."

She frowns at how quickly I answer the question. "Why not?"

"Because children don't belong in Carnage." Don't get me wrong. I'm happy for Saint and Ashtyn, but we were the children raised in that hell, and I don't want any child to have to endure that. No matter who their fathers are.

"What if your Lady wants a child?" she asks, her voice lower than before. As if she's afraid to ask.

"I won't be getting married," I answer.

"Wait." She sits up, and my hand falls from her waist. "You have to take a Lady, and you have to reproduce."

I lie on my back, getting comfortable by propping my head up on the pillow to get a better look at her, but I say nothing.

She goes on at my silence. "Don't you believe in love?"

I snort at that thought.

She surprises me by getting up and straddling my hips. Her hair falls over her shoulder, and I push it back so I can see her body. My cock instantly hardens underneath her. "Then I feel sorry for you," she says matter-of-factly.

I laugh, and she slaps my chest playfully. I grab both of her wrists and hold them captive as her eyes meet mine and soften. "In our world, there is nothing but evil." She licks her lips and sighs. "You are forced to prove you're worthy for them...and once you have proven yourself, they have the power to take it from you at any given moment. Don't you want someone you know will love you unconditionally?"

I just stare up at her, hoping she can't feel my heart racing in my chest.

"Someone who can see who you really are and still accept that?" She tilts her head to the side and smiles. It's a soft one, but it lights up her pretty face. "Who wouldn't want to know love in a world full of hate?"

"That's what you want." It's not a question but more of an observation.

I get it. She had a different life than what the Spade brothers and I had. She wasn't raised in hell. She wasn't beaten because she didn't want to hurt another life. She knows she has to prove herself and is willing to do so, but it's not the same. Letting go of her wrists, I run my knuckles down the side of her face.

Her smile widens, and she corrects me. "It's what I have."

"Who?" *Her fake boyfriend?* I want to tell her that he isn't going to care about her if he ever finds out who she really is. And if he does, she'll have to kill him. If she refuses, I'll do it for her. Because then he'll be a threat to her.

"My mother and my stepdad." Her shoulders are back, and her head held high. She's so proud of that statement.

"Go home...grab your gun and put a bullet in her head while she sleeps." That's what her stepdad told me, and I highly doubt she knows what kind of future she has. Does she even know she's a founder...how much power she truly has? Doubtful.

Her smile falls at my silence, and her eyes drop to my chest, avoiding mine. Sitting up, I cup her face in both of my hands and give her a reassuring smile. "Not everyone is as lucky as you, doll face." I lie, not wanting to burst her bubble that she thinks she's safe in.

That smile returns, and her nails softly run up and down my back, making me break out in goose bumps. "You—"

I push my lips to hers, cutting her off. Enough bullshit talking. If she wants to believe in fairy tales, then that's on her. I don't believe in them, nor do I want one. She's naked in my bed, so why talk when I can fuck her?

CHARLOTTE

I SQUEAL AS HE PICKS ME UP AND THROWS ME ONTO MY BACK. When he kneels between my open legs, I drop my eyes to his hard dick. I could feel him while I straddled him. I've been trying to have a real conversation with him, but it was so distracting.

When I woke up this morning in his arms, he seemed different. He wasn't a Lord or a Spade brother. He was just a man holding me. It gave me a sense of hope. I know what my future holds for me. My Lord will hate me. I thought I had accepted that years ago and only wanted power, but to feel protected, loved? Even if it was false, it fucked with my mind. It made me want that.

"Stop that, doll face." Haidyn's voice breaks through my inner rambling.

"Huh?" I ask, my eyes meeting his as he hovers over me.

He grabs my waist and tosses me over onto my stomach and grabs my hips, pulling my ass up into the air. His knees spread mine wide open, and then he's pushing his cock into my pussy. No foreplay, no ropes, chains, or gags. Just one hand in my hair, shoving the side of my face into his mattress while the other shoves his thumb in my ass, and he fucks my cunt until I'm crying out his name, and my cum covers his pierced dick.

♠

I OPEN MY HEAVY EYES AND LOOK AROUND THE ROOM. IT'S JUST Muffin and me in his bed. Getting to my feet, I use the restroom and put on a shirt before I exit his primary suite. My stomach rumbles, telling me to eat some breakfast. I came twice, and after that, I was nothing but jelly. Haidyn fucked me until I passed out.

Walking down the hallway, I come to the open kitchen and living room where I see Haidyn standing by a kitchen chair in the center of the room. Rope sits on the black leather and so does a syringe. I step back and spin to return to his room.

"It's going to happen, Annabelle."

The name makes my teeth clench. What makes him decide to call me by it? When he's mad at me? Did I do something to piss him off? I thought we shared a moment this morning? Maybe it was wishful thinking talking about love. I mean, I know he's never going to feel that for another woman, but I still felt he had opened up to me just by asking me if I wanted kids. It was a very personal question, and for the first time, it was as if he wanted to know about me. The real me. Not the one I pretend to be because I have to.

"Either you willingly sit down in the chair, or I chase you down, drag you back by your hair, and tie you to it. What's it going to be?"

I shouldn't get excited at the way he explains the things he's going to do to me. But I can't help it. You can only fight for so long, but eventually, it's pointless. Closing my eyes, I silently curse. Goddamn him for doing this to me. Turning back to face him, I lift my chin and walk toward him. When I come to a stop in front of the chair, he lowers his eyes to the T-shirt of his that I wear.

"Strip," he commands, and I feel those butterflies in my stomach that always come when he tells me what to do.

I pull the material up and over my head, tossing it to the side.

"Have a seat, doll face." He taps the leather and picks up the syringe before I do as he says.

Chapter 50

Haidyn

After I finished fucking her, she passed out, and I thought about what she said to me in bed. She knows more than she's letting on, and this is the only way to get what I want out of her.

I take the rope and kneel behind the chair. "Hands behind your back," I command, and she crosses her wrists behind the chair. Once I'm done securing her wrists together, I take the excess rope and bring it underneath the chair where I tie it around both of her ankles. I don't need her in a tight spot because I know she won't fight me on this. I just need her in one place. It's more for her safety than anything else.

I rise and move to stand in front of her and remove the cap off the syringe. She tilts her head to the side for me and sucks in a deep breath. "Good girl," I praise her, and she whimpers. After I push the needle into her neck, I place the cap back on and set it on the kitchen island before returning to her.

I gently cup her chin, forcing her to look up at me, and her eyes go heavy almost instantly. "What do you know about Dollhouse?" I get to the point. I didn't give her as much as last time. I've only got a few questions, so this will wear off a lot quicker.

"Never heard of it."

Bill did say she had no clue what she was meant to do if she fulfills her assignment. "You lied to me in bed this morning about your Lord. Why?" I know he's not dead. That would be too easy. She's meant for someone, especially if she's who Bill says she is.

Charlotte blinks, licking her lips. "Because you have him."

I frown. "What does that mean?"

"He's at Carnage."

Interesting. We have a lot of Lords go in and out of Carnage. The turnaround rate is actually pretty high. Most don't last long. "Who told you that?"

"Bill."

"How the hell would he know that?" Funny that Bill didn't mention that to me during our meetup. I knew he was keeping shit from me.

"He plays golf with his father..."

"Who is your Lord?"

"Winston Garvey."

Hmm. Never heard of that name, so Bill is lying to her or the Lord is going by another name. I'm starting to think anything is possible. "When are you supposed to marry him?"

"A year ago." Her lashes flutter, and I run a hand through my hair. She did tell me she would have already had at least one kid by now.

I want to ask her about breeders, but I don't. She doesn't know anything about it. As a Lord, you're never told what your punishment is for failing an assignment. The Lords want you to be surprised. "What do you know about the founders?" I decide to ask.

Her brows pull together in confusion. "No one knows who they are."

Well, fuck! This didn't get me anywhere. Pulling out my pocketknife, I cut the rope and untie her. Picking her up, I carry her back to bed and pull the covers up over her neck. "It'll wear off within an hour," I say, kissing her forehead gently.

As I walk away, she speaks softly, "May I ask you a question?"

I sit down next to her, brushing her dark hair from her face, and smile. "What is it?"

"Why don't you have a Lady?"

I tilt my head to the side but don't answer.

"Is it because you denied her, or the Lords denied you a Lady as punishment?"

"Why do you think they'd deny me a Lady?" Such a strange word for her to use.

"I got an email about you...under Lady, it said *denied*."

Adam and I have been through her laptop, and any emails she received from the Lords have been wiped clean with no trace of how to retrieve them. So I have no clue what they've sent her. I decide to ask my own question. "If you think I've been denied a Lady, then why did you ask me about getting married this morning?"

"Because everyone deserves someone." She yawns, and her eyes flutter shut.

Four years ago

ADAM AND I ENTER THE OFFICE AT CARNAGE, AND ALL conversation comes to a halt. All four of our fathers are present.

Mine looks at me. "Haidyn, just who I wanted to see."

Must be my lucky day.

"We need to finish that conversation—"

"We did. It's done with." We've already had our vow ceremony. I have a chosen. My father said that Sierra's father owed him a favor, and she was it. I told him that he should fuck her then, and he just laughed. The sick bastard has definitely thought about it.

His jaw sharpens at my words. "It's complicated..."

The door opens behind us, and Adam and I both turn to see a woman enter the office. She wears a red dress that hugs her curves and shows off her large, paid-for chest. Her head is held high, and her eyes sweep over me and Adam for a quick second before she dismisses us both.

"Brothers." She addresses our fathers. Going to them one by one, they each hug and kiss her cheek. "I'm sorry to interrupt. I can come back," she offers.

"Nonsense." My father waves off her concern and pulls out the chair to his desk for her to have a seat. "Come alone today?" he asks, looking back to the door.

"He's here. I left him in the foyer speaking to Jessie."

The room falls silent, and I look at Adam.

"Okay..." Adam starts feeling the awkwardness in the room.

"We're leaving." I feel like they're about to strip her naked, tie her

down and each take their turns fucking all her holes while her husband watches. He probably brought her here for that very reason. And I'd prefer to not have to soak my eyes in bleach tonight.

"Haidyn," my father growls. "We are having this conversation."

"No. We're not."

"Either you listen or we decide for you," Adam's dad speaks.

"What is this about?" Adam looks at me confused.

He has no clue what my dad wanted me to do. I thought I had handled it, and we had moved on.

"Haidyn denied your sister as his chosen," his father states.

Adam looks at me wide-eyed and then back at his father. "You can't be serious. Of course he did. Saint..."

"Would have learned to live with it," Saint's father snaps.

"I have a chosen. Sierra," I remind them as if they all weren't there and watched her bleed on my dick. "And Saint has Ashtyn. The ritual is over. We're moving on."

"You need a Lady." My father squares his shoulders.

"Absolutely not!" I shake my head, knowing exactly where this is going.

"You either take her willingly or we force you," Adam's father says.

"Are you saying he has to marry Ash?" Adam looks from me to them. "Dad?" He steps into his father and after a second he shakes his head. "No. you can't be serious."

"Your sister will marry Haidyn whether they want to or not."

"I won't fucking do it. I won't force her to do it," I growl.

"You love her." The woman speaks, and I choose to ignore her. I don't give a fuck what she thinks.

My father removes a cell from the pocket of his suit jacket and runs his fingers over it before he places it on his desk, propped up facing the room. A video of Saint, Kashton, and I each fucking Ashtyn's ass is playing.

"Jesus Christ." Adam spins around, giving us his back to look away from the video playing of his sister. He throws his head back, closing his eyes and takes a deep breath to try and drown out the sound of Ashtyn's voice begging for more. Adam already had to watch Saint fuck her at the vow ceremony. He sure as fuck doesn't want to see it again.

"He already shares her with you." Adam's father shrugs. "You make

her your Lady, and you can do whatever you want with her. Hell, let them all fuck her if that makes you feel better. Line 'em up."

"I think I'm going to vomit," Adam whispers, running a hand down his face.

"The answer is no," I grind out. How many ways do I have to say it?

"Haidyn," my father growls. "This is serious. You may have refused Ashtyn as your chosen, but she will be your wife."

"I'm not taking her as a Lady," I shout. He's got to be out of his mind.

"There is a bigger picture here," Adam's father snaps. "And we have made sure things are in order for the future of Carnage."

"I don't give a fuck about this place," I argue.

My father throws a glass of bourbon across the room, and it shatters against the wall. "Goddammit..."

"I won't do that to Saint." I shake my head.

"This has nothing to do with Saint. It has to do with you and what we've set up for all of you."

"I don't want her."

"Do you think I wanted your mother?" he snaps. "Do you think I wanted you?" Pointing at me, he adds, "She was worthless, and you're nothing more than a disappointment."

His opinions about my mother and me aren't new. I've never been the son that he wanted—easy to manipulate—and she couldn't give him more.

Sighing, he runs a hand down his face.

Adam's father speaks, "She is the one you will marry. We'll set it up. It needs to be sooner rather than later."

Adam spins around. "Dad—"

"And if you refuse, we'll force you both."

Adam steps toward his father, but I grab his shirt and yank him back. "Do what you have to do," I say and turn to walk out, dragging Adam behind me.

"If she loves Saint as much as you say he loves her, she'll come around to the idea of being your Lady real quick," my father speaks, but I ignore him.

I yank the door open and slam it shut.

"What the fuck, Haidyn?" Adam snaps at me, ripping his shirt from my hold. "Why the fuck didn't you tell me they wanted you to take Ashtyn as your chosen?"

We get into the elevator, and I turn to face him. "Are you fucking serious? You've been running around...being secretive ever since we met with that detective. Fuck, Adam, I can barely get you to answer your goddamn phone. Let alone fill you in on my life," I shout, pushing the button for the basement.

He steps in front of me, and I bow my chest. "What are you going to do? How the fuck do we stop this?"

"I tell Saint." Give him a heads-up and we get ahead of it.

"No." He shakes his head. "He can't find out."

"Are you fucking serious? Did you not just hear what they said? They're going to use him. To make her be my Lady. We have to tell him."

"I'll—"

"Shut the fuck up," I whisper, my eyes avoiding the camera in the elevator. They are probably listening to everything we're saying. "Fill me in later."

THAT WAS THE LAST TIME I SAW ADAM BEFORE TYSON'S PHONE call to Saint, and we had to go save her from her parents' house. Adam was on the run, and we were keeping her hidden. Our fathers' plans for her changed. We either made her a prisoner or Saint took her in as his—initiating her—which got them all off my back about making her my Lady.

CHARLOTTE

HE'S TAKING A SHOWER WHEN I WALK BY AND HEAD TO HIS restroom. I no longer have any dignity or shyness around him. Living with a man changes that. I woke up an hour ago and ate the breakfast that he had fixed for me in awkward silence while he worked in his office. He didn't bring up the fact that he drugged me for answers, and I didn't ask any questions as to why he wanted to know those things.

After I finish, I start to wash my hands and then turn to face him as he stands in the middle of the rain shower. It's in the corner up against the far wall but has no glass or doors. It looks like he's standing in the middle of a downpour, running his hands through his hair as the water falls from the ceiling.

When I watched him sleep earlier this morning in bed, that was the first time I ever got to see him naked, and what a sight it was. He's covered in ink, muscles, and scars. I saw where he had been shot and where I stabbed him. The ones on his back are harder to see, they're long and skinny—like he was whipped. I wonder who did it to him? Was it his father trying to teach him that women mean nothing? It wouldn't surprise me. But men like Haidyn don't like to talk about what they've been through, so I pretended not to see them.

He lowers his head, placing his hands flat against the black wall. I step underneath his outstretched arms, shielding myself from the shower. His eyes open and meet mine. He doesn't look surprised or annoyed, just...empty. I wonder what he's thinking.

The video of him and his dad in that concrete room is still fresh in my mind. I wonder if Ashtyn knows what he did for her. And I quickly push that out of my mind. I don't want to think of those two together in any capacity.

Reaching up, I wrap my arms around his neck, enjoying the feel of the warm water.

I pull him down as I stand on my tiptoes, and he obliges by meeting me halfway. My eyes fall closed as his lips touch mine, and I kiss him. I hate how much I enjoy it. For someone so rough and hard, his lips are tender.

When I pull away and flatten my feet, my eyes drop to his dick. He's hard. My eyes run over the six barbells that run up and down along his thick and veiny dick. "Did this hurt?" I ask, dropping my hand to run my thumb over the ones through the head.

He chuckles softly. "It wasn't for pleasure."

I frown, looking up at him. "It doesn't feel good when you have sex?" It feels good to me. But then again, I've never fucked anyone other than Haidyn, so I've only ever had a pierced dick inside me.

"Oh, it does." He nods, removing one hand from the wall and

cupping my face. His thumb runs over my wet lips, and I shiver even though the hot water covers us.

My eyes go back to his dick, and I lick my lips. Then I'm falling to my knees before him.

"Charlotte," he warns, and I'm not sure if it's for my benefit or his. I just want to taste him. To really take my time and feel it. I'm always tied up and gagged when he fucks my mouth. I want to memorize it.

I place my hand on his muscular thigh and lean forward, the tip of my tongue touching the base of his shaft, and I slowly run it upward. I can feel the barbells on my tongue as I go. One...two...three...four... five...six. Getting to the head, I feel the balls of the others.

Pulling back, I look up at him, and he's got both hands on the wall once again, head down, shielding the rainfall from me with his eyes closed.

I feel powerful kneeling between his legs. This time, I push my tongue all the way out, flattening it against the base, and slowly run it over his dick once again. He groans when I wrap my lips around the tip before sucking.

"Fuck, doll face." His voice is hoarse, and my pussy tightens. My knees shake, and my wet hair covers my face, so I push it out of the way to get a better look before I do it again.

But this time, I wrap my hand around the base when I get to the tip and take more of his length into my mouth. He's so big it makes me nervous. I've had it in my mouth, in my ass, and in my cunt, but I've never got to play with it. I've never held it in my hands and explored it like I want.

I feel his fingers tangle in my wet hair the next second. But he doesn't control my head. Instead, he just holds it off my face as I take my time, learning every piercing and feeling every inch of his dick.

He's so hard for me. I did this to him. No one else is here. No other bitch is getting what's mine.

My free hand drops to his balls, and I squeeze them before letting go.

He repositions his feet wider, and lets out a deep growl as he stands over me. So I do it again.

"Charlotte?" he moans my name.

"Yeah?" I rasp, pulling back and looking up at him.

His heavy blue eyes stare down into mine. "You're going to make me come doing that, doll face." He makes it sound like a warning, but I see it as a compliment.

I smile, proud of that thought, and lean forward, closing my eyes and sucking on his dick while my hand plays with his balls. I don't know what the fuck I'm doing because I've never done it before. He never allows me to have control.

His hips thrust forward, and his hand remains in my hair, but he doesn't force my head down. Is this how he feels when he has control of me? I suck him to the back of my throat, and when I gag, I hold it. He's so long that my other hand is still wrapped around the base.

"Goddamn," he groans, and my thighs clench.

Thankfully, he's bent over enough, leaning against the wall at my back so the water isn't drowning me.

His fingers tighten in my hair, holding on with a fist, and it just makes me want to be better and suck deeper. I suck in a deep breath and take his cock into my mouth and down my throat, taking away my air, and my body jerks involuntarily. I tell myself to relax, opening wider and leaning forward. My hand falls from the base of his dick, feeling the last barbell touch my tongue.

"I'm coming."

Before he can even get the words out, his cock pulses in my mouth. Being the good girl that I am, I keep my eyes open and look up at him, telling myself one more second to swallow his cum.

He lets go of my hair, and I fall back onto my ass, gasping. He steps back from the wall, allowing the water to cover me like a downpour. He grips my arms and yanks me up on my numb legs, and I wrap my arms around his neck. His hands drop to my ass, and he picks me up, slamming my back into the cool wall. He's breathing just as heavily as I am when his lips slam on mine. I kiss him back without thought even though it's not as tender as the one before. His fingers dig painfully into my ass, and I rock my hips against his semi-hard dick, hoping he understands I want him.

He pulls away, and I gasp. "Fuck me." In case my actions aren't clear enough on how desperate I am for him.

Repositioning his hands, he lets go of my ass and wraps an arm around my waist while the other grabs his dick. I'm still trying to breathe as the water falls on us from the ceiling above, so I bury my face into his neck.

"What do you want, doll face?" he growls in my ear while I feel his now hardened cock pressed against my pussy.

"You," I answer, my hands digging into his hair and then gripping his shoulders. Fuck, I can't get him close enough. "Please...I need you."

"Whatever my girl wants." He chuckles at my desperation, and I don't care. I know what it feels like for him to own me, and I want it. Being on my knees for him was like an adrenaline rush. I'm on a high that I don't want to stop.

The breath gets caught in my lungs as he slides his cock into my pussy. I clench around him and his wet chest rumbles against mine. "Goddamn, you feel so good." He shoves my back into the wall to help hold me up while he readjusts his hands as they go back to my ass. "Fucking perfect."

"Please..." I'm almost on the verge of tears, but he likes it when I cry for him. It makes him feel superior as if any Lords aren't.

I loosen my legs around his waist to give him some room, and he takes the hint. His hips start to move, allowing his cock to fuck me while he pins me against the wall. My lips find his once more, and he swallows my cries as I become his desperate dirty little whore.

I have a feeling that's what *Charlotte* was meant to be all along.

♠

Shutting off the water, he grabs the towel off the hook and hands it to me before he gets himself one. "I'm going into town today," I inform him.

He stops, and his eyes meet mine. "No, you're not."

I roll my eyes. "I can't stay here forever, Haidyn. I'll be fine. I have a facial today."

Walking over to me, I watch water run down his chest and over his defined abs before it trails down his large thighs. God, the man is massive in all the right ways. "I'll give you a facial." He wiggles his eyebrows, and I can't help but laugh.

Is he making a joke?

"Your cock fucking my throat until you come all over my face is not nearly as relaxing as Enrique giving me a deep tissue massage." Although I enjoyed what I just did, it's definitely not the same.

He tosses the towel over his shoulder. "Enrique? A man gives you a full body massage?"

"Yep. Has for years now." I smile up at him.

"Not anymore." And with that, he walks into the closet.

I let it go because this is not up for debate. I need a *me* day. That day is today!

I quickly dry my hair. I didn't even wash it, but it did get wet when I joined him. Afterward, I throw it up in a messy bun, get dressed in sweats and a T-shirt, and make my way to the kitchen. I'm craving some more pancakes. I've made myself at home and become pretty comfortable in his house.

He's nowhere to be seen, so I can only guess he's in his gym or his office. I begin reheating the breakfast he made me earlier when the doorbell rings.

I pause, looking up around the quiet house, and when it rings for a second time, I walk toward the double doors. Unlocking them, I open the right to see a man standing on Haidyn's porch. His eyes drop to my bare feet and run up over my sweatpants and T-shirt. When they get to mine, he asks, "Where's Haidyn?"

I cross my arms over my chest. *He's a Lord.* He has to be. They all have that air about them. They think they're untouchable and above you. I'm just a woman who has a pussy for them to use. "Who's asking?" I arch a brow.

"Charlotte?" I hear my name being called out from behind me.

I turn around to see an already sweaty Haidyn headed toward me. So much for his shower. He was in the gym. His eyes are narrowed on mine as if I did something wrong. "What the fuck are you doing?" he barks at me.

"Me?" I point at myself as if he's talking to someone else.

He ignores me and looks at the man standing on the porch. "Hey, man. Come in." Haidyn places his hand on my upper arm and speaks. "Give us a second." Before the guy can say anything, he drags me back into his bedroom. "What the fuck was that?" he demands, slamming the door shut.

"Someone knocked on the door, and I answered. What's the big deal?" I shrug.

"You don't answer the door for anyone," he growls.

"Haidyn, you're paranoid." I think him staying out here in this house has got him on edge. "If someone wants to kill you, they're not going to knock." I laugh, but he doesn't.

He runs a hand down his face and sighs. Giving me his back, he exits his room and slams the door shut as if I'm going to remain in here all day.

I go to open it when my watch goes off. Looking at it, I see I have an email. I wrap my hand around the doorknob and crack it open to see him and the guy walk off toward the back of the house where I know Haidyn's office is.

Shutting the door quietly, I practically jump over his bed, pick up my cell, and rush to the bathroom where I lock the door and turn on the exhaust fan, needing extra sound. Then I pull up my email to see the Lords have sent me a video.

I push play.

It's of a room that has a table and two chairs in it. A woman I know by the name of Laura sits in one of them. She's a therapist and she had a daughter around my age, but we never hung out. My mother wouldn't allow me. Ashtyn sits in the other seat across from her. "Which Spade brother are you the closest with?" Laura asks her.

Ashtyn frowns. "Why?"

"I'm just curious."

"I'm Saint's chosen," she says.

"Yes, but they all three fuck you, no?"

Ashtyn stiffens, and I feel my pulse race at the woman's question.

"A Lord is allowed to share his chosen with whoever he wants," Ashtyn speaks softly.

"Are you being cautious?"

Ashtyn frowns as if she doesn't understand what Laura is asking. I know exactly what she means.

"I doubt Saint would be happy if one of the others knocks you up." Laura goes on.

"Oh, no, that wouldn't happen." She shakes her head.

"And why is that?" Laura tilts her head to the side.

"They..." Ashtyn trails off.

"I see." She writes something down in her notebook. "They don't fuck you vaginally."

I don't know why, but the thought of Haidyn being with her makes me jealous. I know he wasn't a virgin, but I still don't like that he was with his best friend's girl. Maybe it's because she'll always be part of his life. There will be no escaping her. She lives at Carnage now where Haidyn will eventually return to. He'll see her every day. And makes me wonder if Saint still shares her with his *brothers*.

And that brings up another question...will Kashton and Haidyn share whoever they are with, with Saint as well? I just see these women being tied to the Spade brothers' beds while they go from room to room each taking a turn.

"Would you say that you care about Kashton and Haidyn the same as you do for Saint?" Laura wonders.

"What kind of session is this?" she asks defensively.

"It just seems that they are willing to risk their lives for you, and I'm trying to figure out why." She places her manicured nail on her chin. "It can't be sex. Kashton and Haidyn have their own chosens. I'm wondering what you offer them that they can't get elsewhere."

I remember my friends telling me that Haidyn shared his chosen with another. He didn't care about her, but a Lord never does. We're just objects to play with.

Ashtyn crosses her arms over her chest.

"Show her," Laura calls out.

"Show me what?"

A light comes on in the room next door. A window in the wall shows a man hanging from the ceiling. *It's Haidyn.* My wide eyes go to his cuffed wrists that are strung above his head and secured to the chain. He's shirtless just like in the last video they sent me. His jeans are low on his hips, his body stretched while it gently sways back and forth.

My hand covers my mouth when I see the blood that runs from his cuffed wrists. He's covered in sweat, and white pads are stuck on his chest and abdomen. They are connected by wires to a machine that sits on a roller cart next to him. The hood is still over his head, and I bet he's still gagged. How much time has passed since the last video they sent me of him when his father entered the room with three other Lords when they tased him?

His father did this to him. Because of her. He gave her a sedative instead of the adrenaline, and he's the one being punished.

The door opens to the opposite room, and someone new enters with a black cloak and Lords mask on. "Who is that?" Ashtyn asks.

It's Haidyn! How does she not know that?

The guy in the cloak turns on the machine and flips a switch. "Ready for your session?"

Haidyn doesn't move or answer, and I blink, my eyes stinging watching him hang there. I hope he's unconscious.

"Let's turn it up this time. I think your last session was too easy." He turns a knob, and the lights dim as Haidyn shakes, his legs kicking, muscles straining. They're electrocuting him.

"Stop!" Ashtyn says, slamming her hands on the glass. "What the fuck is he doing? Why is he doing that?"

"Actions have consequences, Ashtyn."

The switch is turned off, and Haidyn sags in the cuffs. He sways back and forth, the toes of his boots lightly touching the concrete floor while his abs flex at his heavy breaths.

The guy in the mask turns it on again, and Haidyn's body begins to spasm. Ashtyn bangs on the glass. "Stop. Stop. You're going to kill him."

The man in the Lord's mask laughs at her.

"How do you not know that man doesn't deserve his punishment?" Laura asks Ashtyn.

The Lord slaps Haidyn on the back, and it causes him to spin around in the chains. There are more of those white pads on his back as well, and red marks that cover his tan skin. They whipped him. Now the scars make sense.

"Why?" Ashtyn demands, and I want to punch her in the goddamn face. *It's because of you he's there.* And the sad part is that she doesn't even know who it is. "Why are you making me watch this? Why did you want to even see me?"

Laura gives Ashtyn a soft smile. "This is a reminder, Ashtyn, from the Spade brothers." She must be talking about their fathers. "That you are a guest here, and it will be best to remember that."

The Lord in the opposite room turns off the white patches, and Haidyn hangs in the cuffs connected to the chains. "Until next session," he states before walking over to the door. He shuts off the light, bathing the room in darkness before he leaves Haidyn hanging there.

Shhh...

Chapter 51

Charlotte

I snuck out of Haidyn's house while he was occupied in his office with whoever the Lord was that I answered the door for. After I watched the video, I grabbed my purse and ran.

I spent my day running errands, went by my house, then made it to the spa. Hours have gone by, and I haven't heard from him. It's hard to get in touch with someone when you turn your cell off. But I've kept my eyes open. I've never been more aware of my surroundings than I have today to see if he's following me. But nothing. He's going to be so pissed when I get back to his house, but a part of me is looking forward to it.

I'm being woken up by the nurse as she removes the IV from my arm, and I already feel better, but of course that could have been the nap. I didn't mean to fall asleep, but I also couldn't stop it. Haidyn keeps me worn out. A part of me thinks that's on purpose. She hands me a water this time, and just like the previous drink, I chug it down.

"Enrique can't see you today," she says, and I sit up straighter with a sickening feeling in my gut.

"Why not?" I ask.

"Well..." She nibbles on her bottom lip. "We'll give you a call to reschedule," she answers vaguely and then turns, exiting my room.

What the fuck did Haidyn do? *Shit!* I have to get home. Home? Is his home mine? No. It's more like a prison. One with conjugal visits.

Making my way to the parking lot, I turn my cell back on and go to call Haidyn but stop myself. Why would I call him? What do I have to say?

He's going to lie to me. I know he had something to do with Enrique canceling. I reverse out of my parking spot, stomp on the gas, and race home.

Pulling up to his driveway, I rush into the house. "Haidyn?" I shout, and Muffin meows from the couch as if I've woken her from a nap. "Haidyn?" I run to the garage and see his white bike is gone.

Had he been following me, but I just overlooked him? I mean, he's hard to miss. Sighing, I remove my cell from my pocket, and send a quick text to the group chat. Fuck him. I'm going out tonight.

HAIDYN

I PULL INTO MY DRIVEWAY AND SEE HER SUV PARKED. SMIRKING, I pull into the garage. She came home after her day at the spa. She might have turned her cell off, but I figured she'd make me chase her down.

She's getting more ballsy. I like it.

It's a little past nine in the evening, and I enter the house. It's quiet other than the cat eating out of her bowl in the kitchen. She chomps on the food while she growls at it.

I enter my bedroom just as Charlotte's phone chimes sitting on the nightstand while it charges. Walking over to it, I pick it up to see it's a group chat with some of her friends. I open it up and read over it.

> CHELSEA: I'm so excited about tonight. It's been too long since we've had a girls' night. I need it so badly.

> NIKKI: Yes. Jerrold has been driving me nuts since we moved in together. I need space and time out with my girls. I'm getting fucked up tonight, for sure.

Setting her phone down, I walk toward the bathroom to see if she's in there getting ready. I come to a stop in the doorway when I see her bent over the black marble counter applying red lipstick to her plump lips. She pulls back, placing the lid on and begins to run her hands through her long curls.

She looks absolutely stunning. My eyes drop to her red high heels and run up over her smooth and tan legs. Thoughts of filling her ass with an inflatable butt plug enter my mind as I make my way up to her round ass. She's wearing a white dress that rests high up on her thighs. If she bent over any farther, I'd be able to see what color underwear she has on—if any. The back of the dress has a keyhole out of the middle showing off the curve of her spine. My eyes move to the mirror as she begins to apply more mascara to her already finished makeup. She's got dark shadow on with thick liner and rosy cheeks. She's too busy getting ready to even know I'm watching her. My eyes move to the front of her dress, and it's high on the neck with a built-in collar around her slender neck.

Her phone beeps again, but she doesn't seem to hear it. Or she's just choosing to ignore it. I turn to walk back over to the nightstand and pick it up.

CHELSEA: Me too girl. We're all getting fucked tonight—if we're lucky, in more ways than one.

My girl is getting fucked alright. I type out a message of my own.

Something came up. Can't make it.

Then I hold the power button down until it shuts off completely. The last thing I need is for them to call her. She'll be unable to answer. Besides, her hands will be tied, and she won't be able to speak because her mouth is going to be in use.

My girl deserves punishment for leaving today after I told her she couldn't and then turning her phone off. She has to learn that won't be tolerated.

I pocket her phone, so she's not looking for it. Then I exit the bedroom to grab the things I'll need. *I'm in the mood to play.*

Shhh...

Chapter 52

Charlotte

I take a step back and look over myself in the bathroom mirror. My friends have been begging me to go out for weeks now, but I've become one of those women who seem to drop who they once were for a guy. So tonight, I'm going out, getting drunk, and will probably find myself back here, but at least I'm going to pretend I'm not becoming dependent on a man. The longer I'm here, the more I think I was overreacting. Maybe someone wasn't following me. I was mad at Haidyn, and it made me think it was him.

I start throwing makeup that I have scattered across the counter back into my makeup bag when I see Haidyn enter the bathroom. He comes up behind me and sets a glass of wine on the counter next to my now full bag. It's the first time I've seen him since I left today.

We've both been ignoring one another. I know he did something to Enrique, and he knows I'm aware of it. "Mm, thank you." I pick up the glass and take a sip.

He places his hands on my thighs and runs them up my freshly shaved legs. I choke on the cold wine as I put the glass down. "Oh no," I tell him with a chuckle, pushing his hands away, knowing exactly what he's doing.

His hand wraps around my neck from behind, yanking my head back. My breathing picks up along with my pulse as his free hand yanks the hem of my dress up to my hips, and his hand goes between my legs, cupping my pussy. "Did you just tell me no, doll face?"

I swallow against his hand at the amusement in his voice while staring at the ceiling. "I'm going out," I say, panicking.

"Your plans have changed," he announces in that tone that gives me no chance to argue.

"Haidyn—"

His hand tightens around my throat while the other slides into my thong. "You look gorgeous, doll face."

I moan as a finger softly plays with my pussy. My hips move on their own, trying to get him to touch the spot I crave the most, but have no such luck.

"You really shouldn't have gotten all fixed up for me, but I do appreciate it."

My eyes grow heavy, and my hands fall to my sides as the room sways from the lack of air. But I make no move to stop him. It'd be a useless fight anyway. I'm learning very quickly that I like to lose when it comes to him.

He lets go of my throat, and I suck in a ragged breath. Spinning me around to face him, I almost fall off the side of my heels. He cups my freshly done-up face and waits for my eyes to focus on his before he leans forward and places his lips on mine.

I lift my arms, and they find their way around his neck. Running my hands through his dark hair, I scrape my nails across his scalp. My fingers try to grab the short strands, needing something to hold on to, but he pulls away while grabbing my wrists and pushing them down to my sides.

He reaches around me to the counter, and my eyes drop to his hands to see he's grabbed my lipstick. Popping off the top, he lets it fall to the floor before he grips my chin and tilts my head back. I don't stop him as he presses the tip to my right cheek and then my left. He steps back and smiles to himself. "You've never looked prettier."

Butterflies fill my stomach at his words. I know how stupid it is. That I've allowed him to make me feel this way. I should be kicking and screaming every day at him. I should be trying to start a new life and run as far as I can. But I know it wouldn't matter because he'd bring me back. It'd just make me wet, and I'd find myself crawling to him on my hands and knees, begging for him to fuck my life up.

He steps back into me, and I think he's going to kiss me again, but instead, he grabs my hand. "Come on, doll face. I want to play."

I don't even bother to pull my dress down as I let him escort me out of the bathroom, through his bedroom, and into the living room.

Even with the floor-to-ceiling windows, it's dark in here. It's after nine o'clock, and no lights are on except for the TV that plays, but it's on mute.

He brings me to a stop and turns my back to him. "Hands behind your back. Interlock your fingers," he commands, giving my bare ass a hard smack that makes me moan. I'm confused as to why I'm still dressed even though it's up around my hips. Why didn't he order me to strip?

He wraps something around my upper chest, right above my breasts, and I drop my head to see it resembles a black belt. I hear it snap in place, then he tightens the rough material. He places another one below my breasts, restricting my arms behind my back even more. Another one is around my wrists, securing them in place and giving me no room to move my upper body.

"Bend over. Ass up in the air." He grips the back of my neck and lowers my face down onto the couch while I stand in my heels with him behind me. The position makes it hard to breathe with the tight belts around my upper body.

He places more on my legs. One around my ankles, a second right below my knees, and a third around my thighs.

"Stay right where you are," he states. Seconds later, I gasp when he pushes my thong to the side and two of his fingers enter my pussy. I can't help but push back against them, wanting more.

He's made me greedy. No matter what he gives me, it's never enough.

"Look at you being a whore begging to be fucked." He pushes a third one in, and I'm gasping at the pain and pleasure of how rough he is. Removing them, I sag and take in a calming breath. Then he's running his fingers up and over my ass. He doesn't let me warm up to it. In true Haidyn fashion, he pushes it into me, and I try to get away, but he grips the back of my neck, pinning the side of my face down into the couch, smearing my fresh makeup onto it.

He enters a second, and I cry out, my body trembling at the intrusion. He pulls them out before I feel something pushing its way into me, and I know by the cold and unforgiving metal that it's a butt plug.

It stretches me so wide that I cry, my heart now racing as he holds me in place, forcing me to take it.

Once it's in, he pulls me to a sitting position and orders, "Open wide."

I don't even have to see him to know what's coming. A gag. I swallow, knowing it will be my last chance until he releases me from it. Then I open my mouth as wide as I can, tilting my head back for him.

He leans over my head and slides the cold metal into my mouth, slipping it behind my top teeth first before my bottom ones. I whimper around the metal, having to open wider than I thought my mouth would. I've never worn one like this before.

"You're doing great, doll face," he praises me, and I close my eyes. He stuffs his fingers into my mouth to make sure nothing is pinching. Then he's pushing my head down and buckling it in place. "You're almost ready," he informs me, and I wonder what else he could possibly do. I've learned that Haidyn is very creative when it comes to making my body want more.

"This is going to be a little uncomfortable, Charlotte."

My eyes snap open at his words, but all I see is the couch since he's still standing behind me.

"But you're going to look so beautiful." His hands are in front of my face once again, and I see two small silver hooks drop in front of me before he places them into my nostrils.

I try to move my head, but something sharp digs into my cheeks, stopping me.

"I have you strapped into a spider gag, doll face. It's very restrictive with its O-ring, and four legs that cover your cheeks. If you don't want them to dig into your beautiful face, you'll stay still." The hooks pull on my nose as he connects it to the harness of the gag, snapping it in place.

Drool pools in my mouth already, and I'm gasping through my open mouth, trying to calm my racing heart. The hooks don't hurt my nose, but they aren't the most comfortable thing. I can only imagine how humiliating I look. My nose begins to run, and my eyes instantly start to water.

HAIDYN

I SIT DOWN ON THE COUCH IN FRONT OF HER. "GORGEOUS," I SAY, running my knuckles over her neck and feeling her pulse race.

She blinks rapidly, and I pull my phone out of my pocket. Her eyes widen, and she begins to mumble around the gag when she realizes what I'm doing.

I hold it out in front of her face and snap a picture of her. Then I smile, turning it to face her. She looks at it and mumbles more unintelligible words, making me chuckle. Her wide eyes meet mine, and I smile at her.

"Told you I was going to play with you, doll face." I look over the lipstick and the letters I wrote on her face. T is written in the red color on her right cheek and Y is written on the left. With her painted lips open wide, representing O in the middle.

"You're my *toy*," I inform her, and her eyes close as the first tears fall from her bottom lashes.

I send her the photo. She'll get it later when I return her phone to her, and she turns it on. I start to record and then place mine on the end table next to the couch, facing her. That I'll also send to her later. I want her to see what I see—how beautiful she is when I use her.

Leaning forward, I reach around her and pick up my water off the coffee table and take a sip. I then remove the lemon from the glass before placing it back on the coffee table.

"You're going to kneel until I bend you over and fuck your ass," I tell her, and her shoulders shake in the belts that I wrapped her in. "But until then, I'm going to watch you drool all over yourself." I run my fingers that weren't in her ass over the lemon before I stuff them into her mouth.

Her eyes spring open, and she gags as I push them to the back of her throat. Her mouth is open so wide that she has no capability of swallowing. I grab the back of her head with my free hand and push it down to stare between my open legs.

"I love it when you drool all over yourself, Charlotte. It turns me on to see how much you enjoy being my little whore." She gags again, and I pull my fingers back just enough to run them along the roof of her mouth, then inside either cheek, pushing her tongue out of my way. She lifts her head up, and her watery eyes meet mine. They're narrowed on me, and I like the way that her mascara has already started to run. "You're going to look so pretty after I'm done playing with you. A pretty used-up whore." She closes her eyes, her breathing picking up when she realizes she will spend most of her night this way.

I pick up the lemon, pull out her bottom lip with my free hand, and gently squeeze it. Enough for the juice to fill her mouth. I watch it run over her bottom lip, down her chin and onto her dress. I left her dressed because I love seeing her clothes wet. I make sure no seeds have fallen out and then let go of her lip.

She sniffs, snot already starting to run from her hooked nose.

"The lemon juice is going to make you produce more saliva than usual. And this particular gag is designed to keep your mouth wide open and make swallowing impossible." I reach over next to me and pick up the piece of rope. I lean forward and thread it through the back of the ring on the harness and then bring each end around her head and pull on it, forcing her head down in the process. I bring it around her bent legs that she kneels on and tie it off. "This position—your head down—will also help with the excessive drooling." My eyes drop to see a line already falling onto her legs.

"Punishment isn't meant to be enjoyable, doll face," I inform her, and she whimpers. Her body shakes, and she sniffs again, her nose running as much as her drool.

I sit back, spread my legs farther and turn on the sound to the TV, ignoring her. She'll sit there, gagged and tied with a plug up her ass until I decide to fuck her pretty face before I bend her over and take her ass.

Shhh...

Chapter 53

Charlotte

I crawl out of bed and manage to find my way to the bathroom in the dark. Flipping on the light, I walk past the his-and-her sinks to use the restroom, but I come to an abrupt stop when I see my reflection.

My stomach falls when I see my face. Haidyn bathed me last night after he used my body, but I never got a chance to look at myself. At the time, it didn't matter. I could barely talk, let alone walk on my own.

Stepping up to the countertop, I place my hands on the cold marble, and my eyes widen. Sucking in a deep breath, I shout, "HAIDYN!"

To my surprise, he comes running into the bathroom as if it's on fire. "What?" he demands. "What's wrong?" The panic in his voice would be cute if I didn't want to stab him.

I turn to face him, my wide eyes looking over his smooth and hard chest. He's covered in sweat, which tells me he was working out. His sweatpants sit low on his hips, and his abs flex as he breathes heavily.

"What is it, Charlotte?" He steps forward, and I take a step back. He frowns but comes to a stop.

"My face." I point at it as if he can't see it.

His eyes look it over before they meet mine once again. He says nothing, but he can't hide the smirk that pulls at the corner of his lips.

My hands fist. "How could you...?"

"How was I supposed to know that shit wouldn't wash off?" he asks.

I look back at myself, and my shaking hands come to my cheeks. **T** and **Y** are written on my cheeks in my red lipstick. "It's a stain. The best on the market," I tell him, dropping my head and running my hand through my hair. I had planned on going out and drinking all night. I hate it when my lipstick smears on my glass. So I thought I'd try this.

"Hey." He comes up behind me and turns me to face him. I try to push him away, but he grabs my wrists and pins them behind my back with one hand while the other grips my chin and forces me to look up at him. "I tried to wash it off last night, but you said I was hurting your face."

I snort. "Since when do you care about hurting me?"

He frowns as if I hurt his feelings. I try to step away, but he just tightens his grip on me. "Tell me you didn't enjoy last night."

I say nothing. My jaw is so sore, and I'm dying of thirst, but he's right. I enjoyed kneeling at his feet waiting to be used. That scares me. He could do anything, and I'd get off on it. My body was trained to be a whore. We all are in our world. Sex is used to control us. Manipulate us. We're all made to need it and will do anything to make it happen.

"Use your words, doll face," he orders.

My nostrils flare, and my teeth grind. "I enjoyed it," I say, hoping he doesn't see how much of that was true and more as sarcasm.

The smile he gives me makes me think the latter. "There's nothing wrong with enjoying being played with."

I roll my eyes, and he lets go of my arms, pushing my ass into the countertop behind me. Letting go of my chin, he pushes both hands gently through my hair and pulls my head back to force my chin up and eyes to meet his. "I like it." His voice drops, sounding rougher, and my breath hitches. "The idea of you on your knees, mouth wide open, and covered in your own drool, just begging me to play with you."

"It was a punishment," I say, reminding him of what he said.

He smirks, and I slap his chest. "What did you do to Enrique?"

"Does it matter?"

"Of course it matters," I snap, pushing him out of my way. "You can't hurt innocent people."

"I told you not to go."

I spin around and suck in a deep breath. "So it's my fault?"

"Of course it's your fault."

I gasp at his answer.

He steps into me, tangling his hands in my hair and pulling my head back to force me to look up at him. "Only I see you naked and only I touch you. If any other man does, I'll make sure it's the last thing he does." With that, he lets go of me and exits the bathroom, slamming his bedroom door shut.

shhh...

Chapter 54

Charlotte

Another week has flown by since I've been at Haidyn's house. It seems like home at this point. We might as well be married since we haven't spoken much to one another.

I've been giving him my fuck you attitude, and he doesn't give two shits. We don't need to make small talk. He ties me down and fucks it out of me. The only words I speak to him are *please* and *oh my god* when I'm coming all over myself.

There are worse ways to live.

Haidyn received a call last night that Tyson and Ryat wanted to see him this morning. I didn't expect him to bring me along, but this morning after he fucked me senseless, we showered and got ready. I was prepared to crawl back into his bed because what else is there to do with my life, but he grabbed my hand and ushered me to the garage.

I wasn't going to argue. I haven't heard from the Lords since the video they sent me. It's almost as if they forgot me. A part of me isn't complaining, but the other keeps looking over my shoulder, waiting for them to show up and haul me off to the cathedral for failing.

I feel like the video they sent was a hint that I just can't figure out. Why are they showing me what Haidyn went through? Does it have to do with why he killed their dads? If so, I don't feel sorry for those bastards. I hope Haidyn gave them a slow and painful death.

On the other hand, I think their silence is a good thing. What if they reach out to call it off? What if they tell me to walk away and give me another assignment? Is it possible? Most likely not but then again you can't put anything past them. They want to leave you confused and always guessing. It gives them the upper hand.

We pull up to a house tucked back into the woods. Haidyn comes around to open the door for me and holds my hand with the other on my back. Ryat opens the front door, and we make our way to the living room. I sit with Haidyn on the couch. Ryat and Tyson sit in high-back chairs facing us on the other side of the coffee table.

Haidyn's hand is still in mine, and I have to bite my inner cheek to keep from smiling. I don't know why I care that he's doing it.

Are people who get laid always this happy? Maybe that's my problem. I'm having too much sex. Is that a thing? God, I hope not because we fucked last night and then again this morning, and I could still do it again. It's like a drug. An addiction. My body craves it all the time. I can't get enough of it. And I love when he takes it. I always felt like I was missing out by remaining a virgin, but I didn't know just how much. My body is in a constant state of pain from the positions he fucks me in and arousal waiting for him to use me again. Like now, my thighs ache from how hard I came this morning, but my pussy is throbbing for him to drag me out to the car and bend me over the hood. He makes me a blubbering mess, and I can't even think straight. Then he praises me for not being able to talk, let alone beg.

I watch Tyson's eyes drop to Haidyn's hand in mine, and I blush, looking at anything but him. It's like Haidyn is claiming me. All he needs to do is whip his dick out and piss on me to show them that I'm his. As if his name branded on my ass isn't enough.

"I found this photo a while back. You guys recognize him?" Haidyn asks, reaching into the pocket of his jacket and holding it out across the table to Ryat.

Ryat shakes his head, staring down at it in his hands. "No. But I knew Benny looked familiar from Blackout..."

"You knew him?" Haidyn asks.

"No. I was there one night with Gunner watching the girls when two men made moves on Sarah and Blake. Benny was behind the bar. I didn't know him personally. Just saw him the one time. I asked Blake about it, and she confirmed that one of the guys called the bartender Benny by name."

"He never worked for me, so I don't know how the fuck he got behind the bar," Tyson adds, leaning over and looking at it as well.

"Could have been Beau or Bethany," Haidyn suggests, and I pretend to know what they're talking about. "We know both were working with Luke and were unfaithful to you."

"Maybe." Tyson sighs as Ryat hands it over to him to get a better look. "It just doesn't make sense. If Ash was in Vegas, why was Benny here?"

"To see how close the Spade brothers were to finding her. That's what I would do," Ryat answers, sitting back in his chair.

"You would think he had eyes and ears everywhere, making sure the Spade brothers weren't going to get close."

"The moment you took in Luke and Whitney, his contact was severed. He had to know something was up." Haidyn sighs. "I think he allowed Saint to take her. He wanted her back here and at Carnage."

Ryat nods. "Maybe Ashtyn was just the bonus."

"You think he wanted inside Carnage..." Tyson trails off as a knock comes at the door.

Ryat gets up, checking his Rolex while frowning. He walks over to the door and opens it.

Haidyn lets go of my hand and jumps to his feet as does Tyson.

"What the fuck are you doing here?" Ryat demands, and my eyes widen, noticing the woman.

"Anne?" I ask, standing as well, surprised to see her here. Does my mother have her following me?

Haidyn takes my hand again as if I'm going to walk over to her and squeezes it painfully. "Ow," I whisper, and he loosens just a tad but keeps a good grip on it.

She ignores me and looks around the room. "Haidyn." She acknowledges him, and his body stiffens against mine. "Tyson." She nods, then looks back at Ryat. "I'm here to see my daughter." She goes to step inside, but Ryat moves to block the front door.

"She's unavailable," he tells her tightly.

She seems unfazed. "I just wanted to swing by. When she is *available*, have her call me." With that, she turns, giving Ryat her back, and steps off the front porch.

Ryat slams the door shut and pulls out his cell phone. He places it to his ear, and the house is so quiet we can hear it ringing on the other end before Blakely answers.

"Hey—"

"Your mother was just at our house," he informs her. "Looking for you."

A long silence comes from her end before she speaks. "I haven't heard from her."

"I'm on my way to come get you," he growls. No questions asked, end of discussion.

"Ryat." She sighs. "You can't come get me. I drove. I picked up Lake, and we're on our way to meet Elli for lunch. Then we're going shopping for the babies. It'll be fine. I'll be home soon."

I'm pretty sure she hangs up on him by the way he grinds his teeth when he puts his cell away. "How the fuck do you know LeAnne?" he demands, looking at me.

"Anne?" I ask, correcting her name. Haidyn and Tyson all turn to face me, and I feel like I've done something wrong all of a sudden. "She's my mother's best friend." Haidyn's hand tightens on mine again, and I whimper. I don't even think he realizes he's doing it, or he doesn't care because he doesn't let up like last time. "She met us for dinner weeks ago." I ramble when they all just stare at me. Ever been the only woman in a room full of Lords staring at you like you've wronged them? It's fucking terrifying.

"Weeks ago?" he barks, making me jump. "Why the fuck was she in town?"

"She's looking for a house," I rush out. "She and her husband are moving here..."

"Goddammit," he shouts, cutting me off.

"Come on." Tyson slides his jacket on before handing Haidyn the picture back that he shoves into his pocket with his free hand. "I'll drive and drop you off. You can drive Blake home, and I'll pick up Lake." He's already headed toward the door when Ryat walks toward us.

I want to step back, but the couch is there, and Haidyn still has a tight grip on my hand. Ryat comes to a stop before us, and I swallow nervously as he glares down at me. Surely, Haidyn won't let him kill me, would he? He looks from me to Haidyn. "If you're smart—"

"I know." Haidyn finally speaks, interrupting him.

Ryat nods like they're speaking a different language I don't understand. Then he adds, "Sorry, I have to cut the meeting short."

"No worries," Haidyn says. "We'll finish it another time."

♠

I sit in the passenger seat of my Cullinan as Haidyn drives us back to his house. It was raining earlier, so we chose my car. Of course, the fucker had to drive. Haidyn is the type of man who is always in charge.

My mind is on what just happened at Ryat and Blakely's. "Do you know Anne?" I come out and ask, tired of the lingering silence. He didn't even turn on the radio. I can tell he's inside his own head right now, and it's driving me crazy, wondering what he's thinking.

"LeAnne," he corrects me in a dead tone.

Why do they keep calling her that? My mother has never called her anything other than Anne. Even my father called her Anne. They were best friends before I was ever born. She's in all my childhood memories. She's practically family to us. I'm named after her, for Christ's sake. "I grew up visiting her in Chicago. I think I know her name."

"Well, everyone *thinks* you're Charlotte, and we both know that's a lie."

I whip my head around and narrow my eyes on him while he continues to drive. I don't like his attitude all of a sudden. It's not my fault she showed up and ruined his meeting. "She called Blakely her daughter." He says nothing, but it wasn't a question; it was more like an observation. "You don't believe that, do you?"

"It's a long story," he clips.

"Are you going to tell me?" I snap, getting irritated. Anne didn't even acknowledge me there, but she made sure to point out that she knew who Ryat, Tyson, and Haidyn were. *Why?*

I huff at his silence and cross my arms over my chest, staring out the passenger window. Anne—LeAnne never mentioned having a kid. Her husband was killed a while back, and she was gifted to another Lord, forcing her to move to Texas. Maybe Blakely is his daughter, and

LeAnne is having some kind of motherly crisis since she never had kids of her own.

I don't know Blake personally, but I feel bad for her. Ryat seemed pissed at her. It's not her fault. Then he went and picked her up...how did he know where she was?

I roll my eyes at myself. Of course he tracks her. All Lords track their property. I have one in my neck. Wonder what Haidyn would do if I cut it out? I just might try that.

He pulls into a gas station and brings the car to a stop. "Do you want anything from inside?" he asks, finally speaking to me.

Huffing, I cross my arms over my chest and turn my head away from him to look out the passenger window like a child. *Fuck him!* If he wants to ignore me, then I'll ignore him. No matter how immature it makes me look.

He gets out of my SUV and slams the door shut. I drop my arms and lean my head back against the headrest, letting out a sigh. What the fuck is going on? Why were all three of them so on edge to see LeAnne there? And for her to be Blakely's mom...? If that's true, then why was Ryat so concerned? He called LeAnne her mother when he was on the phone with Blakely, and she seemed...off? Definitely not as shook up as Ryat was but still not excited about the fact that she had been at their house either.

My head is spinning. Surely, I'm missing something. That's something my mother would have told me over the years. When we visited her and her husband, they had family pictures up of the two of them but none of any children.

I did find it odd that they didn't have any since the Lords expect you to give them heirs. LeAnne was high up in the rankings. She is why I wanted to be initiated—after my father took me to the cathedral that night, and I saw her in charge—I just figured they couldn't have them. The Lords don't believe in adoption. Outsiders are not welcome into our society.

My eyes wander to the window again, and I look around the gas station. It looks like a hole-in-the-wall. A mom-and-pop store sort of vibe. Not a well-known chain for sure. It only has four pumps and a small building where you don't even have to go inside to pay. You can choose to go to a small window.

Looking at the side of the building, I see two doors. One says men, the other women. I decide I could use the restroom.

Opening my door, I look over to see Haidyn look up from his phone. He was typing away but stops and a smirk graces his lips, but he has his sunglasses on, shielding his eyes from me. "Change your mind?"

I roll my eyes, not in the mood to decipher his mood swings. "I'm going to use the restroom."

"Give me a second." He looks over at the gas pump. It's crawling. No wonder it's taking him so long. I also didn't offer him my card to put fuel in my SUV. *How gentlemanly of him.*

I give him my back, not sure why I have to wait for him.

"Charlotte?" he barks.

I raise my right hand and give him the peace sign, not bothering to turn around and look at him. I know the bastard is into some weird shit, but I don't need an audience to go pee. He's already seen me do that.

Reaching the women's bathroom, I open the heavy door, making it squeak at my entrance. The place smells musty and the lighting sucks. It's the middle of the day, and there are no windows in here. The floor is dirty and the mirror by the single sink is broken in multiple places—shattered like a spiderweb.

Three stalls are lined up on the right, with the last on the end larger due to it being handicapped. All of the doors are closed, so I bend down to look under them to see if they're occupied. I try to open the first one, but it's locked even though no one is in it. Same with the second. I push open the third stall to find it unlocked when I'm hit from behind, shoved through the door, and knocked onto the dirty floor. Before I can process what's happening, my hair is grabbed, and my face shoved down into the cool tile. I manage to get a scream out before a hand slaps over my mouth from behind.

The taste of salt and dirt makes me gag as I claw at the floor trying to crawl out from underneath whoever is on top of me.

I manage to open my mouth and am able to bite the hand, making them release me. I'm pushed onto my back and look up to a man who has a black ski mask over his face. I start swinging my fists at his mask, trying to yank it off at the same time.

Managing to knee him in the balls, he grunts and rolls off me. I jump to my feet and run toward the door. I don't bother looking back. Instead, I start to scream as loud as I can for Haidyn, hoping he hears me.

Before I can reach the door, an arm wraps around my throat from behind and I'm picked up off my feet. I kick and fight as much as I can as he pulls me back from the door and panic grips my chest as he takes my air away.

"Fucking bitch." He growls in my ear before he spins me around and throws me to the floor once again.

I gasp and cough, trying to breathe as he kicks my side, forcing me to roll over onto my back. Then he's on top of me again. This time, my legs are under his, pinning me down so I can't knee him. I arch my neck, trying to catch my breath and yell, but he cuts me off as his hands wrap around my throat and squeeze as hard as he can.

HAIDYN

I'm on edge. LeAnne showing up at Ryat's threw me off. It makes me rethink why the Lords sent Charlotte to me. She's known her all her life? Her mother's best friend? Why didn't I find that out when I did my research? Bill never mentioned her at our meeting. Is there a reason he left her out of our conversation?

Shoving the door open to the women's bathroom, I start to open my mouth to tell her I'm going to take my belt to her ass for her little attitude, but the sight of her shoes and another set underneath the last stall has any words I was going to say die immediately.

I rush over and kick the door to see man straddling her hips, pinning her back to the floor. His hands around her throat. Leaning over him, I place an arm around his neck from behind and rip him off her.

I pull him backward, and his arms flail as she begins to cough and sputter. Letting go of him, I spin the piece of shit around and punch him in the mask-covered face. He stumbles back into the door before falling into the stall once again. I pick him up and punch him again. Then again.

His body spins around from the force, and I grab the back of his black-masked head and slam the front of his face into the wall. He falls to the floor and lies there, unconscious.

"Charlotte?" I walk over to where she's sitting on the floor, back against the side wall and knees pulled up to her chest. "Doll face." I kneel in front of her, and her tear-filled eyes meet mine. I cup her face and push her wild hair back over her shoulders to get a look at her face and neck. She's got a few marks here and there, but nothing too bad.

My eyes drop to her T-shirt and jeans. She's still dressed, and her shoes are still on. "You're okay," I tell her, and she nods quickly, trying to catch her breath.

Standing, I pull my cell out and send a few quick texts before pocketing it. Then I reach out my hand to her. "Can you walk?"

She takes it without hesitation, and I cup her face once more, forcing her to look at me. She's shaken up but alive. It could have been much worse. I pull her out of the bathroom and hold the door open with my boot. "I need you to get in the car, okay?"

I'm looking down at her, but she's looking at the unconscious man on the bathroom floor. "Charlotte?" I bark, and her watery eyes meet mine. "I'm going to watch you get in the car. It's unlocked. Get in the passenger seat and lock it. Do you understand?" Her car isn't far from where we are, but I can't leave the guy here alone and risk someone walking in and seeing him here. I have to remove him as soon as possible.

She nods again. I lean down and gently kiss her forehead before I guide her out the door. She sprints to the car, jumps in the passenger seat, and slams the door shut. The tint is too dark to see inside, but I know she's locked herself in.

Going back into the bathroom, I throw the piece of shit over my shoulder and carry him out of the bathroom. I have her keys in my pocket, so I unlock it and toss his ass into the back seat before jumping into the driver's seat. I start the car and squeal the tires, getting the fuck out of here.

♠

I pull up to Carnage and bring the SUV to a stop. She hasn't said one word to me since the gas station. I'm letting her process what happened, but she's got her breathing under control.

Getting out of the car, I walk over to the passenger side and open her door. She takes my hand and lets me help her out. Then I drag his ass out of the back seat just as the front double doors open. Saint and Kashton come running down the steps.

"Got your message. What happened?" Saint questions. His eyes go to Charlotte and then to the man.

"Attacked her in the bathroom of a gas station," I answer. "Help me get him inside."

They each take an arm, throwing it over their shoulder, and I take her hand, pulling her inside Carnage. She stays quiet as we ride the elevator down to the basement.

"Is he a Lord?" Kashton asks as we step off.

"We're going to find out," I growl.

"Think it was a hired hit?" Saint inquires, his eyes quickly going to Charlotte again.

They have no clue I'm fucking her. I can tell they're both wondering why I'm with her to begin with. "I don't know." I sigh, but honestly, my mind is telling me no. There's no way anyone would know we were stopping there unless they were following us. But then again, how would they know she'd choose to go to the bathroom when I stopped for gas?

We exit the elevator down in the basement and make our way to an empty cell. I take Saint's place, holding the guy up as he removes a key from his back pocket. He unlocks the cell door so Kash and I can place him inside. The first thing we do is strip him of all his clothing.

"Not a Lord." Kashton observes as we look over the naked man. He lacks the Lord's crest on his bare chest.

"He looks young," Saint adds. "Could mean he just hasn't been initiated yet."

I exit the cell and walk over to the safe that we have in the wall. Putting in the combination, I grab the vial and a syringe and draw it up to the top. Closing the safe, I turn to see Charlotte looking down at her shoes while Kash and Saint both stare at me and then glance at one another.

"Grab the handcuffs and the chains," Saint orders Kashton.

"I won't be needing those," I say, stopping Kash.

Saint huffs but doesn't argue.

Making my way back to the cell, they both follow me. I walk over to the passed-out guy who was going to do God knows what to my girl and look up to see Charlotte now standing in the room as well. Her watery eyes on mine. I look at Saint. "Get her out of the room and lock the door."

"Haidyn—"

"Get her the fuck out of this room and lock the goddamn door!" I shout, interrupting Kashton.

Saint turns and grabs Charlotte's arm, dragging her out of the cell while Kash follows, locking me inside alone with the piece of shit.

Looking down, I place one hand on his chest while the other stabs the needle into it.

Shhh...

Chapter 55

Charlotte

I stand outside of the concrete room, hands on the bars to the cell. My eyes focus on Haidyn. He stands, tosses the now empty syringe to the other side of the room, and reaches up, grips the back of his T-shirt, and rips it off, throwing it away too.

The muscles in his back flex and his hands fist while he watches the guy on the ground open his eyes. He takes a deep breath and jumps to his feet.

Haidyn punches him in the face, knocking him back. The guy begins to swing, getting a hit in on his face.

"Wanna fight?" Haidyn gives a laugh that makes the hairs on the back of my neck rise. "Try someone your own size?" He lifts his fists in front of him, and the guy rushes toward him.

Haidyn steps to the side, and the guy runs right toward me, but before he reaches the bars, Haidyn's arm wraps around his neck from behind, lifting the guy off his feet. Haidyn slams him down onto his back, and the guy rolls to the side and immediately jumps back up.

He's on adrenaline. Why would Haidyn give him that when he's not using it? Is he trying to get his ass kicked?

The guy laughs and swings. But he misses, and the momentum has him spinning out of control. Haidyn kicks him in the stomach, pushing him back into the wall once more. Haidyn grabs his arm and yanks him from the wall.

My shirt is grabbed, and I'm pulled back, forcing me to release the bars just as the guy runs into them. Before he can move, Haidyn steps up behind him, takes his hair, and begins to smash his face into the bars, over and over.

Blood from his face sprays into the hallway and onto us while his grunts fill the basement.

HAIDYN

I PUSH THE GUY TO THE FLOOR. HE'S NOT OUT, BUT HE'S FUCKED up enough that he's done for now. In a few minutes, he'll be passed the fuck out.

Saint unlocks the door, and I step out before he closes it, sealing the guy in once again. I spot Charlotte leaning against the wall with her arms over her chest. Not in an angry way but a protective way. "Hey." I walk up to her and cup her face. Her eyes look up at me through her wet lashes. She was silently crying in the car, but she's stopped since then. "You're okay, doll face."

She swallows, nodding her head. Her eyes sliding to the cell then back to me. They search my face, probably looking at the damage. He got a couple of hits in. I might as well be on adrenaline because I don't feel a fucking thing right now other than uncontrollable rage. He put his hands on my girl, and I'm going to make sure he never does it again.

"Are you okay?" she speaks softly.

I smile at her concern. "I'm fine, doll face."

"You shouldn't have done that." Her brows furrow as if I'm crazy for coming to her defense.

My bloody knuckles run along her jaw down to her neck, and her pulse is racing. "You're ..."

Pushing up on her tiptoes, she crashes her lips to mine, and her arms go around my neck. Without thought, my hands go to her ass, and I lift her off her feet. She wraps her legs around my waist. I press her back into the concrete wall, and she moans into my mouth. Her lips open for me to take control, and I devour her.

My bloody hands grip her hair, and she whimpers into my mouth as if I'm hurting her, but she doesn't pull away. Instead, her legs squeeze my waist tighter.

Slowing the kiss down, she pulls away first, and her heavy eyes open to look up at me. "Thank you," she whispers.

I give her lips a soft kiss this time. Unable to stop. Fuck, I'm so hard right now. Is it bad that I want to open his cell and fuck her right here and now in front of that piece of shit just to show him that she's mine? Rip her clothes off and put her ass up in the air so he can see my name branded on it?

Someone clears their throat, and I look over to see Saint staring at me with an arched brow. Kash nods his head in approval with his eyes on her.

She begins to unwrap her legs from around my waist and I lower her to the floor. "I'm going to take Charlotte up to my room, and then I'll be back down," I state, grabbing her hand.

"Take your time," Kashton hollers with a chuckle as we enter the elevator. "He's not going anywhere."

Shhh...

Chapter 56

Charlotte

I'm shaken up and embarrassed.

I'm supposed to be able to take care of myself. How can I prove to the Lords I can be who I'm supposed to be if I'm not always on guard? Was that a test? If so, I failed. Did the Lords send him because I'm not giving them what they want?

And Haidyn? What the fuck was that? Not only did he save me, but he also beat the fuck out of the guy. I was mesmerized while I watched. The way he moved, the power in his punch. The guy was on adrenaline, and he couldn't hold a candle to Haidyn.

The elevator opens, and I let him pull me down a hallway before he comes to a stop at a door. Putting his finger on a lock, he opens it up, then places a hand on my lower back, ushering me inside.

It's a large room with an Alaskan king-sized bed in the center and a couch at the footboard. There's a set of double doors that look like they open to a balcony and another door on the other side of the bed.

"This is the bathroom." He lets go of my hand and walks over to the door, opening it for me.

I follow on autopilot. I hear him start the sink, and I push my jeans down and use the restroom, not even caring that he's in here with me. Why be shy now? I attacked him after I saw what he did to that man. In front of Kashton and Saint. Why was I so stupid? Now they think of me as any other dumb bitch who lets a dick control them.

Aren't I?

He says jump, and I ask how high. He tells me to crawl, and I say yes sir. Needing to be that good girl for him. Wanting to show I can be the best whore he's ever had. Am I still here because the Lords told me to be or because I want to be?

The lines are nonexistent at this point.

I finish up and go to stand at the other sink. I wash my hands and find myself just staring at my shoes.

He turns to face me and takes my still wet hands. His are now clear of the blood from the basement, but cuts and bruises are already forming. I realize that my hands are shaking.

"Hey, you're okay," he says.

My eyes start to sting, and I bite my bottom lip. Why the fuck am I being like this? I'm not an emotional girl. I cry when I'm mad, but I'm not even sure what I feel right now.

"Charlotte?" His hands drop mine to cup my face, and I pull away, stepping back. But he reaches out, places his hands in my hair, and holds me captive. He's not rough or hurting me, but I also can't pull away. "Talk to me, doll face. Are you hurting anywhere? Can I get you anything?"

I lick my lips nervously, hating how his pretty blue eyes search mine as if he can see how confused I am. I try to shake my head, but his hands prevent it.

"Use your words," he demands in that tone that has my legs shaking for another reason.

"No," I manage to say around the knot that has lodged in my throat. "I'm...okay."

He sighs and lets go of my hair, running his hands through it. "I'll have Devin come and look at you."

"I said I'm fine," I snap defensively.

He frowns, confused by my mood swings, and honestly, I can't explain them either. I've seen a different side of him since I've been sent the videos by the Lords. And how he saved me tonight. But I have to remind myself that he did it because I'm his toy. If I'm dead, he doesn't get to play with me.

"You'll be safe up here. The door automatically locks the moment it shuts. It requires my fingerprint or a code."

My stomach sinks at the thought of him leaving me. A part of me wants to jump him like I did in the basement and beg him to fuck me. The other wants to punch the fuck out of him for making me feel safe.

Maybe I can do both? "How long will you be gone?" I decide to ask instead.

"I'm not sure," he answers honestly, and I let out a huff.

His frown deepens, and I take a step back, needing space to breathe. I can still taste that man's hand on my mouth, and the thought of vomiting still lingers. I want him to kiss me again and make it go away. I want his hands holding me down while he tells me I'm such a good little whore and I can take it. To come all over his cock just so he can flip me over and fuck my ass.

"You can take a shower if you want." It's as if he knows I feel dirty. "I have clothes in the closet that you can change into. Wear whatever you want."

A knock on his door makes me jump. My teeth clench when he notices. I have to get my shit together.

He walks over to the door and opens it. "Haidyn, I got your text."

Jesus! How many people has he texted?

He allows the man to enter and shuts the door behind him. Haidyn begins explaining what happened in the bathroom at the gas station, and the guy I know as Devin suggests I sit down on the couch. I do so to please them both. I don't have the energy to fight them right now. The adrenaline has worn off, and I'm getting tired. And I guess any hope I had of getting fucked is dead since we're no longer alone.

Devin looks me over, shining a light in my eyes and feeling around my head and throat before he gives me some pain reliever and says everything looks good. That I might have a headache, some bruising, and be sore. But I wasn't raped or beaten unconscious. Who knows what the man had planned for me.

Haidyn's cell rings, and he pulls it out of his pocket. "I have to take this," he tells Devin, who shoos him away as he speaks to me. I ignore him and watch Haidyn step out onto the balcony. I try to hear what he's saying.

"Yeah, she's okay...thanks, man...yeah, I'm at Carnage...he's looking her over now. Yeah, I'll meet you down there..." He nods to himself and hangs up.

As he enters the room again, I drop my eyes to the floor, hoping he doesn't notice I was listening. He obviously wanted privacy, but he should have stepped out of the room completely. Maybe he doesn't want to leave me alone. No. That's just me thinking he actually cares. He's about to leave me to go to the basement.

"Everything looks good," Devin reassures him once again.

"Thanks, man." They do a bro handshake half hug, and he walks Devin to the door, letting him out before closing it and coming to kneel in front of me. "I'm going downstairs. I'll be back soon, and we'll head home, okay?"

I don't know if he realizes he called his house *home*, but I hate the butterflies it gives me. "Okay." I nod, feeling awkward all of a sudden. The reminder that I kissed him down in the basement in front of Saint and Kashton. What will they think now? Will they ask him what we're doing? Hell, for all I know, Haidyn has already told them I'm a spy sent by the Lords.

Getting to his feet, he cups my face with both his hands and leans in to kiss my forehead.

Fuck, I hate when he's like this—gentle—and pretends to care about me. As if I'm breakable. It makes me feel weak. As if I need the reminder. I'd rather him strip me naked, tie me down, and gag me while he fucks my ass and calls me his good girl.

That makes me his whore. When he's gentle, it makes me vulnerable.

Without another word, he exits his room, locking me inside, and I find myself falling onto the floor, arms and legs fanned out, staring up at the ceiling and thinking what the fuck do I do now?

HAIDYN

I ENTER THE BASEMENT, STEPPING OFF THE ELEVATOR TO SEE SIN has joined Saint and Kashton. He turns to face me, holding out his fist. "Here you go," he says cheerfully, referring to the phone conversation we had minutes ago.

"Was it hard to get?" I ask.

He drops the USB drive into my hand. I had texted Saint and Kash to be ready for me at Carnage—that I was bringing someone in. I had also messaged Sin to stop by the gas station and grab the footage while I was there with Charlotte. If the man isn't a Lord, I didn't need surveillance of her entering the bathroom and me dragging an unconscious man out of the women's restroom and tossing him into her SUV. I'm just glad we weren't on my bike because we would have had to wait for Sin to show up to haul him here for me.

"Nope. I was either going to pay the guy off or beat the shit out of him," Sin answers.

"Which one was it?" Kash asks, needing to know.

Sin holds up his right hand to show the dried blood on it, making Kash smile. "I did toss him money as I walked out."

"Is Charlotte okay?" Saint asks.

I look up at him, and by the way his eyes search mine, I'd say he's got a double meaning to that question. They saw her cling to me, and I her. Then I shoved my tongue down her throat as if we were horny teenagers. Our dynamic has obviously changed. They just don't know the extent of it. And I don't want them to.

I'm not in the mood to decipher the hidden meaning in his look. "Devin checked her out. She's good."

"Man, between you and Ryat, you guys have had a shit day. Glad the girls are okay." Sin sighs.

"What's wrong with Blakely?" Kash questions, sounding truly concerned.

"The girls were supposed to go shopping, but Elli called me..." His cell ringing saves me from having to come up with a reason to cut him off. Looking down at it, he speaks. "It's Elli. Give me a second. Hey, everything okay?" he answers, walking away from us.

She's pregnant, so he's on high alert at all times. Things always seem to go bad just when you think luck is on your side in our world.

"What happened to Blakely?" Saint asks, while watching Sin on the phone pace behind us. Kashton looks at me, waiting for an answer as well.

"Something about LeAnne looking for her." I shrug, having to say something. In case they speak to Ryat or Tyson about it. I was there when Blakely's mother had shown up. I can't let them know that Charlotte knows LeAnne. All I can do is hope that the others don't say something about Charlotte knowing her. That could lead them to find out who she really is. And they'd have her down here in one of these cells until they got answers to questions that Charlotte doesn't even know about. My talk with Bill helped me understand just how innocent *Annabelle* truly is and what her future really looks like. And I'm going to do everything I can to make sure that doesn't happen.

"What the fuck?" We hear a man groan, and I smile. The adrenaline doesn't last long especially when in a fight. He went down pretty quickly, but I knew he'd be up just as soon.

We walk over to the cell, and Saint opens the door. All three of us step inside as the man gets to a sitting position, rubbing the back of his head. His face is bloody, and his right eye is already swollen shut. I've fucked him up two times now. This isn't about bloodshed; this is about answers.

"Who the fuck are you?" His one good eye looks around quickly, going among the three of us. "What...what did you give me?" His bloody hand goes to his bruised chest. The adrenaline has a kick to it. When you wake up from it, there's a lingering pain throughout your entire body.

"Who are you?" I ask, ignoring his second question. "No cell and no ID," I add. "Wearing a ski mask over your head and attacking my girl in a public bathroom." Stepping forward, I ask what I already know. "Just what were you planning on doing with her?"

He looks away from me, and his jaw clenches.

"He has nothing to say. Maybe you should have Devin wire his mouth shut," Sin says as he joins us in the room.

"Want to be a Spade brother?" Kash asks, looking over at him. "Seriously, I feel like we could adopt you."

Sin laughs, thinking it's a joke, but Kashton has become quite fond of Easton, and I'm pretty sure Kashton would have him and Elli a room ready to go by the end of the day.

"Fuck you." The guy spits blood onto the concrete floor. "Your girl isn't anything special." His one good eye finds mine.

I kick him in the face, needing to move this along. I saw how Charlotte looked at me upstairs. She didn't want me to leave her but was either ashamed or too afraid to ask me to stay with her.

The bastard's head snaps back, and blood sprays across the concrete floor he lies down on before rolling to his side, holding his bloody face. Without the adrenaline, he's going to feel it a lot more now.

I shove him onto his stomach and order, "Tie his hands behind his back."

Kash comes to kneel beside him as I push my boot into the back of his neck, holding the man down. He doesn't even fight him as Kash pulls his arms behind him and secures them with a pair of handcuffs. I remove my boot, and Kash steps back, kicking him back onto his back. I place my boot at his throat this time. "Last time and I start cutting. What were you going to do to my girl?"

He coughs, spit flying from his mouth and splattering his busted face. "She...was...random," he says between gasps.

"So you don't know who she is?" Saint questions, wanting to make sure he stays consistent with his answers.

He tries to shake his head, and I press my boot further into his neck, cutting off his air. "Use your fucking words!" I demand. Loosening my boot, he coughs once more.

"N-ooo," he cries out. "I swear."

"So were you going to rob her or rape her?" I ask.

A part of me doesn't believe him. Another part wants to because if he's lying, then I have another problem on my hands. It's not uncommon for a Lord to hire someone outside of the society to do their dirty work. Or he could have been a Lord who didn't make the cut.

"Both," he says through gritted teeth, spit flying from his bloody mouth.

"At least he's honest." Kash shrugs, looking at me.

Yeah, after I've beat the shit out of him twice. "What do you know about the Lords?" I demand, wanting to know more. No matter what he does and doesn't know, the bastard will die here.

"Fuck the Lord! I'm not religious," he snaps.

Sin throws his head back laughing, and Kash chuckles. Saint and I don't find it funny. "Lords aren't religious either, but we do believe in hell." I remove my boot from his neck, and he rolls back onto his side to relieve the pressure of his arms underneath him. "And today you start serving three devils."

Shhh...

Chapter 57

Charlotte

I was just getting out of the bathtub when Haidyn returned to his room. I didn't want to wash my hair, so I opted for a bath rather than a shower. I washed my mouth out with mouthwash and then cleaned my body.

I feel a little better but tired. The clock on my dash says it's only six o'clock in the evening. It started raining at some point while we were at Carnage.

As we were leaving, I couldn't help but think that my future husband was in the same building as me. Hell, I was in the basement. He could have been right there, and I had not known it.

But I know what happens there. If he's a prisoner, he's as good as dead, meaning any future we have is no longer an option, which makes me wonder why I'm even doing an assignment. What other future do they have planned for me now?

When we pull up to Haidyn's house, he parks in the garage and opens the door for me. He hasn't told me what he did when he left me in his room, and I haven't asked.

"Would you like anything to eat?" he asks as we enter his house.

"No, thank you," I say softly. "Jessie fed me at Carnage." He had brought me some soup and crackers, informing me that Devin requested he bring me something to eat due to the meds he had given me.

He nods. "I'm going to take a shower." With that, he enters his bathroom and shuts the door.

I find myself pulling his T-shirt and sweatpants off my body and crawling into his bed naked. I didn't have any clean underwear at Carnage, so I chose not to put mine back on. The sheets are cool and feel good on my bruised skin. Lying on my side, I watch the rain hit his wall of windows. It's not nighttime yet, but the storm makes it appear to be at this time of day.

I try to fight a yawn, but fail, knowing if I fall asleep now, I'll be up way too early in the morning. But what else is there for me to do?

Lightning illuminating the room has my eyes opening. Seconds later, the sound of thunder shakes the walls.

The bathroom door opening has me sitting up, and I see Haidyn entering the bedroom. He has a towel sitting low on his hips, wrapped around his waist. He walks toward the door when I speak. "Will you lie with me?"

He comes to a stop and turns to face me with a look of surprise on his face.

I'm not even sure why I asked. I just feel...alone. I want his hands on me. I want my legs wrapped around his waist, not his towel. The moment we shared at Carnage is still fresh on my mind and my body is begging for him.

Lightning fills the room once again, and he walks toward the bed. I lie down at the sound of the thunder that follows and watch shamelessly as he removes his towel and lets it drop to the floor before he pulls back the covers and crawls into his bed with me.

I had felt him hard at Carnage, but of course he's not anymore. Something tells me it wouldn't take much to get him there again.

He holds the edge of the covers up. I take the hint and scoot over into his side, placing one leg over his waist and an arm over his chest. He lets them fall, and darkness covers the room as the rain hits the windows.

His right hand slides under the covers to rest on my thigh that is over his waist. His thumb gently rubs back and forth, and I feel my body instantly heat. All of a sudden, I'm getting hot, and my breathing picks up.

I swallow nervously and break the awkward silence between us. "Did you find out anything?" My voice is softer than I meant it to be, and his silence makes me wonder if he even heard me.

After a long second, he lets out a deep breath, making his chest rise and fall. "No."

He's lying. I want to be mad, but maybe he's protecting me? Trying to ease my mind about what could have happened in that bathroom. "I'm sorry I didn't listen to you," I say, my voice louder than before but still on the softer side.

His thumb stops on my thigh, and his hand moves up over my hip, my side, and then to my face. Cupping my cheek, he forces me to look up at him. I can barely see him in the dark room, but the lightning helps a little. "You're okay," he assures me.

"Why did you want me to wait on you?" I ask, needing to know.

His eyes search mine as he answers. "Because men will camp out in a women's bathroom to attack them as they enter. They will rape and kill them. Then leave them there to rot as they get away."

"Is that what you think he was going to do to me?"

He sighs but doesn't answer the question. Instead, he says. "Why do you think he picked a gas station right off the busiest highway?"

I frown, not understanding.

"Because it's loud. That highway has a lot of traffic coming and going—each way. Men are able to do whatever they want, and no one can hear the women screaming for help."

"I screamed for you," I whisper. "Did you hear me?"

I feel his heart pounding under my hand that rests on his chest. "No."

"So...why did you come in there?" I ask.

"To check on you," he replies simply. "I'm sorry it wasn't sooner."

"I..." Debate on whether to tell him this but I decide after what I saw him do to the guy that I might as well. "I checked underneath the stalls but saw nothing. I was just looking to see which ones were open, not thinking a man was hiding in them. But he obviously was." I give a rough laugh, and he frowns. "I didn't see any shoes, but they were locked. He must have been standing on the toilet. Hovering to go unseen. He had two doors locked knowing I'd have to use the only one available. I wonder how long he had been in there waiting for someone to enter."

He remains quiet while I tell him what happened. He hadn't asked for specifics, and I felt like they didn't matter to him. He saw what was happening, and that was enough to make the guy pay for putting his hands on me in any way. But I wanted him to know. If I had not been throwing a fit and had listened to him...

I stop that train of thought because I did throw a fit and didn't listen to him.

The lightning flashes again, and I get a look at his eyes on mine. He's already looking down at me. His blue eyes appear so soft and caring, yet it's an illusion. I'm feeling vulnerable and horny as fuck. Tonight could have gone very differently. I could have been raped, killed, or both. This man has proven that he's going to protect me.

I lean up without thought and press my lips to his, not knowing if he's going to push me away or kiss me back. When his hand slides to my hair, I moan against his lips, praying he's going to make me his whore. Because I almost became someone else's, and that terrifies me.

I thought the Lords were the ones to fear, but I forgot that there are monsters outside of our world as well. And they will tear you apart for no other reason than because they can.

HAIDYN

I PUSH HER ONTO HER BACK, AND SHE PARTS HER LIPS FOR ME while her legs wrap around my waist. I lower my hand and slide it between our bodies, needing to be inside her. I jacked off in the shower, needing a second. I wasn't sure she wanted to be touched after what happened.

She was obviously grateful when she kissed me at Carnage, but that could have been the adrenaline alone. Time has passed, and I wanted to give her whatever space she needed, but the way her nails dig into my tatted back tells me she needs me right now as much as I need her.

I screamed for you.

Fuck, I never heard her. It was pure anger that had me entering the bathroom after her. I was going to tell her off for not waiting. A woman has to always be on guard. I'm not one of those men who live in a world that think the women aren't different than the men. Maybe it's because we're brought up to see them as vulnerable at all times.

Perhaps it's because we're the ones who are always watching their every move. I did it before I made her mine. She was oblivious to almost everything around her. Hell, I was in her house at the same time as her, and she never even knew it.

"Haidyn." She pulls her lips from mine, gasping my name and pulling me from my own thoughts.

"I know, doll face," I say breathlessly, pushing the head of my hard dick into her soaked cunt. Fuck, getting myself off in the shower didn't help.

She arches her back and neck, her voice ringing out into the dark room as I push myself inside her like she was made for me.

Clenching my teeth, I push my cock balls deep, holding it there as I reposition myself. I lower onto my forearms, my hands gripping her wrists and pinning them down by her head.

I start to move, loving the way her body reacts to me. She's panting, and I'm already out of breath. I lower my lips to her bruised neck and kiss her racing pulse tenderly. Letting her know that I can fuck her while leaving her begging for more.

"Fuck, Charlotte." Her body shivers against mine. "Tell me, doll face...who do you belong to?"

"You." She gasps.

"Whose little whore are you?" I demand, thrusting harder, forcing the headboard to hit the wall.

"Yours," she cries out.

Letting go of her wrists, I sit up. My hands grip her narrow hips, holding on so tight that I'll leave more bruises than the bastard gave her, and I begin to move. Thrusting harder and harder as her voice fills the room along with the lightning and thunder.

Her pussy clenches down on my pierced cock while she comes, and I'm panting as I slam into her as if I have a line of men behind me watching me try to knock her up.

My eyes drop to her stomach. The thought of Bill enters my mind. I imagine her tied up and ready for men to line up to fill her full of their cum to see who can knock her up first. A breeder...is what he said she'd be if she failed her assignment.

Fuck that! Annabelle Marie Schults belongs to me. So I will make sure whatever it is the Lords want her to do, she passes. Because once the birth control shot I had Gavin give her wears off, she won't be getting another one. The only babies she'll be having are mine.

Her hands get my attention as they reach up and grab my hair. She pulls me down, wanting my lips on hers again, and I don't deny her.

She opens up for me, and I pull away to place my arms under her knees, spreading her legs wide open. Then I reposition myself back down on top of her to kiss her, cutting off her cries.

♠

I'M WALKING UP THE STEPS INSIDE THE CATHEDRAL TO FIND A MAN turning to face me. He zips up his jeans and winks at me. "Good luck, man. May the best man win."

He throws his shoulder into mine in passing, and I see ten more men standing single file and a woman strapped down to a breeding bench. Her legs spread with her ass and pussy up in the air. There's a butt plug in her ass to make sure no one uses it. That's not what this is for. I walk around the front of the structure to see she's bent over; dark hair covers the floor. I get a sickening feeling in my gut when I bend down and grip her hair to lift her head. Pretty blue eyes meet mine and widen when they see me. It's Charlotte. She's got duct tape over her lips, and her muffled screams fill the room as another man begins to fuck her.

A hand hits my shoulder, making me jump up and turn around. "Get in line, Haidyn. But just know your odds are pretty low. She's already been here for five days." The guy chuckles as he walks away.

I open my eyes to the sound of the rain still hitting the wall of windows. I'm on my side with one arm draped over a sleeping Charlotte. The other underneath her neck. My cock still inside her cunt.

Looking at the clock on the nightstand, I see that I've only been asleep for an hour. The nightmare woke me up.

Very gently, I remove my arm from underneath her neck and then slowly pull out of her. She moans in her sleep but doesn't wake.

Getting out of bed, I slip on a pair of sweatpants before making my way to the kitchen. I need a drink. Something alcoholic and strong.

I flip on the light, thinking I see a figure sitting in the living room. I come to a stop when I see who it is. Fuck, I should carry a gun on me at all times. I have them all over this house, but not one on me at this very moment.

"Haidyn." She gives me a smile, standing by the windows. "I was wondering how long it'd take for her to pass out." Her eyes slide to the hallway that leads to my bedroom.

"Leave," I order.

She slowly walks toward me. Her hands drop to the trench coat, and she opens it to reveal she's naked underneath. "I thought I'd come by and offer a little help. Ya know...let me show her how it's done."

My jaw clenches. "Get the fuck out of my house," I growl.

"What? Don't think she'd be into it?" She places a finger on my chest, and I step back. "You could blindfold her; I'll tie her down," she offers. "Tell her it's your fantasy...two women at once. She won't be able to resist. She hasn't told you no yet, has she?"

I slap her, making her gasp in surprise. Her hand rises to her cheek, and she lowers her head as her heavy breathing fills the silent house.

I step forward, pressing my body into hers. "Last chance. Get the fuck out of my house."

Her head snaps up, and her eyes burn holes into mine. "Do you feel threatened, Haidyn?"

"Not at all." I chuckle. "You're an annoying little bitch who needs to know her place, and it's nowhere in my life."

"Do you honestly think she'll stay with you when she finds out about us?"

"She knows I've fucked whores in the past." I shrug. Charlotte isn't going anywhere. I'm not going to let her.

She huffs, finally yanking her trench coat closed. I step out of her way. "Now get the fuck out of my house before I go wake her up and tell her everything."

"Are you threatening me?" she demands.

"I'm promising you. Stay the fuck away from us."

Her eyes widen at my choice of words before she straightens her posture and gives me a bone-chilling smile. She's good at those. "History has a way of repeating itself, Haidyn. Remember that." Turning, she walks out of my house and slams the front door shut as if she just won a bet.

I don't like that feeling any better than knowing she was in my house and around Charlotte. The slamming of the door has me returning to my bedroom to check if it woke her up. Charlotte's still sound asleep on her side. One arm under my pillow and the other where I lay. Just how I left her.

I knew there was a bigger picture as to why the Lords made *Annabelle* insert herself into my life. If I'd been honest with myself, I would have known the reason this whole time. But even I couldn't deny her. It was as if I pushed the big red button that says DON'T PUSH just to see what would come of it.

My concern is why now? What benefit does *she* get from me knowing she's aware Charlotte is in my bed? Do I think Charlotte will walk away? No. She's too attached. I haven't forced her to be with me since the beginning. I gave her an out, but she came back. *Because she had to*, I remind myself. The Lords gave her an ultimatum, and I was her choice.

She's working for the Lords, but I haven't given her anything to use against me. And I never knew what they wanted until now. Now I know.

Turning, I make my way to the home gym. I need to let off some steam.

shhh...

Chapter 58

Charlotte

Stretching my back, I groan. Fuck, I'm so sore. My entire body hurts. There's a dull ache at the back of my head, and my side hurts. Whatever Devin gave me back at Carnage has worn off.

I open my heavy eyes and reach out my arms across the bed. My eyes pop open when I feel I'm alone.

Typical.

He fucks me and then leaves me. Rolling onto my back, I stare up at his dark ceiling. The sound of the rain still falls outside on the windows to my left. It's soothing. I love it when it storms. The only thing to make it better would be if I woke up with Haidyn still inside me.

I tense. *What the fuck, Charlotte?*

A phone beeps, and thankfully, I don't have to dig deeper into that thought. I roll over and pick up my cell off the nightstand and see it's an email from the Lords. I open it up, and there's a video. My eyes go to the bedroom door as it slowly opens farther, and then a second later, Muffin jumps up onto the bed and settles on Haidyn's pillow.

Getting up, I grab my earbuds and lie back down again under the covers and push play on the video.

It's not like the other videos they've sent me. This one is different. It's of a large bedroom with guys standing around. Some have beers in their hands; others have mixed drinks. One guy is smoking a cigarette while the other is getting high. It looks like a college frat party of sorts. But they all have one thing in common—a cell phone in their hand—and they are all recording something in the room.

A door opens, and Saint exits first as he pulls Ashtyn out of what looks like an en suite bathroom. It's old because he's missing the snake tattoos around his neck. She's naked from the waist down. He brings her to a stop, spins her around, and he places his hand on her face, kissing her.

Her body melts into his as she moans into his mouth. He pulls away first and pushes her onto the bed. He flips her onto her stomach and yanks her ass up in the air. Haidyn comes into view, and I sit up straighter. My eyes shoot to the open bedroom door, but it's still just me and Muffin.

Saint reaches his hand out, and Haidyn hands him a belt. Saint quickly ties her arms behind her back, and she wiggles her ass against his jeans. Saint laughs. "Oh, you're getting fucked, sweetheart. Remember the rules...no coming for them."

My heart picks up at his words. Surely, Haidyn isn't going to fuck her in this room full of guys?

Saint gets off the bed and moves to either side of the footboard and ties her ankles to it. Her legs are wide open, and the guy recording the video walks over to look at her smooth pussy. She's soaking wet. Digging her face into the bed, she whimpers. "Saint...?"

He undoes his jeans and pulls out his dick as he yanks her to the edge. Kashton hands him a bottle of lube, and Saint pours it all over her, letting it drip down her legs. He begins to fuck her ass.

My eyes shoot to Haidyn's bedroom door, turning down the volume all the way even though I've got earbuds in as the video continues to play. I don't want to watch Saint fuck her. It feels... wrong.

I stare out the bedroom door into the dark hallway, expecting...no hoping that Haidyn comes into his room. Because I want a reason to have to turn off the video. I don't want to see what I already know is coming.

But like a train wreck that you can't look away from, my eyes drop back down to my phone, and I see Saint pulling out of her ass. He leaves her lying there tied face down, and Haidyn steps up at the end of the bed.

My heart starts hammering in my chest as he undoes his jeans and pulls out his hard dick. I turn up the volume as he speaks, "You love having our cum leaking out of your ass, don't you, baby girl?"

Baby girl?

"Haidyn..." She whimpers his name, rocking her hips back and forth, and the blood rushes in my ears.

"Don't worry. We're all going to fuck you like the whore you are, Ash," he assures her, and the men in the room laugh.

He takes the head of his cock and runs it up over her pussy, smearing it with her wetness, lube, and Saint's cum before he pushes it into her ass.

She cries out his name as he reaches forward, grabbing a hold of her dark hair and holds her face down into the bed as her back arches, and he starts to fuck her. His free hand on her bare ass, his fingers digging into her skin. Her moans fill my ears as she rocks back and forth against him.

"That's it, baby girl..."

I shut off my phone and throw it across the room, unable to watch anymore. Tossing the covers off, I get to my feet and rip my earbuds out and hurl them as well before I begin to pace. I'm trying to catch my breath. It feels like someone just punched me in the stomach.

Why? He's not mine. Not like he was hers.

He loved her, I remind myself. She was supposed to be his, and he gave her away to Saint.

Laura had said that she was sleeping with them, and Ashtyn said they never fucked her vaginally. Knowing it and seeing it are two very different things.

I'm sweating, my pulse racing. Why do I fucking care so much? I don't want him. I knew going into this there was no future. But the way he fucked me when we got home...it fucked with my head.

And that video...I run my hands through my tangled hair.

I've got to get out of this house. It's making me insane.

My skin is hot, and my head is pounding. I'm so fucking pissed. Why did they send me that? Do they think I'm getting too close? They want to push me away from him? They want me to know he'll never belong to me. I'll never be her. The one he let go.

FUCK!

I pick up a T-shirt on the floor and yank it on and storm out his bedroom. Coming into the living room, I can hear "Coming Undone" by Korn filtering down the hallway, and I know exactly where it's coming from.

Making my way toward the back of the house, I shove the gym door open to find him standing in nothing more than a pair of sweatpants facing away from me lifting free weights. I shamelessly watch the way his back muscles flex before he notices I've joined him.

His eyes meet mine in the mirror, and I cross my arms over my chest, waiting for him to stop the music.

"That's it, baby girl..."

My teeth grind at the words echoing in my mind.

He sets the free weights down and turns to face me. He picks up his cell and lowers the music but doesn't turn it completely off. "What are you doing awake?"

I don't like his tone as if I'm not allowed to be up and out of bed this time of night. As if he knows that I was just watching him fuck another woman.

After I was attacked, and when we got back here, he fucked me...I felt something that I've never felt before—loved. But it was an illusion. I was emotional, and he was the one there for me. He was still typical Haidyn—rough and needy. But it was also the gentlest I think he's ever been. There were no handcuffs, no ropes, and no toys. Just him and me. It was just as amazing as any other time he's made me his. But I want a fight right now. I want to slap his fucking handsome face and then kneel like an obedient dog and beg him to fuck my mouth. I want to prove to him that I'm not Ashtyn. That I can be better than her. I don't belong to anyone else. He doesn't have to share me with another man. I'm all his. Fuck, I'm so goddamn stupid, even I know it's pathetic.

"I'm leaving," I inform him, lifting my chin. I'm still trying to catch my breath.

I'm shaking I'm so fucking livid. At him. At myself. At Ashtyn. A part of me says it wasn't her fault. Saint was the one who passed her around to his friends. *A Lord can share his chosen with whoever he wants.* That's what she had told Laura. It wasn't like Ashtyn crawled to him on her hands and knees and begged him to fuck her. *In that video.* Who knows how many are out there like that.

"No. You're not."

"I'm not your prisoner, Haidyn." I can leave whenever I want. "Find another whore to use." I can think of at least one.

He's across the room before I can even turn to leave. His hand wraps around my throat and I rise to my tiptoes. "You're the whore I want to use, doll face."

I fucking hate that it makes me feel special. It's just another lie.

His eyes search mine, and I hope he can see how much I hate him right now. "Do I need to start tying you to the bed before you fall asleep?"

"Fuck you, Haidyn," I grind out, my hands gripping his muscular tattooed arm, but the thought sounds so good. That he wants to keep me here. Even if it's as a pet. No. I saw the video…I know I'm just the current whore in his bed. I'm sure there's a line of them waiting for him. Hell, I'm sure they text him all the time. Just like the woman at the clinic. The way she looked at him—mouth watering and ready to beg.

His jaw sharpens, and he lets go of me and commands, "Remove your shirt."

My breath catches but my teeth clench. I hate this give and take. My mind wants to give him whatever the fuck he wants. My body wants him to take it.

"No," I tell him, and the threatening smile he gives me replaces the doubt that I'm not good enough and fills my stomach with butterflies. "I'm leaving." With that, I turn, tossing my hair over my shoulder and hoping it hits him in the face.

An arm wraps around my neck, pulling me to a quick stop. "Haidyn—" I growl, trying to fight his hold.

His free hand drops between my legs, and his fingers find their way to my already wet pussy. He shoves two inside me, and I gasp, pressing my back into his front and feeling his hard cock against my ass. "You have a choice, doll face," he informs me. "Remove your shirt, or I drag you down to the basement and chain you to the wall."

I groan, hating that I'm turned on at the sound of the second option. *He wants me to stay.*

"Make a decision," he orders, his fingers playing with my clit.

My hips rock back and forth, wanting him to enter me, but he slaps it, and I cry out. He releases my neck, and I stumble forward to turn around and face him. I'm fucking pissed and turned on at the same time. I want him to fuck me because if his cock is in me, it's not in someone else, right? That someone else being Ashtyn. We both seem to be in shitty moods, and it makes me wonder what happened for him to be in one.

"You have five seconds," he informs me. "One...two..."

Reaching down I grab the hem of my shirt and rip it over my head. Then I throw the wadded-up material at his chest. He lets it fall to the floor.

"Go put your hair up and meet me back in here."

I storm out of the gym and walk through his house naked with my head held high. I'm pissed and excited at the same time. Fuck, I hate him. I hate the way he makes me feel. Now I can add jealousy to that list. Jealous of a woman married to his best friend. Haidyn probably gets to use her whenever he wants. Well, everything except for her pussy.

That's something I can give him though. Fuck, I'm already making excuses as to why I would be the better fuck.

Entering the bathroom, I quickly brush my teeth. If he wants my hair up, he's going to fuck my face. He likes to kiss me after he comes down my throat. Afterward, I throw my hair up in a high pony as he instructed and stomp my way back to his gym.

He's sitting on a bench with a bag at his feet that wasn't in here before. "Is this good enough for you, sir?" I can't help it. I want a fight. He needs to dominate, and I want to submit to him. He's just going to have to force it out of me. He wants a whore? I'll give him one.

"Come here," he orders, ignoring my attitude. Or maybe he's going to fuck it out of me.

One can only hope he'll take my mind off the brunette that I just watched him fuck in the ass.

I make my way over to him, and my pussy begins to tingle as his eyes devour my body. The man has seen me naked every day since he forced me to come live with him, and he continues to look at me like it's the first time. "Remember what I told you sarcasm will get you?"

A face fucking. "I do." I lift my chin, and his satisfied smile makes my heart race.

He unzips the black duffel bag and pulls out several pieces of black rope in various sizes. I bite my lip to keep from moaning, my pussy soaked. Anything to take my mind off that video.

"Arms behind your back."

I do as I'm told, and he wastes no time as he starts to take the longer piece and begins to tie my wrists together. Then I feel him start to wrap it around my arms a little higher but underneath my elbows. It pulls my arms back farther than before. It gives me even less movement, and my breathing picks up. Once secure, he moves the rope up higher and above my elbows and does the same process. It pushes my chest out, and I moan at the lack of movement. It's so tight, and I love it.

He turns me to face him, and he takes the rope over my shoulder and down the inner side of my breast. I turn side to side for him as he instructs as the rope rubs against my skin. Securing the rope around my chest as well.

When he's done, he grips my ponytail and yanks my head back. I'm panting, my lips parted as I stare up at him, my eyes already heavy and pussy throbbing. I fight the rope, but it's tied too tight. I can't fucking move my arms an inch, and it makes me moan and my nipples harden.

"There's my girl." His free hand comes up to run his knuckles down my throat over my racing pulse.

My girl. They're just words. She's his *baby girl...*

"Hai-dyn." My voice is rough at the position of arch in my neck. I try to swallow, but it's hard.

He leans down and presses his lips to mine. I open my mouth, letting him slide his tongue into mine and control the kiss like he does my body. His hand drops from my throat and falls between my legs.

Yes! I spread them wider, and his fingers play with my swollen clit. I should be embarrassed by how wet I am but I'm not. He knows how much tying me up turns me on. I'd be more embarrassed if I wasn't soaking wet.

He pulls his lips from mine along with his hand, and my head falls forward when he lets go of my hair. He shifts me to the left before he grabs the bench that sits in the middle of a huge workout station and moves it out of the way. He grabs the bar that runs across the top of the workout bench and lowers it, locking it into a new spot.

Then he turns to face me, and both hands go to my face as he forces me to look up at him. "How do you feel?"

Like I want to punch you in the fucking face. "Fine." I don't want him to care how I feel. I want to be his good little whore. I want to let him do whatever the fuck he wants to me. I can keep him satisfied. I've given him everything I have. He wasn't her first. Not like he was mine.

Haidyn pulls me over to the bar that he just moved, my hips resting against the cold metal.

"Spread your legs," he commands, crouching down.

I stare at myself in the mirrored wall in front of me and watch him grab a new piece of rope from the bag. He wraps it around my ankle and ties it to the corner post before repeating the process with the other, spreading my legs wide open.

He stands behind me at his full height, and I watch him mesmerized as his hands run up and down my bare thighs. I lean over a little and shake my ass and spit falls from his lips landing on it. I used to gag, but now I moan, knowing what's to come.

He doesn't make me wait. His thumb pushes into my ass, and I gasp at the feel of it. "Haidyn," I whimper, needing his dick. *Fuck, why am I so desperate?* So needy for him? Is it him or me?

It's me. I'm just not sure if I'm trying to prove a point to him or myself. Maybe both.

My hips start to hurt as they grind against the metal bar, and my upper body is tired of having to hold itself up.

He removes his thumb, and I growl in disappointment. Laughing, he picks up his cell and props it up on the floor against the mirror. I see it's recording us. My breath catches, knowing he'll send it to me later. I like to watch what he does to me almost as much as when he fucks me. It's so when we're done, I'll have something to remember him by.

A part of me hopes that the next whore who comes along finds our videos so someone can be jealous of me.

Going back to his bag, he picks up the lube, a butt plug, and two black rubber clips connected by a chain. I'm gasping and dripping wet, ready for him to fuck my ass. The thought reminds me that I haven't had an enema since the first one and I need to get the courage to ask when he'll give me another.

Coming to stand back behind me, he pours it all over my ass, and I feel it run down my pussy and thighs. Then he's fingering me again. I moan, pushing back against it. "Please..." I trail off, needing more.

He slaps his name branded on my ass, and I cry out from the sting. Then he's pressing the butt plug into me, and I rise on my tiptoes, pulling on the rope that keeps my legs open as he watches it go in.

I push back against it, unable to stop myself. Just like the first time he fucked my ass in my basement. When I let him take what he wanted.

"That's it, Charlotte." He slowly fucks my ass with the butt plug. "Good girl." His free hand drops to rub my thigh. "Feel good?"

I nod, sniffling, and he slaps my outer thigh for not using my words. "Yes. It feels good," I add. "But your dick would feel better." I know what he likes, and I want to give it to him.

He laughs, pushing it in. My body trembles as he steps back, shoving his sweatpants down his hips, and his hard cock springs free. I did that. Not some video of him fucking someone else. Not another bitch moaning his name. Me. His doll face.

"Look at you needing to have your ass fucked. Next time I decide to fuck it, you'll crawl for it," he promises.

"Yes." *Anything.* I agree. At least it means this won't be our last time.

He's not going to let me leave.

Coming to stand before me naked, he begins to play with my breast, and I lean into him. My lips part, wanting another kiss.

He leans down and my eyes close, but I yank on the ropes in frustration when he only kisses my forehead.

"So impatient." He smiles, playing with my left breast while his right hand holds the chain and two black clips. His fingers pinch my nipple, pulling me forward, and I gasp at the pain. "You have such beautiful breasts, doll face. They're fucking perfect."

Letting go, he opens up one of the black clips and grips my breast in his hand, pinching the clip down on my nipple.

I cry out, pulling back as the bite sends a shock straight to my pussy. "Haidyn..." I yank on the ropes, my eyes instantly tearing up. It takes my breath away, and I bounce on my toes, waiting for the sting to lessen.

"You're doing great, doll face." He encourages me and then grabs my other breast. He places that clip on as well and my body trembles as wetness leaks from my pussy. "So beautiful." Stepping into me, he grips my face and lowers his lips to mine.

I kiss him desperately, needing him inside me. Fuck, I've never wanted to be fucked more than I have right now. He pulls away, and I suck in a ragged breath as he orders, "Open wide."

My trembling lips part, and he lifts the chain, pulling on my breasts, and he places the center of the chain in my mouth. "Don't drop it."

He steps away, and I look at myself in the mirror through watery eyes and see the clamps pulling my breasts up and my nose begins to run. My teeth bite down on the cold metal, and the rope wraps around my chest like a harness.

He guides his cock into my soaked pussy, and I suck in a sharp breath through my clenched teeth at the sting of his size stretching me. Fuck, it feels so good. Especially with the added butt plug. He reaches out and grips both of my breasts. He massages them, and it pulls on the chain in my mouth, but I bite down on it no matter how much it pulls on my breasts.

"Good girl," he growls. His eyes meet mine in the mirror. "Watch yourself, doll face. You're going to come all over my cock and then lick it clean, do you understand?"

I nod the best I can, sucking in deep breaths through my nose. He begins to fuck me hard and fast, not wasting a second, and each thrust has my boobs moving enough that it pulls on the clamps, making me wetter and wetter.

He grips my ponytail and shoves me forward. When he yanks my head back, it pulls the chain taut, making it slip from my drooling mouth, and I cry out.

Shaking his head, he reaches around with his free hand, slips his three middle fingers through the chain, and shoves his fingers into my mouth, forcing me to hold the chain.

I rise on my tiptoes and spit flies from my mouth as he gags me.

My shoulders shake and my thighs clench as his cock fucks my soaked cunt. My breathing comes in short pants, and my skin gets flushed from the pain caused by the clamps.

"Come on my cock, doll face. I know you want to. I can feel how close you are." He smiles at me. "You love being my fuck toy."

My eyes grow heavy, and my pussy clenches down on his pierced dick as I come all over it.

HAIDYN

I PULL OUT OF HER PUSSY TO SEE MY COCK COVERED IN HER CUM. I remove my fingers from her mouth, and she gasps. Taking a new piece of rope, I connect it to the single column tie on her wrists and tie the excess to the upper bar, and it puts her at a ninety-degree angle—bent over the metal bar at her waist.

The room fills with her heavy breathing as she tries to come down, and I retrieve a one-pound dumbbell. When I bought the set, I wondered what the hell I'd do with one pound, but it's going to come in handy for my girl. Placing it on the floor below her, I grab a piece of rope and drape it over the chain connecting the nipple clamps and pull on it gently, watching her tied arms stretch just a little.

"HAIDYN," she cries out.

"Almost done, Charlotte. Then you get what you want." She wants to be fucked. Again. She can't get enough, and neither can I. And it has nothing to do with the bitch who was naked in my kitchen just an hour ago.

Charlotte whimpers, her eyes tightly shut as I tie off the rope to the dumbbell that sits on the floor.

"Oh my god." She gasps. When she pulls her upper body up, it lifts the dumbbell off the floor, tugging on her breasts and making her cry out.

"Life is about choices, doll face," I tell her, and she lifts her head to look at me.

Tears run down her pretty face. I reach up and cup her cheek, and she leans into my hand. "I...please..." She closes her eyes tightly.

I let go of her face and stand, then pick up the last piece of rope and wrap it around her throat. After making sure she has plenty of room and won't choke, I reach up and tie off the extra to the bar at the top of the workout equipment. "This is what they call predicament bondage," I explain. It's the same thing I did with the anal hook, but I will admit this one is a little more advanced. "You either choose pain or choking."

She sucks in a deep breath.

"You can let your nipples rest, but the rope will tighten around your neck when you drop the weight to the floor. Or you lift your chest to loosen the rope around your neck to breathe. But in doing so, you pick up the dumbbell, which will pull on your nipples. The choice is yours, doll face."

She's trembling, gasping, and crying. I won't leave her like this for long. She's not experienced enough. My point isn't for her to choke herself—I didn't make it that tight. I don't want her passing out on me.

I walk behind her body and admire my work. I didn't tie her arms to the top bar too tight because I don't want to restrict her movements too much. I want her to choose nipple pulling or choking, and her upper body needs movement for that.

Then I look down at her pussy and smile. "You're soaking wet, doll face. Look at yourself. It's running down your legs." I run the back of my knuckles down her inner thighs to gather her wetness and then lick my knuckles clean. "I've got one more surprise for you."

Reaching into my bag, I grab what I need and walk back in front of her. I bend down and wave the dildo in front of her tear-streaked face. Her heavy eyes find it and her lips part.

I smile. "Want my cock in your mouth, doll face?"

"Ple-ease?" She licks her wet lips.

I hold it out in front of her, and she licks the tip of it like it's ice cream. She lowers the dumbbell to the floor, and the rope tightens around her neck. Her lips part, and I slip the tip of the dildo into her mouth. She sucks on it.

"Spit on it," I order and pull it out.

She does so, then parts her lips again. I push it back in, and she lifts her upper body, pulling the one-pound weight off the floor, and fresh tears fill her eyes. Her cheeks hollow out as she sucks on the dildo.

"That's a good girl." I take my free hand and push a single piece of hair behind her ear that fell out of her now loose ponytail. "Suck on it, Charlotte. Take your mind off the pain."

She pulls her head back and removes the dildo from her mouth and sucks in a breath. Crying out that the simple movement forced the dumbbell to swing and pull on her nipples.

"It's a lot, I know." I tell her, and she leans forward, wrapping her lips around it again. "Open wide."

Doing as she's told; I slowly fuck her mouth with it. In and out, holding it in front of her face and forcing her to move her head side to side to lick it and suck it. "You're such a desperate whore. Look at you trying to get this dildo to come as if it's a real cock."

She sniffs as the snot runs from her nose like the drool from her open mouth.

"That what you want, Charlotte? Want me to fill your dripping pussy with this dildo while I fuck your face?"

She blinks and mumbles around the cock. I pull it out, and she leans forward trying to keep it in her mouth. I laugh and stand. Walking behind her, I take the drool-covered dildo and slowly push it into her cum-covered cunt. She groans as her thighs shake uncontrollably.

"I want you to see how pretty you look." I tell her coming to stand in front of her once again. I lean back against the mirrored wall watching her struggle. The dumbbell is on the floor, and her lips are parted as a line of drool falls to the floor.

"Haidyn...please?" She gasps, body trembling.

I push off the mirror and step into her. My hard cock is right in front of her face. I reach up, placing my hand on the bar above me, and speak, "You want it, doll face? It's right in front of you." It's still got her cum all over it.

She whimpers, lifting her head and chest, which pulls the dumbbell up off the floor. Her open mouth tries to wrap around the tip of my cock, but I move my hips from side to side.

Her open mouth follows it before she's able to wrap her lips around the tip. I want to tease her because the more she moves, the more stimulating it'll be.

She sucks on my cock so hard that it takes my breath away. "Fuck, doll face," I growl. "You're so greedy."

As she sucks me into her drooling mouth, my legs start to buckle. *Jesus!* "You're so worked up." I grind out. "How's your ass and cunt feel, Charlotte? Must feel really good by the way you're swallowing my cock."

She mumbles around my pierced dick before she opens her mouth wider, and I push farther down her constricting throat.

"Goddamn." I throw my head back loving the way it feels when she gags.

"You like having something in all your holes? Like feeling full?" This is the only way she'll know how it feels. No other cock will fuck what's mine.

I drop my hands and place them both under her throat, sliding my fingers between her neck and the rope, lifting her head even more and she cries out around my dick.

Her body trembles, and she pulls on the rope that keeps her tightly in place. I pick up my pace, fucking her mouth as if it's her pussy. The force of my hips has her body rocking back and forth and the dumbbell swinging between my parted legs. Between gasps and whimpers, she's crying. "You're doing so good, doll face," I growl. "That's it." She blinks, looking up at me through watery lashes. Her bloodshot eyes are heavy, and I wonder how many times she's come so far. "Open up for me. Let me fuck you like a good little whore while you come all over the dildo stuffed in your cunt."

Her body jerks, and she gags as I slam my cock into her mouth. My balls start to tighten. I don't want to come yet, but between her cunt and her mouth—she feels too good. My hands can feel the bulge of her throat from my dick going in and out. She's gasping for breath as her drool runs down my legs and the dumbbell sways back and forth, pulling on her nipples.

I push forward one last time, holding my cock at the back of her throat as I come. I pull my semi-hard dick free of her swollen lips, and she hangs her head, letting the dumbbell fall to the floor. She holds her breath.

I quickly untie her neck, remove the nipple clamps, and release her arms and legs. Then I remove the dildo and butt plug. "Come on, doll face. Let's get you cleaned up and back in bed." I pick her limp body up in my arms and carry her through the quiet house and to the bathroom.

Setting her in the bathtub, I begin to fill it with warm water and cup her tear-streaked face. "Look at me, Charlotte."

Her heavy eyes open, and she slowly blinks, her wet lashes fanning her cheeks. "You did so good for me." I smile, and her eyes fall closed. She's shaking uncontrollably, and I lean over the side of the Jacuzzi tub, kissing her passionately. She doesn't reciprocate it. She's too far gone.

I'll wash her and put her in my bed. Where she'll stay. In my house. With me. Even if I have to do this to her every night, I will. I wasn't lying when I said I'd either tie her to my bed every night or chain her up in my basement. Either way, she's not leaving this house.

No one is going to take her away from me.

After I finish, I carry and place her naked body in my bed next to a purring Muffin. As I turn to step away, I see her phone and earbuds on the floor over by the windows. I pick up her cell and open the screen and see she's in her emails, and it's paused on a video.

Looking down at her, I watch her sleep. The Lords sent her something that pissed her off. Why else would she all of a sudden want to leave me?

I press play, and I don't need audio to see that it's me fucking Ashtyn in the ass. It was our senior year at Barrington at the house of Lords. That was the night I overheard Sierra talking shit to Ashtyn in the bathroom. I shared my chosen with Hooke. Then Saint gave Ash an enema and fucked her mouth while she held it in. After he let her relieve herself, he fucked her ass and then let Kashton and me take our turns.

Find another whore to use.

That's why Charlotte stormed into the gym in such a pissy mood. Aw, my girl is jealous. It's cute.

My eyes drop back down to the phone and see Kash step up to take his turn and the video ends. Then it disappears. Gone as if it never existed. Why are the Lords sending her this? Why did they want her to see that? Do they want her to leave me? Or do they want me to force her to stay?

She's not going anywhere. I don't care how many videos they send her or how much it pisses her off.

Setting her cell on the nightstand, I lean down, kissing her forehead, and whisper, "Get some rest, beautiful," then go to take a shower myself.

Shhh...

Chapter 59

Charlotte

I'm not technically released from Haidyn's house arrest after I was attacked in the bathroom, but I'm also no longer fighting to stay at my house either. I feel stupid about my outburst. We both know I can't walk away from him. The Lords can send me whatever they want. I can't call quits on this assignment.

I needed a break and was surprised today when I told him I had a few errands to run and all he did was kiss me bye and went back to his office. Today is my IV appointment. I almost canceled, considering I haven't been out lately, but who knew that sex was just as exhausting as getting hammered?

Last night after dinner, he tied me down and started with my mouth. Then moved onto my pussy. Fuck, I was in tears due to how sore my body felt. I wanted to beg him to stop just so I could have a break, but of course I was gagged. So like his good girl I am, I had to take it. And he reminded me every second how good it felt. I came three times.

Getting out of his bed this morning was a challenge. That's when I knew my *me* day couldn't hurt.

I'm sitting in the room with the IV in my arm, and I go to turn my phone on silent so I don't have any interruptions when it dings in my hand.

I open it up to see it's a message from Haidyn.

Sushi or Italian?

I smile and respond.

Sushi.

The three little dots bounce around until it goes off again.

Whatever my girl wants.

I shut my phone off without responding. Hating and loving the way my pulse races. Why does he have to say shit like that? Why does any text from a monster make me smile?

I'm getting in too deep. This is why my father had me remain a virgin for so long. My mother told me no man would ever know my body as good as I'd know it myself, but she was wrong. Haidyn knows it better than I ever could.

It's getting confusing. Who he is in my life and what I'm supposed to be doing. My emotions are getting the best of me. The fact that he saved me from the attacker in the bathroom makes me think he actually cares about me. But then I tell myself, he can't play with me if his toy is ruined.

An hour later, the nurse returns and removes my IV. I thank her and make my way to my car. When I turn my cell back on, it chimes with an incoming message.

UNKNOWN: Bring Haidyn to this location 10:00 sharp. Tonight or else…

I toss the phone across the car like it's on fire and hear it hit the passenger floorboard.

"Fuck!" I shout, hitting the steering wheel. "This can't be happening." I run my hand through my hair, gripping a hold of it.

This is it. This is what they wanted me to do all along. Turn him over to them. But why? What has he done to them that they want to punish him? And why me? Why give me this assignment?

And if I don't…I fail. I told Haidyn if it was ever him or me…I'd choose me. Every time. But now? He saved me. That guy in the bathroom could have raped and killed me, but Haidyn didn't let that happen.

Is this why they sent me the video of him and Ashtyn right after he saved me? Because they know I'm getting attached and want me to hate him?

My phone rings and it makes me jump. Taking in a deep breath, I lean over and pick it up off the floor to see it's Haidyn. For a second, I think about not answering, but I can't ignore him. That would throw up red flags. "He-llo?" I clear my throat and try again. "Hey."

"Doll face." His deep voice fills my ear, and my thighs clench closed, hating how much my body responds to him.

"What...what are you doing?" I stumble over my words and want to punch myself in the face. Taking a deep breath, I try to calm my racing heart.

"You okay, Charlotte?"

His question makes my chest tighten that I'm that readable, and he's not even looking at me. He can tell by my voice alone that something is wrong. "Of course," I answer, giving a soft laugh. "I just finished up my IV," I add. "The sessions always make me jittery afterward." *Lie.*

"Okay." He buys it, and I let out a sigh of relief. "I just wanted to let you know reservations have been made for dinner. Eight o'clock." My stomach knots at the fact I have to turn him over two hours after that. "I have to go into Carnage, but I'll pick you up from your house, okay?"

I had told him that I wanted to grab a few more things from my house today. I need more clothes. At this point, I might as well just move in with him. The thought makes my stomach knot because after tonight, it won't matter. I nod my head to myself and answer him softly, "Yeah. Sounds good."

He hangs up, and I drop the phone on my lap. Going into this, I told myself I'd do whatever I had to do to make it in this world. But I never thought I'd have to give up the one thing that makes me feel like our world isn't so bad.

HAIDYN

I enter the office at Carnage. Saint and Kashton both look up at me and then at each other.

"Hey, man." Kash gets up and walks over to me, giving me a handshake hug as if I didn't just see him two nights ago. "What's up?"

"I came to look at something," I answer and drop into my chair at my desk, avoiding Saint's stare. We haven't had the talk yet to explain what and why I did what I did. I'm not in the mood right now. I have something to figure out.

Placing the USB drive into the computer, I pull up the surveillance footage from the gas station that Sin grabbed for me. I didn't have time to watch it because I spent the evening inside Charlotte. Then my guest arrived, throwing me off. I ended up fucking Charlotte in my gym.

They plan on taking her away from me, but it won't be happening. I have a plan of my own, but I've also got something else to handle at the moment.

Sitting back in my chair, I cross my arms over my chest and watch the screen. It has five different angles. One shows the four pumps, the second shows the off-ramp and busy highway. The third shows the front door and the window that you can pay at right next to it. The fourth shows the back, an empty parking lot with one car—which I'm guessing belongs to the employee. The fifth one shows the bathrooms.

I set it to three minutes before I know we arrived and push play. My eyes scan the one that shows the off-ramp, and her SUV appears after a couple of minutes. As I pull up to the pump, something catches my attention, and I see a black motorcycle exit the highway.

I sit up straighter. It pulls into the gas station as I get out of the car to pump her gas. I don't even see it. On the screen, my attention is on the pump while I know my mind was on Charlotte. I was pissed at her attitude and thrown off by LeAnne showing up at Ryat's.

The guy gets off his black R6, removes his black helmet and hangs it on his mirror, then removes his black gloves and jacket. He tosses them over his seat, and I notice he already has his ski mask on. He was wearing it under his helmet.

The blood rushes in my ears as I watch the passenger side door open. I know Charlotte and I exchange words, and then, just like I remember, she enters the women's restroom.

He rushes to enter behind her.

She had told me she checked the stalls. That she thought he had set her up to use the last one, but he entered after her. She was targeted. He was there for her and her only, which means he knows who she is.

It shows me cussing out the damn pump. It was taking forever. I eventually give up and storm over to the restroom. I had every intention to rush in there and fuck her ass. Maybe take my belt to it. Whatever I had to do to prove to her that the attitude wasn't going to go unnoticed or unpunished. But seeing him on top of her changed everything.

The door opens on screen, and my eyes go to hers. She looks terrified. I can see how much she's shaking while I order her to get in the car. I was on high alert. It wasn't about trying to calm her down; it was about getting her the hell out of there as soon as possible.

I watch myself throw the guy in the back and get into her SUV, driving off. My eyes go back to the black bike that sits there in the parking lot, and my blood boils at the sight of it.

"Motherfucker!" I slam my hands on the desk and jump to my feet.

"Haidyn?"

I ignore Saint and rush out of the office, and I don't even bother with the elevator. Instead, I take the stairs down to the basement. Hearing their footsteps shuffling behind me, I shove the door open and grab the set of keys out of my back pocket. I approach the cell we've got the naked guy in and unlock it.

He jumps to his feet and lifts his arms to defend his face, but I grab the back of his neck and shove him out into the hallway before I drag him into the open room. Walking past the pits, I bring him to the center and reach up, pulling on the chain that hangs from the ceiling and wrap it around his neck three times.

The guy yells profanities at me, but I ignore him as I yank on the excess chain, forcing him up to his tiptoes. "Don't worry, it won't choke you," I inform him.

Then I go to the far corner, ignoring Saint's and Kashton's concerned looks. If they want to stay for the show, then they're more than welcome. But it would be best if they shut the fuck up and let me work in peace.

I open the cabinet and pull out the things that I want, placing them all on a rolling cart while I hear him struggle behind me. Once I have enough, I roll the cart over to him and pick one up. I press it to his face, and he tilts his head back, trying to get away while his hands grip the chain wrapped around his neck.

"You lied to me."

He tries to shake his head. "Nnnnoooo." Spit flies from his mouth. "I didn't..."

"Why have you been following Charlotte?" I use her fake name to see if he corrects me.

I have no clue what this guy knows, but she had called me and told me that *I* had been following her on my bike. It wasn't me. She wouldn't see the difference between mine, an R1, and his, an R6. His is blacked out like mine, so to her, it was close enough. The question is was that on purpose or coincidence? Funny thing is...I don't believe in coincidences.

The moment I saw it on the security footage, I knew it had been him. *She wasn't random.* He was hired to follow her. The question is was he supposed to just watch her or hurt her? And if so, why make a move when she was with me? Why not have done it when he knew she was alone? Did they want me to find her dead?

"I don't..."

I shove a knife into his upper thigh.

He screams, his hands lowering to the handle, and he feels around it but doesn't pull it out.

"These won't kill you." I hold one up and examine it. "The two-inch blade has inverted cuts, so once inserted, it locks into your skin. I mean, they can be removed, but..." I put my hand on the handle and give it a little tug, making him cry out. "Yeah, it hurts." I let it go.

Picking up another one, I speak. "Why were you following Charlotte?"

"I was hired to watch her," he rushes out.

I stab the second knife into the opposite thigh, and his body jerks as he sobs. "The more information you give willingly, the better your odds," I inform him, not in the mood for this shit.

"A man," he rushes out. "I don't know his name. He came to me..." He pauses. "Told me to watch her. Keep an eye on her..."

"Rape her," I add, slamming another one into his stomach.

"FUUUCCCKKK!" he screams. His shaking hands go to it, and he tries to pull it out on his own but stops himself with a sob.

"How long?" I growl, getting impatient.

"I...I don't know..." he rushes out. "Maybe a few months."

I step back from him as if I was just hit by a man twice my size. They've had someone on her for a few months? That's how long she's been seeing me? *It's the Lords.* They want to make sure she gets the job done.

"Leave him," I snap to Kash and Saint, who are still being nosy bitches and watching the show. I storm out of the room and take the stairs once again to the first level. Shoving the door open, I'm walking toward the front double doors when a hand grabs my arm and brings me to a stop. I whirl around to see it's Saint. I rip my arm from his hold. "Don't..."

"What the fuck is going on, Haidyn?" he demands.

"It doesn't concern you," I growl, giving him my back once again.

"Yeah, well, my wife didn't concern you," he shouts, and I come to a stop and turn back to face him and Kash. "But you didn't care about that, did you?"

My teeth grind, and I want to put my fist through his face. We've still got unresolved issues regarding Ashtyn. But his words just remind me that this is about him right now and how I betrayed him. And I don't have time for that. Charlotte is my main concern.

"Haidyn?"

My head snaps up to see Ashtyn standing at the top of the grand staircase. "Oh my God, Haidyn." She rushes down the stairs, and my eyes remain on Saint's as she jumps up and wraps her legs around my waist and her arms around my neck. "I'm so glad you're back."

"Hey, baby girl," I say softly, hugging her back. Gently, I push her away, and she gets the hint, lowering herself to her feet.

Silence fills the large foyer, and I finally look away from Saint and down at Ashtyn. I give her a soft smile, and she licks her lips, her eyes filling with tears. She understands I'm not staying. She thought I was officially living back here at Carnage, but that's just not the case.

With that, I turn and walk out of Carnage, knowing what I need to do.

shhh...

Chapter 60

Charlotte

I spent the day shopping with the girls. The ones who know who I really am. I'm struggling to know the real me. I like who I am with Haidyn—Charlotte—but I like the life that Annabelle gets to live. She's not a fake. She's part of a secret society, but she knows where she belongs.

Charlotte is the lie. She has a fake life and fake friends, but she has Haidyn. He's the realest thing I've ever had in my life.

It's getting complicated and harder to differentiate between the two people I'm supposed to be. Why can't I have both?

Then the text. I've been trying to decide who I want to be for the rest of my life because I have to choose at ten o'clock tonight.

Give him up or myself.

I needed to clear my head and buy myself some time, so I went shopping. I spent all day blowing money, thinking it would help me. It's by far the dumbest thing I've ever done, but I needed to try something.

Pulling my SUV into the garage, I get out and pop the hatch. It takes both hands to grab all the bags, and even then, it's a struggle. I even leave the back open and garage up as I get them into the house. I place them all on the kitchen island and turn on the light.

I pull a bottle of wine from the fridge and open it before pouring it into a glass. Checking my cell, I see that I have two hours before Haidyn will be here. He was the only thing on my mind while shopping today. I bought outfits for him, which sounds so stupid in the long run. Not because he doesn't care what I wear, but because I'll never see him again after ten o'clock.

I'm trying to convince myself that they just want to talk to him. But even I laugh at that thought. But what if it's just a test for me? I show up, and they say they just wanted to see if I'd do it?

I take my previous statement back. That was the dumbest idea I've ever had.

Tossing back the wine, I swallow the cold liquid, hoping it will drown me and make the decision for me. I feel like turning Haidyn in is betraying me now. But can I live with myself, not knowing what will happen to him? I've seen the videos and how he stood up for Ashtyn. What he's been through. What if he's just misunderstood?

I can be that woman for him, right? I've handled him so far. I want him to see me differently. Again, so fucking stupid.

Making my way to my bedroom, I pass the living room and come to a stop when I see someone sitting on my couch. The lights are off, but I can see the shadowy figure. I want to be afraid, but instead, I smile that he's here. I flip the switch on the wall. "You're early..."

My words trail off when the light illuminates the room, and the man who I thought was sitting on my couch, isn't. "Wesley?" I ask, my heart is now racing. "What are you doing here?" I look around the room and see he's alone. Not like I expected him to be with someone else. It's just become a habit.

He's sitting on the couch, leaning forward with his elbows on his knees, looking down at the coffee table. My eyes follow his, and I take a step back when I see the small jewelry box sitting on the glass. The same one that Haidyn tied me to weeks ago, and I came all over. Back when I thought he was my biggest threat and now I'm his.

My mind always goes to him. He's consuming my life. *It'll be over tonight.* I immediately stop that train of thought.

"Where have you been?" He looks up, and his eyes glare at me.

I straighten my shoulders, not liking the accusation in his tone. The Lords made me date him. I didn't want a boyfriend. "I was shopping," I answer honestly. The last time we texted was three days ago. I had sent him a Photoshopped picture of me. He never responded, and I never gave him another thought.

"You can't answer your phone." He arches a brow.

"It died earlier." *Lie.* I turned it off, needing to clear my mind. I know that Haidyn is tracking my every move with the tracker in my neck, but I didn't want him to be able to reach me because of how I acted during our phone call earlier. I couldn't let him know that something was going on.

"I know you're cheating on me."

His words are a relief. "I'm—"

He laughs, interrupting me. "You can save your lies."

"I wasn't going to lie," I whisper. "I was going to say sorry."

"Sorry?" His laughter grows. "You think that word means shit to me?" he screams, jumping to his feet.

I take another step back.

He holds up his right hand, and in it is the notebook I gave Haidyn for our sessions. He opens it up and reads it out loud. "Haidyn's dirty little whore. Over and over..."

I step to the side as he throws it toward me, missing my face.

"I told you all about Sally. And how she cheated on me. And you do the same?" He picks up the box and throws it across the room as well. It hits the wall; the box opens and then slides down the hall.

"Wesley—"

"I knew you'd be another fucking whore."

My stomach knots at his words because they're true. I'm a whore. Haidyn's whore, just like I wrote in the notebook. Swallowing the lump in my throat, I say, "I told you that I wanted—"

"To be fucked?" He gives another rough laugh. "And we decided to wait. To have a relationship based on love and respect. Not sex."

I wrap my arms around myself and bow my head. Haidyn always tells me to use my words. To speak what I want. I did that with Wesley, and he didn't listen. Or he did and just didn't like what he heard. Being with Haidyn has taught me a lot. I've always known sex was a big factor with the Lords. My mother raised me to believe that it's big in any relationship. Lords or not—you see sex everywhere you look. Billboards, books, magazines, social media. There's nothing wrong with that.

"You decided." I look up at him through my lashes. "You decided for us that I didn't need it." His jaw sharpens. "But I told you how I felt. I wanted that connection with you." I couldn't be more grateful that he turned me down that night. I'm glad Haidyn was my first...at everything.

"So it's my fault that you're a cheating whore." He nods to himself. "Got it. Just like Sally and blaming me for your infidelities."

"No," I say. "I chose to do that on my own." *But did I?* I didn't have a choice. First, the Lords tell me to remain a virgin, then they tell me to give Haidyn whatever he wants. I'm nothing more than a piece of the puzzle they can place wherever they want to make the story fit. Now they want me to be part of getting rid of the man I think I'm falling in love with.

"I have been faithful." He points at his chest. "Do you know how many chances I've had to fuck around on you, but I didn't? I knew we had something special."

"Wesley—"

"I knew that what I wanted was long term with you," he screams.

I don't know what to say to that because it was never meant to be more than what it was. He was a filler in my life. A stepping stone to get to where the Lords want me to be. "I'm sorry, Wesley. I really am."

He snorts and pulls his suit jacket on, buttoning it closed. His eyes drop to my tennis shoes and run up over my leggings and hoodie. When they meet mine, I see the anger and betrayal I've caused him. "Now you're just like every slut there is out there." He comes over to stand in front of me, and I swallow nervously. "When he's done with you, he'll throw you to the side, and you'll realize I was the better man." With that, he turns and walks past me out the front door, slamming it shut.

A part of me is relieved. That's a lie I no longer have to keep up with. But it doesn't help my conscience with what I have to do with Haidyn. I down the rest of the glass of wine.

HAIDYN

I PULL UP TO HER HOUSE TO SEE HER GARAGE DOOR OPEN AND her SUV parked inside with the hatch up. I park my bike inside next to it, shut her hatch, and close the garage door when I enter the house.

She's been ignoring me all day by keeping her phone off. And although I've been tracking her, not being able to speak to her is unacceptable. Especially since I know someone had that guy watching her. Since the guy is locked up at Carnage, they will hire someone else to follow her.

Walking down the hallway, I see an open box on the floor. I pick it up to see it's black and the interior is padded with a light blue satin. I close the box and open it back up. It's for a ring. But it's empty. I close it and place it in the pocket of my leather jacket.

I make my way into the kitchen to see bags piled up on the kitchen table. Being myself, I start to open them up to find lingerie. A sexy black lace teddy. A pair of black Christian Louboutin heels. Some more lingerie and then underwear. Another pair of heels.

She spent the day shopping.

Leaving everything, I head to her bedroom and find the bathroom door open with her phone on the counter. Spotify is open, and she's blaring "Dirty Thoughts" by Chloe Adams.

She's got her dark hair up into a messy bun on top of her head, and a bottle of wine sits on the side of the tub. It's halfway gone. The tub is filled to the brim with water and so many bubbles that they're sliding down the side of the tub to the floor. Her head rests on the fluffy white pillow, and a washcloth lays over her eyes.

I crouch down next to the tub and pick up the corner of the washcloth, slowly pulling it off her face. Her head rolls to the side, and her eyes open to meet mine. "Rough day, doll face?"

She sighs and turns her head to stare up at the ceiling but says nothing.

"What happened?"

"Wesley found out about you."

I frown. "Who is Wesley?" As I ask, it comes to mind. "Ahh, the boyfriend."

"As if you ever cared that I had one to begin with."

"I didn't," I say, and she gives a rough laugh. "What did he have to say?" I'm guessing she means by found out about me is in regard to fucking her. If it was Lords related, she'd be freaking out because he's part of her fake life.

She lifts her left arm from the tub. A diamond sparkles on her bubble-covered hand. "He was going to propose."

Now the jewelry box in my pocket makes more sense. "Kinda small, isn't it?" I joke.

"Funny how he thought I would marry him." She gives another laugh. "He didn't even know me. Not the real me."

I remember our conversation in bed when she said, *"Don't you want someone you know will love you unconditionally?"*

Looking at my watch, I see it's almost seven. "Come on." I stand and grab her towel. "Dinner is in an hour. We need to get going soon."

I see her tense, and her breathing picks up at my reminder of our plans tonight. She reaches for the bottle of wine and begins to down it. Then she stands, and I notice her eyes can't meet mine. Instead, she stares at my T-shirt while allowing me to wrap the towel around her.

"You sure everything is okay?" I ask, cupping her face and forcing her eyes to mine.

She blinks, her lashes fanning her cheeks before she swallows nervously. "Yeah, just tired."

I frown at the lie but let it slide. She's keeping secrets but so am I. I'm not going to tell her what I did today or that someone had hired that man to follow her. I don't want to scare her. There's nothing for her to worry about. I have it taken care of.

Shhh...

Chapter 61

Charlotte

I'm freaking out. Fucking terrified at what I'm about to do. As of right now, I'm turning him over to the Lords.

And that changes everything.

He's on to me. He knows something is wrong. I can't hide it, so I'm going to have to convince him something else is bothering me. Or allow him to take my mind off it for a little while.

"Can we skip dinner?"

His frown deepens. "Of course. What else do you have in mind?" he asks.

I wrap my arms around his neck, causing the towel to drop to my feet, and his eyes fall to my chest. My nipples are already hard, and my heart pounds. I want him to fuck me. Maybe I'll get lucky, and he'll fuck me to death. Then I won't have to make a decision.

"I want you to fuck me," I say, lifting my chin.

His eyes meet mine, and a smirk plays on his gorgeous face. "I love it when my girl uses her words."

Wetness pools between my legs, and I try to ignore the way my heart skips a beat. We're on borrowed time. I want to ask him to make love to me. So I know what it feels like once in my life, but I can't make the words come out. That would throw up too many red flags because I'm his whore, not the love of his life.

I reach up and press my lips to his. His hands drop to my ass, and he picks me up. My legs wrap around him, and I devour his lips. Like I'm on death row and this is my last meal. Which, in a way, it is. Possibly for both of us.

This will be our last time together. I'm going to let him do whatever the fuck he wants to me. I'm his offering. He just doesn't know it.

He's carrying me to the bedroom, and we fall onto the bed, him on top of me, his lips still devouring mine. My hands go to his shirt, and I grip the material. He gets the hint, pulling his lips from mine just long enough for me to rip his shirt up and over his head.

I moan into his mouth as my hands go between our bodies, and I fumble with his belt for a few seconds before I get it undone.

He pulls away from me and stands while I lie on the bed, panting and impatiently waiting. His hands go to his jeans and he removes them before yanking his belt from the loops and then tosses them to the far side of the room. "Roll over," he orders, and I gladly oblige, placing my hands behind my back, knowing what he wants. He secures the leather belt around my wrists and then flips me back over.

I stare up at him, my arms restrained underneath me as he crawls back onto the bed. His knees spread mine wide, and he takes his hard cock into his hands, guiding it into my soaked pussy.

Arching my back, I cry out, and his hands wrap around my throat. He stills, cock buried into my cunt as he lowers his lips to mine and whispers, "This what you want, doll face?" He gently kisses my parted lips, teasing me.

"Yes, please..." I beg, my body fighting him trying to get him to move inside me, but he holds still, liking the way I squirm.

"You're so desperate." His lips smile against mine.

I groan impatiently. I need him to own me. To take me to that place where my mind stops. "Fuck me..." I swallow against his hands. "Please, Haidyn."

He sits up, his hands tightening around my throat, cutting off my air, and my pussy clenches down on him. Yes! This is what I want. Fucking choke me out.

His blue eyes are on mine as I look up at him with heavy lashes. He slowly pulls out of my pussy, and I part my lips. My body's natural reaction is to try to breathe, but I get nothing. He smiles down at me before his cock enters me once again painfully slow.

The room starts to spin, and my eyes flutter. This is how I'm going to go. Letting him kill me sounds better than giving him up.

He slams his hips forward, and my eyes roll back into my head. "That's it, beautiful," he says. "That's what my whore likes." He pulls out and slams into me again. My chest heaves, trying to breathe. "Come on my dick, doll face. Remind me that I own you."

My body shudders as my vision fades to black. I'm not sure if I'm passing out or dying, but my body involuntarily jerks, begging to breathe while I come.

His hands let go of my neck, and I cough. Spit flies from my open mouth, and I realize I'm crying as he leans down and kisses my cheeks.

"Good girl, Charlotte." His hands slide into my hair, and he yanks my head back to expose my neck to his lips. He tenderly kisses my racing pulse while his cock continues to fuck me rough and hard. Smashing my arms underneath us. I can no longer feel them. Nothing else matters except for him right now. He pulls away and orders, "Eyes on me, doll face. I want to see you while I come inside you."

My heavy eyes find his, and it takes everything I have to keep them open.

"That's it. That's my good little whore." The sound of our bodies slapping fills the room, and he lowers his lips to mine, kissing me passionately, burying himself deep inside me and pulsing as he comes.

♠

I'M LYING ON MY BED NAKED, COVERED IN SWEAT, AND TRYING TO come down as I watch Haidyn dress. His back is toward me, and he's pulling up his jeans over his black boxer briefs. Once he fastens his belt, he turns and walks over to the side of the bed and picks up his shirt off the floor. I watch shamelessly as he pulls it on, and my eyes are fascinated by how his muscles flex with each movement. My eyes catch sight of the scar from when he was shot before his shirt covers it, and I get a pain in my chest.

It makes me wonder what he's been through. From the videos the Lords sent me—slitting his wrists to being electrocuted and whipped—I feel sorry for him. And men like Haidyn don't want pity. They want respect.

What do the Lords want from him? Why send me to do it?

He leans over the side of the bed and plants a soft kiss on my forehead, and I want to wrap my arms around him and pull him back into my bed. We're safe here. When he's inside me, nothing else exists.

When he pulls away, I open my eyes. "Can we go for a ride?" I ask before I lose my nerve.

"You want to go for a ride?" he asks.

I sit up, nodding. "Yeah. On your bike." I have to make him think he's in charge and can control things.

"Of course." He smiles at me, and my stomach sinks. I feel like I'm going to get sick. "Get dressed. We'll go back to my house and grab a helmet and jacket for you."

I wave him off. "I don't need that stuff."

He snorts. "You're not getting on the back of a bike unless you're wearing some kind of gear."

"I've never seen you wear *gear*," I state, whatever that entails.

He smirks. "I don't care if I die."

His words are like a slap in the face, and my breathing becomes labored. As he leans over once again, his lips gently touch mine as he speaks. "I don't want something happening to you." With that, he walks into my bathroom.

I take the second alone and bury my face in my hands. I've never hated the Lords more than I do right now. They did this on purpose. They put me in his life to take him away from me. I shouldn't care about this monster as much as I do. I should want to give him up. But I want him to be mine. And I want to be his.

He cares about me. I'm not saying it's love, but it's more than what it started out as. Slowly, I get out of bed and walk to my closet to get dressed, still trying to think of a plan to save us both.

HAIDYN

TWENTY MINUTES LATER, WE'RE AT MY HOUSE. I'M PULLING MY bike into the driveway while she parks her SUV in the garage. I walk over to the wall and grab a helmet and a jacket. They're too big for her, but it's better than nothing. I was being honest when I said that I didn't care if I died. I've seen too many riders die due to a lack of gear.

She walks over to me on autopilot, and I slide her arms into the jacket and over her shoulders zipping it up. "Have you ever ridden on the back of a bike?" I ask.

She shakes her head. I want to spank her ass with my belt for not using her words, but I'll let it slide this time because I have bigger plans for her.

She's quiet. More than usual. My eyes look over her jeans and tennis shoes, and I watch her nibble on her lip. Her hands have a death grip on her phone, and her eyes stare straight ahead. Her back is rigid, and she still wears the ring that dipshit gave her as if it means something.

I pretended to be surprised that she canceled dinner, but I wasn't. She's getting easier to read. Unable to hide what she's thinking from me.

She wanted to feel something from me, so she chose sex. She wanted me to erase her mind of the fake boyfriend. Even though it wasn't real, he still made her feel bad for what we're doing. Fuck that piece of shit.

I wanted to fuck with her head in her bed. I wasn't gentle, but I wasn't as rough as I've been with her body. I wanted her to feel me, and I wanted her to understand how she felt when with me. The Lords teach that a mind is a powerful thing. And when you start to second-guess yourself, it all goes downhill.

"Do you trust me?"

"Yes." Her brows furrow, and I can't tell if she's surprised by that answer or confused that I asked.

"Hold on to me and follow my lead." She's never ridden before, but I'm not going to do anything drastic with her on the back. I want her to feel safe. She already seems to be terrified. "It may feel awkward or scary, but I've got you, okay?"

"Okay." She nods, dropping her eyes to the garage floor, and a silence lingers.

"Are you sure you're okay, Charlotte?" I ask, reaching out and cupping her face.

"Yeah." She jumps, surprised at the contact, and nods. "I'm good."

"Is there anywhere in particular where you want to ride to?" I ask, wanting to keep her in conversation.

"No," she answers softly.

I press my lips to hers, and she instantly melts in my hands. Her body presses into mine, and I slap her ass to keep it light. "Let's go," I say, pushing the helmet onto her head and buckling it for her.

Shhh...

Chapter 62

Charlotte

He turns his back to start his bike, and I slide the cell phone the Lords gave me into one of the pockets and zip it up. I'm breathing heavily inside the helmet, and I'm already shaking.

Haidyn slaps the back of my helmet. "Get on, doll face." He holds out his hand, and I quickly rub mine on my jeans to wipe off the sweat, hoping he doesn't notice before I put it in his.

I get on the back and try to adjust myself, getting comfortable. But I quickly learn that bikes aren't meant for comfort. We take a corner, and I hang on to him, leaning with his body and giving him full control just like he said.

Closing my eyes, I push the helmet into his back and tighten my arms around his waist. Maybe we'll have a wreck, then I won't have to turn him in. Maybe we'll get hit by a car and both die.

I wasn't raised in church. Lords believe they are the only gods, and most Ladies don't believe in a higher power either.

He places his left hand on my thigh, and his fingers dig into my jeans, giving my leg a squeeze. I break out in a sweat, my heart racing. All of a sudden, I can't breathe. "Haidyn?" I call into the helmet, but he can't hear me.

I pull back, push up the visor, and tap his back. "Haidyn? Stop!"

The bike slams to an abrupt stop as he pulls off the main road, my ass coming up off the seat, my body slamming into the back of his. I manage to get off the bike ungracefully and almost fall on my ass. I frantically try to push the helmet off, but it's stuck, choking me.

"Charlotte," he snaps, grabbing my arm and pulling me to him. He shoves my head up and undoes the buckle and pulls the helmet off.

I lean over, hands on my thighs, and suck in fresh air as excessive drool fills my mouth. I'm going to get sick...

"What's wrong?" he asks, rubbing my back. "Are you hurt?"

I shake my head and step back, not wanting to be touched. His concern pisses me off. That taste of vomit begins to burn my throat, and I gag.

"Charlotte," he barks. Grabbing my arms, he forces me to rise to my full height, and my tear-filled eyes meet his blue ones.

"I can't...I can't do this," I whisper, my bottom lip trembling, and I swallow down the bile that rises.

"Do what?" He looks from me to his bike, then back to me. "I promise you, it's safe," he adds. "I was joking earlier. Nothing is going to happen to us." His eyes soften, and he runs his knuckles down my cheek. "I wouldn't put you in a situation where you could get hurt, doll face."

The tenderness of his touch and his choice of words do me in. My body jerks involuntarily as I spin around and give him my back just in time so I don't vomit on him and drop to my knees.

"Hey." He steps up behind me and gathers my hair with one hand while the other rubs my back. "I'll take you to Gavin." His hand leaves my back while the other still holds my hair, and I begin to dry heave.

Standing, I rip my hair from his hand and turn to face him. "I'm not sick," I rush out.

He frowns, removes the phone from his ear and looks down at my vomit. I step in front of it to hide the cobb salad that I had for lunch while out with my friends. It tasted awful coming up. I should have eaten the soup of the day instead.

Pocketing his cell, he steps into me. "What's going on? Talk to me," he urges.

I blink, and the first tear falls down my cheek. His eyes follow it. "I..." Sucking in a deep breath, I swallow. "I got a message from the Lords," I whisper, and his body stiffens. "They want me to take you to a location."

His face hardens, and I take a step back. Lifting my hands, I placate as another tear runs down my cheek. "I promise I didn't know..."

"When did you receive it?" he demands.

The urge to vomit returns when I answer. "Earlier today."

He runs a hand over his hair and lets out a growl of frustration.

My chest tightens. "I'm sorry, Haidyn."

"When were we supposed to be there?" he snaps.

My shaking hand unzips the pocket of the jacket, and I remove the phone to see it's 9:59. "Now."

He looks around the dark road. "How far are we from the given location?"

"I don't know..." I have no clue where he took us to ride. And a part of me knew I wasn't going to turn him in because of that.

The clock hits 10:00, and I hold my breath, looking up at him. Not sure what to do now. Time slows as we stand on the side of the road, both staring at my cell. The moment it changes to 10:01, it begins to ring in my hand.

I drop it and take a step back, my throat burning at the need to vomit once again. He goes to pick it up, but it immediately stops after one ring. Then it alerts us of an incoming text. "What's...what does it say?" I ask, swallowing the knot in my throat while he reads over it.

"You have failed your assignment, Annabelle. You are to report to the cathedral tonight at midnight. Alone," he says tightly.

My legs give out, and I kneel on the side of the road in the grass, knowing this is it. I failed because I couldn't give up a man who saved me. Why does it have to be one life or the other? Why can't we both live and just move on without each other? But even I know the answer to that. I can't walk away from Haidyn. If I wasn't willing to give him to the Lords, I'm not willing to give him up to anyone.

HAIDYN

"Charlotte?" I pocket her phone and kneel in front of her. She's bent over, gasping for breath. I pull her to her shaking legs and hold her face, afraid she may get sick again. "Breathe for me, doll face. You're okay."

She shakes her head. "I'm so-sorry."

"Hey, you're okay," I reassure her.

"Please." She tries to pull away, but I tighten my hold.

"I'm not going to hurt you, Charlotte. I promise. You're okay. It's okay." I'm so fucking proud of her right now. She was given an order and couldn't follow through. *Fuck, that's my girl.*

I pull her to me, and she wraps her arms around me, burying her face into my chest. "You're okay." I rub her back. "I'll fix it," I assure her.

She pulls back, and I allow it. "How?" Her wide, tear-filled eyes look up into mine. The poor thing is terrified. Her body trembling. She got herself so worked up that she made herself sick.

My hand drops to her left hand, and I raise it between us to see the cheap little diamond. "Marry me."

She takes another step back, and her hand falls to her side. Her lips part on a small gasp, but she says nothing.

"Think about it, Charlotte. If you're my wife, the Lords can't touch you." The Spade brothers don't have the same rules as the other Lords.

If I make her my Lady, only I can hand her over to them. It changes everything. I will have full control of my wife. It won't matter what assignment she has; it'll void it. So her assignment won't be a fail on her end. It'll be the biggest *fuck you* to the one pulling the strings. I'm in charge here, not *her*. They'll never see it coming. I'm definitely doing it for my own sick reasons, but it's fucking perfect. I should have done it sooner.

"But...how's that save you?" Her shoulders shake. "I don't know what they want from you...if I marry you, they'll just send someone else."

I snort. "I'm not worried about me, doll face." If they want her, they'll have to get through me. And I'm not a Spade brother for nothing. "What do you say, Charlotte?" I step in, cupping her tear-streaked face. "Will you marry me?"

She slowly nods and whispers, "Yes."

Shhh...

Chapter 63

Charlotte

We pull back up to his house, and he helps me off the bike and leads me inside. I haven't spoken since I said I'd marry him.

I honestly don't know how we got to this point. Where I became so weak for a man I was supposed to use to get me where I wanted to be in life.

Was it the sex? Most likely. Men can fuck without getting attached. Women have too many feelings. We associate sex and love. Maybe I'd have been better off if he had shared me with others. Then I'd know my place.

"I'm going to make a phone call," he states as we enter his room. Pulling me to a stop, he spins me around and cups my face. I stare up at him, and he lowers his lips to my forehead, gently kissing it. "I'll be right back." With that, he exits, and I plop down onto the couch.

My face falls into my hands, and I try to calm my racing heart. I'm giving up on Annabelle—the one who had big dreams. Now I'll be Charlotte—Haidyn's whore—until the day I die. I mean, it's not a bad life to live. It's just the fact that I've let everyone down. The ones that doubted me. I proved them right.

The door opens, and I look up to see him enter once again. This time, he has bags and suitcases in his hands. "Here's your things." He sets them down and turns, exiting once more.

I fall to the floor and open one of the suitcases. I should have known I wasn't going to give him to the Lords because after Wesley left, I went into my closet and packed more of my things knowing I was coming back here.

Opening the second one, I see the white dress folded on top. It just feels right to wear it one last time.

Getting to my shaking legs, I slowly undress out of my jeans and T-shirt and slide the dress on. Then I numbly make my way to the bathroom and freshen up my nude lipstick and blush. A fresh coat of mascara. I never dreamed of a big wedding, so it's not like I had expectations on what this day would be like.

I take a step back and look at myself in his floor length mirror. I hate how much I want to look pretty for him. That I want him to remember this night. Not as the night I was going to hand him to the Lords but the night that I gave myself to him.

Feeling eyes on me, I turn to face the bathroom entrance. He stands there in the doorway, hands shoved into his jeans and heated eyes running over my body.

I run my hands down the soft fabric. "I..." I clear my throat. "I didn't know what to wear." My voice is soft, and I shuffle from foot to foot as he just stands there staring at me in silence.

He wants to change his mind. Licking my lips nervously, I try to come up with a reason for him to marry me. "Haidyn—"

Stepping into the bathroom, I trail off as he comes up to me. His muscular body presses into mine. His hand cups my face, and I hold my breath waiting for the inevitable. He's going to change his mind. Maybe he'll hand me over to them instead. His lips part, and I hold my breath as he speaks.

"You're a gorgeous bride, Charlotte."

My eyes sting, and my pulse races. The blood rushes in my ears. *Bride.* I'm going to marry this man. I'm going to be his Lady. That thought makes me excited and terrified. I'm not sure if I want to cry or vomit. Right now, I'm trying not to do both.

HAIDYN

"Thank you again for making it on such short notice," I say, showing the Lord toward the front doors of the house.

He nods. "Of course, and congratulations."

Closing them behind him, I make my way back into the living room to find my wife standing at the floor-to-ceiling windows overlooking the woods as it pours rain outside. We barely made it home on the bike before it started.

She wears the dress. The same one from the night that I first laid eyes on her. I was in complete awe when I found her in the bathroom earlier dressed in it. I don't believe in signs, but it felt like one. That she was meant for me. Little Miss Priss to my pretty little whore. I've never had something that was all mine. Men like me don't get what they want. They get what the Lords want them to have. What have I done to deserve her? Abso-fucking-lutely nothing. But that doesn't mean I'm not going to take advantage of the beautiful brunette who just took my last name.

She holds a glass of scotch, gently swirling it around as the ice clanks. Bringing it to her lips, she takes a sip, grimacing.

"You know it's poor taste to get drunk at your wedding," Adam jokes, coming to stand next to her. He holds Muffin in one hand while the other scratches her head.

Charlotte sighs heavily and tosses the drink back, sucking in a sharp breath at the burn. I'm not sure if she's ignoring him on purpose or just doesn't care.

My eyes drop to her heels and slowly run over the white dress. I wanted to get her out of it years ago, and now I get my chance. It'll be on my floor tonight. Her dark hair is down and wavy, and I know she wears very little makeup. We rushed right back here to sign the documents. A few signatures, and a witness and she has become my wife. No chapel, no tux, no flowers, and no guests. Just me, her, and Adam. She hasn't even asked who he is. I think she already knows.

Annabelle Marie Schults is mine. Forever.

Crossing my arms over my chest, Adam turns to see me. He gets a smile on his face and pretends to hold a microphone to his lips. "Ladies and gentlemen...I introduce Mr. and Mrs. Reeves." He then acts like he drops it and picks up the remote on the coffee table, pointing it at the TV and pulls up his Spotify account. He picks one of his sappy playlists, then "You Are The Reason" by Calum Scott flows from the speakers. The man is as much of a hopeless romantic as he is heartless.

Charlotte turns to face me, and I'm already headed toward her.

Her eyes drop to her heels as she shuffles from foot to foot. *She's nervous.*

I come up to her and reach out my right hand. "Dance with me, Mrs. Reeves?"

She looks up at me through her dark lashes as I take the drink from her left hand and set it on the end table next to the couch. Then I grab her right hand and pull her to me.

Shhh...

Chapter 64

Charlotte

I'm married!

I'm officially Mrs. Reeves. We signed some papers, and the guy who I'm pretty sure is Adam signed as our witness. It was as if we were buying a car while sitting at the kitchen table. All it took was our signatures.

It wasn't the wedding every little girl dreams of, but Haidyn was right—it's the only way to save me. As much as we've been through, I trust him. I protected him, and he's done the same for me. Now I owe him my life.

I'm a Lady. Fuck, that feels weird to say. Haidyn's Lady.

Getting married was a loophole I never thought of until Haidyn mentioned it. Then it all made sense. The Lord I was supposed to marry no longer exists to the world, and I was no longer saving myself for marriage. No Lord would want me after belonging to Haidyn. But does it even really matter? I don't think so.

This Lord wants me. Even if it's not for the right reasons, it's good enough for me.

My husband holds me tight to his muscular body as we dance around the living room while the rain hits the house, and I close my eyes, trying to get my emotions under control. I feel like I just cheated death. In a way, I did. But I also failed at what I was supposed to do.

I've let down my father and my mother. What will she say when she finds out what I did? I took the cowardly way out. I don't deserve to be a Lady, let alone belong in this world. But now I've tied myself to a Lord—a Spade brother at that. One who doesn't want children. I guess it's for the best. Who wants to bring a child into this world, knowing what they'll have to go through once they grow up? There is no end to the Lords. Just another generation to come.

I pull away from Haidyn, and I'm surprised he lets me go. We stand in the middle of the living room staring at one another. My heart hammers in my chest at the thought of belonging to him for the rest of my life.

His blue eyes search my face before dropping to my heels and slowly run up over my body.

Licking my lips, I reach down and gather the dress in my hands, slowly pulling it over my head and throwing it to the floor. I want to be his in every way. This is what a devoted Lady does—she gives herself to her Lord. And that's exactly what the rest of my life will consist of—being my husband's whore. I step out of my heels one by one.

"Charlotte—"

I gently push on his chest, and he sits down onto the couch. Pushing my thong down my legs, I crawl onto the couch and straddle him. His hands go to my thighs, and I remove my bra before cupping his face and lowering my lips to his, kissing him.

His fingers dig into my thighs, making me moan, and I rock my hips back and forth. The sound of a door closing is heard over the music playing, and I assume it's Adam leaving us alone to make it official. As if I haven't belonged to Haidyn since the Lords gave me him as an assignment.

Pulling my lips away from his, I grab his T-shirt, and he sits up straighter, allowing me to pull it over his head. Then my lips are back on his as my hands drop to his jeans, undoing his belt, button, and zipper.

Hovering up on my knees, I manage to pull his hard dick out of his boxer briefs, and he groans in my mouth when I squeeze it. "Fuck me," I breathe.

His hand drops between our bodies, and he rubs his pierced dick against my wet pussy before lifting his hips and pushing it inside me. "Whatever my wife wants," he whispers roughly against my lips.

I whimper at his words while lowering myself onto him. He stretches me to accommodate his size, and it takes my breath away. His hands go to my hair, and he pulls my head back as his lips fall to my exposed neck, kissing it tenderly.

My body shakes while I ride him, listening to the thunder outside as the song changes to "Silence" by Marshmello and Khalid.

"Tell me that you're mine, doll face," he demands.

"I'm yours." I gasp rocking my hips back and forth, clenching my pussy around him.

He lets out a growl, making his hard chest vibrate against mine, and I swallow before sucking in a deep breath. I'm starting to sweat, my skin tingling as he holds me tightly to him while I ride my husband on the couch in the middle of the living room.

He lowers my head, and his lips capture mine as my fingers dig into his hair. Fuck, I can't get close enough to him. I want him to swallow me up. Is it bad that I want to lose myself to him? That I no longer want to be who I was?

Gone is Annabelle Marie Schults. Now I'm Charlotte Reeves. His Lady. Did I ever really know who I was? Who I wanted to be? I'm not really sure. I thought living a loveless marriage was going to be so horrible that I was willing to kill another to gain power. But Haidyn has taught me that you don't need to be loved in our world. Just protected.

Pulling away from his lips, I place my forehead to his while we both take a second to catch our breath, my hips coming to a stop with his dick still inside me. "I vow to be yours, Haidyn. Forever." I tell him. Anyone can sign a piece of paper. I want him to know that I'm in a hundred percent. Whatever he wants, I'll give it to him, including my soul. A Lord demands nothing less.

He lifts his hand and cups my cheek. His thumb runs along my parted lips as a smile tugs at his mouth. "You vow to be mine, doll face."

"We vow," we say in unison, and then his lips are back on mine, devouring me like the monster I thought he was.

HAIDYN

She tastes like the scotch she downed as if she needed the liquid courage to hand her life over to me. Whatever makes her feel better about being my wife.

My hands drop to her hips, and I help guide her pussy to fuck my cock. I want to pin her down, put a vibrator in her cunt, and watch her come over and over while I tell her how pretty she looks. But not tonight. I've got the rest of my life to do that. No matter how long or short that will be.

She throws her head back, and the house fills with her moans. I let go of her hips, grab her arms, and shove them behind her back. I use one hand to wrap around her tiny wrists holding them parallel to each other on her back while the other finds its way to her long dark hair. I force her head down so she has to meet my stare. "Eyes on me, doll face. I want to watch my wife come on my dick."

Her heavy eyes search mine while her soaked cunt clenches my pierced dick. Her hips rock back and forth, and I gently kiss her parted lips. Her breath catches, and I smile at the way her lashes flutter. "That's it, Charlotte. Come for me, doll face."

"Hai-dyn," she gasps, and I lean in, capturing her lips with mine, and this time, I kiss her forcefully. My mouth dominates hers as she does exactly what I want. Pulling away, she sucks in a breath.

"That's my good girl." I let go of her wrists, and her arms drop to her sides.

I stand, holding her to me. My hard cock is still inside her wet pussy covered in her cum as I carry her to our bedroom. Crawling onto the bed, I push her hair from her face. Her heavy eyes find mine, and I take her shaky legs and shove her knees to her sweat-covered chest. Then I grab her arms and cross them behind her bent knees. I hold them in place while I watch my cock slam into her cunt over and over.

Her body fights my hold, but I don't let go. I fuck her as if she's a whore I paid for and not the woman I just married. "Fuck, Charlotte." I groan, my teeth clenching at the way her pussy hugs my dick. "You feel so good." I never knew sex could feel like this. I've always wanted something different...something new. That's why I chose to pay for it. One woman for the rest of my life? It sounded boring. Mundane. My wife is anything but that.

"Please...?" her soft voice begs, fighting my hold.

I shove her legs to the left, putting her on her side, but I still hold her in place. My pierced cock slams into her, filling our bedroom with her soft cries. My free hand reaches up, grips her hair, and I yank her head back so I can lean down and kiss her soft cheek. Her body stiffens, and I smile against her face. "That's a good wife. Letting me use you like the whore you are for me."

She's gasping, body trembling, and I sit up, slamming into her a few more times before I come inside her.

When I let go of her, she cries softly as she stretches her body out underneath me. A quick look at the clock on the nightstand tells me I have to leave if I'm going to make it to the cathedral on time.

"I have to go, doll face."

As if I just threw cold water on her, she widens her eyes and sits up. "I'll get ready." She tries to get up from underneath me, but I grab her wrists and then pin them down by her head. "Haidyn—"

"You're staying here," I tell her.

"What?" she gasps. "Haidyn, no—"

"Yes." I interrupt her. "You're not going." With that, I pull out of her cunt and get up off the bed. The Lords are already fucking up my marriage and sex life.

She jumps up off the bed on shaky legs and glares at me. "They want me there. Not you."

"Well, they will have to deal with me." I pull on a pair of boxer briefs followed by a pair of jeans.

"If I don't show, they'll think I'm a coward." She lets out a huff.

Leaving my jeans undone, I walk over to her and cup her face, forcing her to meet my stare. "You're not a coward."

She snorts rolling her eyes. "I married you to save my own ass. That's the definition of a coward."

She married me to save *my* ass and I'll do whatever it takes to save hers as well. "I'll tell them I forced you."

"Haidyn—"

"You had no choice," I push some brown strands behind her ear. If only she knew how far I'd go to get what I want.

Her eyes narrow on mine. "You told me we always have a choice. The Lords will know that I chose to save myself."

"I'll tell them that I drugged you, flew you to Vegas, and made you my wife." I reach down and run my hand over her little diamond that she still wears from dipshit.

She pulls her bottom lip between her teeth and nibbles on it.

Leaning forward, I plant a kiss on her forehead. "I'll be back soon, doll face." Letting go, I turn around and give her my back and finish getting dressed. I have somewhere to be.

Shhh...

Chapter 65

Charlotte

I'm lying in Haidyn's bed, staring up at the ceiling. I feel like I could get sick at any moment worrying about what the Lords will say to him. I just keep reminding myself that I trust him. He wouldn't have married me knowing he had to turn me over to them... he said it was our only option.

Getting out of bed, I begin to pace the room, needing movement and trying to clear my mind and keep the bile down that burns my throat. My stomach is in knots. Adam's playlist still blasts in the living room, filtering into the bedroom and echoing through the large house. His song choices are a total contradiction of who I expect him to be. Right now, it's "Always Remember Us This Way" by Lady Gaga. I go to leave the bedroom to turn it off, but the sound of my phone beeping gets my attention.

I rush over to it, wondering if it's Haidyn to tell me how it went, and see it's an incoming email from the Lords. The clock reads 12:10. Why would they send me this afterward? Haidyn is supposed to be there. Hell, I hope he's already done and on his way home.

Taking a deep breath, I open it up and push play.

A concrete room comes into view and there's a rectangular metal-like table in the center. Chains hang on the back wall in various lengths and sizes along with rope. It's Carnage.

The sound of a door opening fills the large space, followed by an altered voice, making my pulse race. "Put him on the table."

Two guys come into view next, and they're dragging Haidyn. Each one under an arm. His head hangs forward, and blood drips onto the floor as his combat boots smear it while they haul him to the center of the room. They've beaten him unconscious.

My hands begin to shake at the sight of him, and my skin grows hot. *Why is he at Carnage?*

The thought has crossed my mind that this was a setup, and they wanted him at the cathedral alone tonight. It takes four Lords dressed in cloaks and masks to get his body onto the table.

A groan comes from his busted lips as they begin to strap him down with black leather belts, buckling him in place. The first one goes over his ankles securing his legs together at one end of the table. The second below his knees and the third over his jean-clad thighs.

My throat tightens, making it hard to breathe at the thought of them hurting him in any way. He was trying to save me.

A Lord steps into view and places a towel under a faucet, getting it wet, and Haidyn coughs up blood.

"Wake up." One slaps the side of his face. His eyes don't open, but he groans again as if in pain. "Wake up, Spade. Come on. It's time for your punishment."

Punishment? What did he do? They're punishing him for making his whore his wife. It's all my fault. I jump to my feet. My hands go to my mouth when I feel the bile burning my throat. Rushing to the bathroom, I manage to make it to the toilet on time as I throw up. My stomach tight and shoulders shake.

Falling down onto my ass by the toilet, my eyes drop to my phone on the floor and see that I didn't pause it. I go to stop it, unable to watch anymore when they rip his shirt off and move his arms down by his sides. And begin to do another belt over his hips, waist, chest and last his neck. His large muscular body takes up most of the narrow table.

I let out a shaky breath when my eyes scan his chest and see his Lords crest, but he doesn't have the 666 branding or any other tattoos that I can see from here, but he's covered in bruises. Some look older than others. I place my hand over my mouth to hold in a sob when I realize this video is old. Much older, considering his lack of tattoos as well. But I have a sickening feeling this isn't his first time with these Lords.

My chest pounds, my heart in my throat as I watch one of the

Lords roll a cart to the side of the table. They put sticky pads on his chest and turn the machine on. A beeping sound fills the room, and lines begin to pop up on the screen—they're monitoring his heart rate. It's slow and steady at the moment, but I'm guessing that's because he's unconscious.

Tears sting my eyes, and I blink rapidly to clear my blurry vision.

"We shouldn't have beaten him," one altered voice speaks.

Another laughs. "No way he would have willingly gotten up on this table."

"He'll come around. And when he does, we'll be ready."

The screen goes black, and I grind my teeth. My watery eyes continue to scan the screen, but nothing is there.

I bring my knees to my chest and try to calm my breathing, wondering why they are sending me this. I lift my shaking hands and wipe the tears from my face. That acid taste is still in my mouth, thinking I'm going to get sick again.

My phone beeps once more, and I pick it up, immediately opening up the new email they sent me, unable to stop myself. I need to know what they do to him and why.

This video is identical to the previous one. Haidyn still lies on the table, but his swollen eyes are open, and he's looking around aimlessly as if he's just waking up. He seems unfazed by the sound of his heart rate. How much time passed between the two? Was it hours... minutes? I wish it'd tell me.

"About time, Spade." One of the Lords comes into view, laughing.

Haidyn doesn't say anything.

The guy comes to the head of the table and taps the side of Haidyn's bloody face. "You took away our chance to play with our toy outside so *she* said we can play with you." Laughter fills the room and my stomach drops.

Toy? What toy? It's a woman. Has to be what he's talking about.

"Fuck...you," Haidyn says, and my skin breaks out in a sweat at the sound.

"Boys, let's begin." He pushes a button that he has in his hand and the table begins to move, lowering Haidyn's head while his feet rise. Not much, just enough that his head sits lower.

The towel I saw them wet in the previous video is thrown over

Haidyn's face and the sound of his heart rate accelerates in the concrete room.

"Let's see how long you can hold your breath." One says before he walks over to a hose that's hangs on the wall. He uncoils it and turns on the faucet. Water flows from the end. "Hold the towel tight." He commands to no one in particular.

One steps to the right of the table and grips each end of the white towel, pulling it tight across Haidyn's face.

"Someone start the timer," he orders, and a third guy goes over to the counter and flips an hourglass as the one with the hose holds the end over the towel, and water begins to cover Haidyn's face.

They're waterboarding him.

My heart lodges in my throat at the sight. Haidyn fights the restraints, his fight or flight kicking in, but he's strapped down too tight. There's nowhere for him to go. Water splashes onto his body and the concrete floor as they wait for the hourglass to run out of time.

I blink, tears stinging my eyes before they fall down my cheeks as I hold one hand over my mouth while I watch.

Pulling away the towel, he's sputtering and gasping for breath. His heart rate has picked up and is now echoing throughout the room at a fast pace.

"That's one." The man standing at Haidyn's head laughs and places the towel back over his face, doing it again while one resets the timer. "Do you know why they use a towel?" He makes it sound like he's talking to Haidyn, but since he can't speak, another one bites.

"Why?"

"Because it allows the water to enter the airways, but at the same time, it prevents them from expelling it."

Fresh tears fall from my eyes as I sit and watch them torture my husband.

By the third time, Haidyn's heart rate is less consistent. The sound is much slower and less often than it was as he lies strapped to the table. And one of the Lords speaks. "Take it easy, man. She said to punish him. She'll do the same thing to you if you kill him."

"I'm not worried." The Lord taps the side of Haidyn's wet and bloody face. His body is shaking uncontrollably while he tries to breathe. You can hear the water gurgling in his lungs while he chokes on it. "Don't worry, Spade. I'll bring you back." He tosses the towel over Haidyn's face once more. "I've never been waterboarded before, but I hear it's painful." He goes on. "You put them at an incline, so the water fills the sinuses. It also keeps the water from filling the lungs. But your breathing becomes labored, and you panic because your body thinks it's drowning, and you can try to hold your breath as long as you want, but it's impossible not to inhale it."

Another. Then another.

I'm sobbing, and my entire body shakes as I slowly watch them kill him. Just when I think they'll stop and let up, they do it again.

During the seventh time, the sound of the beeping finally stops, and Haidyn's body goes limp as the guys remove the wet towel.

I blink rapidly and choke out a sob into my hand when one of them speaks. "Fuck, man, I told you..."

"I got it under control," the one who's been torturing him says.

He walks over to a counter and picks up a syringe. Removing the cap with his teeth, he bites it off and returns to the table and stabs Haidyn in the chest, shoving the plunger.

Haidyn gasps, the beeping returns, and it's faster than it previously was. They gave him adrenaline.

"Look at that." The Lords all laugh. "Welcome back, Spade." He leans over the edge of the table, his face hovering over Haidyn's while he continues to choke. "You should have just let us rape her, man. That's all bitches are good for. They're meant to be used. Especially chosens. You robbed us of that opportunity when you killed her. Now we get to play with you instead."

He stands to his full height, and I watch Haidyn's chest rise and fall, trying to catch his breath. His body is tight, veins popping out of his arms and neck. His restrained hands fist tight at his sides. It's the adrenaline. On top of trying to drown him, they've shot him up with speed. His heart monitor is beeping so fast I wouldn't be surprised if he has a heart attack.

"Now, where were we..."

The screen goes black, and I stare at it waiting for another to pop up, but nothing happens. Blood rushes in my ears, and I drop the phone next to me, cupping my face and trying to catch my breath.

"Charlotte?" I hear Haidyn's voice in the bedroom.

I open my mouth to tell him that I'm in the bathroom, but nothing comes out. That burning sensation returns, and I crawl over to the toilet once more, where I begin to dry heave.

"Charlotte." His voice is closer this time, and he grabs my hair as tears spill down my cheeks while he kneels behind me. One hand rubs small circles on my back, and when I have nothing left to get out, I flush the toilet and fall onto my ass.

"Hey, doll face." His soft voice makes me cry harder, and he pulls me into his lap as we sit on the marble floor. "It's okay, Charlotte," he assures me. "I took care of it. You're safe."

Of course, he thinks I'm worried about myself and his meeting with the Lords tonight. That's how this night started out, but that's not it now. Not at all. It's what I just watched this man go through. Who was torturing him? And why? One had said that he took away their toy. What did they mean? And who was the *she* that said they couldn't kill him? Who did Haidyn kill to keep from being raped? The Lord had mentioned a chosen. Was it Sierra? My friends had asked what happened to her? And that they didn't know.

There are worse things than dying.

I have so many questions that I can't ask him.

"You're safe here, doll face. I'll protect you."

I throw my arms around his neck, and he wraps his arms around me tightly, holding me to him while I try to hold back a sob. I let him think he's reassuring me. I'm okay, but I hold him, knowing he's home safe. Something actually worked how we wanted it to.

"Shh." He rubs my back. "You're okay."

I need him. There's an ache between my legs and a pain in my chest. I need him right now. As his wife, as his whore. What I saw on those two videos was only ten minutes of his life. What else has he gone through? How many other times did they punish him? Was it because of Ashtyn or someone else? Pulling away, I gasp, needing to breathe, and he cups my face with both of his hands.

"I'm...sorry." I manage to say through the lump in my throat.

He gives me a soft smile, running his hand through my hair. "Don't be sorry, doll face."

My husband thinks I'm apologizing because I almost turned him in. And I don't correct him.

. . .

HAIDYN

"Come on." I help her up and walk over to the bathtub. I turn on the faucet, and she goes over to her sink and brushes her teeth, followed by mouthwash. She's still silently crying, but she's not sobbing anymore.

She's got herself so worked up that she's made herself sick again. Poor thing.

I grab a towel and place it on the counter and then help her into the tub. She pulls her knees to her chest and stares down at the water as the tears fall down her cheeks.

"I'll be right back," I say and then make my way to the kitchen. Grabbing her a bottle of water, I return and set it on the edge of the Jacuzzi tub. "You need to drink something."

She stays silent while I bathe her. Her tear-filled eyes remain on the water while I wash her hair and then her body. She doesn't even ask me how it went at the cathedral. Which I'm glad. I don't want to have to lie to my wife, but I will if she asks. I don't want to upset her more than she already is.

Rinsing the conditioner out of her hair, I grab her hands and help her stand on her shaking legs. Then I dry her off and cup her face, forcing her eyes to meet mine. "It's all going to be okay," I assure her.

She nods as if she believes me, but we both know she doesn't. And why should she? I've blackmailed her for my own selfish reasons. More than she knows. I'm almost sorry for what I've done to her. But like I once told Charlotte, I have no regrets. That's still very true.

"I have something for you," I tell her.

Her large, tear-filled eyes meet mine. I hate to see her so upset, but her eyes are gorgeous when she cries. She swallows nervously before licking her lips but says nothing. I drop mine to her left hand and remove the small ring the fake boy toy gave her earlier tonight. I feel sorry for the fucking bastard. That he'll never get to have her...not like I'll get to. I'm a proud enough man to know what I have, but I'm too selfish to let anyone else experience it. I set the ring on the black marble counter with the reminder to throw it away later.

Reaching into the pocket of my jeans, I remove the box and open it up. Her eyes drop to it, and she gasps when I remove the ring and slide it on her finger. "You deserved more," I tell her.

"What…how…?" Her eyes go from mine to the wedding ring and back to mine again. "Haidyn it's…gorgeous."

"Just like you," I say, pushing wet strands of dark hair behind her ear as my eyes search hers. "I want you to see what I see every time I look into your eyes."

Her breathing picks up once again and I take her face in my hands. "Hey, it's okay." She's starting to panic…regretting her decision to be my wife. It's too late. She can have second thoughts all she wants. She belongs to me now and I'm not going to let her go.

"Can I have a minute, please?" she asks softly.

I lean in and kiss her forehead. "Of course," I say and then exit the bathroom, closing the doors behind me and letting her do whatever she needs to do alone. Tell herself what she needs to hear to assure herself she did the right thing.

I need a drink. For some reason, my chest is bothering me more than usual tonight.

Shhh...

Chapter 66

Charlotte

"I want you to see what I see every time I look into your eyes."

My hands tremble as I look down at the ring he just slid on my finger. It looks massive on me. A large sapphire diamond in the center with two tapered baguettes on either side of a silver band. Something tells me it's platinum. The center stone has to be over five carats and it makes me sick to my stomach. What I almost did to him. How differently tonight could have gone.

Swallowing the knot in my throat, I go over and pick up my cell off the floor and make sure that the Lords deleted the emails they sent me. Just like usual, they're gone. Never existed.

Sighing, I enter the closet and see the bags that are full of the things I bought today while shopping that Haidyn had brought in when we arrived back here to get married. Along with my two suitcases that I still need to unpack. But it all can wait.

Looking over his side of the closet, I reach up and remove a white T-shirt off the hanger and slide it on, inhaling his scent. It immediately calms my nerves.

I enter our bedroom and frown when I don't see him in here. I make my way to the living room in nothing other than his T-shirt. All that money I spent on designer lingerie today and I'd rather wear a shirt of his than anything else. No matter how unattractive he may find it.

I'm now his wife. If I ever forget, the ring he gave me will serve as a reminder that I have the rest of my life to dress up for him.

"Broken" by Seether and Amy Lee filters through the house as the music continues to play on the TV. I make my way down the hallway, and I see the door to his office open. I come to a stop at the doorway to see him standing in front of his minibar. He pours himself a glass of bourbon before he throws it back. Setting the now empty glass down, I watch him reach up and rub his chest as he closes his eyes and sighs heavily.

"Hey?" I step into his office. "You okay?"

"I'm fine," he states and begins to fill up the glass again.

I bite my bottom lip, knowing he's lying, but I'm not sure what I can do to fix it. The video is still very fresh on my mind. What they did to him...that was just one time. How many other times has the man died and been brought back to life? That can't be good on anyone. It has to leave some sort of lingering effects. Not only mental but physical too.

Is that why he tried to commit suicide? Because he wanted to end it on his terms? His way? I can see Haidyn being that type of man and taking matters into his own hands.

He finishes making his drink and then sits down at his desk. I exit his office to head back to the bathroom. I catch sight of the ring Wesley gave me on the counter. Picking it up, I toss it in the drawer and grab what I need before returning to his office.

Coming to stand next to his desk, I hold up the bottle of lotion that I brought from my house. He looks at it and then me. "Want to watch me rub one out, doll face?" The corner of his lips twitch with amusement.

The idea of him sitting there, legs spread wide and wearing nothing as he jerks himself off isn't a bad image at all. But I shake my head. "Come here." I take his hand, and he lets me pull him up and over to the black couch. "Have a seat," I say.

He plops down. Placing his hands on his jean-clad thighs, he smirks up at me. "Doing this again?"

I frown, not understanding what he means.

"Where you try to get me to lay down and spill all my secrets," he explains.

"No." My frown deepens. "I want you to tell me things because you want me to know. Not because you think I'm going to use them against you," I say truthfully. I'm no longer the woman I was when I walked into Carnage under false pretenses.

The smirk drops off his face, and I ignore it. Tossing the lotion onto the couch next to him, I reach forward and grab the hem of his shirt and pull it up and over his head. Thankfully, he helped me by raising his arms.

"Your turn," he orders, his eyes going to the shirt of his that I wear.

"This is all I have on," I say, motioning to the thin material.

"Even better." He stands and grabs the shirt and doesn't even give me the chance to fight him before he throws it across the room.

I cross my arms over my chest. "This isn't supposed to be about sex."

"Then what's it supposed to be about?" he asks, placing his hands on my waist and slowly running them up over my ribs. My body instantly heats.

As my eyes search his, I get a lump in my throat thinking of that video the Lords sent me. I don't know why I'm so emotional. Why I can't seem to keep my shit together. I've never been this way before. Yet I've also never been blackmailed by a man and forced to hand him over, then decided to marry him to save my own ass either. I just keep telling myself to breathe. This is new for the both of us.

"I just want to take care of you," I whisper. I want to do something no one else has ever done for him.

He frowns at my response. As if he's trying to decide if I'm tricking him.

That's my only job now. For the rest of my life. I'm on summer break from Barrington. I doubt he'll let me return to the university in the fall. And a job...career? Men like Haidyn don't want their wives to work. They want you devoted to them a hundred percent of the time. He doesn't want kids so he will be the only person in my life. I'm not complaining. For once, I can see my future, and it's just the two of us. There are no what-ifs anymore. I weighed my options when he asked me to be his Lady, and I made the choice to take him as my Lord.

"Okay, Charlotte." He nods to himself and reaches down removing his shoes and socks. Then he undoes his belt before pushing his jeans down his legs along with his black boxer briefs so we're both naked. Sitting down on the couch, he grabs my arms and pulls me onto him.

I straddle his legs, and my hands go to his broad shoulders.

"Do your worst, doll face." He smirks. "But you'll do it with my cock inside of you."

His hand drops between our bodies, and I rise up to allow him to position his pierced dick against my pussy. He runs it back and forth, just teasing me for a few seconds, feeling how wet I already am for him.

My hips begin to rock back and forth, my want for him to fuck me growing hotter. When the head of his cock starts to push into my wet pussy, I lower my forehead to his and take in a deep breath.

He groans as I slide down onto his long and hard length. I go to rise up but his hands on my hips prevent it. "When I'm ready to fuck you, I will," he states. "Until then, you'll sit here on my lap with my cock inside your wet cunt. Understand?"

"Yes," I answer and lick my lips.

"Good girl." He sits back, his arms fanning the back cushions of the couch.

My eyes drop to his smooth and tatted chest, and I see the bullet wound. "When were you shot?" I come out and ask. "Was it recently?" The scar looks messy and new.

"Yes." Is all he answers.

"Since you've met me?" I dig deeper. Haidyn isn't the type of man to go into detail. You have to keep it simple with yes and no answers to get any information out of him.

"Yes."

My eyes lift to meet his. "Is that why you left Carnage?"

"Yes and no."

I don't understand what the fuck that means but it makes me wonder if he did it himself. Maybe after the second try he was too ashamed to stay there with his brothers. But a part of me, a bigger part of me tells me it has to do with Ashtyn. And I hate that my mind immediately goes to her when I think of him getting hurt in any type of way.

"Does it hurt?" I question.

"No."

He's lying. I saw him rubbing it when I walked in here before he took two big glasses of alcohol. I don't see him drink very often.

It could be because you almost handed him over to the Lords tonight.

I ignore that voice in my head and lean over, pick up the lotion and pump it twice into my other hand. Then toss it back to the side. Running my hands together, I try to warm it up before I place my hands flat on his chest and begin to massage it in.

He instantly relaxes into the couch; his head falls back and his lips part on a moan. "Goddamn."

I make my way over to the scar where he was shot and gently rub the lotion over it. Not sure if I could hurt it or not. The feel of his cock jerking inside of my soaked pussy makes me rock my hips.

"Thought this wasn't about sex?" He chuckles.

I ignore him and run my hands up his exposed neck, loving the way his Adam's apple moves as he swallows. It takes a lot to make a man like Haidyn vulnerable. I want him to open up to me. I'm his wife. I should know things about him that no one else does.

The Lords have already shown me more than Haidyn will ever tell me, though. Will those stop now that I'm his wife?

My eyes follow my hands as they run over his hard and muscular body. He has a skull tattoo on his right pec. It looks like it's melting, dripping down his chest. The left eye is where his Lords brand is—circle with three horizontal lines through it. He has the 666 brand on the other. A shattered hourglass below it. "What does this mean?" I wonder, running my nails over it. "Why is it shattered?" I clarify, looking over the pieces of sand that cover his skin. It looks so real. As if I could run my hands through it. The details are amazing.

He's used them a lot with me when I'm being punished.

Lifting his head off the back of the cushion, his eyes meet mine when he speaks. "It's a reminder that nothing lasts forever." He removes his arms from the couch and places his tatted hands on my bare thighs that straddle his lap. "No matter how bad things are, they'll eventually end."

I get an instant pain in my chest as his words. He means being tortured in Carnage, right? They used one to track time when they were waterboarding him.

Reaching over, I pump lotion into my hand again and this time I start to massage his right arm and his eyes fall closed once more. "Fuck, doll face. I could get used to this."

"I quite enjoyed it. Until you killed Enrique." I say changing the subject. I can tell I've gotten about as much information as he wants to give me tonight. So I'm moving on to the next thing I want to talk about.

He smirks but doesn't open his eyes. "Don't worry, Charlotte. I'll be more than happy to strap you down to a table and rub all over your body while your ass and cunt is filled with a vibrator and your mouth stuffed with a gag."

I let go of his hand and slap the side of his arm playfully. "That's not relaxing."

"I would definitely enjoy it." He chuckles.

Before he can stop me, I lift my hips and slam down on his cock, catching him off guard.

He sits straight up, his hands gripping my thighs and his fingers painfully digging into my skin making me whimper. "Hai—"

"Want me to fuck you, doll face?" He arches a brow.

I try to rock my hips back and forth, but he keeps me in place. It's what I need. Him on top of me. Showing me what a desperate whore I am for my husband.

HAIDYN

I'M HARD AS FUCK. MY WIFE SITS ON MY LAP NAKED WITH MY cock inside her. Of course, sex is the only thing on my mind. Although, the rub down she gave me was feeling pretty amazing as well.

I've been thinking of fucking her since I returned home, but I didn't think she'd be in the mood when I found her on her knees in the bathroom. She's proving to me that it doesn't take much to get her begging.

She tries to move her hips, but I don't allow it. "You want it? You know what to do."

Letting out a growl, she throws her head back, and I smile. How quickly I was able to turn her train of thought from wanting to know about me to wanting me to fuck her. It's not that I don't want to open up to her; there's just not much for me to share.

I like this Charlotte—desperate for me. If she were to know the truth—what I've done and what I plan on doing— she'd hate me. She won't want to rub on me. Instead, she'll be holding a gun to my head like she's done twice before.

"Why..." She lifts her head, and her heavy eyes meet mine. "Why haven't you given me an enema other than that one time?"

"There it is." I smile at my girl. "I was wondering how long you'd wait before you begged for another one." Letting go of her with my right hand, I run my knuckles down her delicate neck. "Is that what you want, doll face? Want me to fuck that tight ass of yours?" If I were keeping track, I'd say my dick has been in her cunt and mouth more than her ass, which is new for me.

"Please," she begs, and I don't think I'll ever tire of hearing it.

"Whatever my wife wants." I've got everything here at my house down in the basement to give her one. "I'll tie you down...but this time, I'll put a vibrator in your pussy and watch you come all over yourself while you take the enema."

"Yes."

"Tomorrow," I tell her.

Her shoulders slump. "But...I want you to fuck it tonight. Right now."

I don't care about it being messy. "It'll be much more painful without any prep." I usually put a butt plug in at first to get her ready to take my dick.

"Maybe I want it to hurt," she whispers.

"Remember what I told you last time you wanted me to fuck your ass?" My hand drops between her parted legs, and I rub my thumb on her clit while she remains sitting on my cock.

Her breathing picks up before she answers. "That I'd crawl for it."

A good listener and using her words. "That's what I want to see.

My wife on her hands and knees crawling to me while she begs for me to fuck her in the ass like the whore she is."

"Okay." She grinds her hips, her pussy clenching on my pierced dick.

Gripping her hips, I pull her off my cock, and she groans in protest as I set her onto the couch, and I stand. Walking over to my desk, I open up the top drawer and pull out the bottle of lube. Leaning up against the surface, I cross my arms over my chest. "What are you waiting for?"

She slowly gets off the couch and falls to her hands and knees. She crawls across the black rug in the center of the room with her head held high and those gorgeous blue eyes on mine wearing nothing other than my ring on her finger.

I've never been more turned on. To watch this woman who was innocent—no other man had ever touched—to see her so desperate for me. To know that she's my wife and that she's going to let me do whatever the fuck I want to do to her.

When she first came into my life, I wanted to ruin her for any other man who came after me. Now I know I'll be the only one to ever have her. She'll beg me; she'll cry for me; she'll come for me like the dirty little whore I've made her become.

She comes to a stop in front of me, tilts her head back, and her heavy eyes fall to my hard dick.

"You're so goddamn beautiful, Charlotte," I tell her.

"Haidyn...please..."

"Turn around and put your ass up in the air," I order.

Turning around, she places her ass up in the air, arching her back. Her hands go behind her and she spreads her legs to give me a view of her smooth, wet cunt and ass.

Pushing off the desk, I open up the second drawer and grab what I need. Then I walk back over to her and cuff her small wrists behind her back, loving the way she tries to fight them.

"That's it, doll face." I lower myself between her already trembling legs. I pop the top on the lube and pour it all over her ass and pussy. Then my fingers start to work on her ass.

She rocks back and forth as her moan and whimpers fill the room.

"Remember you wanted this to hurt." I remind her and she pushes against me as I enter a second into her tight ass.

Pressing down on her lower back, I position the head of my cock up against her, and she pushes back against me.

I stay where I'm at, enjoying the way she silently begs for it. My cock in one hand. Her branded ass cheek in the other. I should make her fuck it herself. Make her show me how much she wants it, but she already did that, and it was a glorious sight.

Leaning forward, I push the tip into her ass, loving the way it opens up to let me in. She cries out, digging her face into the rug. "I'm going to give you what you want," I tell her and push farther into her, loving how tight it is.

"Fuuuccccckkk," I groan over the sound of her cries. "You feel so good, Charlotte." I pull out and thrust forward again, forcing her body to rock back and forth on the rug. "That's it, doll face. You're doing so good for me."

I pull out, making her slump against the rug, and I toss her onto her back, smashing her cuffed arms underneath her and spreading her legs wide as I position my dick at her ass once again. I push into her, loving the way she arches her neck and back, letting out a cry. "You're taking my cock so well, beautiful."

I lean over her shaking body, place my hands on either side of her face, and push her hair from it as I tenderly kiss her lips. "Look at me, Charlotte," I command.

Her watery lashes flutter open as her tear-filled eyes meet mine, and I pause, my cock halfway inside her ass.

"Haidyn?" She gasps. "Ple-ase?" Her body rocks back and forth on the rug while her heels dig into my ass as she tries to get me to move. To fuck her harder.

I smile at her, pushing my hips forward stretching her tight ass to accommodate my size. "You're amazing." I kiss her lips again as she sucks in a ragged breath from my movement. "So fucking amazing." Pulling back, I press forward, and she trembles.

"Please don't stop," she begs in the sweetest voice, and if I wasn't already on my knees, I'd fall to them for her.

"Never," I promise and begin to move more forcefully. Giving my wife what she wants. I couldn't stop myself if I wanted to.

She arches her back, holding her breath and her body stiffens under me. "That's my good girl," I say, not bothering to stop or slow down.

I sit up, wrap my hands around her delicate neck, and slam into her ass, loving the way her heavy eyes stare up into mine. My breath comes in short pants, and my balls tighten. I can't hold out any longer. Slamming forward, I bury my cock deep into her ass and come.

Shhh...

Chapter 67

Charlotte

I wake to the sound of glass breaking. My eyes pop open, and I go to speak, but a hand slaps over my mouth. I blink rapidly, trying to see, and my hands come up to push whoever it is off me.

"Shh, you're okay, doll face," Haidyn whispers, his lips by my ear. I can hear his steady breath over my heavy breathing. "Do you understand?"

I nod the best I can, and he removes his hand from my face and jumps up off me. I'm trying to get my brain to catch up with what's happening. A light flips on, and I see Haidyn standing naked beside the bed. He's pulling on a pair of jeans and slipping a T-shirt over his head. Then he yanks his nightstand open and removes a gun. He pushes the slide back, cocking it.

My heart picks up, realizing I wasn't dreaming. Someone is in the house. "Haidyn?"

"Stay here," he whispers.

"What...?" I jump out of bed. "No—"

"Stay in here," he whisper-shouts at me, then rushes out of the room, softly closing the door behind him.

I pick up a shirt of his from a chair and slide it on with a pair of my underwear I find on his floor. Then I rush into his closet and grab the baseball bat he has sitting against the wall. Running back into the bedroom, I flip off the light and press my back into the wall, trying to calm my breathing. Where is my gun when I need it? I know he has them all over his house, but it's not like he's shown them to me. Probably because I've tried to shoot him twice before.

My hands are sweaty, and I strain to hear what's happening on the other side of this door. Seeing the doorknob slowly turning has me adjusting the bat in my hands, preparing me for whoever is about to enter.

What if Haidyn missed whoever it is? This is a big house. Whoever broke the glass could be in one room while Haidyn is in the other and they missed one another.

The door opens, and I step out from behind it, seeing a figure enter the room and I step farther into it, swinging at the intruder. The bat connects across their upper back.

"Fuck," a familiar voice groans.

"Haidyn?" I flip on the light and see him turning to face me. The bat falls from my hands, landing on the bedroom floor. "Oh my God..."

"What the fuck, doll face?"

An arm wraps around my neck from behind, yanking me off my feet. My wide eyes go to Haidyn as he lifts the gun in his hands. "Let her go!" he demands.

"Go ahead." A man laughs in my ear. "Shoot us both. It will make my job easier." His laughter grows, and I take a second to lean forward as much as I can and then throw my head back, knocking it into his face.

His arm loosens just enough to give me space to place my arm between it and shove him away. I run toward Haidyn, but the guy reaches out and grabs my hair. Spinning me around, he yanks me to him before knocking his face into mine.

HAIDYN

It happens so quickly that by the time I realize I have a shot, she's on the floor, and he's running out of the room.

"Fuck." I drop the gun to my side and kneel next to her. "Charlotte?" I look over her bloody face. He hit her hard. "Charlotte, look at me. Come on, doll face."

She blinks, and her tear-filled eyes are unfocused.

"What the fuck is going on?" Adam barks, entering my room and looking around. He's naked and half asleep.

"Someone was in the house," I answer, not taking my eyes off hers. "He got away."

He runs out of the room, and I cup her face. "Look at me, Charlotte." She blinks, but her eyes find mine. "That's it, beautiful. Talk to me."

"Hai-dyn." She blinks once more and lifts her hand to hold the side of her head. "Ow." She winces.

I let out a deep breath and help her to her feet. Guiding her over to the couch, I set her down on it and leave her to go the bathroom. Once I grab her some painkillers out of the cabinet, I get her a water from the fridge. Returning to our room, she looks up at me and sniffs. "I'm sorry—"

"Don't apologize." I interrupt her.

"I didn't realize it was you." She goes on.

I take her shaking hands in mine. "Hey, don't worry about it, doll face. I'm fine. Promise." I give her a reassuring smile that she doesn't return. "Here take these." Handing her the painkillers and water, she takes them just as Adam appears back at our bedroom door. "I'll be right back." Stepping into the hallway, I shut the door behind me. "See anything?" I ask Adam.

He shakes his head. "Whoever it was, they're long gone."

Fuck! "Okay. Thanks for trying."

"Of course." He snorts and places his hands on his hips, and I notice he's still naked. I've never met a modest Lord. "Sorry I didn't come sooner."

I run a hand through my hair.

"Who do you think it was?" he asks.

"Could have been anyone," I answer honestly.

Slapping my shoulder, he suggests, "Take her to Carnage for a couple of nights. Let me see what I can find out."

"No—"

"It's your best bet, Haidyn." He interrupts me. "Carnage is the safest place for both of you."

"They don't know who she is," I remind him through gritted teeth. Adam knows everything. He was the one I contacted when I found her SUV on the side of the road. He was the one who was able to find out the information that I couldn't.

"Then don't tell them," he counters, making me huff. "No one needs to find out who she is. Just give me two days to figure out what happened, and I'll let you know the moment I find something out."

I nod, knowing he's right. It's not a coincidence that I just made her my wife, and someone broke into our house. One that very few know I own. "Okay." I nod.

Entering the bedroom, I find her lying back in bed, the covers up to her neck, and her eyes staring up at me. She looks more alert now and sits up. Her eyes go to the door as I close it.

"How do you feel?" I ask, walking over to her side of the bed.

"I have a pounding headache," she answers softly.

I push her hair from her face and cup her jaw gently turning her face to look at it. He managed to hit her pretty good. She's got a bruise, but the skin isn't split anywhere. Her nose was bleeding, but it's stopped. "We're going to go stay at Carnage for a couple of days," I tell her.

She nods, not even bothering to argue or ask why. "I'll get dressed," she says and pushes the covers back as she gets to her feet. Before she can make her way to the bathroom, I grab her arm, bringing her to a stop, and gently kiss her forehead. Then I let her go.

Shhh...

Chapter 68

Charlotte

I'm so tired and have a pounding headache. My ears are still ringing. I packed a bag, and we were out of the house within ten minutes.

We pull up to Carnage, and as we enter, Saint and Kashton are already standing right inside. They pay me no attention. Haidyn had called them on our way, and they were way more concerned that we were attacked than the fact that Haidyn mentioned I was with him.

"I'll meet you in the office," he tells them both, and they turn, heading to the stairs. Haidyn places his hand on my shoulder and turns me to face him. Cupping my face, he kisses my lips tenderly. "Go up to my room and try to get some rest, okay?"

"How long will you be?"

"I don't know." He sighs, and I know that's as good of an answer as I'm going to get.

"Okay." I pull away and choose to use the elevator. I have one of Haidyn's duffel bags over one shoulder and Muffin in my arm. I didn't want to leave her behind, and Haidyn didn't argue when I put some cat food in a to-go container, cleaned out her litter box, and grabbed some extra litter. Adam comes and goes, and I didn't want to be here worrying about her there. And what if whoever broke in goes back, and she's there all alone? I can't take that chance.

I purposely kept my left hand shoved into Haidyn's hoodie to hide my ring when we entered. I feel like there's a reason Haidyn hasn't brought me to Carnage and has chosen to hide out at his house. We've been forced to be here. I understand why, but I'm going to lay as low as I can.

I'm in the elevator, making my way up to Haidyn's room while he's in their office explaining what happened and trying to find out who is after him. Muffin jumps out of my hand just as the door slides open, and I go to run down the hallway after her.

I come to a stop when I see the door at the opposite end of the hall open, and Ashtyn steps out. Her dark hair is up in a messy bun, and she's wearing a pair of cotton shorts and a tank top as if she was in bed and woken up. She looks the same as she did in the pictures and videos that the Lords sent me except her hair is a little darker.

"Hey there, pretty kitty." She bends down and picks up my cat. "How did you get in here?" Ashtyn scratches between her ears, making her purr.

"Her name is Muffin," I speak.

Ashtyn looks up and gives me a warm smile. "Hi." She begins to walk toward me. Her eyes quickly scan my busted face, but her smile doesn't falter. "I'm Ashtyn. I've seen you before but haven't had the chance to introduce myself." She reaches out her right hand to me. "I'm Saint's wife."

"Charlotte," I say, placing my right hand in hers while removing my left one from the front pocket of my husband's hoodie. "Haidyn's wife." That's something she'll never be to him.

Her smile falls, and her blue eyes widen as they drop to my left hand. Her hand falls from mine, and I reach out, taking my cat she has tucked into her left arm. "Oh, uh..." She stumbles over her words. "I didn't know Haidyn was seeing anyone."

"Several months now." Not a total lie.

She nods her head as if she's supposed to know this. "Congratulations." Her eyes meet mine, and she gives me a forced smile.

"Thank you," I say. "It was nice to meet you." With that, I put in the code to Haidyn's door. Entering the room, I place Muffin on the floor. She immediately runs and jumps on his bed, and I quickly remove her stuff from Haidyn's duffel bag, setting up her things in the corner. Then I undress and crawl into his bed as well, sighing as his cool sheets envelop me.

I probably shouldn't have said anything to her because I doubt

Haidyn has told his brothers that we're married. But I wanted her to know that he has me. I've already protected him more than she ever did. And I'll do whatever he needs in order to protect my Lord. I'm not going to turn my back on him. Instead, I'm going to prove myself to her or anyone else who challenges our marriage.

HAIDYN

I ENTER THE OFFICE TO SEE KASH AND SAINT SITTING AT THEIR desks. Their conversation dies the moment their eyes meet mine, and I know they were discussing my wife being here with me.

"So Charlotte—" Saint starts.

"This isn't about her." I stop him from finishing that sentence. I have a feeling it is, but they don't need to know that. I'm just here because I'm buying time for Adam to do some digging. I'll send Saint and Kash on a wild goose chase in the meantime.

"Did you get a look at him?" Kash questions.

"He was wearing a mask," I answer.

"A Lords mask?" Saint asks.

I shake my head. "A black ski mask."

"Hmm." Kash speaks. "Like the guy who attacked Charlotte in the bathroom?"

I lean back in my chair and cross my arms over my chest. "Yes," I answer, getting a sickening feeling in my stomach as they exchange a look. It's not uncommon for a criminal to cover their face, especially nowadays. Cameras are everywhere. The fact that there was no car in the driveway makes me wonder how far he walked to get there. Or was he dropped off from down the street? I hate having to rely on Adam to figure it out. But if anyone can, it's him.

"Anything new from Benny?" I inquire, trying to get their minds off my wife.

Saint shakes his head, and Kash just snorts.

"What if I have something that could work?" I offer. While Charlotte dressed and packed a bag for Muffin, I packed a few things of my own.

Saint sits up. "Whatever it is, let's try it."

We make our way down to the basement and I follow them both past the cells and to the last one on the right. Saint unlocks the door, and we step inside. Benny lies in the center of the concrete box; he's missing an entire arm from his elbow down and one eye is swollen completely shut. His right leg looks to be broken. Saint has spent some time fucking the man up.

I pull the syringe out of my pocket and bite off the cap. Once I inject it into his neck, I stand and step back, giving him a few seconds for it to kick in.

His head falls from side to side before his chest heaves through a cough. "Why are you here?" I question, testing the waters.

"Because...of Ashtyn."

I look at Saint, and he frowns at me. "What the fuck did you give him?"

"Truth serum," I answer.

We're not ones to use that shit here. Carnage is about torture, but it's obvious Saint's beat him quite a bit, and the bastard still refuses to talk. So we're going to consider this desperate times call for desperate measures.

Saint walks over to him and taps his steel-toed boot into his side. "How did you gain access to Carnage to kidnap my wife?"

His one eye looks around aimlessly, and he licks his busted lips. "She...she let us in."

"Who the fuck is she?" Saint snaps.

"Costello," he mumbles, and I stiffen.

Fuck! I was hoping it wasn't possible and that Kash was wrong when he told me his theories.

"Why the fuck would she let you into Carnage? What does she get from it?"

"All of you," he answers, and I run a hand down my face.

"She wanted us dead?" Kash asks.

He nods. "Yes."

I shake my head. He can't be lying, but I think that's just what he was told and made to believe. Otherwise, we'd already be dead.

"How did you know where our trackers were?" I ask. We've had ours since after our training, but Saint gave Ashtyn hers when he brought her back recently.

"Em-emerson," he answers.

Saint steps forward. "How the fuck would he know where Ashtyn's tracker was?"

"I-I don't know..."

"I do," I say and they both look at me. "That day you had Emerson escort her to the office. He had ripped open her robe, and you could see the bruise on her hip," I say.

Saint runs a hand through his hair. "I should have killed him instead of cutting off his hand. Thankfully, I can remedy that mistake."

I pull the picture out of my back pocket and show it to Benny. "Who is in this with you?"

He's staring at the picture, but I don't think he's really seeing it. Saint grips his hair and yanks him to sit up. Grasping the back of his neck, he holds Benny in place so he can look at it. "Answer the fucking question," he shouts, shaking him.

"It's...it's my cousin," he slurs.

"What's his name?" I demand. I figured they were related somehow.

"Hudson Owens," he whispers.

Saint shoves him to the ground, and I sigh. "Well, at least we have a name," I offer.

"Where the hell did you get that?" Saint asks me.

"After I left, I went to Vegas. Benny had someone set his place on fire, wanting everything destroyed. I guess in case we found out where he lived. He didn't want anyone leading him to Ashtyn. But the picture survived. I've been searching for answers."

"Why didn't you give this to me when you found it?" he snaps.

"I'm giving it to you now," I argue. "You almost beat him to death." I point down at Benny. "Obviously, you wouldn't have gotten any answers."

"You don't know that," he shouts.

"Guys." Kash steps forward, placing a hand on each of our chests to push us apart.

I turn to head upstairs and crawl into bed with my wife. The idea of being buried balls deep in her pussy is already helping my sour mood, but Saint ruins it when he speaks next.

"How'd you get Charlotte into your bed?"

I come to a stop and turn to face him. "Excuse me?"

He smirks, and Kashton runs his hand through his hair, growling, "Saint."

"What the fuck does that mean?" I demand, stepping back toward them.

"I'm just curious." He crosses his tatted arms over his chest, widening his stance. He's mad at me and wanting to start a fight.

"You know if it wasn't for us, she wouldn't be in your life."

"Goddammit," Kash hisses, giving us his back.

I highly doubt that, but I'll bite. "Meaning?"

Saint steps into me. "We made a deal with the Lords."

His words make my pulse race. I look at Kash, and he's avoiding eye contact with me as he paces the hallway. "What kind of deal?" I demand, getting a sickening feeling that they know who she really is. Did they find out that she was lying about her identity? If so, what are they going to do about it? They can't turn her in. She's my wife. They just don't know that I made her my Lady, and I'd prefer it to stay that way.

"We make sure you see a therapist, and they make sure you don't end up down here in a cage," Saint answers.

I frown, not understanding what he means.

Kashton sighs, his eyes finally meeting mine, and he softly speaks. "The Lords wanted us to lock you up, Haidyn. Not in a prisoner kind of way, but to protect you. After..." He swallows. "To make sure you didn't off yourself."

I grind my teeth. "I didn't try to kill myself." I'm really fucking tired of having to say those words.

"*She* hated you for what you did." Kash states the obvious about the bitch who moved in to train us. "She saw our training as a chance to get revenge. And you took the most punishments—"

"I did." I step closer to them. My narrowed eyes go to Saint's. She hated me for other reasons, but my brothers didn't deserve what she had planned for them. "Because I was the one who helped Ashtyn escape." He stiffens at my confession although this isn't fucking news to him since Benny ratted me out. "I did my best to keep her attention on me because it was my fault the Lords sent her," I growl.

"Haidyn—"

"But I never tried to kill myself because of it," I spit. "You guys can believe whatever the fuck you want but tell the Lords the deal is done. I don't want Charlotte involved." It could cause them to dig into her deeper. Or the Lords may out her to them, hoping that my brothers take care of her. I won't let them near her. It's one of the reasons I've kept her as far away from here as possible. "And whoever I choose to fuck is no one's business."

"And apparently where you are and whether or not you're alive is no one's business either." Kash snaps getting mad at me. "Where the fuck have you been, Haidyn?" he demands.

I look at Saint. "Saint knows where I've been. Don't you? He dropped by my house the other day and said hi." It's a cheap shot but I'm ready for a fight. I'm also testing him to see if he mentions Adam being there. If he'll add fuel to this fire or try to put it out.

"What the fuck, man?" Kash turns to face him. "His house? How the fuck did you know where he's been?"

Saint's jaw sharpens but he doesn't answer. Instead, he just glares at me. *Good choice.*

Kashton turns his attention back on me. "Has it all been about her? Have you two been shacked up somewhere just so you can fuck her?" He scoffs at his own question. "As if you've ever needed privacy to fuck a woman."

I step into him, and it takes everything I have to not break his goddamn nose. "What I do with her and how I choose to do it, is none of your business. So back the fuck off, Kash." He needs to drop this conversation about my wife right now before he goes too far.

His nostrils flare and his chest bows out. I'm not in the mood for this shit. Not tonight.

Kash takes a step back, shaking his head as if disappointed in me. He's not the first and definitely won't be the last.

Giving them my back, I exit the basement and make my way to the birdcage to find Charlotte and Muffin asleep in bed.

After undressing, I crawl in next to her. She rolls over to face me, her arm going to my chest, and I run my fingers up and down it while I stare up at the ceiling.

"Everything okay?" she whispers.

"Everything's fine, doll face. You're safe," I assure her and turn onto my side, kissing her forehead. "Go back to sleep."

Chapter 69

Haidyn

I wake to the sound of a knock on the door. Sliding my arm out from underneath my wife, I pull on a pair of boxer briefs that are on the floor and open my door. Kashton stands in front of me, both arms on the doorframe. His eyes slide to a sleeping Charlotte before they come back to mine.

"The Lords texted us." His clipped voice informs me he's still mad at me after what took place down in the basement.

My phone died hours ago, and I didn't bother to charge it. "We don't do assignments." I go to shut the door, but he stops it with his foot.

"We've been scheduled for a pickup and delivery back here to Carnage."

I sigh, running a hand down my face. Can't we get one night without someone fucking it up? "I'll meet you downstairs in ten." I slam the door shut and walk back over to her.

Running my fingertips over her cheek, I push her dark hair from her bruised face. I have never been paranoid before, but everything seems suspicious regarding her. Like this? Are the Lords summoning me to leave her alone so something can happen to her here while I'm away? Surely not. They know she's my wife. She's not technically untouchable, but it does make her important—more so than she already was. And no one wants to see what I will do if they decide to target her.

Her eyes flutter open, and she looks up at me. "Come back to bed." She reaches out and wraps her hand around my wrist.

I kneel next to the bed. "I'll be back, okay?"

"Where are you going?" She yawns.

"The Lords need me, but I'll be right back."

"Wake me up." Her eyes flutter shut, and I smile.

"Of course." I kiss her forehead and stand. Shutting the door behind me, I make my way to the first floor and out the door.

The hearse that we use for Carnage sits running in the circle drive. Knowing Kash is inside, I open the passenger side door and fall into it.

Thankfully, he remains silent. We haven't spoken since we were down in the basement and Saint admitted they made a deal with the Lords, other than him just coming to get me. I have nothing else to say about it. And I meant it when I told him to tell the Lords to fuck off.

The radio plays "Anywhere But Here" by Five Finger Death Punch and Maria Brink. I close my eyes and lean my head against the headrest. I'm tired. My body has gotten accustomed to lying next to Charlotte every night with my cock inside her. She helps me sleep, and I hate how dependent I've become on her. I never knew my body could get that much rest.

The car coming to a stop has my eyes opening, and I sit up to see we're at the cathedral. Getting out, we make our way into the double doors and walk down the long aisle, passing rows and rows of pews toward the Lords altar.

A man lies on his back, arms and legs tied to each corner—spread eagle. He's naked and bleeding from cuts and gashes all over his body. Confessionals are always getting dirty.

They secure the Lord to the altar, and then one Lord gets to do whatever he wants to get the Lord to expose all his secrets. It's up to the higher-ups if he is to be left dead or alive. We've been summoned to take him back to Carnage. Poor bastard would be better off dead.

A woman stands in front of the altar with her back to us. She's dressed in fishnet tights, a pleated black miniskirt that sits high on her slim waist and a white crop top with black chunky boots that lace up the front. Her bleach-blond hair is up in a messy bun, and she hums a lullaby as she dunks a sponge into the bucket beside the altar next to her feet. Soaking the sponge, she lets the water drip from it before she washes the man off.

He screams into the gag secured in his mouth by the leather harness wrapped around his head. Kashton and I make our way to the front of the aisle and sit down in the front of each pew.

Her humming echoes throughout the open space, and I look at Kash to see him leaning forward in the pew, his elbows on his knees and chin in his hands. His eyes are zeroed in on her ass while she leans over, washing the Lord.

She knows someone was called to collect him and we're here. She just doesn't care. When she's finished, she'll let us know.

The woman's voice grows louder, and instead of humming, she sings the words to "Hush, Little Baby." I have to admit she has a pretty voice. The hauntingly beautiful sound fills the cathedral.

She takes her time, carefully cleaning him as if he's made of glass and requires tenderness. When she drops the sponge into the bucket, water splashes over the edge, and she turns to look at Kash. "A little help, please?" She holds out her left hand.

He gets up and walks over to her. Taking her hand, he helps her get up onto the altar where she straddles the guys waist. "Hand me that basket." She points at a wicker basket on the floor next to the stairs.

Kashton picks it up for her and places it next to the man's head. He steps back, shoving his hands into the pocket of his hoodie and watches to see what she's going to do.

The woman lifts the guy's head and undoes the buckle on the gag. Ripping it from his mouth, she tosses it to the floor, and he begins to scream.

"You fucking crazy bitch!" He yanks on the ropes and tries to buck her off, but she holds steady, digging into the basket.

Pulling a roll of duct tape out, she rips the corner piece free and places it over his lips. Then she grips his hair and lifts his head off the altar as she wraps the duct tape around his head several times before leaning over and ripping it off with her teeth.

She pulls out a small blowtorch from the basket and turns it on. She places the flame against the tape while his muffled screams fill the room. "That should keep it in place." She smiles and taps the side of his face as she speaks to him. "Those who spill secrets will be silenced."

She goes to get up, and Kashton rushes over. Grabbing her waist, he helps her down off the altar. She thanks him before walking around to the opposite side of the altar. Her green eyes meet mine before she looks over at Kash. "He's ready for you." She gives us a chilling smile. Her bright white teeth are a noticeable contrast to her black eye shadow and red lips.

The man's screams grow louder, and he fights the rope harder. She looks down at him with that smile still on her face. She touches his cheek, and he arches his back, trying to pull away.

I stand and walk over to the altar, and as I get closer, I notice she had sewn him up prior to cleaning him. It's nothing professional. Just a needle and black thread. Scanning his body quickly, I count at least fifteen different places from head to toe. Some around five inches long, others shorter.

"Nice work," I tell her.

"Practice makes perfect." She grabs the pleats of her black skirt and curtsies. Her green eyes slide from mine to Kash, and she winks at him. Then they drop to the Lord on the altar. He still wears his brand. *That's our job to remove.* Reaching up, she taps the side of his bloody, snot-covered face. "If you're lucky, I'll come visit you in hell." With that, she spins around and walks out the side door.

Kashton watches the now closed door while he speaks. "Do you believe in coincidences?"

"No," I answer.

"Me either."

CHARLOTTE

I'M EXITING THE BATHROOM AND STEPPING INTO HAIDYN'S bedroom at Carnage when I hear the doorknob turn before it opens. He goes to step in when someone calls his name.

"Haidyn?"

He pauses while still in the hallway, but the door remains open while I stand in his bedroom.

"What's up, Ash?" He sighs, running a hand down his face.

He left me in bed in the middle of the night when Kashton came to get him. He said the Lords needed him. I don't know where he went or what he did, but judging by the blood on his shirt and jeans, I'd say someone is either dead or wishing they were.

"I wanted to talk to you," she says softly.

I can't see her from where she stands because she's not in the way of the open door, but I can hear her as clear as day. Haidyn stays silent, facing her.

"I just wanted to tell you that I love you too," she rushes out.

My stomach drops at her words, confused and instantly irritated.

When silence stretches between the two of them, she continues. "So much happened so fast. The wreck...you got shot..." She sniffs. "Those four days... thinking you were dead and then you were alive. After everything unfolded with Benny, you left." She steps closer to him, coming into view, and I watch her start to wrap her arms around his neck, but he reaches up and grabs her wrists, stopping her.

Her shoulders slump, and he releases her before they drop to her sides. "I'm sorry, Haidyn, for everything. Just know that I do love you." She stands up on her tiptoes and kisses his cheek before he can pull back, turns around, walking away. The sound of a door closing tells me she returned to her and Saint's room.

Haidyn turns to enter his door and comes to a stop when he sees me standing by his bed, holding the towel wrapped around my body and hair dripping wet. I got tired of waiting for him to come back, so I took a shower.

He slams the door shut and then silently walks past me, entering the bathroom and shutting that door as well.

I stand staring at the now closed door to his room. I can hear the blood rushing in my ears and feel my heart pounding in my chest. My skin is hot. I decide that I hate her fucking guts. More so than I did when I watched him fuck her ass in that video.

I don't care what kind of past they have or what kind of future we lack. She knows I'm here with him. She knows that I'm his wife! Why confess her love now? He did so much for her in the past. She had to have known how he felt about her, right? Was she stupid, or just didn't care then? Four years she was gone and now that she's back and Haidyn has a wife, she cares? I don't buy that.

Spinning around, I shove the bathroom door open. The steam has already started to fill the large space from his shower. I yank that door open and cross my arms over my chest. "What was that about?"

He has his back to me. Turning around, he opens his eyes and looks down at me. "Nothing."

"Nothing?" I give a rough laugh. "She tells you that she loves you...*too,* might I add, and you call that nothing." I understand we're where we are at because of the Lords. But what I just saw makes me want to cut a bitch. My mother and Anne said he loved her, and that's why he killed their fathers for her. But I never really thought about it until now. Seeing it and hearing it are two very different things. I'm becoming attached to my husband, and I will make sure anyone who tries to take him knows I'll do whatever it takes to keep him.

"It's not what you think." He blows it off.

I snort. "So you're saying you've never told her that you love her?" He remains silent. "Let me guess, you're also going to tell me that you've never fucked her?" When he doesn't respond, I growl. "That's what I thought." I know the truth; I just didn't want to think of it.

Maybe that video meant more than I thought it did. I know Haidyn has been with other women. Hell, he probably couldn't even give me a body count if I asked. I'm the dumb one who had to save herself for him.

I go to slam the glass door shut, but he grabs my hand and yanks me into the shower, instantly soaking me and my towel. "Haidyn," I hiss, wiping the water from my face so I can open my eyes.

He pushes my back into the cold wall, and I shiver as he presses his body into mine. I glare up at him. "So she's with Saint because she didn't want you." I can't help but keep talking. Maybe I want to piss him off. Perhaps I want him to wrap his hand around my throat and choke me out. Maybe I want him to fuck me so hard that I scream his name so she can hear it from across the hall. Isn't that what a man is supposed to do—make other women jealous of you?

"No," he says calmly. "She's with Saint because I didn't want her." His right hand comes up and pushes the wet strands of hair off my cheek. "You're the one I chose to marry—"

"Because you had to." I interrupt him. We're not going to pretend that we got married because we love one another. "Are you still fucking her?" I'm not even sure I want to know the answer to that. A part of me wants him to say yes so I can have a reason to hate him. As if I don't have enough already. Another part of me pleads with him to lie and say no. Surely, Saint doesn't allow that. I almost laugh at myself. Of course, Lords share their wives. Wearing a ring and hearing I love you means nothing to them.

Chapter 70
Haidyn

She slams her palms into my bare chest, trying to push me out of the way. I stay where I am.

"Move," she snaps, glaring up at me.

"No."

"Get out of my way, Haidyn," she shouts.

"I said no."

"HAIDYN!" Her fists hit my chest.

I grab her wrists to keep her fists from making anymore contact. "I said no, Charlotte. I'm not still fucking Ashtyn."

She's breathing heavily, and her hard eyes glare up at me. I like this side of her. Although I'd rather not have had that conversation with Ashtyn, I do like Charlotte's reaction. It shows me that I'm not going crazy alone. She's jumped headfirst into this forced marriage with me, and I'm not the only one attached.

I did something that can't be undone when it comes to my wife. And given the chance, I'd do the same thing again.

This is exactly how she reacted when the Lords sent her the video of me and Ashtyn at the house of Lords. I haven't told Charlotte that I know about it, and she hasn't told me. It'll stay that way. I can play their stupid game and pretend I never saw it. But I'm going to prove to my wife that Ashtyn doesn't matter to me. Not the way Charlotte thinks anyway.

I didn't even know Charlotte was listening when Ashtyn stopped me in the hall, or I would have shut down that conversation before it started. I pushed Ashtyn away because I have to establish boundaries with her. Things are different now. I'm different now. And my priority is my wife and how she feels.

Letting go of Charlotte's wrists, she drops them to her side, and I cup her face. "I haven't fucked her in years."

"Bullshit," she snaps.

I chuckle. "Don't believe me, doll face?"

"No. I don't," she growls. "But let's go ask her. I bet she won't lie to me." Pushing me back, she goes to step around me, and I grab her arm, spinning her around and pulling her against me. I have one hand in her wet hair and the other wrapped around her body.

"I haven't fucked her since she and Saint got married," I say truthfully.

"And when was that?" she demands.

"Four years ago," I answer.

Everything went to shit not long after that. I never wanted Ashtyn like Saint did. Not like I want Charlotte. I didn't need Ashtyn to tell me she loves me to know how she feels. I never told her that, needing to hear it back. I just wanted her to know that I was there for her.

Charlotte nibbles on her bottom lip, and I cup her face, my thumb pulling it free. Her pretty blue eyes look up at me through her wet lashes. "How many have you fucked since you started fucking me?" Her voice is so low that it's almost hard to hear over the shower.

I like how nervous she is. How much she wants to know, yet is still afraid of the answer. "No one." I drop my hand to run my knuckles over her chest. "You've been the only one, doll face." My girl keeps me satisfied. I've never been a one-woman kind of guy, but it's different with Charlotte. I wouldn't have married her otherwise. "I've also never kissed anyone until you," I tell her. It's the truth. That day she stood in her kitchen after giving herself over to me, I did what I had wanted to do for so long. Kissing is too personal—intimate. I wanted to make her mine in every way.

She takes in a shaky breath.

"What about you? How many men have you fucked?" I joke, knowing damn well no one else has touched her. They'd be dead if so.

She rolls her eyes and grabs my left hand. "We need to get you a ring."

"I don't wear jewelry."

She huffs. "You've got like eight piercings in your dick and another in your nose. Not to mention you wear a watch. I don't think a wedding ring will kill you."

I can't help but smile and shake my head. "Not happening..."

"Then I won't wear mine." She goes to remove her seven-carat Harry Winston cushion-cut sapphire wedding ring, but I grab her hands and lift them above her head. Crossing her wrists, I hold them with one hand while the other grips her chin and forces her head up to meet my glare.

"Don't you dare take that off, doll face." I warn.

The growl from her pretty lips makes my smile grow. Her eyes narrow up at mine as she tries to pull her wrists free from my hold.

She's mine, and I'm going to make her understand that. When we started this game, I was determined to win no matter what it cost. Now I understand that it might take everything I have because I already know how this will end. This is why the Lords sent her to me. I believe her when she says she doesn't know what they want from me, but I know. There's only one thing that they want me to give—my life. And I'm going to make sure it's worth it.

Allowing myself to fall in love with her is madness. No matter how I try to justify it, the ending will be the same. I can only hope I have time to leave her with something that will remind her of me.

She doesn't understand that our worlds have been intertwined for years now. The Lords put me in her life in the most unforgivable way. And she'll never see me the same when she finds out what I've done.

I've taken a lot from her. Some things she's aware of; others she's not. But she'll see the pain I've caused her once the truth comes out. I can only hope I will no longer be here when she discovers the truth. Because I don't know how I'll face her once she realizes what I've done.

"Maybe I want the world to know you're mine too," she states, lifting her chin.

"Jealous, doll face?" I like it.

Huffing, she says, "I'll just brand my name on your chest."

I laugh, and it just pisses her off more. Letting go of her, I watch as her hands fall, slapping her bare thighs. She can brand, tattoo, or carve whatever she wants on me.

"Fuck you, Haidyn." Her small hands shove my chest, and I step back, chuckling. Reaching down, she grabs the soaked towel, picks it up, and exits the shower, slamming the glass door shut so hard I'm surprised it doesn't break.

I'm rinsing off when she returns and yanks the door open once again. I turn around to see her standing outside the shower still naked, hair dripping wet with her right hip pushed out. "What the hell are these?" She holds up a clear rectangular container that holds a pair of blackout contact lenses. "Something tells me they're not a part of a Halloween costume."

"Been going through my things, doll face?" I knew she would. Not like I'm hiding anything from her. I've ordered all the toys I've used on Charlotte specifically for her. I've got tons of shit here at Carnage because this is where I live. This is where I fucked the random women I paid for all the time. Hell, sometimes they would bring their own sex toys for me to use on them. The question is...is she only bringing them to my attention because of the conversation I had with Ashtyn? Or would she still have the balls to say something to me if she wasn't mad at me?

She huffs. "How many have you used these on?"

Stepping forward, I place my hands on either side of the shower glass door and ask, "Does it matter?" I want to piss her off because I'm loving her attitude. I'm in the mood to rile my wife up, pin her down, and fuck her senseless.

Spinning around, she tosses them onto the counter and slams the bathroom door on her way out.

I quickly finish up and get out. Picking up the blackout lenses, I toss them into the trash with no plans of ordering a new pair. I won't be using them on her. Covering up her pretty eyes would be a crime that even I would never commit. Plus, she likes the humiliation of having to watch me record the things I'm doing to her. She gets off on it as much as I like to watch her cry.

I make my way to the open bathroom door, wanting to make sure she's not in Saint and Ashtyn's room. The last thing I need is to pull my wife off a pregnant Ashtyn. I'd rather not have to have that conversation. Plus, it would throw up red flags to the guys.

She's standing next to the bed, pulling her thong up her legs, getting dressed. I was gone all night and am tired as fuck. I could use a nap after I'm done fucking her. My wife's attitude has me as hard as a rock. Coming up behind her, I wrap an arm around her waist and pick her up off her feet.

"Haidyn," she growls, kicking her feet out.

"It's cute when you fight, doll face." I say, and it just makes her struggle harder.

I toss her onto the bed face up and grab her thong, ripping it off her hips. She whimpers as the thin lace leaves a mark on her flawless skin. Then I flip her onto her stomach and pull her ass up in the air. I slap it, making her yelp. Then I do it again before my hand rubs the red spot.

Kneeling between her legs, I shove them open and take my hard cock in my hand rubbing it against her wet cunt. I smile to myself that even though she's mad, she's still wet. "I love that you're always ready to be used, doll face."

She moans as she puts her hands on the bed to push herself up onto all fours. I slide my cock into her, slamming balls deep, and she cries out; her body begins to shake. Grabbing her arms, I bring them behind her back, forcing her to fall onto the side of her face. I hold her wrists captive in one hand.

"That's it," I say, watching the length of my pierced cock go in and out of her soaked pussy. "Spread your legs for me, Charlotte." I push them farther apart, forcing her to arch her back more. "Fuck, doll face. You feel so good."

"Haidyn...please..." Her hips rock back and forth, wanting me to fuck her harder.

I slap her ass again and slam my cock into her, making her cry out.

I've been around women long enough to know how they think. My wife wants to stake her claim on me. As if the ring she wears doesn't prove she belongs to me.

I'm going to fuck her until she screams out my name. She wants Ashtyn to know she's mine. And I'll let Charlotte think she's accomplishing that even though I know Ashtyn can't hear her. These walls are soundproof for a reason.

But like everything else I've done regarding my wife, what she doesn't know can't hurt her.

. . .

CHARLOTTE

We lie in his bed, and I stare at the ceiling. He's on his side, arm across my stomach. Muffin lies on Haidyn's pillow by his head, purring loudly. It's midday, but I know he's tired from getting woken up in the middle of the night. I am, too, if I'm being honest. It's gotten to where I can't sleep without him next to me. I tossed and turned after he left. I think it's also because we're at Carnage. I never want to spend more time here than I have to.

His breathing evens out, and I see he's fallen back to sleep. I sigh; my thoughts are still on him and Ashtyn. I can't shake it. I know I shouldn't care, but it bothers me. Part of me thinks she knew I was right there and could hear her, so she told him. Did she want him to say it again in front of me?

The other part tells me I'm just being a bitch, and she had no clue I was right there and able to hear her. She was genuine and wanted him to know where she stood. I mean, she is married, for fuck's sake. But she was also with Saint when Kashton and Haidyn both fucked her.

I'm going in-fucking-sane. I could wake Haidyn up and make him fuck me again to get my mind off it. But what would that do? Afterward, it'd be back on my mind. The fact that I went snooping through his things while he was gone didn't help. Forget a beginner's guide to bondage, the man has everything to supply a BDSM club in his closet. I had decided to let it go and not say anything, but Ashtyn confessing her love to my husband threw me over the edge. You can tell yourself it doesn't matter as many times as you want, it doesn't make it true.

A cell phone rings, and Haidyn wakes up and pulls away from me to pick his up off the nightstand where he has it charging.

"What's up, man?" he asks, answering sleepily. "You did? Sounds good...thanks." Hanging up, he puts it down and turns back, snuggling into me.

I lick my lips. "Who was that?" I ask.

"A friend. They got the guy who broke into the house."

He means Adam—the guy hiding out at Haidyn's house. For some reason, he doesn't want me to know who Adam is. Have I not proven that he can trust me? "What does that mean?"

Yawning, he answers. "We're going back home when we wake up from our nap."

"Is the guy dead?" I ask, wanting to know.

He kisses my cheek and whispers, "He will be."

Chapter 71

Haidyn

I didn't say goodbye to Kashton or Saint before Charlotte and I left Carnage. After I fucked her, I passed out. Then when I woke up, she was sound asleep, and it was dark outside.

After a quick visit from Devin to administer a new tracker, I woke her up, and we left. I wanted her back at our home, in our bed. Adam comes and goes a lot, so for the most part, it's just her and me there, and I like that.

Plus, I wanted to get her away from Ashtyn. That whole situation was...awkward. Charlotte has nothing to worry about, but she's not going to believe what I have to say because I haven't proven it to her. But I will. I'll make her understand that no other woman can compare to her.

I'm in my home gym when the door opens and Adam enters. I put down the weights and grab my towel to dry off my face. He wasn't here when we got home earlier this morning. "What'd you find out?"

He straddles one of the benches and looks up at me. "Found him five miles from here. Holed up in an abandoned cottage. His target was me."

I frown. "You?"

He nods. "Went through his cell, and all he had was my name and this address. So I think he just assumed you were me, and he planned on taking both you and Charlotte out. Leave no witnesses sort of thing." He stands and pulls his cell out of his pocket. "I have somewhere to be." His eyes meet mine again. "I'll be away for a while."

I nod, enjoying the idea of having the house to ourselves. He walks out and I turn toward my weights to get back to it when the door opens again. I turn expecting it to be Adam, but my wife enters, dressed in a pretty red sun dress and a pair of heels. She's got her hair down and curled with her makeup done. Her matching red lips make me want to tie her up, push her to her knees and fist her hair while I smear the lipstick all over my cock.

The only thing I want her wearing right now is my ring and maybe a gag in her mouth while she drools all over herself. "Where do you think you're going?" I ask her.

I don't want my wife to feel like a prisoner in our home, and the guy who was following her is locked away inside Carnage. Someone sent him to follow her so how many more are watching every move she makes? It still makes me nervous to think of her being out of my sight. Knowing that someone could hurt her. But this house is no longer safe if Adam has a hit on him, and they know he lives here. I'll hire security, add more cameras all over the property, and make sure that this place is on lockdown twenty-four seven. The thought of taking her back to Carnage comes to mind, but I push it to the side.

Maybe I'll take her out of town? Snowed in at a cabin secluded in the mountains sounds nice. Her tied to a wooden four-post bed begging me to fuck her. But so does the thought of my wife lying naked on our own private beach while she's tied to a lounge chair with a vibrator in her cunt and a plug in her ass. As she comes all over herself, I sit next to her drinking a scotch and watching the sun set while I listen to her moan into the gag.

"*We* are going out today," she states, crossing her arms over her chest and interrupting the visuals I just gave myself.

I smirk, loving her attitude. It's so cute. She's had one since I woke her up at Carnage last night. "And where are we going, doll face?"

"To get you a wedding ring," she says matter-of-factly. "Then we're going to lunch to eat like a normal married couple." Giving me her back and heading for the door, she adds, "You have thirty minutes before I leave. And your ass better be ready."

I laugh as she slams the door shut. My girl wants to claim me as hers by wearing a ring. I won't tell her that I already have one in a drawer in the closet. I just haven't put it on. I didn't think she'd care that much about it. But if she wants to take me to get one, then I'll let her.

CHARLOTTE

I pull up to my house and park. We've been married for two weeks, and I'm officially moving in with Haidyn. He told me last night that he's hired a moving company. I didn't put up a fight. He said they would handle everything, but I wanted to pick up some more of my clothes. He had to run to Carnage and said he'd meet me here.

I enter my house with a smile on my face. It's weird, actually, how happy I have been lately. It's Haidyn. As much as I want to deny it, I can't any longer. He makes me love Charlotte more than Annabelle.

Flipping on the light to the kitchen, I see a bottle of wine on the island and a glass already filled next to it.

I laugh, putting my purse on the counter. "You're an hour early," I call out, picking up the glass and taking a big drink. Setting it down, I turn around to see him sitting at the kitchen table. Just like he did the first time he broke into my house.

Smiling, I pick it up and take another sip. "Trying to get me drunk to have your way with me?" I arch a brow. "We both know that's not required."

He sits there dressed in his cloak and mask, and my body tingles with excitement of what's to come. I take another drink, stepping closer to the table. "Going to chase me around the house again one last time?" I look up at the ceiling and tap my chin with my free hand in thought. "Maybe drag me down into the basement." I tip the wineglass and finish it off. "I'm up for any one of those." I laugh at my own words. As if Haidyn would let me decide what he does to me.

I turn around at his silence to pour another glass, but I drop the wineglass when I see another Lord standing in my kitchen. The hairs on my neck instantly rise and so does my heart rate. I take a step back but run into something. An arm wraps around my waist, and another covers my mouth.

Kicking my legs, I try to scream into the hand and pull it off, but I'm too weak. What the hell? My vision blurs, and it's getting harder to breathe.

"Relax," an altered voice speaks into my ear. "Give it time to kick in."

My watery eyes go to the second Lord who stands in front of me still dressed in his cloak and mask, just watching. He picks up the wine bottle and drops it to the floor, the glass shattering and the wine covers the tile.

There was something in it. I can feel my body slacken; my arms feel heavy and fall to my sides.

"That's it." The person behind me loosens his hold on me, and I drop to the floor like the bottle of wine, unable to hold myself up.

The side of my face lies in the wine and the side of the kitchen island goes in and out of view.

My arms are grabbed, and I'm rolled onto my back. One of the Lords comes to stand on either side of my hips. Everything seems to be in slow motion. The guy pulls a syringe out of his pocket and a clear vial. My head lolls around, my vision going in and out. I try to speak but can't seem to make my lips work. I feel like I'm about to pass out.

I feel a sting on my face, and my eyes manage to open to see the man leaning down into it. His mask is inches away from my blinking eyes. "Don't worry, Annabelle. This..." He holds the now full syringe in front of my eyes. "Is for later."

My body jerks involuntarily, and I begin to cough.

"There it is," one of them says.

I can't breathe. My throat closes, and my back bows off the wine-covered floor. Panic grips my chest, and all I can think is to get ahold of Haidyn. But nothing works.

Hands grab my face and hold it in place while my body goes into spasms, flopping around out of control.

"No need to panic," the mask that hovers over me says calmly. "It's all part of the plan."

I'm dying. I can feel my chest heaving, trying to breathe, and I get nothing. And thankfully, everything goes black.

Chapter 72

Haidyn

I enter her house and remove my jacket. I go straight to her bedroom but don't see her in there or her bathroom. "Charlotte?" I call out, knowing she's here. Her SUV is in the driveway.

Walking through the living room, I still don't see her. "Doll face?" I holler. "I know you're here," I add with a smile. Is my girl playing a game with me? I'm more than willing to play hide-and-seek. "When I find you, I'm going to..."

My words die off when I enter the kitchen. She's lying on the floor, face up, in a puddle of broken glass and wine. "Charlotte?" I rush over to her and drop to my knees. "Charlotte?" I place my fingers on her neck and hold my breath as I feel for a pulse. Panic grips my chest when I don't feel one. Which can only mean one thing... "FUCK!" I rip her shirt down the center and press my palms to her chest.

"I wouldn't do that if I were you."

My head snaps up to see a Lord enter the kitchen. I pick her limp body up in my arms and place her on the island. "What the fuck did you do to her?" I demand, refusing to believe what I already know. Placing my hand over her lips and nose, I pray she takes in a breath. Some kind of sign that I'm not too late. She's not purple or ghostly white, nor is her body stiff. I feel for her pulse again. Silently counting in my head, I don't feel anything. But then...yeah, there it is. I hold my breath, waiting for another one, but they're too far apart.

He holds up a syringe in his hand that's full of a clear substance, and my stomach drops, knowing exactly what it is. My eyes go back to her, and I reach up and yank my shirt over my head to lay it over her exposed chest and stomach since I ripped her shirt. "What the fuck do you want?" I growl.

Pulling out a seat at her kitchen table, he sits down in it and removes his Lords mask. My pulse races at the sight of the man who I've been carrying around a picture of. "How do you know Charlotte?" I demand.

"You mean Annabelle?" He arches a dark brow, and I grind my teeth. His laughter fills the room. "You were so consumed with her that you had no clue what was right in front of you." Standing, he walks to the island, and I move to the end of it, blocking him from getting any closer to her.

"Get to the fucking point!" I shout, losing my patience.

I need what he has in his hands, and I need it now. Who knows how long she's been in this position. She could have arrived hours before I got here. I was at Carnage and knew we had plans to meet here, so I never thought to look at her tracker to see when she arrived at her house.

"I give you this, but you give something in return."

"Anything," I snap. "Just name it."

He smirks. "You have forty-eight hours." His eyes drop to Charlotte and then come back to mine. "You'll get a text of the location." With that, he hands it to me.

I go to grab it, but he pulls it back out of reach. I want to ram it into his fucking eye. "Yes?" I ask through gritted teeth.

"You'll have an hour to respond. If you don't..." He leaves the consequences hanging in the air, but I know what he means.

I always knew it would come down to this. But he was right. I got caught up in a life with her and kept thinking it would last longer. That I'd have more time to spend with her and figure out a plan for our future. But that's what love does to you—dream. It's all a lie. There is no such thing. It's a small crack in a ship's hull that slowly fills with water until it can no longer stay afloat.

Nothing lasts forever.

He holds out the syringe, and I yank it from his hand before he even has the chance to take it back this time. With that, he places his mask back on and walks out of the kitchen, leaving me alone with my half-dead wife. I remove my cell from my pocket, thankful I have Gavin on speed dial. I'm placing it on speakerphone when he answers.

"Haidyn..."

"I need you at this address immediately," I rush out, texting it to him.

"What do I need?" he questions with no hesitation.

"Whatever you can fit into your bag." I hang up and toss the phone to the opposite counter, not needing it anymore. "Come on, doll face." I pick her up off the island and carry her limp body to her bedroom. Laying her on top of the comforter, I remove my shirt that covers her and put the syringe beside her on the bed for a second.

I tie her hands above her head to the bed with rope before I remove her heels, undo her jeans, and yank them down her legs along with her underwear.

Then I get off the bed and open her nightstand, grabbing what I need. I crawl back onto her petite body and straddle her narrow hips once again. I pick up the syringe, and my free hand goes to her chest. My teeth clench, hating the fucking bastards who are making me do this to her.

"I'm sorry, Charlotte. This is going to hurt," I say, then shove the needle into her chest and push on the plunger, filling her body with some of the liquid. She's not a three-hundred-pound man. Her body doesn't need nearly as much as someone like I would.

Her eyes pop open, and she gasps, her body arching up off the bed. I toss the half-used syringe across the room, making a mental note to pick it up later.

"Charlotte!" I cup her face, and she pulls on the rope that keeps her wrists tied down. "Charlotte, look at me, doll face." I place my hands on her upper arms to help keep them in place, so she doesn't hurt herself. "Look at me!" I shout, starting to panic, but then her blue eyes focus on mine. "There you go. That's it, doll face. Look at me."

She's gasping, trying to catch her breath. "Hai-dyn..."

"Shh," I say. "You're okay. It's me." Her eyes are wide, her chest heaving while her small body fights me. "Breathe," I say, taking in a deep one myself. "Come on, beautiful. I know it's a lot."

She looks around the room. "Eyes on me," I command. "I need all your focus on me. Ride it out."

"Wh-at—?"

"Don't talk." I interrupt her. "I had to bring you back, Charlotte. I gave you a shot of adrenaline."

Tears instantly fill her pretty eyes.

"Hey, you're okay. I promise. You'll be okay. Just breathe for me. Can you do that?"

She nods quickly, blinking rapidly.

"That's my good girl. Deep breaths." I know her body wants to fight. It can make you feel invincible. But I need to keep her here until I know it's wearing off. I don't want any more harm caused than what has already happened. If we're lucky, he didn't rape her while she was out. The fact that she was still dressed doesn't ease my concern.

"Please?" she cries, arching her neck to look at her restrained arms. "Haidyn..." Her voice cracks, and it makes my chest tighten.

"I can't stop it, Charlotte. We have to let it run its course," I tell her.

She begins to cry, her hips bucking underneath me.

I get up off her and position myself between her legs, spreading them open. I slap her smooth cunt. She screams out at the contact, and I do it again. Pushing a finger into her, she's not even close to being wet. But this is the only plan I have. When we're given adrenaline, we've either exhausted ourselves or fight until we kill our opponent. Why not fuck it out of her?

"Hang on, doll face," I say, unzipping my jeans and pulling my dick out. I'm not even in the mood to fuck, but I need to do something. This will help.

I pour the lube over her cunt and ass. So much that it runs down and covers the comforter. Then I coat the toy. Any other time I'd enjoy her writhing and crying underneath me, but given the circumstances, I'm not. "Deep breaths," I remind her, pushing the vibrating butt plug into her. "That's it. Almost there," I say over her gasps and smile when all I can see is the base. I turn it on, and the sound of it vibrating fills the room, and she squirms for a different reason.

"Oh...God..."

"That's it," I say, running my hands up both sides of her waist and to her breasts. "Feel that? Focus on that, doll face."

Her hips continue to buck but for a different reason. She looks up at me, and her lips part. I lean down and kiss her. My lips attack hers, and I rub my cock back and forth against her lube-covered cunt, teasing her.

CHARLOTTE

I SUCK ON HIS TONGUE, AND HE MOANS INTO MY MOUTH. FUCK, I feel like I could run a marathon and beat a world record. My skin is on fire, nerves tingling, and my heart races.

He gave me adrenaline.

I'll have to ask later what the fuck happened. Last I remember, I was lying on the kitchen floor thinking I was dying, and now I'm tied to my bed naked with a vibrator in my ass and Haidyn's lips on mine.

He pulls away, and I rise up, trying to keep the kiss going, but my tied wrists above my head stop me. I groan, pulling on them. "Haidyn?" I growl.

I've done drugs before. Weed, ecstasy, and coke once. None have ever made me feel like this. I just want to run or fight...either sounds good right now.

His hand goes between my legs, and he turns the toy up. The vibrating gets more intense, and I arch my back, my breath getting caught in my lungs. It feels like an electric shock pulsing through my body.

"I have to wear you out, doll face. Best way to bring you down faster."

I don't know what the fuck he's talking about. *Bring me down?* I feel fantastic.

He grabs my legs, bending my knees, and shoves them into my chest. "HAIDYN." I gasp, my body fighting harder, but he's got me pinned down just how I like it. I'm starting to sweat, and goose bumps cover my skin, making me shiver.

His cock pushes its way into my pussy, and he doesn't take it slow or allow me to accommodate his size. He throws my legs over his shoulders, bends down, and places his lips back on mine, then begins to fuck me.

Even though my eyes are closed, I see flashes of light in all different colors as I devour his lips.

He pulls away again, and my eyes spring open, glaring up at him. "Count for me, beautiful."

"Count what...?" The vibrator gets more intense, and my breath catches once more as his pierced cock thrusts into my pussy.

"That's it, Charlotte." His eyes search mine, and my back bows off the bed.

My mouth opens, but nothing comes out when I try to scream. Instead, Haidyn shoves three fingers into my mouth, making me gag. I think he's going to remove them, but he holds them there instead and uses them to pull my head down so I have to look up at him as I come. Spit flies from my mouth, and my nose runs.

"Good girl." He removes his fingers and slaps my cheek. My pussy clenches around him, and he does it again.

"Haidyn..." *Gasp.* "Please." I yank on the rope, hoping to touch him.

"Again." He places his hand over my mouth this time. "Eyes on me," he growls, his thrusts picking up once more and I blink rapidly to clear the tears in my eyes so he can come into focus.

His cock hits just the right spot while the vibrator in my ass remains on high. I'm gasping for breath through my nose when another wave hits me, and it feels like a brick wall falls on top of my body, weighing me down.

When he removes his hand from my face, I part my lips and gasp.

"That's it, doll face. You're being such a good girl for me," he praises me, and I whimper, my body starting to feel more tired than energized.

"Nooo." My voice is rough, and my mind is starting to get foggy. I want that high. It was glorious. Like I'm floating up above the world looking down over an endless ocean of pretty blue water.

"Yes, beautiful. Give me another."

The sound of his voice has the image disappearing. "Hai—"

His hand slaps over my mouth once more, and this time, he also covers my nose, taking away my air. My eyes widen, and I try to shake his hand off, but his fingers dig into my cheeks, latching on.

He lowers his face to mine, "I'm wearing you out, beautiful." His blue eyes are soft as they search mine. "When it wears off, you'll pass out."

Panic grips my chest when I try to suck in a breath but can't.

"Do you trust me?" he asks.

I nod the best I can. Blinking, my vision clears, and I feel fresh tears fall from the corner of my eyes. My arms pull on the rope, but I'm losing my fight. Quickly.

"I'm going to make it better, doll face," he assures me. Then his soft eyes turn hard, and his thrusts turn more forceful. "You're okay. It's going to be okay."

I shake my head, arch my neck, and try to buck him off, but nothing works. A burning sensation begins in my throat, and my body convulses under him as my pussy clenches his dick. A rush like no other flows through my veins, and it feels like the life was just sucked out of me as my heavy eyes fall closed. I hear him say *good girl* one last time before everything goes black.

Chapter 73

Haidyn

I stand in her bedroom, my arms crossed over my chest, looking at her passed out in the bed while Gavin checks her over.

"Everything sounds good." He turns to look at me. "She'll be okay."

I run a hand down my face. *Fucking exhausted.* "Thank you for making the trip."

"Of course." He walks over to me and slaps me on the shoulder. "You did the right thing." I told him everything that happened from when I walked into her door to fucking her while taking her breath away. She's been out for over an hour now.

But I don't feel like I did the right thing. First, I stabbed her in the chest with adrenaline, and then I forced her to pass out. Usually, we'd both be into that. But neither of us were. I didn't want to hurt her. Not like that. Not at all. I'm in love with her. She's my wife. That's not supposed to mean something in our world, but it does to me.

I walk him out and close the house up behind him. Entering the kitchen, I pick up the spilled wine and broken glass, cleaning everything up for her. After taking out her trash, I pick up my phone off the counter and pull up the contact I want. I stare at it for a few seconds, trying to calm my racing heart. Fuck, I hate this bitch so goddamn much. But this has to be done.

Hitting call, I place the cell to my ear and pace Charlotte's kitchen.

"Hello, Haidyn." The woman answers on the first ring. "I knew you'd come around eventually."

"I want your word," I demand, ignoring her statement. This is what she wanted.

Her laughter makes the hairs on the back of my neck rise.

"Give me your fucking word!" I bark, not in the mood for her bullshit games right now.

She clears her throat. "You're not in any position to..."

"You want me? Then you fucking promise me that you don't touch her!" I know what's coming. And I'm willing to do what she wants as long as it guarantees my wife is safe.

"You have my word," she states. "Annabelle won't be touched."

I hang up and slam the phone down onto the counter. I was never meant to live a long life. That's why I never understood why Saint wanted marriage and kids. It's something he'll leave behind for others to take care of. And I would trust only a handful of people to care for Charlotte. And when the time comes, I'll have to make that last call to ensure her safety.

♠

I'M STILL IN THE KITCHEN WHEN I LOOK UP AND SEE HER entering. "Good evening, doll face." I give her a big smile, glad to see her up and walking around.

She looks up at me through her wild dark hair that falls over her shoulder and down the front of her bare chest. Her bloodshot eyes are hard, and her face tight.

I go over to the kitchen table and pull out a seat for her. She sits and buries her face in her hands. Putting some food on a plate, I place it in front of her. "Eat up."

"Not hungry," she groans.

Coming down from an adrenaline shot can be rough. Especially after what she was originally given to knock her out. Her body needs time to heal. Lots of rest. "How do you feel?" I ask, reaching out and touching her forehead.

She pushes my hand away and demands, "What the hell happened, Haidyn?"

I sigh, rubbing a hand over the back of my neck. I've been waiting very impatiently for her to wake up but also dreading it knowing she'd want an explanation. "What do you remember?"

"Don't do that." She shakes her head, her voice sounding exasperated. "Only fill in what you think I deserve to know."

"Charlotte..."

"This is my fucking life!" she shouts. Jumping up from her chair, she picks up the plate and throws it across the room. It hits the floor and shatters; the food goes flying across the tile and splatters against parts of the wall. Taking a deep breath, she pushes her wild hair from her face and sits back down. Her tired eyes meet mine. "I came home and there was a glass of wine on the counter." She nods to the island before bowing her head once again. "I thought it was you. That you had beat me home and had it out and ready for me. I downed it. There were two Lords here..." She pauses, and I frown. *Two?* I only saw one when I arrived. "Next thing I knew, I was lying on the floor thinking I was dying. Then I woke up, naked and tied to my bed. You fucked me, and I passed out." Her eyes meet mine again and there's a challenge in them that I wish I could ignore. "So you tell me, Haidyn...what did I miss?"

I pull out a chair and sit across from her. Out of range of her fist and I made sure to hide all of her knives and the gun I found hidden in a drawer. If she kills me, I can't protect her. "I found you on the kitchen floor. I thought you were dead but that's how you're supposed to appear." Her eyes narrow, not understanding, but I continue. "I called Gavin, and he brought me adrenaline to bring you back..."

"Bring me back from where?" she demands, not second-guessing what I'm saying. Why would she? She's proven that she trusts me with her life. My wife doesn't expect me to lie to her, but I can't tell her everything that took place while she was out. Because then I'd have to explain who was here and what I had to do in order to save her.

"You were given a drug that slows your heart rate to the point where it makes you appear dead. The only way to bring you back is adrenaline."

"How do you know that?" she asks.

"Because I recently needed to appear dead."

CHARLOTTE

"THOSE FOUR DAYS... THINKING YOU WERE DEAD, AND THEN YOU were alive."

Ashtyn's words come to mind when she stood in the hallway at Carnage and told my husband she loved him too. "Let me guess, you did it for Ashtyn? Your *baby girl*." I roll my eyes. "Why am I not surprised?"

He frowns at me, and I shake my head. Pushing my chair back, I get to my feet and sway a little. He jumps from his to come to my aid, and I push him back. "I don't need your help."

"Charlotte—"

"Did you take that bullet for her too?" I joke but his silence makes my stomach drop. "Why?" I demand. "Why did you risk so much for her? She wasn't yours."

He looks away from me, jaw sharpening.

I hate how much he cares for her. I know I'm not supposed to. That it's okay for them to have a past, but I've only ever belonged to him. It's not fair that another woman was supposed to be his. "If you want her, then go get her." I go to storm out of the kitchen, but he grabs my arm and spins me around, forcing me to face him. My hands come up, and I try to push him away, but I'm still too weak.

"I don't want her." He reassures me, holding me in place.

"Don't touch me," I snap.

"Calm down, doll face," he growls. "You just woke up and still need to take it easy."

Tears sting my eyes, and I don't know if I want to kill him or kiss him.

"It's okay." He reaches up and pushes my hair behind my ear. I drop my face to hide, but he cups my chin and forces it up so his eyes can meet mine. "I'm here with you. I married you. You're the one I want."

"I...I don't know what's wrong with me," I admit softly.

He sighs. "You've been through a lot, Annabelle." I flinch at the use of my real name. He said it softly, almost as if he feels sorry for me. "It's going to take a toll on you. But you will be okay. It's all going to be okay."

The way he says it has me questioning everything, but I can't seem to make my lips work. I'm just tired. So instead of fighting him, I push myself into his muscular body and wrap my arms around his chest, burying my face into his shirt and inhaling his scent. It's become my home. My safe place.

He pushes me away, and my stomach sinks, reminding myself that I'm not Ashtyn. I'm just some whore forced to marry him. But he reaches down and slides an arm underneath the back of my knees and picks me up, cradling me to him. I swallow the knot in my throat as he carries me back to my bed.

When he lays me down, I force myself to release him, thinking he's going to leave me, but he crawls into bed next to me and pulls me against him. I allow my eyes to fall closed as he holds me and kisses my forehead while his voice reassures me that I'm his. As if words mean something in our world.

Chapter 74

Haidyn

She cries herself to sleep in my arms. The clock is ticking, and the hourglass is running out of sand. Closing in on the time I have left with my wife. I wish I could rewind our past. I'd change so many things about our relationship...or lack thereof. But isn't that what life is all about? You live and learn.

I've learned that it's okay to love someone no matter how little time you get with them.

I kiss her forehead, my lips lingering for a few seconds, feeling how warm she is. She'll start to feel better by morning. That will give me one more day with her, and then she'll live a full life without me. But at least she'll be alive and well taken care of.

Closing my eyes, I try to dream of the future we could have had if we were born into a different life—where our kids play in the backyard with their puppy while my wife sits on my lap on the back porch with my arms wrapped around her and a smile on her face. I've never been one to dream, but she makes me believe it's possible. Some dreams feel real but so do nightmares. What you see in the dark will come to light. So instead of opening my eyes, I choose to keep them closed and fall into a depth that not even the devil could pull me out of.

♠

My eyes spring open, and I sit up when I see I'm alone in her bed. "Charlotte?" I shout, my heart instantly racing. "Charlotte?"

"What?"

I look over to see her standing in the doorway of her bathroom, her hair wet and a smile on her face.

"Fuck, doll face." I let out a long breath. "Give me a heart attack." I drop back down on the mattress.

She walks over to the bed and jumps onto it, straddling my hips. She's got a naughty smile on her face and a towel tucked underneath her arms.

I reach up and yank it free, tossing it away. Throwing her head back, she laughs. "I didn't want to wake you." Her face goes serious for a second, and she whispers, "You look so peaceful when you're asleep."

"How do you feel?" I ignore what she just said.

"Much better." She drops her eyes to my bare chest as her fingers lightly trace the Lords crest and then the 666 brand we got during training. Then they move to my bullet wound. Her eyes meet mine, and I see the apprehension in them. She has something on her mind, and she's going to tell me. "Let's run away together."

There it is, and it makes me smile. "We can't." I refuse to give her a life like Adam has. Once you start running, you can never stop.

Rolling her eyes, she sighs heavily. "You said that it was up to me how long I'm with you. That I got to choose."

"I did," I agree, remembering that time in her kitchen. It feels like years ago that I decided she'd be mine.

She holds up her left hand, showing me her sapphire wedding ring. Then I meet her stare as she speaks. "I choose to be with you forever."

I want to remind her that she didn't choose me, but instead, I sit up, cupping her face, and speak. "To some, forever is only a matter of seconds." Then I press my lips to hers, ending the conversation. My mind is made up. I've failed at protecting everyone who had ever meant anything to me. I won't make the same mistake with Charlotte. My wife deserves better. The love of my life deserves the world, even if that means I'm no longer part of hers.

She opens her mouth and wraps her arms around my neck. I slide my hands into her hair, tightening my fingers into the silky strands. She moans into my mouth.

My time with her is limited, but I consider myself lucky. Not everyone knows when they'll leave this world. I do, and I'm going to spend every second buried inside her. Savoring her scent, the feel of her soft touch, the sound of her voice. So when I'm locked in a cage surrounded by nothing but darkness and silence, I'll have her on my mind. I'll have memories to remind me that I was once a man who loved a woman who deserved better. They won't be able to take that away from me, and that's what I call a win.

CHARLOTTE

He's pulling away from me. I can't pinpoint what's going on, but I can feel it. A woman's intuition is the only thing that never fails her. When I woke up in his arms, I had this sickening feeling in my stomach. I got out of bed and made it to the bathroom just in time to vomit. I tried to tell myself that it was just the past twenty-four hours that finally caught up with me, but that was a lie.

I brushed my teeth and took a shower, trying to wash away everything and start fresh. I had just got out when I heard him calling my name. It just solidified that something is coming. If he's worried, then I need to be terrified.

I dig my fingers into his hair, and he moans into my mouth. Fuck, I'm desperate for him. My hips start to rock in his lap, and he pulls my lips from his with his hands in my hair. His lips trail along my jawline and to my neck. He sinks his teeth into my sensitive skin, and I shiver, my pussy clenching as I rock my hips. "Please?" I beg shamelessly.

"Use your words, doll face," he orders. His hand drops to my ass, and he gives it a hard smack.

I groan, needing more. "Please fuck me." My voice is as needy as my body. "I'm your whore, Haidyn. Use me however you want."

"Fuck," he growls. His free hand drops to my neck, and I look up at the ceiling, giving him full access. He can choke me out or bite me. I've become a woman who will accept whatever he decides to do to me.

A Lady gives her Lord whatever he wants. "I'm yours," I say breathlessly, hoping he understands I mean more than just sex.

"Yes, you fucking are, doll face." His lips trail along my jaw, and I roll my head to capture them. Needing to feel them on mine and he takes my breath away.

♠

I FINISH USING THE RESTROOM AND ENTER THE ADJOINING primary suite to see he's gone. "Haidyn?" I call out. He doesn't answer, so I grab his T-shirt from my floor and pull it on.

Exiting my room, I enter the living room to find him standing with his back to me staring out the floor-to-ceiling windows showcasing my backyard. My view isn't nearly as gorgeous as the one he has at his place, but it's still pretty. I frown, seeing he's put his jeans on.

Walking past my coffee table, I notice that my cell phone is on it, and I make a mental note to plug it in. I'm sure it's dead. "What are you doing?" I come up behind him and wrap my arms around his waist, pressing the side of my head into his bare back, inhaling his scent. I try to tell myself that I'm just overreacting, but I know something is coming, and I can't stop it.

He turns around in my arms, and I look up as he gently brushes his knuckles along my cheek, pushing my hair from my face. I smile up at him, but he doesn't return it. Mine falls, and a sickening feeling returns to my stomach.

Reaching down, he picks up my left hand and runs his thumb over my wedding ring. That feeling intensifies, making me swallow nervously. "Do you regret it?" I whisper.

His silence makes my stomach drop. He steps into me, cupping my face with both of his warm hands and forces me to look up at him through my watery eyes. "I don't regret marrying you, Charlotte. What I regret is why you married me."

I sniff. I've fallen in love with this man, and the thought of him deciding he no longer wants me makes it hard to breathe. "What do you mean?"

"You only married me because you felt you had no choice." He sighs.

I place my hands on his muscular chest and feel his steady heartbeat. "You didn't marry me because you loved me." I give a soft laugh to try to lighten the mood.

He doesn't say anything about that. Instead, his eyes search mine, and I grab his hand and begin to pull him to the bedroom. "Come on." I try to change the subject. "Lets go to bed. I'm tired."

Chapter 75

Haidyn

She's passed out and tucked into my side. I have one arm under her neck while the other sits on my bare chest. I stare up at the ceiling as the sun slowly rises, illuminating her bedroom. Charlotte finally fell asleep about an hour ago.

I should have let her sleep sooner, but I couldn't stop. I needed her. And like the good girl she is, she allowed me to take whatever I wanted. It'll never be enough, but all good things must come to an end. And my time is up.

Removing my arm out from underneath her, I slide out of bed and look over her. She didn't move. The poor thing is exhausted. I want her to remember me. The me who loved her. Not the me who blackmailed and treated her like shit. Not the me who is about to leave her as if she never meant anything to me.

The alarm on my phone begins to buzz, and I pick it up off the nightstand, turning it off. It was set just in case I managed to fall asleep. I didn't. I'll have plenty of time to do that for the rest of my life. However long that may be.

By the clock on my phone, I have an hour to get to where I need to be. I bend down, reaching up underneath the bed, grabbing what I need and unzip my bag. I remove the contents and begin to attach them to each corner post of the headboard.

Then I sit down on the bed next to her. Gently, I brush her dark hair from her face before pushing her onto her back. She lets out a soft moan, and I can only pray that she's dreaming of me.

First, I grab the pillows and toss them to the floor. I need everything out of my way for what I have planned. Grabbing her right arm, I pull it to the corner post of the bed, and I begin with a single column tie around her tiny wrist before I secure it with a Burlington bowline. She can pull on it all she wants, and it won't collapse. Then I walk around the bed and do the same with her left arm.

"Haidyn," she whispers, arching her neck, but her eyes remain shut. She gently pulls on her outstretched arms that are secured to each corner post of the headboard.

"You're going to be fine, doll face," I tell her, moving to the end of the bed. I grab her ankles, straightening her legs, stretching her arms a little farther. I need it to be as tight as possible. Otherwise, she's going to hurt herself.

Crossing her ankles, I secure the third piece of rope around them, tying her legs closed. Then I crouch down and secure it to the bottom of the bed.

"Wh-at?" Her heavy eyes open, and she tries to move her arms but realizes she's tied down. A soft smile appears on her face. "Haidyn, I can't...I'm too tired."

She thinks I'm going to fuck her again. If only I was that lucky. Walking back over to the side of the bed, I sit down next to her and cup her face. Her pretty blue eyes blink as the sun shines through the windows.

"Close your eyes, doll face. Go back to sleep." Just then, my cell vibrates once more, and I realize I pushed snooze on the alarm instead of turning it off.

"Haidyn?" She tries to sit up, sounding more awake now. She knows our time is up. I should have left before she woke, but I'm selfish and needed more time with her. "What are you...? Untie me, Haidyn," she demands.

"I'm sorry, doll face. But that's not going to happen." I get up off the bed.

"HAIDYN!" Her voice rises, and she yanks on the rope. I can see the panic in her big eyes. "Untie me, Haidyn. Right now."

"Charlotte—"

"Please, Haidyn...don't do this."

When I say nothing, she arches her back and screams at the top of her lungs. She's yanking so hard on the rope that the bed shakes.

"Calm down, Charlotte." I cup her tear-streaked face. "Shh, you're okay." She tries to shake her head, but I hold it in place. "You're going to be okay."

"Nnnnoooo." She sobs and sniffs, taking a deep breath. "Please..." She licks her lips. "Please untie me."

"I can't," I say softly.

Fresh tears fill her eyes, and her lips tremble. "Please," she cries desperately, and my chest tightens at leaving her here like this.

"Okay, doll face. Okay," I say, and she closes her eyes tightly. "Just breathe. Deep breaths." I need her to calm down.

"Untie me..." She looks up at her wrist while yanking on it.

"Okay. Just calm down. Can you do that for me?"

She nods quickly. "Yeah." She lets out a long breath and repeats, "Yeah."

I turn and open her nightstand, removing the two things that I need. "I'm sorry," I say because I didn't want to do this. "You've left me with no choice." I rip off three pieces of the duct tape and place the tip of them on the edge.

"HAIDYN!" she screams, arching her back. Tears instantly fill her eyes, and she yanks so hard on the rope that the bed shakes. "You promised!" She begins to cry again. "Please don't leave me...don't do this...."

I shove the wadded-up thong into her mouth, and she arches her neck, trying to get her face away from my hold. I slap my hands over her full mouth while my free hand grabs one piece at a time, securing them on her mouth. I use more pieces than I normally would because her face is wet. I'm hoping between all of them, they'll stick.

Her gagged sobs start to fill the room. Getting up off the bed, I pick up my cell to make a call. Placing it on speakerphone, I set it on the bed next to her and grab my jeans off the floor to remove my pocketknife while it rings for the second time.

"Hello?" a familiar voice answers.

"Hey," I say in greeting. She screams into her gag, but it's too muffled that even he can't hear it.

"What's up, man? Where the fuck are you? I tried calling you last night..."

"I was at Charlotte's," I answer. No reason to lie. He'll figure it out anyway. "I need a favor," I say, moving this conversation along. I have somewhere to be. When I came up with this idea, I knew that I couldn't leave her here like this for very long. I needed someone to come get her and take care of her like I would.

"Name it," Kashton tells me.

I take the knife and place it on my skin at the back of my neck and press the blade into it, feeling the skin cut and the warm blood run down my back as her screams grow louder. "I need you to come get Charlotte. She's at her house."

"And where are you?" Kashton asks.

"I have somewhere to be," I answer, squeezing the skin until I feel the tracking device pop out. I had it replaced but can't take the chance of them looking for me. That will put her in jeopardy. I made a deal, and I will honor it.

"Haidyn—"

"Tell Saint I'm sorry." I interrupt whatever he was about to ask.

"What the fuck is going on, Haidyn?" Saint barks, letting me know that Kashton also has me on speakerphone, and he was listening in.

"Nothing," I lie as my eyes drop to a sobbing Charlotte while she thrashes on the bed, tears falling out of the corner of her eyes. "I just need you to understand that I'm sorry for what I did." If anyone took my wife away from me, I'd lose my mind. It took me falling in love with Charlotte to see that I only hurt him. I'm glad that he was able to find his way back to her.

"Haidyn," Saint snaps.

"Charlotte is at her house. I'll send you the address." I end the phone call and send them the information they need. Then I pull up another number and send one last text before I delete it along with the text that has the address I received so no one can read them before placing it on the nightstand right next to hers. I made sure to wipe out all calls and messages last night so they wouldn't be able to find anything on my phone. I know my brothers, and they will dig through it for any hints. There will be none.

Then I catch sight of my wedding ring. I take it off and turn to the bed. I cup her tear-streaked face and lean over her trembling body. "Just know that it was real for me, and I hope that one day you can forgive me, beautiful."

She blinks, her nostrils flaring as she breathes deeply through them.

My thumbs rub the tears away, but they're falling too fast to keep up with them. "In a world where it's either you or me...I'll always choose you, doll face."

Sniffling, she shakes her head, remembering the words she once said to me. I nod. "Yes, it'll always be you. I love you," I say, leaning down and giving her forehead a soft kiss, ignoring her sob. "Remember that, Charlotte."

Then I turn, place my ring next to my cell, and give her my back. I get dressed before walking out of her house, listening to her muffled screams. Jumping onto my motorcycle, I rev the engine and drive to my destination. I received the text last night where I needed to be just as he said I would.

Pulling into the unfamiliar private airport, I shut off my bike and get off when I see the jet on the tarmac. It can only be here for one reason—me.

I make my way up the stairs and board the plane. A woman sits in a white leather seat, one leg crossed over the other.

"Haidyn." She smiles, getting to her eight-inch heels. "It's been too long." Her eyes drop to my combat boots and slowly run up my body before they meet mine. "Boys?" she calls out, and four men appear from a sliding glass door behind her wearing cloaks and masks. "Strip him."

They step forward, and I reach above my head, grabbing the back of my T-shirt. I lift it over my head and toss it to the side before I undo my belt, unzip my jeans, and shove them down my legs along with my boxers. I know the rules. *How could I forget them?*

I stand naked in front of her and the four men. She arches a brow, her eyes on my soft cock. She licks her lips. "It'll be like old times, baby." She steps into me, reaching out, and her hand lands on my bare chest. Her blue eyes lift to meet mine; she's no longer wearing her green contacts. "Did you enjoy her?"

I don't answer. I'd rather give her silence because I know how much she hates that.

She steps back and lets out a frustrated sigh, proving my point. "Take him to the back and put him in the cage." Her lips pull back into a nasty smirk that I know all too well. "It's time to go home, Haidyn."

CHARLOTTE

THE RINGING IS LIKE NAILS ON A CHALKBOARD. HAIDYN'S PHONE continues to go off where he set it on the nightstand.

"Haidyn?" a voice shouts from inside my house.

I lift my head the best I can and scream into the tape, yanking on the ropes that tie me down. I can't feel my hands anymore. I've managed to pull the rope tighter with my fight.

"Haidyn?" My bedroom door is kicked open, the wood splintering before hitting the interior wall and I close my eyes as I see Kashton and Saint enter. "Jesus Christ," Saint hisses.

"Hang on, Charlotte," Kashton tells me as they cut me loose.

I don't even care that I'm naked. Or embarrassed that I'm tied up. All I care about is Haidyn. We've lost time. How long ago did he leave? It felt like I've been lying here for hours. How far away is he by now? I knew this was going to happen. I should have done something when I had the chance. Now it may be too late.

The tape is ripped from my face and the thong yanked from my mouth. Drool falls from my lips as I'm pulled to a sitting position. Saint's hands grip my soaked face. "Where the fuck is Haidyn?" he demands. "What happened?"

"I...don't know," I rasp through a sob. My voice is already hoarse from screaming into my gag. I feel like I'm going to be sick.

"Fuck!" Kashton shouts.

"What?" Saint looks over at him.

"Haidyn's tracker." Kashton holds up the bloody device before throwing it to the floor. Then he picks up his wedding ring. "What... what the fuck is going on?"

"Start from the beginning." Saint looks at me.

I open my mouth, but I can't speak. Instead, the bile starts to rise, and I scramble off my bed and fall to all fours on the floor.

"Shit," Saint hisses over me.

I'm too weak to even stand. After being drugged, the two-day fuck-fest and then Haidyn leaving me tied to a bed for who the hell knows how long, my body is exhausted. A burning sensation intensifies deep in my chest. "I'm…going…"

"Let me help you," he says, knowing what I'm trying to say, and ushers me into the bathroom. I fall to my knees in front of the toilet, and he pulls my hair back for me while I throw up like I've been partying my ass off on a two-day bender instead of losing the love of my life.

Just know that it was real for me, and I hope that one day you can forgive me, beautiful.

Sitting back on my heels, Saint reaches over and flushes it for me. "You okay?"

I nod, wiping the back of my hand across my lips, and he helps me to stand. He remains by my side while I take a sip of water from the sink and rinse my mouth with mouthwash. Then we return to my bedroom where Kashton waits for us.

Saint sits me on the edge of the bed, and my watery eyes look over the ropes that they cut to get me free.

He left me. I never thought that Haidyn would do that.

Saint begins to hand me my clothes, and I take a calming breath, trying to stop the tears. If anyone can help Haidyn, it's his brothers. I begin to tell them everything I remember and what Haidyn had told me happened that filled in the missing spots.

"Who were the Lords that were in your house?" Saint demands.

"I don't know. I never saw their faces."

Saint looks at Kashton, probably trying to decide whether they believe me.

"Obviously, whoever it is has to be connected to her."

The way Kashton says *her,* makes my chest tighten. "I tried to get him to stay." A fresh tear runs down my cheek. I love him. I would have done anything for him except give him up. Except live a life without him. Didn't I prove that to him when the Lords made me choose between me and him? Haidyn knew that I thought it was real. That I chose him.

"Come on." Saint grabs my underwear that he had tossed on the bed next to me and crouches down to slide them onto my legs. He pulls me to stand, yanking them up. I fall back down onto the bed and allow him to dress me.

I'm numb and heartbroken. How can Haidyn do this to me? To us? I didn't even want him in my life, and now he's left me with a hole in my heart. Completely devastated. How do I function in life without him? I've become dependent on him for everything.

"Let's go," Kashton growls, already leaving my room.

It doesn't even matter where they're taking me. I have better luck seeing Haidyn again if I'm with them than being here alone. I'm the one he walked away from after all. I can't bring him back, but they can drag him back to me. Then I'll show him how fucking crazy a woman in love can be because I'll never let him out of my sight again.

Saint pulls me to stand, then sweeps me up into his arms. I'm shaking, and that bile taste returns, but it's not as strong this time.

"Are you going to get sick again?" he asks as if he knows.

"I...I don't know."

"Just let me know and I'll pull over," Saint assures me.

Kashton opens the back door to a black Escalade for Saint, and he places me into the SUV. He then takes the driver's seat while Kashton gets in the passenger seat.

I try to calm my breathing. If anyone can find the man I love, it's them. I rub my sore wrists. They've already started to bruise.

"What are you doing?" Saint asks Kashton.

"I'm going through his cell. There has to be someone in here who knows something."

"Adam," Saint states, giving him a quick look before driving onto the highway. "Look for Adam in his contacts."

Kashton shakes his head after a second. "There's no Adam, but hang on..." He quickly scans through them. "There's a contact under Ghost."

"Give it a try." Saint shrugs. "Can't fucking hurt."

He places the call on speakerphone and holds it out so they can both hear it ring. It stops on the second ring before a man's voice fills the SUV. "Hey, man—"

"Adam?" Saint barks.

Silence comes over the line.

"Listen, we don't have time for this shit." Saint goes on. "We need help finding Haidyn."

"What do you mean finding him?" the familiar voice on the phone asks, confirming what I already knew.

"He's left," Kashton hisses. "Cut out his tracker and took off. About an hour ago."

An hour? It feels like so much longer than that. But still, he can get far within an hour. Especially if he took the Spade brother's private jet. Maybe they can track that if he's on it.

"Fuck," Adam shouts.

"We need your help." Saint growls, already impatient. "We're on our way to Carnage. How long until you can get there?"

He's silent for a long second before he speaks again. "I can't..."

"This is for Haidyn!" Saint snaps. "Come and help us. No questions asked. Once we find him, you leave like last time." It's more of a statement rather than a question.

Saint gives Kashton a quick look, who is staring out his passenger side window.

"Kashton?" Adam questions.

"Yeah," he finally speaks, voice rough. "After we find him, you can leave. Again. No questions asked."

"I can be there in twenty minutes." The call ends.

I sink into the back seat, closing my eyes and trying not to lose my mind. He left me. I mean, I shouldn't be all that surprised, right? I was just hoping that I could change his mind last night. I thought I could will him to want to be with me, to stay with me, but it wasn't enough. He ended up leaving me after all.

Why marry me if he never intended on being with me? To humiliate me? He told me he loved me. Was that true? Or just another lie.

"Is there anything else you remember?" Saint asks me.

So much about the past two days are a blur that I'm sure there is something... "Gavin," I say forgetting to tell them about that part.

"What about him?" Kash demands, turning in his seat to glare at me. I get it. I'm the enemy. I took their brother away from them. I'm the reason he left them…again.

"Haidyn told me that he had called him…Gavin brought him adrenaline to bring me back."

"Call him. Tell him to get his ass to Carnage. Now. Maybe he can fill in the spots that Charlotte can't remember," Saint orders Kashton.

Shhh...

Chapter 76

Charlotte

We pull up to the front of Carnage, and Kashton helps me out of the car. My legs are wobbly, and my body shakes. I'm not sure if it's from the fuck-fest last night, the sobbing, or the lack of sleep. But my knees go to give out and Kashton picks me up with an arm behind my knees and the other around my back.

I bury my face into his chest and try to stop crying. "We'll find him," he assures me, but I have my doubts. He could be anywhere by now.

When he's setting me down onto a couch, I open my eyes and see we're in their office. My eyes go straight to Haidyn's desk. My chest tightens at how vacant it looks. It's a haunting sight.

The door swings open, and I look over at the guy who enters. His eyes immediately meet mine, and my heart races.

"What do you know?" he demands, looking at Kashton and Saint.

I lower my eyes to the floor and cover my face with my hands, having to remind myself to breathe.

"Not much," Saint answers. "She filled us in that she was drugged. Seems she was given the same drug that *you* gave Haidyn when he pretended to die. And Gavin brought her back with adrenaline. She said he didn't give her much information. He called Kash to go get her. We found her tied to her bed and him gone."

Adam looks over at Haidyn's desk and then back to me. "I know who has him, but I don't know *where* they have him."

"Who the fuck is it?" Kashton snaps.

Adam's eyes meet mine as he says, "Bella Marie Costello."

The room falls silent—Kashton and Saint both go stiff where they stand. I find myself getting to my shaking legs. "No," I whisper, shaking my head. "That's not possible."

Saint is the one who whirls around and glares at me. "You know her?"

I swallow the knot that forms in my throat. "She's my mother." *Costello is her maiden name.*

"WHAT?" Kash shouts, making me flinch. Before I can blink, he's in front of me, and he's got my back on the couch, staring up at him with his hands around my throat, cutting off my air. "What the fuck do you mean she's your mother?" He's shouting in my face.

"Get off her!" His hands are removed from my neck, and I roll off the side of the couch onto the floor where I cough and curl into a ball.

The door opens. "Saint..." I close my eyes at the sound of Ashtyn's voice. "What's going on?" she asks, obviously not up to speed on the situation.

They all ignore her.

"Bella is Isabella—"

"I know who she is." Adam interrupts Saint. "But you can't hurt Charlotte."

"Saint?" Ashtyn's voice has gone from curiosity to concern, yet they still ignore her.

"We'll do whatever the fuck we want with her," Kashton growls, pushing Adam off him. "You weren't here!" he screams in his face. "Her mother..."

"Haidyn married her. Charlotte is his wife," Adam snaps as I sit up and push my back into the front of the couch, pulling my knees to my chest. That feeling of nausea has returned tenfold, and I feel everyone's eyes now on me. Including Ashtyn. I guess she's kept that to herself by how surprised Kash and Saint are because I had told her I was Haidyn's wife out of spite. Because I felt threatened. Now it seems so silly.

Both of their eyes drop to my left hand, and they notice my ring for the first time. Kashton digs into his pocket and pulls out Haidyn's ring that he had left on my nightstand. I didn't know Kashton brought it with him.

"You have to be fucking kidding me," Kashton growls. "And let me guess, you're her guardian?"

"No. You are," Adam answers, and Kashton's face tightens.

"What's a guardian?" I ask, panic bubbling in my chest. Kashton obviously wants me dead, so him being a *guardian* over me doesn't sound like anything good. But just like Ashtyn, everyone ignores me.

Saint turns and punches the wall, making Ashtyn take a step back, and I lower my forehead to my bent knees. My hope that we'll find Haidyn is dwindling because if they're mad at him for marrying me, they might not care to find him. Is that why he married me? Did it have to do with my mother? How does he know my mom? I don't understand how they're connected.

The door opens once more, and I look up to see Gavin enter. He squares his shoulders, and I wonder if he can feel the tension in the room. "You wanted to see me?" he questions.

Saint is pacing, and Kashton is glaring at me. It's Adam who speaks. "What did Haidyn tell you?"

"Nothing."

"Bullshit!" Saint snaps and points at me. "He called you to give Charlotte adrenaline. Why?"

Gavin frowns. "I didn't give her adrenaline. Haidyn had already given it to her before I arrived, so he wanted me to check her out. He informed me that when he arrived at her house, she was lying unconscious on the kitchen floor. She had been given a drug to make her appear dead, and he administered the adrenaline himself. I checked her over, and she was well. Unconscious but would make a full recovery."

A silence falls over the office again. I swallow the taste of vomit and whisper, "He lied to me."

Saint snorts as if that's the least of my problems. Kashton rolls his eyes, and the man who I know as Adam looks at me with sympathy. Ashtyn stares at her twin brother with a look of confusion and surprise to see him in the same room as us. No one is on the same page right now. So many secrets and lies between all of us.

"I'm sure there's several things he's lied to you about," Saint says coldly. His eyes drop to the ring on my finger before they meet mine again.

"Saint," Adam snaps, his green eyes hardening.

Saint ignores him and walks over to the couch. I push my back into the front as he places his fists on either side of the cushions against my back, leaning over and caging me in. His cold dark green eyes search mine as he says, "Did Haidyn tell you that he killed your father?"

I shake my head. *What?* He must be mistaken. "No—"

"We were all on his yacht that night..."

"Stop!" Adam yanks him away from me, but he pulls himself from Adam's hold. "Let it go, Saint," he barks.

"Let it go?" He snorts. "This bitch's mother..."

"This isn't about her or her mother. This is about Haidyn," Adam shouts, interrupting him. "Charlotte is his wife." Adam's soft eyes meet my watery ones. "He's in love with her. He gave himself up for her." Then he points at Ashtyn who stands with her back to the wall. "He gave himself up for your wife. For you." He jabs a finger into Saint's chest. "And you." He glares at a pissed-off Kashton. "All of us. You called me and here I am. Now shut the fuck up and help me come up with a plan to get our brother back!"

♠

I SIT ON THE FLOOR STARING AT HAIDYN'S DESK. A SMALL hourglass sits on the surface. All the sand fills the bottom. If I had any energy, I'd break it. I'd get up, throw it against the wall, and watch it shatter like my fucking soul.

I wish I could stop time like that. Make the world halt while we look for him, but it doesn't work that way. Instead, the seconds slip through our fingers like sand. Every minute he's gone is another we can't get back.

Saint, Kashton, and Adam have been fighting for I don't know how long now. Ashtyn hasn't moved from the wall that she clings to. Gavin hasn't spoken since he revealed the truth of what happened.

"What about her?" Kashton says over the ringing in my ears.

"What about Charlotte?" Adam barks.

"How do we know that she's not part of this?"

"N-o." My voice cracks. I would never. "I chose him over the Lords," I add as everyone glares at me. Mine find Adam's. "Ask him.

He'll tell you." Adam was at the house; I didn't tell him the specifics, but I'm sure Haidyn did. They're close.

"What the fuck is she talking about?" Saint demands, turning to face him.

Adam runs a hand through his hair and sighs. His silence makes me nervous, and I get to my feet. "The Lords wanted me to hand Haidyn over to them. And I didn't," I rush out.

"You're working for the Lords?" Kashton growls.

Shit! "No. Adam, tell them...please." I beg him. He has to know that I'd never hurt my husband.

"It's a long story," Adam says, and I take a step back when Saint turns to face me.

"Last time an outsider was in Carnage, they had a bomb inside of them. I don't put anything past her bitch of a mother. I say we cut her open."

"What?" I shriek. "No. I'd never—"

"Why waste such a pretty thing?" Kashton interrupts me. "Let's search her." His eyes drop to my shoes and then run up over my body, making my panic rise even more. "Strip her naked and hold her down. I'll look."

I'd beg them not to if I could speak. I can't even catch my breath right now.

"What the fuck, Kash?" Ashtyn pushes off the wall to step forward. "Absolutely not. Saint..." She looks at him, and his hard eyes meet hers. "No—"

"She's not a threat!" Adam shouts, placing his hands out and moving to stand in front of me. I reach up and grip the back of his T-shirt, holding on for dear life. "You're not fucking touching her."

"Until she proves she's innocent, I'm with Kash," Saint states.

"I love him," I say defensively.

Saint snorts, and Adam turns around. Prying my hands from his shirt, he helps me to sit down on the couch.

"Her phone," Kashton announces.

My shoulders shake, knowing there's nothing on it that will prove my love for Haidyn because I have no proof that I didn't do this. All the emails I've been sent from the Lords were immediately deleted. There's nothing to prove my loyalty to him. The only things I have on my phone regarding Haidyn are the videos and pictures he would send me after he fucked me.

I'm about to say I don't even have my phone with me when Kashton pulls it out of his pocket. I guess he grabbed it when he picked up Haidyn's ring and phone.

I swallow the taste of vomit once again. Not only have I lost my husband but now I'm also going to be stripped naked, cavity searched, and thrown into a cage in their basement.

You can't reason with Lords. Once they make up their mind, you're just fucked. I stare at the floor silently while they go through my phone.

"Think I've found something," Kashton says.

"What is it?" Saint demands.

"Haidyn."

I jump up to my feet at Kashton's answer. A second later, Haidyn's voice fills the office. "Hey, doll face..."

"Haidyn?" I yank the phone from Kashton's hands and look at the screen to see it's a video. He's sitting on my couch, dressed in nothing but a pair of jeans. The phone is propped up against something on the coffee table.

I place my hand over my mouth to hold in my sob at the sight of him. This was last night...when I saw my phone on the coffee table when he stood in front of the floor-to-ceiling windows in my living room.

"This isn't how I wanted to tell you goodbye. But in our life, we rarely get what we want." A soft smile tugs at his lips. "You were my exception."

He bows his head, his right hand twirling his wedding ring around his finger as he looks at it. "I knew that you were too good for me the moment I first saw you. That I'd never live up to the man you'd deserve. So I let you go...but when you were placed back in my life, I couldn't stop myself." He looks back at the phone and gives a soft smile.

Back in his life?

"I've done a lot of unforgivable shit in my life, but the best thing I ever did was make you my wife. I wish I could have done it differently. You deserved so much more than what I gave you. I should have gotten down on one knee and begged you to spend the rest of your life with me. I should have told you how much you changed me. That you showed me what being alive truly felt like. I always felt like I was missing something...my life was boring. Same thing over and over. And then you walked into my life with that amazing smile and when I looked into your eyes—I saw a future that I never thought existed...not for a man like me, anyway."

A lump forms in my throat, and I blink to clear the tears from my eyes so I can see him on the screen.

"I knew you'd never give a man like me the chance at forever. So I forced your hand. I had to have Adam help me." I look up at Adam, and his green eyes are already on mine. Blinking the fresh tears away, I drop mine back to the phone. "Because I knew that'd be the only way I'd ever get you. And I just couldn't pass up the opportunity to be your husband." He looks away from the camera as if he can't look at me, and my chest tightens.

How dare he leave me this memory? Why break my heart twice? When I found him in the living room and asked if he regretted marrying me...he had just left me this video. He knew then exactly what he was going to do.

His blue eyes come back to the screen, meeting mine once again. "I'm sorry I couldn't give you the forever you deserved, doll face. But I promise I gave you all I had left to offer."

The knot grows in my throat, and I can't hold back the sob anymore as I remember what he said when I told him I chose to be with him forever. *To some, forever is only a matter of seconds.*

"Please know that I loved you more than anything in this world... and when I walk out this door, I'm leaving a piece of myself behind with you because nothing short of forever would have been enough." He smiles, and I try to catch my breath. "You'll be safe at Carnage and my brothers will protect you." He leans forward and picks up the phone before speaking. "I love you, Charlotte."

The screen goes black, and I fall to the floor. My knees no longer able to hold myself up and the room fills with the guy's voices, arguing back and forth as my trembling hands push play again.

HAIDYN

The screeching of the steel door has my heavy eyes opening. I was placed in a steel cage while on the plane. It seemed like a short flight. Too short to even require a plane ride. Once we landed, I was blindfolded and taken to an undisclosed location.

When it was removed, I was in a concrete room with no window. Locked inside a new cage as if I was in the basement at Carnage. But it doesn't feel like home. They put a needle in my neck, and when I woke up, I had an IV in my arm. I don't know what the fuck it is, but I feel like it's draining me of everything I have.

"Come on, Spade. She wants to see you." My arms are grabbed, and I'm pulled to a sitting position. Several of them yank me to my feet, and I groan. Fuck, I've never been so weak in my life.

They pull my arms behind my back and use handcuffs to secure them in place. Then I'm shoved forward. "Walk," one barks.

I follow one, while three trail me.

A set of double doors are open, and the guy in front of me comes to a stop once we're in the room. "On your knees," someone behind me commands.

I grind my teeth. "Fuck you—"

The back of my legs are hit, knocking me to my knees. The one in front of me turns around, grabs a chain on the floor, and hooks it to the thick metal collar around my neck. It pulls me forward, forcing me to arch my back.

"Hello, darling." I hear her sing.

"What the fuck do you want?" If I'm lucky, she'll leave me in that concrete room until I die.

Her laughter echoes through the large room before she enters from a door on the right. She comes to stand in front of me dressed in an all-black floor-length dress. It has a deep V showing off her massive tits. Her face is done up as if she's twenty-one and headed to the club to party her ass off. "You look like shit, Haidyn."

"What are you giving me?" I demand.

She grips my face, her long, pointy nails digging into my skin, and I try to pull away, but the chains are pulled tight, so it's pointless. "Some people pay a lot of money for what I'm giving you for free," she answers. "The Lords wanted me to give it to you and your brothers back when I was 'training' you guys, but I thought better of it. Now that I have you to myself..." She smiles. "Do you ever wonder how so many in the world live to be so old? How they're able to hold their 'positions' for so long? No illnesses, none die at a young age other than the occasional freak accident...or the Lords put a hit out on them?"

"You're drugging me to live longer?" I ask skeptically.

I mean, I wouldn't be surprised that such a drug exists because I have had those thoughts before. People in power like to remain in power. It's why we have so many older Lords all around the world.

"I had high hopes for you, Haidyn. I'm giving you a gift."

I snort, and she lets go of my face.

"In fact, I still do." She falls down into a chair in front of me. "I knew you wouldn't be able to resist a pretty face." My heart accelerates at the mention of my wife. "Hudson?" she calls out, and a man walks into the darkly lit room. My eyes narrow on him, knowing exactly who he is. I remember him from Charlotte's kitchen when I found her lying on the floor thinking she was dead.

Walking over to her, he says, "Yes, Mommy?"

I pull my lip back at his pet name for her. I'm not one to kink shame because I like some fucked-up shit, but the fact that he's calling his ex-girlfriend's mother, *Mommy* grosses me out. Sliding his hand into the V of her dress, he grabs her breast and leans over, kissing her.

"You fucking—"

"All a part of my plan." She interrupts me, pulling away from him. "I made sure she had you as an assignment, but it wasn't going anywhere." Rolling her eyes, she continues. "Then Ashtyn returned, and you left—Benny almost fucked all of that up. I wasn't sure what to do. But Hudson came up with an excellent idea. He called his friend and had him follow Annabelle while she sat outside of your house. He waited for her to leave, pulled her over, and roughed her up before taking her to jail. Where the only person she thought she could call was him." She smiles, and I'm shaking, staring at the fucking bastard. I should have killed him in her kitchen, but I was too concerned with waking up my wife. "You, of course saw her car and made the call to look into her. You couldn't resist wanting to see her once you realized who she was." He lights a cigarette and hands it to her. "You're a fucking soldier, Haidyn, but you have too big of a heart." She frowns, taking a drag. "It's not a good quality in a Lord but predictable. After everything you did for your brothers and then Ashtyn, I knew you wouldn't be able to turn down a damsel in distress. So...he roughed her up a little bit and sent her back to you."

"We have a deal," I grind out.

"Oh, I'm a woman of my word. You remain here; she remains untouched."

Hudson laughs. "Well, I wouldn't say *untouched*." He smiles at me. "I've enjoyed watching everything you've done to her. After seeing how much she liked it, I have plans for her."

I yank on the chains, making them rattle along with the cuffs, trying to pull them from the floor, but I'm too weak. "You touch her..."

"You left her vulnerable. The poor bitch actually fell in love with you." He laughs. "I'll sweep in, pick her up, and give her a shoulder to cry on. Slowly, I'll take over her mind. It won't be hard to break her, not after what you did to her. But don't take my word for it. I'll have the chance to prove it when she moves in here."

I look at Isabella, waiting for her to say something. To elaborate on what he means by *moves in here*. Our deal was me, not her. If he drags her here, then she's breaking it.

"Do you know how the Lords started?" She tilts her head in thought with a smirk on her face.

I don't answer. There are theories, but nothing has ever been proven. I never cared to dig into it because I knew I'd never get the truth. And what the fuck would it change? Nothing.

"All men are the same. They think because they have a dick, they own the world. But what if I told you that women started the Lords centuries ago?"

Hudson laughs as if it's a joke, and she glares up at him. He begins to cough, trying to cover it up. I say nothing.

"See...look at you right now." She crosses one leg over the other. "Chained up like a dog."

My cuffed hands fist.

"Do you really think a man would put another man in this position?" She throws her head back laughing. "You go through three years of initiations to weed out the weak. You're told you can't fuck. What man would decide to go without pussy for so long?" She takes another hit from the cigarette. "Women run this fucking world, but we have to let men think they're the ones in control. Without us, your legacy would die. Your name forgotten." She chuckles. "Part of the rules—everyone must serve. You are put to the test. Fight to your death so to speak. Our daughters have to spread their legs..." She shrugs. "As if that's hard to do. But you, the men...three years without sex and then given someone to fuck? You're like a kid on Christmas morning. You parade her around like the trophy you've won, and it makes you feel like a man again."

This isn't my senior year at Barrington, and she's not my chosen. I knew Charlotte was her daughter the moment I found out her true identity. I wanted revenge and saw an opportunity. Even though I knew it was a setup. I couldn't deny I wanted her since the day I saw her on her father's yacht.

Four years ago

I WAS KEPT IN A CELL—STARVED AND DRUGGED—FOR WHO KNOWS how long. Four men had entered, and I didn't even bother to fight. What's the point? I'm not saying I'm giving up, but I refuse to give that bitch the satisfaction of watching me lose a fight when she's stacked the odds against me.

I woke up after that, thinking I was buried alive. I couldn't see, my nose was plugged, and I couldn't move—the space so small. The only source of oxygen was through a tube that I could feel in my mouth. At times the airflow was cut off, forcing me to panic, no matter how hard I tried not to. I was burning up—my body on fire and sweating to death. I'm pretty sure I was hallucinating, unable to see or hear anything and unable to control the body spasms.

I knew it was the pits. I don't know how long I was in there—felt like days—but I eventually lost consciousness, and the next thing I knew, I was waking up in a hospital bed.

Now, I'm returning to the basement for more torture, more training.

I'm shoved through the plastic curtains by the Lords who remain covered in cloaks and masks. I immediately come to a stop. Saint and

Kashton both hang from their tied wrists secured to the ceiling in the center of the room. It's the first time I've seen either one of them since Ashtyn shot my brother. How long has it been...days, weeks, months? Time doesn't exist down here. At least they're both alive.

Kash looks like fucking shit. Bruised, cut, and bleeding, he's on the brink of death. His skin ashen and breathing labored. Scanning Saint's body, I see he's got a fresh 666 brand not far from his bullet wound. He hasn't been down here long. Maybe a day. At the most two.

"Oh, you're back." The bitch turns and smiles at me. Slapping Saint's fresh brand, he grunts. "Told you Haidyn would be okay," she tells him.

"What do you want?" I ask. It's a stupid question, but for us to finally be seeing each other, there has to be a reason. It's all about mind games with her.

"I'm here to teach you to be men."

Kash snorts and spits blood from his busted lips onto the floor.

"I feel like we've gotten off to a rough start. Let me introduce myself. My name is Isabella, but you can call me Costello."

"Fuck you, bitch." Kash groans, his head falling back to look up at his restrained wrists as his body hangs from the ceiling. "I'm not calling you shit."

She sighs, shaking her head. "Do you know why I chose to move into this hellhole for six months?"

We say nothing, and she steps into me. I bow my chest and fist my hands that want to rip her head from her body. Too many of her men are here, and they outnumber us. Kash looks as weak as I feel, and who knows how Saint feels since his surgery or what they've done to him.

"I wanted to be part of making the next generation of Spade brothers "good boys," but the real reason is for revenge."

Giving me her back, she claps her black Versace heels on the concrete floor, splashing the puddles of blood and water as she walks over to a rolling cart that contains scissors, knives, and pliers. "You..." She picks up a knife, running her fingers up and down the rusty-looking blade, and her red lips turn up. "Killed my husband."

"Fucking...lying...bitch." Saint gets out, finally speaking. "The Lords wouldn't allow you to come here for revenge."

"As you'll learn during our time together, I can be very convinc-

ing." Her smile grows. "They knew I'd get the job done. Plus, revenge is the best motivation."

I slowly approach her, and she doesn't even flinch as she tilts her head up to meet my glare. "If I did kill your husband, he deserved it."

Her face turns red, and she slices the blade against my upper thigh, cutting me.

I grind my teeth. "Goddammit." I hiss under my breath, placing all my weight on the other as I assess the damage, watching the blood run down my leg. It's not deep or anything. My main concern should be an infection due to how filthy it was.

"When I leave Carnage, you will remember Isabella Schults as the one who taught you how to be men."

"Schults?" I repeat out loud, my pulse starting to race as I recognize it. Fuck, our initiation last year...the yacht that was named Isabella, and her husband owned it.

"Let them down." She waves her hands toward Saint and Kash. "Put them in the pits. They deserve a time-out."

"No!" I growl, and she turns to face me once again.

She holds the tip of the nasty bloody knife to my neck, and my nostrils flare as my eyes look down my nose at her. "You want me? I'm right fucking here." I won't make my brothers pay for something I did. Especially when I was just following orders from the Lords.

"We're only sixteen days in, Haidyn. Let's not get ahead of ourselves."

My shoulders are screaming from my arms being pulled behind my back, and my knees are killing me from kneeling on the concrete. Her voice is making my ears ring. I just want to go back to my room. "What does that have to do with Charlotte?" I snap.

Isabella's eyes narrow at her daughter's fake name. She stands and takes the few steps, closing the space between us. "She was always meant to be great." Holding her arms out wide, she adds, "Annabelle will one day take over for me. And you will answer to her."

"To us," Hudson adds.

My eyes shoot to his and back to hers. Bill told me that Charlotte wouldn't be happy with what the Lords give her if she fulfills her assignment. But he never said *what* it was. Hell, I still don't know what Isabella's talking about exactly.

She gives me a soft smile. "She will marry Hudson."

I shake my head. "She'll never do it." I leave out the fact that Charlotte is my wife. I'll save that for another day. Since I'm going to be here until the day I die.

She throws her head back, laughing. "You think I'll give her a choice?" My chest tightens at the thought of her not having any control over her life. After everything she went through, she'll hate where she ends up. It was for nothing. "But just like you and the other Spade brothers, Hudson and I will prepare her to take over here when I'm done. And she will do whatever the fuck she is told to do." Her eyes look me up and down with a smirk. "Something tells me she won't be as hard to *train* as you and your brothers were." Smiling, she turns and goes to walk hand in hand with Hudson.

"How many?" I ask, my heart now racing, knowing the shit that she'll put her own daughter through.

Charlotte is strong but not that strong. I will burn this place down to the ground with both of us in it before I sit back and watch this bitch train my wife. All I can do is hope that my brothers keep her hidden from the world.

Isabella stops and turns to face me. "How many what?"

"How many of you fucking bitches run this society?"

She smirks and takes a step toward me. "There's power in numbers," she says vaguely. "Just like women are given medications to be fertile."

I frown. That's not something I was aware of. But after what Bill told me about the breeders, it too makes sense. Fuck, why didn't I put all of this together sooner?

She laughs, seeing the confusion on my face.

"There's a rumor going around that Lords are given enhancements to produce twins." She throws her head back, her laughter growing louder. "And you actually believe it. They are given...supplements, yes, but it's the women who determine twins. Not the men. Take your friend Ryat, for example. His wife, Blakely. She comes from a founder. She's about to give him twin boys, right?"

LeAnne. Now it all makes sense. Charlotte said her mother is best friends with LeAnne. I should have known.

"Who knows how many more kids they'll have. Or their kids will have...see, Haidyn, it's the Ladies who keep your legacies alive."

"Except for you." Hudson laughs like he knows a secret. "You'll be here until you die, and well, let's just say you won't have a legacy to leave behind."

I wish now more than ever that I hadn't had Gavin put Charlotte on the shot. I would give anything to give my wife what she wanted—a family. Not because of the Lords. *Fuck them!* But because that's what she wanted, and she deserves everything.

"A life span of a man in the United States is around seventy-seven years old. With my help, you will exceed that. Think of it as a gift from me to you—you'll get to see Annabelle every day for a long...long time." She looks behind me. "Return him to his room. Remove the IV and get him prepped for stage two of his initiation." Then she turns and exits the room with his hand on her ass.

Shhh...

Chapter 77

Charlotte

It's been a week since Haidyn told me he loved me and left me tied to my bed. A week of absolute torture.

Life has a way of laughing at you. My first thought when he appeared in my kitchen that night was that he was going to drag me to Carnage, place me in a cell, and leave me to die. It's happened, just not in that way. I'm trapped here at Carnage while he's somewhere else.

I lay here in his bed, just staring up at the dark ceiling trying to remember his touch, his body holding mine, the way he fucked me.

I've never been more dependent on another person in my life like I am Haidyn. He inserted his life into mine in every way. Then he just leaves, and he expects me to go on with mine. *How?*

I love you, Charlotte.

Adam took my cell phone from me. He got tired of me watching the video that Haidyn left me over and over. He blamed it on the battery and said he'd plug it in for me. It was just another lie.

The door opens, and I remain staring up at the ceiling. I've gone numb. They don't have any clues as to where he is. At first, I would listen to them argue back and forth. I even felt bad for Ashtyn when she would cry and beg Saint to find him. Now, I tune them all out. I know it's selfish, but no one in this hell loves him like I do. At least that's how I feel. If so, they wouldn't have abandoned him. Given a choice, I know I'd never leave him. I'd never pick another soul on this planet over Haidyn. At some point, all of them have. And Adam was right; my husband gave himself up one time for every single one of us.

"Anything?" Saint asks.

He's speaking to Adam. After he arrived, Adam called another Lord and had them go get Muffin and grab a few things of his and mine from Haidyn's house. I've been in Haidyn's room with the two of them ever since. Adam hasn't left my side. I think he believes I'm suicidal. Honestly, it'd be better than this. Or it could be because Saint and Kashton still haven't warmed up to me. Pretty sure they want to kill me, and I wouldn't fight them. I deserve that.

I fell in love with the man who killed my father. Am I a horrible person because it doesn't change the way I feel about him? Most likely. That's why my mother has him—because he took someone she loved. So she's punishing me for loving him in return. It's the only plausible explanation I can come up with since they won't tell me anything.

"No," Adam answers, typing away on his laptop.

Saint sighs. "How is she doing?" He speaks as if I can't hear him.

"Devin and Gavin should be here any second."

I roll over, giving them both my back, and close my eyes. Maybe they'll sedate me, knock me out so I can get some sleep. At least I can dream of being in Haidyn's arms again. Dream that I belong to him. That he's still here. Anything would be better than the hole I have now.

My entire body aches. My chest is so tight it hurts to breathe. I'm not eating anything Jessie brings me. Because I know wherever Haidyn is, he's also not eating. Why should I get what he isn't? Is he being tortured? I'm sure. I hate that no matter what my mind comes up with, I know it's worse. What could my mother possibly be doing with him?

The door opens again, and I hear Adam get up from his chair in front of the double doors that lead to the balcony. It's where he works on his laptop and phone endlessly. But he needs energy drinks to help him pull all-nighters and function throughout the day.

"What do you need?" Devin asks.

"I need to know my options," Adam says.

"With?" Gavin asks.

"Her." I imagine he's pointing at me while they stand at my back. "She's refusing to eat, drink...I don't think she's gotten up to use the restroom in over twenty-four hours. She's got to be dehydrated at this point." Adam sighs.

"Charlotte?" A hand on my shoulder wiggles my body, but I ignore it. "Charlotte?"

I'm pulled onto my back, and I place my eyes on the ceiling as one of them shines a bright light into them. I'm not even sure I could talk if I tried. My throat is too sore from all the sobbing I've done. Can you run dry? Like you cry so much that you can no longer produce tears?

I think the worst part is the unknown. It's been seven days. Even if they find Haidyn, how will he feel about me now? Adam said Haidyn gave himself over for me. Why? We could have had a chance, but he wouldn't listen to me. Now, what am I supposed to do with my life? It's meaningless without him in it.

"Nothing," Adam barks. "I'm telling you to do something."

"Haidyn wouldn't want..."

"Haidyn isn't fucking here!" Adam shouts, interrupting Gavin. "I'm telling you to do something. She's hurting herself."

"I say let her do whatever she wants." Kashton sounds amused. I wasn't even aware he was in the room. "We don't force the prisoners to eat. If she wants to die a slow death of starvation, then let her."

"Kash." Adam growls his name in warning. "You're her guardian, for Christ's sake."

I still don't know what that means, and I'm no longer sure I want to.

"I didn't sign shit." Kashton laughs like it's a joke.

"We can move her over to the hospital." Devin speaks next, trying to come up with a plan.

"That's a start. Then what?" Adam lowers his voice.

"Feeding tube," one suggests.

"She'll just pull it out." Saint chuckles at their Band-Aid for a life-threatening illness.

As if he even cares what happens to me. Honestly, I'm not even sure I have the energy for that.

"Restraints," Gavin adds. "They'll keep her from being able to harm herself or remove the feeding tube."

"Restrain her to the bed?" Adam repeats, liking the sound of that option.

A moan escapes my cracked lips at the thought of being tied down. Not because I'm horny but because it makes me think of Haidyn. *"Are you a rope bunny, doll face?"* I can hear his voice ask me that question. If they blindfold me too, then I can pretend he's in the room. Just being his typical dickhead self and making me wait to get off until he thinks I'm ready. Making me use my words and beg him.

He's trained my body and my mind to need him. And then he just leaves me and expects me to go on with my life like I imagined him this whole time.

"None of that will be happening," a woman's voice states.

"Ash—"

"Help me get her to the bathroom, Adam." She interrupts Saint. "Now."

"I don't think..."

"I don't give a fuck what you think, Adam," she shouts. "Give me twenty-four hours with her." No one says anything to that, and she repeats, "Help me get her to the bathroom."

"Come on, princess," Adam says softly before arms roughly slide underneath my body. He picks me up, and my head hangs off the side of his arm as he enters the en suite bathroom.

My eyes are open, but I don't see anything. Not really anyway. Just blurry shapes and bright, shiny lights. Unless he takes me to see Haidyn, it doesn't matter.

The sound of running water fills my ears, and I'm set on the side of the tub. The room spins as if I've been drinking for days, but I know it's because I've been depriving my body of what it needs to survive.

"I'll give you ten minutes," Adam tells Ashtyn. "If it doesn't work, then we do it my way."

"You don't get to show back up out of nowhere—again—and start giving orders, Adam." She gives a rough laugh.

"Haidyn wouldn't want her to live like this," he argues.

I want to say he left me, but it doesn't matter. They all know that.

"I also know Haidyn wouldn't want her drugged, tied to a hospital bed, and fed through a tube," she snaps. "Now, get the fuck out." She shoves his chest, slamming the door shut in his face before locking it.

She places her hands on either side of my face, forcing me to look at her. I hate how pretty she is. And that all I see when I look at her, is how much Haidyn cares for her. Would he have left her like he left me? Why didn't he try to run with me like I asked?

"I'm trying to help you. Help me in return."

"Doesn't...matter," I whisper. It's the first thing I've said in days.

Instead of arguing with me, she slides off Haidyn's T-shirt that I wear and my underwear. I don't have the strength to fight her or care that she sees me naked. Everyone else has, so what's one more person?

She takes my hand and helps me into the Jacuzzi tub as it fills with warm water. I slide down into it, waiting for the water to get high enough to just drown me.

"They'll find him," she speaks softly. "And you need to look your best when you see your husband again."

My head falls to the side, and I look at Haidyn's bathroom counter. His cologne, a toothbrush, and a soap dish are all that's on it.

"After your bath, I'll have Jessie get you some food." She continues.

At the mention of eating, I feel the need to vomit. It's been a few days since I did that. My hand goes to my mouth, and I swallow it down.

She pauses, shampoo lathering in her hands. Her eyes meet mine when she asks, "Are you pregnant?"

A pain in my chest makes me flinch. "No," I answer, dropping my eyes to the water filling the bathtub.

"Are you sure?" she questions.

My teeth clench, and I growl. "I'm on the shot. Have been since before the first time he fucked me."

She drops her eyes to her hands and goes back to lathering the shampoo before washing my hair. I close my eyes and let her take care of me as if I'm incapable of such a small task.

HAIDYN

I'M BEING KEPT IN A ROOM WITH NO WINDOWS, SO I HAVE NO idea how long I've been here. At first, I was keeping track of the days by how long they keep the lights on. It's like prison—lights on and off at a certain time every day and night. Then they started keeping them on for a full twenty-four hours. Then they switched it up and kept them off just as long.

They either did it to confuse the hell out of me or they want me to go mad. Either way, it's working.

I'm still weak as fuck, and I'm also starting to hallucinate. I'm not sure if that's from what they're giving me or lack of food and water.

They won't allow me to die but want me to remain on the brink of death. It's a tightrope to walk, but something that me and my brothers do at Carnage. It's a physical and mental mind game. It's the same shit that her and her men put us through during our "training."

My mind stays on Charlotte. All I can think is that she's at Carnage. Alive. That my brothers are taking good care of her. Isabella and Hudson can't touch her there.

After Benny was able to get in, we locked that place down. My brothers won't allow them to get to her. Anyone who tries will be shot on sight. I don't care how important Isabella is. Her daughter is safe and far away from her. Plus, the longer she plays with me, the longer she forgets about Charlotte.

Then the thought that I try to push to the back of my mind creeps up—what if Kash and Saint find out who Charlotte really is? Would they still protect her? Will they know that I'm in love with her? That I gave myself up for her to live a different life?

I'm only one man and needed another who I could trust. Do you have any idea how hard it is to know you can't protect the one person you love?

I feel like I've traded one life of hell for her for another. What kind of life is worth living when you're a prisoner at Carnage? She'll have to remain there the rest of her life.

I don't care. Anything is better than what Isabella and Hudson have planned for her. Charlotte being his wife makes me want to vomit—physically ill. Knowing what I've done to her—how does he even know? Rage, unlike anything I've ever known, eats at me.

She's mine, and they expect me to watch it? To see her every day and not kill them? I know my girl. She won't want him, so he'll have to force her. I'm sure he'll do it in front of me.

Or Isabella will hold her down. I know what that woman is

capable of. None of it good. It won't matter that Charlotte's her child. The woman cares about nothing.

The metal door to my room squeaks open, and I squint when the room lights up from the hallway. A man enters and comes to stand next to me while I lie on the hospital bed. I've been restrained to it since my operation. Not like I could walk anyway, given the drugs they keep pumping into me. My mind stays foggy and my body heavy.

"Come on, Spade. Time for your meds." He laughs, and my jaw tightens, knowing they're about to shove another needle into my arm. At least I'll get some rest. Last time I had a "round," I slept through most of it and was able to dream of the life that my wife wanted us to have. The one that she deserved.

Shhh...

Chapter 78

Charlotte

This afternoon, I found myself getting out of bed. I'm pretty sure I gave Adam a heart attack when I sat up and told him I was hungry. He immediately jumped to his feet and called Jessie in to feed me.

The food tasted like paper, and the water was sour. My body doesn't know what's good for it anymore, but my talk with Ashtyn last night made sense. They are going to find Haidyn, and when they do, he'll need me.

I've taken a life before. The least I can do is live mine. If what the Spade brothers think is true, I'm going to fight for my life just to spite my mother. When I see her again—if ever—I'll have questions. And she won't give me anything if she thinks I've gone weak. I still have to prove myself. For my husband.

The elevator opens, and I step off with Adam and walk down the hallway. After I ate, I brushed my teeth and got dressed. I didn't have to say a word to him. He just knew that I needed to get up and move. So he let me lead him through Carnage and I find myself walking aimlessly. He follows a few steps behind, and I can hear him typing away on his cell. I don't know what he does for a living or why he left the Spade brothers, but I'm not sure I even want to know. Lords are raised to rule, so I hope whatever life he finds is worth being on the run.

I come to a stop and spin around to face him.

"Charlotte," he grunts, almost running into me since his attention was on his phone. "Need something?" Adam pockets his cell.

"What did Haidyn mean by you helped force me to marry him?" My voice is still rough from lack of conversation.

"You made a choice," he says.

You always have a choice, doll face. "How did he do it?"

Adam steps forward and grabs my left hand. He runs his thumb over the sapphire ring while his green eyes search mine. Instead of answering my question, he asks his own. "Knowing what you know now, would you have married him?"

He means my father. Would I turn my husband over to the Lords if I had known that he was the Lord who killed my father? No. I can't say that I would, so I bow my head, avoiding his stare and his question.

"So this isn't about revenge?" Haidyn had asked me the first time he drugged me. I thought it was weird, but he meant revenge on my father. He was under the impression that I knew what he had done.

"Sometimes love needs a little push." Adam drops my hand. "And when a Lord decides he wants you, he makes sure he gets you one way or another."

My eyes go to his left hand, and I don't see a ring on it, but looking closely, I can see a tan line where one has been. If he's not going to give me any information about my own marriage, he's for sure not going to tell me anything about his love life. So I change the subject.

"What is a guardian?" I ask since I have him alone and in conversation.

"If Haidyn dies, he has left another Spade brother in charge of you."

I flinch at the thought of my husband dying. *No.* He wouldn't do that to me. I know how the Lords work and how my mother was regifted to my stepdad. "You mean regifted me to someone else?"

He shakes his head. "Spade brothers are different. Therefore, our rules are different. A Lady is regifted to another Lord because she can't be let out into the world. She has to stay within the society to keep our secret. Same happens to a Lady of a Spade brother. You will belong to Kash but not in the way you think. You won't become his wife or his whore, but you will be his responsibility. You will belong to Haidyn until you die."

My husband left me to a man who currently wants me dead. "Why didn't he choose you?" I whisper.

"I wasn't an option," he answers, and I wonder if it has to do with him not living at Carnage.

Giving him my back, I continue down the hall and open the door to their office.

Conversations instantly come to a halt when we enter. Saint and Kashton both glare at me before looking at Adam. Ashtyn sits on Saint's lap, and she gives me a big smile of encouragement. She's become an ally that I never thought I'd have. But I guess in a world full of men, you have to have the women's backs.

As much as I hate that she and Haidyn have a past, she's not my competition. She's a woman who loves a man and knows how far a woman is willing to go to keep him.

A man has his back to me, and as the room falls silent, he turns to see who entered. I take a step back when a set of familiar eyes meet mine. Adam places his hands on my shoulders, making me jump.

"It's okay." The guy lifts his hands out to his sides. "I'm here to help."

Saint snorts. "How do we know we can trust you? You're married to the enemy."

Bill looks at him and sighs. "You just have to take my word for it." His eyes meet mine, and he gives me a soft smile. "Haidyn did."

I step forward. "You spoke to Haidyn?" Hope fills my chest, making my pulse pick up at the thought of seeing him again.

He nods. "I've been looking for him." Running a hand over his head, he takes a deep breath.

"Well...did you find him?" It's Ashtyn who asks what we're all wondering.

"I have an idea where he is, but..."

"But what?" Kashton snaps when he trails off. Everyone is on edge. Tired of waiting and not getting anywhere. We've had no leads and no tracker. My husband just vanished as if he never existed.

"Gaining access won't be easy."

Saint taps Ashtyn's thigh, and she removes herself from his lap so he can stand. "Just tell us where the fuck he is. We'll blow the goddamn place up if we have to."

I want to smile that his brothers are going to do everything they can to bring him home. Even if I know it's not for me. For all I know, they plan on trading me for him, and I'm okay with that. As long as I get to see him one last time. I never even got to tell him that I love him. He robbed me of that opportunity. I had tape over my mouth when he said those three words. Like a true Lord, he didn't care what I wanted to say or how I felt.

"You're going to need help." Bill goes on.

Saint snaps his fingers at Kashton. "Make the call. Tell them to get here. Now."

Kashton nods and pulls his cell from his pocket as he exits the office, wanting to make his call without us eavesdropping.

"If he contacted you, what took you so long to come here?" I ask. Haidyn left his phone behind, so he had to have reached out before he left me.

Bill's eyes meet mine before they drop to my stomach. My hands go to it instinctively. His eyes rise to mine once more. "There's a lot you don't know about, Annabelle."

"My name is Charlotte," I correct him.

I'm who Haidyn knows me to be. I want nothing to do with the life I had before him. I might as well erase everything I thought I knew. It seems to have all been a lie. Haidyn is real. My life with him is real. The love I have for him is real. And the future I know we're going to have is real.

He nods. "Charlotte."

The door opens behind me, and Kashton enters. "They're on their way," he announces.

Bill looks at Saint. "Get the jet ready. It's not far, but it'll be quicker." Then his eyes go to Adam. "You'll want to bring Devin and Gavin with you."

♠

LESS THAN THIRTY MINUTES LATER, MORE LORDS ARRIVE, AND we're on our way out the front doors when Ashtyn comes running down the grand staircase just like the first time I saw her here. But this time, it's me she's yelling at. "Charlotte?"

I walk over to her, meeting her at the bottom of the last step.

Her wide eyes go from mine over my shoulder and then back to me, lowering her voice. "Should you go...?"

"I'm not staying here." I give her my back, and she reaches out, grabbing my arm.

"Char—?"

"I'm going to get my husband," I snap, spinning back around. Reaching out, I place both of my hands on her upper arms and give her a soft smile, softening my voice as I see the unshed tears in her eyes. "I'm going to go help bring him back," I promise her.

Ashtyn sniffs but nods softly. I pull her in for a hug, and then my shirt is grabbed, and I'm yanked away. A quick look over my shoulder tells me it's her husband.

"Saint," she snaps at him, and he just rolls his eyes.

"We're in a hurry, sweetheart. We'll be back as soon as we can," he tells her, pulling me through the front doors before they slam shut.

"Don't grab her like that," Adam barks while standing on the porch. He pulls me from Saint and isn't any gentler if you ask me.

"Get her in the fucking car, and let's go," Saint growls, walking over to a car that Sin and Ryat stand next to. Tyson is also over there, pacing back and forth, his head down with his cell phone in his ear. Everyone is trying to get a plan of action together so no one gets killed during this rescue mission.

"Come on, princess." Adam takes my hand and ushers me down the steps and over to an SUV. Holding the back door open for me, I climb in, and he shuts it.

I'm sitting in here alone, and my legs start to bounce. Rubbing my sweaty hands on my thighs, I try to dry them off. I'm a nervous wreck. What if this doesn't work? What if he's not there and it's a setup for the rest of the Spade brothers? I'd hate for Haidyn's brothers to be in danger. I don't want anything to happen to any of them.

The door on my left opens, and Bill hops in next to me. He scans the circle drive before he turns to look at me. "Are you willing to do whatever it takes?"

His question reminds me of the conversation I once had with my father outside of the cathedral.

"You will one day marry your Lord, but he will not define you."

Giving me a soft smile, he adds, "But a sacrifice must be made in order to get to the top."

"What do I have to sacrifice?" I ask.

He looks away from me, staring out the windshield, and the silence lingers among us before he answers, "Whatever they want."

My life is no longer about having power or being at the top. Now it's all about the life I want to live with my husband. And I'll give up anything for him. My father lied because my Lord does define me. I'm nothing without him.

"Absolutely." I swallow the knot in my throat. Not because I'm nervous but because I know it will require a lot. My mother isn't going to hand him over. Especially to me.

"The others aren't really going to care, but Adam..." He shrugs. "He cares what happens to you."

"I'll do whatever it takes," I reassure him, and he pats my thigh.

Bill pulls his hand back just as both front doors open. Kashton hops in the passenger seat while Saint takes the driver's side. The door on my right opens, and Adam jumps in, smashing me between him and Bill. His eyes drop to my shaking legs and then my eyes.

I look ahead and try to even my breathing out. Getting myself worked up won't do any good. My mom will smell my fear.

We pull up to an airfield that's close to Carnage, and a private jet awaits us and another car. The front and back doors open, and four men jump out. They begin talking to Tyson, who gets out of the car following us with Sin and Ryat.

Bill gets out, and I go to follow, but I'm grabbed and jerked through the opposite door. Then I'm pushed up against the side of the SUV. A hand wraps around my throat, pinning me in place as Adam presses his hard body into mine. Lowering his lips to my ear, he whispers, "Don't leave my fucking side, princess. I don't trust him; do you understand me?"

"Everything okay?" Bill calls out.

Adam drops his hand from my neck and steps back. We both look over to see everyone standing on the tarmac staring at us.

"Yeah," I say to Bill, trying to give him a reassuring smile. Then I look at Adam and nod. "Yeah." I'm hoping he understands I'm answering his question.

Adam grabs my hand and yanks me from the SUV and pulls me toward the plane.

"If I didn't know better, I'd say you're in love with your friend's wife." Bill speaks as we walk by him.

"You don't know shit." Adam snorts.

shhh...

Chapter 79

Charlotte

I've never been surrounded by so many Lords at once in such a tight space. I mean, the jet is huge, but the last time I was with this many was during my initiation at the cathedral.

Not to bring any attention to myself, I sit quietly next to Adam, listening to them go over their options. Tyson's men brought plans to a place they keep referencing as Dollhouse. I've never heard of it other than that one time Haidyn asked me about it.

They think my mom runs it, and I want to argue, but the fact that Bill has remained quiet has me keeping my mouth shut. It's obvious he knows more than me. I'll just add it to the list of things my mother has been lying to me about.

"What if he's not there?" Sin asks. "If we need to, we can split up and hit another place at the same time," he offers.

"He's there," Bill assures him. "She wanted him. This is the only place she'd be able to keep him without my knowledge."

Saint snorts. "Then how are you so sure?"

"I have someone on the inside. I couldn't prove it or risk going to you all until I got the confirmation this morning. They informed me she's keeping him in the dungeon. Total isolation and drugged."

A dungeon? My mother has one of those? Fuck, even Carnage just calls it their basement. And drugs? What kind of drugs could my mother have access to? A sickening feeling makes my stomach roil.

"Same thing she did to him during our 'training.' Fuck, I hate that goddamn bitch." Saint hisses.

Training? What are they talking about training? Since when do

Lords go through that? The video comes to mind that I've been sent where he's strung up, bleeding and being tortured. The one where they waterboarded him...was my mom the *she* they were referring to?

"I hate to be a Negative Nancy here..." one of Tyson's men speaks. I remember him introducing himself to Bill as Colton before we boarded the plane. When Bill asked him if they were able to get access to the plans of the address, he had given them. "But what if he's dead?"

I slap my hand over my mouth to keep in a sob at that thought, and Adam grabs my other one, giving it a firm squeeze.

Kashton bends over, dropping his head between his legs as his hands come up and interlock at the back of his neck.

"Doesn't matter..." Saint says, shaking his head.

"Colt isn't wrong..." Another by the name of Alex starts. "What if you guys are willingly walking into a fucking trap. You"—he points at Adam—"have been MIA for four years. Benny didn't get to execute whatever fucked-up plan he had for you guys, but this is the perfect opportunity to get you all four in one spot and..."

"It doesn't fucking matter," Kashton yells, jumping to his feet. "Like Saint said, it doesn't matter if Haidyn is dead or alive." He lowers his voice. "We know the odds. And either way, we bring our brother home...where he belongs." With that, the plane falls silent. Kashton walks over to a minibar, opens a tiny bottle of vodka, and downs it.

Bring our brother home...the thought of burying him has the bile rising once again, and I jump to my feet.

"Charlotte?" Adam calls out to me.

I ignore him and run to the back of the plane, shoving what I'm hoping is the bathroom door open just in time to throw up into a toilet. I can't stop. Tears run down my cheeks as I hover over, trying to hold my hair back until someone else grabs it for me. When I'm done, they flush it and help me back out of the tight space.

I fall into a seat at the back of the plane and bury my face into my hands, unable to stop crying. He's been there for eight days now. There's no telling what he's been through in that amount of time. How many times have they killed him and brought him back like they did when waterboarding him? And how much can his body take until it gives up?

"Here you go," Kashton says.

I look up through tear-filled eyes to see him holding out a glass of water to me, but when I go to reach for it, Adam takes it from Kashton and turns, tossing it into the bathroom sink.

"I didn't poison it," Kashton growls at Adam as he comes back to stand next to me.

"Are you pregnant?"

Everyone looks toward the front of the plane when Devin asks. He turns to look at his twin brother who sits next to him. "Did you run a test because I didn't think of it."

Gavin shakes his head. "There was no need. I administered the shot per Haidyn's request. She's not due for another one yet."

Devin nods in understanding, and everyone goes back to their previous conversations, and I catch sight of Bill. His eyes drop to my stomach as if he thinks otherwise, and I jump up, pushing Adam out of my way, and return to the bathroom.

"I'll grab her another water," Kashton offers over my dry heaving.

♠

Bill was right; it was a quick flight. It seemed by the time we were up in the air, we were already descending. Adam takes my hand and leads me to the front of the plane. We're the last to get off. We walk down the stairs, and the warm night air hits my face.

Several blacked-out vehicles are parked on the tarmac, and all the Lords stand around going over last-minute plans.

I'm not sure what they will do, but I keep telling myself that if anyone can save my husband, it's these men. They didn't get to where they are because they're weak or afraid.

They're all ruthless and the best at what they do. And nothing will stop them. I'd put all my trust into one Lord—I like Haidyn's odds with eight of them, plus Tyson's four men. These twelve men are going to rescue my husband. All I can do is hope that he's still alive.

"Load up," Adam barks, making me jump.

He takes my hand again and pulls me to a black Cadillac SUV

when my other hand is grabbed. "She needs to ride with me," Bill says, pulling me away from Adam.

"I don't fucking think so."

Bill stops, and we both turn around. I expected it to be Adam who protested, but to my surprise, it's Kashton who spoke. He steps forward, grabbing my upper arm and pulls me into him. They're ripping my fucking arm off.

Bill walks toward us, but he stops when Saint and Adam surround Kashton and me. Even Sin, Tyson, and Ryat step closer to us.

"We don't have time for this," Bill growls. "My wife doesn't expect Charlotte to walk right in on her own because Charlotte doesn't even know this place exists. She needs to come in with me through the main entrance while you guys go in the back."

"You said *you're* not supposed to know where it is," Saint argues.

Bill sighs. "She contacted me today, and she knows that I'm bringing her."

"I'm not letting her go with you." Kashton shakes his head and then drops his gaze to me. "I don't fucking like you, but my brother married you." He looks away, and his jaw clenches before they return to mine. "He chose me to be your guardian, and because of that, I will protect you."

Bill is right. If my mother knows it's an ambush, who knows what she'll do to Haidyn after what I've seen him go through in the videos the Lords sent me. I look up at Kashton. "It'll be okay," I say, nodding. I promised Bill that I could do whatever it takes, and I meant that. "We're all here for the same reason," I remind him.

I take a step back from Kashton to test the waters. Thankfully, he doesn't follow me. He fists both of his hands, and his jaw sharpens as he looks over at Saint. Adam runs a hand down his face, and the others just stare, as if they're waiting for the sign to attack Bill and drag me back to them.

Bill opens the passenger side door to a sedan.

"Charlotte?" Kashton calls out, and I stay where I'm at as he walks toward me. He reaches into his leather jacket and removes a gun from his shoulder holster. Pulling back the slide, he cocks it—chambering a bullet and holds it out to me. "Do you know how to use a gun?"

"Yeah."

"Don't ask questions. Just point and shoot. Don't stop until you run out," he orders me, then his eyes slide over my head to glare at Bill before returning to mine.

I smile, remembering the second time I pulled a gun out on Haidyn in his living room, and he said practically the same thing. "Got it." I take the gun from him.

"It's loaded and has a factory safety delete—meaning there is no safety. So be careful. Don't shoot yourself."

I nod. "Thank you."

Then I turn and slide into the passenger seat. Turning, I see them all watching as Bill closes my door and gets in, starts up the car, and drives away. I rest my head against the headrest and close my eyes, sighing.

"11 Minutes" by YUNGBLUD and Halsey softly fills the speakers, and my eyes start to sting.

"How long have you known about Dollhouse?" I ask, needing conversation. I'm tired of living in my head.

"Since before your father passed. Your mother has been running it for years. After she passed her assignment her senior year at Barrington."

"Saint told me..." I bow my head and stare at the gun in my lap. "That Haidyn killed my father."

Bill nods. "He did." Then he quickly looks over at me. "But your father knew he was coming. Trent fucked up and knew the Lords would send someone after him. He was Haidyn's initiation. I was on the deck with your father when Haidyn walked out onto it. Your father suspected it was him because we were...acquaintances with the Spade brothers and knew that their sons were in the middle of initiations. Plus, Haidyn wasn't on the attendee list for the party."

"What did he do?" I ask, running my sweaty hands on my jeans, wanting to know. My mother never wanted to talk about my father's death. She said it was too painful.

"Haidyn took a second. He paused..." His eyes slide to mine quickly. "It was you."

"Me?" I frown.

He laughs softly. "Haidyn saw you with your friends. You were laughing and drinking champagne. You caught his attention, and he watched you long enough that he forgot why he was there."

Haidyn had seen me that night? Why hasn't he told me that? I never knew he was there. Or that he had seen me before our first meeting at Carnage. Not until he left me the video...*back in my life.*

"Your father didn't want there to be a scene." He goes on. "Because although he knew Haidyn was there for him, he didn't know how he would do it. Usually, the order is to make it messy. And he didn't want you to see it happen. So he walked over to you, hugged your friend, kissed your cheek...he put himself in Haidyn's line of sight to get his attention back on him. It worked, and Haidyn followed him to his office."

"Where he shot him," I whisper, lowering my eyes to my lap again, and I stare at the gun that Kashton gave me. I wonder how many people he's used it on. How many lives it's taken. Were they all Lords? Did they all deserve it?

"You can't blame Haidyn for doing what he was brought up to do, Charlotte. Otherwise, you'd have to take a look in the mirror."

I run a hand through my hair and stare out the window at the passing trees and sink into the warm seat, knowing he's right. "We're all evil," I mumble. "I killed someone and never considered who they left behind."

He chuckles. "We live in a world that's kill or be killed. You just have to be the first one to pull the trigger."

HAIDYN

I'M STANDING ON MY WRAPAROUND PORCH OUTSIDE MY BEDROOM, looking over the woods. It's the middle of the night, and I have a cigarette in my right hand. My cell in my left. I have the sliding glass doors open to my room behind me. It's a beautiful night. It's been raining for hours, and it doesn't look like it's going to let up anytime soon.

The moans and whimpers get my attention, and I turn around to see Charlotte in the bedroom.

I put out the cigarette on the railing and enter the room. She's gasping while she wiggles in the ropes that bind her in the ball-like position while she hangs from the ceiling. I told her that day at Carnage I was going to string her up and have a cigarette while cum leaked from all her used-up holes. Like the worthless whore she was meant to be. Tonight was the night.

I wouldn't say she's worthless, though. She serves a purpose. One that gets me off. Fuck, I can't get enough. The moment I'm done, I can go again. And again. She's been living with me at my house for three days now, and I don't plan on letting her leave anytime soon.

I walk over to her pussy and ass. She's got a vibrator in both. I turn them up on my phone loving the way her hoarse voice carries throughout the room. Her knees are bent to her chest, making sure they're both easily accessible. Her arms are around her legs, secured at the back of her bent knees.

Then I move to where her head hangs and run my fingers over her parted lips. "You look more beautiful than I imagined," I say softly, and her heavy eyes open. Her pretty face is covered in her drool, tears, and my cum.

I fucked her cunt first—she came twice.

Then her mouth—that way, she could taste herself on me. I wanted to remind her how much she enjoyed it.

Saved her ass for last.

"Hai-dyn?" She gasps, her small body trembling in the ropes.

"Yeah, doll face?" I ask, my hand moving to rest at the back of her head, and I lift it a little so her watery eyes can meet mine while I look down at her. "Tell me what you want, Charlotte."

She licks her lips like an obedient toy needing to be played with. "Please?" she begs.

"You just love being used, don't you?" I laugh softly, and she squeezes her eyes shut tightly.

I slap the side of her face. "Eyes open, doll face."

Her eyes pop open, and she sticks her tongue out, staring heavily at my jeans. My cock is right at eye level with her. I unzip my jeans and pull out my hard dick with a smile.

She's been hanging here for quite some time now. After I was done with her ass, I took a shower and had a cigarette. So I'll give her what she's so sweetly begging for, then I'll untie her, give her a bath, and put her in bed for the night. Then I'll start my day tomorrow using her again.

I OPEN MY HEAVY EYES AND LOOK AROUND. ALL I SEE IS darkness. So I close them again. Wanting to get back to when I was with Charlotte. When she was mine and I was hers. And we had more time. I kept thinking that the hourglass was going to run out, and it has. All I can do is hope that my brothers are keeping her safe, even if that means locking her up in the basement.

Her mother can't get to her. Not now. Not ever. What Isabella and that piece of shit boy toy of hers will do to my wife is far worse than anything they can put me through.

My shoulders scream and my back aches as I hang from the ceiling with my arms above my head by the chains. It's their go-to position. It keeps you the most vulnerable. They can get to your front and your back at any time.

I've lost count of how long I've been in this position, but once again, my hands have gone numb. They came in, dragged me out of bed, and strung me up, then left me in the dark.

The door squeaks open, and I flinch at the harsh light that fills the room, rapidly closing and opening my eyes. So much for getting back to dreaming about my wife. A cart is pushed into the room, and on it sits a syringe that is already filled.

Isabella enters and picks it up. "Tilt his head back," she orders.

My hair is grabbed and yanked back forcing me to look up at the ceiling. Then I feel a prick in my neck.

Next, my arms are free, and I drop to the concrete floor like a dead weight. I groan, rolling onto my side and the lingering pain. *Fuck!*

"Get him dressed. Meet me outside," she orders as if I can't do it myself.

"Come on, Spade."

I'm lifted to my feet, and two men hold me up under my arms while another helps get my jeans on. Then they dress me in a T-shirt and shoes. I don't know why I'm all of a sudden getting to wear clothes, but I'm not going to argue. I'm tired of being so damn cold.

The stuff that they pump into me through my IV always has me freezing.

Thankfully, I'm able to walk on my own, which is surprising, considering I have no clue how long I've been caged in that concrete room with very little food and water.

"What did she give me?" I ask, rubbing my neck where she stuck me with the needle.

Of course no one answers.

I don't feel sluggish or tired. I know it wasn't adrenaline, but it's got my blood pumping. I feel jittery, and my heart races. I take a quick look around when we step outside, and nothing looks familiar. But it also doesn't look different either. We're in the middle of the woods and the sun is starting to set. I can tell we're still in Pennsylvania. The flight wasn't that long.

Looking ahead, I see several people standing over by a chain-link fence. My breath catches when I see there's a woman tied to it with barbed wire. I'm having déjà vu—she's got a hood over her head, but I'd know that body from anywhere.

"What the fuck...Charlotte?" I run to her, but a man steps in front of me and points a gun at my face, forcing me to stop. "What the fuck are you doing?" I shout at her mother. How did she get here? This has to be a trick. No. I don't believe that's my wife.

Isabella doesn't answer. Instead, she walks over to her daughter and rips off the hood. My stomach drops when I see the bruises on her beautiful face. She's got duct tape over her mouth, and she screams into it when she sees me, pulling on her limbs. She twists and turns, and just like before, blood runs down her body from the barbed wire digging into her skin.

"What the fuck do you want?" I shout.

This is what she did to me and Kashton with our chosens. Same scenario just a different woman. This isn't someone the Lords are forcing me to fuck. This is my wife. Her daughter. What could she possibly want? I've already given myself over to her in order to save Charlotte.

"I'm testing you, Haidyn. Let's see if you pass." She crosses her arms over her chest. "You can either kill her or watch my men have her."

Charlotte's wide eyes go to me.

I step toward her, not knowing what to do but knowing I have to do something. I'm not going to kill her, and I'm sure as fuck not going to let them rape her. But the man with the gun in front of me, hits me with it in the face, knocking me down.

"Cut her loose," Isabella orders.

They cut her ankles first, then her neck, and last, her wrists. She falls to the muddy ground and rips the tape off her mouth. "You sick fuck," she screams at her mother.

Isabella just smiles down at her. "You knew what kind of world you wanted to be a part of. The world that you *killed* someone to prove yourself worthy." Then she looks at me. "What's it going to be, Haidyn?" She glances at her Rolex watch. "You've got one minute."

My eyes go to my wife, and she's already staring up at me as I get to my feet, trying to hear her over the blood rushing in my ears. "Please, Haidyn." She's gasping to catch her breath. Her dark hair sticking to her bloody and tear-streaked face. "Don't let them do this."

I've never felt more helpless in my entire life. I might as well be tied to that fence like she was. My heart is heavy, and I feel sick to my stomach. I could never hurt her, let alone kill her. And her mother knows that. I gave myself for her. "We had a deal," I growl looking at Isabella.

"Things can always change, Haidyn. You know that," she says.

"Take me." I place my arms out wide. "Punish me." I don't care what they do to me as long as it saves her.

Isabella gives me a big smile. "I am, darling."

"Haidyn?" Charlotte yells my name to get my attention. "Please, Haidyn." Her gaze drops to the gun that the man still holds aimed at my head. "Do it...please..."

She's insane. What have they given her to make her beg for death? What have they already done to her that I don't know about?

Her bloodshot blue eyes scan the men surrounding us before they meet mine again. "Please, Haidyn. You said you love me."

My chest tightens to the point I can't breathe at her words. *I do.* More than life itself. But I can't take hers. I turn back to her mother. "What do you fucking want from me?" I scream, stepping into her, and one of her men shoves me back. "Huh? Let her fucking go! I'm right here." I'm shouting, my body vibrating with desperation.

My hand is grabbed, and I go to yank it away, but something heavy is placed in it. Looking down, I see it's the gun that the Lord in the mask was pointing at my face.

"You're running out of time, Haidyn," Isabella reminds me.

I don't even think. I turn, lift the gun, and aim it at her head, pulling the trigger just as I'm hit from the side and knocked to the ground.

BANG!

The gunshot ricochets through the trees, making birds fly off in the distance, missing the bitch.

Isabella still stands right where she was giving me a cruel smile. All the men laugh, and my stomach sinks when her eyes drop to her watch, and she speaks. "Time's up."

I look up at my wife from where I lay and see she's up on her feet ready to run and one of the guys tackles her to the muddy ground.

We're outnumbered.

"Don't fucking touch her!" I scream, trying to knock off the man who has a knee in the back of my neck, pinning the side of my face down into the ground. When he removes it for just a second, I think this is my chance, but then I feel a sting in my neck, and I'm paralyzed. Unable to move.

Charlotte is dragged back by her ankles as she fights them, kicking her legs and swinging her arms. She screams, and the man who's got ahold of her barks, "Help me out."

I lie helpless on the ground, forced to watch when a man kneels beside her, holding a gun to her head and speaking to me. "You made your decision."

Hudson walks over to her—he's the only one not in a cloak and Lords mask—and she kicks and screams as he drops to his knees and grabs her legs. He pushes them to her bare and bloody chest and takes her arms, pulling them underneath her bent legs. He ties off her wrists, locking her legs in place. He stands and the guy who tackled her stands as well. They both stare down at her, admiring my very naked and helpless wife.

"Pl-ease." She sobs, rolling onto her side and pulling on the rope. "HAIDYN!" she screams my name.

I'm...sorry. Not only am I paralyzed, but I also can't speak. I'm fucking useless. One more person in my life who I've failed.

The man still kneels beside her with the gun pointed at her head as if I could do anything to them to save her. I can't let him take her from me. Not like this. Not here in this hell. I can help her through it.

Hudson drops to his knees and unzips his jeans. He pulls out a pocketknife and flips it open. He grips her ass cheek in his hand and cuts off my name I branded onto her. I gave her that with plans to send her back to her mother. A show of ownership that I had over her. A way to rub it in Isabella's face that she fucked with us, and I fucked her daughter. Now it's a way to cause her pain.

Charlotte lets out a blood-curdling scream, and he tosses it to the side as blood flows from the chunk now missing.

"Go ahead and take that gun she gave you and shoot yourself afterward," he tells me. "Because it won't matter that you're too much of a coward to kill her. She'll never be the same after I'm done." Then he begins to rape my wife.

She's screaming and sobbing. So loud, that I hear her even over the ringing in my ears. I look down at the gun they gave me that was knocked out of my hands. It's close enough to reach if I could move. I could have killed Hudson instead of Isabella. But I guarantee there's only one bullet in that gun. The one they wanted me to use on Charlotte, and I wasted it on her bitch of a mom. If I killed him, they would have killed me. And I can't die. She's going to need me after this. Now more than ever.

"Hai-dyn." She sobs, and a lump forms in my throat while he pins the side of her face down into the mud.

I'm sorry, doll face.

Hudson grunts, pushing deep inside her, and comes. He gets to his feet and laughs down at her as she holds her eyes tightly shut, gasping for breath.

"Next," her mother calls out, and another man falls to his knees. She fights the rope that's got her tied in place. "It's just sex, dear," her mother tells her. "We've all been through this. It will make you stronger."

"Ple-ease," she begs, and it kills me. "Haidyn, stop them... help me!"

I'm sorry.

She closes her bloodshot eyes, unable to look at me. They're doing this to her because of me. It's about torturing me. My wife is innocent and was never given all the facts about the life she thought she wanted.

I've betrayed her. I've failed at the one thing I told her I'd do—protect her. Instead, I'm allowing men to line up and rape her like an offering to the Lords while I lay on the ground unable to move and forced to watch it happen. To remind me that I have no say in what happens to her. She belongs to them now, and they're going to do whatever they want.

When the last guy is done, Hudson throws the knife down, and it lands blade down in the mud next to her head. Everyone leaves us alone out by the fence, and I'm finally able to move again.

I crawl to her, grabbing the knife and cut the rope that binds her wrists behind her bent knees. Then I pick her up and take her straight inside to a bathroom, where I lay her in the tub. I start the water and set the drain.

She's covered in dirt and blood. She's bleeding in multiple places—wrists, ankles, and her neck where she fought the barbed wire. Her ass where Hudson removed her brand. I turn to the cabinets and yank them up, slamming them shut. I find three washcloths and duct tape. I wrap one around each of her wrists as tightly as I can and then place the tape around each one, making sure the washcloths stay in place to help stop the bleeding and not to get wet while she's in the tub. Then I fold the last one and place it around her bleeding neck, holding it tightly to her throat.

My eyes go to hers and see they're dead, lifeless. There's nothing there. Those dark blue-sapphire eyes that I fell in love with no longer exist. She stopped crying during the third guy and shut down. Went numb.

"You're okay, doll face," I tell her, knowing it's a goddamn lie. This is what they wanted. Her broken and compliant. The water fills the tub as the dirt and blood swirl around her. "I'm sorry, Charlotte. I couldn't kill you. I love you." I couldn't do it. I know it's the most cowardly thing I've ever done. But I just can't let her go. It doesn't matter what she's been through; I'll love her the same way and take care of her. She's my wife. I took vows.

A single tear falls from the corner of her eye before she speaks. "I hate you."

I blink, and she's gone. I'm no longer in the bathroom. She's no longer in the tub. "Charlotte?" I bark, starting to panic when I see nothing but darkness. "CHARLOTTE!"

"How was it?" A woman's familiar voice fills my ears as a light turns on, blinding me.

"What the fuck did you do to her, you fucking bitch? Where did you take her?" I'm gasping for air, trying to get up, but I can't move. I blink rapidly needing my eyes to adjust to the harsh light.

"Haidyn, you're hallucinating," Isabella speaks.

"No—"

"Yeah, that's what the drugs do to you. Nothing is more terrifying than a mind. It knows your worst fears. You can't escape it. And I was in yours for six months. I know how it works."

"History has a way of repeating itself, Haidyn. Remember that." She had said to me when I found her in my house while Charlotte was in my bed. She wanted me to remember what she made me do to Sierra and put Charlotte in the same position.

"For the next several days, you'll have hallucinations. It's poetic, really. You're going to drive yourself mad, putting the woman you love through so much pain and suffering because we both know your biggest fear is living without her." She snorts. "And although I tell you it's not real, it'll feel real. Every single time."

I blink, trying to get my breathing under control. My jaw is sore from being clenched so tight.

She walks over to the bed, and I wonder if any of it was real? Was I ever hanging from the ceiling in this concrete box? If so, when did she cut me down and secure me back in the hospital bed?

Her hands touch my chest, and I stiffen as she runs her pointy nails over my Lords and 666 brands. "She'll be here soon..."

"No." I don't believe anything she says. How do I know that wasn't real and this is the hallucination? One of my fears is her being locked in this place.

Isabella gives a rough laugh. "Oh, she's on her way. Did you really think hiding her out at Carnage would stop me from getting my hands on my daughter?" She makes a tsking sound. "I've let you keep these." She pinches my Lords brand. "Because that will be her first task. You're going to get to see just how much she loves you, Haidyn. If she chooses to hurt you or take a punishment for herself." With that, she walks out, bathing me in darkness again.

I arch my neck and let out a scream of frustration as I yank on the restraints that keep me tied to this bed. Breathing heavily, I sink into it, knowing I'm not getting out. I knew when I left her tied to her bed, that this is where I'll be until I die. Charlotte will choose the right thing. And if she doesn't, I'll cut them off myself to keep her from being punished because of me.

In a world where it's either you or me...I'll always choose me. I hope my wife still feels that way.

Shhh...

Chapter 80

Charlotte

We rode the rest of the quick drive in silence. As he pulls into a drive, he orders, "There's a hoodie in the back seat. Put it on."

I turn and lean over, grabbing the black hoodie and pulling it over my head. It has to be a man's large due to how big it is on me. It makes me think of Haidyn.

He comes to a stop and puts the car in park. "It has to look real."

I swing my head to look at him just as his fist connects with my face. He knocks my head back into the window. Tears instantly fill my eyes, and my breath is momentarily taken away before the pain takes over, making me cry out. An instant headache throbs behind my eyes.

My shaking hands go to my face, and I lean forward as blood drips from my nose and fills my mouth.

He opens his door and slams it shut. I realize I'm crying when he opens mine. He pulls me out by my hair and shoves me to the ground. I try to crawl away, but he grabs my hands and pulls them behind my back. He places me in handcuffs and yanks me to my feet. "You fucking..."

He slaps a hand over my mouth. "Save your energy, you're going to need it." He leaves me to stand there by myself on shaking legs as he gets back into the car.

Yanking up my hoodie, I feel him slide something into the back of my jeans and then he puts the hoodie back down covering it up. "You'll need this too." He shoves something into my back pocket. "Let's go." He grips my upper arm and yanks me up a set of steps.

I try to even my breathing out and calm down, but I'm having a hard time walking in a straight line. I feel dizzy, my face is throbbing, and I'm spitting blood. I can feel it running down my chin. He opens the front door and pushes me inside. I fall to my knees and cry out.

Fuck, Haidyn's brothers are going to kill me if Bill doesn't do it himself.

"Bill," a familiar voice sings. "What did you bring me?"

My hair is grabbed, and my head yanked back. I grind my teeth to try to keep quiet. But my stomach drops when I see a set of brown eyes.

"What?" I gasp. "No..."

He kneels in front of me. His eyes search mine before they drop to my bloody hoodie. He reaches out to touch my face, and I pull away, dropping my chin to my neck to avoid him.

He yanks my head up and grips my tear-streaked face. It makes my already throbbing cheeks hurt. "I thought you'd miss me, *doll face*." He calls me by the nickname that Haidyn gave me, and I flinch.

"What...are you doing here?" I ask breathlessly. So confused. Bill didn't mention Wesley being involved.

He laughs loudly. "Did you really never question my involvement in your life? The fact that I wouldn't fuck you?" His laughter grows. "Your mother made me promise that I wouldn't touch you. And it was so hard to do when you begged me like a whore."

I flinch and try to pull away, but he just tightens his grip, making me cry out.

"And your brand...didn't you wonder why I never brought it up when I saw you naked?"

"Nooo," I say as my cheeks dig into my teeth from his tight grip.

"You're such a naive little bitch." He laughs in my face.

"Where's my wife?" Bill asks, sounding bored.

Wesley lets go of me and stands to his full height, but his eyes remain on mine when he smirks. "She's in the middle of something."

"What am I supposed to do with Annabelle?" he demands as if babysitting me is putting him out.

"I have an idea." Wesley bends down, grabs my hair, and yanks me to my feet. He's got me bent over at the waist so all I can see is our shoes as we walk on old hardwood floors, and then we're going down a flight of stairs, and the floor changes to concrete.

I'm brought to a stop and shoved into a wall. The side of my face smashes into it as my wrists are freed. The sound of steel squeaks, and then I'm shoved to my knees once more. "She'll be fine in here until her mother is ready to see her. She has him to keep her company." He nods behind me.

Looking up, I see a hospital bed shoved into the far wall of a small concrete room. "Haidyn?" I gasp, scrambling to my feet before running over to him. "Haidyn...oh my God." I cry as I see him lying on the bed. His eyes are closed, and I quickly look over the restraints that keep him secured to it. He has an IV in his right arm, and a bag of fluids hangs from a nail on the wall next to him.

"What did you do to him?" I demand. "Haidyn?" My hands shake his bare chest. Oh my God, he feels so cold. "Haidyn, wake up."

"Pathetic, isn't it?" Wesley laughs. "This could have been avoided if Isabella had just let me slit his throat."

I spin around, my hair whipping my tear-streaked and bloody face. My stomach drops at his words. Stepping forward, I ask, "What did you say?" My voice trembles just like my body.

He smirks, placing his forearm on the inside of the door. Popping a hip out, he speaks. "Didn't you watch the video I sent you?" He laughs and adds, "When he *tried* to commit suicide."

I step toward my once fake boyfriend, tears running down my face. "Why would you...?"

"How about all the other videos?" he smirks and I'm having a hard time catching my breath. "See...it was all a test. One to see if you were that easy to manipulate." He laughs like it's a joke. "I knew you'd fall for it. You wouldn't be able to *not* feel sorry for the tortured man. Didn't matter how shitty he treated you. All of you bitches are the same." He places his hands under his chin and speaks in a high-pitch voice. "I can change him." Then his eyes go hard, and he takes a step closer to me. "No matter how many times your mother has told you that you're special, I promise you, you're not special, Annabelle. Especially to a Spade brother." He throws his head back laughing. "He's here for your mother, Anna, not you. And when she decides he's served his time and you're ready to take her place—she'll make you kill him." He steps back and grabs the door.

"No," I say, running toward it, but he slams it in my face. "Wesley?" I shout, slamming my fists on the cold steel. I hear the locks set in place as we're covered in complete darkness. "Haidyn?" I ask, spinning around and blinking rapidly, trying to adjust my eyes to get my vision back. "Haidyn?" I reach my hands out to feel my way. I come to a stop and remember that Bill put something in my back pocket that he said I'd need.

My shaking hands go to my jeans, and I feel my phone. I pull it out, sobbing with excitement. My trembling hands almost drop it before I can open it up to the flashlight. Turning it on, I make my way over to Haidyn and prop it up on the bed so I can see the medical restraints. I unbuckle his wrists and ankles, and I rip out the IV, knowing whatever is in it can't be good.

"Haidyn, please wake up," I whisper, wondering if they have cameras in here. If so, how long until they return? Until they realize this is all a setup? "Haidyn, please...I need to know you're okay." I sniff, and it hurts since I'm pretty sure my nose is broken. "Please... Haidyn." I shake his bare chest with my free hand.

He's cold to the touch, so I reach up and feel for a pulse. It's weak, and it makes me cry harder. "Please don't die. Please don't leave me again," I beg, yanking the bloody hoodie up and over my head and laying it over him with shaking hands. "I love you." Tears fall from my eyes and drop on his cheeks. "Did you hear me?" I scream in his face, needing him to open his eyes. "Look at me." I gasp, trying to catch my breath. "I love you. Please, Haidyn...don't do this to me...to us."

HAIDYN

I CAN HEAR HER VOICE. IT'S AS IF SHE'S RIGHT HERE WITH ME, but I know that's not possible. She's at Carnage with my brothers where she belongs. Isabella was lying. She wants me to think she won.

"Haidyn, please?" my wife begs, and it feels like the room shakes.

I don't know what she's begging for, but whatever it is, I'd give it to her.

"HAIDYN!"

Her voice is louder, and then there's a bright light in my eyes.

"Please wake up. I need you to wake up."

"Char...?" I cough, unable to finish saying her name. It's not real. It's a trick my mind is playing on me. My own personal hell. Any second I'm going to have to choose...watch her mother's minions torture and rape her or kill my wife. Even though I know it's not real, I can't kill her. I can't live if she doesn't. I'm a coward.

"Yes, Haidyn. It's me. Wake up. Please..."

My heavy eyes crack open, and I expect to see nothing but the black room, but there's a light by my head. It shines on the opposite wall next to the bed.

"Oh my God." I hear a voice sob. "Haidyn."

I turn my head to the left, and the light moves, shining on my face, and I blink rapidly.

She crawls onto the bed and lies down next to me. I wrap my arms around her and pull her against me. My one hand tangles in her soft hair while the other holds her waist. She's crying. Her small body shakes against mine. "You're okay, doll face. You'll be okay." Fuck, I can smell her. Strawberries and cream. It's as if we're lying in our bed back at home. "Take the brands." I tell her. "Can you do that for me, doll face?"

"Haidyn—what...?" She sniffs.

"Do whatever they want you to do. I'm so sorry I let them hurt you. I promise that I love you. Just do whatever they want you to do. Can you promise me that, Charlotte?"

"Haidyn," she cries softly. "No...I love you..."

"Shh, it'll be okay." I want her to know that no matter what, she'll be okay without me. "I love you," I whisper.

Somehow, I feel a little more at peace. I had already made up my mind that I was going to leave her, but I didn't know until now that I needed to hear her one more time. I was already willing to give up my life for hers. Now I can without them hurting her in the process. She shouldn't have to prove who she is. Not when I can show her who she can be.

Maybe this is what hell is. I've had it wrong all these years. It's not

Carnage or physical torture. It's the mind games. The what-ifs...what could have been...

I wish I could say that I'm stronger than this, but I'm not. If I'm dead, then they won't have anything to show off for. They won't force her to do shit against her will if I'm not here to witness it.

I don't need a gun and a bullet to end it all. I just have to let go of her.

Shhh...

Chapter 81

Charlotte

His body goes limp against mine just as the door opens. I jump off the bed and spin around to see two tall figures enter the room. I can't make out who they are because I've been in a blacked-out room, and the light from the hallway behind them is blinding.

I reach into the back of my jeans, pulling the gun out that Bill put there after he dragged me out of his car. I point it at them, stepping in front of the end of the bed that my husband lies on, blocking him.

"Wait!" One throws up their hands. "Charlotte, it's Kash and Saint."

I lower the gun and sniff. "Something's wrong with him," I rush out, stepping to the side. "He was talking to me, but I couldn't get him to wake up." I can't explain it, but he wasn't really here. "Then he went limp."

They both run past me and over to Haidyn. "Is there a goddamn light in here?" Saint snaps.

I turn the flashlight back on my phone and shine it on the wall, searching for some kind of switch, but see nothing. I go out into the hall and search the wall. I see a few switches and flip them on and then rush back to see if they've worked.

It did. The room has a single bulb hanging from the ceiling, and both of his brothers are leaning over the bed, speaking into his face and shaking his shoulders. Nothing.

"Let's get him the fuck out of here," Kashton barks to Saint.

I wrap my arms around myself. "Where is everyone?"

"Tyson and his boys are searching for your mother. There's another guy..."

"I'm right here." My hair is grabbed, and my neck yanked back to stare up at the ceiling.

"Let her go," Kashton demands. "And I won't blow your fucking head off."

Wesley laughs. "Do you really think I'll let you drag me to Carnage? That I'd ever go back to that god-awful place?"

"What the fuck are you talking about?" Saint barks.

He doesn't answer and the room falls silent, and I try to wiggle free of his hold. I'm so tired, and my head pounds. I just want to crawl back into bed with my husband. He needs me. We're wasting time.

"Wesley..."

"My name isn't Wesley,'" he shouts, shaking me.

I feel the heavy gun in my right hand, and I point it down at the ground, not taking a second to think about it. I pull the trigger, momentarily going deaf as it echoes in the tight concrete box. Wesley shoves me forward, and I turn around to see him step out of the room. His mouth is open, and he's screaming, but the only thing I hear is the sound of my ears ringing from the first shot.

Lifting the gun, I shoot again, and he falls to his knees as blood covers his jeans.

The gun is ripped from my hands, and I'm pushed to the concrete floor onto my back. I look up to see Kashton straddling me. His hands grip my wrists, holding them down as he looks over to the right. His mouth is moving, but I can't understand what he's saying.

That ringing is still there. I don't even try to fight him.

He lets go of me, gets up, and yanks me to my feet. Placing his hands on either side of my face, he searches my eyes as his lips move but still nothing. Picking me up, he carries me out of the room, and my head hangs off his arm as I see Ryat and Sin rush into the room and help Saint pull an unconscious Haidyn out of bed.

♠

I'M CARRIED ONTO THE PLANE AND SET ON THE COUCH. I HAVEN'T

spoken to anyone. My ears finally quit ringing, but my face is still pounding.

"Fuck," Kashton hisses. Pushing my head from side to side, he examines my face. "I think you broke her fucking nose," he growls.

"I had to do something," Bill growls, walking on next.

"Haidyn is going to kill you." Kashton goes on.

"He has to live first," Bill snaps. "Now get over here and help us."

Kashton leaves me to walk back over to the open door. Next, I see Sin, Ryat, and Tyson helping Saint carry Haidyn onto the plane. He's still unconscious. I sat next to him in the car holding his cold hand. I would pray, but there is no God. Not one who listens to a murderer.

I jump to my feet and rush over to them.

"Stay back, love." Kashton picks me up and carries me back over to the couch where he sets me down. "Let them work."

Gavin and Devin step onto the plane, and the door instantly shuts as the engines roar to life.

"Where are your guys?" Sin asks Tyson.

"They're on the ground. They got Hudson and Isabella. They're going to meet us back at Carnage. We didn't want them on the plane with us, so they're driving."

They lay Haidyn on the floor, and Gavin and Devin instantly dropped to their knees next to him.

"Why...isn't he awake?" My voice cracks because my throat is so sore from sobbing. I feel sick to my stomach again, but I've managed to keep it down.

No one answers me. Instead, they speak as if I'm not right here.

"His pulse is weak," Gavin informs Devin.

His skin is so pale.

"He's fucking dying. Do something," Saint orders.

I begin to crawl over to him, but I'm picked up off the floor. "No!" I cry as Kashton carries me to the back of the plane. I kick and scream, but it doesn't do any good as he takes me into the back bedroom. He tosses me onto the bed and straddles my hips, pinning my arms down by my head.

I arch my back and scream, "HAIDYN?" hoping he can hear me. That he can wake up for me.

"Hurry up," Kashton snaps, looking over his shoulder.

"I'm sorry, Charlotte. But this is for your own good," Adam states as he fills a syringe with something from a clear vial.

I kick my feet and buck my hips, but Kashton has no trouble holding me down. Adam grabs my face and pushes it to the side before I feel a prick in my neck. My body instantly betrays me, and I go limp.

"That's it, love," Kashton says softly.

I blink, my eyes heavy as I stare up at him. He lets go of my wrists, and I try to move my arms but can't. He pushes my hair from my face and gives me a soft smile. "It's going to be okay." Then he looks at Adam who still stands by the bed. "What did you give her?"

"It was a very small dose of sedative. It's not going to knock her out completely. Just makes her lethargic."

"Hai-dyn." I try to say my husband's name but even I can't understand it. How can they do this to me? If he's dying, I want to be in his arms. I want him to hold me. I want them to kill me. I can't live without him.

The past week has been hell. I refuse to go on without him.

Shhh...

Chapter 82

Charlotte

I'm being carried into Carnage and taken straight to Haidyn's room. Kashton is laying me in his bed when the door bursts open, and Ashtyn enters. "What the fuck is wrong with her? Where's Haidyn? Where is Saint?" She starts asking questions.

"Haidyn is being taken to the hospital wing. Saint is with him. And I gave her a sedative," Adam answers.

My head falls to the side, and I blink, seeing Ashtyn come to sit next to me. "Why? What happened?" She grabs my hand and holds it.

"Haidyn was dying, and she was distraught. It was a very tight space, and I had to do something to give Devin and Gavin room to work."

"So you drugged her?" she snaps.

He rushes over to his bag that he keeps on the floor by the table he has taken over as his desk and unzips it. He starts pulling things out, one of them being a needle.

"What the fuck are you doing?" Ashtyn snaps. "Leave her with me. She'll be fine."

"I'm going to start an IV. The meds will pull her out of her current state, and she'll be back to herself."

"Who the fuck are you, Adam?" she demands, and he doesn't answer. "Where did you learn to start IVs?"

He comes over and pushes the needle into my arm and then tapes it off before he places the IV bag up. "Come here and hold this," he barks at her.

She lets go of my hand and jumps to her feet. Then he and Kashton start to walk toward Haidyn's bedroom door.

"Where are you going?" she demands.

"Tyson's guys should be here any moment. We've got to help with her mother and Hudson since the others are in the hospital with Haidyn. Don't leave this room until you hear from us." With that, they leave, slamming the door shut.

HAIDYN

I SIT UP IN THE HOSPITAL BED, MY HEAD FOGGY AND BODY extremely weak. It's taking everything I have to hold my head up. Slowly, I pull a shirt over my head and shove my arms into the sleeves, forcing a groan out of my lips.

"You need to rest," Gavin tells me.

"A few days should be enough," Devin adds.

"He'll take as much time as he needs," Saint informs them, and I roll my eyes.

"I'm fine." I don't feel bad, just tired.

I've been awake for maybe thirty minutes and already want to go back to bed. I begin to put on the sweatpants that Saint brought me, and Devin steps over like he's going to help me, but I shoo him away. I'm fucking capable of dressing myself. It might take me a minute, but I'll get it done.

The moment I woke up, Gavin and Devin had me chugging fluids and electrolytes like it was vodka and I'm an alcoholic.

The door opens, and I look up to see three men enter the room. The first thing I asked when I came to was where was Charlotte. I was informed that she was with Ashtyn and was on her way to my room. The second thing I asked for was to see Sin, Tyson, and Ryat. I was surprised to find out they were already here at Carnage.

"You look like shit, man." Sin is the first one to speak.

Tyson nods and agrees. "I have seen you look better."

Ryat remains quiet. All three come to stand by the side of my bed while Gavin and Devin stand on the other. Kashton sits in the window, looking out at the courtyard. He hasn't spoken to me since I came to. Saint leans against the far wall, glaring at Adam standing beside him. Everyone seems to be on edge, and no one has filled me in on how they saved me yet. I have plenty of time to hear that story, but this is important.

"What do you need?" Ryat finally speaks.

They think I've asked them to come here to help me out with something. If only that were the case. "I..." Pausing, I'm not sure where to start. What I have to tell them will change their lives.

"Haidyn has been given some new information." Saint fills my silence. "And it involves your wives." I've just finished explaining it to my brothers since it involves Ashtyn.

"What the fuck is it?" Ryat is the first one to ask to step forward.

I wouldn't have led with that but okay. "I was given something..." I gesture to my right arm. "Some kind of drug that helps you live longer."

Sin snorts. "Like vampire shit? Come on, Haidyn, you're not supposed to believe everything you read online."

I give a soft laugh. "Isabella told me that the founders were given enhancements."

"You mean like the kind given for twins?" Tyson inquires.

I don't ask if he means the women or the men. I'll fill them in on that later. One surprise at a time. "Kinda." I shrug. "I was given medication that will keep me from getting sick." They all frown. "No cancer, no common cold. Obviously, I can still die, but it won't be from an illness."

"I don't understand what that has to do with us or our wives," Tyson speaks.

"Isabella also informed me that women started the Lords, and if those founders were given the drug..." They look from one another and then back to me, so I continue. "Then they had children...and their children..." They get the picture.

"You think our wives came from founders?" Sin is the one who asks. His voice tells me he doesn't want to believe me. But the way he rubs the back of his neck tells me he's considering it.

I know for a fact that Blakely is. Isabella told me so, and Ashtyn...

my father told me in his office that I was lucky he found *another one* when he had Bill in his office. I now understand that he was talking about Ash being from a founder. And then Charlotte was one as well. "I can't be sure, but they should be tested," I say. That's what Devin and Gavin are for.

"What if they did, and they have this shit, and we don't?" Ryat looks at Gavin. "You can give it to us, right?"

"Guys..." Gavin raises his hands out to his sides in surrender. "We don't know what it is."

"But—"

"And we don't have access to it," Devin finishes, cutting off Tyson.

"I can get it," I assure them, understanding how they feel. I'll go back to Dollhouse and turn that place upside down to find it. When the guys dragged me out of there, I was unconscious. Otherwise, I would have had them get it before we left.

"What do you need? From our wives?" Sin asks.

"Blood work," Devin answers. "I can let you know the results as soon as tomorrow, assuming we can get a sample tonight."

"And if they have it?" Ryat speaks up. "You'll give it to us immediately." It wasn't a question.

"No." Gavin shakes his head.

"Are you fucking serious?" Sin demands. "If my wife has something that I don't, I'm fucking taking it." He steps forward.

The thing about a Lady is that if your Lord dies, she is regifted to another. I'm not sure about Laikyn and Ellington, but I'm positive that Blakely will test positive for the enhancement.

"We don't know what it will do to you." Gavin points at me. "Look at him. He's weak. Tyson doesn't have assignments, but you two do." He looks from Sin to Ryat. "The last thing I'm going to do is shoot you up with God knows what and then send you on your way. What if you get called on an assignment the following day and are too weak to fight and are killed? Then you have your wives regifted to another Lord. Is that what you want?"

"Fuck no!" Sin snaps, running his hand through his hair.

Ryat drops his head, rubbing the back of his neck as he contemplates his options.

"The first time I had an IV in my arm for a good twelve hours," I say. "Longer the second time." I look over at Gavin. "What if you give them an hour's worth a day? See how they react to it?"

I look back at Ryat, Tyson, and Sin. They each have their eyes on Gavin, waiting for his approval. Finally, he nods. "We can try it."

"Did she tell you the founders' families?" Tyson looks at me.

I shake my head. "No. But not very many women we know have pull over the Lords, so I'm guessing those that we know of, is a good place to start."

"I can see that," Tyson agrees.

"Fucking bitch," Ryat growls. "God, I knew LeAnne would be a pain in my side. Should have made sure that Matt killed her."

Gavin looks at Sin. "I've already pulled a fresh blood sample from Laura, and it's at the lab. I put a rush on it and should know by morning."

"But Laura wasn't important," Sin states. "She only had the position she did because of her marriage to Nicholas. Which means the Asher name was the one from the founder. Not Elli's mother."

Gavin shrugs. "It doesn't hurt to check. Especially since your father is the biological father of Laura's child. If they both come back negative...we've got options."

Sin nods, leaving it at that. He'll have that conversation later with his wife.

"What about our children?" Ryat questions. "If our wives have it, what does that do to the babies?"

"We've kept a close eye on the pregnancies and haven't seen a reason to be concerned yet. Of course, we'll have to do blood work once the babies are delivered, but I don't see any reason to panic. We'll test the wives first and then monitor the babies even closer until delivery."

Silence fills the room as they let all the new information sink in and think about their options, which aren't many. Their wives either have the enhancement or they don't.

I look over at Adam who hasn't spoken to me. I'm surprised he's even here. "You know what this means?"

His blank stare meets mine.

"If Ashtyn is from a founder, then so are you," I state the obvious.

Saint is the one who lets out a sigh as if he hadn't thought of that. His mind has been on his wife, not his brother-in-law.

"Doesn't matter." Adam shakes his head. He knows where his future is going, and it has nothing to do with the Lords.

"Adam—"

"I said it doesn't matter, Kash," Adam snaps at him.

Silence falls over the room once again, and after a few minutes, I clear my throat. "There's one more thing."

"What is it?" Tyson sighs.

"They gave me several different drugs, and I'm not sure which one it was...but one of them made me hallucinate." If they're going to take something, they need to prepare themselves.

"Hallucinate how?" Sin asks.

I'm not sure how to explain it. "Think of worst-case scenarios."

They all nod as if understanding, and then everyone filters out of my room to go get the tests done. Kashton hovers, and I know what's coming before he even opens his mouth.

"Just say it," I tell Kash, watching him pace. It's going to come sooner or later, and I'd rather it be now.

He comes to a stop and lets out a frustrated sigh. "Not suicidal?" He gives a rough laugh. "That seemed pretty fucking suicidal to me, Haidyn." His hard eyes glare at me.

"Charlotte—"

"Don't tell me you did that for her, Haidyn!" he shouts, interrupting me. "Do you have any idea what kind of state she was in? She's not my favorite person, but Charlotte was practically comatose. She fucking shut down on all of us. Hell, Adam wanted to tie her to a hospital bed and sedate her with a feeding tube." My hands fist at that thought. "Fuck, man." His eyes soften, and his shoulders slump. "How many times do I have to think you've killed yourself? Hmm? How many times do I have to lose a brother?"

The sincerity in his voice makes my chest ache.

He steps closer to the bed and shoves his hands into the front pockets of his bloody jeans. He hasn't changed since they found me. "We've already said bye to Adam twice. And we're going to have to do it again. But how many times are you going to leave us?"

"I'm not going anywhere."

He snorts, not believing a word I say. "You've been MIA and got married. FUCKING MARRIED!" Kash screams. "You had Adam there. What about us, huh? What about me?"

"I made you her guardian," I inform him.

"How was that possible, Haidyn? Hmm? Because I wasn't fucking there to sign off on that."

I run a hand down my face. "I had Adam sign your name."

He throws his arms out to his side and then lets them fall, slapping his thighs. "You should have just had Adam sign his."

"I wanted you."

"I—" The sound of the door opening cuts me off, and I see Charlotte step into the room.

I stiffen when I see she's got black eyes and a cut on her face. "What the fuck happened?" My wide eyes go to Kash.

He turns to see her standing there and speaks, ignoring my question. "We'll finish this conversation later," Kash tells me and then walks over to her. Placing his hands on either side of her bruised face. "Give him hell, love." He then releases her, reaches into his pocket, and pulls out a ring. *My wedding ring*. Handing it over to her, he exits, leaving us alone.

She shuts the door and leans back against it, crossing her arms over her chest.

"Doll face?" I lower my voice. "What happened to you?" Fuck, I never thought I'd see her again, and I have the urge to pinch myself to make sure I'm not hallucinating or dreaming.

Her gaze drops to her shoes while mine looks over her yoga pants and my oversized T-shirt, before her tear-filled eyes slowly look up to meet mine.

I sigh. "Charlotte—"

"You left me naked...tied to my bed." She pulls her bottom lip in to nibble on it nervously.

"I had no..."

"Choice?" She gives a rough laugh, looking at my ring in her hand. "You're the one who told me we always have a choice. You just *chose* to leave me!" Her voice rises.

I expected everyone to hate me. That was the point. They were supposed to despise me and move on with their lives while I rotted in there.

"I needed you, and you left me." The sound of her voice breaking makes my chest tighten.

"I left for you."

She sniffs, and her eyes look around the room, unable to meet mine. "I...I'm sorry for what she did to you."

I'm not sure if she's referring to four years ago or this past week. I'm afraid to even ask how much Kashton and Saint have told her, so I say, "Charlotte, it wasn't your fault."

"But that's why you wanted me, right?" Her tear-filled eyes meet mine, and I realize she's referring to back then. "When you found out who I really was. Because of her...because of what my mother did to you and your brothers? I was your revenge."

"Yes," I answer her honestly.

She nods her head, her bottom lip trembling.

"But then I fell in love with you," I add. "And none of that mattered."

She gives a rough laugh. "How can you say none of it mattered? She tortured you. She tortured your brothers...you should have let her take what she wanted."

"She wanted you," I growl. That was her endgame. She wanted my wife to take over her fucked-up operation. I was just a bonus. Bill was right; Charlotte would never be the Lady that Isabella wanted her to be. She knew she needed leverage, and I was it.

"Come here, doll face," I order softly, but she stays leaning up against the door. Pushing up off the bed, I get to my feet, wanting to walk over to her, but I sway a little and sit back onto the bed.

She's in front of me the next second, scolding me. "Be careful."

I part my thighs and pull her to stand between them. Her blue eyes narrow on mine. "You tricked me. *Again.*"

I link my fingers behind her back, holding her in place. I'm weak right now, but I feel like I can still hold her. Now if she pulls out a knife to stab me or starts swinging, she'll win. "I did what I thought was right. When put in any kind of situation where it's either you or me, it'll always be you." *I'll always put her first.*

Taking in a deep breath, she places her small hands on my face as her eyes search mine. Fuck, I never thought I'd see them again any other time than in my dreams. But that'll never compare to the real thing. "Why do you always give yourself up for everyone else?"

Jesus! How much have they told her?

"I didn't want you to save me."

"That's my job—"

"My life doesn't matter if I don't have you in it." She interrupts me. "Don't you get that?"

Unlinking my fingers, I reach up and brush her hair back from her face, watching her pretty eyes swim in the tears that refuse to fall. "You said you wanted to spend forever with me. Do you still mean that?" I ask even though she's stuck with me. We took vows, and she wears my ring. My name is branded on her ass, for fuck's sake.

"To some, forever is only a matter of seconds." She throws my previous words back into my face.

A smile tugs at my lips, and she frowns. How can I possibly find that funny? Lifting her left hand, I look at her wedding ring. "There is no amount of time that will be enough with you," I tell her, my eyes meet hers again to see the first tear fall over her bottom lashes. I brush it away from her cheek. "But I promise to be yours until the day that I die." Thanks to Isabella, that might be longer than I originally had.

She holds up my ring between us. "If you put this back on, you better never take it off again."

I smile, taking it from her, and slide it on my finger. "Never," I promise, wrapping my arms back around her so she doesn't pull away. "Tell me, doll face. What happened?" My eyes roam her face, looking for any other sign of trauma.

She licks her lips. "Bill punched me in the face..."

"He did what?" I shout, my body instantly shaking at her words, making her flinch. My blood pressure rises to the roof immediately.

Placing her hands gently on either side of her face, she adds, "It had to look real. I couldn't just walk into Dollhouse..."

"You were fucking there?" I snap. This isn't getting any better. My hands go to her yoga pants and yank them down, turning her to look at her ass. I release a sigh when I see my name branded on her ass. Hudson didn't cut it off. It was just a hallucination.

"Haidyn." She frowns, pulling them back up. "Yes. I was lying in bed with you. Spoke to you."

When the fuck was she in bed with me? "Char—"

"I wasn't going to stay behind while your brothers went to save my husband." She places her forehead against mine and closes her eyes. "I'm glad you're okay, Haidyn, but if you ever leave me again, I will throw another knife at you, and I will kill you myself."

I chuckle and then flinch due to my soreness. "When I die, I want it to be by your hands, doll face."

Chapter 83

Haidyn

"Be careful," my wife scolds me as we enter our bedroom at Carnage.

"I'm fine," I assure her, although I'm having a hard time keeping my eyes open.

I was able to convince Devin and Gavin to let me sleep in my own bed with my wife tonight, but only if I allowed them to give me a shot in the ass. Whatever it is, it's made me tired as fuck.

"You guys need my help?" Adam asks, pushing a wheelchair. Gavin and Devin tried to make me sit in it, and I told them to fuck off. They seemed satisfied enough when Adam volunteered to follow us with it.

"We'll be fine," I tell him.

"Thank you." My wife smiles, encouraging his help.

He nods and backs out into the hall. "If you need me, I'm right across the hall." Then he shuts the door, leaving us alone.

She helps me into the bathroom, and she turns the faucet on to the tub. "No. I want to take a shower."

"Haidyn—"

"I'm taking a shower, Charlotte." I leave no room to argue. Honestly, I'm not sure I can get back up if I sit down in the bath, but I won't tell her that. I hate looking weak, especially in front of her.

Huffing, she shuts off the faucet and opens the shower door, turning it on while I remove the T-shirt and sweatpants before we enter the shower.

I allow her to wash me while I sway back and forth on my feet. She makes it fast, knowing that I'm fading quickly.

She helps dry me off, and I enter the bedroom to see her over by the door about to turn the light off. "Leave it on." It has nothing to do with spending eight days in a blacked-out room and everything with wanting to see my wife.

Spinning around, she looks at me tilting her head as if to question how we will sleep with the light on, but she just nods and walks over to the bed.

I crawl in on my side—closest to the door—and she gets in, cuddling up next to me. I wrap my arms around her and hold her to me as tight as I can, which isn't much, considering how weak I still am.

Her body begins to shake against mine, and then she sniffs. Lowering my head to hers, I kiss her forehead. "It's okay, doll face. I'm here."

She sniffs again, and her arms tighten on me. "Promise me—"

"I'll never leave you." I interrupt her, knowing exactly what she was going to say. "I promise."

Closing my eyes, I hope that when I open them, she's still here... with me...in our bed. I hope this isn't another hallucination.

♠

My heavy eyes open, and I close them immediately at the harsh light. I reach out and feel nothing but blank space.

I open my eyes and sit straight up, flinching at the sharp pain that takes my breath away. "Fuck," I growl, reaching up to rub the back of my neck.

"Haidyn." The door to the bathroom opens, and my wife exits, rushing over to me. "Hey, are you okay?" She sits down on the bed next to me.

I reach out, grab her hand, and lie down, pulling her on top of me. Her giggle fills the room. Fuck, I never thought I'd hear that again.

"You need to take it easy," she says and sits up, straddling my hips.

I look up at her, and she's smiling down at me. She looks absolutely stunning, even with her black eyes and bruised face. Reaching up, I push her hair from her face. "How do you feel?"

"I'm fine. Don't worry about me. How do you feel?"

"I'm fine."

"Lie," she deadpans. And her face falls as her eyes look me over. "Seriously. How do you feel? Need me to call Devin or Gavin to come check on you? Need some pain pills?"

I shake my head. "No."

"Haidyn." She huffs. Crossing her arms over her chest she looks away from me, her eyes scanning the room.

Reaching up, I undo them and bring her left hand to my lips, kissing her knuckles. Her eyes drop to her wedding ring. "You tricked me." Biting her bottom lip, she brings her eyes back to mine.

"You'll have to be more specific," I say, knowing exactly what she means. I was hoping she'd forget the video I left her, but of course she didn't. "That could describe many things."

She holds up her left hand, arching a brow. "Our marriage. Just how did Adam help force me to marry you?"

I grab her hips and push her onto her back to where I'm kneeling between her legs. I ignore the pain that runs up my side and grind my teeth, hoping she doesn't notice. But when that giggle comes from her perfect lips again, it was totally worth it.

She wraps her legs around my waist while I run my hand up and down her smooth thigh. "I had Adam go through your laptop."

She rolls her eyes dramatically. "Well, I didn't think you needed a Mac. Pretty sure you can afford to buy your own," she jokes.

I don't laugh. "While I had Adam looking through it, he found two devices that were connected to it. An Apple watch and a cell phone."

The smile drops, and her wide eyes search mine. *I have her attention.* "The very same that you had been contacting me from." I knew that the Lords had given her a "fake" life. I just never stopped to think how deep that went. "I had him send you a text from an unknown number after your appointment about turning me over to the Lords."

Her body stiffens under mine, and her breathing picks up, but she remains silent. I wait and let her collect her thoughts, trying to remember how it all went down. "No—"

"I called you after he sent the text to gauge your mood. I even asked you if you were okay when you seemed flustered." It's the only reason I let her leave my house that day. I wanted her to have some alone time while she debated what to do.

Her eyes narrow, and she tries to get up, but I grab her arms, wrapping my hands around her tiny wrists and pin them down by her head. "Haidyn," she growls, fighting me. "What the fuck—?"

"I left you alone all day with your thoughts deciding on if you wanted to turn me over to the Lords or not. Then I arrived at your house, and you pretended to be upset about your fake boy toy." I snort. "I never even had dinner reservations because I knew you wouldn't want to go. You'd be too worked up."

"But...but you left me that night after we signed the marriage license. You went to the cathedral for me. The Lords had texted me to be there or else..." She trails off again.

"Also, Adam." I nod as she puts two and two together.

"Then where the fuck did you go that night?" she snaps.

I smile down at her. "I went and picked up your ring." A friend of mine was holding it for me. It's also why I made her stay behind at the house. If I had let her leave with me like she wanted, she would have known it was all a setup.

Her pretty features soften at my words, and she swallows. "So," she whispers, "you went to all that trouble to trick me into marrying you to piss my mother off."

"No." I frown. "I married you because I love you," I say truthfully.

"But—what if I had taken you to the location that *you* gave me? Then what?" she asks, still confused how I managed to pull it all off. "Huh? I would have known it was a setup."

"I had two plans," I admit shamelessly. "You know the results of one." My eyes slide to her left hand that I still hold pinned down by her head. "The second was you delivered me to the location that I sent you—what you thought were the Lords. Adam would be there waiting for us, dressed in a cloak and mask so you wouldn't see his face. We would have been *ambushed*. He would have placed a hood over your head and handcuffed you, making you think you were being taken. Then Adam would have left us alone after that—done with his part."

Her eyes search mine as if she's looking for the lie. She won't find it. Not anymore. I've been given a second chance at the life she wants. I'm not going to waste it. Telling her the truth won't change the fact that she's my wife and I'm her husband. And she belongs to me and I to her until we die.

"I was going to drive you to a secluded location where I would have stripped you naked and tied you up." My eyes drop to her pretty pink nipples to see they're now hard, and seeing her body react to my plan makes me smile. Our relationship started off with me forcing her to be my good little whore. I want it to stay that way. "I would have left you tied with the hood over your head. Wouldn't want you seeing me too soon. I'd make you assume that you were left there alone wondering what was going to happen to you and what happened to me." I shrug. "Did they kill me and take you for themselves? Your guess is as good as mine."

She bares her white teeth at me while her arms fight my hold, and I tighten my hands around her small wrists making her whimper. Her hips lift off the bed. I'm not back to myself but I'm stronger than I was yesterday, which means whatever Devin and Gavin gave me is working. I'll have them shoot my ass up again with that shit today.

"After a day or two of watching you cry and listening to you beg your kidnapper to let you go, I'd come in as me to kill them and save you." Then she would have married me.

She's panting, her chest rising and falling quickly. I release her wrists, and she reaches up and slaps me, making me laugh. It feels good to know she cares. "You were going to be mine, either way, doll face."

"Fuck you," she spits out, and I wrap my hand around her throat, holding her down onto the mattress but not choking her.

My free hand drops between her parted legs while I sit between them and feel her pussy. She's soaked. "Does the thought of me kidnapping you turn you on, beautiful?"

She arches her neck and moans, and I push a finger into her cunt. "Words, Charlotte." I remove it and slap her shaved pussy.

"Y-yes," she cries out.

"Good girl," I say and slap it again. Goddamn, I missed her. Not just the sex. Everything about her. "Want me to take you to a secluded location, strip you naked, and tie you up?"

"Yes." She nods the best she can.

"Want me to make you beg to be fucked, doll face?"

"Please..." She trails off when I slide two fingers into her this time. I never thought I'd get to be with her again.

Her hands wrap around my wrists, and my fingers pause as her heavy eyes open and meet mine. "You do owe me a honeymoon."

"Yes, I do." And I add, "Whatever my wife wants."

I knew it was wrong, but I didn't give a fuck. I was going to marry this woman, even if I had to make her think her life was in danger. I wasn't sure if she would give me up or not, but I was willing to take that chance, and that's why I had a backup plan. Either way, the result would be the same.

CHARLOTTE

It's been two days since Haidyn was rescued and brought to Carnage. Being with him twenty-four seven is the closest thing to heaven that I'll ever know. He doesn't leave my side. If we're not in his bed, we're in his shower or out on the balcony. If we're not fucking, he's holding me. We can't keep our hands off one another.

My dependency on him has grown more than I thought possible. We need to talk about so many things, but I'm just not ready. Things are going so well, I'm afraid to tell him what I know. That it'll push him away from me. *"In a world where it's either you or me...I'll always choose you."* But what if what he finds out changes everything? It's not something that can easily be overlooked or forgotten. Things have changed, and I don't want him to see me differently.

So I put that thought out of my head for the time being. Like right now, it's a little after noon, and we just got out of bed. His cum still leaks from my ass, soaking my underwear. We were about to get into the shower when Kashton knocked on Haidyn's bedroom door. He told us to wake the fuck up and meet them down in the basement.

I'm tucked into his side, one arm wrapped around the front, the other his back, my fingers linked together, holding on for dear life. Thankfully, he doesn't seem to mind with an arm draped over my shoulders, holding me to him. It's not the easiest to walk like this with him because of our height difference, but I'm afraid to let go.

After I passed out last night, I had a dream that he left me. I woke up in a panic and he was there, holding me, talking to me, fucking me. Reminding me that I'm his good little whore and I belong to him. I fell asleep on my side while he held me tightly with his dick still inside me.

The door to the elevator opens down in the basement and we step out walking through a set of clear plastic curtains. They remind me of a meat department at a store. I half expect to see blood-covered pigs hanging on hooks from the ceiling once we go through them.

But instead, Kashton, Adam, and Saint stand in the center of a room while my mother is chained to a wall. *Close enough.*

She starts screaming into the gag that's secured around her head, making her drool all over her naked body.

My eyes drop to the floor unable to meet hers. All the lies that I believed—I'm so fucking stupid. I thought she was the one thing that was real in my world. Turns out, I had to make up a fake life to find something real.

A cell beeps, and Kashton pulls his out of his pocket before he speaks. "They're here."

I want to ask who else is coming, but I guess I'll find out soon enough.

Turning my back to Isabella, Haidyn pulls me into him, wrapping his arms around me, and I dig my face into his shirt, inhaling his scent. It helps calm me. My breathing evens out, and my body relaxes into his muscular one.

The elevator alerting us to our guests' arrival has me pulling away from him so I can see who it is.

The plastic curtains separate before Ryat and Sin enter the basement. Then Tyson walks in behind them. None of them are known for their kindness but right now they look very pissed, and it makes me wonder what Isabella did to all three of them for them to be here to witness whatever the Spade brothers plan on doing to her.

"The gang is all here," Kashton states. "Let's get started. Haidyn..." He looks over at my husband. "The honor is all yours."

I step away from him, my arms falling to my sides. Instead, I step closer to Adam, who stands off by himself. I still don't know their full story, but all the Spade brothers seem to be mad at one another right now. I've just tuned them out and put all my focus on my husband.

He's started getting his strength back—at least it seemed that way when he tossed me around like a rag doll last night. He held me down and made me beg for each orgasm and I gladly obliged.

Adam places an arm over my shoulder, and I lean into him watching Haidyn step up to my mother. He takes a knife out of his pocket, flips it open, then runs the tip of the blade down her cheek. He cuts the leather strap from the gag, so it falls free of her mouth, but it also slices her cheek open.

A shrill scream comes from her lips, and I cover my ears as the blood drips onto her drool-covered breasts. Adam's arm tightens on me in a protective state. "You get one chance..." Haidyn starts. "Anything you want to tell us?"

She sucks in a deep breath, her body fighting in the chains.

He raises the knife and does the same to her other cheek. The scream that follows seems louder than the last. "I can cut you all day," he tells her.

"The Lords allowed me to train you, but I had to get intel." She's gasping to catch her breath.

"Intel on what?" Haidyn questions.

"They told me that I couldn't kill you but to do whatever was needed to get you to confess," she answers through gritted teeth.

No one says anything, so I ask, "Confess to what?"

"Killing our fathers," Haidyn answers, not turning to face me.

"You killed them for that fucking whore!" she shouts, referring to Ashtyn. Saint goes to step forward, but Kashton grabs his arm, pulling him to a stop. They need information more than her death right now. "They had made deals that they still needed to fulfill."

"You mean like the one they had with Laura?" Sin spits out already knowing that's one of them.

I knew Laura but had no clue just how evil she was. She's Sin's mother-in-law and sold her soul and her daughter to the devil in exchange for her husband to be a prisoner here. Haidyn caught me up on things I needed to know over the past couple of days. I thought how horrible it would be to have a mother that evil. Now I kinda know what that feels like.

Haidyn laughs, making the hairs on the back of my neck rise. When you fall in love with the devil, you see him differently. But I forget just how dark he can be. I like this side of him just as much as I love the other sides of him. Haidyn can be whoever he needs to be when it comes to the situation. As can I.

My mother looks at Sin, and even though she's chained to a concrete wall, she's smiling at him. "You should thank Laura for your wife. It's because of her that Elli begs you to fuck her like the worthless whore she is."

Sin runs toward her. Tyson tries to grab him, but he manages to shrug him off and punches my mother in the face, knocking her head into the wall.

Haidyn wraps his arm around Sin's neck from behind and yanks him off her. "Calm down," he tells Sin as he fights Haidyn. He lets go of him and pushes him toward Tyson who grabs him, pulling him farther away from the wall while Ryat steps in closer to help if needed.

She spits blood out of her now busted lips, and some of it dribbles down her naked body.

We all turn around to see my stepfather joining the party, and Adam pulls me over to the side. He still doesn't trust him, and I wonder if he knows something that we don't.

"Oh, thank God." My mother begins to cry, and I turn to look at her. Physical tears run down her bloody face, and she pulls on the chains, pretending to be helpless.

It's as if I've been blind all my life and can finally see her for who she really is. I never doubted the Spade brothers when they said how awful my mother is, but seeing it is different.

"Bill, get me out of here." She sniffs.

I turn back to look at Bill, and he's staring at me. His eyes slide to Haidyn's before they meet mine again. Stepping into me, he cups my face and gives me a warm smile. "Your father would be proud of you."

His words make my chest tighten.

"He would hate you," my mother shouts, realizing that Bill isn't here to save her. "Haidyn killed your father!" she screams. "He took him away from us."

I turn and look up at my husband, and his eyes search mine. He doesn't know that I've already been told this. It's one of the many things we've both avoided. "Charlotte—"

"Trent knew he was going to get killed." Bill interrupts Haidyn, repeating the same words he told me when we were in the car to Dollhouse. "He knew what he was doing and that there would be consequences. He didn't care." Bill looks over at Haidyn and then back at me. "It wasn't Haidyn's fault that the Lords wanted your father dead. He betrayed them, and it was going to happen regardless."

"You can't be fucking serious!" my mother screams, and I step back into Haidyn as Bill walks over to stand in front of her. "Get me out of here!" she demands.

He crosses his arms over his chest and stares at her.

"WILLIAM! Do something!" She's gasping while fighting the restraints.

"I married you because of Trent," he tells her. "He was my best friend and when he made the deal that we both knew would one day catch up with him, he asked me to take you in as my Lady, but it wasn't because of you. It was for Annabelle." He turns and looks at me over his shoulder. "He knew the path you'd put her on, and he wanted to make sure that she had one parent who would put her first."

"I'm her mother," she shouts as if that means something.

He snorts. "And now you belong to them."

My mother's scream makes my ears ring. She's throwing a tantrum because no one cares about her. *Not anymore.*

She sucks in a deep breath, and her narrowed eyes land on my husband. I stiffen at the way she smiles at him. "Have you told her about us?"

"Us?" My head snaps to Haidyn.

He runs a hand over his hair.

"Yes, Annabelle." I grind my teeth at the use of my name. "I've fucked him."

"We've all fucked you," Saint speaks, surprising me.

"Not like we had a choice," Kashton adds.

Haidyn wraps his arms around me, and I allow him to pull me into him. I will not let my mother control any part of my life anymore. And I can't hide the smirk on my face when she lets out a huff.

"It won't last." She tries to change tactics. "Before you know it, you'll find yourself down here just like the rest of their women. Women mean nothing to them!" she shouts. "They're all disposable."

The one thing in my life that I'm a hundred percent sure of is that my husband loves me. And the only way I'll end up down here, chained to the wall is if I'm naked and begging him to fuck me.

I hold up my left hand and don't even have to say anything. The way her face falls and turns ghostly white says it all. Then like the evil bitch she is, she gives me a bloody smile as she speaks. "Have you told her yet?"

I don't want to let her words affect me because I know she's just trying to get to me, but feeling Haidyn's body stiffen against mine has me pulling away and turning to face him. "Tell me what?" I demand. "Haidyn?"

His eyes drop to my stomach, and I instinctively place my hands on it. Stepping into me, he takes my hands in his, and mine begin to shake. We haven't discussed what he went through while he was gone. He hasn't offered it, and I don't want to bring up something he's trying to forget.

Licking his lips, he takes a deep breath that makes his muscular chest bow out. "I..." His face softens, and the hairs on my neck rise in alert. If he's upset about it, then it's bad.

My mother's laughter fills the basement, and the sound claws at my skin like razor blades. "What is it?" I ask, my throat tightening.

His jaw sharpens, and he looks away from me. I know I won't get anything out of him, but my mother is more than willing to do so. "While he was recently under my *care,* he had a procedure."

"Fuck," Saint hisses.

My watery eyes go to him and then Kashton to see he's got his head down, rubbing the back of his neck. My eyes shoot back to Haidyn's, still not able to put the pieces together. "What did she do to you?" I whisper.

"She gave him a vasectomy." Adam answers me, and my head whips over to see him come to stand next to us. His green eyes on my mother. "A long time ago, the Lords used to do it to the lower-level members to weed out the weak—end those families altogether. But then they realized it was a punishment for the higher-ups to do so. It was just another way to control us. The most degrading thing you can do to a man is remove his chance of having an heir."

"They're not supposed to get married and have a family," my mother snaps. "You all lost that chance when you killed your chosens."

Kashton steps into her, but Saint pulls him back. "You didn't give us a choice," Kashton spits at her.

"You always had a choice!" she screams. "You chose the cowardly way out." Her eyes move to Saint. "That's the only reason the Lords let you keep your whore of a wife is because you married her behind their backs."

Kashton and Haidyn both killed their chosens? Is that the video I saw? My mother let those four men torture Haidyn because he killed Sierra instead of letting them rape her.

I realize I'm crying when Haidyn runs his tatted knuckles down my cheeks. "I'll get it reversed," he tells me.

My pulse races with hope, and my tear-filled eyes search his. "You want children?" He didn't want them before.

"Of course." He frowns as if I'm crazy and imagined the whole conversation that we once had in his bed. "You're my wife, and I want to give you a family."

A sob escapes my lips, and I slap my hand over my mouth.

He pulls me in for a hug, and I cling to him. "I'm so sorry, Charlotte." He presses his hand to the back of my head, holding me to him, and I cry harder. "So sorry."

"Haidyn?" I pull away, and he lets go of me so I can look up at him.

"Yeah, doll face?" he asks, his pretty blue eyes searching my watery ones. "You can tell me...what is it?"

"I'm pregnant."

Chapter 84

Haidyn

"What?" I ask. My ears hear her, but my mind doesn't believe her.

"Don't lie to him!" her mother snaps from behind me.

"I'm pregnant," my wife repeats, ignoring her as if she's not in the same room with us.

"It's impossible!" Isabella shouts. "She's lying to you. Trying to trick you. It's probably someone else's."

I'm the only man Charlotte has ever been with. If my wife says she's pregnant, then she's pregnant. I place my hands on her flat stomach, and she covers her mouth trying to quiet her sob but fails. "When…? How…?" I have so many questions. It hasn't been three months since she received the shot.

"I don't know." Charlotte sniffs. "I've been sick. I thought it was just nerves. But Ashtyn had me take a test, and it was positive."

I've seen her sick. I've held her hair, rubbed her back, and bathed her when she was sick. I thought she was just stressed.

I smile at her, and she laughs softly as fresh tears fall from her bottom lashes. The smile on her face is breathtaking, and I wish we were alone so I could show her just how much I love her and how excited I am that she's having my baby.

"I can answer those questions." Bill speaks up, joining the conversation once again.

He looks at her mother and then at me. "I'm the reason Anna… Charlotte," he corrects himself. "Is pregnant with Haidyn's baby." The room falls silent, and he looks over at his wife. "And you helped me make it happen."

"None of you know what you're talking about," Isabella yells.

"You had her set up at your spa." His eyes go to Charlotte. "And when you two got into that argument, Charlotte confessed that she had sex with Haidyn for the first time and that he put her on the shot. I was able to change out her IV bag at her next spa visit and had it filled with a solution to counteract the shot until Gavin administered the next one. It was only a matter of time before he knocked her up."

Her mother screams, and I watch my wife's face fall. "What is it?" I ask, cupping her wet cheeks. "Are you okay?"

Charlotte's wide eyes search mine. "I...I wasn't thinking."

"What is it, doll face?" I ask, wondering why she's panicking all of a sudden. This is great news. I hated the fact that I had Gavin put her on birth control and that Isabella took that opportunity from us.

"Only Ashtyn knew. I haven't told anyone else...she promised..."

"Calm down. Take a deep breath, beautiful." I interrupt her rambling. "What is it?"

Taking in a shaky breath, she whispers, "The Lords at my house... you said they gave me something to appear dead...then the adrenaline. I just realized..."

"We'll have Devin check on the baby," I assure her. I don't want her to panic or think the worst. So much is happening. We'll take one thing at a time.

"I didn't even think about it," she rushes out. "I made Ashtyn keep it a secret because I didn't think you wanted kids. I've been trying to think of how to tell you..."

"Charlotte," I command, stopping her. "It's okay." I don't want her to regret her decision. I understand she felt abandoned and did what she thought was right.

She nods, looking around aimlessly. "Okay."

I look up at Kash. "Can you...?"

"Go. Go." He waves us off.

I take her hand and pull her out of the basement and to the elevator. Isabella isn't going anywhere; the guys can have her tonight. I'll get everything I need from her another time.

Thirty minutes later, we're entering our bedroom in the birdcage, and I lie her down on my bed, cuddling up next to her. "Talk to me, doll face," I urge, pushing her hair from her tear-streaked cheeks. "How long have you known?" As I ask the question, my hand drops to her flat stomach, and I push up her T-shirt. Thoughts of her pregnant belly come to mind. How beautiful she'll look. Devin did an ultrasound and assured us the *babies* are fine. And that he's more than willing to let us see them whenever we want. "Use your words, doll face."

She sniffs before licking her lips and whispers, "Two days ago. You were still in the hospital. When we got back from Dollhouse and the sedative wore off, I got sick again, and Ashtyn talked me into taking one of her tests."

I sigh, dropping my forehead to hers. Both of my hands cup her soft face. I hate that I left her tied to her bed all alone and had no clue that she was pregnant. To raise my children. "I'm sorry, Charlotte." What would Isabella have done to her and my babies if they hadn't pulled me out of there when they did?

"I'm the one that's sorry, Haidyn. I promise..." she rushes out. "I swear I didn't know."

I shut her up with my lips crashing onto hers. I hate hearing her apologize for something she had no control over. She opens her mouth for me, and I deepen the kiss as her hands go to my hair. She digs her fingers into it, pulling tightly.

Did I want a child? No. Not before she came into my life. But just like Isabella put Charlotte in my life, her stepfather made sure she always remained a part of it. I was willing to give my life up for hers. Now she's giving me life. Nothing could be better.

I pull away and she sucks in a deep breath. "I love you, Charlotte," I tell her. I hope she knows that by now, but I want her to hear it. I was taught that words mean nothing, but she's made me realize they are important.

She blinks, fresh tears falling from the corner of her pretty blue eyes. "I love you, Haidyn."

Chapter 85

Haidyn

We all sit in our office, including Adam. He stands over in the corner. I'm thankful he stayed here with Charlotte to take care of her. I called Kashton and Saint to pick her up from her house because I knew they could protect her at Carnage. I never thought to ask Adam. He's always coming and going, and I didn't want her on the run like he is. But like the brother he is, he stepped up and helped take care of my girl. I owe him for that.

After I found out that my wife is pregnant, we spent a few hours in bed and then Kash told us that our presence was needed. So here we are. She sits quietly on my lap with my arms wrapped around her waist, holding her in place.

"Did you get anything else out of Isabella?" I wonder.

Kash shakes his head. "She just kept saying you killed our fathers and you deserved to be punished." He adds chuckling, "And she yelled at Bill a lot."

Ashtyn is sitting over at Saint's desk, and at Kash's words, her head pops up, and her eyes go to mine. "Why did you kill them?" Her voice sounds hopeful. As if I'm going to tell her that I killed them for her.

I hate to disappoint her. "I—"

"I don't know why you kept it a secret all these years." Saint interrupts me. "Not like we give a fuck."

He says that now, but I remember what it was like after they were found dead. We were ordered to go into "training" for the following six months. We all hated our fathers for different reasons and wanted them dead, but Isabella made us hate life when she took over.

Adam steps forward. "I killed them," he announces, and I run a hand through my hair. I wasn't going to admit it, but I was also planning on taking his secret to my grave.

Ashtyn pushes herself to her feet. Her hand going to her growing belly. "What?" she whispers. "Why...?"

"Bullshit!" Saint snaps. "You were long gone by then."

"Whose getaway car do you think Ash used the night she ran?" Adam asks Saint, and the room falls silent while Saint's body grows rigid. Adam's eyes slide to his sister's. "I was trying to make it right." Walking over to Saint's desk, he steps in front of Ashtyn. "I regret not being able to save you the night Tyson called me. I know you don't believe me, and you owe me nothing, but I've been trying to make up for that night ever since."

Ashtyn shakes her head softly trying not to believe him but the way her eyes start to water tells me that she thinks he makes sense. She just never thought of putting two and two together. "No...that night in Saint's room after everything went down here at Carnage with Benny, you told me you heard I had run—"

"I lied." He interrupts her.

"You lied then, or you're lying now?" she demands. "Because it's hard to tell."

"Fuck, Ash." He sighs, rubbing the back of his neck.

She pulls her lip back with disgust. "I can't believe anything you say."

"You couldn't even stand the sight of me," he yells at her. "How could I tell you the truth when you didn't want to hear it?"

I told her to run. I gave her the key to the tunnel, and I knew that Adam was inside Carnage, and his car was on the other side. The keys were in it.

It wasn't like we had a plan that night. She wasn't supposed to find them or be a part of it, but the plans changed, and we had to wing it.

"I had found out what happened to you and the fact that Dad knew Benny had raped you...and that he also knew Saint had cheated at the vow ceremony...it didn't sit well with me." Adam sighs. "Please know I didn't choose to leave you, Ash. I was just doing what I thought would help."

"Why didn't you tell us this? That Adam was involved that night?" Saint demands, looking at me, knowing I had to be the one who told Adam everything. No one else inside these walls knew that I was still in contact with Adam at the time.

"I told her to run. The alarm was sounding, and our fathers were dead. I wasn't a hundred percent sure what was going on. Then I ran into her in the hallway after she shot you," I say, and Ashtyn drops her eyes to the floor. "By the time you woke up, Isabella had already arrived. Kashton and I were two weeks into training. Six months later, it just seemed too much time had passed." I look at Adam. "He had followed her that night and knew where she was. He told me she had a new life. She was happy. I didn't want what we did to be for nothing."

"That wasn't your call to make," Saint snaps.

"Would you have brought her back if she had a child?" Adam asks, and Saint glares at him. "Hmm? If you had found her four years later and she had a child, would you have kidnapped them both?"

"She lost the baby," Saint argues, and Ashtyn flinches at his words. "I could have been there for her, and he took that from me." He points at me. "He's her guardian, for fuck's sake," Saint yells, and I feel my wife stiffen on my lap. "He was supposed to take care of her for me. Not take her from me."

"Don't blame Haidyn." Adam shakes his head. "I asked him to help her. For me. He gave her a life! The life that I wanted her to have," Adam screams. "A better one...one that she deserved."

Saint snorts. "She was a stripper fucking for money. Some life."

Ashtyn's head snaps up, and she glares at him. He lets out a long breath and reaches out for her, softening his voice. "Sweetheart—"

"Fuck you, Saint," she snaps, storming out of the office and slamming the door shut. He rushes after her.

The room falls silent, and I run my hand down my wife's leg, trying to reassure her, but I'm not sure of what exactly. That I'm here for her? That all the lies and deceit are over?

This is what brothers do—they fight. But once again, we're all back here at home where we all belong.

CHARLOTTE

Haidyn is Ashtyn's guardian. I'm not mad. I actually expected it, and it makes sense. He did so much for her then and now.

My mother was right about one thing—my husband has a big heart and will do anything to protect someone, even if that means giving his own life.

We all leave the office and me and Haidyn make our way up to his room. We enter, and I close the door behind me. Leaning up against it, he turns and comes back to me.

"Hey," he says, softly cupping my cheek. "Talk to me."

I look up at him with a sigh and admit, "I feel bad."

"Why?" He frowns. "None of this is your fault."

"Because..." I step away, and his hands fall to his sides. "I was jealous of you and Ashtyn, and then I heard about how much she went through...I should have never—"

"Stop, Charlotte." He interrupts me, stepping back into me once again. "It's okay to be jealous. It's okay to feel how you felt. What Ashtyn went through doesn't change what me and her once did." He refers back to when they had sex. "But I do want you to know that you are the only woman in my life. You are the only one for me. My past with her doesn't dictate my future with you. Do you believe that, doll face?"

I nod, licking my lips. "I do." I can't change their past. Ashtyn isn't the only woman he's ever slept with. I also know that my mother is one of them, but Kashton had said they didn't have a choice.

I understand that I'm the problem in this scenario. That I'm the jealous bitch who gets to call this amazing man my husband. But moving forward, I will kill any bitch who tries to take him from me. I fight for what I want, and he's it for me.

♠

Haidyn and I were up all night in bed. It started out with him making love to me and then he flipped me over and fucked my ass like the dirty little whore he's turned me into. Then I spent an hour on my knees in the bathroom while he held my hair.

Gavin said the morning sickness will eventually stop, and it can't come soon enough. When I was finally finished, Haidyn carried me to bed, and I passed out with his dick inside my pussy.

We weren't asleep for long when a knock came on the door and busted our bubble. Twenty minutes later we were loading into a car and following the others back to where my mother was holding Haidyn.

Ryat, Sin and Tyson were already here waiting for us. They're looking for some drug that my mother gave Haidyn. On the way here, my husband explained how I already have it, along with other Ladies.

We're founders.

And it made me feel sick. Just another lie that I would have never found out if I had not given my life over to Haidyn.

Bill had taken me to what he called Dollhouse when we were looking for my husband. I didn't get to pay much attention to my surroundings at the time. So when Haidyn pulls up to a mansion on top of a mountain, I whip my head to look at him.

"What are we doing here?" I ask.

It doesn't seem familiar. What I do remember was old and smelled rotted. Instead, a fancy gate sits at the entrance off the road. There is a pond on either side of the long driveway, and each has a fountain lit up at night.

"Bill is meeting us here." He brings his car to a stop, turning it off. "Dollhouse is on the same property, but he says this house has what we're looking for."

House? Reminds me of an extravagant resort of some kind.

Getting out, he opens the passenger door for me, and I stay silent as he immediately starts talking to the other Lords as we make our way up the steps and inside.

I take my hand from his and walk around, taking it in. It's only what the wealthy would accept as a home. Crystal chandeliers hanging from cathedral ceilings, Persian rugs, cream-colored marble floors with what looks like real gold flakes. The size alone tells me it's worth millions.

My mother owns this? I've never been here before.

An arm wraps around my side. "Are you okay?" Haidyn asks.

I nod. He's been worried since I got sick. I know it's the pregnancy, but I also think it's my nerves. I'm terrified something is going to happen to the babies. I want to think happy thoughts, but my mind tells me that there's always going to be someone out to get my husband.

"The guys and I are going to go meet Bill in the basement. Will you be okay up here by yourself?"

Looking up at him, I give him a reassuring smile. "Yes."

Leaning down, he places his lips on mine, giving me a soft kiss before he pulls away and walks away with the others.

The sound of a door opening to my right catches my attention. I see Ashtyn stepping outside onto the back porch, and I follow her. Making my way down the concrete steps, I continue to walk through the backyard, past the Olympic-size swimming pool, and we approach the woods.

She comes to a stop and stares at the trees. I look over the metal bar high up in the branches. A piece of rope hangs from the center and two cinder blocks are on the ground. They too have rope wrapped around them.

Ashtyn stands quietly staring at it as I watch her. The soft wind blows her dark hair around and I hear her sniff.

I go to turn around and leave her alone...to give her a second when her voice stops me. "He kept me tied up for four days."

Turning back to face her, my stomach drops at her words. I lick my lips. "I'm so, so sorry..."

She turns to face me and cuts me off. "I'm not like them."

"Who?" I ask, wondering who she's referring to exactly.

We know that Benny is connected to Hudson and my mother, but we don't know the extent of it. My mother refuses to talk, and Benny is practically dead. No one has spoken to Hudson yet. He's been in the hospital since I shot him twice.

"Our husbands...our parents...the Lords in general." Her eyes go to the house behind me before they find mine again. "I'm not going to blame you for who your mother is. Or what part she played in my life...no matter how big or small." Her hand goes to her stomach before she walks over to me, closing the small space. "I'm not going to pretend I know anything about your marriage to Haidyn." Reaching down, she takes my hands in hers. "I bet he put you through hell." Giving me a small smile, she adds, "But I do know he fell in love with you. And I can't tell you how happy I am that he found you and to have a sister." She pulls me in for a hug, and I feel her shoulders shake.

I hug her tighter as my eyes land on the rope that hangs from the metal bar in the trees. Swallowing the knot that lodges in my throat, I promise to be a better person to her. Because she's right, our husbands are *brothers,* making her my *sister*.

Chapter 86

Haidyn

We've moved her mother to a cell, and today is the day we bring out Hudson. He's strapped in the same spot as Isabella was several days ago. He's remained silent. Tyson's men brought him back with them, and he's been in the hospital. It was the first time I saw Kash actually smile since they rescued me from that hell. His face lit up when he told me my wife shot Hudson. He was so proud of her.

My wife stands next to me while Adam stands on the other side of her. Saint and Kash stand by Ryat, Tyson, and Sin. Bill is still here as well.

"What can you tell us that Isabella can't?" I ask.

He purses his lips and lifts his chin. I've slept beside my wife the past few nights, wanting to put a fucking knife through his chest but have refrained. I know what he was going to do to her, and it makes me sick to even think about it.

I know what I hallucinated wasn't far off. He's a sick fucking bastard.

"He asked you a question, motherfucker!" Kash steps forward, and I grab his shirt, pulling him back.

"I know something." My wife speaks, and everyone in the room turns to face her.

"You don't know shit, bitch." Hudson laughs at her. "You didn't even know that I was in on it. You thought that I was actually interested in you. You're pathetic," he spits.

She turns to face me, ignoring him as she speaks. "He was the one who slit your wrists."

I stiffen at her words, and Kash spins around to face him. "You what?" He looks back at my wife. "How the fuck do you know that?"

"He told me when he and Bill threw me in the cell with Haidyn at Dollhouse. He was bragging. Said that my mother should have let him slit your throat..." Her eyes fill with unshed tears, and she adds, "I just put two and two together."

Saint steps up to him. "So you were here...? In Carnage with Isabella when she was training us?"

He gives us a cruel smile.

Saint punches him, knocking his head to the side. He spits blood from his split lips. All this time, this piece of shit had been with my wife long before I even knew who she really was. Isabella told me that he set her up for me to find her car on the side of the road. Once I got that call from Adam informing me of who she was, I spent the next two weeks setting up cameras in her house, preparing her basement... he knew all of that. That's why I never saw him on the cameras. I had her tell everyone that she was going out of town, and it gave him an excuse to stay away, and she never questioned his distance. Then he showed up pretending to be mad when he found her notebook. He had to give her a reason to walk away. To make her feel like she betrayed him. He was just playing with her mind, adding to her mother's bullshit game. And I never took the opportunity to check the cameras when she told me he had been there while she sat in her bathtub. I was too busy making sure she married me that night. If I had just checked them, I would have seen him in her house. I would have recognized him. I never showed her the picture I had of him in my pocket. She never saw it when I showed Ryat and Tyson. LeAnne showed up, and my wife was attacked. It just never seemed important.

"Who is this?" I demand, stepping forward holding out the picture of him and Benny. "How do you fucking know him?" Benny already told us, but I want to hear him say it.

Hudson just laughs.

A cell phone goes off, and Adam pulls his out of his pocket. He reads over something and then sighs.

"What is it?" I growl.

"It's Gavin. The results are back..."

"And?" Kash snaps when he trails off.

"Benny was telling the truth. Hudson is Benny's cousin."

"That's how Benny got inside Carnage," Kash whispers. "If you were here with Isabella, then you knew how to get in and out."

"But...but you didn't have a Lords crest." Charlotte frowns, just now learning the information that we already knew.

"That's because he never passed the initiation," I add. Not surprised both Benny and Hudson failed.

"Then how the fuck did he get so close to Isabella? No way she would have brought civilians to help her. The Lords would have never allowed that."

Hudson's laughter fills the basement. "They let her do whatever the fuck she wanted."

Kash runs a hand down his face with a growl.

Getting a thought...I walk down the hallway to the cells and unlock the one that holds a prisoner. Opening the door, he shrinks back into the corner, shielding his face from the harsh light. "Let's go." I grab his hair and yank him to his feet and drag him out into the room, shoving him forward.

He cries out, his knees and hands slapping the concrete floor. "Do you know him?" I grip his hair and yank his head up to look at Hudson.

"Yeah. Yeah." The guy rushes out. "He's the one who hired me."

"Shut the fuck up, you son of a bitch," Hudson barks. "Fucking snitch."

"Tell me everything you know, and I'll make it quick." I promise him.

He whimpers, closing his eyes tightly before they open and look up at me. "He—"

"Shut your goddamn mouth!" Hudson screams, yanking on his restraints.

"I'll give you one minute to decide your fate." I inform him, letting go of his hair.

He bows his head taking in a shaky breath. "He came to me. Showed me a picture of her. Gave me her name and address. Told me he'd pay me to keep an eye on her and would give me further instructions once I was ready. When I questioned what he meant by ready… he gave me a cell that had an app that tracked hers." He rocks back and forth, hugging himself.

I nod my head in understanding. That's how this motherfucker knew we were at the gas station that day. Her cell phone. They gave her that new cell, laptop and watch in order to monitor everyone she spoke to, everywhere she went. There was no way for her to escape them. "And?" I cross my arms over my chest.

"And…" he looks up licking his busted lips. "That day I followed you guys to the gas station…I had gotten a text earlier that morning giving me the green light."

"Green light for what?" It's Kash who demands when he doesn't elaborate.

"He…he sent me ten thousand and told me I was able to do whatever I wanted to her. Make it rough…and messy."

"Rape her?" I clarify, my skin on fire at the thought. "Why the gas station?" As much as the thought of him succeeding makes me fucking rage, his actions don't make sense. If he had the resources to hurt her, why do it when she was with me? Why chance getting caught?

His shoulders shake and he leans forward, bowing his head once more and whispers. "He said it had to be done when she was with you."

"He wanted you to leave her for me to find." Looking up at Hudson, I see he's glaring at the man on his knees. Reaching down, I grip the man's hair once again and yank his head back to look up at the ceiling as I pull the pocketknife out of my pocket. Flipping it open, I bend down and slide it across the man's exposed neck, pushing the blade deep into his skin. Blood instantly pours from the split skin, and I shove his body forward where he lies at Hudson's feet and the blood puddles around the now dead body.

I hear my wife gag but I ignore her. I'm too wound up. I want to kill every single mother fucker that has ever had ill intentions against my wife. Taking a deep breath, I remind myself that death is the easy way out. It's too quick.

Ignoring the dead guy, I place my attention on Hudson.

"Who went to Charlotte's house with you?" That's another piece

I'm still missing. Charlotte said there were two guys there when she had the wine and I found her practically dead in her kitchen.

I went back and watched the cameras for that night. I needed to know if they had raped her. What had happened between her passing out and me showing up. Along with how much time had passed. The other guy never took his mask off to show his face.

He just laughs, and I find myself losing my patience.

"At Dollhouse, you told me that you had watched everything I did to her. How did you see it? I had cameras all over that house, and you were only ever there that one time." The one time my dumb ass didn't check them.

"We gave her that phone," he answers with a bloody smile. "Every text, video, or picture that you sent her, I saw."

He looks at Charlotte, and his laughter fills the basement. "You were so stupid, bitch. Your mother was actually worried that you wouldn't crawl on your hands and knees to Haidyn. I knew you'd be easy, though. I assured her that she didn't need the added hormones to your IV treatments. But she said it couldn't hurt. That she would do anything to make sure you were his willing whore, begging him to do anything to you."

My teeth grind, but I let him talk. I want him to run his mouth. He knows we've caught him, but he thinks he's won when it comes to my wife. I'll let him continue to think that.

He looks at me and goes on. "You also set up cameras all over her house, and I was able to connect to them."

Motherfucker. I never thought to have Adam secure the ones I installed in her house. Why would I? I thought that I had the upper hand.

CHARLOTTE

I lean my back against the wall. My eyes shoot from Saint to Kashton and then my husband. He's got his back to me, facing the opposite wall that has Hudson chained to it.

He licks his bloody lips and just smiles.

Haidyn shifts his stance, getting irritated. The Lords ignore the dead guy lying naked at Hudson's feet.

"Haidyn?" Tyson speaks up and holds out a phone to my husband. "My guys found this in his pocket when they loaded him back at Dollhouse."

Haidyn takes the phone, and I look down at it as he skims through contacts before going to his pictures and video. He stops on one and presses play.

My voice fills the basement from the phone in my husband's hand. "Pl-ease," I cry.

Haidyn's voice is heard next. "Please what?" he demands.

"Please...fuck my ass." I sob, and Haidyn ends the video before anything else can be heard.

The phone begins to shake in Haidyn's hand, and he looks up at Hudson.

"I saw it all," he says, laughing.

"When I decide I'm done with you, you will have no dignity left. All you will know is me. All you will want is me." Haidyn's words echo in my mind from the day we returned to my house after the enema. He was right. I no longer have any dignity because it didn't bother me at all that the other Lords in this room just heard me begging Haidyn to fuck my ass when we were in my basement.

Haidyn tosses the phone to his right, and Tyson catches it midair. Haidyn rushes over to Hudson and begins to untie him from the wall. Hudson tries his best to run off, but Haidyn wraps an arm around his neck from behind.

I'm pushed back into the wall by Kashton who comes to stand in front of me in a protective manner.

"Help me secure him," Haidyn growls and tosses him onto a metal table in the center of the room.

It's the same one that I watched them strap Haidyn to before they waterboarded him. I swallow the awful taste in my mouth, refusing to miss what is about to happen. I'm going to prove to these Lords that I can see what they can dish out.

Saint and Tyson both go to the end of the table and secure Hudson's ankles, then his thighs along with his stomach, arms, chest, and last, his neck. He's screaming and fighting as Haidyn steps away and goes over to a wall lined with cabinets. He opens and closes several of them, obviously looking for something.

After a second, he turns and walks back over to stand at the head of the table, and he grips Hudson's face with one hand while the other holds something to his eye. It looks like some type of medieval device that holds your eyelid open—a speculum.

Ryat picks up the second one on the counter and walks it over to Haidyn because he was the closest and Haidyn mumbles his thanks as he does the same to the other—keeping them both wide open.

Then Haidyn goes back over to the counter and fills a syringe that can be none other than adrenaline. "Don't want you to pass out," he says, stabbing Hudson in the chest and pressing the plunger.

I take a quick look around to see all the guys watching my husband. No one looks as sick as I feel. They've seen this before. They've been this way before. I'm pregnant and can't even keep fucking toast down, but by God, I'm not leaving this room without my husband. The awful smell down here alone is enough to make me vomit every time I get off the elevator. I avoid looking at the dead guy lying in a pool of his own blood, shit, and piss. The body expels its waste once it dies.

Hudson's entire body goes rigid as he pulls on the restraints from the rush of the adrenaline. Haidyn tosses the used syringe onto the counter, then leans over Hudson's face and digs his fingers into his eye.

I place my hands over my mouth when I realize what he's doing.

Hudson lets out a blood-curdling scream that makes the hairs on the back of my neck rise. Haidyn's fingers dig into Hudson's eye socket before his eyeball pops out.

My knees go weak, and I swallow the vomit down, not wanting to embarrass myself.

Haidyn holds up the bloody eye with one hand while the other grabs his bloody knife out of his pocket that he slit the other guy's throat with and flips it open. He cuts off the nerves that still hold it in place. Then he hovers it over Hudson's good one and squeezes his hand into a fist. It pops the eye in his hand and blood squirts all over them.

My body jerks involuntarily, trying not to vomit again, and Kashton steps back into me as if my knees are going to give out.

"There's one." Haidyn's voice is as cold as this basement. He digs his fingers into the other one and the table rattles while Hudson's screams continue to fill the large space. It echoes off the concrete walls and ceiling, carrying down the hallway.

Haidyn rips the other one out just the same, and I gulp down the acid taste that fills my mouth as he pops it in his hand just like the first. My husband slaps his bloody hand over Hudson's mouth to muffle his screams and speaks. "I hope your memory is better than your eyesight because that's the only way you're going to see my wife."

I push off the wall, unable to swallow it down anymore. I don't even go to the elevator; I won't make it. I shove open the door to the staircase, bend over, and vomit on the concrete floor.

♠

After I finished puking up my guts, I made my way to Haidyn's room. I had called down to Jessie and apologized profusely that I had gotten sick in the stairwell, and he told me it was okay.

I went straight to the bathroom and brushed my teeth and washed my mouth out and am splashing my face with cold water when I hear the bedroom door unlock.

Straightening my back, I wipe the water off my face as Haidyn enters the bedroom. He comes to a stop when he sees me through the open bathroom door. He's washed his hands, face, and tattooed-covered arms, but it's still on his shirt, neck, and jeans.

He takes one more step into the room and stops. His eyes search mine as if he's unsure what to do. I look weak and pathetic. As if I can't handle whatever he can do. I hope he knows it's the pregnancy. I'm not scared of what he'll do to me or judge him for what he'll do to others who threaten our family.

I exit the bathroom and rush to him. I throw my arms around his bloody neck, and he wraps his around my waist. I hug him, and he holds me to him.

"I'm sorry, Charlotte." He sighs. "I wasn't thinking."

I pull back, placing my hands on either side of his face. "I love you, Haidyn Jamison Reeves."

He frowns at my words, and it makes my stomach drop at the thought he could ever second-guess how I feel about him.

I once asked him—don't you want someone you know will love you unconditionally? I want him to know that he has me. No matter what the Lords throw at us. "I love you," I repeat.

He runs his knuckles down my cheek while his eyes search mine. I thought I knew who Haidyn was when I agreed to marry him, but I was wrong. He's more than I could have ever imagined. He's got a heart of gold and will protect who he loves fiercely. I want to do the same for him.

His hand moves to cup my face, and I push up on my tiptoes to press my lips to his. He grips my ass and lifts me. I go to wrap my legs around his waist, but he's already got me on the bed, hovering over me.

My hands go to his belt, and he pulls his lips from mine, then sits up. He yanks his bloody shirt up and over his head while I unzip his jeans and pull his hard dick out.

I want him to pull my hair, drag me to the floor, shove me to my knees, and fuck my face while I look up at him with tears in my eyes. But we've got plenty of time for that. Right now, he wants to show me that he loves me too. He thinks I'm too sensitive to see who he really is. Thankfully, I've got the rest of my life to prove him wrong.

Chapter 87

Haidyn

"I'm so sorry, doll—"

"Shut up and fuck me." She breathes, interrupting me.

If I wasn't so worried, I'd laugh. She's avoiding the elephant in the room. That elephant being me and what I just did. I forgot she was even with me while down in the basement. The bastard got off easy when I slit his throat. But Hudson? Taking his eyes was just the beginning. He'll live. I'll make sure of it. After I realized she had run out, Saint called Devin to come and return Hudson to the hospital for medical treatment while I washed myself off the best I could. I needed to find her.

All I could think about was everything I've done to her…the photos and videos I sent to her cell. Hudson watched them. He saw her beg me, come for me. He saw her in the most vulnerable positions and got off on them. His threat at Dollhouse could not go unpunished. If he had access to her phone, then he knew that I had sent her the text about turning me over to the Lords. Which also meant he knew that I married her. Why did he choose to keep that a secret at Dollhouse when Isabella said she'd be forced to marry him? Maybe he was going to use that information for himself later down the road? Ammo to make Charlotte compliant?

"Haidyn." Her grip tightens on my hard cock, and she lifts her hips, wanting me to fuck her, bringing me out of my thoughts.

My eyes search hers, and she licks her parted lips. Rising up, she gently kisses my lips before she lays her head back down. "I want you."

I didn't kiss her back. My head is a fucking mess, my heart racing. I wanted to stay downstairs and rip his limbs from his body, but I needed to check on her. Make sure she was okay. The thought of her being afraid of me terrifies me. "I'd never hurt you." I feel the need to tell her.

Letting go of my dick, she places both hands on either side of my face. Frowning, she lets out a long breath. "I'm not afraid of you, Haidyn. I love you. The real you."

I lower my forehead to hers, and she removes her hands from my face to wrap around my neck. "I love you," I whisper. My mind tells me to forget the bastard who tried to take her from me and realize she's here—in my bed, under my body wearing my ring, carrying my children.

"I love you, Haidyn."

My lips find hers, and I push the thought of anyone but my wife out of my mind as I grab my cock and slide into her soaked cunt.

Her nails dig into my back as her cries fill our room. I'm rougher than I should be, but she doesn't tell me to stop. No. Instead, she begs me for more, and I'm more than willing to make her my dirty little whore.

Chapter 88

Haidyn

It's been a week since my brothers saved me. Things seem to be getting back to normal around here if that's even possible. Nothing about our lives is ever normal. But I have my girl here with me and in our bed every night. Nothing could be better than that.

"Where are we going, Haidyn?" Charlotte asks as we walk through the hospital at Carnage.

Staying quiet, I open a door for her and usher her in with my hand on the small of her back.

"Finally. What the fuck is going on, Haidyn?" Ryat demands, jumping to his feet. His wife remains sitting in the seat beside him.

I look over at Devin and Gavin and nod my head to them. Devin begins to pass out a paper to Blakely, Charlotte, and then Ryat. I don't need one. I already know. Found out this morning while Charlotte was sleeping next to me and immediately messaged Ryat that I needed him and his wife to meet us here.

"What is this?" Blakely asks, reading over the paper in her hand.

Ryat's body goes stiff while reading his before wadding it up in his hand.

"While we were running the blood tests on all the wives, Haidyn thought it would be a good idea to run another test." Gavin addresses everyone. "And as you can see looking at the results, there's a match."

"I don't understand." Charlotte's brows pull together as she looks up at me. "What does it mean by fifty percent match?"

"Goddammit." Ryat sighs, hanging his head.

"What?" Blakely gets to her feet, her paper falling to the floor. "Ryat, talk to me."

"Your mom..." He pauses, looking up at her and the color drains from her face.

"What about LeAnne?" she asks slowly. I know enough about their relationship to know that they're not close. And if Ryat had his way, her mother would be dead.

He cups her face and lets out a long breath. "She's a twin."

"What?" Blakely steps back, and his hands fall to his sides. "No. I would have—" She cuts herself off because she realized she doesn't know jack shit about her mother. "What does that mean?"

"It means that you and Charlotte are related," I answer. Charlotte and Blakely both spin around to face me. "LeAnne has a twin...and it's Isabella, Charlotte's mother."

♠

Ryat and I leave our wives to speak while we step out into the hallway. He begins to pace, and I shove my hands into my pockets. "I thought they deserved to know."

I had Adam do some digging, which led to him finding out that both Isabella and LeAnne legally changed their last names while attending Barrington. My question is why? What happened that they needed to sever any connection that could prove they're related?

Ryat nods more to himself than me. "I just...I don't understand." He turns to face me. "You told us that Charlotte had an initiation...she was branded, and you were her assignment." He runs a hand down his face, feeling the past week. It's weighing on all of us. I'm going to crawl into bed with my wife and pass the fuck out after I fuck her. "The Ladies are all from founders, but the Lords didn't make Blake finish her second initiation and Elli had one, but no assignment. Of course, Lake didn't have to do anything because of what Ty had negotiated. But it still doesn't answer why the Lords didn't require more from the other Ladies like they did Charlotte."

I filled them all in the other day on everything that Charlotte went through, and they were all as confused as me. "I can't answer that question," I say honestly, hating that I don't know everything.

"I can."

We both turn to see Bill walking toward us with Tyson, Sin, and Saint. We haven't kicked him out yet due to how much help he's been. Without him, I'd still be locked in a cage, and my wife would be getting raped and beaten on a daily basis.

They come to a stop in front of us.

Ryat nods his head. "I'm listening." He sighs, tired of the bullshit games.

"Blake's mom was never part of her life. Her stepmom set up that deal with Matt and his mother. If you hadn't intervened with Blake, who knows what would have happened."

Ryat fists his hands, imagining the possibilities of the life his wife could have had.

"Then of course, Elli..." He turns to face a pissed-off Sin. "They wanted to prove she was mentally unstable. They didn't want to give her any initiations to prove she could pass. But you marrying her changed the game. Once the Lords realized she was your wife, they had to give her something to at least prove her loyalty to you."

Sin runs a hand through his hair, dropping his eyes to the floor.

"And Laikyn—her father didn't want her to be part of the Lords because he was going to sell her."

Tyson's jaw sharpens at his words.

Bill goes on. "Anything can change the course the Lords want you on. Nothing is set in stone," he goes on. "And Ashtyn. Nothing went as planned with her. When you denied her, things changed."

Fuck! I close my eyes. Not this...

"Wait. What do you mean when *he* denied Ashtyn?" Saint asks.

Opening my eyes, they land on Bill, and he mouths, "*Sorry.*"

"It's nothing," I tell Saint.

He shoves Bill out of the way and steps into me. "Don't give me that shit, Haidyn!" he snaps. "I'm not in the fucking mood." His voice rises. "Tell me the fucking truth."

"Saint?" Ryat barks, grabbing his arms and trying to pull him back, but he doesn't budge.

"No," Saint shouts in my face. "You fucking owe me that!" His finger pokes my chest.

"He doesn't owe you anything," Adam's voice calls out as he comes down the hallway.

"Adam—" I raise my hand to tell him it's okay and look at Saint. "Ash was supposed to be my chosen." The moment the words leave my mouth, I feel lighter. I've been carrying around a secret for so long I didn't know how much it weighed until now.

"Fuck you, Haidyn!" He goes to swing, but this time, Sin steps in as well, and they're both able to pull him back.

A part of me is disappointed. A fist to the face sounds good right now. So I step forward, closing the space. "I didn't want her," I shout, getting pissy but not sure why. Maybe because it's like them thinking I've been suicidal all this time—no one fucking believes me. "I knew how much you loved her, and I'd never take her from you," I add.

"Bullshit..."

"It's true."

Sin and Ryat let him go and he turns around to see a very sleepy-looking Ashtyn standing in the hallway. Her watery eyes go from mine to her husband's.

"You knew this?" he asks her in disbelief.

"I've always loved you, Ashtyn," I tell her while on our way to dinner.

"Haidyn—"

I feel I need to explain. I didn't take her out to dinner to make her uncomfortable. "Not in the sisterly love sort of way because that would be gross. Considering I've fucked you." My eyes drop to her crossed legs, and she shifts in her seat. "Also, not enough to want to spend the rest of my life with you." She frowns, and I chuckle. "Romantic, right? You were supposed to be my chosen."

Ashtyn nods, answering her husband. "I did."

I never had the chance to finish that conversation we started in the SUV before we were hit and both kidnapped. But I know she believed me. I'd never lie to her about something like that.

"Why didn't you tell me this?"

She gives Saint a soft smile. "Because it wouldn't have changed anything." Her hands go to her growing belly, and she's telling him the same thing he said to her. If one of the babies isn't his, it won't change their future—their family.

He turns to look at me and then back at her. "That doesn't excuse Haidyn—"

"Goddammit, Saint!" Adam interrupts him.

"Adam." I shake my head. Enough has been said.

"No." He looks at me. "I'm so fucking tired of this shit." Adam turns to face Saint. "If you need to blame someone, blame me."

"I already do, Adam. But while we're on the subject, how the fuck did you know so much?" he demands, stepping toward Adam, but Ashtyn wraps her arm around his waist to keep him back. "You sure know a lot of shit for someone who has been MIA for so long."

"Because I was here when all of our fathers told him that he would take Ashtyn as his Lady, and he denied her. He refused. Over and over." Adam's voice rises. "And they gave him no choice. Told him they'd force them to marry if need be."

"Lady?" Ashtyn looks at me wide-eyed.

Well, this is just getting better and better. I was never going to tell her that.

"He wanted to tell you, and I told him I'd take care of it."

"No." Saint runs his hand over the back of his neck, confused. "That doesn't make sense...your father let me take her as a chosen... why would he allow that if he was going to make Haidyn marry her?"

Saint always had plans to marry her. We all knew he'd spend the rest of his life with her.

"He set you up, Saint," Adam growls. "Quit being pissed off for two fucking seconds and think about it." Saint narrows his eyes on his brother-in-law. "My mother had her raped, and my father told you...he wanted you to cheat on the vow ceremony." Saint swallows, starting to see the situation for what it was meant to be. "I think it was a way to get you out of the picture. I don't know if they were going to kill you or make you their prisoner but definitely deny you as an option at her being your Lady. I'm telling you, they all wanted Ashtyn to marry Haidyn. All four of them were in on it."

"It's true," Bill speaks, jumping in.

"How the fuck would you know?" Saint barks.

"LeAnne."

"Bullshit—"

Adam interrupts Saint. "LeAnne knew because she was here in our father's office that day Haidyn and I met with our fathers." He sighs and adds, "At the time, we didn't know that Ashtyn had been raped and that you cheated. Then I was forced into hiding, and you ended up marrying her in secret before our fathers could force Haidyn to do it. It wasn't long after that Haidyn messaged me that Ash was pregnant, and she was freaking out because Laura had told her she was raped, and you cheated at the vow ceremony. She said the baby wasn't yours. If Laura knew she was pregnant, then my father knew, which meant all the fathers knew. I had to do something. To save her... to save you..." He trails off. "It was just another reason I had to kill them."

Saint turns his attention on me, and his green eyes look tired, but I can still see the hurt in them. It may always be there. We may never be the brothers we once were, and I take all the responsibility.

"Saint?" Ashtyn tugs on his arm.

"Yeah, sweetheart?" He looks down at her.

"I love all of you." She reaches up, cupping his face. "But you're my husband. The only one I want to spend the rest of my life with. I just want all this fighting to stop." The first tear slides down her cheek, and he leans forward to kiss her forehead. "I just want it all to end so we can move on. Please, Saint."

"Of course, sweetheart," he assures her.

The door opens to my right, and my wife walks out of the room with Blakely. I reach my arm out moving over to her, and she immediately cuddles up to my side as I hold her tightly to me. Leaning down, I kiss her hair and catch sight of the smile that she and Blakely exchange as Ryat goes to his wife. At least one good thing came out of that bitch other than my wife.

"How do we find out how many founder families there are?" Tyson asks, and I couldn't be more thankful for a change of subject.

"We don't," Bill answers. "The only advice I can give is to test everyone the Spade brothers currently have here at Carnage and everyone in the future that the Lords send them. Keep a record." He looks at me.

Kashton crosses his arms over his chest. "There could be five or there could be thousands. All the bitch does is lie. I don't trust anything she says."

"Did women even start the Lords?" Saint asks Bill, letting out a long breath.

He's over this fucking day, and truthfully, so am I. I'm over this past week. I think we all are. Ashtyn's idea of letting it all go and moving on sounds pretty damn good.

"Yes and no," Bill answers.

"It's one or the other." Saint snaps, and Ashtyn reaches out to take his hand in hers, giving him a soft smile to calm his nerves.

"I believe that she believes that's how it started," Bill says.

Chapter 89

Haidyn

I'm sitting at my computer and look up across the room to see my wife curled up on the couch, facing me. She passed out the moment she lay down. Saint and Ashtyn have gone to bed, Kash left to go somewhere with Sin and joked for me not to wait up for him. Honestly, makes me a little nervous. If any two Lords could fuck some shit up, it'll be them. Especially together.

The door opens to the office, and I sit back in my chair, crossing my arms over my chest as Bill shuts it behind him. "You wanted to see me?" he asks, looking at Charlotte.

"Have a seat." I gesture to the one opposite my desk.

He pulls it out and sits down, running a hand down his face.

"You punched my wife." I haven't had the chance to speak with him alone until now.

"I did what I had to do." He shrugs. "You'd do the same."

"No." I shake my head. "I'd never hurt..."

"So you're saying you've never done anything to her that you regret?" He arches a brow in question.

My teeth clench because there's lots of things that come to mind that I did wrong when it came to Charlotte. "How'd you know?" I change the subject. I wanted us both to get answers, but I'll fill my wife in later. She's exhausted. I'll let her get her answers some other time. He's not going anywhere. We've got his wife, and we told him he can visit as often as he wants.

"That you'd fall in love with her?" he questions.

"That I wouldn't kill her," I growl. He knew how much we hated Isabella. "Why risk her life if you were supposed to protect her?"

"One man can only do so much." He chuckles. "And Isabella wouldn't allow me to interfere in Charlotte's life. Well, her plan for Charlotte's life. It was set in course long before you killed her father." His eyes soften when he speaks again. "And of course Ashtyn."

"What about her?"

"What you did for her, helping her escape. My wife called that soft and weak. I call that a man." He rolls his chair back so he can look over at Charlotte sleeping. "Not very many men in our world actually care about their wives." He looks back at me. "I knew it the moment you saw her on the water that day."

I frown.

"She hasn't told you?"

"Who hasn't told me what?"

"I'll let your wife tell you that story." He laughs softly and I wonder when he had the chance to talk to her alone. "But we both knew if given the chance, you'd take it."

"I don't know what you're talking about," I say honestly.

He stands. "Everything happens for a reason, and I guess it was a good thing you turned my offer down that day in your father's office."

I stiffen knowing exactly what he's referring to. If Charlotte would have been my chosen, would I have been forced to kill her or watch her get raped by Isabella's men? I know what I'd choose because while in her hell, I saw it. I lived it. It was a hallucination, but it might as well have been real. "Do you think she would have made her daughter live the same fate as Sierra?" I ask.

He nods. "Absolutely. Isabella would bite her own nose off to spite her face. A child..." he shakes his head. "To her that's a justified sacrifice."

"Why did you come to my father? Why try to make her my chosen?"

"Isabella wanted revenge. She was willing to put her in your life to make you pay for killing Trent." He shrugs. "But I told her you refused, and she said she'd get another chance. The woman may be the antichrist, but she has the patience of a saint."

"She wasn't even of age to be a chosen," I add with a growl and quickly do the math in my head. "Hell, she was what, sixteen when I killed her father?" Fuck, she looked every bit of twenty-one and was drinking champagne that night on his yacht. I never thought to question her age because I knew nothing would come of it. That would have made her seventeen when he went to my father to try to make a deal for her to be my chosen.

"Legal age of consent in Pennsylvania is sixteen." He shrugs, and I don't bother to ask why he knows that.

I huff. "Charlotte said that you told her her future husband was a prisoner here at Carnage. I've looked the name up you gave her, and he's never existed."

"She wanted information..."

"So you lied?" I growl.

"Of course." He huffs. "That day she came over to the house..." he runs his hand through his hair. "Charlotte was different. She had confidence and was asking too many questions. Isabella was putting on a show for Charlotte and slapped her."

"She what?" I bark. "Why would you allow that?"

"I had a part to play." His eyes narrow on mine. "Just like you. Charlotte needed something to keep her interested in Carnage. If I didn't push her, Isabella would have—especially since she was aware you took her virginity. Isabella was excited. She was finally getting something from you, you were claiming *Annabelle* as yours." He shakes his head. "It was finally going how Isabella wanted it to go, and I didn't want to fuck that up."

"And Hudson?" I question. "What part did you play in that?"

"I didn't know that Hudson was helping her. I had my suspicions that he was involved but couldn't prove it. Then I found some messages on Isabella's phone that he was her fuck boy. I knew then he was involved."

"Why didn't you kill him? He was fucking your wife." It could have solved several of our problems with one less piece of shit after my wife.

"I didn't give two shits about her then, and I give less now." He shrugs. "If he kept her busy, she was out of my face. Plus, I could have killed you for the same thing."

I sigh, hanging my head and ignoring that last part. I did what I did because I had to. It wasn't like I wanted to fuck her. She gave me a choice, and I picked what I thought was best.

I try to think back if I have any more questions to ask him. I have a feeling he's not going anywhere anytime soon. He will always look after and check on my wife.

He turns to the door. "Take care of her."

"Wait," I say, and he pauses. I look at her, she hasn't moved, and then move my gaze back to him, frowning. "That's the same thing her father said to me before I killed him." I trail off thinking of what Bill just said about the day on the water. "I thought he meant the yacht." I scratch the back of my head.

He chuckles. "He hated that damn thing. Isabella wanted it. Why do you think it was named after her?" The room grows silent, and he exits.

I close down my computer and walk over to the couch. Leaning over, I slide my arms under her and pick her up. She remains a lifeless doll all the way to our room, and I lay her on the bed, then gently undress her until she's naked. I help her under the covers and undress myself before I get in beside her.

Her body is so warm, and I cuddle into her, holding her tight and kissing her forehead.

CHARLOTTE

I open my heavy eyes to see I'm lying in bed with Haidyn back in his room. Last I remember, we were in his office, and I lay on the couch because I could barely keep my eyes open.

Snuggling closer to him, he turns on his side, and I look up to see he's already staring at me. "Why are you awake?" I whisper. What time is it? A quick look around tells me it's still nighttime.

"I like to watch you sleep," he admits shamelessly.

I understand what he means because I enjoyed watching him sleep that one time I woke up and he was next to me in his bed. "You need to rest," I tell him.

His soft laughter makes his chest rumble against me. "I've got plenty of time for that."

"Can I...?" My eyes drop to his Lords crest, trying to get the courage to ask what I want to know.

"Use your words, doll face," he says, running his hand up and down my thigh that lies over his hip.

"What happened to your mother?" My eyes meet his.

He's never talked about his mother or his father. But then again, Haidyn and I don't have any conversations about his childhood. I don't know what it was like, but I can guess it wasn't pretty. I know what kind of man his father was from the one video Hudson sent me but nothing about his mother. So many secrets and lies have been uncovered in the last couple of weeks regarding my mother that I want to know about his. His father was such an awful man, but his mother had to have been good, right? For Haidyn to turn out how he did? To have a heart as big as he does.

"She left when I was ten," he answers.

"Left?" like walked away from him and his father? That's not an option. "The Lords regifted her?"

He rolls onto his back, and I run my hand over his hard chest, feeling the slow rhythm of his heartbeat. I go to move my leg off his waist, but his hand grabs my thigh, holding it in place.

"No. My mom was your typical Lady—did whatever my dad said and hated her life." He sighs. "We had a house, but my father practically lived here at Carnage. All of our fathers chose this place over their homes. One morning, I woke up at our house, and she made me breakfast. Then she grabbed her bag that she had packed on the counter and just walked out the door."

"But...in the Lords email I received, it said your parents were deceased."

"My father treated her like shit," he continues like I didn't speak. "He wanted a big family of boys—an army, as he called it. I remember her being pregnant with their second child. I was so excited to get a brother. Complications during the pregnancy resulted in losing the baby. I remember words like hemorrhage and emergency hysterectomy. He hated her after that. Thought she was worthless."

My chest tightens at his words, but I'm not surprised.

Turning onto his side once again, he reaches out and pushes a few strands of my hair behind my ear. "A part of me always thought that he killed her. He never seemed surprised that she didn't come home that night. He went on with life like she was never there to begin with. I wasn't sure until you told me that day in your kitchen that both of my parents were deceased. If the Lords know she's dead, then my father killed her."

I sit up, my chest aching. "Haidyn...I'm so sorry...I shouldn't have—"

"Hey," he sits up and places both hands on my face, giving me a soft smile. "Quit apologizing for something you had no control over, doll face."

I swallow the knot in my throat. "I should have never told you—"

"I drugged you." He interrupts me. "You couldn't have lied even if you wanted to." Placing his forehead on mine, he sighs. "I should be the one telling you I'm sorry, Charlotte."

I shake my head, and he nods his. "Yes." Pulling back, he searches my eyes and gives me a soft smile. "I'm sorry, Charlotte."

"No," I argue, not accepting his apology. I know what he did was wrong, but I also understand that this man saved me from a life damned to hell. Not all Ladies are as lucky as me. They don't find a Lord who protects them, falls in love with them, would give their own life for them.

"No?" He chuckles, and I don't understand how he can be laughing right now.

I frown, and he straightens his shoulders, taking in a deep breath. He pulls my face toward his, and his lips give me a soft kiss. "I'm sorry for everything I did, Charlotte."

"I don't care," I say honestly. None of it matters. Not anymore.

He pulls back, and his eyes search mine as if to ask if I'm okay. How I can possibly dismiss it all. I love him. That's what matters now. The why and how we got here doesn't matter to me. It's our future that does. Our marriage, our children, the life that we're going to make.

"Charlotte—"

I cut him off by placing my lips on his, and he kisses me back without hesitation. He pushes me onto my back, and I spread my legs for him to kneel between them. My hands slide to his hair, and he lifts his hips as he adjusts his cock so he can fuck me.

Pulling my lips from his, I arch my neck and suck in a breath at the feel of his hard dick entering me. The growl from his lips vibrates my chest, and his lips go to my neck as I wrap my arms around him, clinging to him. "Please?" I beg, needing more of him.

"I know, doll face." He places soft kisses on my neck as he begins to fuck me like the whore I want to be for him.

He's rough. His hands move to wrap around my neck and my arms lay lifeless out to my sides, letting him have his way with me.

His pretty blue eyes are on mine, and I drown in them.

My husband has taught me that there are two different kinds of love in this world. The first is selfless—you would give your life for another person. He was willing to give his up for me so I could live mine. And I respect that, I really do, but if he ever tries to leave me again, I'll stab him in both of his legs so he can't walk or run. Because I'm not like Haidyn. I'm the second—selfish. I refuse to live a life where he isn't by my side every day and lying next to me every night. He's my husband...my Lord. We're a team, and I'll remind anyone who comes after us exactly that.

Chapter 90

Haidyn

I sit at my desk while Kashton sits across from me at his and Saint stands in the middle of the room talking to Adam when the door to our office opens. Sin enters like he owns the place.

"Hey, Sinny." Kashton smiles up at him, and Sin snorts at his nickname. "Have you decided to come home?"

"I'm here on Lords orders," Sin states, and the air in the room instantly changes from light to heavy.

I stand, and so does Kashton.

"What kind of orders?" Saint questions.

"I was given an assignment last night to deliver a Lord to Carnage," he answers, his eyes on Saint's. "I have an hour left."

"Who?" Kashton demands, knowing this isn't going to end well.

Sin looks from Saint to Adam, and I stiffen when he speaks. "You."

"What the fuck, Easton?" Kashton barks, coming out from behind his desk. Adam places his hand out on Kash's chest, stopping him from taking Sin to the floor.

"This is my fault," I growl. Adam was in hiding, and I brought him out when the Spade brothers called him to help save me. "I'll speak to the Lords."

Sin raises his shirt and removes his holstered gun from his belt. He sets it on Kashton's desk. "I'm willing to tell them you refused to go, and I put a bullet in your head instead."

Adam ignores Sin's proposition to kill him. *This isn't a game.* If Sin has an assignment, it has to be completed. Meaning we either take our brother in as a prisoner or we watch Sin kill him right here, right now.

Adam looks at me. "You didn't make me kill our fathers."

"No, but I should have..."

"I did what needed to be done in order to protect my sister," Adam snaps before looking at Sin. "And I'll do it again." Then he turns to face Saint. "I'm sorry after all I did, I still failed her. And you."

Saint swallows nervously, and I hope this isn't his goodbye for good. He's told me he'll die before he turns himself over to the Lords in any way. He left that life behind years ago, and he'll never go back.

"Wait. Wait." Kashton raises his hands. "Let's think about this for a second. We've got an hour."

"That's not enough time." Saint growls. "You should have come sooner," he barks at Sin.

"It's fine," Adam assures him. "I'll go downstairs."

"We're not putting you in a cell." I shake my head.

"We will if it'll buy us time," Kash argues.

I run a hand through my hair and sigh.

"I'll go downstairs for now, and we'll figure it out. Sin..." He picks up the gun and hands it back to Sin and nods to the door. He and Sin exit the office.

"This is bullshit!" Saint slams his hands on the desk when the door closes, giving us a few seconds to discuss what the fuck we're going to do with our brother.

"I say we keep him locked up. I mean, whatever makes the Lords happy." Kashton throws his hands out to his side. "Otherwise, he'll always be on the run."

Saint sighs and nods. "I agree. Ashtyn...wants him around," he says tightly, letting us know that he's still very angry with Adam but wants Ashtyn to have some sort of relationship with her brother.

"We'll figure something out," I assure them.

We make our way to the elevator, and right before the door closes, we hear a loud noise. "What the fuck was that?" Kash demands.

"Sounded like a fucking gun," Saint growls, already hitting the button on the elevator to open the door before it can even come to a stop.

We all three rush out once it reaches the basement to see Sin on his knees, blood running from his busted nose, and Adam on the floor lying next to him.

Sin looks up at us, raising his empty hands as he speaks. "He took my gun."

Chapter 91
Haidyn

It's a gloomy day at Carnage, and I'm not just talking about the weather. "Meet you at the Graveyard" by Cleffy softly plays from a small speaker.

I stand dressed in a suit and tie. My black Pradas sink in the muddy ground from the rain we've had for the past two days. I've always loved rainy days, but today is different. My heart is heavy as we say goodbye to our brother.

Ashtyn's cries turn to sobs as Saint has to help hold her up. She and Adam were never close, but have you ever been given a second chance at something and have it taken away before you could see where it goes? That's how she feels. Plus, with her pregnancy, her hormones are off the charts. She knows that Adam did what he thought was best for her, but she'll never get to ask why.

A soft hand squeezes mine, and I look down at Charlotte standing next to me in her black dress. My free hand holds the umbrella over us. The words she told me last night echo in my mind. *"It's not your fault."*

But it is. I made a deal with the devil to protect my brother, and it ended up costing all of us everything. So much could have been avoided if we had come together years ago. I did what I thought was right, but now that I have Charlotte, I see it was all wrong. I could have saved a lot of people, a lot of heartaches. But here we are. It's too late to turn back. I have a wife and children on the way.

We can only move forward and try to live with the losses we've been dealt.

"He wouldn't kill himself," Ashtyn cries as the rain covers her once curled hair. Now it sticks to her shoulders and face. Her umbrella is open and on the ground. She gave up holding it long ago.

"Ash—"

"No." She cuts off Saint. "I don't believe it." She pulls out of his arms and runs to the casket. She pushes it open and screams when she sees what's left of her brother. We chose a closed casket for a reason. Saint didn't want her to see him that way—what was left of him. Should have sealed the damn thing shut.

"Jesus." Kashton grabs the lid and slams it down as Saint picks up his wife. Her legs no longer able to hold herself up when she falls into the mud.

Saint carries her to their car he has parked by the entrance of Carnage. He's taking her back to the main building.

"Goodbye...brother." Kash speaks brokenly before leaning over, kissing the wet casket, and walks to his car.

"Kash?" I call after him, but he jumps in the driver's seat, slams the door, and turns the opposite way as Saint did. He squeals his tires, exiting the gates, and leaves Carnage.

I remain where I am, unable to say goodbye. The last time I stood here was after our six months of "training." I finally had a chance to breathe and came out here where our fathers were buried. I wanted to tell the bastard goodbye. That I wasn't sad he was killed. And that I hope he rots in hell. One that is far worse than Carnage. But now I can't seem to move.

"Haidyn?" Charlotte says in a soft voice.

I look down at her, and she gives me a sad smile squeezing my hand. Giving a quick look around, she sees we're alone, then turns to face me. "Let's go home." Her eyes are bloodshot from crying, and her makeup has run a little.

I look back at the casket and the headstones that surround it. Our fathers are buried in the cemetery here, and now the first one of us. One by one, we'll all be placed in this ground. Even in our death, we won't be able to escape this hell that we've created.

That's the point—you're born a Lord; you die a Lord.

I turn around and pull my wife toward the car. Opening her door, she gets into the passenger seat, and I close it. Walking around the front, I get one last look over the hood at my brother before I slip into the car.

CHARLOTTE

I'm surprised he didn't take us back to his house in the woods. He chose Carnage. Maybe because it was closer. Or perhaps it's because he wants to be near Saint and wait for Kashton to return. I'm not sure.

We get out and make our way inside and up to his room. I sit on the end of the bed, and my mind wanders to Ashtyn. I feel sorry for her. I know we've had our problems, but that doesn't mean I want her to suffer the loss of a brother.

My mother isn't dead, but she might as well be. I can't say I feel sorry for her being down in the basement. She deserves that. After everything she did to the Spade brothers, and that's just what I now know. I shouldn't be surprised, though. Everyone in this world is evil. Even my husband.

I look down at my ring, and a smile tugs at my lips. The sound of the shower turning on gets my attention, and I see he's left the bathroom door cracked. I get up, unzip my dress, and remove my muddy heels.

Making my way into the bathroom, I go to open the shower door, but the sound of his phone buzzing on the counter gets my attention. Walking over to it, I see a text flashing across the screen.

UNKNOWN: Midnight tonight. Airfield.

I bite my bottom lip as the screen goes black, wondering who the hell sent that and what they could possibly want with my husband. *It could be anybody.*

Deciding to circle back around to it later, I open the shower door and step inside. I wrap my arms around him from behind as he faces the sprayer, and I squeeze him.

He removes my hands and turns around in them. I reach up and place them around his neck instead. I can see the regret in his pretty blue eyes. He blames himself, and I hate it. I wish I could take his pain and loss away, and deep down, I know I can't. But I'll try.

Rising up on my tiptoes, I press my lips to his. His hands drop to my ass, his fingers dig into my skin, and he picks me up. Wrapping my legs around his waist, he deepens the kiss. He knows I'm here for him. My Lord can use me however he wants. I'm his toy, his whore. And if he needs to use me to make himself feel better, I'm all for it.

Pulling away, I take a deep breath and speak. "I want to change my name."

He frowns at my words. I've been thinking about it for quite some time, and I want him to know who I am. Who I really want to be. "Legally," I add. "To Charlotte. For you."

Slowly, he releases me, and I unwrap my legs from around his waist to stand. His large hands cup both sides of my face. "I love you. Annabelle...Charlotte...the name doesn't change who *you* are."

"I want to be who you fell in love with," I whisper. I was named after my mother and her best friend—twin sister. I want nothing to do with that life and family. I'm going to start my own with this amazing man, and that starts with who I want to be.

He smiles at me. "You are, doll face. You're my wife. You're going to have my babies. None of those things change because of your name." I open my mouth, but he's quick to speak. "But if you want to change your name, then change it. Just don't do it for me."

In our world, we're kept as secrets. You can't talk about who we are or let anyone find out about the society. But Haidyn taught me to use my words. To say what I want and how I feel. I love who I am with him more than I ever loved who I was before he entered my life.

Charlotte Reeves is who I was always meant to be.

Epilogue 1

Haidyn

I gently turn the doorknob to my room and step out into the hall so I don't wake Charlotte. Turning to walk down the hall, I pause when I see Saint and Kashton doing the same thing. It makes me wonder where Kash went after Adam's service and when he returned.

We look at one another and then down at our phones.

"I got a text," Saint states.

"Me too," Kash adds, and when they both look at me, I nod.

"Come on. Let's see what the fuck is going on." Saint begins to walk toward the elevator. Taking it down to the garage, we decide to take the bikes. It's been a while since we've all gone for a ride, and tonight seems like as good a night as any. Thankfully, it stopped raining at some point.

We choose to wear our helmets. That way, we can speak to one another if need be. We ride out of the gates of Carnage and down the curvy road. My eyes catch sight of the driveway that I saw my wife's SUV sitting, and it's crazy to think of the events that led us to where we are now.

Arriving at the airfield where we were instructed to meet, we come to a stop at a black private jet to see a matching SUV parked next to it. "Who the fuck could it be?" Kash inquires as we climb the stairs onto the jet.

"What the fuck?" Saint barks out when we see two familiar faces sitting on one of the leather couches.

They were in the middle of speaking and came to a stop when

they heard Saint. Bill picks up his scotch and takes a sip while he holds his cell in the other.

My eyes look at the man sitting next to him and frown. He has a manila folder in his hand and is wearing an all-black suit with a matching tie. Just like the last time we saw him—four years ago.

"How the fuck do you two know one another?" Kash demands.

"Have a seat, gentleman." Bill gestures to both couches on either side of the aisle facing one another and purposely avoiding the question.

"What do you want?" I ask, looking at the one we haven't seen in years. *Why now?*

"Brothers." He acknowledges us.

I sit down on the one on the right while Kash and Saint pick the one across from me.

A cell ringing breaks through the silence, and I look down to see a phone light up with a picture of the detective and a girl. She's dressed in a black graduation hat and gown; his arm is over her shoulders pulling her into his side and they're both smiling. He declines the call, turns off his cell and flips it over.

I look up as he clears his throat nervously and Bill looks from the phone to the detective with narrowed eyes. "Why is...?"

"Later." The detective cuts him off.

What the fuck is that about?

A woman walks out from the back, fixing her blouse as if she just picked it up off the floor and stumbles to button it up. She comes up next to them.

"Tell my pilot we're ready." Bill gestures to the air. "And get these men whatever they want to drink."

"Of course." She smiles at him and then drops her eyes to her shoes as she makes her way to the cockpit.

"What the fuck are we doing here, and where are we going?" Saint demands, looking at his watch. Kash doesn't have anyone back at home in his bed as far as I know, but Saint and I do. And I'd much rather be balls deep in my wife than here with these two men.

"I'll let you know once we're up in the air." He sits back in his seat as the engines start.

We get comfortable knowing they've got something to tell us that we obviously need to hear. What else could Bill have to say that he hasn't already filled us in on?

The flight attendant takes our drink orders, which is just Kash. He wanted vodka. Pretty sure he's been drinking all night since we buried our brother. Saint and I opted out. The last thing I want is to be drugged. We're still Lords, so anything is possible. Plus, in a one-on-one fight, I'm not sure how well I'd be able to perform right now. I'm still not a hundred percent myself yet, and all the energy I do have, I use on my wife.

The plane levels out, and Saint begins. "Okay. What the fuck are we..."

The back door opens—the same one the woman came from—and we all jump to our feet.

"No fucking way!" Kashton gasps.

"What the fuck?" Saint demands.

I just stare at the man who has a smile on his face. "Brothers." He spreads his arms out wide.

Kash is the first to embrace him in a tight hug, slapping his back. "What in the fuck, Adam?" He laughs, shoving him. "How many lives do you have?"

"I'm like a cat," Adam jokes.

I chuckle and embrace him next. When he pulls away, he turns to face Saint, and he crosses his arms over his chest.

Adam sighs. "Sit, please. We have a lot to fill you in on, and I don't want to have to keep you all night."

"We buried you," Kash states the obvious. "Your body...It was cold." He points at me. "It wasn't like Haidyn's fake death where he sat in a morgue. You fucking shot yourself...you had no face."

Adam runs a hand over his dark hair. "Yeah." His green eyes meet mine. "Although it wasn't my body. We had to pull some strings."

"We?" I ask, and my eyes shoot to the two men also on the plane with us. They say nothing.

"So, what...you're a detective or a cop?" Kash wonders, looking at Adam. "CIA?" Then jokes. "Hitman?"

"Not necessarily." He shakes his head, chuckling.

"Then what the fuck are you?" Saint growls, tired of fake deaths and games.

He slaps the detective on the back. "He's my boss. For the past four years, I've been undercover working in a top-secret division that specializes in human trafficking," Adam announces, and the plane falls silent. He licks his lips and continues. "After we had our meeting senior year at the house of Lords, I began to investigate the disappearance of the girl I was accused of killing." His eyes drop to his hands in his lap. "At first, it was to prove my innocence, but then it became more than that, and this has been my life ever since."

"This whole time?" Kash smiles at him as if a proud dad. "You've kept this a secret? Why not just tell us?"

Adam sighs and ignores that. "The Lords want me dead."

"No shit." Saint snaps, "But why?"

"They—"

"The Lords are part of the problem." Bill finally speaks and I was wondering why he's even here. We all look at him. "They want Adam dead because he knows too much. To them, he's turned on the society and betrayed his oath."

"And you?" Saint arches a brow. "I'm confused...are you part of the Lords right now or have you too betrayed them?"

"I'm whoever I need to be," Bill answers vaguely.

Saint snorts, not liking his answer.

"So what does that mean exactly?" Kash asks, looking back at Adam.

Adam drops his head once again, and Saint gets to his feet. "Goddammit, Adam," he growls. "Your sister thinks you're dead."

"I'm protecting her." Adam's green eyes snap up to glare at him.

"Bullshit!" Saint argues. "She's a fucking wreck..."

"They will come after her!" He jumps to his feet. "I'm trying to do something here! I'm trying to fix a problem that we've helped create!" He shouts and adds, "Your wife was raped. Again." His words make Saint flinch. "My sister..." He pokes his own chest. "Raped...again. And she's carrying that fucking bastard's child! AGAIN! I'm trying to prevent another mother, sister, or someone's daughter from having to go through that."

I get to my feet and touch his arm. "Adam," I say softly, trying to defuse the situation. He doesn't need to bring up what we all know. It's not going to change the past. Plus, I haven't asked or heard if it's been confirmed whether Benny is the father to one of Ashtyn's babies. I'm just guessing Adam assumes the worst.

Adam steps back and falls into the seat between his boss and Bill. He opens up a briefcase and pulls out another manila envelope and slaps it down on Saint's lap that reads TOP SECRET across the front.

"What is this?" he asks, opening it.

"It's not just here," Adam states.

"What's not?" Kash questions.

Adam's boss goes to speak, but Adam beats him to it. "The girls… the disappearances."

"Tyler Cason Crawford." Saint reads the name out loud.

I look at Adam. "Any relation to Tyson?"

"Not that we've found," his boss answers.

"Is this Tyler guy a Lord?" Saint goes on, and his brows crease as his eyes skim the report.

"Not that we can tell." Adam shakes his head.

"Eight cases—car abandoned on the side of the road…wallet and purse left behind." Saint closes the folder and hands it over to me. "Why are you showing us this?"

I open it up and read over it myself as Adam speaks. "These are strikingly similar to the case that I was accused of being a part of. But those eight in Indiana were not made as public as those that took place here in Pennsylvania. Certain things were kept hush-hush."

"They have to be connected." Kashton nods in understanding.

"But those took place first," Bill adds, gesturing to the folder in my hands.

"Indiana is about seven and half hours from here," I state.

"It's only three and a half hours from Chicago," Bill announces.

I look up at him and frown. "LeAnne's been in Chicago." Lived there with her husband until Ryat killed him and she moved to Texas. Now she's supposedly moving here, according to my wife.

"It would make sense that she's involved in these young women disappearing. She's Isabella's twin," Saint agrees.

"So you think they've been involved since the beginning?" Kash asks.

"I found it odd how Isabella had Sierra tied to the fence that night," I admit.

"I thought it was some twisted joke referencing Adam." Kash refers to his chosen and leans back in his seat. "The use of barbed wire...knowing Adam was on the run for the girls that were found brutally murdered. I thought she was just being a sick bitch."

I toss the folder onto the table and run a hand down my face. It all makes more sense the more I think about it. And how Charlotte's SUV was left on the side of the road for me to see. Isabella knew it'd catch my attention, and I'd be unable to ignore it. And she also knew that I'd call Adam, wanting him to freshen my memory on the cases from four years ago because it involved him.

"Adam—"

"I've got to do this, Saint." He interrupts whatever he was about to say. "It doesn't end because Ashtyn is back at Carnage with you." Saint's jaw sharpens, and he looks away. "I know you can take care of her, but who is going to take care of the others?" Adam points at the open folder on the table. Hanging his head, he runs his hands through his hair aggressively. "It won't always be this way," he says softly. "One day I won't have to play dead."

"And if it is?"

He looks up to meet Kashton's stare, answering his question. "I'll keep in touch. I'll message you but only those present here. Ashtyn will remain thinking I'm dead until I say so." He looks at Saint, who gives him a nod, dropping his eyes to the black-and-white carpet.

"And if something happens to you, then what?" I ask.

"Then I'll be calling you," his boss answers, and I get a chill down my spine. *Our brother will be dead.*

"So this is what...?" Saint asks, hands out wide and sitting back in his chair. "A final goodbye?"

"This is me not wanting any more lies," Adam responds softly.

His boss leans forward, placing his elbows on his slacks. His eyes land on mine. "You and your wife opened up a new door when you discovered Dollhouse."

I snort.

"We've been looking for their operation for years."

"Whoa?" Saint points at the open folder on the table. "Are you saying that Dollhouse was a stash house or some shit for sex trafficking?"

I look at Bill, and his eyes are already on mine. I look away, getting a sickening feeling in my gut.

"Benny was holding Ash there at the house." Adam growls and Saint gets to his feet and starts to pace as Adam adds. "It makes sense they're all linked."

Adam's boss nods and answers Saint's previous question. "They run women and men through Dollhouse like it's a revolving door. They have auctions and parties all the time."

Saint comes to a stop and sits back down in his seat.

The plane falls silent, and Adam looks at me. Then I notice his boss is also glaring at me. Another look at Bill and I huff. "What?" I ask feeling awkward at their stares.

Adam sighs, glancing at his boss and then back to me. "We think Isabella was going to use you."

I give a rough laugh. "Use me how?" Of course she was going to make me her toy. An experiment for her to play with. That's what she did when she was running Carnage.

"As a sex slave." Bill is the one who answers.

My laughter grows. "You're joking, right?"

"Think about it, Haidyn." Adam starts. "She gave you a vasectomy. That way you couldn't knock anyone up. She was going to sell you out to the highest bidder as long as you were alive."

My laughter dies, and that silence returns.

"But he's a Spade brother," Saint argues. "Why give him a vasectomy when he could give her children that will be just as powerful as she wanted Charlotte to be."

"You just answered your own question," Bill states.

Saint runs a hand down his face. "Explain it because it's been a long week, and I'm really fucking tired."

"Because of Charlotte." It's Adam who speaks. "She was willing to give Haidyn a vasectomy to make sure Charlotte couldn't have his children. And that makes him perfect for Dollhouse."

"Goddammit." Kash sighs, and I look over at him. "It does make sense."

"I've seen some shit over the last four years and believe me when I say you guys have no idea what kind of evil is out there. The Lords are involved, but it also goes way beyond that. And the women can be just as sick as the men. And Charlotte—?"

"What about my wife?" I interrupt him.

At the mention of Charlotte, Bill throws back what's left of his drink, and I wonder just how much he knows that he's never going to tell us.

Adam is the one who answers. "I think she had more plans for her daughter than she wanted you to know about."

"Meaning what?" Kash questions.

"For one...a breeder..."

"No." I slam my fist down on the small table and stand.

"What do you mean by breeder?" Saint asks, reminding me that I haven't filled them in on that yet. Bill frowns at me as if I've had plenty of time to tell them everything. I ignore him.

"Anything is possible. They bring in big money." Adam goes on and my teeth clench, knowing he's not wrong. "Children are not only being given to the Lords, but they're being sold."

Saint puts up his hand. "Are you saying children within the society are being sold outside of the society?"

"It's been happening since the beginning," Bill states. "But they were able to keep it under wraps for a while."

Adam nods to Saint's question and adds to Bill's statement. "You have to be born into the Lords, but people are getting desperate. Word has gotten out, and they want an opportunity to join. When they realize they have no chance at being a member themselves, they try to buy their way in. Thinking their 'adopted' children will then reproduce in the future."

"Wait..." Saint gives a humorless laugh. "So they what...'adopt' children from the Lords and then force them to breed with their biological children later on down the road so their bloodline is crossed with a Lord?"

"Pretty much," Adam agrees.

I sit back in my seat and let out a deep breath.

Adam's boss hands him the manila folder that he and Bill had when he came on board, and he holds it out to me. I look at him skeptically before I take it and open it up. There's a picture of a woman.

She's tied to a chair, hood-covered head down, blood covering her naked body and floor. "Who is this?" I ask.

"Next page," he says.

I turn to the next one, and Kashton speaks before I can. "What the fuck, man. That's your chosen."

"Yeah." Adam sighs, and I look up at him.

"I don't understand." I hand the folder to Saint, so he can look at it.

"When I was searching through Charlotte's laptop, I came across some information that I looked into a little more."

"Meaning?" I growl because, as far as I'm concerned, he never found anything.

"She was Charlotte's initiation."

I shake my head. "No. Charlotte would never—"

"She didn't know." Adam interrupts me. "It's not Charlotte's fault what happened. Hell, every single one of us have done what the Lords wanted with no questions asked."

"What happened to her?" Saint asks. I haven't filled them in on what all Charlotte did. They know of an initiation and an assignment but I left out the details. "What was cut from her upper back?"

"Lords brand," Adam answers.

"What's on her inner thigh? What does it say?" Saint lifts it closer to his face to read it.

"It's a barcode. All slaves at Dollhouse have them," Bill answers.

"Did you brand her when she was your chosen?" Kashton asks.

Adam shakes his head. "Wasn't me."

"Why would she have the Lords crest?" Kash inquires.

"I don't know the story. I can only guess. You and Haidyn were forced to kill your chosens, I was already gone. Ash was on the run, but technically, she was already Saint's Lady by that time. So I think they had our chosens taken out."

"Have anything you want to tell us?" I bark at Bill. "What do you know about the brand and barcode?" My wife was branded for initiation. Maybe Adam's chosen was from a founder? No. That can't be because they would have made her a breeder, not killed her at such a young age.

Bill shakes his head, and I fist my hands. "I told you; my wife kept me in the dark."

"Forgive me that I don't believe you," I snap.

"When was the last time you saw her?" Kash continues, staring at Adam's chosen in the photo.

"It's been a while," Adam answers vaguely.

I let out a long breath. "So you're saying that my wife killed an innocent woman." I thought that it was weird that Charlotte even had an initiation to begin with. And that it didn't make sense that she removed her brand and then had Charlotte kill her. I thought it had more to do with Charlotte than the mystery woman.

"Yeah."

"I shot her," she says softly. "And every time I close my eyes, I see her."

"Charlotte can never know about this," I tell him, and they all nod. This will destroy her. She did what she thought needed to be done.

Bill looks at me. "You had a deal with Isabella."

"You had a deal with her?" Saint barks.

"What the fuck, Haidyn?" Kashton snaps. "For how long?"

Bill raises his hands to both of them.

I keep my attention on him. "I did." My eyes slide to Adam for a brief second, and he sighs heavily.

It was right after we finished training, and she showed up unannounced at my house and gave me the ultimatum—me or Adam. I gave her me. It only lasted for a couple of years. She'd come over, and I'd fuck her. It took everything in me not to kill her. But the Lords already thought I killed our fathers, so if I killed her, I was afraid they would send someone new to Carnage to put my brothers through hell, and I wouldn't do that to them. *Not again.* Now I realize she came up with a better plan—Charlotte. "What about it?"

"Her 'death' means that deal is now void. She kept her word." I snort at that because that's the only one she's ever kept. "That's why Adam had to fake his death. It didn't need to be a big show. Just one that was believable."

"I'll make a new one," I say. "I'll talk to the Lords."

"No." Adam shakes his head. "You've done enough for everyone else, Haidyn. I've made my own deal this time."

The plane falls silent. No one dares to ask what he's done, but we all know the answer is sitting right in front of us. He went to Bill and offered up something he couldn't refuse.

I run a hand through my hair.

"What's Dollhouse have to do with you?" Kash asks Adam. "If you guys didn't know where it was, then how can the Lords connect it to you?"

"They can't necessarily. But the Lords got wind that I'm not 'missing' like I've been pretending to be for the past four years. So we had to do something..." Adam adds, gesturing to shoot himself in the head.

"How do we know that you weren't the one to rat him out?" Saint asks Bill.

"You don't," he answers.

Adam shakes his head. "He didn't." He assures us.

"And Sin?" Kash asks. "What about his assignment?"

Adam nods. "That's another reason we have to keep quiet about my existence. Sin knows I'm not dead..."

"Now I feel bad for beating the shit out of him," Kash mumbles. "FUCK!"

"It was for show." Saint gives a humorless laugh. He sounds as tired as I feel. "You guys set us up."

"We had very little time and very limited options." Adam doesn't agree or disagree. Or elaborate on how he managed to get a body and make it look like him. "I'm trying to do the right thing. The one thing I couldn't do for Ash..." Adam trails off. "I just...wanted you guys to know that I'm still here."

Kashton gets to his feet and walks over to Adam who also stands. He slaps his back, hugging him again. "You're still my brother, no matter what you do or where you live. And you'll always have a room ready at Carnage if you ever want to come home."

"Thanks, man." Adam smiles, pulling away. "You can't get rid of me that easy," he jokes.

I stand and dig into my pocket, removing my keys. I pull the one off the ring and hold it out to him. "Here."

"No..."

"Take it. I bought that house for you. It's always been yours."

He takes it and pulls me in for a hug. I hate that we've ended up where we are, but I'm proud of Adam standing up for what he believes in. A lot of men we know would never do that. Especially against the Lords. Once you have a target on your back, it's hard to avoid it. This could be the last time we ever see him.

"Thank you." He places it in his pocket.

Saint stands and turns to face him. "Don't get yourself killed," he says.

Adam laughs. "That's the only plan I have." Saint pulls him in for a hug.

"Here. This is for you." Bill hands me another manila envelope, and I take a second before I open it. What else could he possibly have for me tonight? Removing the contents inside, I look over the picture of the man and then back at Bill arching a brow.

"What happened to him?" he asks, and I have a feeling he already knows.

"I killed him."

Bill looks over at the detective, who snorts and mumbles, "Fucking Lords."

"Why does it matter?" I inquire.

"We think he was working with my wife," Bill answers. "Isabella owns the spa that she had Charlotte going to."

"Son of a bitch," I hiss. The fucking bitch was running everything in Charlotte's life. But it makes sense. That's how Isabella was able to control the contents that went into her daughter's IVs. It also explains how Bill was able to change one out to counteract the birth control.

"Who is this and why did you kill him?" Kash asks, taking the envelope from me.

"He was a massage therapist who rubbed on my wife," I growl. "I made it quick." If that makes it any better.

"We think she was using the spa to pick women for Dollhouse." The detective states, nodding to the envelope Kash hands to Saint. "We had surveillance on the place, trying to get answers, and you killed one of our main suspects."

I sit back crossing my arms over my chest. He's not going to get an apology from me. I wanted the bastard dead because he had his hands on my wife. I know it was a little over the top, but I sure as fuck don't regret it. Now I wish I had made it slow and painful.

The detective sighs at my silence before Adam speaks. "Okay, let's talk business."

"Business?" I ask, arching a brow. "What kind of business?"

His boss leans back in the seat, placing his left ankle on his right knee, and speaks. "We're going to need your help." Then he looks over at Bill, who nods.

Saint beats Kash and me to it. "Name it."

♠

On the way home, there is nothing but awkward silence. We all wore our helmets so we could communicate, but none had anything to say. It was all said on the jet that we flew around on for over an hour.

Saint and I exit the highway, and Saint's voice fills my ears when we both see Kashton isn't following us.

"Kash—?"

"I've got somewhere to be." He interrupts Saint, pulling his front tire up off the pavement and riding off in a wheelie.

"Fuck." Saint sighs, his helmet shaking.

I understand we all have a lot to think about, and he needs some time alone.

Pulling into Carnage, Saint and I park the bikes in the garage and make our way to the birdcage. As we step off the elevator, he speaks. "Are you leaving in the morning?"

I turn to look at him, my hand on the door. "I'll see you in the office. Seven o'clock."

"Seven o'clock." He agrees and goes to enter his room but pauses. Taking in a deep breath, his eyes meet mine. "They were going to force you to marry Ashtyn." It wasn't a question, so I don't say anything. "Were they going to use her or me?"

It doesn't matter. "Saint—"

"Me." He nods to himself, answering his own question. "Of course. If they knew how much she loved me, they would have used that against her to make her comply. Just like Isabella was going to use Charlotte's love for you against her at Dollhouse."

It makes sense. Isabella knew our fathers' plan—whatever it was—

so she decided to use some form of it. She had four years to come up with hers, though. "I would have never let it get that far," I assure him. "I would have done something...anything...before I would have let them force Ashtyn to be my wife."

"Good night, brother," he says, and before I can say the same, he's entered his room.

I enter mine just as quietly as when I left. I'm removing my shirt when the bedside light turns on. I spin around to see my wife sitting up, arms crossed over her naked chest and narrowed eyes on mine.

"Where have you been?" she demands as if she just caught me cheating on her.

I take a minute to try to come up with an answer. I hadn't thought this was what I would come home to.

"I saw the text earlier while you were in the shower, Haidyn." Her eyes lower to the comforter, and she uncrosses her arms. "Are you in trouble?"

"No," I say, dropping my T-shirt to the floor and crawling onto the bed still dressed in my jeans. I prop myself up next to her on my side.

She lies down and turns her head so her pretty blue eyes meet mine. "Would you tell me the truth?"

"Of course, doll face."

"Are *we* in trouble?" Her hand goes to her flat stomach, and I hate how worried she is. How everything that we love could so easily be taken from us.

"No." I place my hand on her stomach over hers. She sighs, placing her other hand under her neck, and she stares at the ceiling. "Everything is okay," I assure her. "You're okay. Our babies are okay, and we're okay."

Her watery eyes come back to mine, and I give her a reassuring smile. For once, I'm not lying to her. My brothers and I are going to keep Adam and Sin's secret. None of us will jeopardize what we have, what we've built here. Adam is doing good, and we'll take any chance we can to help him finish what he started. No matter how long that takes.

"Promise me no more secrets. No more lies."

"I promise." Immediately breaking it. I can never tell her about the woman she killed. I'll take that to my grave. It was for nothing. None other than her mom putting her through some sick joke or trying to send Adam a message.

"I love you," she whispers.

I get up, and she spreads her legs, allowing me to kneel between them. I'm still half dressed, but my wife is naked. Just how I left her. Placing both of my forearms on either side of her head, I slide my fingers into her dark hair, and I pull her head back so I can lower my lips to her delicate neck. "I love you, Charlotte."

She groans, her nails running up and down my sides. My lips trail up to her jawline and to hers. She opens up for me, letting me dominate her mouth as her hips rise, begging me for more.

Pulling away she smiles up at me. "You still owe me that honeymoon."

I return it and say. "Next..."

She slaps her hand over my mouth and shakes her head. "I don't want to know next week, next month, or next year. I want it to be a surprise." Removing her hand from my mouth, she wraps her arms around my neck.

"Whatever my Lady wants," I tell her, already having a plan.

Things are going to change around here. Babies are on the way—not only my wife but Ashtyn as well—and soon this place we call hell will be filled with laughter and little feet running up and down the hallways. We've always said Carnage is no place for kids, but it will prove us wrong.

It's not what I thought my life would be. It's way more than I could have ever dreamed.

Epilogue 2
Haidyn

EIGHTEEN YEARS LATER

Her bitch of a mother injected me with shit to make me live a long and healthy life. I'm not sure how much I took or how long it added to my life, but every time I look at my wife, my chest tightens, thinking of having to live a day without her. She has it too... but that doesn't mean either of us is bulletproof.

I used to never care if I lived or died, but now death is often on my mind. The one thing I keep coming back to is if she dies before me, I'll put a fucking bullet in my brain the day I lose her. But then I look at our children. They would need me. Our kids are strong, but to lose both parents on the same day? And one of those being due to suicide? I'd hate to leave them to the Lords to fend for themselves.

I've never been sick. Not a cold since they dragged me out of that place. Not a single gray hair. I'm in my home gym at least five days a week. I feel great, and I hate it. I push myself every day to do more and lift heavier—I'm the biggest and strongest I've ever been—to try to hurt myself but nothing happens. And Charlotte? She's more gorgeous than ever.

She gave me three sons, and if it were up to me, I'd keep her knocked up forever. But carrying triplets wasn't easy for her, even with the founder's enhancements. She was on bed rest for most of her pregnancy, and the boys came early via emergency C-section. Devin and Gavin both assured us that wasn't uncommon when it comes to triplets, and we knew early on that it wasn't going to be a vaginal delivery. It didn't ease my worry for my wife and children.

I had my vasectomy reversed two months after my brothers saved me. Charlotte and I have never stopped trying to have more kids, but it just never happened. Gavin said that it wasn't a guarantee. That the percentage of it to take was ninety to ninety-five percent. Unfortunately, I didn't have those results. That doesn't mean I'm not thankful for what we do have.

Our house has been full of laughter and craziness. Raising three boys—future Spade brothers—hasn't been easy, but I couldn't have found a better partner to share it with.

All three of our sons want to join the Lords. Of course, Charlotte isn't totally thrilled about it, but she told me she expected it. They're all reckless and unapologetic like I was at their age.

"How is it?" I ask Devin as I stand with my arms crossed over my chest, looking at one of our demons.

"It's looking good," Devin answers, eyeing the stitches in my son's thigh. "Healing nicely." He rolls his chair over to the cabinet, and my son sits up on the table, then jumps off. He pulls his jeans up over his boxer briefs and zips them up.

"I told you guys it was no big deal." He shrugs carelessly.

"Two inches to the left, and it would have severed your femoral artery." Devin glares at him. "You would have bled out."

My son's blue eyes meet mine as he smirks, and I shake my head. *That's a boy in love.* "You know your mother once stabbed me." I chuckle at the memory.

His lips pull back with disgust. "Gross, Dad. I don't want to know about any kinks you and Mom have."

"You know they say sexual fetishes are hereditary," I add.

He makes a gagging sound, and Devin just laughs.

"Come on." I slap my son's back. "You're late for school."

He slides his leather jacket on and thanks Devin. Our boys are good kids, but I'm not going to say that they don't destroy shit on a daily basis. They've been unstoppable since the moment they learned to crawl. Charlotte and I have been chasing them ever since.

His phone rings, and he removes it from his pocket. "Hello?" he answers. His eyes meet mine for a brief second before he rushes to hang up. "I'll call you back."

"Who was that?" I ask, knowing he didn't want me to hear his conversation.

"It was Sawyer." He fixes the collar on his leather jacket. A sign he's lying.

"Oh yeah? What did your brother have to say?" I check my watch. It's almost ten. "Shouldn't he be in class?"

"He's running late." He waves me off, doubling down on his lie.

"I see," I say, letting it go. "Well, have a great day at school," I holler as we exit the double doors of Carnage.

"See ya, Dad." He jumps into his car and squeals his tires taking off. He's in a hurry to get to wherever he's going, and I'm not sure if that's school.

The boy's mind is only on one thing, and it's a girl. I can't blame him, though. Mine is always on his mother. Charlotte gave me a life I only ever thought existed outside our world.

Walking down to my car, I get in and exit Carnage. Taking the short drive across the street to the opposite gate. Getting out, I enter the house my wife and I built years ago. She loved my house in the woods, so she designed one like it, but only bigger and better. She filled it with color and life.

A picture of us hangs in the grand foyer. She's wearing the white dress she wore the first night I saw her, and I'm in a black tux. It's from our tenth anniversary when we renewed our vows. I can't go back and change the night we got married but I tried to give her something... more. Even when she told me she didn't need it. What makes it even better is our three boys—Adler, Keller and Sawyer—are in it with us.

She still has the dress. And once a year, she wears it for me. I take her out to dinner and show my wife off to the world. I'm proud to call her mine. The following morning, I surprise her with a honeymoon trip. She never asks what I have planned or what I'm going to do to her. She trusts me with her life, and I love to keep her guessing. As much as I love to see her dressed up, I also love to see her begging and crying for me to fuck her like a desperate little whore. And she loves it too.

"Doll face?" I holler, removing my jacket and tossing it over the round table in the grand foyer, knowing she'll get on to me later for it.

"In the bathroom," she calls out.

Smiling, I make my way to our primary suite. Entering the bathroom, I find her standing at the counter, wearing nothing but a white towel tucked under her arms. Her long dark hair is up in a messy bun, and her makeup is done on the light side. The bathtub gurgles as the water and bubbles drain.

"How was Adler's appointment?" she asks, her pretty blue eyes meeting mine in the mirror.

"Good. Devin said everything looks great." I come up behind her and undo the towel, letting it fall at her feet. Her body is still wet in some areas from her bath, and she's got bubbles on her shoulder.

My hand massages her ass cheek that still has my name branded on it. I promised I'd never take my wedding ring off, but I broke that promise shortly after I made it. I removed it to get her name tattooed on my ring finger. She had told me that she wanted to legally change her name to Charlotte. I wanted her to know that I supported her decision.

Charlotte Bailey Reeves is the name she chose. Bailey was her father's middle name. She wanted him to still be a part of her life.

Pulling away, she turns to face me and throws her arms around my neck, wrapping one leg around my hip. "I don't have to be back at the spa for a few more hours." The pregnancy took a lot out of my wife and after the boys arrived, she wanted to spend as much time as she could with them. She eventually took over the spa her mother owned and made it her own. "How long before you have to go back to work?" she asks.

I lower my hand to grab her ass and push my lips to hers, whispering against them. "I'm going to spend my day watching you get off, doll face."

"Haidyn," she groans, pushing her hips into mine. I'm so fucking hard for her. "I have to go in later..."

"No. You don't." She has a great team that works for her. They can handle the day without her. "How's that sound, Charlotte? Want to be my good girl coming all over herself?" I love forcing her to come over and over. My wife is gorgeous, but there's just something so fucking sexy watching her turn into a blubbering mess while she's covered in cum.

"Yes. Please." She leans forward to kiss me, and I pull away, making her growl in frustration.

My free hand drops between her legs, and I run my fingers over her pussy. She's wet. Not as much as I want but I'll get her there. Letting go of her, I slap my name branded on her ass. "Rip everything off the bed except the fitted sheet. I'll be right there."

I turn and enter the closet and then press a code to open the secret door. Entering the room, I grab my bag and drop it onto the table in the center of the room and then go to the wall and grab everything I need. My wife designed this house just how she wanted it. And we knew we had three kids on the way. So she made sure we had a private room where I could do whatever I wanted to her. Even after the boys move out, I'll still use it to play with her.

Going back to the bedroom, she sits on the edge of the bed, waiting on me like the good girl she is. Her workday long forgotten. I drop the bag at her feet and kneel. I grab the first item and hold it up to her face.

Her breathing picks up as her heavy sapphire-colored eyes meet mine. "Don't want me to beg?"

I give her a smile. "Oh, you will."

She opens her mouth for me, and I push the black rubber ball into it and buckle the back. Looking over her beautiful face, I run my thumb over her pretty pink-painted lips while her heavy breathing fills our room. Leaning down, I give her forehead a soft kiss and instruct her to lie on the bed.

Taking my time, I tie her in place, loving the sound of her muffled moans and whimpers. Once I'm done, I stand back and admire my wife.

She's lying in the center of our bed—doggy position—her legs spread wide, each ankle tied to either end of the footboard. Her back is arched with her smooth ass and pussy up in the air. Her arms are underneath her. Wrists tied together with the excess rope tied to the center of the footboard.

Her head is to the side, facing me. Big, watery eyes look up at me with a ball gag in her mouth. She's not going anywhere. I grab the last thing and lean over the bed. She speaks unintelligible words into the gag, and I smile, showing her what I've got in my hand. "I'm going to stuff your cunt with this, Charlotte. And you're going to lie here face down, tied to our bed for an hour." Her eyes widen, and she pulls on the rope. The movement makes her lashes flutter, and she moans at the lack of movement the rope allows her. *My little rope bunny.* "Then I'll remove the gag and let you beg me to fuck your ass."

I kiss her cheek and then slowly insert the dildo into her now soaked cunt. Then I place the hourglass on the dresser in her line of sight. Having to watch time makes it drag on. And then having to count her orgasms on top of that...she'll be a mess by the time I fuck her.

My cell rings and I get off the bed and pull it out of my pocket. Looking at the caller ID, I open the double doors to the wraparound porch and hit answer, walking out onto it. "Hey, man. What's up?"

"I know you're busy, so I won't keep you long," he says in greeting.

"You're fine. I've got all day." I smile, turning to watch my wife squirm, hearing me speak. She'll spend all day being my whore. Then I'll take her out to dinner and show off what's mine.

"My wife just informed me that we'll be in town this weekend, so I was wondering if you guys will be available for dinner?"

"Yeah," I tell him. "Of course."

"Perfect. I'll tell her to reach out to Charlotte, and they can plan it."

"Sounds good, man," I say, and he hangs up.

Walking back into the bedroom, I go to the app on my phone and turn on the vibrating dildo that's in her pussy, and she begins to moan. Her ass rocks back and forth as if she's fucking my cock. "That's it, doll face." I rub her ass. "Feel that?" I turn it up, and her legs begin to shake. "One hour," I remind her. "You're to lie here and come all over yourself for me, Charlotte. Make sure you count each one."

I hear her cell beep, and I go to the bathroom to pick it up and see it's a message in a group chat the wives have.

J: Who is free this weekend for dinner?

I lock the screen and place it back down. My wife can respond later tonight. She's booked for the day.

Going back to the bedroom, I walk over to the mini bar. I pour myself a glass of scotch and sit down in one of the chairs over by the open French doors. Taking a sip, I watch her struggle, loving the muffled sounds that come out of her gagged mouth.

Men like me aren't lucky. We see what we want, and we take it. As I look at the photos she's framed and hung up of our family over the years, I see the life that I never knew was possible. I guess it doesn't matter when I die. Charlotte gave me a life that I didn't deserve, and even if I'm lucky enough to spend forever with her, it still wouldn't be enough.

LORDS TREE

THE RITUAL

RYAT ARCHER — BLAKELY ANDERSON

REIGN ARCHER | ROYAL ARCHER | RYANN ARCHER

THE SINNER

EASTON SINNETT — ELLINGTON ASHER

BREXTON SINNETT | ANNALEIGH SINNETT

THE SACRIFICE

TYSON CRAWFORD — LAIKYN MINSON

HALSTON CRAWFORD | HARTLYN CRAWFORD

Carnage

SAINT CARTER — ASHTYN PRICE

TINSLEY CARTER | BERKELEY CARTER

Madness

HAIDYN REEVES — CHARLOTTE HEWETT

ADLER REEVES | KELLER REEVES | SAWYER REEVES

WORLD CROSSOVERS

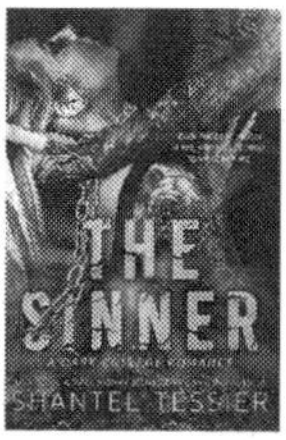

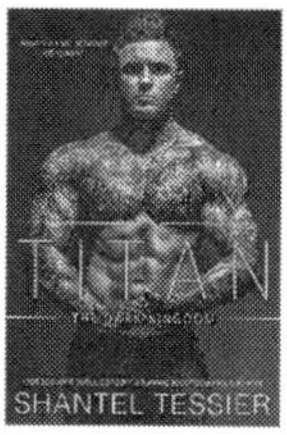

CONTACT ME

Facebook Reader Group: Shantel's Sinful Side

Goodreads: Shantel Tessier

Instagram: shantel_tessierauthor

Website: Shanteltessier.com

Facebook Page: Shantel Tessier Author

TikTok: shantel_tessier_author

Store: shanteltessierstore.com

Shantel Tessier's Spoiler Room. Please note that I have one spoiler room for all books, and you may come across spoilers from book(s) you have not had the chance to read yet. You must answer both questions in order to be approved.